The Paladin

Also by George Shipway

George Shipway

THE
PALADIN

HARCOURT BRACE JOVANOVICH, INC., NEW YORK

Printed in the United States of America

Library of Congress Cataloging in Publication Data

Shipway, George, 1908–
The paladin.

1. Tirel, Walter—Fiction.   I. Title.
PZ4.S5575Pal3   [PR6069.H5]   823'.9'14   73-9887
ISBN 0-15-170740-5

First American edition 1973
B   C   D   E

To
L. B. S. and F. W. S.
In loving and grateful memory

BOOK ONE
The Paladin

'The Normans are a turbulent race and, unless restrained by a firm government, are always ready for mischief. They are eager for rebellion, ripe for tumults, and alert for every sort of crime.'

Orderic Vitalis (1075–1141), monk
and chronicler of St Evroult.

NORMANDY, FRANCE AND MAINE   c. 1090

0   50 km

BESSIN

Coutances

Torigni

O

Courci

N

Falaise

Grantm

Genets

Avranches

Mont St. Michel

Arderon

Dol

A

Fougères

F

BRITTANY

MAINE

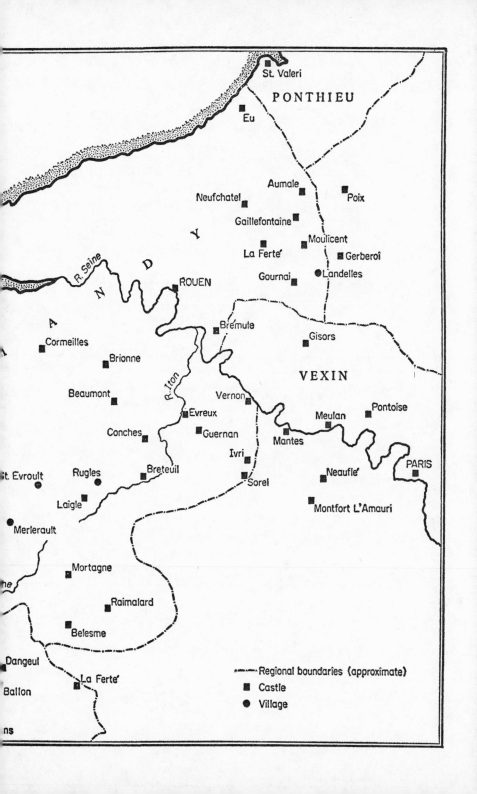

Author's Note

This tale is fiction embroidered on a historical patchwork.

Very little is known of Walter Tirel's life before he emerges in English history as William Rufus's reputed assassin. Although he was certainly the third Lord of Poix, a chronicler mentions a Walter Tirel who was son of Dean Fulk of Evreux – two contradictory accounts which I have tried to reconcile. Tirel married, at some date before 1085, Adelice of Clare, and acquired in her dowry Laingaham in Suffolk. Beyond these meagre facts we know virtually nothing about him before that fatal day in the New Forest in 1100.

With the exception of Richer the Saracen, the main characters are historical. But to Isabel of Montfort's shade I offer shamed apologies. The chronicler indeed relates that 'she rode in knightly armour when the vassals took the field, and exhibited much daring among knights and men-at-arms'. He also mentions 'her sinful wantonness'. Nevertheless there are no authentic grounds for making her the kind of woman portrayed.

The chronology of events in Normandy at this period is often obscure. The accepted sequence has been generally retained, with one exception of no great significance: Mabille Talvas was actually murdered at Bures in 1082, not at Raimalard in 1078.

Chapter 1

1070–71

The crab-apple tree leaned from a gap in Evreux's ancient rampart where the palisade had rotted behind Dean Fulk's timbered house. The roots clutched the earthen bank and sucked life to a gnarled trunk clothed in mildewed bark, and a branched canopy which spread a sun-dappled shade in summer. By September the tree always bore a few wrinkled, black-spotted apples; we harvested them greedily and pretended to enjoy their bitterness.

It was a quiet, sheltered place, set in an angle where the ramparts met at a stone bastion which we were forbidden to climb, for the masonry was broken and crumbling: a trap for childish limbs and a home for vipers. The palisade rose to a bowman's stave arm, too tall for us; from the apple-tree's gap alone could we look out from Evreux, down the brambled slope to the moat – a still, weed-scummed tendril of the river Iton – across meadows, sheep pastures, copses, cornfields and scattered steadings to the forested hills, an hour's ride distant, which girdled the town like a blue-green sea.

Dean Fulk's house, sheltering beneath the abbey's grey stone walls, enclosed this wasteland corner and created a haven from the grown-up world. Boulders jutted from grass-patched gravel: several bore incised letters and outlandish carvings. Dean Fulk had once proposed a chapel on this ground; the villeins digging for foundations came upon stone coffins, broken jars, a scattering of bones. The dean traced the eroded inscriptions with his fingers, and muttered to himself. 'An ancient burying ground,' he said. 'These were Romans, the same who built the bastion yonder. A pagan people, but their gods once were powerful. It might be unlucky to disturb them.' He signed the air above a yellowing rib-cage, countermanded his orders, and so preserved our sanctuary. When he had gone we burrowed laboriously beneath a stone, set it on end, rubbed away the soil to reveal a carven warrior wearing a strange, short-skirted hauberk. Fromont, boastful of his learning, pretended to read the letters engraved below, and declared the slab a memorial to a man-at-arms, a centurion or some such thing. Fromont always professed more than he really knew, and I may have remembered the expression wrongly, for it was a long while ago. I was barely ten years old at the time.

This was our playground, where my memories begin.

My companions were Dean Fulk's sons: Hubert, the eldest – a man more than twice my age – and young Fromont, both of whom I then believed to be my brothers. The dean, on Hubert's knighting, had given him seisin of Guernan's castle – a neighbouring fief his family held from the Dukes of Normandy. Affliction came on Hubert within a month of his inheritance. Scuffling with Ascelin Goel's men before the tower of Ivri, five leagues south-east of Evreux, a sword-blade cleft his helmet and his skull. They carried him on a litter to Evreux, where from Christmas until Candlemas he lay senseless in Dame Orielde's chamber, while she and her women tended him and the household's clatter stilled. Understanding of a kind returned at last to the empty eyes which stared at the raftered ceiling; and Hubert, lifted from his pallet, sat long hours in the sunlight, his head swathed in linen, and watched the town's traffic pass beyond the churchyard fence: pedlars leading donkeys, peasants homing from the fields, scythes and pitchforks sloped upon their shoulders, a fisherman with his catch suspended from a pole like silver leaves, sergeants and men-at-arms singing bawdy songs and clanking to the castle. One day Dame Orielde unwound the bandage and we saw, awestruck, that his hair was white, a dead-white like a viper's belly, except for a sable streak which marked the scar.

When, in autumn, the days grew shorter and Our Lady's church shadowed the yard, Hubert followed the sun to our sanctuary, and watched us playing beneath the apple tree. At first his presence constrained our games; soon we grew accustomed to the quiet figure seated on a stool, and almost forgot him. Hubert smiled and nodded, and seldom spoke. Imperceptibly he became a friend, and suggested new diversions to our games. He taught me to whittle a child-size bowstave from an apple branch, and plaited a string from linen threads. 'Though apple wood, Walter,' he said, speaking slowly, for the wound had caused some impediment in his speech, 'will never make a proper bow. Some day I will find you a length of yew or limewood.' I found it difficult to avoid staring at the tattered gash across his scalp, fringed by its peculiar black-haired margins; once he allowed me, greatly daring, to trace the wound where it crept below the hairline to his eye. The puckered skin gave like a jelly beneath my touch; furtively I wiped my fingers on my breeches.

Hubert was kind, and slow, and very gentle; but never again would he ride with knights in battle. Dean Fulk gave Guernan to Warin, his second son – a stern, black-browed man, short of speech and temper, whom we feared. He kept a sharp hold on his fief, and came seldom to Evreux.

2

A child's mind absorbs the colour of his surroundings, as a moth merges with the gold and russet of an autumn leaf. Therefore it is difficult to describe Evreux as I saw it through childhood's eyes, to disentangle adult memories from the natural acceptance of a background which I knew when young. The town then seemed a monstrous place, a warren of streets and houses, always crowded, always noisy. Evreux is indeed considerable and holds two thousand people, but it was never so vast as I imagined. The ancient ramparts, whose circumference I once tried to follow on flagging seven-year legs, enclosed the town in a furlong-sided square. Above a sepia sea of rooftops, thatched and shingled, two buildings soared like dominant crags: Our Lady's church and Count William of Evreux's castle, set at diagonal corners like weights that balanced Evreux's scales of power. The castle donjon reared foursquare upon a grass-grown mound; the lowest storey's mortared stone supported two more storeys hewn from oaken logs. From the mound's foot flowed the ward, a ditched and palisaded apron which enclosed a hidden world – a world of barracks, stables, armouries, Count William's timbered hall, and the iron menace of his knights and men-at-arms. The inhabitants of this fortified home seemed remote as a distant star: we saw the count ride out, a merlin on his wrist, or spear in hand and tawny boar-hounds at his horse's heels, and the gaily cloaked, imperious cavalcade that followed.

William of Evreux – a small man, hair grizzled beneath a fur-trimmed cap, face beaked like an ageing falcon – once passed me near the Vernon gate and, as I bent my knee and bowed my head, sent me a hard, examining look. I trembled, and wondered how I erred. He said nothing and rode on, and I glanced beneath my lashes

3

at his lady, the beautiful Hawise, and the esquîres in his train – careless youngsters, arrogant in bearing, some no older than myself. A gawky, long-legged girl usually attended my lady Hawise, a dark-eyed, brown-faced creature dressed all in brown: leather doublet and breeches, a black cock's feather in her leather cap. She sat her palfrey like a warrior, and wore a sulky look. I thought her ugly, and never troubled to inquire her name, since women held no interest for me then.

My interests were, in truth, remarkably confined. Dame Orielde controlled our daily lives. She was not easily crossed: a tiny, bustling woman whose emaciated face, finely boned, had once been beautiful. Her commands, given in ripped, staccato tones like a sergeant's drill-snap, we seldom disobeyed. The abbey's precincts, the chapter house and the deanery's palings enclosed her world; there also she preferred to confine her children's comings and goings. Evreux's narrow streets and the muddy market-place by the Vernon gate were territories forbidden to our wanderings. On holy days she sometimes allowed Fromont and me to go in Hubert's charge beyond the walls, to the fields where sun-tanned villeins tossed the hay, to a sandspit below St Taurin's chapel where they dipped the sheep, to lie belly-down in wind-rippled rushes at the river's edge and watch excitedly our fishing lines and the chicken-bone hooks which Hubert delicately carved. But these excursions were rare: Dame Orielde was always restless for our homecoming. She seemed haunted by a dread of the world beyond the ramparts, by a nagging fear I did not understand.

Dean Fulk insisted that with Fromont I should learn to read and cipher, and engaged his chaplain to teach us letters. The monk was a humourless man, and I found his lessons tedious. Fromont absorbed his learning easily, and was pompously contemptuous of my backwardness. Destined for St Evroult's cloister, he owned ambitions to become its abbot. His round face and serious demeanour earned our instructor's approval – in fact they were much alike. I often found it hard to believe that Fromont was his father's son, for Dean Fulk was a lean, engaging man whose eyes twinkled easily on the world he had renounced. He had fought in the Conqueror's wars, and bore a livid sword-scar on his cheek. Yet his tolerance had limits, as I soon discovered. Bored beyond endurance by my lessons, I once gave an insolent answer to my tutor, which Dean Fulk heard – and promptly thrashed me with an ash-rod. Though the beating hurt much more than Dame Orielde's whippings I managed to endure

4

and forbore to snivel. In the end he cast down the rod and scrutinized me thoughtfully. 'I think,' he said to the monk who watched complacently, 'our Walter is not made for learning. A different kind of blood flows in his veins. You will bear upon him lightly, brother Eudo.' Afterwards my periods of instruction were diminished; I spent fewer hours in the sunless hall where Eudo scratched a pointed stick on a space in the earth-floor cleared of rushes. The time thus gained I spent with Hubert in our playground, learning from his slow-spoken words of warfare and the ways of knights in battle, watching his dexterous fingers shape bowstaves and arrows, earning his approval of my marksmanship. One day, to my delight, Dean Fulk gave me a palfrey, a shaggy skewbald no bigger than a pony, and bade Hubert teach me proper horsemanship. 'For,' he said enigmatically, 'I foresee the way his course is set.' I did not understand him, nor did I care; thereafter when the weather was fair Hubert, riding a safe ambling rouncey, took me beyond the moat to a level meadow where he taught me the elements of knightly combat: my lance a fishing-rod, my sword a wooden stave, my shield of plaited wattle taken from a sheep pen. I learned, as I have said, the elements, because Hubert could not engage me: his movements were lumbering and awkward since his wound.

On days of rain and wind – they seemed few enough; in my youthful memories the sun always shone – I often wandered in Our Lady's abbey, for this was Dean Fulk's domain. Unlike the castle – forbidden ground, a lair of mystery and terror – the church was familiar to me from earliest childhood: an awesome place within, huge, where the altar's candled splendour dazzled my eyes and shrouded the dark aisles in deeper gloom. Stone pillars thick as tree-trunks climbed to a cavernous ceiling; the roof-beams interlaced like twining boughs; black monks and silent priests moved stealthily in the shadows. I thought it a perfect setting for our game of catch-thief; nor do I think Dean Fulk, an easy man, would much have minded. Fromont, of course, disapproved; and I played solitary games in the darkness, creeping cautiously from pillar to pillar and pretending the clerks were dragons.

Among such frivolities the seasons passed until my tenth year, until the day we nearly lost our apple tree, and my life was changed.

Hubert sat in the sunlight, busy with knife on wood. Smilingly he handed me a new arrow, fletched with mallard wing, the shaft fined to a point – he never allowed me to use steel broadheads. Gaily I braced my bow and checked the fistmele.

'Measure a score,' Hubert said in his slow, soft voice. 'Mark for that moss-patch below the withered branch.'

I paced the distance, notched and flexed, sighted over the pile and drew the string steadily to my chin. All this – position and stance and draw – Hubert had taught me over the months. From there an instinct took command, an inborn skill that has been mine since first I rested stele on stave, a flair which I cannot explain. From the soles of my feet a current flows, a thrill like a tensioned wire, through spine and shoulder, arm and wrist, to fingers and string and shaft. It leaps, an invisible arc from barb to mark, and signals deflections for wind, corrections for range, in the third of a heartbeat, without thought or awareness. I become one with the stave and the stele, the mark an infallible lodestone.

My bow was knotted apple wood, my arrow, crude and unbalanced, of whittled elm. The barb thumped in the moss-patch. I sighed and lowered the bow, and heard the thudding of hooves.

'Good shot, boy!'

I turned, and saw Count William, and bent my knee. Dean Fulk walked at his stirrup; a little cavalcade clattered behind: a swarthy knight, a stranger, clad in a calfhide jerkin, deerskin breeches and long, supple boots. A fair-haired boy of my own age rode at his sword arm; I knew him by sight: Amauri of Montfort, the count's nephew. A moon-faced, chinless youngster in foppish clothes, all velvet and silken tassels, talked to the long-legged girl who rode like a soldier. The sulky look had left her face; dark eyes swept me from head to foot. I flushed, stared back defiantly, and saw her smile.

I suppose, looking back over the years, it was then that I fell in love.

Count William spurred to the broken palisade, and examined it gloomily. 'No doubt you'll want this repaired,' he remarked to the swarthy horseman.

'Better so, my lord,' the knight replied. 'It is the fourth weakness we have noticed in our circuit. Gaps in a rampart attract an enemy like kites on carrion.'

Count William felt his rein. 'Very well. See to it, Fulk: it's in your demesne. That tree will have to come down.'

Fromont's lips drooped at the corners; he seemed ready to cry. I know not how I looked, but my heart echoed his dismay. Hubert tried to speak, fighting his affliction to find words. Amauri thoughtfully watched our faces. The count had already turned his horse when the boy said, 'Could you not spare the tree, my lord? You can replace the broken stakes and close the gap.'

Count William paused, surprised. 'Hey? Why so, Amauri?'

Amauri nodded in my direction and said lightly, 'It's a bowman's butt, my lord. Where else may our archers practise?'

'Children's games!' the stranger knight rapped impatiently. 'We waste time, my lord count.'

Count William sent him a glance of cold dislike; then pensively surveyed our stricken faces. 'Where else, indeed? Well, why not? New timber, Fulk – that's all you need. The tree may stand. Now, Morin, let's inspect the bastion – a sorry ruin, I'm afraid.'

He signed to the children to stay, and rode from the yard. The knight followed, lips compressed. Amauri slipped from his saddle and laughed.

'A narrow escape,' he said.

Rather diffidently I introduced myself. He was a denizen of that sinister castle, an associate of frightening knights and bray-mouthed men-at-arms. Fromont regarded him in silent suspicion, finger to lips. So, like puppies disturbed at play, hackles raised, we examined each other a moment; and Hubert, whittling an arrow shaft in the background, smiled to himself.

Amauri said gently, 'Walter, will you teach me the use of your bow?'

The frost dissolved. Amauri presented his companions: his sister Isabel, who now grinned at me widely, and Ralph of Conches, who afforded a distant nod. Briskly, and not without importance, I taught Amauri to set his feet, present his heart-ribs to the mark and draw the string, right elbow cocked and stave-arm braced. He obeyed patiently; I fussed around him, shifting his position and altering his hold, until he grew restive and lowered the bow.

'When can I shoot?' he inquired plaintively.

I explained haughtily that stance was everything; then relented and notched an arrow. I showed him the primary draw – which you can use only for a weak bow – and watched critically while he loosed. The pile nicked the moss patch. Isabel clapped her hands.

'Well done, brother.' She jumped from her palfrey, 'Now let me try.'

She began handling the bow. I could hardly credit her incompetence – all children, even girls, play at archery from the cradle – and began to think it feigned. Finally she fumbled her nocking and dropped the arrow.

'Teach me.'

I set her left hand on the stave, reached round her shoulders, squeezed her fingers on the string and drew. Thus I held her from behind in a light embrace. Isabel pressed her body against mine. I could not see her face. Mine was flaming.

We were not innocent, we youngsters. We had listened to kitchen sluts and scullions, heard the coarse jests of men-at-arms, seen farmyard animals in rut, tripped over coupling peasants. We knew a good deal about venery. But our knowledge was theoretical; and I was ignorant and shy. When Isabel's buttocks stroked my thighs I flinched like a startled hare. The bowstring twanged. The arrow quivered in the apple tree. Isabel turned her head.

'Have I hit the mark?' she inquired guilelessly.

I was instantly aware that the question had nothing to do with archery. My cheeks flushed a deeper red. Amusement kindled tiny sparks – amber flecks in jet – in the eyes that looked into mine. I thought her shameless – a judgement I have never altered through the years.

I mumbled, 'You have – first time. You need no tutoring from me.'

I sat beside Amauri on a Roman tombstone. He seemed not to have noticed his sister's wanton prank; though Ralph of Conches scowled and chewed his lip. For want of prattle to cover my blushes I said, 'Who was the knight riding with Count William?'

Amauri grimaced. 'Morin du Pin, from the Duke of Normandy's mesnie. He has brought the Duke's writ, and knights and men-at-arms, to garrison the castle.'

'I thought it already guarded by the count's own men.'

'It was. Save for a few household knights they have been dispersed. I don't understand why. Duke William seems to doubt my uncle's loyalty – which has made him angry.'

Hubert said, 'Nor is he the only discontented baron. The Duke sends his garrisons to all important strongholds.' He put his knife away and brushed shavings from his lap. 'One cannot really blame him. In England rebellion seethes; Anjou foments trouble; Normandy is restless, and war is in the air.'

He gazed absently across the town, to the donjon thrusting like a fist above the rooftops. His hand lingered for an instant at his girdle, on the left hip where a sword-hilt might have rested, and he sighed a little. 'We have seen no harrying in Evreux's marches for many years – beyond your memory, Walter.'

Amauri said proudly, 'I have seen war.'

'That I know,' Hubert replied. 'Your father is at odds with his neighbour the lord of Neauflé. Montfort L'Amauri is no place for children – which is why you were sent here.'

'And very dull it is.' Isabel stood before us, and handed me my bow. 'I have remembered to unbrace it, and here is your arrow.'

I avoided her gaze, thanked her and found myself stammering. Isabel laughed, turned on her heel and stood beside Ralph's palfrey, fondling his knee and chattering gaily. A smug look crept over Ralph's features; he almost smirked. Amauri watched them, frowning.

'A mannerless hussy, my sister,' he observed. 'Twelve years old – it's time she learned to behave.'

The Count of Evreux swung into the yard, talking over his shoulder to Morin du Pin. 'You'll have to put a working party on the bastion – the stones are mostly rubble. I'll find you masons and a labour gang. Well, that finishes the business. Get mounted, Amauri, and you, Isabel.' He seemed in a sunnier mood, looked at me and added jovially, 'And here's our young archer, bow in hand. Let's see if you can repeat your hit, my boy – I'll wager it was a fluke!'

Hauled thus into the forefront, like a jongleur before his audience, I trembled and glanced appealingly at Hubert. He nodded reassurance, chose three arrows from the bundle he had carved and put them in my hand. 'They'll fly true,' he murmured. 'Twenty paces – and send them fast!'

I braced the bow, slipped two arrows in my belt, took stance and notched the third. With the touch of nock on string my nervousness departed. The shafts thudded in the tree like three successive heart-beats – and my palm could have covered the fletchings. Count William's bowmen grunted acclamation; the count bellowed, 'Well hit, indeed! A marksman, a sharpshooter – a veritable tirel!'

And so I earned my nickname, which has lasted all my life. The cavalcade departed from our playground; Isabel waved a hand and smiled wickedly.

'Farewell, Walter . . . Tirel.'

4

The trio returned to Dean Fulk's house next day, and often afterwards. Amauri became my friend: an attraction of opposites, as Hubert remarked. He was gold-haired, fair-skinned, blue-eyed, fresh and open in his manner, bubbling with life. My hair is black, my face pale and thin; I am often moody and inclined to brood. Isabel came also; I sometimes wondered at the freedom she enjoyed; I did not then realize that Isabel made her own laws. Although she occasionally teased me her conduct was more restrained – perhaps Amauri had rated her in private. Ralph of Conches proved a milksop: he fussed about his frippery clothes, botched the games we played – catch-thief or snatchsticks – and snivelled when we hit him. A year older than Isabel, he assumed towards her a possessive attitude which, to my secret fury, she cordially encouraged. Ralph, first-born to the lord of Conches and Toesni, a kinsman by marriage of Count William, had been sent to Evreux for training in the duties of esquiredom – this being a prevalent custom among noble families. Amauri once mentioned to me a mutual understanding between the Houses of Montfort and Conches that Ralph and Isabel should eventually be wedded: after hearing this I bullied Ralph with extra vigour.

Since I no longer held these young castle-dwellers in respectful awe, my visits to the castle in their company caused no misgiving. Nobody took any notice of us. We entered Count William's hall and saw him and his lady at the high table conversing genially with lounging knights in fur-trimmed cloaks. An esquire strummed a lute; Countess Hawise's slender fingers marked the rhythm. I gaped at her beauty, and whispered admiration. 'My aunt,' Isabel answered flatly, 'is a barren, domineering bitch who will never give Evreux heirs. I loathe her.' Amauri quickly shushed his sister; Ralph looked shocked. The count discursively related an anecdote concerning the battle we call Hastings and the English Senlac; the knight to whom he spoke looked as though he had heard it often before, and swallowed a yawn.

The donjon we did not enter. Amauri regarded it thoughtfully.

'We used to run races up the ladders from floor to floor. First to touch a battlement merlon won. Not any more,' he added regretfully. 'Morin du Pin put a stop to it. A grim fellow, the Duke's castellan – thinks of nothing but soldiering.'

One gusty April day they came on horses to Dean Fulk's house, two mounted sergeants following; and Amauri proposed that we should ride out together to Guernan's forested borders. I sought Dame Orielde's sanction, and met steadfast opposition. Even the sergeants' presence, helmeted and sworded, failed to move her. Almost in tears I begged, until Dean Fulk sauntered into the courtyard, listened to my plea, and gently overrode his wife's objections. 'All is safe, lady: that I promise you. No enemies ride near Evreux's marches.' (Afterwards, remembering the Dean's intervention, I asked a question. 'It happened at Sorel, in the autumn of '58,' he answered sombrely. 'Talvas's men, returning from a raid to Breteuil, came suddenly from the forest. We closed Sorel's gates in time, and shut out Fulk, my first-born, playing in harvest fields across the stream. He was seven years old. I found his body afterwards. It was not pretty.') Dame Orielde yielded, and ran weeping into the house. Happily I saddled the skewbald pony.

On a blustery morning we rode south-east over the water meadows, flushing snipe and nesting mallard, beyond the vineyards and across the fields where peasants ploughed, past the furthermost steading and a hermit's ruinous hut to scattered coppices, outriders of the great forest which reached envious fingers to the cultivated lands; and saw in the far distance Guernan's wooden tower thrusting above the forest's wind-thrashed trees like a rock amid raging waters. A half-trained merlin perched on Isabel's wrist; rashly she cast it at an errant ringdove. The hawk, wind-battered and confused, missed her stoop and sought sulky refuge in a beech-tree's topmost branches. Hopping awkwardly from bough to bough, jesses trailing, she refused to answer the lure; we rode beneath, faces skywards, following the bird deeper into woodland where twigs scraped our noses and brambles raked the horses' flanks. Amauri acidly pointed out the folly of casting merlins in a gale; Isabel snapped, Ralph tut-tutted, and we all became bad-tempered. Eventually the fugitive entangled her jesses and hung head-down in yellow-eyed fury.

'She's your bird, sister,' Amauri said brutally. 'Fetch her down!'

Before I could quit my stirrups Isabel swarmed lithely up the trunk. She retrieved the merlin, descended, and set the hawk again upon her wrist.

'She's come to no harm,' she said defiantly.

'No thanks to you,' Amauri snapped, 'and you've set her training back a month!'

We were all tired and cross. I gestured to the forest, and said

11

pacifically, 'Guernan is not far. Let's visit brother Warin. He'll not grudge us a bite of food.'

Ralph said, 'That surly man? No. Anyway, he's no more your brother than I am.'

I stared at him. Isabel said sharply, 'Ralph, guard your tongue!'

'What are you saying?' I asked. 'Explain yourself!'

He began gobbling like a ruffled cockerel – which was always his way when disconcerted. A sergeant spoke gruffly. 'We'd better return, master. Rain is on the way.'

Amauri said quickly, 'Yes, come on. We don't want a soaking.'

Nevertheless he got one. Amauri left the wood at a canter, stretched to a gallop across a patch of open grassland. I followed, still wondering what Ralph meant, and saw Amauri ride full-tilt into a green-splotched bog. We dismounted and heaved him out, dripping, muddy and quarrelsome. Nobody consoled him.

'You'll get a whipping for this,' I promised, surveying his ruined clothes.

'I?' Amauri inquired haughtily. 'Never! No one will touch me. I am Montfort.'

I grunted dubiously. My family was also noble, Dean Fulk from the House of Laigle. There are no degrees in nobility – only, as I discovered later, disparities in power – and a man whose lineage is unsullied, priest or pauper, is held respectable as Normandy himself. My pedigree, however, had never shielded me from Dame Orielde's strap, nor Dean Fulk's supple ash-rod. Amauri's vaunted immunity sounded unlikely.

The rain which the sergeant foretold descended in wind-lanced gusts and soaked us very thoroughly during the long ride home. We approached Evreux's outlying steadings, overtook peasants driving cattle and pigs, goats and sheep, their women staggering under household chattels. From every tenement they straggled towards Evreux like ants to a lump of dung. We looked at them incuriously – villeins are strange creatures, who behave in peculiar ways – but the sergeants frowned, rode over to them and spoke. They returned with urgency upon their faces.

'The alarm is out! Hurry, masters!'

We spurred our horses. A struggling welter of rank humanity and cattle and loaded carts choked the drawbridge. The sergeants whipped a passage; we entered the gate and heard horns braying from the donjon: a noise that blended raucously with the church bells ringing for vespers. Dame Orielde, white-faced, anxiously awaited my return, and said bitterly to her husband, 'You promised me no enemies today, my lord!'

'And none is with us yet,' Dean Fulk answered mildly. 'We take precautions, lady – that is all. King Philip and the French may come this way.'

5

Evreux's gates were closed, the bridges raised; sentries stalked the ramparts, spears glittered on the donjon. The town seethed, packed beyond capacity: peasants from surrounding farms lived, ate and slept in the streets; their animals crammed the yards. I peeped excitedly through the gap beside our apple tree – the new palisade bulged crookedly, obstructed by the trunk – expecting every day to see helmets gleaming from the forest, mailed horsemen riding the fields, smoke writhing from burning huts. The land lay empty, deserted save for a few animals abandoned to the enemy. But the enemy gave no sign and, somewhat disappointed, I questioned the dean.

'Disaster in the north,' he said. 'Baldwin of Flanders dead; his sons Arnold and Robert the Frisian fighting for succession. King Philip of France supported Arnold, called on Normandy for aid.' Dean Fulk smiled wryly. 'The Duke does not like being reminded he is France's liege. He sent a mere ten knights under William fitzOsbern, Governor of Normandy. Robert flayed Philip's army at Bavinchove, killed Arnold and fitzOsbern. A defeated rabble returns to France and may cross our marches. Count William – and Morin du Pin – are taking no chances.'

'They will sit inside Evreux and let Frenchmen ruin our lands?'

'Idiot boy! You have no idea of Count William's power – he commands formidable forces.' Dean Fulk spat, and wiped his hand across his mouth. 'If Philip burns a single byre he'll have a battle on his hands.'

Pent within the town after my newly-won freedom, I soon grew restive, and welcomed the return of Amauri and his friends. We haunted the apple-tree playground, played loggerheads and handball and took turns to practise with my bow – wherein lay the seeds of disaster. Though Isabel quickly became adept, and Amauri competent, Ralph of Conches was notably unskilful. We pretended to

13

take cover whenever he notched an arrow, and baited him remorselessly when he missed. One day – the sixth of our confinement –
infuriated by our teasing, he loosed so wildly that the arrow flew
over the palisade and vanished across the moat.

'My best arrow!' I shouted. 'You clumsy dolt!'

Ralph's rabbit-mouth quivered; tears started to his eyes. 'That
from you, you bastard brat! Go seek your shafts!' Before I could
move he snatched two more and despatched them over the ramparts.

Amauri dropped him with a swinging backhander, and he fell
squealing. I ran to the gap, peered through. Isabel crouched beside
me. We saw the arrows' banded crests flaunting like scarlet reeds on
the wet meadowland.

'I must recover them.' I set foot in the notch between tree and
stake and began to climb. Isabel pulled me down.

'You won't get far.' She pointed to a man-at-arms who leaned
negligently against the palisade, yawning and scrubbing his face.
Another watched from the bastion on our left. 'The sentries will
have you back. And how would you cross the water? Can you
swim?'

I looked at the stagnant, reed-fringed strip, ten paces wide. 'No –
but it's not deep. I have seen villeins wade across.'

Amauri came up, rubbing his knuckles, and jerked a thumb at
Ralph, gone blubbering to Hubert for consolation. 'He'll think twice
before doing that again – but you've lost your shafts.'

'I have not,' I asserted stubbornly. 'I shall fetch them after dark.'

Isabel looked at me, her eyes alight. 'You wouldn't dare!'

That was enough, as she well knew. I gritted my teeth. 'I'll go
tonight. It will be full dusk by compline; when the bells ring I shall
start.'

Amauri said, 'Don't be a fool. You'll get a throwing-spear in your
guts – the sentries are edgy after dark.'

'They always challenge first. Anyway, I'm going.'

Excitement danced in Isabel's face. 'You promise?'

I glowered at her. Amauri's chilly reminder had already cooled
my ardour; I was beginning to have doubts. You teasing bitch, I
thought – you'd be thrilled to see me spitted.

'Of course,' I answered loftily.

I cowered by the apple tree and looked into the dark. Bells clanged from Our Lady's tower; the versicles of compline droned faintly from the church. The night was warm and windless; stars pricked the sky, shed a dim silvered light that painted blacker shadows on the ground. Lights studded the town behind; the voice of a crowded populace murmured like distant surf. The sentry on my right hawked in a dry throat and stamped his feet; he was fifty paces away and hidden in the night. I breathed deep, gripped the palisade's top and set my foot in the crevice.

A hand felt my shoulder. I jumped like a prodded cricket and released my hold. A voice whispered, 'Let me go first, then you can help me up.'

'Isabel!'

I gripped her arms, and felt her riding garb: short tunic and leather breeches. She chuckled softly.

'Quiet, Walter! You'll alarm the watch.' She felt for the stockade's edge. 'Now lift me.'

I obeyed numbly, questions jostling in my mind. Why had she come? How had she evaded the castle guards, and made her way unescorted through the streets? The young of noble Houses did not wander unattended; a sergeant or at least a servant always accompanied the castle children to Dean Fulk's house. The questions went unanswered. I did not, then, quite appreciate Isabel of Montfort.

She vanished over the stakes. I followed, and crouched beside her on the grass. We wriggled like weasels down the bank, and reached the soggy margins of the moat. She put her lips to my ear.

'We'll have to strip.'

This, in my own plans, I had foreseen: I wore only a linen shirt and knee-long breeks. Thankful for the darkness, I shed my clothes, heard the faint rustle of leather alongside. I parted the reeds and slid cautiously into the water, shuddering at the icy shock. A hand grasped mine. We edged forward, a handsbreadth at a time, legs calf-deep in slimy mud. The water crept upwards, from navel to nipples to gullet. I checked, afraid. Isabel drew me on.

We reached the farther reeds, climbed from the water and lay on the bank, yearning to gulp air but afraid to breathe. Isabel's lips fluttered on my cheek; I felt her nakedness on mine.

'You've marked the arrows?'

'Yes. A little to our left.'

I crawled from the embankment's lip to the meadow beyond. Evreux's ramparts were a black blur behind us; her scattered house lights blended in a wan aurora. Moving on hands and knees, my body torn by brambles, stung by springtime nettles, I gathered two arrows, could not find the third. I went farther, heard Isabel following, hunted fruitlessly in bushes and tussocks.

'No good,' I murmured. 'We'll leave it.'

'We've come a long way,' Isabel said. 'They can't see us here.'

She stood, and I beside her, both hot and panting from our long, laborious crawl. Her body was a pale wraith in the starlight; she smelt of rank marsh water and warm girlhood. I knew an odd prickling beneath my skin, a sensation like a myriad minute needles. I gulped noisily.

'We must go back.'

She said, 'Not yet. Let's enjoy our freedom while we may. There's a copse beyond the meadows, across the sheep-folds, where we can be secure.'

She went, and I trailed after. Hand in hand we stumbled over the pasture, climbed wool-flecked wattle hurdles, entered the margins of a coppice whose bare-branched birch trees wove complicated traceries against the stars. She came to a small hollow, a moss-grown, grassy dell.

'We can rest here before returning.'

We lay together supine on the couch of moss, and gazed at the sky. We were warm from our exertions; the air was mild as a midsummer's noonday, the copse quiet and still save for a roosting pigeon which fluttered on a branch above our heads. Isabel pointed.

'Can you read the heavens, Walter? Is that the star called Venus?'

She dropped her hand, and touched me on a place I will not specify. I shuddered, and put my arms around her. A twig cracked sharply in the undergrowth. We froze, lay quiet as voles disturbed by a prowling cat.

A horseman threaded his way between the trees; the hooves trod noiselessly on winter's leafy carpet. He reined on the lip of the hollow and stared towards Evreux. I could have touched his horse's fetlock with my hand.

Starshine lighted a pointed helmet, glinted on the nasal which masked his features, reflected from the mail discs of his hauberk. A long shield dangled on his back; a pennon drooped limply from the lance athwart his body; the spearhead glittered like a pale blue flame. He was still as a graven statue – and I knew I looked upon the image of war.

We lay rigid, the breath choking in our throats. The destrier, aware of our nearness, sidled and fretted. He gentled it, still gazing towards the town. Then the lance-head dipped, and pointed in my face.

'Up!' he rasped.

We clambered to our feet, and stood shivering. The man peered into our faces, examined us from head to foot, and laughed.

'Full young for the joys of swiving! Whence do you come?' The voice was deep and resonant; the tones carried a youthful ring.

'Evreux,' I muttered miserably.

'Ha! Which is where I go – but not too near.' He paused, considering. 'You shall be my heralds – and decoy unfriendly arrows. Lead on!'

The point pricked my ribs; I took Isabel's hand and stumbled from the copse. We crossed plough-furrowed fields and sodden meadows, and saw Evreux's pallid halo. The warhorse plodded at our heels; the lance-head nudged my spine. A bowshot from the Vernon gate the knight halted, and urged us on.

He said, 'Go closer. Let's test the alertness of Count William's watch.'

We crept forward, hand in hand, shaking with fear, aware fully of our danger. The gate guard's challenge grated. The knight called loud and clear, 'Hola! My salutations to Count William! I restore you a brace of unfledged nestlings, fallen from your coop.'

The guard shouted. I heard the clang of arms, and men running to their stations. Arrows whirred like hornets. We flung ourselves flat and nuzzled the earth like burrowing fieldmice. The knight laughed.

'A gift from Robert of Belesme!'

Hooves thudded into the dark.

We called our names and pleaded with the guard. Our childish trebles offered reassurance; torches flared; after much commotion they lowered the bridge and opened a postern. Footsore, naked and ashamed, we shuffled through, trying not to hear the sniggers of the men-at-arms.

Dean Fulk, panting, dropped the rod.

'That for a start!' he snapped. 'A beginning only – I know not what the end may be. A disgusting business!'

I wept bitterly. The flogging – the worst I ever suffered – had broken my endurance. Blood trickled from the weals that scored my back.

'Stay here. I go now to the count, to learn his will. My honour in this matter is at risk!'

He took the horn lantern from its hook, and left the room. I stayed on hands and knees, and dribbled on the floor. Dame Orielde came, lit candles, found an ewer and washed my wounds. Tight-lipped, she smeared a salve; then brought fresh garments from a press. My shoulders cringed from the wool.

I stared blearily into the candle flames, fought against sleep, strove to forget the pain. Horns sounded the third watch before Dean Fulk returned. His face was lined and haggard; he spoke tiredly, the anger gone from his voice.

'The count is pleased to be lenient – but your time here is at an end. I am astounded at his clemency: you have publicly disgraced his House and the House of Montfort.'

'Father, I did not —'

He raised a hand. 'So you have sworn. I believe you – you are, I think, over young to achieve carnality. And, Walter, I am not your father.'

The candles wavered in a wandering wind-breath, a mouse scuttered beneath the rushes, a sound like dead leaves rustling. The words held no meaning for my weary mind.

'Count William bade me tell you.'

Dean Fulk dropped exhaustedly upon a stool, propped elbows on knees and gazed at his hands. 'Your story begins in the castle of Poix, on a day eleven years gone when Lord Walter wedded Albreda, daughter of Ralph of Gacé – him they call Tête d'Ane – who is uncle to Count William. A guest attended the festivities, a personable knight – I shall not name him; he is dead – and stayed a while after-wards in Lord Walter's mesnie. Like other household knights he paid court to the young bride: no more than the usual dalliance to beguile idle hours, poems and chansons and vows of devotion, lightly given and soon forgotten. The Lady Albreda was virtuous: she allowed no liberties.'

A trumpet bellowed faintly from afar, signalling the changing of the watch. Dean Fulk plucked a frayed thread on his sleeve.

'Lord Walter, even in those days, was a strange man, aloof and brooding. He watched his lady's innocent dalliance in bower and arbour, frowning and pulling his chin. At last, his jealousy erupting, he expelled from Poix the handsome knight. Soon afterwards the Lady Albreda bore a son.'

He looked at me under his eyebrows.

'You are that boy – Walter of Poix.'

I was beyond astonishment. Sleep tugged my eyelids; the tunic chafed the crusted weals upon my back; I clenched teeth on a yawn.

'Lord Walter professed to find a likeness in your infant face which was not his own. He led his men against the man he swore had fathered you, surprised his castle and slew him with his own hands. The knight, before he died, swore on the Rood his own guiltlessness and Lady Albreda's. Men on the threshold of eternity do not perjure their immortal souls. Everyone – save the lord of Poix – believed him. You are no bastard, Walter.'

He snuffed a guttering candle. The movement collected my senses, and I lifted a nodding head.

'The matter did not end there; the consequences linger yet. Lord Walter returned from his empty vengeance and drove from the castle his wife and new-born son. Lady Albreda fled to her kinsman, Count William of Evreux, who received her kindly. But the travails of a journey in midwinter, soon after childbed, brought a sickness on her so that in a little time she died. Count William, enraged by the slur upon his House, sent armed companies against Poix – but the castle is strong, Lord Walter at that time a resourceful knight. The count harried the lands and departed, lacking his full revenge. Then Duke William summoned him to Hastings and a kingdom's taking, and he has since let the matter slide. Poix, after all, is five days' march from Evreux. To Dame Orielde and myself he entrusted you, his infant relative.'

I said sleepily, 'Why have you not told me this before?'

Dean Fulk smiled sadly. 'The count decided your childhood should not be marred by knowledge of a bloody history. Circumstances – and your own foolery – have advanced the telling.'

'And Lord Walter, my . . . father?'

He sighed, and scratched pensively at a blister on his palm. 'He lives in Poix, aged beyond his years, a recluse who stirs seldom beyond the castle's pale. Poix is France's vassal, a marcher lord. King Philip, mistrusting a hermit's competence to guard his frontiers, sent to command the garrison one Baudri of Pontoise – a hard man, lacking scruple or remorse.'

A cock crowed lustily from the darkened town. Dean Fulk lumbered to his feet, stretched his arms till the sinews cracked. 'Nearly dawn – and time you found your bed.' He laid a gentle hand upon my shoulder. 'So that's who you are, Walter: Count William's kin and, through him, blood relative to Normandy himself. Heir also to Poix's lordship, your inheritance denied by a man who is not quite sane. Your future, with God's help, is in your hands. For you must leave Evreux. At noon I take you to the count, to hear his purpose.'

A remembrance twitched my mind. I opened smarting eyes. 'That knight who found us – Robert of Belesme . . .'

'A worthy scion of the House of Talvas,' Dean Fulk said grimly. 'Roger of Montgommeri's son by his witch-wife Mabille.' Involuntarily he signed himself. 'A cruel and wicked woman, a poisoner and enchantress – I pray that you may never cross her path. Robert is still a youth – I'd have thought him too young for knighthood.'

'He intended that Isabel and I should die.'

'He did. A typical Talvas twist – to contrive the death of children by their kinsmen's hands. Your Saints were vigilant.'

He snuffed the candles.

'Sleep well, my son. I shall not rouse you before terce.'

I tumbled to my pallet, and slept without dreams.

8

Even after all these years I can remember the terrified anticipation of my audience with Count William of Evreux.

Dean Fulk led me to the hall; we stood silently before the count, awaiting his attention. Dust motes danced like gilded fireflies in the shafts of sunlight lancing through lean windows. At the doorway a man-at-arms lolled on his spear; two knights indolently rolled dice on a trestle table, conversing in undertones; a mastiff snuffed for bones among the rushes. Count William, enthroned on the dais, scrabbled testily among parchment scrolls which littered the high table, and argued with Morin du Pin. His lady sat beside him, idly fingering a missal, turning the illuminated pages without interest. I trembled, and swallowed my spittle.

Count William and his castellan hotly disputed some detail concerning the distribution of guards on gates and ramparts. The count, plunking fragments of wheaten bread on the table top, defined his dispositions. Morin, black brows frowning above his swarthy face like a sable bar, stubbornly disagreed. The count swore roundly and swept his hands outwards in an explosive gesture, scattering parchment on the floor and crumbs on the spotless tunic I wore for the occasion. His watery blue eyes rested angrily on my face, blinked and cleared. He seemed glad of a diversion.

'Ha, Fulk!' Count William said. 'He has been well scourged, I trust?'

Dean Fulk answered gravely, 'Yes, my lord. I myself laid on the stripes.'

The count scratched his cheek; the bristles rasped. Morin du Pin sent me an irritable glance, took up again the interrupted wrangle. Count William forgot me, and disputed with him vehemently. The Lady Hawise tapped the missal on her lips to hide a yawn.

'The boy, my lord count,' she murmured.

'Hey? Ah, yes, the boy. A moment, Morin.' He leaned elbows on the table, and glared into my eyes. Oddly, there was no anger in his look. 'Listen to me, you shameless child!'

He summarized my character in scathing terms, said he had proposed despatching me to St Evroult, to the disciplines of a monastic house. But the dean had pleaded my lack of learning, that I had no bent for the religious life. 'Therefore,' the count blared, 'I shall not inflict on the good abbot an illiterate and lecherous novice.'

Countess Hawise seemed absorbed in her psaltery. I wondered what 'lecherous' meant.

Nor would he take me into his household, and so condone my precocious lewdness. In fact, the count continued, his leathery wattles quivering in simulated rage, he had considered kicking me from Evreux to find a living as best I may. Only my noble blood and extreme youth had saved me.

His lady lifted her lovely eyes and said tranquilly, 'Also the testimony of that wanton hussy who led him astray.'

'Isabel!' the count snapped. 'She returns to Montfort L'Amauri so soon as the roads are safe. Her brother with her – they are two of a kind. And you, boy – you shall go to Duke William's court, to learn an esquire's duties and discipline of a kind you never dreamed!'

He leaned back, drummed fingers on the table and looked at Dean Fulk. Although he scowled, the whisper of a smile was on his lips. 'The lad is my kin: I shall provide for his needs. Now take him away!'

9

The backwash of the defeat at Bavinchove, which had caused our confinement and consequent disgrace, never crossed Count William's territory. Only a small cortège passed mournfully beneath our ramparts, a sorrowing procession bearing William fitzOsbern's body to burial at Cormeilles. Evreux's gates were opened; three days later I rode for Rouen, escorted by a sergeant and a brace of servants.

I had not again seen Isabel, and wondered sadly whether she too was whipped.

Chapter 2

1072-74

The sergeant-of-arms spat heartily and filled his lungs.
'On guard! Cut right! Recover!'
The hilt twisted in my sweat-slippery hand. The sergeant strolled between the extended ranks, halted in front of me and leaned on his sword.
'Slow, master – very slow. I think you are idling. Let's have it again. Guard!'
My companions furtively watched me repeat the motions. My arm ached from fingertips to spine. The blunted practice blade – a man-size weapon: no concessions were granted to youthful muscles – weighed heavy as an oak-bough. Sweat trickled from my forehead, stung my eyes; the Tower's ward danced blurredly, like a picture glimpsed through rain. The sun had not yet risen; a river-mist hazed Rouen's rooftops; wagons rumbled distantly across St Sever's bridge. A watering party led horses through the castle gates. A pair of knights, one tall, one short and stout, reclined on hay bales and watched our drilling; they chewed grass stems and loudly criticized our clumsy strokes.
The sergeant finished commenting on my performance, marched to the front of the squad and surveyed us coldly. 'Your sword-cuts, masters,' he observed unkindly, 'are soft and harmless as an old man's prick. We have worked for barely an hour – how would you last a battle, fighting from prime to none?'
The rasp returned to his voice.
'Guard! Point left – lunge! Hold!'
The sergeant turned his back, sauntered away, discovered absorbing interest in a crow flying overhead. We crouched immobile, feet apart, knees straddling an imaginary saddle, swords extended in the lunge. The moments crawled; the blades dragged heavily, began to quiver. I sighted my sword point against a wood-knot on an

23

armoury door, strove to hold it there, saw the sword tremble and begin to sink.

The tall knight plucked a grass stalk from the bale, and nibbled it ruminatively. 'I'll wager you two deniers,' he said lazily to his friend, 'the brat in the green jerkin crumples first.'

'My money's on the black-haired clod in front,' the other answered. 'See – his blade is already sinking.'

I was the black-haired clod in front. The sweat coursed down my face and tickled my ribs. My arm shook; inexorably the point sank lower. The sergeant lost his crow, turned and examined us intently.

Iron clattered sharply. Someone, exhausted, had dropped his weapon. The sergeant snapped, 'Recover!' Wearily we rested blades on shoulders. He strode to the culprit. 'Unfit, that's what you are, master – unfit. You need exercise. Five circuits of the ramparts – run!' He watched the boy depart, smiled grimly, and ordered, 'Remainder – rest!'

We propped ourselves upon our swords. The knight spat out his straw and said, 'You owe me two deniers, Lisiard. Come to the stables – I'm tired of watching this horrible crew.'

They strolled away. The sergeant said, 'Attention! We will now practise the parry and cut nearside. Watch me. You flex the right wrist, thus...'

A chapel bell tolled prime. We screwed ourselves up to endure, for we would not rest till terce. Three hours to go. St Mary Jesus' Mother, I prayed silently, please send me strength.

2

The Tower of Rouen is a replica of London's Tower, which the Duke modelled on his Norman stronghold: those who have seen one will know the other. Stone-built, foursquare, four storeys tall, each floor holds a spacious hall whence lesser chambers – store-rooms, closets and passages – branch in complicated patterns; and stone stairways spiral in the thicknesses of walls. At first I was lost in this echoing maze, a sombre, gloomy citadel wherein daylight oozed reluctantly like coins from a miser's fist. Save for the topmost floor, where Duke William and his lady had their council room and bowers, the halls were always crowded, always noisy, resounding to the voices of knights and soldiers, varlets and scullions, to clanging mail and weapons and rattling pots and pans. I remembered Count William's wooden donjon at Evreux, and wagged my head in wonder.

The Tower's ward and ramparts confined a little world whose latitude extended to the riding school and tiltyard beside the Seine. For three strenuous years I saw little of the city, and heard its ferment from afar. Once, sent on an errand to the guard commander, I climbed the stairways to the battlements, and beheld Rouen spread below me like a map. Evreux was but a village in comparison. Walls of chiselled rock, hewn and bastioned by the Romans, stretched like enclosing arms eight hundred paces long; rooftops clustered close as pebbles upon a shingled beach; spires charged like spearheads to the sky. Vessels nudged the wharves and, sails bellying in the breeze, trailed arrow-heads downriver to the sea. Suburbs spilled beyond the river, across St Sever's bridge, a straggle of huts and hovels, unwalled and unprotected: a hostage, the guard constable said severely, following my gaze, to accidents of war. Then he cuffed me for an idle lout and sent me down.

The Bastard of Normandy – a secret name: they were starting to call him Conqueror to his face – was often in the Tower, more often not; affairs of state called him frequently to England or to Maine. I was nothing in his eyes: a maggot in the Tower's crawling flesh. I served him on bended knee at meals when he sat enthroned, his barons on either hand, and flinched from the flint-grey eyes, the frown on his balding forehead. Prince Robert, ripe for knighthood, was permitted to sit at table; Prince William Rufus waited at his father's shoulder: the torchlight flushed his face a deeper red. Henry the youngest I seldom saw: six years old, he stayed in his mother's bower. The barons also I knew by sight and title – I had to: you spoke to them by name when offering food – so that Montgommeri and Meulan, and Grantmesnil and Breteuil (of whom the last pair were my future companions in fortune and adversity) became familiar to my eyes as the moon and stars – and equally remote.

The tables were always full, the faces constantly changing. Noblemen and prelates brought their problems to the Duke, and waited on his judgement, for Rouen was the centre of an empire. An esquire in waiting had to register their faces in his mind and remember their styles and titles. Ralph of Mont-Pinçon, the Duke's steward – a plump, unctuous man we all disliked – used to assemble the esquires on duty before the meal. Peering the length of the smoke-hazed hall, we listened to his roll-call and tried to join names and faces: a matter of importance, since an error meant a whipping. Thus, about two months after my coming, I linked lined and haggard features to Count Simon of Montfort L'Amauri, and saw Amauri standing behind him.

He and I talked hastily at the kitchen door, taking dishes from the scullions.

'Why are you here?'

'To enter the Duke's household.'

'The Saints help you!' I said fervently. 'Listen: meet me at the well-head in the ward, and bring your baggage. Then I'll find you sleeping-space within the hall.'

The company dispersed, the lords to chambers in the Tower or quarters in the city, the knights and men-at-arms to rest wherever they could: beneath or upon the trestle tables, in passages and garderobes. The hearth fire crumbled gently into ashes. The ceiling was a canopy of smoky darkness, the floor a hummocky sea of sleeping men who snored and muttered in their dreams, their bodies huddled in rows like corpses after a sack. Draughts stirred the rushes, swayed the tapestry behind Duke William's empty throne. I shivered and drew my wolfskin closer. Amauri stirred beside me.

'Can't you sleep?' he murmured.

'No.'

'Nor I. Your bedchamber stinks like a privy.'

'That's what it is.'

For winter sleeping I had found a niche carved for some forgotten purpose in the outer wall, adjacent to the privy's vent – which is why no one wanted it. I was not fussy; and the little cave protected me from feet stumbling in the dark. Here I had led Amauri, and helped him unbind his bundle. Like all of us, he brought few possessions: a cloak and a change of garments, riding boots and a bearskin coverlet. The less you owned the less you had to lose: thievery was rampant.

I whispered, 'I'm glad you've come. I thought you'd stay in your father's house until you were knighted.'

'No. He was furious when Count William sent me from Evreux. No fault of mine.' He sounded cross. 'All due to that hoyden Isabel. And you, of course. I have been brought to Rouen to learn discipline – as a punishment.'

'I also. A heavy penance, Amauri.'

'Is it bad?'

'Bad enough. We are driven like beasts from dawn to dusk.'

'We? How many more?'

'Thirty or so, children of noble Houses in Normandy and Maine. A few from England. None older than fourteen.'

A rat ran over my hand. I slammed it with a wood-stave that I kept, and heard it squeak.

Amauri said, 'How long will our training last?'

'Three years. Until we're fourteen. Then, if I'm lucky, some baron will accept me in his retinue. I suppose you'll go back to Montfort.'

Someone shouted in his sleep and threshed his arms. His neighbour, cursing, thumped him.

I said hesitantly, 'Isabel – what happened to her?'

Amauri grunted. 'The Countess Hawise talked to her alone in her bower. I don't know what happened – Isabel wouldn't say. She hardly spoke for days.' He yawned. 'A strange person, my sister. The best horseman I know, and nearly as good with a bow as you are, Walter. More boy than girl. If I hadn't seen her stark' – straw rustled as he turned his head; I knew he grinned in the dark – 'I'd sometimes doubt her sex.'

A man crept near the entrance to our den. I lay quite still, eyes probing the gloom. In the past I had been twice awakened by a crouching figure dim in the firelight, jerky breathing and groping, sweaty hands. They were always knights – no base-born sergeant would have dared to touch us – hoping for complaisance and an hour of love. It was easy to repulse them, threatening uproar – my stave was not kept solely for killing rats. The Duke dealt hardily with sodomites; they could not afford discovery.

The man went by; we heard him void his bowels in the privy. The sickness in my belly eased; I swallowed bile. Amauri squawked, and beat with his hands.

'Hell-spawned rat! It bit my ear!'

'You'll get used to it. There's worse than rats in Rouen.'

'Yes.' His voice was subdued. 'Our tutors. Walter, have they – the knights and sergeants who instruct us – ever made you blubber?'

It was not what I had meant. I said, 'No. I've been near to it.'

'I thought not. You're not the crying kind. I wish I were as tough.'

He turned on his side and pulled the coverlet to his ears. 'You'll help me, Walter?'

'There's no help for anyone here,' I answered heavily, 'save in himself.'

The farrier said, 'One of the Duke's stallions – so watch yourselves!'

A rope knotted to an iron ring secured the roan's forehand. Two esquires gripped the headstall; the horse sawed his head, almost lifting them from the ground. I wore a blacksmith's apron, over-large for my meagre frame, which drooped to my ankles, and grasped a heavy rasp in a hand too small to hold it. Cautiously I bent to lift the near hind foot. The animal snorted, lashed out; the hoof scraped my cheekbone, sent me flying across the forge. The farrier laughed; his mate, pumping a bellows which roared the furnace, grinned sardonically. I picked myself up and wiped blood from my face.

'Try again,' the farrier grunted. 'Face his tail and run your hand from hock to fetlock.'

I obeyed. The stallion flattened his ears, rolled his eyes: the esquires clung to his head. I lifted the hoof, straddled it quickly as I was taught, scraped rasp on horn. The leg heaved and plunged beneath me. Encouraged by the puny weight, the destrier straight-ened his hock with a vicious jerk that hurled me headfirst through the open door. Gravel ripped skin from palms and forearms; I lay in the dirt and gnawed my lip to restrain the tears. A hand descended on my shoulder and hauled me to my feet.

'Twice is enough,' the owner said. 'You're too young to cope with that brute. Riou,' he told the farrier, 'start him on a kinder animal, or you'll have a dead esquire on your hands.'

A smile lighted the differently coloured eyes – one blue and one amber – and creased the round red face which gave him the name of Rufus. Duke William's son and namesake, two years older than myself and lately escaped from the purgatory where the younger esquires lived. We admired him from a distance, his burly muscular frame, his skill at arms and horsemanship, and revered him as a paladin. He seldom cuffed or kicked us like others of his kind.

'I'll show you how it's done. Give me your rasp and apron.'

Riou the farrier said anxiously, 'Better not, my lord. The stallion has never been shod.'

'Yet you inflict him on these babies,' Rufus answered cheerfully. 'I also am an esquire – and need no privilege.'

He slapped the horse's muzzle hard, ran a hand from withers to rump, lifted the fetlock and gripped it between his thighs. The

animal humped and tried to kick; Rufus danced on the leg, rolling a
rich stream of oaths, and went on rasping. He finished, examined
the hoof, and dismounted from his plunging perch.

'There,' he said. 'The horn's level and true. Now fit the shoe.'

I tonged a shoe from the furnace, lifted one-handed the dangerous
leg, felt muscles contract for the kick. Rufus slapped the muzzle
again, hauled on the horse's ear.

'Go on,' he urged. 'He'll stand quiet.'

Hot iron pressed on horn; a bitter burning stench pervaded the
smithy. I inspected the scorch-marks; the shoe fitted exactly. The
farrier took the pincers and plunged the shoe in a bucket. Water
hissed and steam-clouds wreathed. Rufus released his hold and
patted the destrier's neck.

'An amiable slug,' he said breezily. 'You'll meet worse than him
before you've done. Walter of Poix, aren't you? Mark this, Walter:
never be afraid of a horse – they know at once. And there's a deal of
nonsense talked about gentling horses. If you meet a savage, treat
him like one.'

He lurched from the smithy – Rufus moved like a mariner walking a storm-tossed deck – and waved farewell. I watched him go,
gratitude and reverence contending in my mind. The farrier brought
me sharply to my senses.

'Wake up, master. You've still to nail the shoe. Three things
young gentlemen must learn before their knighting: ride a horse,
groom a horse, shoe a horse. You've a long way to go for the
last.'

I found hammer and nails; and firmly slapped the stallion's nose.

4

The Tower's armoury was a large and gloomy chamber where light
strained through slender arrow-slits in twenty-span-thick stone walls.
Mail coats drooped on racks like grey skins flayed from corpses;
spears leaned against the walls; arrow-sheaves rested on shelves;
battle swords and the short dirks used by men-at-arms dangled from
hooks. A cresset sputtered sulkily; the wavering flame flashed a
galaxy of light-sparks from blade and point and edge.

'There are sixteen hundred discs or rings in the average hauberk,'
said the sergeant armourer. 'Each must be sanded separately till it's

bright as a baby's bum. And be careful of this mail coat – it belongs to the Count of Breteuil.'

I bent over the beechwood table where the hauberk lay spread-eagled, dabbed my dampened deerskin in sea-sand heaped on a platter and scrubbed a disc. A rust fleck yielded, the grime dissolved, the disc glittered like a star. The armourer inspected it critically.

'Good enough,' he grunted, 'but you'll have to work faster than that or you'll take all day. An hour to clean a hauberk – that's the standard. Wipe those sand grains from the gambeson.'

He stumped away, a squat, leathery man, an eye-socket shrunk and shrivelled, his nose crushed flat by a mace. Thirty esquires polished thirty mail coats at the long low table. Nobody spoke very much – the sergeant discouraged chatter. The work was finicky and laborious, tiring to hand and wrist; the sand rubbed our fingers raw, our eyes smarted from strain and torch-smoke. The air was warm and oppressive – in winter bitingly cold – and we were thirsty; our bellies rumbled, for we were always hungry. But we would neither eat nor drink until the hauberks, scoured to diamond brightness, passed the armourer's ruthless scrutiny. That done, and every speck of sand removed, we wiped the discs with an oily cloth – good olive oil. Not finished yet – we rubbed mutton fat inside the leather gambesons, then wiped them clean: an awkward, fumbling job, since the coats could not be turned inside out. Then they were hung once more upon their racks.

The helmets remained: more scouring, polishing and oiling. A few were gaudily painted to distinguish the wearer in battle: a custom then beginning to prevail. These we handled gratefully – they could not be scoured. The armourer scowled, swore that paint corroded iron, the habit a mere foppery, a mark of decadence since Hastings.

Then the tall shields strung in rows. We oiled limewood frames, greased hides and enarmes, polished copper rivets. Sometimes the bosses were painted or the frames picked out in colour; the sergeant contrarily approved and, were the blazons chipped or faded, insisted we renew them. The hours passed; the torch smoked vilely; our eyelids drooped and stung.

The swords. We scrubbed blades with soft dry leather – you do not use sand on swords – burnished hilts and pommels. The armourer thumbed the edges, ground nicked or blunted blades on the big grey stone while two of us worked the treadles: he would not allow tyros to whet the swords of knights. The dirks we sharpened ourselves: he stood over us blaspheming, dripping water on the stone, damning our crass ineptitude and doubting our noble ancestry.

We finished, put away cloth and leather, oil and fat, swept up the sand, cleaned table and floor. The sergeant found imaginary blemishes, demanded last-minute tasks. At last he let us go. We stumbled wearily down a winding stairway to the Tower's single portal, and blinked like fledgling owlets in the sunlight's westering rays.

5

The younger knights played a game with us that they called 'Middens'.

The Tower's privies, set high in the walls, streaked slimy fans on the stone and vented ordure into the dry fosse below. The years since Duke William's building had piled mounds of excrement within the ditch; and it amused our seniors to corral stray youngsters in the fosse and throw them into the muck.

The game had rules. You were given an old spear-shaft for defence – these relics of former contests littered the ditch – and your opponents carried horse-whips, long plaited leather thongs. The battle was unequal, for you were outnumbered, your adversaries older and stronger, and the whips outreached the staves. If you escaped from the ditch you were safe – otherwise, the midden.

They cornered Amauri and myself one April afternoon and hustled us into the fosse. We snatched up staves and faced the enemy, a dozen brawny oafs who laughed and flicked their whips. Relentlessly they herded us towards the stinking, steaming mound that climbed the wall.

'Hola! Close for the kill!'

For an instant the daylight went; I stood naked in a springtime night and cringed from the whirr of arrows. A rider whose mailcoat gleamed in the starshine, a musical bell-toned voice.

This was the man.

Black-haired, green eyes in an ivory face, pale lips thin as knives. Tall, wide-shouldered, lean. A black velvet tunic, gold-embroidered, and supple Cordovan boots. He swung his whip negligently; then lashed for my eyes like a striking snake.

I ducked and charged.

31

Thongs scorched my face and shoulders. I lunged at the velvet tunic. A foot crashed into my belly, and I fell retching on the grass. Amauri straddled my body, spear-shaft lifted.

'Enough, Robert!'

I finished vomiting, and raised my head. Rufus stood on the lip of the fosse, frowning, hands on hips, his hair a golden halo in the sun.

'You kicked him. Against the rules. The boy has earned his sanctuary, so let him go.'

Belesme slowly ran the whip through his fingers. 'I have never believed in rules,' he said carelessly. 'They get in the way.' He struck Amauri down, and lifted me effortlessly above his head. He laughed and straightened his arms. I squelched in the ordure.

Rufus descended the slope, setting his feet carefully on slippery grass. His hand crept to the dagger at his belt, rested on the hilt. Belesme, unmoving, watched him coming. Our tormentors drew away and gathered in a group, silent and serious: one did not lightly defy the Conqueror's sons.

Belesme said, 'Be careful, William.' He sounded amused.

Rufus glared. Anger tripped his speech. 'A p-pity duelling is forbidden to esquires,' he stammered. 'If I were a knight I'd f-fight you sword to sword.'

Rufus had lost his temper, and in doing so shed his dignity. Later, when manhood and authority lent him stature, he was fearful in his rages; at this moment Belesme's easy demeanour seemed more impressive. He answered lightly, 'You'll have to wait a little. Meanwhile, why quarrel over a crapulous brat?'

Deliberately he turned his back, and sauntered away. His companions followed. Amauri reached me a hand; I struggled from the filth and tried to clean myself. I felt sick and humiliated, and strangely disappointed. The paladin I revered was somehow worsted.

Rufus met my eye, and read my thoughts. The anger went from his face and left it sullen. 'Should have used my dagger,' he muttered, half to himself, 'and rid the world of a Talvas. Insolent —'

'My lord!'

A priest stood at the top of the bank. Rufus said, 'Come down, Ranulf.'

The man descended the steep scarp, moving gracefully as a cat. We knew him well: Ranulf surnamed Flambard from the flaming thatch which surrounded his tonsure. Luminous deepset eyes surveyed Amauri and me briefly and dismissed us, rested thoughtfully on the prince.

'By your favour, my lord, a word with you.'

The Duke, they said, appointed Flambard as his son's spiritual mentor after Lanfranc went to England: if so, it was an odd choice – a more unlikely clerk I never met. He was talkative and witty, his manners gentle despite his breeding: the father a low-born Bayeux priest, his mother reputed a witch. He drew Rufus apart, talked rapidly, his hands gesturing in emphasis.

'. . . can't afford to quarrel . . . Montgommeri safeguards Maine . . . more politic, my lord . . . risk the Duke's displeasure . . .'

Rufus listened, eyes on the ground, his full lips downturned at the corners. I knew him to be impatient of advice, and awaited an explosion. Instead he nodded, smiled, and slapped Flambard's shoulder.

'Very well, Ranulf. I must learn to curb my temper.'

He looked at me and grinned.

'Walter,' he declared, 'you stink. Come to the bathhouse.'

6

The grey palfrey owned an iron mouth, a spine-jolting trot, and an inexorable resolution to follow the animal ahead. The saddle-flaps were cracked and hard, my stirrup leathers much too long. Straw dummies and swinging quintains dotted the exercising field beyond Rouen's eastern gate; thirty esquires circled the riding track in single file. Dust whitened our clothes and drifted over the Seine.

'Walter of Poix – circle right!'

I pulled the rein; my spurless heels drummed the grey's serrated ribs. He snorted and bore straight on, muzzle to rump of the chestnut trotting in front. I tugged without effect; and yearned for the skewbald pony who grazed on Evreux's meadows far away.

'Ride – halt!'

The grey stopped instantly at the command; the saddle's pommel stabbed my crutch. The green-eyed knight who instructed us left the centre of the ring and walked his horse towards me.

'Well, dog-turd,' Belesme said pleasantly, 'have you never forked a saddle before?'

We had all ridden since we could remember, which he well knew. This did not seem the moment to remind him. I kept silent.

'Answer me, carrion!' A backward sweep of his cutting-whip slashed my face. Blood trickled from a broken lip and salted my tongue.

'I have,' I muttered. This was a hazard we endured in the riding school, where the instructors were always knights. A sergeant would never have dared strike you – but horsemanship was too important to be taught by sergeants.

'So? Not ignorance, then – just sheer incompetence. You all need waking up.'

He cantered away, reined and swung about.

'Ride – dismount!'

We dropped to the ground, stood by our horses' heads.

'To the front – mount!'

Each of us raced to the palfrey ahead, scrambled to the saddle.

'To the front – mount!'

Down and up. Again and again. Down and up. Belesme cracked his whip and shouted. We bobbed from saddle to saddle like dummies jerked by ropes. Somebody's fingers scrabbled hopelessly on leather, at a saddle too tall for his mounting. He fell and lay there sobbing. Everard of Rai, it was, as I remember – a pleasant boy, light-boned and frail, barely twelve years old. Belesme flogged him as he lay.

'That,' he observed impassively, 'should rub the sleep from your eyes. Mount!'

The work continued, trot and canter, circle and turn. The saddle skinned my thighs, the reins blistered my fingers. The dust-misted riding school, the trees that fringed the river, and the frowning grey-stone curtain of Rouen's walls began to tremble ominously before my eyes. Sweat stung my blood-caked lips. Everard fell again, stayed motionless and disregarded; our horses cantered over and around him.

'Turn – left! Circle – right! Halt! Rein back! Canter-r-r!'

He halted us at last; we held our horses' withers and fought for breath. Belesme surveyed us coldly. 'You think you need a rest. You don't – but your horses do. Dismount. Lead to the Trojan Horse.'

We plodded wretchedly to a lofty wooden dummy, a contraption made from a wine-cask mounted on wheels. An ancient battle saddle was strapped across the cask; some humorist in days gone by had nailed two rounded pebbles in a bag between the after legs. Why the thing was named as it was we never knew.

'Four of you ready to push, and you' – his finger pointed – 'take the lance and mount.'

I sat coffined between pommel and cantle, legs straight, feet thrusting on the stirrups, toes pointed down, cantle rammed on spine. The lance – a headless ten-foot shaft – I tucked in rest beneath my arm. (Older knights who saw us puffed their lips contemptuously. They still preferred the overarm thrust they had used at Hastings.) I levelled the point at the target: a solid oaken block on top of a rigid stake.

'Charge,' Belesme ordered.

Four youthful shoulders shoved the heavy machine; the wheels creaked; the Trojan Horse trundled twenty paces towards the target. My lance point gouged the wood; the shock jarred spine on cantle, strained arm and shoulder. The wheels crunched to a standstill.

The whip cracked viciously. 'Push!'

I clenched my jaws. This was a torture inflicted by our more venomous tutors: normally, if you resisted the first shock and forced the 'horse' to a stand, the stint was ended. Now for endurance. The pressure increased: the cantle bruised my back, my muscles quivered. The lance slid through my fingers.

'Useless! You'll never withstand the brunt of a charge if you can't do better than that! Next one up!'

It was that same morning, I believe – or maybe another: my memories of those testing months are blurred, like nightmares half-remembered after waking – that Belesme drove us to the river to swim our horses. Though the passage to the Island of the Cross was a hundred paces wide, only fifty were beyond the horses' depths, for the banks shelved gently. It was enough; few of us could swim. We kicked our mounts girth-deep into the water, slipped from the saddles and trailed alongside, gripping manes and pommels, steering the animals by splashing their faces. Belesme led us, disdaining to dismount, riding like a centaur half submerged. Spluttering and thankful, we reached the island safely; the trouble happened on the journey back. Young Turgis of Medavi lost his hold and disappeared. None of us could help him; our own struggles kept us busy. Belesme saw, turned his horse and plunged again into the river. Turgis surfaced briefly, once, beyond his reach, then vanished.

They found his body below the bridge on the following day.

So Turgis left us, and some thought him lucky: he had gone without dishonour. There was no easy escape for boys who aspired to knighthood, no way, when committed to esquiredom, to retrace one's course without disgrace. Everard, I recollect, fled by night from Rouen and returned to Rai; he was sent at once from Normandy to an abbey at Limoges, and bade the world farewell from a monastic cloister. Another youngster, unable to endure – we had watched him cracking for weeks; it needed only Belesme to drive him over the brink – also vanished from our company; years later, it was said, someone saw him with a band of strolling players. A few died by accident or disease – the summer in Rouen brought a bowel flux, the winter a wasting sickness – and the rigours of our training drove some to a mindless stupor, so that they existed like mummers' puppets, dancing to the strings of custom and command. Thus the weaklings were ruthlessly winnowed – which I suppose was the intention – but our numbers remained constant: ten- or eleven-year striplings flowed unceasingly to Rouen. Some came from recalcitrant barons, as hostages for good behaviour. But entry to Normandy's household was eagerly sought: an esquire might attract Duke William's notice, be knighted at his hands, gain his favour and, perhaps, a fief. The harshness of his discipline was notorious throughout Neustria, the prizes of survival well worth winning.

I survived, and Amauri also. The savage routine of days and months and years stripped puppy-fat from our bodies and softness from our minds. We learned to wield lance and sword, ride the fiercest stallions foaled, endure wounds and agony without complaining. We were arrogant in success and merciless to failure. We trod the brutal pathway to fulfilment of ambition, to acceptance in a brotherhood which embraced all Christian nations, to be one of those terrible fighting machines which men call knights.

7

The war in Maine did not concern us; we were too young to go campaigning. Nor did we have much chance of learning why it happened: we were far too busy. Rufus, since the incident during the game of 'Middens,' often sought me out: I gained the impression that he thought I needed protection, and a friendliness developed between us. From him I gathered vaguely that Geoffrey of Mayenne, restive under Normandy's rule, persuaded Count Fulk of Anjou to expel Duke William's garrisons in Mans. The Angevin John of La Fleche called for the Duke's help; Count Hoel of Britanny supported Fulk. It all seemed very complicated. An army mustered at Rouen, tents and pavilions sprouted like toadstools on the meadows, and stranger barons thronged the Tower. Ralph of Mont-Pinçon ordered yet more tables to be set in the hall – a feat I did not think possible – harassed the cooks and scullions, and chased the young esquires like a sheepdog herding ewes. Duke William held great state; every dinner was a banquet. He allowed his duchess and her ladies to sit at the high table, a privilege normally kept for feast days such as Pentecost and Easter. We spent breathless hours scurrying between board and kitchen, carrying heavy silver dishes: swans roasted whole in their feathers, herons garnished with leeks and chervil, venison in honey sauce, salmon stewed in wine. We poured clove-spiced wine and metheglin, cider and ale and must. If the ovens had been on the battlements, as was usual in lesser donjons, our task would have been impossible; but Duke William's kitchens were in the ward – he kept separate top-floor ovens for heating missiles.

The feasting remained quite decorous until the women withdrew; then the wine flowed faster, the minstrels' songs became bawdy, their jests obscene. The Duke sat a little longer, drinking watered wine from Auvergne, conversing with his vassals, the granite eyes roving restlessly from face to face. When he rose from the table the bishops also departed; and the knights at the trestles grew rowdier. Some became maudlin, or fell and sprawled snoring; a few were quarrelsome. One night a dagger flashed in the torchlight, blood spurted from a throat. The killer was too drunk to flee; next day his body dangled from Duke William's gallows.

The Count of Evreux brought his mesnie to Rouen. In the three years since my going the count had aged; he was greyer and more shrunken. He did not recognize me when I served him; bashfully I spoke my name, and thanked him for the fustian cloak he sent at Martinmas, the calfhide shoes at Christmas. He put fingers to my chin and turned my face to the candles.

'Ha! The fledgling chick has become a fighting bantam!' He prodded my chest and felt my biceps, like a coper inspecting a horse. 'Hard and tough, and you've grown a span! Still handy with a bow, hey?'

'I practise when I have the time, my lord.'

'Good, good! Simon,' he said to his neighbour, 'this lad can put three arrows in a handsbreadth before you can breathe twice. They call him Tirel, as I remember.'

The Count of Montfort L'Amauri dropped his mutton bone on a platter and wiped his fingers. 'So? Is this the boy? Amauri has spoken

often of his skill.' He glanced at Count William, and smiled wryly.
'The cause, if I have the story right, of my daughter's sudden return
to Montfort.'

I flushed, and fervently wished myself elsewhere.

'Tut!' Count William looked embarrassed. 'That was a long while
ago, and maybe I was hasty.'

'Water under the bridge,' Count Simon agreed tolerantly. (Much
later I realized that the greater the baron, the less fidgety on points
of honour: they fought for things that really mattered: land and
castles, wealth and power. Only petty lordlings battled over
niceties.) 'And the girl is safely bridled now – betrothed to Ralph of
Conches. They shall be wed when he is knighted.'

The pitcher dropped from my fingers, wine dribbled on a patterned drugget woven by Spanish Moors. Count William fumed;
an esquire pushed me aside, muttering, and dabbed his linen napkin
on the mess. I knelt beside him, pretended to assist.

Amauri was in the kitchens, and nodded glumly when I told him.
'I know. The match has always been intended. A shrewd alliance;
Ralph is heir to Conches and a dozen fiefs besides.'

He eyed a varlet pouring broth into a brazen bowl. 'Not over-full,
halfwit,' he snapped, 'else how shall I carry it? Isabel,' he continued,
'has come to Rouen in my father's train, and lodges at the house of
Conan. She leaves for Montfort at prime tomorrow.'

'Where does this Conan live?'

'Don't be a fool, Walter. We parade at dawn – you won't have
time. Anyway —' He looked at my face, and sighed. 'As you will.
It's a big gabled house, next to St Peter's church in the Street of
Cutlers.'

8

I slipped through a postern gate in the darkness before sunrise. The
guard knew me well, believed my story of an assignation and
bawdily wished me luck. I crept through unfamiliar streets, found
the building easily and waited beside the portal. A streak like burnished copper washed the eastern sky and paled the stars; a cowled
monk went by, muttering over his beads; an ox-cart rumbled past
me in the gloom; peasants departed for St Sever's fields, silent figures
shadowy as ghosts. Voices called from Conan's shuttered courtyard;

torches flared and horses stamped and sidled. The great bell of the cathedral tolled for prime: the clangour rolled like thunder over the roofs. I crouched beside the gatepost and shivered in the dawn-wind's icy breath.

The gates creaked open; horsemen clattered beneath the arch-way, men-at-arms and bowmen, an armoured knight. A man richly garbed – ermine edged his cloak, gold glittered in the texture of his tunic – walked beside a palfrey. The rider stretched a hand and gave farewell. 'My thanks to you, master Conan.' I ran to her stirrup.

Stooping from the saddle, she peered into my face, and held me eye to eye for one long instant. Her face was thinner than my memory pictured, the cheekbones higher, eyes blacker, slanting at the corners, the lashes longer. Her lips parted in a smile, white teeth gleamed in the sun-tanned face.

'A moment, messire Conan.'

She slid from the saddle, gripped both my hands and laughed delightedly. She was tall as I, slim and lithe; the leather doublet and breeches clung to her like a skin. All the pretty speeches I had invented fled from my mind like dreams at cockcrow, and I stood there stuttering.

'After all the years, no word for me . . . Tirel?'

I squeezed her fingers hard, and found my voice.

'Were you . . . whipped?'

The question probed three springtimes gone: she nodded and answered at once. 'Twice. By that hell-bitch Hawise, and then my mother. They both hurt.'

'I am sorry. The fault was mine.'

'I've no regrets. Wasn't it worth it, Walter?'

I remembered her touch on my body, and flushed. 'I would venture again, with you. Anywhere, with you. Isabel —!'

'Hush, Walter. They are listening. I know what you would say. Not now, not here. Our time will come.'

'How is it possible? You are betrothed.'

A sunbeam brushed the housetops and lighted her face. The smile was gone. 'That jackanapes? Ralph will be my husband – never my master.'

I shook my head. Women did not speak so of the men they married. Isabel, I decided, was still young, untaught, unaware of the code that ruled our world.

I had much to learn.

She leaned closer and spoke softly. Her breath was warm upon my cheek. 'Walter, you must find me again. Will you swear it?'

Like a knight swearing fealty to his suzerain, I held her hand between my palms. 'I promise. You have my oath and faith.'

'Farewell... Tirel.'

Isabel swung quickly to the saddle, motioned her escort on. The cavalcade clattered beneath the arch; she did not look back. The man called Conan surveyed me quizzically; a smile twitched the corners of his mouth. 'You keep early trysts. Whence do you come, boy?'

He was young, gold-haired, handsome, a merchant by his manner, and clearly wealthy. Prince Henry, many years after, threw him to his death from Rouen's Tower.

'From the donjon, my lord.'

He laughed. 'An escapade, I think. You'd better return quickly, else you'll meet trouble.'

I arrived late for sword drill, pleaded a gripe in the bowels, and was duly thrashed.

9

The Duke departed with his army into Maine, and stayed all summer. Rufus went with him: I missed his scarlet face and yellow hair, his friendly humour and companionship. The Tower seemed nearly deserted; echoes clanged from pillar to pillar and rebounded from vaulted ceilings. In truth Duke William left an adequate garrison, mostly mercenary soldiers whom he could trust – men who served for money and lacked ambitions to grasp the rungs of power in his absence. In July my rigorous training ended, and I had leisure to mingle with these knights. They were iron men, chiefly Bretons and Flemings, a few from Gascony or France, landless, their fiefs escheated by rapacious lords or ruined by the ravages of war. Most were gently bred, some not. Their calling stamped them with a common brand, a likeness in appearance and behaviour. All were shaven close on lips and jowls and neck; all wore the 'cloven hoof,' a sunbrowned segment from brow to mouth which coif and helmet left exposed, cleft by pale noses which the nasals guarded. They were taciturn when sober, expansive when in wine; and I heard grisly histories of siege and sack.

During these last months of training we learned an esquire's duties to his lord in war and peace. We were taught to cook, both in the Tower's ample kitchens and the field, where we brewed simple dishes over fires built of twigs. We knew how to look after armour: now we discovered the arts of cleaning and pressing garments, the correct folding of a mantle, repairing shoes and breeches. We learned to make all sorts of beds, from fur-lined feather mattresses to bracken pallets for campaigning. In battle, we were told, you followed your lord at a wary distance wherever he rode, remounted him were he unhorsed, gave him your horse if his was killed, dragged him from the fray if he were wounded. It sounded more perilous than in fact it was: no proper knight would knowingly kill an esquire – retaliation was too simple – unless, of course, he broke the rules and joined the fighting. There was always the risk of arrows or a blood-maddened man-at-arms; but you wore a haubergeon, carried a sword and burned candles to your guardian saint.

We enjoyed this routine's leniency after three years' savage discipline. We wandered the streets and market, and gaped wide-eyed at the hucksters shouting their wares – wax and pepper and spice, braided belts and cloth of sendal – the money-changers offering jewels and plate, the fiddlers and singers and wandering mountebanks leading leopards and dancing bears. We entered taverns, drank raw unwatered wine and were sick in the gutters.

We discovered women.

Here I must make plain that our lives under Duke William's rule had hitherto been ascetic as a novice's penned in a cell. Women we indeed encountered, on three different levels: the highborn ladies who attended the Duchess; their attendant tirewomen; and the sluts infesting castle-ward and kitchen. The ladies ignored us totally: we stood lower in their regard than the vermin they plucked from their heads. Some of us played furtively with kitchen-maids in saddle-rooms, and afterwards related lurid lies.

Now, according to a custom which reigned among Rouen's esquires, we were ritually deflowered. Four drunken louts – rough bumpkins who attended Flemish knights – hunted Amauri and me through alleyways and herded us to a brothel near the Gate of Apollonius: a thatched and wattled stew where tumbled blankets heaved in corners and cobwebs hung like grave-clothes from the rafters. They stripped my breeches, forced me to a grinning doxy sprawling, thighs spread wide, on the feculent floor. I was angry and ashamed, quite unable to perform; but the wench was kind and lustily proclaimed my prowess, rolling her eyes and gasping in pretence. The esquires beat my back and cheered; someone emptied a winecup over my head. Then they grabbed Amauri. He shrugged himself free and loftily demanded that a table should be brought. He threw the slut on the greasy planks, disdainfully did the swiving that was needed, looked coldly at our tormentors and stalked from the room. I stumbled after, yearning miserably for a tenth of his composure.

'Did you . . . succeed?' I asked him later.

Amauri grinned. 'Why not? One must always find *some* pleasure in adversity.'

10

In September Duke William returned to Rouen. Rufus found me at the butts where I practised daily, and eagerly described the events of his first campaign. The Duke had crossed the marches of Maine in the south-east, stormed Fresnai after a stubborn leaguer and cut off his prisoners' sword-hands: a measure which so depressed Fulk's garrison in Mans that they surrendered without a fight. At Mayet south of the Loire the Angevins offered battle, but Count William of Evreux, at the Duke's bidding, led an embassy to Fulk and arranged a truce. 'Spoiling sport, I call it,' Rufus growled. 'I was hoping for the biggest fight since Hastings. However, my father was probably right. Battles are chancy affairs – you can never tell how they'll go.' The truce lasted, and led to a treaty of peace. Fulk of Anjou ceded his lands in Maine to Robert, heir to Normandy, in return for the latter's homage. Robert the prince became Count of Maine – and in so doing altered my life.

I have said nothing of Duke William's eldest son because he had hitherto never touched on my petty affairs. I saw him about the Tower, at the tiltyard, or riding from the gates with hounds and hawks, and attended him at mealtimes. He was short and florid – but not so red as Rufus – boisterous and sullen by turns and, as esquires who served him realized, a faithful friend to wine. Often at table I saw the Duke gaze thoughtfully at his heir when Robert, in playful mood, threw beef bones at his friends or challenged them cup for cup. A mutual dislike divided father and son. The Duke never sent him those rare smiles he bestowed on Rufus, whom he loved; Robert seldom showed his father the attractive charm and friendliness he displayed to others. The Duke in a rage once sneered at his stumpy legs, and dubbed him Curthose: a name which stuck. Robert hated it; none used it to his face. But so I shall call him, for there are too many Roberts in my history.

'The County of Maine ought to soothe Robert's ruffled feathers,' Rufus continued. 'He's always grousing because, at eighteen, knighted, and heir to Normandy, my father gives him no responsibility, not so much as custody of a wooden castle. Walter, you're shooting at sixty paces – a trained bowman's range. You'll never carry.'

I drew and sighted. The arrow thudded in the dummy. 'Yet Curthose returned with the army. Why? You can't rule Maine from Rouen.'

'That bow's got a powerful draw. Let me try it. Why? The Duke wants the county to settle down, be certain it's really peaceful before Robert takes over. He doesn't trust him to run a kitchen, let alone a gang of restless barons. No – it's quite a light pull. How do you get the range?'

'Light arrows. More velocity,' I answered briefly. 'What happened to that other Robert, black Robert of Belesme? I haven't seen his ugly face around.'

Rufus scowled. 'He fought well at Fresnai, repulsed a sally. My father appointed him castellan after the place surrendered. Another fortress in the hands of Talvas. At least it keeps him out of Normandy.'

'I wish,' I said viciously, 'that earth-sack was his body.' A second arrow thumped beside the first. 'I've accounts to settle with Belesme.'

'Don't be silly, Walter. He's a knight and a royal castellan. Beyond your reach. You'd better give some thought to your future. What are you going to do?'

I shrugged. 'My three years' training is ended. I don't know. Return to Evreux, I suppose, and attend Count William. I can hardly go to Poix.'

'Hardly. I know your story.' Rufus's voice was kind. 'Why not serve Curthose? He'll have to gather a household before he goes to Maine, and I can bring you to his notice.'

I unbraced the bow, strolled to the butts to recover my arrows, wandered back. In that short journey – six score paces – I pondered Rufus's proposal and unwillingly made a decision. On the face of it, what better prospect could be offered to a young esquire than service with the man who one day must rule Normandy and England? I did not, at fourteen, covet power, but I realized that from Curthose, the hub of power, would radiate the spokes that led to land and riches. Why, then, should I hesitate, and think wistfully of Count William and Evreux?

Maine was a long, long way from Conches. Evreux was not.

I returned to Rufus, who argued amicably with a bowman on the merits of light arrows. 'No penetration, my lord,' the sergeant said respectfully. 'You must have weight to kill.' I grimaced at the man, and showed him an arrow soil-marked to the crest. To Rufus I said formally, 'Lord William, I thank you for your kindness; and I offer my humble service to the Count of Maine.'

Next day I knelt before Curthose, and put my hands in his.

II

I exchanged my habitation on the Tower's first floor – the main hall where for thirty-nine months I had lived and slept – for quarters on the storey above, in a draughty passage outside Curthose's chamber. The count's new dignity had brought him a room to himself, a small windowless cell once used as a store for wine-casks. Curthose, it was said, enjoyed the smell.

I missed Amauri's company. Together we had managed to evade much of the kicking and buffeting which were the lot of young esquires; now I found myself vulnerable to persecution by a small coterie of knights and older esquires. As the youngest of Curthose's retinue I naturally inherited the heaviest tasks; for a time I lived as harshly as in my earliest days in Rouen. Rufus rescued me. Although he served the Duke, he mingled with his brother's entourage enough to see my misery. I think he spoke to Curthose; certainly he once stopped Joscelin of Rupierre, a crusty knight ten years his senior, in the middle of a beating, and rebuked him in a manner quite unfitting an esquire, however royal. Joscelin flinched before Rufus's stammering rage – and finished the thrashing when the prince had gone. Nevertheless my life became easier.

Amauri returned to Montfort to serve Count Simon. Rufus to some extent replaced him in companionship, and often sought me in my leisure hours. Together we rode the woods and cast our hawks, schooled our lords' destriers in the riding yards, wandered the riverside bow in hand and tried to shoot flushed mallard on the wing. The Duke's son naturally had many friends; yet in my innocence I did not think it strange that he should prefer the company of a boy two years younger than himself. The hero-worship I had first accorded him, based on respect for his bodily strength and courage – Rufus, to the end, excelled most men in feats at arms – yielded during these weeks to devoted friendship, an affection as deep as I felt for Amauri of Montfort.

I came to know well Rufus's close companions, some genuine friends like Hugh of Avranches and Robert fitzHamon, others arrant hangers-on hoping for future favours. Flambard was often there, watching quietly in the background, his handsome, fine-boned face expressionless, his thoughts unreadable. None of us liked him, despite his charm; many were jealous of his influence over Rufus, and slandered him to no avail. Rufus merely said, laughing, 'No one else cares so little whose hatred he brings on himself, provided he pleases me.'

And now, unhappily, I must tell how a friendship withered, and I departed from Rouen.

It happened on a hot August afternoon. The city drowsed in heat; cattle in the meadows swished their tails beneath the trees; and the Duke had ridden hawking with his court to the forest beyond St Sever. The men-at-arms on duty reclined in shade, languidly rolling dice or sleeping, arms across faces; sentries on the battlements sweltered in sunlight and screwed their eyes against the shimmering glare. In Curthose's gloomy cell I resentfully tidied garments strewn on stools and floor, for I had been left to clean his chamber while his retinue rode to the woods. I was shaking out the rushes, I remember, when footsteps clattered up the stairs. A shadow at the doorway blocked what little light there was: I looked up and saw Rufus.

'What, loitering like a night-owl in the dark on a day like this? Come on, Walter – let's cool ourselves in the river!'

I spread a crimson drugget beside the bed, smoothed a crease and answered sourly, 'Not yet awhile. I have work to do.'

Rufus sat on the bed and hugged his knees. 'Joscelin is a hard taskmaster. I must scold him again.'

'Let be. He visits his resentment on my head. Why have you not gone hawking?'

'Can't ride – got a boil on my arse. I must get Gislebert the leech

45

to lance it. Stop fussing around, Walter. Come and sit down.' He patted the coverlet: a costly patchwork, miniver and vair. I looked at him irritably.

'Now you've rumpled the bedspread – and I shall have to iron the creases. For the love of God —'

'Ah, quit dithering!' Rufus pulled me down beside him. 'You worry too much. Let us be peaceful.' He put an arm around my shoulder. I felt him trembling.

'Walter, my sweet friend —' His voice was hoarse.

I tried to rise. Rufus pressed me down. I smelt his body: a feral stench like a bitch in heat. A sweat-bead coursed his cheek.

Then Rufus gripped me in a wrestler's hold. Fingers scrabbled my thighs. Panic clutched with ice-cold claws; I tore at his wrists and rolled sobbing on the floor, crawled to the door on hands and knees. I found the doorpost and tumbled through. Hands seized me like an armourer's vice; I yelped in terror. A voice said, 'Be quiet! Come with me.'

Flambard.

He hauled me to the stairway, helped me down, thrust me into an alcove where the night guard slept. I collapsed on a straw pallet and covered my face.

Flambard said, 'You will say nothing of this to anyone.' His voice was level and full of menace. 'Do you hear? Attend me, boy – stop snivelling!'

The priest pinched my jaws between thumb and fingers, and lifted my head. His eyes, dangerous as spears, glared into mine. 'Your life, I promise you, depends on silence. Is this understood?'

'I shall not betray him,' I said drearily. 'He was my friend. But Rufus —! I would never believe —'

'Providence has so created him. Who can oppose the will of God?' He added contemptuously, 'You make a deal of pother over very little. I cannot believe you to be so innocent.'

I remembered the hall on winter nights, and hands that groped in the dark. Flambard said impatiently, 'Take hold of yourself. Your troubles are unimportant. Nor need you flatter yourself that you alone have attracted Rufus.'

I said dully, 'This has happened before?'

Flambard nodded. 'A stable lad and a sergeant's son. Both are dead: one drowned in the Seine, the other slain in a tavern brawl. Accidents, Walter of Poix, are easy to arrange. For esquires as for stablemen.'

46

'I don't need your threats,' I answered wearily. 'You have my word.'

Flambard said tautly, 'Keep it, if you value your life. My sole concern is to ensure Duke William never learns of his son's . . . foible. Therefore you'll have to leave Rouen quickly.'

He stroked his nose and pondered.

'Tomorrow Curthose sends a baggage train to Mans, an advance party to prepare his quarters. I shall arrange for you to travel with it. Make ready to depart at daybreak.'

I climbed to my feet. Flambard watched silently and, as I turned to leave, said with surprising gentleness, 'Your hero is disgraced, his image soiled. Perhaps it is better so – Rufus will never change, and your love has turned to loathing. But remember, Walter: one blemish on an apple's rind need not destroy the fruit.'

At dawn I rode for Maine, and strove throughout the week-long march to banish thought.

Chapter 3

1076–77

Robert Curthose tapped a fingernail on the drink-horn's silver rim. He said, 'More wine, Walter.'

I stopped polishing the scabbard and filled his cup from a wine-cask in a corner of the tent. A storm-wind thrashed the walls, flapped the doorway curtain, gusted raindrops through the slit, whipped tattered clouds across a darkening sky. Although it wanted an hour to none I had lighted a lantern. The swaying light planed shadows on the faces of the knights.

Ivo of Grantmesnil stretched his arms and yawned. 'The siege lines have been set for a week, and Dol still stands. These Bretons are obstinate men.'

'The Duke has miscalculated.' Curthose gulped wine; his words were a trifle slurred. 'His forces may be enough to leaguer Dol, but are certainly too small to bring Brittany to heel – which is what he wants.'

Ivo grunted. He was an enormous man, a burden to his destrier, fond of food and argument. His craggy, square-jawed face ended in a chin which jutted like a battering-ram; the vintages of ten summers since his knighting had flushed a high-bridged, prominent nose. Life and living amused him: he smiled easily, the skin crinkling at the corners of his mouth and eyes.

He said, 'Yet he has called you to his standard all the way from Maine.'

'There's no mystery there. My father plays me like a fish: Maine was the bait I swallowed. Now, after two years' freedom, he's reeling in the line. I doubt I shall see Mans again.'

'You misjudge him, Robert,' William of Evreux said quietly. The cross-straps inside a helmet worn in twenty years of warfare had rubbed sparse patches on his greying hair. 'Maine has been tranquil under your rule. It is merely politic to draw troops from a peaceful demesne.'

An arm thrust the door-flap aside. Rain pattered on the mud-streaked straw which covered the floor, wind wavered the lantern. Robert of Belesme stooped under the lintel, unloosed his cloak and shook it. Water glistened on his helmet, beaded winking jewels on his hauberk. He bowed to the Count of Maine and said disgustedly, 'The entrenchments are half drowned, the men thigh deep in water, the horse lines flooded. No hope of storming Dol in these conditions.'

'You have informed the Duke?'

'He bade me tour the siege lines; and so I have reported. He said the rain can't last for long, and we have plenty of time.'

'And where, meanwhile,' inquired Joscelin of Rupierre, 'is Count Alan of Brittany?'

Curthose clicked finger and thumb. 'Wake up, Walter – wine for Belesme. Count Alan? Gathering an army, presumably, to relieve Dol. Meanwhile we sit in the wet and wait.'

I filled a cup and gave it to Belesme, who sipped and made a face, and spat. 'A sour brew. Can't you do better than this, Robert?' His gaze wandered round the tent, the sodden straw and sagging roof, a rent whence water trickled, a saddle humped like a broken throne, gaping panniers that spilled crumpled clothing, a truckle bed raised on planks. 'I've seen more luxurious quarters on campaign, and cleaner. Your esquires' – his eyes flicked disparagingly across my face – 'need a boot in the crutch.'

'Not their fault.' Bad-tempered lines furrowed Curthose's face. 'They do the best they can with the little they get. I don't own your resources, Robert. You have revenues from wealthy fiefs: Belesme and Alençon, Domfront and Seez. I haven't.'

'God's blood, you've all the revenues of Maine!'

'Don't you believe it. They go straight into my father's coffers. I receive a pittance, a mercenary's wage.'

Belesme set down his goblet, lifted the helmet from his head, let it dangle by the coif upon his back. He said, 'The Count of Maine a pauper? Difficult to credit!' Again he scanned the squalid tent. 'Is this how Duke William's heir fights Duke William's wars – in quarters which might make a sergeant shudder?'

'You're trying to inflame an ulcer till it bursts!' Count William snapped. 'Permit my lord of Maine to nourish his own grievances – they need no fostering from you!'

Belesme smiled. 'I venerate your age, my lord, and bow to your experience. You are Duke William's man – so are we all – but I don't think you've arrived in Count Robert's mesnie to scatter seeds of wisdom. You have another purpose.'

'True enough. To spy on me, and tattle to my father if ever I disobey,' Curthose gabbled, the words tumbling from his mouth like pebbles from a bucket. 'I can't decide a lawsuit without the Duke's writ, quell a riotous vassal unless the Duke approves, spend a denier from my treasury until I have his permit. I'm not even allowed to choose my friends!'

Aimeric of Villerai tried to scratch his armpit, found himself frustrated by the mail rings, and said uncomfortably, 'That's not true, my lord. I, and the others here' – he looked at the listening faces, pale in the shrouded light – 'Ivo and Joscelin and William of Breteuil, follow you willingly at your behest.'

They growled assent. Joscelin of Rupierre said sombrely, 'Some of your mesnie have other loyalties, as we know.' Count William looked at his hands; his mouth was grim. 'It is time, my lord, you reclaimed your rights.'

'The revenues of Maine —'

'A place in the Duke's council —'

The voices clacked like pigeons' wings; a rain squall hurled its slingstones on the tent. I squatted in a corner, scrubbed mildew from the scabbard. Two years in Count Robert's household, serving him at Mans – and my fortunes were no more forward than the raw esquire's in Rouen. I ate the count's victuals, lodged in his donjon, wore his discarded clothes. My tunic was patched at the elbows, frayed at the hem; my shoes leaked water in the wet and grit when dry. Only the haubergeon he had given me – it hung beside me on the armour stand – was in good repair: an armourer's masterpiece, close-lapped six-sided scales. It had been altered to fit my form: Curthose was burlier than I.

'Duke William is growing old. He can't support two kingdoms on his shoulders indefinitely.' Belesme sniffed his wine, poured it disdainfully on the floor. 'You, my lord count, should demand the governance of Normandy – thus assuming your own birthright and relieving your father's burden.'

'Quite so. Precisely.' Curthose nodded owlishly. 'Unfortunately the Duke is adamant; and I have neither money nor men to enforce my claim.'

Nothing at all, I reflected: nothing for yourself, nothing for me. A dozen knights who call themselves your friends, who may or may not stay staunch in crisis. What would they bring you? Possibly four hundred swords, all told, and a little silver. Strongholds? Most were already garrisoned by the Duke's retainers, men like Morin du Pin at Evreux. Curthose, you are derelict – and if you raise your hand against the Duke he'll crush you like a louse.

William of Evreux said thinly, 'Your words, my lord of Belesme, touch the edge of treason.'

Belesme laughed. 'You exaggerate, Count William. I merely urge Count Robert to assert his rights.'

I finished the scabbard, strapped it to the baldric and hooked it on the armour-stand beside Curthose's hauberk. The Count of Maine, I thought, asserted only his rights to wine and wenches. A kindly man, generous so far as his slender purse allowed – but not hardy enough to wager a throne on a hazard of arms. I had chosen to serve him, and believed I erred. What hope had I of winning a fief when I was knighted? Curthose had none to give. Was I to remain a household knight, a landless soldier? Intrigue, I decided, was simmering; Belesme was warming the stew. Perhaps it was time to stir the pot and see what came up in the steam.

I refilled Count Robert's cup, and said, 'Be careful, my lord. The Duke has other sons.'

Belesme looked at me as if a mouse had spoken. 'You keep a peculiar household, Robert. Do your esquires often offer their opinions?'

Curthose patted my arm, and hiccuped. 'I won't have you angry with Walter. He's my friend, and an intelligent lad. He gives me sound advice.'

This, in its way, was true. Frequently in the bed-chamber when I disrobed him, maudlin with wine, Curthose mumbled his perplexities and I offered him what comfort I could find. I doubt he remembered much when he awoke.

Count William snapped, 'He talks sense. Can't you see the danger?'

A trumpet called from afar, its voice faded by the wind. The knights listened, suddenly tense. Ivo said, 'All's well. Guard change – not an alarm. What danger, my lord? The Duke can't break his public oath and forswear his barons – who have all done homage to Count Robert as heir to Normandy.'

'Normandy, yes,' I said. 'There's also England. No one is promised England.'

'Christ's wounds!' Belesme exploded. 'Robert, you averred the boy had sense. How can the Duke —'

51

'A divided heritage,' Count William said. He studied me with surprise. 'The years are bringing you wisdom, Walter. That's exactly what I meant.'

A horseman thudded past the tent, hooves squelching in the mud. 'Someone in a hurry,' Ivo murmured. 'Who'd ride abroad on a day like this? I don't follow you, my lord. The Duke won't split his dominion. It would be madness.'

I took my master's helmet from the rack, examined it beneath the lantern, found a rust-fleck and plied my leather. 'My lord of Belesme,' I said gently, 'you advocate rebellion – for reasons beyond my feeble understanding. Duke William hates disloyalty. Also he loves Rufus. If Rufus is given England, where then lies your fealty?'

Curthose swore. 'Holy Rood! I wouldn't believe —'

'The boy's insane!'

Trumpets shrilled. Voices called confusedly, feet spattered in the puddles. Ivo surged to his feet, lumbered to the door, lifted the flap and called urgently.

'General alarm! Arm at once!'

The knights ran out. Belesme, already armoured, leaned negligently against a tent-pole. Curthose plucked the laces of his tunic: I untied the bows, pulled the doublet from his shoulders, lifted his hauberk from the rack and held it by collar and hem. He extended his arms, plunged into the mail-coat like a diver, emerged red-faced from the coif. I settled the helmet on his head, drew tight the thongs, buckled the ventail across his chin.

'The lad's handy with armour, if a little wanting in the head,' Belesme drawled.

A corpulent figure, helmeted and mailed, burst through the doorway. I bent my knee; Belesme inclined his head.

'Hasten, Robert,' Duke William grated to his son. 'Get to horse.'

'Why the alarm?' Curthose puffed. 'A sally? Surely —'

'The leaguer's ended. We march for Avranches forthwith.'

I draped the baldric across Count Robert's shoulder, belted the sword on his hip, knelt and fastened the spurs. Duke William watched impatiently, his fingers tapping his sword.

'Count Alan has marched from Fougères to relieve Dol,' he barked, 'and with him Philip of France. Five thousand men only five leagues distant.'

'You'll not give battle?'

'Don't be an idiot. We're pinched between Dol's garrison and a much stronger force which, if we don't hurry, will cut our line of retreat to Avranches and Normandy.'

Curthose held out his arms and I wound the bullhide straps from wrist to elbow, tied them neatly.

'Very well. Walter, summon servants, strike tents and load the baggage.'

'Baggage!' the Duke snarled. 'We haven't time – nor do we crawl at a wagon-train's pace. We leave all standing, and run! Come on!'

Curthose followed him from the tent. Quickly I slipped the guige over his head, arranged the shield upon his back. The Duke stood, hands on hips, and gazed at the prize he had lost. A desolate, rocky scrubland unrolled to Dol's torn ramparts, to blackened mounds which once had been a town. Beyond them the donjon climbed, inviolate, to the tendrils of scudding clouds. Soldiers filtered from the siege lines, assembled under bannerets and marched away. A mangonel, abandoned, reached tall timbers to the sky like supplicating arms. Voices shredded faintly on the wind; the dying daylight glinted on spears and helmets.

A conroy gathered behind the tented camp; sodden pennons flapped upon their lances. Duke William faced his son, and pointed. 'The rearguard. You take command. Wait here till all have marched, and watch the castle – the Bretons may risk a sally when they see us going.'

He stamped away, bellowing for his destrier. A varlet brought Count Robert's horse; he climbed heavily to the saddle. I ran to the tent to arm myself, and met Belesme lounging against the door. His eyes followed the Duke, and he smiled.

'The Bastard is beaten,' he said. 'His first reverse for over twenty years. Is this, I wonder, a portent for the future?'

I made no answer, and pushed rudely past him, hating the man. The lantern had gone out; I groped in the half-dark for my haubergeon.

This was my first campaign, and it ended in defeat.

2

The downpour yielded to a misty drizzle. Wind-squalls flailed the trees which bordered a rutted road and showered the heads of the men who marched beneath. The column uncoiled in the dusk like a long brown winding worm. I rode with the rearguard, three files behind Count Robert's burly back, and heard him jest with Ivo, and put a wineskin to his lips. He seemed in excellent humour: the garrison of Dol had not hindered our retreat.

'A word with you, Walter.'

William of Evreux came alongside and drew me from the ranks. We plodded through a miry field, mud sucking the horses' fetlocks. He seemed hesitant to speak; his cheeks were drawn and hollow; the helmet shadowed his eyes. At last: 'Walter, I think you had better return to Evreux.'

I said, surprised, 'But why, my lord, should I quit Count Robert's service?'

He stroked his nose beneath the nasal. 'You are my kin. I have some obligation to save you from disaster.'

I bowed my head. 'I am grateful, my lord count, for your guidance and your gifts throughout the years – but now I do not understand you.'

Count William compressed his lips. 'You're not a fool, boy – as I have seen. You know full well that Curthose treads a dangerous path.'

'He listens to evil counsels,' I answered warily, 'but has not followed them.'

'Not yet. Curthose is weak-willed; he can't much longer resist that devil Belesme, nor the mad suggestions which those fools around him make – Grantmesnil and Breteuil and the rest.'

'You have striven against them, my lord.'

'I have.' The count's voice was tired. 'Curthose believes his father set me in his household as a spy. Not so. Duke William realizes his bent, and sent me to counter the evil that surrounds him. I think I've lost the fight.'

He gripped my wrist, and said fiercely, 'Robert Curthose is hell-bent on rebellion. Must he drag you also to destruction? Leave him, and come with me!'

My palfrey stumbled in a greasy furrow; abstractedly I hitched the rein, collected him between bit and spur. The last rays of twilight faded from a stormy sky. I said, 'Can you, my lord, bestow on me a fief when I am knighted?'

'A moiety, perhaps – no more. My castles are already held, as you should know.'

I visualized his offer: a few arpents of shrivelled vineyard, a thatched and ruinous hall, my companions the parish priest and a drunken bailiff. I am Walter of Poix, I thought, arrogant in youth and folly; blood-relative to Normandy. The world must give me more than this.

Count William said earnestly, 'Why do you hesitate? I promise you land and a dwelling-place. Remember also you are heir to Poix – and your father can't live for ever.'

I stared between my palfrey's ears. 'Lord Walter doesn't acknowledge me as his son. Moreover, France holds seisin of Poix; King Philip could revert my claim. No, my lord. I am ever thankful for your generosity – but I follow the Count of Maine.'

Count William lifted a hand, and let it fall resignedly on his thigh. 'Curthose has less to offer than I,' he muttered. 'I can't comprehend you. This, Walter, is a decision you'll regret.'

He turned his horse and cantered to the road. The drizzle stung my eyes and beaded drops upon my cheeks.

3

The galloper from Fresnai, five leagues north, arrived at Mans on a wintry dawn, and insisted that I rouse my lord of Maine. The knight who guarded his bedchamber chuckled and jerked a thumb. 'You won't be welcome in there,' he said. 'The count has company.' I entered the darkened room and opened the shutters. Curthose sat up, knuckled his hairy chest and said sleepily, 'Curse you, Walter – it's barely day. What is the hour?'

The woman in his bed coyly drew the coverlet over her nakedness. She was wife to a wool merchant in Mans: a complaisant husband, for the count had kindly remitted the octroi duties on his fleeces. I said, 'Past prime – and news from Fresnai, my lord. Viger of Dangeul has crossed his own march and ravages the seigniories of Ballon. Belesme is taking the field against him, and needs your help. A hundred swords, he says, should be enough: Dangeul is a paltry donjon.'

'The devil take Viger! He brought his plea for Ballon's seisin before my council; I heard the cause and decided against him. Must I now campaign in the midst of winter?' Curthose absently fondled his doxy's breasts; she sighed and snuggled against him. An icy wind-gust rattled the shutters: the count shivered and slid beneath the bedclothes. 'No. I have business in Mans: there's that dispute over the abbey's vineyards to be settled. Tell Ivo to take a constabular to Fresnai.' He grinned maliciously. 'You go with him, Walter. You know I hate being wakened before terce.'

I bowed and withdrew. My message pleased Ivo of Grantmesnil, who found the winter months in Mans lugubrious; the city's stews and taverns, he declared, failed to recompense for the closed season for campaigning and his favourite sport of war. He stumped cheerfully from the hall and bellowed orders. By noon six knights and five-score mounted sergeants marched in whirling sleet, crossed the Sarthe at dusk and entered Fresnai.

Belesme was icily impatient. 'Have you been gathering flowers by the wayside? Four hours for seven leagues! If you'd come sooner we'd have caught Viger in the open. He'll be safely inside Dangeul by morning, and we'll have a lengthy leaguer on our hands.'

Belesme was wrong. Our constabular, strengthened by thirty men from Fresnai's garrison, clattered over the drawbridge in the darkness before dawn and took the forest track to Dangeul. It was full light when we left the trees and saw on the plain ahead Dangeul's wooden tower above the village. Horsemen filtered between the huts; men-at-arms escorted laden wagons, herded straggling cattle and prisoners roped in files – the loot from Ballon's devastated steadings. Diminished by distance to the size of ants, they converged on the castle gateway; like ants they scurried when they saw the dawnlight gild our spears.

'Bowels of Christ!' Ivo roared. 'We've got him!'

He flourished his lance. A trumpet howled. The column cantered, formed a long, uneven line which bulged and bellied. Ivo's enormous shoulders heaved in front; he sang a wordless chant, the melody drowned by the thundering hooves. Chunky boulders pocked the ground; horses swerved and collided; gaps opened in the line. As befitted an esquire I took post behind the ranks, three careful horse-lengths back, and drew my sword. My palfrey stumbled; I jerked the reins and cursed, and felt a dryness in my throat.

Some thirty men in mail had turned to meet us. At half a bow-shot's distance their lances swooped and levelled, and they smashed into our centre like an avalanche of steel. Our wings closed in, the swords came out, and a whirling mellay raged on the stony plain.

I watched and waited.

From the welter of fighting horsemen a knight rode straight towards me. He held a splintered lance, his shield flapped loosely on the guige, his rein-hand clutched his face. Blood sprayed between the fingers. Riding blind, he passed at an arm's-length distance. I stood in the stirrups and swung my sword at his neck.

He toppled from the saddle, rolled over and lay face-down. I caught his destrier and returned to the prostrate knight. The unequal battle was ending: little knots still circled and fought, a remnant galloped for survival to the forest. Bodies mottled the ground; riderless horses wandered head in air. I saw Ivo break from the turmoil, collect a dozen sergeants and ride for Dangeul's gates. Others pursued him, avid for Ballon's plunder. Wagons, beasts and men still throttled the drawbridge. The fight had not lasted long.

Belesme approached on foot, followed by men-at-arms, turning over bodies and looking into faces. He said savagely, 'We've lost Viger. Either he's escaped or didn't ride in the charge.' He looked at the prone figure beneath my palfrey's feet. 'Who's that you've got?' He turned the body over with his foot, wiped blood from the broken face, and whistled between his teeth.

'Viger of Dangeul. At last. Did you kill him?'

'I struck him down. He was already wounded.'

Belesme wrenched off the helmet. The man moaned. Belesme clapped his hands together. 'God's bones! He's still alive.' He said to a sergeant, 'Strip him!'

They tore the hauberk from his body, peeled tunic and breeches and left him naked. Viger lay on his back, stared sightless at the sky. Blood dripped from a cut that bared his jawbone; a red pool welled where my sword had cleft him. He made small noises, like a baby crying.

Belesme drew his dagger. His face wore a greyish pallor, spittle dribbled from his lips and smeared his ventail. He bent over the naked man.

I said, 'Viger of Dangeul is my prisoner. I want his ransom.'

He stared at me blindly, and I quailed from the mad green eyes. He sliced off Viger's ears, stabbed out his eyes and hacked his crotch. The body squirmed, and uttered shrill animal cries. The sergeants stood in a group, silent, their faces still. I spewed down my palfrey's shoulder.

Belesme straightened, breathing deeply. He looked calm, relaxed, like a man after loving a woman. He plucked a tuft of grass and wiped clotted fingers.

Viger moaned softly, once, and died.

Belesme said lazily, 'He gambled and lost the hazard, and deserved a felon's death. You may take his horse and armour.'

He sauntered away. I wiped my mouth and forced myself to look on Viger. I had helped to kill him: the first of many I would kill. I had seen death since I could remember: men and women dangling from gallows, starved villeins dead in ditches in the winter, reeking bundles sprawled in steadings after a raid. I had not witnessed cold, deliberate butchery – and cursed my qualms. This was war. I would be a knight: knights were made for war, and war for knights. I must learn to be less delicate.

I was taciturn during the ride to Mans: Ivo of Grantmesnil, bouncing hugely on his destrier, rallied me for my sulks. 'Cheer up, Walter. At least you've gained a hauberk and a horse.' (Viger's charger, mail-coat roped to saddle, trotted beside my palfrey.) 'Can't fathom Belesme,' he continued ponderously. 'Viger would have brought a tidy ransom. He's done this sort of thing before, I remember: captured young Goulafre when he took Mesnil – then killed him slowly. Seems to enjoy torture. Very wasteful: the man's got no money sense.'

I nodded morosely, my thoughts elsewhere, revolving an idea that formed in my mind. A knight must own a warhorse and coat of mail: extremely expensive articles which his fief's revenues provided or a wealthy suzerain bestowed. I owned no fief; Curthose, perpetually scraping deniers, was unlikely to equip me. I had acquired horse and hauberk: why should I not be knighted?

When we had reached Mans I put the question bluntly to Count Robert. He scratched a pudgy jowl and laughed.

'No reason at all, Walter – though I'll hate losing you: you're the best esquire I've known. What's your age? Seventeen? Old enough: I got my spurs a year sooner. Kneel down, lad.'

He glanced round the hall. Knights lounged at tables; a minstrel plucked a mournful tune upon his lute; Ivo of Grantmesnil idly rolled dice from hand to hand. Curthose beckoned him.

'Ivo, I want you as witness.'

Ivo lumbered over, stood beside me. Count Robert raised his palm, lowered it on my neck, and intoned the accolade:

'Itel valor deit aveir chevaler
Ki armes portet e en bon cheval set;
En bataille deit estre forz e fiers . . .'

He clasped my hands and raised me to my feet.

'Be a knight, Walter of Poix, and show courage in the face of thine enemies.'

And so, in slaughter and a homely ritual, I left my youth behind.

Belesme came frequently to Mans, and laboured to incite Curthose against his father. He worked on Count Robert's vanity, emphasized his lack of power, land and wealth, insisted that all Normandy, wanting a change of rule, yearned to follow the banner of Duke William's son. I listened in dismay; my protests were shouted down. The knights of Curthose's mesnie supported Belesme: their motives were easy to read: they wanted simply war. They were knights, and war was their life. But Belesme was no impulsive firebrand; behind that ivory face and those restless eyes lurked a calculating, ruthless brain. I tried to probe his purpose, and was baffled. Belesme had so much to lose: his father, Roger of Montgommeri, had long since gone to rule an English county; the son now held Montgommeri's lands and twenty castles crowning seigniories from La Ferté to Falaise. Would he endanger his possessions to test Duke William's might?

Curthose listened willingly to his friends' persuasions, became scarlet and excited as the hour grew late and wine cups emptied, thumped the table and swore he would have his dues. The morning and an aching head usually cooled his ardour; during these early hours, before he broke his fast, I often sought him privately and counselled caution. The count listened gloomily, blinked bloodshot eyes and glumly calculated his father's power, the troops he led and castles he commanded; and clutched his temples.

I had bound myself to Curthose: if he should lose his heritage my visionary fortunes vanished as well.

Had it not been for Rotrou of Mortagne's revolt, which led to the affair at Laigle, Curthose might have vacillated thus for ever. Duke William, doubting Rotrou's loyalty – not without reason – disseized him of Mortagne and sent a company to garrison the castle. Rotrou closed Mortagne's gates, repulsed Duke William's men and drove them from his marches.

The Duke was enraged. For years no Norman vassal had lifted a sword against him: Rotrou, he decided, must be taught a lesson. To his liegemen in Maine and Normandy he sent summons of array, and appointed Laigle five leagues north of Mortagne as the mustering-place. Five thousand lances gathered – the Duke had learned from Dol the folly of paltry forces. Knights and men-at-arms thronged Gilbert of Laigle's donjon, barons bickered over billets in the town, pavilions sprouted on the fields beyond the paling. The Duke brought his retinue from Rouen, eyed Gilbert's dumpy oak-trunk donjon, his grimy hall, and quartered himself in Robert of Calcege's house, the only considerable mansion that Laigle boasted. Rufus was with him: I saw his yellow hair and ruddy features when they crossed the drawbridge. My skin crawled at the memory of those groping hands in Count Robert's bedchamber – and yet I knew a sense of sadness and of loss. It was easy to avoid him: Laigle was like a warren, even more densely crowded as the days went by.

Curthose secured lodgings for his mesnie in the house of one Roger of Caux; there we waited, drank and gambled while Duke William's vassals marched from distant fiefs. We found little enter-tainment in Laigle – a miserable town, no better than a village – and small use for hawk and hound, since Rotrou's senseless harryings had rid the woods of game. The arrival of fresh contingents broke the tedium: we waited by the gate to watch them enter, and criti-cized their horseflesh and accoutrements. So, on a sunlit summer noon when sentries hailed a company's approach, I sauntered to the gate and saw Ralph of Conches lead forty knights and sergeants over the bridge.

Ralph had not changed much over the years: the same plump cheeks, thick petulant lips and protuberant eyeballs. He noticed me and raised his hand, and spoke to a slender, youthful knight who rode at his side. The young man wore peculiar armour, a supple, shimmering hauberk which clung to his body like silk, fashioned in a manner entirely strange. Wrist-long sleeves, I noticed: how did he bend his sword arm or guide his horse? He passed so close that, curious, I touched his skirt: interlinked rings in a close-set mesh. Very odd.

'Tirel!'

The ground rocked under my feet. I looked up, met laughing eyes in a suntanned face. I stuttered and struggled for words.

'Will you constantly be mute whenever we meet?'

She touched slender fingers to my head, a feathery caress, a fleet-ing benediction. I clung to her hand and pressed it against my cheek.

'Stay close to me, Walter. You must not lose me again.'

I followed in a maze of wonder, walking like a man who dreams. I knew Isabel was wedded; I had pictured her in Conches' donjon, idling with her ladies in the bower, pointing embroidery, listening to romances of Roland and Roncesvalles, tinkling plaintive tunes upon a lute. She would supervise her handmaids laying linen in the presses, count the napkins and fret about a threadbare shirt. When the weather was fair she might ride sedately to the woodlands with her lord, a merlin on her wrist and hounds trotting at her heels. Every twelvemonth she would lie in childbed. This was how the chatelaines of castles lived: I had not imagined Isabel could break the shackles.

Now she rode armed and armoured to war against Mortagne.

I found her near a granary, picking a pebble from her horse's hoof. She dropped the foreleg, straightened, and gave me a long, searching look. We sat together on a pile of baggage. The helmet dangled on her back; her hair, cropped shoulder length, shone like a raven's wing in the noonday sun.

'You're changed, Walter. All the softness gone. Hard and dangerous: a sword-edge restive in the scabbard.'

'I changed?' I gestured incredulously to her mail-coat. 'And you? The Lady of Conches attired like a knight, riding to battle in full panoply of war?'

She put a hand on my knee. 'Must I live immured in a bower, numbering my beads and suckling infants? That life is not for me. So, after some argument, I persuaded Ralph.'

'He must be easily convinced.'

Isabel said curtly, 'Ralph can refuse me nothing.'

'A doting spouse,' I agreed bitterly. 'Yet he must care little for your safety.'

'I am well protected.' She called softly: 'Richer!'

A man who loitered nearby came quickly over. He wore meshed mail like Isabel, a thin, curved sword on his hip, and a small round shield, the boss a needled spike. An unbraced bowstave dangled from a shoulder. I studied this outlandish armour, and wondered whence he came.

'Richer the Saracen, a knight of Spain,' Isabel said.

'Rashid, in truth – a name the Frankish tongue can't compass,' the man said, smiling. Brown, liquid eyes twinkled in a face the tawny shade of a chestnut sprung from the husk. The clinging link-mesh defined wide shoulders and narrow hips. 'My lady is courteous: I am merely a horse-dealer and not, by your reckoning, a knight.'

I answered politely, wishing him elsewhere. He read the impatience in my eyes, smiled again and bowed, retired a little distance and waited, leaning on his strange curved sword. Isabel regarded him pensively.

'Richer brings Moorish horses every spring from Spain, drives them north from Gascony and sells them on the way. He sold the last at Conches, a few months since. And there he has remained, a stranger in an alien land – to become my devoted follower, who guards me night and day.'

I sent Richer an unfriendly glance. 'No more than that?'

'No more,' Isabel answered soberly. 'I am, perhaps, less wanton than you suppose – and Conches is a hard place for dalliance.'

'No more difficult than Laigle in a muster of array,' I said savagely. 'How can we meet alone in a crowd five thousand strong?'

'Patience, my friend.' She gave me a look provocative as a gage of challenge. 'You are in Count Robert's mesnie?'

'Yes.'

Isabel sighed. 'I must persuade Ralph to wait upon the count, and perhaps seek quarters in his household.'

I said carefully, 'Attachment to Curthose may be unwise. He does not stand high in the Duke's regard.'

'That I have heard. I believe I can bear to risk the Duke's displeasure.'

Ralph came from the donjon, shouting for his destrier. Isabel patted my hand, rose and went to her lord. His flabby features lightened when he saw her; he laid a possessive arm around her shoulders. Isabel spoke to him quickly; Ralph listened, pulling his ear, playfully tweaked her hair and climbed to horse. Isabel nodded to me across the ward.

I strode to Roger of Caux's house to make all ready for my love.

5

Duke William, gnawing his lip, impatiently awaited Count Stephen's contingent from faraway Aumale, the last of his vassal lords to reach the muster. Had Stephen started earlier, or marched a little faster, we might have gone from Laigle before Robert Curthose lost his temper and Belesme's plot exploded.

The knights of Count Robert's mesnie lounged beneath a lime tree which shaded the gravelled forecourt of Roger of Caux's manse. The meal was done; servitors placed honey cakes and sweetmeats on the table, replenished winecups and departed. Beamed and plastered house-walls surrounded three sides of the yard; the fourth was a gated paling that opened on a street. A thatch-roofed gallery projected from the wall above our heads – a convenient place for loitering when the day was wet or cold. We basked in a watery sun-light and listened to Belesme.

'This is your chance, my lord count.' He rapped a knuckle on the table. 'Now or never. All the troops in Normandy have gathered at Laigle. The barons also, and the Duke himself. Rouen waits for the taking.'

Ivo of Grantmesnil yawned. 'By whom? Our conroys are here as well.'

Belesme smiled. 'We must ride secretly – and fast.'

'We shall be instantly pursued,' Curthose complained, 'and cut to pieces if we're caught. I think the risk too great.'

'Rouen is not unguarded,' I warned. 'Roger of Ivri commands the garrison.'

'A weak one,' said Aimeric of Villerai. He was a spare, ferrety man, his hair fiery as his temper. Excitement sparked pale blue eyes. 'Ivri, moreover, would surely open the gates to the Count of Maine.'

Ralph of Conches flicked hunted glances at the speakers, and licked his lips. 'I don't like this scheme, my lords. The Duke is not so easily outwitted. And if we fail our seigniories are forfeit.'

'You were less hesitant three days ago,' Belesme said scornfully. 'I told you of our plans – I had to, since you've forced yourself on Count Robert's household. You swore an oath of secrecy, and promised your support.'

'I promised —'

'Our own castles will be defenceless, open to Duke William's troops,' Aimeric of Villerai interrupted. 'What if he lets Rouen go, and takes our donjons one by one?' He scraped a finger down a bony cheek, scored by an arrow-scar from chin to temple. 'I don't think I'd exchange all Villerai for a moiety of Rouen.'

Belesme slammed a hand on the table, rattling the flagons. 'How can he? Rouen is the key to Normandy, the kernel and the hub. With Rouen in Count Robert's keeping, the scales of power weighted in his favour, all Normandy will rally to his standard. We are not alone in resenting Duke William's rule!'

There, I reflected sourly, he's probably right. Many restless lords would willingly exchange Duke William's iron hand for Count Robert's flaccid fingers.

Curthose drained his goblet, kicked back his stool and paced the forecourt, pulling his chin. The gravel crunched beneath his feet. Belesme examined him through slitted eyes, his knife-edge lips clamped tight. Curthose muttered, 'Why not? I demand only what the Duke's already promised – my rightful heritage. And yet —' He scuffed the pebbles with his toe. Belesme shrugged, and poured more wine.

A clamour sounded from the street, the noise of angry altercation. None paid attention: clashes were common in crowded Laigle. The paling gate burst open; Rufus thrust aside the man-at-arms on guard.

'Back, half-wit! Am I not allowed to visit my brother?'

A grin split the crimson face, and he swayed on his feet. I saw at once that Rufus was slightly drunk. Prince Henry and a knight-attendant followed. Curthose greeted them and led them to the table, offered wine and sugared figs. Rufus dropped heavily on a stool, stared hazily around the table, pointed a finger.

'Belesme, Breteuil, Grantmesnil, Rupierre, Villerai and Poix – my brother's keepers. Good day to you! Ha! – and Ralph of Conches: a new vulture in the flock. Planning the campaign against Rotrou – or have you other designs?'

Belesme said blandly, 'May I add water to your wine, my lord?'

Henry said, 'Be quiet, Rufus.' He spoke softly, yet the words cut like swords. I looked at the prince in surprise: esquires do not rebuke knights – and Henry was barely eleven years old. His features were round and heavy, like all of the Tanner's blood. There the likeness ended: Robert and Rufus were red-skinned men, he was sallow; emotions rippled his brothers' faces like wind on tranquil waters; Henry's was flat, expressionless, the eyes like hard wet stones.

'You forget yourself, William,' Curthose spluttered angrily. 'Have you come to insult my friends?'

Raindrops pattering lightly on the lime tree gave me an excuse to intervene. I gestured to the gallery above. 'Let's take shelter, my lords. There's a barrel of wine in the upper room, a gift from Robert of Meulan's vineyards.'

'Never a poor vintage there. Come, Rufus!' Henry stood briskly, guided his brother to the ladder, followed him up. I climbed after and saw what happened.

A pitcher stood on the balustrade, put there by a servitor to cool. Rufus lurched against Henry, whose elbow knocked the pitcher. Water cascaded on the heads beneath. I heard a bellow of fury.

Curthose, water dripping from his hair, pelted up the ladder,

Rufus met him at the top and kicked him in the face. William of Breteuil and Ivo swarmed up like stormers at an escalade. Henry grabbed a heavy stool and smashed it on their heads. The brothers stood at the ladder's top and fought like wildcats.

The knight-attendant – he alone of all the company wore armour – doubtfully fingered his sword. I caught his eye and shook my head. He tapped home the blade, ran to the balustrade and knocked Aimeric back. Shouts and war-cries clanged between the walls. I saw the daggers come out, and retreated quietly from the railings: there was no profit to be gained in taking sides between Duke William's sons.

Robert of Belesme leaned calmly against the tree, popped a sweet-meat in his mouth and smiled contentedly.

The paling door swung open. Men in armour thronged the fore-court. The fighting stopped. Curthose clambered sullenly down the ladder, sucking a gash on his wrist. Duke William stalked through a corridor of shields, and stood glowering in the centre of the yard. Anger flushed the bald, high forehead, his lower lip jutted, his ponderous belly curved before him like a prow.

'Splendour of God!' Duke William breathed. 'I am called from council because my sons behave like peasants brawling in a tavern. I, William of Normandy and England, am summoned like a nurse-maid to quell the drunken bickerings of ill-begotten children!'

'I am not drunk, my lord,' Curthose said.

The Duke turned on him. Nobody stirred a finger.

'So much the worse! If, sober, you act like this, what will you do in wine – your usual state? If you can't control your own wild temper, how can you attempt to rule the realm which – the Saints forgive me! – I promised you years since?' His voice rose. 'Tell me, you drunken, whoring sot – how can you of all men govern Normandy?'

He said much more to Rufus and to Henry, shouting above the noises in the street. No one answered, and no one moved. The Duke turned abruptly, strode from the yard. Curthose stared at the house-tops, his face working, tears glistening on his cheeks. Belesme, lithe and quiet as a hunting cat, moved close and whispered in his ear.

'Yes,' said Curthose. 'Yes. We ride tonight.'

Rain pools glimmered in shreds of starlight, shattered like broken glass beneath the hooves. Tree-trunks moved in the darkness, clustered like silent foemen waiting in ambuscade. Rugles was left behind, a dim scattering of cottages, a rushlight glimpsed through a window, a peasant's frightened shout. The forest closed. The track narrowed to a pallid wandering channel amid the trees. Horses skidded on wheel-ruts, squelched in mud, stumbled over flints and fallen branches. The files bulged and tapered, broke in scattered fragments, crashed through scrub and undergrowth, scrambled back to the road. The pace was fast, a long jolting trot which made for hard collisions in the dark, sent men and horses sprawling in the mud, scarred flesh and temper.

Three hundred lances rode for Rouen, twenty leagues away.

We had left Laigle after compline, stealthily, like murderers quitting a corpse. Belesme took command, sending secret messengers to the encampment in Laigle's fields, to the mesnies of Count Robert's knights, bidding them arm and saddle when the dusk of evening fell. The separate retinues departed by different paths, casting wide circles round the town, and assembled at a hamlet which Belesme appointed. We were not certain we went unseen; the Duke's sentries were alert, his spies diligent. We trusted to our speed to evade pursuit, to outstrip any courier who might bring Rouen warning.

I had started the march with Curthose, had lost him in the journey's checks and collisions, and rode half-way down the column amid stranger knights and sergeants – perhaps from Grantmesnil's troop: I heard Ivo swearing loudly in the gloom. Mail rings clinked and rustled, leather creaked, scabbards thumped on saddles, bridles jingled, hoofbeats hammered like hail. A stirrup irked my instep, the plastron chafed my chest. The stallion I had taken from Viger of Dangeul proved a lumbering beast, heavy on the forehand and unbalanced: he tripped frequently in ruts, started at shadows. I kept him up to the bit, nursed him over the crawling miles, sweated beneath my hauberk. I felt drowsy despite my vigilance, and forced myself awake – a moment's lapse on this nightbound road could mean a fall.

Something sounded different in the perpetual clink and clatter, a tiny alien noise nearby, a soft metallic whisper like the rubbing of silk on steel. I listened, half asleep, and tried to place the sound, elusive as a melody heard and lost.

After marching miles in darkness the hallucinations start. You seem to swim rather than ride. Your horse's legs are invisible; you see nothing but the dim shoulders of the man ahead and a swaying lance. Soon the delusions begin: bright flashes at the edge of sight make you turn sharply and there's nothing but blind blackness. You hear sounds like distant horns and quick staccato shouts and voices from empty air.

I endured them all, that night. Glad I was when morning dimmed the stars and I saw tree-shapes leaning greyly on the sky. Unfriendly phantoms of the night took colour and shape, resolved into tired riders on mud-spattered, flagging horses. The strange rustling persisted; I turned my head impatiently: nightmares should go at dawn. A slender, chain-mailed horseman met my look and smiled. Daylight splashed harsh shadows beneath her eyes.

I said dourly, 'Is it necessary that you should risk your head for Robert of Maine?'

'Count Robert? He signifies little to me.' The small light-boned grey she rode matched an easy canter to my destrier's shambling trot. 'I follow my liege lord, as do you all.'

'Ralph? He condones your presence here?'

Isabel made a weary gesture. 'Not Ralph. Walter, will you never understand?'

Richer the Saracen untied a small wineskin from his saddle-arch and gave it to his lady. She drank, and a faint colour touched her cheeks. I tilted back my helmet and scrubbed my nose.

'I understand nothing,' I said roughly. 'You, a woman, don armour and a sword' – I looked contemptuously at her slim curved scabbard, the twin of Richer's – 'and attend Duke William's muster. That alone is sufficiently fantastic. But to ride to war with this array —! I don't think you realize fully what we intend.'

'I know it all.' She touched my hand. 'Years ago, Walter, you promised to find me. I grew tired of waiting.'

I stared at her, bemused. Richer said softly, 'My lord, we approach a town.'

The trackway coiled across scrub-spotted heathland to a donjon frowning above clustered rooftops. The sunrise winked on spears, a far-off trumpet wailed a muted warning.

'Beaumont,' I said. 'Nearly halfway.'

The head of the column swung from the path and skirted the

palisade well beyond bowshot: old Roger of Beaumont held fierce allegiance to Duke William. When the donjon's battlements had sunk below the trees the column halted, eased girths and watered at a shallow brook. Bannerets collected retinues which had been dispersed by speed and darkness, and bellowed for absent faces. Someone called my name.

'I must go,' I said reluctantly. I looked at the Saracen. 'Guard her well, Richer. My sword is at your call.'

He stroked his bowstave, and smiled. 'I will, my lord.'

I led my laggard warhorse to the van. Curthose anxiously examined his destrier's leg. 'Overreach,' he muttered. 'Hope the brute lasts out.' An esquire bent and smeared a salve on the wound. Belesme stood, hands on hips, listening to reports from bannerets, his face grim. 'Forty missing,' he said curtly, 'and fifteen horses lamed to a hobble. Can't these rascals ride?' Ivo of Grantmesnil shrugged barndoor shoulders. 'Twenty-five miles at breakneck speed in the dark. What else do you expect?' Belesme snapped: 'More speed and tighter discipline. We must reach Rouen before vespers, before they close the gates.'

Curthose slung his shield aback, climbed to the saddle. 'If you force the pace too much we'll be left with a handful against Ivri's men.' His face was puffy and drawn, the eyes bloodshot. 'We hazard our lives, my lord – a stake you lose only once.'

Belesme sneered, and gave the sign to canter.

I prefer to forget the details of that daylong ride. Belesme, erect in the saddle, moving easily to the rhythm of his horse, set a searing pace. The sun glared from a cloudless sky; the road crossed open uplands, beyond the sheltering cool of copse and woodland. We sweltered in our hauberks, the metal too hot to touch. Hooves crumbled mud into dust which swirled in clouds and gritted our mouths and powdered men and horses to the semblance of daylight ghosts. The shield-rim rasped my back; I slipped the guige and rode enarmed. The ventail scoured my chin; I loosed the buckle and let it flap. My awkward destrier could at least endure: doggedly he pounded on, head down, snorting through his nostrils. Sweat runnelled his dusty hide in a hundred tiny rivers. The column lengthened, lost cohesion: men cantered in scattered groups, in pairs, alone; many faltered by the way, stumbled to a halt, dismounted and plodded on foot or stopped exhausted by the roadside.

We halted once, where the Seine curved near the road, and quenched raging thirsts. Belesme would not allow the horses to drink. 'The winning-post's nearly in sight,' he grated through dust-caked lips. 'You don't water horses in the middle of a race.' We continued at a trot, since our mounts could raise no more, and plunged through the ultimate forest before St Sever's fields. The trees cast giant shadows, birds were twittering to roost. The forest fringes faded on ploughland and open pastures; St Sever's spired crucifix pierced a sky drenched with gold. The last lingering rays of sunset gilded Rouen's walls and turrets. Labourers and wayfarers speckled the road, thronged the bridge three bowshots distant, and hurried into Rouen for the night.

The gates of the town were open.

Belesme halted in the churchyard. 'Keep under cover. Beyond this we can be seen from the Tower's battlements.' He watched the glow fade from the western sky, and waited a little while for stragglers to catch up. All the barons arrived, Grantmesnil and Breteuil and the rest: they owned sturdier horses than the mounted sergeants. Ralph of Conches sat slumped in the saddle, Isabel and Richer beside him. I was astonished and dismayed: one certainty had consoled me through the scorching day – the fragile lightweight animal she rode could not reach Rouen. What breed of horseflesh was this?

Belesme surveyed the company sardonically. 'A hundred or so – it should be enough. Count Robert, henceforward you must lead – Ivri will open to you, and you alone. We must ride full pelt and enter the Tower before they take alarm.'

Curthose went to the front, his face set and, for once, determined. The spurs went in and we left St Sever's shelter, rode loose-reined, thumping lance-butts on our destriers' ribs, forcing the foundered beasts to a sluggardly gallop. People scattered from the track; we swerved round carts and oxen, drove headlong for the bridge. Planks drummed beneath the hooves. We plunged through the gate; a startled gate-guard watched us pass, eyes starting and mouths agape. Curthose turned right-handed; the squadron threaded a narrow street that wound between leaning houses, burst from the street to an open space which fronted the Tower and ward. The bridge was down, the palisade gate open.

Belesme shouted, 'Ride for your lives!'

The drawbridge heaved and lifted.

Helmets flickered behind the palisade, men ran to their battle stations. The bridge thudded on its lintel, and crossbars clanged in the sockets. Belesme pulled up on the edge of the moat, stroked his destrier's neck and whistled soundlessly between his teeth. Curthose halted beside him and brandished his lance.

'I am Robert of Maine!' He tore the helmet from his head and showed his face. 'Open!' His voice cracked. 'Open, in the Duke's name!'

A man climbed the wooden watch-tower beside the gate, and leaned from the embrasure. He carried a shield and a naked sword, but wore no armour. So nearly had we surprised them.

'Roger of Ivri at your service, my lord,' he called. A square, rugged face and wary amber eyes. 'If you show me Duke William's token I shall willingly lower the bridge.'

Belesme gathered his rein, turned his destrier and picked a way through the silent horsemen who clustered at the lip of the moat. Curthose shouted, 'Token? What need have I of tokens to enter the Tower? Do you not recognize me?'

'I know you well, my lord. Yet without your father's signet I cannot let you in.'

I touched Count Robert's arm. 'It is useless, my lord. You have lost the throw. Better that we should go while we have the chance.'

Curthose's lip quivered. 'Go? Go? Surrender what we have? The city is ours.'

I said wearily, 'What use to us is Rouen without the Tower? Come, my lord.'

Belesme waited at the city gates, pensively studying the sunset. Clouds streaked across a flaming sky like the banners of charging squadrons. A lone star glittered in a blue-black vault. The gates had been shut behind us, the gate-guard fled. Sergeants dismounted and heaved back the bars. We crossed St Sever's bridge, riding slowly, tired beyond thought or speech, gathered silently on the farther bank and let our horses drink. The river plucked and eddied in the rushes; a water-rail croaked dismally, a cry like a mocking laugh.

Belesme said bleakly, 'We have failed. Now we are forsworn, outcast, traitors for Duke William's vengeance. Count Robert, I await your orders.'

Curthose crouched over his saddle. His shoulders heaved. 'What shall we do?' he mumbled. 'Where can we go?'

I left him weeping in the dusk, and went to find Isabel.

Chapter 4

1077

By morning, a depleted company, we reached the outskirts of Brémule.

Joscelin of Rupierre had gone, taking his liegemen, likewise William of Breteuil with his retinue. Both bade courteous farewell to Count Robert and departed for their own domains, hoping to forestall Duke William. (Joscelin was caught and killed near Courci; William regained his castle and, much later, came to terms with the Duke.) All the barons had considered what they should do. Aimeric of Villerai puckered red-rimmed eyes and wrinkled his nose, looking more like a ferret than ever. 'I could make a dash for Villerai,' he said, 'but I'd have to fight to get in. The Duke's castellan there will know we failed at Rouen.' Ivo wiped a huge hand down his face and grinned. 'Grantmesnil's a long ride across the heart of enemy country. I don't think I'd reach it. My neck will be safer with you, my lord count.' Ralph declared sulkily that he would make for Conches and trust that his liegemen would open the gates. Isabel said flatly, 'In that case you ride without me, my lord. I do not abandon the Count of Maine in his hour of need.' The barons looked at her in wonder. All were aware of her identity: her advent as an armoured warrior had stirred Laigle's gossips like wood-smoke puffed in a hive, and outraged the priests. But a woman's eccentricities were the business of her lord: everyone was curious, no one interfered. Public defiance was another matter: the men waited for Ralph to chastise his insolent lady. He shrugged sullenly and stared at his hands. Isabel put an arm around him and whispered in his ear; Ralph smiled unwillingly and nodded. 'I follow you, Count Robert,' he decided.

I said nothing. For me there was no alternative.

Robert of Belesme had listened impassively. Then he said, 'We need a fortress stout enough to resist Duke William's leaguer, garrisoned by men who will let us in, then fight on our behalf. My

71

mother the lady Mabille holds Raimalard. The Duke has his garrison there, of course; but the castellan, Hugh of La Roche d'Igé, is her . . . friend.' He smiled a little. 'He will admit us, and for a time at least we shall be safe.'

'Raimalard? A long journey,' Curthose objected.

'Four days, with luck,' Belesme replied impatiently. 'Do you know a stronghold in Normandy or Maine which will shelter rebels who have failed? What other choice have we?'

Clearly none. We walked the exhausted horses through the night, and at daybreak halted within a copse somewhere near Brémule. There we faced the practical necessities of food and forage: the bread and meat in the saddlebags were finished, the wineskins dry; the horses had not eaten since leaving Laigle. Belesme took four sergeants and departed to investigate a village standing among cornfields beyond the copse. I posted sentries – who drooped on their spears and fell asleep standing – and went to find Isabel. Most of the men already slept; Ralph snored beside her; Richer sat at her feet with his sword across his knees, eyes sunken in his head, and gazed broodingly into space. Isabel lifted heavy eyelids and said drowsily, 'You are not rid of me yet, Tirel. Come to bed.' I was too tired to be shocked; I lay down, closed my eyes and tumbled into slumber and those quick haunting dreams which utter exhaustion brings.

A distant scream jolted me awake. I met Richer's look; he pointed towards the village. Again the scream, a voice of agony beyond endurance. 'My lord of Belesme,' Richer said, his voice flat and empty.

I remembered Viger's dying, and clambered to my feet and ran. Twice in the glade I tripped on recumbent bodies which grunted but did not stir; and fell again in the soft ploughland. In a sprinkling of wattled hovels and leaf-thatched byres the sergeants thwacked spear-shafts on the backs of cowering villeins who loaded a cart with barley sacks and oats and a slaughtered calf. A crudely painted crucifix crowned a rickety wooden building no larger than a cottage. An oak tree shadowed the church's door. Suspended by the ankles from a branch, a figure writhed head down; a threadbare robe flopped over the face and left the body naked.

With his sword point Belesme carved intricate designs on belly and ribs.

'Enough!' I said roughly. 'Must you raise the countryside about our ears?'

Belesme's face was rapt, his eyes glazed. He lowered his sword and scanned his work, a craftsman enthralled by a masterpiece. The tip of his tongue, like a peeping lizard, flickered between his lips.

'Merely an obstreperous priest,' he murmured. 'The rascal dared to resist.'

My sword sliced through the rope. The man tumbled on the grass and moaned. 'Have you lost your senses?' I shouted. 'We plunder peasants because we must – we're starving. But wantonly to torture a priest —! Will you raise every man's hand against us? Are Duke William's hunters not enough?'

The vagueness was gone from Belesme's eyes, they focused and glittered green. We faced each other sword in hand. Slowly he enarmed his shield; I had forgotten mine.

'Our cockerel knight is ruffling his feathers,' he said softly. 'Time his comb was cut.'

His sword point flickered, feinted at my throat. I parried and disengaged. He cut fiercely at my shieldless side; I warded, point down, blade vertical. My guard was slow, my wrist unbraced. The force of the slash spun the hilt from my hand. I bent quickly to retrieve the weapon. Belesme rested his sword point on my lips.

'You're not a very good swordsman, Walter of Poix,' he said in a voice like ice. 'Now make your peace with God.'

Kneeling upon one knee, my body trembling and my mind empty, I waited for death.

'Keep still, my lord of Belesme.'

Belesme lowered his blade. Fearfully I turned my head. Richer's bowstring was drawn to his ear; a mirthless smile twitched the corners of his lips. Belesme thoughtfully considered the arrow-head that pointed at his throat, languidly sheathed his sword and kicked me in the chest.

'Go away and live. Perhaps you've learned a lesson.'

He turned his back and surveyed the huddled body of the priest, who lay motionless and moaned no more. I went shakily to Richer, and tried to control my quivering knees. Together we crossed the plough, overtook sergeants hauling a laden cart to the copse. I said, 'I was a dead man if you had not come.'

'You can thank the lady Isabel,' Richer said. 'She sent me after you.'

'Why?'

Richer shrugged. 'I do not probe my lady's motives, nor question her commands.' The singsong accent of his French grew more pronounced – I learned later it signified anger. 'You crossed Robert of Belesme – and forgot your shield. Are you tired of living?'

I was still too shaken to resent his tone, and answered nothing. Richer continued, 'I am strange to your Frankish customs; I do not fully understand the morals of your race. Women in my country don't ride armed to war, nor knead their lords like tallow in their hands, nor pursue another like a bitch in heat —'

'Enough, Richer!'

He went on as though I had not spoken. 'I neither understand nor can I help myself: Allah has ordained that I should love this woman. To what end? I have become her servant, and perhaps her friend. No more. If I, an alien and an infidel, so much as touch her hand I die – sliced in a hundred pieces by outraged Christian swords. You have but one to face. Ralph of Conches,' he added bitterly, 'wields a blade less formidable than Belesme.'

'I should fear your arrows also, Richer.'

He said tiredly, 'You have no need. My lady loves you, and I cannot oppose her will. But I promise you, my lord of Poix, I shall do nothing to help your cause.'

I reflected sadly that, hunted by Duke William's conroys, my cause was unlikely to prosper. We entered the coppice. The sergeants roused the sleeping men; fires were lighted, barley ground and baked, the calf's flesh roasted, horses fed. I ate greedily and, between mouthfuls, told Isabel of my deliverance. She smiled kindly upon Richer, and gave him a gobbet of meat between finger and thumb. He took it reverently, like sacramental bread.

At noon we saddled the horses, and found the road for Raimalard.

2

Belesme gave all the orders, made the decisions. Curthose, sunk in apathy, stared for the most part at his horse's ears. Through desertions and lamed animals we lost more men on the way. The road hugged the French marches, and Belesme, whenever he thought prudent, crossed the border and rode across territories whose lords owed homage to King Philip. He avoided Vernon and Sorel, marcher castles which Duke William garrisoned, and hid in coppices or forests when spears twinkled in distant dust-clouds; and brought us on the fifth day to Raimalard.

The fortress gripped the knoll of a spur which dominated a desolate landscape. It was a solitary castle, black and forbidding, without a protectorate town or village nestling at the foot, without a field or steading in the valley. I saw it first on a summer noon, when the sky was blue and cloudless – but the sunlight seemed to lose its warmth when it fell on Raimalard.

Belesme parleyed for a little at the gate; then we crossed a cavernous fosse which was hewn from the rock and entered a ward encircled by embrasured walls. On one side was a row of stables, granaries and haylofts; on the other barrack huts and armouries; a hall stood in the centre. All were built of stone, the roofs stone-tiled – Raimalard was proof against fire. The square donjon, three storeys high, all stone, surmounted a tall, steep-sided mound which commanded the rocky spur. There was none of the motley litter common in castle wards; all was tidy, orderly, bare as a spinster's bed.

You might starve the castle out; you'd lose a thousand men in a storm. We had found a strong enough bolt-hole, and yet I felt unhappy. The fortress's inhabitants did nothing to soothe my doubts. The men-at-arms were taciturn and unfriendly to our followers – but their armour shone like silver, their weapons were honed and burnished. All were bearded, like Englishmen or Bretons, which I thought peculiar. The three garrison knights were hired men, foreigners from Gascony and Aquitaine, silent and reserved to the fringes of discourtesy. Silence, in truth, brooded over Raimalard: nobody sang or shouted, men spoke in undertones. At first our vassals chattered and jested happily in relief at the journey's end. The eerie quiet – and perhaps an intangible chill which troubled me also – soon subdued them. They off-saddled almost in silence, and forbore to hiss and blaspheme when they rubbed the horses down.

Mabille Talvas and the Duke's castellan, Hugh of La Roche d'Igé, awaited us up in the donjon.

The legends of Mabille, murderer and witch, were as familiar to every knight as the lacings of his hauberk. They said she had poisoned Gislebert, her husband's brother, and Geroi of Courville and William of Montmirail. They said a child had sucked her nipple and later died in agony. She disinherited Arnold of Echoufour, then killed him with a cup of envenomed wine. I expected to find a monster, a ghoulish, wizened hag: instead I saw apple-red cheeks and beaky features, grey hair and emerald eyes – the Talvas brand – a diminutive silk-clad lady vivacious in her manner, talkative and fluent.

'My lord count,' she welcomed Curthose, 'you must be weary after your travels. Wine, Anfrid, quickly! Try these sugared quinces, or medlars boiled in honey. The barley cakes, I promise you, are excellent – I saw them baked myself.'

Even Curthose hesitated. Belesme took a quince and put it in his mouth. 'I can guarantee the purity of your victuals, my lord,' he said dryly.

'Of course they're pure, Robert, and very tasty,' Mabille prattled. 'I keep an excellent cook at Raimalard, as you should know. Dear me! Such a pother all over the countryside – Duke William's soldiers racing round like berselets tracking a hind. Only the other day a cheeky banneret arrived with a conroy and wanted to search the castle. I ask you! We had to be quite firm with him, didn't we, Hugh?'

'An arrow through his arm discouraged him,' Hugh of Igé agreed. 'The next may be less easily repulsed.' He was a fair-skinned man, black haired; thick black brows met over a broken nose. His eyes, sunk deep in his head, were dark and haunted.

'Nonsense!' Mabille said briskly. 'The Duke won't try. Everyone knows Raimalard has never been taken. I account it an honour, my lord of Maine, that you are here.'

'I hope you may not repent,' said Curthose mournfully. 'My presence can't be kept a secret, and my father will spare no pains to hunt me down.'

Ivo of Grantmesnil examined his empty wine-cup. 'What happened at Laigle? Did the Duke besiege Mortagne?'

'Oh, no. He made terms with Rotrou, and then divided up his army. Some he sent to Villerai,' Mabille said brightly, smiling at Aimeric. 'Others stormed Grantmesnil' – Ivo grunted – 'and the siege lines are set round Conches.' She glanced sympathetically at Ralph, who looked despondent; she saw Isabel at his shoulder and her eyelids flickered. 'My dear young lady, you must be *most* uncomfortable in all that iron! Do let me give you a robe and mantle!'

'Thank you, my lady. I have grown accustomed to armour.' Isabel did not return Mabille's wide smile.

'As you wish, my dear. I must confess I didn't expect *another* woman in my austere donjon.' Mabille complacently surveyed the forbidding room which occupied the donjon's second floor: a living-hall in peace, a fighting chamber during war. A miserly daylight filtered through the arrow-slits; a shaft of sunlight slicing through the doorway revealed damp hewn-stone walls, a bare planked floor, spears and bowstaves racked in rows and arrows bound in sheaves. 'You'll find the hall in the ward *far* more pleasant – all of you.' She smiled upon us sweetly. 'Hugh, I'm sure, has arranged everything for your comfort.'

Mabille dismissed us, nodding and pecking her pointed nose like a sprightly hen. I went to the ward where varlets served meat and wine and spread palliasses and furs for sleeping – we lacked everything except the armour which we wore. A tiny bath-house lurked between an armoury and stable: I stripped my hauberk and contemplated bathing – but remembered I had washed myself at Laigle. Ivo wallowed enormously in a half-cask and cursed the servitor who scrubbed his back. 'Where's the washer-girl?' he demanded. 'Careful – you heavy-handed lout!' I realized then no women lived in Raimalard – no washerwomen, kitchen sluts or sergeants' doxies – the usual feminine tribe which pervaded every castle.

Richer hung a blanket in a corner of the hall to make some privacy for Isabel and Ralph. He knotted the cords firmly, and said, 'There, that's done. I shall find you a pallet, my lady.' He looked at me seriously. 'I don't like this place, Lord Walter.'

Nor did I – but it was unnecessary to alarm Isabel. I said briskly, 'Why so? Mabille has a reputation – we have forty armed retainers. She can't hurt us – and I must say she doesn't look much like a witch.'

Isabel said, 'Walter, you're asleep. Can't you *smell* the wickedness?'

3

The summer ambled by in sun and wind and rain; the days began to wear a mantle of routine. Belesme despatched patrols at dawn which scoured woods and tracks for enemy troops. They declared the neighbourhood clear, ventured almost to Mortagne, four leagues away northwards, reported an armed encampment beneath Duke William's banner – news which depressed Curthose, who loitered daily in the hall, withdrawn and brooding, a flagon at his elbow. At evening, fortified by wine, he grew more cheerful and wove optimistic schemes for luring discontented vassals from the Duke's allegiance. He found a sergeant who could write – oddly, there was no priest in the castle, nor chapel in the ward – and dictated compulsive letters to powerful barons: Anjou and Aumale, Montfort and Meulan. The messengers departed, riding by secret ways – and never returned. The count's retinue steadily shrank: a scant thirty lances of the three hundred who had ridden from Laigle were now left.

I found Raimalard oppressive. The castle's absolute solitude, like a lone vulture brooding from its eyrie on a cliff, was in itself unnatural. A village clustered at the foot of every fort I had known: yet from Raimalard's battlements you could not see another dwelling. Nor, as I rode on patrol, did I find anywhere a byre or steading or any mark of husbandry. The demesne seemed totally deserted. I discovered by chance some overgrown mounds which might have been huts, and weed-rank clearings that might have been ploughland, and some mildewed skeletons mouldering into dust. I once smelt wood-smoke in a forest and tracked it to the embers of a fire and a crude bough-and-bracken shelter, but saw no living being.

Patrols were welcome; they broke the monotony. Otherwise I walked the ramparts and gloomily surveyed a sombre landscape, or lingered in the hall and gambled away my scanty deniers. I had nothing else to do. There were no mews in Raimalard, no liamhounds or berselets, not a scavenging cur dog.

'What do you expect?' Ivo's vast paw scooped up my stake. 'A typical Belesme stronghold, perhaps a bit worse than most. No more money, Walter? I'll lend you half a mark. Your throw. They're all like this – all the ones I've seen – Sorel and Alençon and La Ferté. Permanently stripped for war, fireproof, always mobilized. Nothing extraneous: neither women nor hawks nor dogs. Dull as a monk's dinner. A deuce to my nine – you're unlucky today.'

'What about supplies?' I objected. 'There's not a village or a cultivated field on the entire fief.'

'Friend Robert saw to that. Destroyed everything when he gave Mabille the castle.' Ivo rolled the dice. 'Two treys. You should beat that. Everything – corn, wine and fodder – comes from Belesme three leagues away. Robert holds his mother in a noose and can throttle her at will – simply by cutting off Raimalard's rations.'

'Are you saying that Robert doesn't trust his mother to hold one of his own castles?'

'Of course. Can't blame him. Would you trust a Talvas – especially one with a record like Mabille's?'

I lost my borrowed stake, left him and joined Isabel and Richer on the ramparts. The stony hillside dropped to a stream which twisted along a wooded valley. The valley climbed to a desolate moorland, gnarled by rocky outcrops, which stretched like a vast brown blanket to the horizon's forested rim. I scanned the scene silently, thinking unpleasant thoughts. Raindrops spattered from a leaden sky. Isabel shivered, and said, 'Walter, when can we leave?'

'We can't leave,' I said. 'There's no other haven for us in all Normandy. Here we stay until Duke William finds us.'

'And afterwards? What can the future hold?'

Not a great deal, I reflected drearily. If the Duke took Raimalard we would hang; if he wearied of a siege and marched away we were no better off than now – proscribed traitors hunted by his vengeance. Raimalard could withstand a lengthy leaguer; we might be penned in this black stone fortress for months or maybe years. I quailed at the prospect – our wanderings in the bleak wilderness outside alone made life endurable.

I said gruffly, 'Duke William won't kill his eldest son. Therefore he must, in justice, spare us also.'

Isabel smiled – she seldom smiled in Raimalard: nobody did – and said, 'You're trying to comfort me, dear Walter. I'd like to believe you – but the Duke isn't famous for his mercy.'

Richer moved closer, and rested a hand casually on his sword. 'The lady Mabille,' he murmured.

Mabille came towards us on the rampart walk, talking briskly to Belesme and Hugh of Igé. She paused and stared Isabel up and down, patted her arm affectionately.

'You look just like a boy, my dear, in your leather gambeson and calfskin breeches. Such an advantage of this peculiar mail' – her finger pecked Richer's hauberk – 'it doesn't have to be stitched to the gambeson: you can easily slip it off. Don't you agree, Walter? You must find it wearing to live all the time in armour.'

'I have no other garb, my lady.'

'Yes – you did arrive in rather a hurry, didn't you? So very inconvenient. Hugh, can't you possibly find some clothes for these poor people?'

Hugh of Igé's haggard features twitched; he mumbled a reply and tried to smile. Mabille descended to the ward; Isabel eyed them musingly.

'Hugh of Igé, Duke William's man, has become Mabille Talvas's dog. He would beg at her command.'

'The woman's a sorceress,' I said dourly. 'I think he's bewitched.'

We leaned against a merlon and watched the evolution in the ward below: a custom whose daily performance had blunted surprise. The garrison paraded, fully armed; Mabille walked down the line, showing no interest in accoutrements, peering into faces, occasionally caressing a beard and whispering, so it seemed, inaudible endearments. The men stood rigid, staring into space. Invariably, at the end, she stood in front of them as though considering; then beckoned with her finger – a perky, birdlike gesture – and a soldier left the ranks, marched stiffly into the donjon.

'Choosing her stallion for the night,' Isabel observed venomously. 'I'd have thought the bitch too old for whoring.'

Richer shook his head. 'It's not as simple as that.'

'What do you mean?' I asked.

Richer let the question hang. 'You sleep too soundly, my lord. Haven't you noticed our men are never detailed for night guards? Don't you know that nobody sleeps in the donjon save Mabille and her son, Hugh of Igé and a single soldier? Have you never heard the noises after dark?'

I looked at him perplexedly. 'Are you afraid of treachery, Richer? Surely —'

'No, my lord. Our bodies are safe from harm.' His fingers brushed his forehead: had he been Christian I'd have thought he signed himself. 'I fear for our souls.'

4

On a morning dark with cloud we woke to find Belesme and his retinue gone from Raimalard. This looked very like desertion: I roused Curthose and suggested we seek an explanation from Mabille. We got small satisfaction.

'How should I know what Robert's doing?' she asked brightly. 'A *dear* boy – but hardly a dutiful son. He never confides in me, you know, and went off without a word. *So* secretive!'

Hugh of Igé stared on the ground, and said heavily, 'I think he's gone to Belesme, hoping to surprise the castle.'

'Of course! Of course!' Mabille chattered. 'How clever of you, Hugh! And if Robert can seize Belesme there'll be another stronghold to oppose the Duke, who'll have to divide his forces. How *very* ingenious! There's your answer, my lord of Maine!'

When we quitted the donjon I said, 'What do you think, my lord?'

Curthose scratched the bristles on his chin – the man-at-arms who shaved us wielded a jagged knife. 'I don't like it, Walter, but there's nothing we can do. How many of our men are left?'

'About a score. The garrison now outnumber us three to one.'

He stared. 'You don't believe—'

'I believe this: Hugh of Igé spoke his piece by rote – and the words were not his own. We should set a watch at night, my lord.'

'Within the castle? Against Mabille's men?' Curthose wagged his head dubiously. 'Surely unnecessary. Our liegemen share the guards by day, and ride on patrol. When will they sleep?'

I left him in the hall, nodding over his wine, found Richer and gave him bald instructions. He listened silently and said, 'My lord of Belesme's departure has made us doubly vulnerable. Now we are in danger both by day and night.'

'Why? I don't follow you, Richer.'

He said cryptically, 'When a wolf deserts his lair look for lions in the offing. Guard yourself well on patrol, my lord.'

With Ivo and a brace of sergeants I crossed the valley and fol-lowed a wagon-way leading to Belesme. Bracken and thorn-scrub yielded to oak and ash; midsummer foliage darkened the daylight seeping through low grey clouds. The path narrowed, became a faded rusty ribbon guiding our horses' hooves. I rode ahead with Ivo, striving to discern the track. The dead leaves of a hundred winters muffled our hoofbeats; and we entered quietly upon a little glade dimmed by the overhanging trees.

A fire showed the naked bodies of men and women who pranced and postured in a ring. Beyond the fire something white writhed on a moss-grown crag. Over it stooped a black-robed shape which held a knife: the blade was dulled, wet-crimson.

A deathly fetor pervaded the glade, a mingling of corruption and a rancid animal stench, goatlike and unclean.

For three heartbeats we stood unmoving. Then the picture dis-solved. Naked bodies fled to the trees, squealing as they ran. The black-robed creature crouched motionless and watched us. I forced my trembling destrier forward, and saw what lay on the rock.

It had been a girl, no more than a child. Now she lay gashed and voided, a mangled travesty. Her eyes were open. She still lived.

'Christ in mercy!'

Ivo's sword hissed from the scabbard, flashed and struck. The child's head jumped from the stone, rolled on the dead-leaf carpet. Blood gouted briefly, stained the moss dark purple.

The thing with the knife cackled.

I dismounted, plucked a brand from the fire and held it high, and crept to the stone. I looked on a grey-white face, old and wrinkled, a mesh of dirt-crusted furrows. Wide green eyes gleamed above a falcon's beak, and bloodless lips grimaced over rotten teeth. White hair clung to her shoulders, and vermin crawled in the strands.

The crone spoke. 'Greetings, Walter of Poix.'

I recoiled violently and dropped the brand. She slipped lithely as a fawn behind the stone, and vanished in the dark. Ivo swore, spurred his horse, lifted his sword. I seized his rein and pulled him to a stand. We both saw something disappear among the trees. It was black and furred, and moved silently. It went on all fours.

We heard voices, hoofbeats and the clink of mail. The sergeants rode into the glade. The light was dim, the fire dying; but they saw enough to strike them dumb.

Ivo slid from the saddle, scratched his sword-point on the lichened stone, averting his eyes from the sacrifice that lay above. He said, 'This is an altar. Look!'

I bent closer. Lettering was there, deeply incised, unintelligible; and an eroded carving, a horned and bestial head.

Ivo sighed and sheathed his sword. 'I have seen the like before, deep in another forest, far away in Périgord. The god of an old religion, half man, half goat, remembered only by forest dwellers, the descendants of his worshippers from ages long ago.'

The smell still lingered. Ivo said, 'Why did you stop me killing her?'

I closed my eyes and waited till the sickness passed.

'Didn't you ... recognize it?'

5

On the edge of the moor I set up marks, took a sergeant's bow and quiver and occupied myself with archery. Ralph of Conches, for want of something better, occasionally came and practised likewise. The borrowed bow was hazelwood, the limbs unbalanced; the arrows aspen, stiffly spined and apt to yaw. I made poor shooting;

Ralph showed no improvement since the days when he shot at the apple tree.

He loosed a shaft twenty spans wide, lowered the bow and said without relevance, 'That infidel Richer.'

I glanced at the Saracen, who stood clear of the mark – farther since Ralph began shooting – and collected arrows after we had shot the round. I said, 'What about him?'

'He attends over-closely on my lady.'

'Why complain? Isabel has assumed the guise of knight, Richer her esquire. A devoted one: he guards her well.'

'Too devoted. I begin to fear for my honour.'

I smoothed the fletching of an arrow which Ralph's clumsiness had ruffled, and nocked it to the string. 'Kill him, then,' I said indifferently, 'or send him away.'

'A course I have considered, and rejected. It would expose my lady to a greater menace.'

'Which is?'

'Yourself.'

I raised the bow and drew, sighted over the pile on Richer's breast, sixty paces away. 'Explain, Ralph.'

'You understand my meaning very well.'

I altered aim and loosed. The arrow thumped the packed-earth target. 'A span low,' I murmured. 'The shafts twist in flight. Ralph, I know this: you trouble yourself unduly. I can promise you Isabel's virtue is safe from Richer.'

'And from you?'

I leaned on the bowstave and stared at the ground. 'You're thinking of that ancient scandal of our childhood days, at Evreux years ago. It was nothing – you had best forget it.'

A sullen frown settled on Ralph's plump face, the slack lips pouted. 'You're trying to evade the issue. I'm not blind. I've seen you look at her, and she at you, since the day you met at Laigle.'

I said quietly, 'I have not horned you, Ralph.'

'You say it. How can I know the truth? There has been chance enough in the flight from Rouen – and here at Raimalard.'

'True. Chance enough.' I nodded towards Richer, busy gathering arrows. 'There is your custodian, Ralph.' I added thoughtfully, 'I may even have to kill him myself.'

Ralph gobbled; his face flushed scarlet. 'Shameless —! So you declare openly your lust!'

I unbraced the bow. 'This you had better know, if you have not already guessed. Before you were betrothed to her I loved Isabel. I love her still. If ever we leave Raimalard alive I shall try to take her from you. Until then you have my word: she, and you, and your piddling honour are all safe from me.'

I turned to Richer, who strolled towards us carrying a sheaf of arrows. 'Those are wayward shafts – no wonder our bowmen so often miss. Show us, Richer, something of your skill.'

He braced his bow – a double-curved, light stave, the belly goat's horn, the back of polished wood – and nocked an arrow from his quiver. A raven flapped across the sky. Richer swiftly raised the bow and loosed in one fast motion. A crumpled mess of sable feathers thudded to the ground.

I grinned at Ralph. 'You see? Stop worrying, man. I'm not bent on suicide.'

Richer studied our faces curiously; then went to retrieve his shaft.

6

I was slumbering heavily and dreaming vividly.

I dreamed that a monstrous cat crouched over a child and licked her face. The tongue flickered in rhythm with the claws that ripped her bowels. The child squirmed hideously and shrieked my name. The shrieks died to a whisper close to my ear, and I struggled to the surface of awakening.

'Walter! Walter! Come.'

Richer's voice. I pulled on a cloak and followed him from the night-dark hall, stepping over pallets and the bodies of sleeping men. He took my wrist and guided me to an alley between hall and barrack. A shard of moonlight severed a notch in the clouds and lit a recumbent figure, snoring heavily, propped against a wall.

'Our sentry.' Richer's voice was grim.

I bent and shook the man. His head lolled loosely; I smelt the wine on his breath. 'The drunken rogue,' I muttered savagely. 'I'll have him flogged in the morning!'

Richer drew his dagger and pricked him under the jaw. The sentry mumbled incoherently, but did not wake. 'There was more than wine in his cup,' he whispered. 'No toper ever slept so sound. Leave him.' He beckoned, and I followed to the ramparts. The fleeting moonlight silvered stone-tiled huts, painted merlons and embrasures in patterns of black and grey. The night was quiet, profoundly still. The ramparts were deserted.

'Where is the watch?'

Richer shrugged, and pointed to the gate. We walked quietly, treading carefully, avoiding noise. The gate yawned wide, the drawbridge down. There was no guard, no sentry in the watch-tower, nobody at all. Raimalard seemed lifeless as a citadel of the dead.

I looked at the hulk of the donjon. A yellow gash gleamed from a topmost arrow-slit, like a candle burning through a weary night. We returned along the rampart walk, climbed the mound and stood in the tower's shadow.

Richer whispered, 'Listen!'

We heard the cry from the donjon, a bubbling moan, then silence, and a howl like a plea for mercy from the nethermost depths of hell. A voice bedevilled, a man's voice – or what remained of a man.

I shivered, although the air was warm, and felt sweat-drops trickling on my spine. We slipped quickly down the motte, returned to the ramparts. I rested my forehead on a merlon; the cold hard stone soothed like a healing balm. Richer roused me, hand on shoulder, and pointed into the night. Firelight flickered far away, in a tentacle of forest across the valley's shadowed chasm, beyond the heathland's ghost-grey wastes. The flame waxed and waned, dimmed and glowed, like an ember fanned by breathing.

'I have seen such fires these many nights past,' Richer said.

Fantasy began to smother my mind. I thumped my knuckles on my temples, and strove to regain reality. 'The castle is defenceless, the sentinels gone. We must rouse our followers and post a guard.'

Richer shook his head. 'No need. There is nothing of this world that threatens us tonight. Stay here, and watch.'

The cloud-veil shredded. Moonlight flooded the ward; black, sharp-edged shadows flowed from the skirts of hall and hutment. The distant fire faded and died. Faint as a brief sigh of death, a voice called once from the donjon. A man-at-arms stumbled from a barrack, relieved himself against a wall: the padding of his footsteps rang loud as a clash of arms. I was chilled and frightened, and prayed wordlessly for God's protection against terrors which I did not understand.

A stone rattled on the hillside. Richer put a finger to his lips, drew me beneath the shadow of a watch-tower.

Mabille came through the gate. Her face was calm and peaceful, the eyes half closed, her arms hung loose at her sides, she glided over the ground like a small grey ghost. Her hair, unbound, flowed down to her waist. The stains which streaked the front of her robe shone wetly under the moon.

Behind her, two by two, walked her knights and men-at-arms. Their eyes were glazed and vacant, they moved slowly, shuffling like men in a trance. A moist stickiness matted their beards and dappled their mail.

I crossed myself and abjectly invoked the Saints.

Hugh of Igé entered last. His head was lifted to the sky, and I saw the clotted smudges that caked his lips and chin. The haunted eyes were pits in an ashen face, a face with the desolate look of a damned soul doomed to perdition. He muttered softly to himself, and pulled his fingers as if cleansing them.

The procession crossed the ward, disappeared inside the huts. Mabille and Hugh climbed slowly up the mound, entered the donjon. The light in the arrow-slit vanished.

We crept to the hall and spoke not a word – the horror transcended speech. A bulky figure loomed at the doorway, and I felt for my dagger. A sword blade pressed my wrist, and Ivo said, 'Steady, Walter.'

I looked at him numbly.

'I saw you go,' he said, 'but lacked courage to follow you. No mortal should walk abroad on this of all nights of the year. Midsummer Eve, Walter,' Ivo added gravely. 'A bad time to be out.'

7

Three days later Duke William's men caught Aimeric of Villerai.

Aimeric's fiery impatience had led him into rashness. He enjoyed leading his patrols to the marches of Mortagne, within sight of the Duke's encampment around the castle, and afterwards boasted of his forays. 'I watched them having a tournament once,' he said complacently, 'and was tempted to join the mellay. Don't think they'd have noticed – the place is more like a hunting camp than a warlike muster. They manage to enjoy themselves, which is more than we do here.'

Nevertheless Mortagne kept watch, and Aimeric was sighted and chased. The first we saw were minute figures crawling over the plain, strung out and riding hard. Hugh of Igé sounded the alarm:

horns brayed, men armed themselves and ran to battlements and ramparts. The bridge came up and the gates were closed. Lacing my helmet as I went, I sprinted to the gate.

'For the love of Christ! Don't you realize that's Aimeric's patrol? You can't shut them out!'

Hugh's eyes met mine, and slid away. He said stonily, 'I'm responsible for Raimalard's defence. I won't take risks.'

This needed more authority than I possessed. I hurried to Curthose, who gloomily watched the chase from the ramparts. The riders hurtled down the moorland slope to the stream. Aimeric led – I recognized his yellow helmet – and then two sergeants on failing horses who dropped back at every stride. The pursuers – a dozen armoured knights and sergeants – were closing the gap. Triumphant war-whoops travelled on the wind.

I said, 'My lord, Hugh of Igé has closed the gates.'

Curthose regarded me blankly. 'What? What? The man must be mad! Tell him to open!'

'I have. He refuses.'

Curthose astoundingly lost his temper. His face went scarlet and he whipped out his sword. 'Ivo! Ralph! Get your men mounted! Make a sally and bring Aimeric in! Walter, follow me!'

He ran across the ward, waddling absurdly on short bandy legs. Hugh of Igé saw him coming, rapped an order. We reached the gateway and faced men-at-arms and a line of levelled spears.

Curthose spluttered an obscenity, and charged.

This was no way for the Count of Maine to die. I thrust my sword between his legs and brought him down. Hugh snarled at his men; the hovering spearheads checked and lifted. I raised Curthose to his feet, retrieved his fallen sword. He was very angry.

'Walter, I'll have your blood —!' He saw Hugh, and roared, 'Open the gates, you spawn of hell! Will you stand here idly and see my vassals killed?'

Curthose lifted his blade. Hugh of Igé backed a pace, fronted his shield and stood on guard. A voice called from the rampart.

'You've no call to fight, my lords. Duke William's men eradicate the causes of your quarrel.' Mabille gestured prettily. 'Come and look.'

We stared from an embrasure. Aimeric's sergeants were gone: a riderless horse cantered over the moor, another thrashed belly-up in the heather; horsemen milled around two wriggling bodies, and hacked and thrust. The yellow helmet fled to the stream. I could see the destrier's foam-flecked neck, the bloody rowels that scarred his ribs. A knight on a sorrel stallion thundered in his wake, lance in rest, spurring his horse and shouting. Aimeric swerved for the ford, flung away his lance and tugged at his sword.

He hit the stream at a gallop which sprayed water like slivers of crystal. The horse stumbled, fell to his knees. Aimeric twisted in the saddle, cut backwards with his sword. The knight took his lance from rest, raised it high and stabbed and let it go. The point plunged deep in the spine, the shaft swung in a shining arc. Aimeric screamed, threw wide his arms, and rolled slowly into the water.

I licked dry lips. Curthose muttered, and signed himself. Hugh of Igé, like a man exhausted, leaned on the quillons of his sword and bowed his head. Mabille sighed deeply. Her eyes were bright, excited, and she smiled.

'*What* a pity!' she trilled. 'He was such an *entertaining* man! Well, there's no need to open the gates now, is there?'

She pattered away. Curthose looked at Ralph and Ivo, who waited, mounted, in the ward. 'Off-saddle,' he said tiredly. 'They've caught him.' I watched the enemy lift Aimeric's body, rope it across his saddle like a hog, and ride away. A hopeful bowman flexed and loosed; the arrow fell far short and a sergeant rated his folly.

The day passed, and another night. Aimeric's end discouraged the patrols we sent out; they did not venture far and brought scanty information. The little they said was bad: the Duke's outriders were active in the forests and probed constantly to Raimalard. I paced the ramparts, staring at the horizon which hid Mortagne; Ivo grew terse and lost his humour; the sentries' eyes became red with watching. Then, like a wolf-pack which has tasted blood, Duke William's army came, a moving forest of spears and pennons, a sea of shining helmets. Pavilions like gaudy flowers blossomed on the sad dun moorland; a mangonel's stark skeleton slanted beyond the stream.

They dug entrenchments, and the siege of Raimalard started.

8

A siege that was not a siege.

The Duke's men fashioned gabions and mantlets, picketed the tracks which led to Raimalard, hacked a fosse across the spur the castle gripped. They built three mangonels, carted stones and piled them beneath the timbers. They made a battering-ram, shielded beneath a hide-covered roof and mounted on wooden wheels. 'Though how they propose to haul that machine up here,' said Curthose, eyeing the precipitous slopes below the ramparts, 'is beyond my understanding.' Then, the siege lines formally set, the Duke sent a herald to demand surrender. Curthose returned a polite refusal, and sent greetings to his father. The knight bowed, and called, 'My lord says also this: Hugh of Igé, to whom he entrusted Raimalard, is proved traitorous and forsworn. The Duke promises him no quarter.' The herald dipped his lance, leaf-garlanded in sign of truce, and rode down the stony path. Hugh gave a twisted smile. 'The man could have saved his breath. That much I already know.'

We posted double sentries day and night; the garrison slept armoured, weapons at hand. Nothing happened. The power-ropes of the mangonels stayed slack, the ram steamed damply in the rain, the storming parties rested behind their mantlets. We scratched our heads and waited. Isabel and Richer had had no experience of siege warfare. Curthose, Ralph and I had taken part in leaguers; we had never been besieged. Ivo had. After a week he began to grouse. 'There's something wrong about this,' he stated. 'Unlike the Duke to be so inert. The whole business stinks like a fish market on a hot afternoon.'

'Perhaps they're trying to starve us out,' Curthose suggested.

'Impossible. Hugh says we've rations for a year. Fodder's a problem – may have to eat the horses.' Ivo bit his thumb and added thoughtfully, 'I wonder what has happened to Belesme?'

He was answered within days. A sentinel called a warning; we manned battle stations, saw a fresh contingent join the besiegers' camp. There was no mistaking the elegant form of the knight who led them, nor the piebald thoroughbred he always rode. We watched Belesme enter the Duke's pavilion, stroll amicably with him through the horse lines, talk earnestly and gesture to the castle. Clearly they discussed an escalade. Curthose ground his teeth and swore.

'Misbegotten bastard son of a leprous sow! Not only has he played me false – he's betrayed his mother! What answer can Mabille produce for this?'

She said, for a change, very little, and without her usual pertness. 'I am not responsible for my son's actions, my lord count. He goes his way, and I mine.'

Curthose said furiously, 'How may I know whom to trust?

You're of the same blood, my lady – do you wonder that I doubt your loyalty?'

Mabille regarded the hands folded in her lap. 'You hold Raimalard, my lord. Is that not sufficient proof?'

She would say no more; Curthose, fuming, left her. I told him glumly that Hugh of Igé, pleading the stresses of siege, had mingled our own retainers with the garrison, allocating sentry posts and battle stations haphazardly by night and day. The men, thus scattered, could not speedily be gathered to our aid at need. Strangely enough, I pointed out, the donjon, save for a lookout on the battlements, remained unoccupied.

'And what do you infer from that?' Curthose snapped. 'That Hugh of Igé can't be trusted? Obvious as the blazon on his shield!'

Belesme's arrival stirred activity. Artillerymen manned the mangonels: for three days we endured a battering. The castle's elevation prevented serious damage: the boulders, flung in high curving arcs, had weight but little velocity. A horse was killed, a sergeant crushed and rooftops smashed. No arrows came, for the siege lines were placed beyond bowshot. More worrying were the evident signs of an imminent escalade: entrenchments fully manned, ladders poking from the ditches, bannerets rehearsing storming parties, bowmen practising in squads. Even the cumbrous battering-ram was manhandled to the front. Ivo assessed these preparations from the ramparts, and spoke from the depths of hard experience.

'I reckon they'll attack tomorrow,' he said definitely.

That night I slept in snatches, and woke quickly when I heard the noise – a muffled shouting from the donjon, a scream abruptly snapped. I roused Ivo, snatched sword and shield, ran from the hall and scrambled up the mound, Ivo swearing breathlessly behind. The ladder to the donjon door was gone, the portal closed. I hammered my sword hilt uselessly on stone, leaned panting against the wall. Ivo gripped my arm.

'What is it, Walter? What do you fear?'

The echoes of the scream still rang within my head.

'Treachery,' I said. 'Perhaps devilry.'

A storm-wind soughed in the embrasures. Camp fires in the plain below glimmered like scattered rubies. The donjon door creaked open. A torch flared in the portal. A man leaned from the opening, framed blackly against the light.

'Who comes there?'

'Walter of Poix. Ivo of Grantmesnil.'

'Enter.'

The ladder dropped. I raised my shield and climbed, expecting I knew not what. Hugh of Igé waited in the hall, torch lifted high. I examined him warily in the wavering light. His face was grey and shrunken, the skin shrivelled on the bones. He beckoned with his chin.

'Come!'

We followed him up the steps, thrust aside a curtain at the top and entered the upper chamber. Tapestries covered the walls; figures of men and animals and the shapes of bestial creatures danced on the embroidery. A drugget on the rushes wore strange ciphers and designs. A brazier smoked in a corner. The air was heavy and foul, and smelt of ordure. On a bed against the wall lay a naked body.

It had no head.

Blood was everywhere, soaking the coverlet, splashed on the tester, dripping to the floor. I looked at the shrivelled breasts, the old, wrinkled thighs, and leaned, swaying, on my shield. Ivo breathed gustily through his nose. Hugh of Igé watched us, his eyes dull marbles in the pits of a corpse-like face.

'A man can endure so much, and then no more.' His voice was a croak. 'My soul is damned to eternity, my honour lost and gone. I have killed the goddess I worshipped. Grant me, my lords, the mercy of your swords.'

'You have rid the world of a virulent witch,' Ivo said roughly. 'Why should I kill you? Out, man! I can bear no more.'

We stumbled from the chamber, down the ladder from the donjon. The wind breathed cool and pure, scented by earth and rain. Ivo filled his lungs, like a man coming up from the depths.

He said, 'What now? Will the garrison obey you now she's . . . gone?'

Hugh said in an iron voice, 'No. The men are her creatures – as was I. I shall leave Raimalard.'

'How?' Ivo swept a hand to the dying fires that ringed the castle. 'Have you wings?'

'There is a way.' Hugh crumpled to the ground and held his head in his hands. 'And you, my lords, had better follow.'

'Abandon Raimalard? The Duke will attack at dawn.'

'A farce,' Hugh answered wearily. 'The gates will open when the stormers reach the ramparts. It is planned. Robert of Belesme and . . . Mabille.'

'Betrayal,' said Ivo softly. He tapped his shield and stared into the night. A pale coppery sheen smeared the eastern horizon, a faint sigh of colour, fragile as mist on a mirror. Ivo stood up decisively, 'We haven't much time. Show me your way.'

Hugh led us to a granary, opened the door. Corn crunched beneath our feet, grain-sacks climbed to the roof.

'Help me.'

By the starshine's light through the open door we lifted sacks, cleared a space on the floor, scooped aside loose corn. Hugh bent, grunted with effort, heaved up a square flat flagstone. A black pit gaped in the earth. Ivo peered into the hole dubiously.

'Where does this lead?'

'It emerges at the bottom of the hill.'

'Within the siege lines? Useless. You can't —'

'It opens on a ravine which will cover our escape.' A hint of desperation tinged Hugh's toneless voice. 'Hasten, my lord, if you are coming.'

Ivo unhurriedly drew his sword, rested the point on Hugh of Igé's breast. 'You must wait a little while, my friend,' he said amicably. 'Walter, go quickly to the hall. Rouse Curthose, Ralph and his lady. Bring them here. The rest,' he added regretfully, 'must take their chance with the Duke. Tell them to surrender when the escalade begins.'

I did as he commanded. My whispers were urgent, the explanations short. The knights and esquires we abandoned understood Count Robert's peril, that his life was forfeit while their own were safe – they owed fealty to their suzerains, not to the Duke of Normandy. They accepted with relief the prospect of surrender. Curthose grumbled, half asleep, and hunted clumsily in darkness for his baldric. Ralph said nothing; I could feel his shaking, sensed his fear. Isabel silently donned her hauberk; the chain-rings rustled in the quiet like leaves shaken by the wind. We crossed the ward, keeping to the shadows, stepping cautiously as cats. Richer, without a word, came after us.

Hugh dropped into the cavity, and Ivo followed, sword mistrustfully in hand. We entered an enclosed blackness, a narrow sloping corridor carved through solid rock. The sides scraped my shoulders; I crouched beneath the roof, and shuffled downwards step by step. In places the passage was so low that I went on hands and knees, cutting my palms on sharp-edged stone. The darkness enfolded us, absolute as blindness, the only sounds the scrape of feet, a rasp of iron on stone, and laboured breathing. After a while you did not know when the channel curved or straightened, whether you climbed or fell. My nerves thrummed taut as a bowstring; time stretched to an eternity endless as the tomb.

Hugh said something in a muffled voice; I heard him pant and strain, his muscles crack, and the creak of wood. Light flooded the chamber, a pallid whisper of dawn, harsh to our dazzled eyes as a noonday glare. We crawled under a tangled trellis of thorn and bramble which hid the outlet, and for a time lay still. Ralph joined his hands before his face and prayed, whether in thanksgiving for deliverance or invoking mercy for the future I could not tell. Hugh signed us on; we followed the bed of a deep ravine choked with elder-scrub and hawthorn, hiding us from sight of watchers who lurked above. We passed beneath the outposts, heard a tired sentry welcome his relief, a horse snort and whinny; and cringed at the threat of challenge.

Hugh stopped at last in a shadowed copse where bracken blanketed the ground. Daybreak paled the camp fires; then a sun-beam like a golden sword brushed Raimalard's sombre tower.

He said, 'I have brought you out, my lords. Now, by your leave, I must depart.'

Ivo looked at him beneath his brows. 'You will not accompany us further?'

Hugh smiled crookedly, a grimace like a grin upon a death's-head. 'You seek merely to escape Duke William's vengeance. I, for my crime, shall be hunted till I die by the brood of Talvas. I leave you to judge who must run fast and farthest. Farewell, my lords.'

He turned and walked unsteadily from the grove. I watched his shape grow small and disappear – to begin a journey which took him to Apulia, and then, when Belesme found him, to Outremer and death.

Ivo of Grantmesnil slapped his hands on his knees and lumbered to his feet. 'Well, my friends,' he said, grinning hugely, 'here we are, free to go wheresoever we will – with neither horses, provender nor home. No destination either.' He slung his shield aback and loosened his coif. 'Let's start walking.'

Chapter 5

1077-78

Knights are unused to walking – they ride wherever they go. Nor is armour made for the exercise, which revealed muscles I had never known existed. We went slowly and then more slowly.

We headed away from Raimalard, keeping roughly north, seeking cover in trees and undergrowth, feeling dangerously exposed when we traversed open ground. Shortly after daybreak a murmuring travelled on the wind. Ivo lengthened his stride.

'The Duke's attacking the castle,' he said curtly. 'Soon they'll find we're gone, and start searching.'

We rested at noon in a wood, and sheltered in a dell beneath birch and holly, and drank thirstily from puddles. Already my feet were sore, my thighs ached. Curthose thankfully removed his shoes and dabbled his feet in water. Isabel wiped her face with a wetted kerchief. Nobody said very much. I rested my head on my knees and tried to think, to concoct some plan for our travelling, a mode of existence. First of all, and sooner rather than later, we had to eat.

Richer lifted his head. 'Listen!'

We heard the drumbeat of galloping horses. Ivo made urgent downward motions with his hand; we lay flat in the bracken. A dozen armoured riders hurtled past the rim of the dell, led by Robert of Belesme. I glimpsed the blazing fury in his face. The hoofbeats died in the distance; sunlight filtered through the trees and gilded the dust-haze of their going.

'Chasing Hugh of Igé,' Ivo said soberly. 'God send him aid and us as well. Come on – we can't stay here.'

At sundown, dragging our feet, we arrived at the edge of a clearing. Two wooden huts, a byre and a corral overlooked a narrow field sown with beans and barley. Sheep grazed on withered grass, swine rooted among the trees, a woman milked a goat. A bearded peasant stirred a pot hung over a fire, and children played nearby. A ploughman drove a wooden plough behind a heifer; he wore a coat of cary cloth, the hood full of holes, frayed mittens and patched knobbly shoes. His tongue peeped out as he followed the furrows; mire beslobbered him and he wallowed in mud to the ankles. A woman wrapped in a winnowing sheet walked barefoot alongside, wielding a long goad. In a wicker basket at the end of the field lay an infant wrapped in rags; two small children sat on either side; all were crying. The ploughman sighed deeply, and said, 'Children, be still.'

We stood in the fringe of the forest, examining the place cautiously for signs of danger. The steam from the pot spread a savoury smell, and my mouth watered. Drawn as by a lodestone, I moved forward; Curthose held me, and fumbled beneath the skirts of his hauberk.

'Wait. I have money: we must pay for what we take. If we rob they'll betray us to the hunters.'

His prudence was unavailing. At the sight of armour the woman screamed, grabbed a child and fled. The ploughman and his wife, mouths wide in fright, seized their children and ran after her. We were left with the animals and an infant too young to walk, who sucked his thumb and stared round-eyed.

'Might have known they wouldn't wait,' Ivo grunted. 'This is Belesme's country, after all. The peasants expect nothing but killing and rape.'

Curthose said, 'Be quick. Collect what food we can carry, and get away fast.'

We found black bread, some grain in a mud-lined hole in the floor of a hut, and a handful of dried beans. We killed two goats and slung the carcases across our shoulders. Hastily we swallowed the simmering pottage, and scorched our lips. Curthose left deniers in the cauldron. Then, following paths that seemed to meander endlessly and led nowhere, we plunged deep into the forest and kept walking until dark. When we halted, almost spent, Richer skinned a goat, made a fire and roasted meat. Voraciously we ate the burned and half-raw hunks; and afterwards sat round the fading flames and fought despair.

Ralph said, 'Unless we find horses I, for one, can't go much farther in my mail.'

Ivo stretched his arms. 'I agree. My shoulders are rubbed raw. We'll have to shed our hauberks.'

'Go unarmoured,' Curthose muttered, 'hunted as we are? I'd feel naked.'

'You can have my mail, my lord,' Richer said quietly, 'It's lighter and more flexible than yours.'

Curthose surveyed Richer's slender figure, looked down at his own stout chest. 'Wouldn't fit. Ivo, you may be right, and for a different reason: we may have to depend on villeins for our victuals – and they're terrified of men in armour, as we saw today. We'd do better if we went unmailed.'

'Travel in shirt and hose?' I asked. 'All right by day – but the nights are cold.'

Isabel said, 'Cut away your rings and mail-discs, and keep the gambesons.'

We gaped at her – astounded, I think, by a woman's sense. Slowly we pulled out daggers and, by the fire's uncertain light, began hacking at thongs and laces. Ivo dug a pit with his sword; discs and rings and helmets were shovelled in; Isabel sadly dropped her chain-mesh hauberk on the pile.

'What about shields?' Ralph asked.

'No shields,' said Ivo firmly. 'Every thorn-bush, every twig we've passed, has plucked at mine all day. We keep only swords and daggers, and travel light.'

The shields were hidden in deep undergrowth, beneath a tangled filigree of briars. Curthose broke a deadwood branch, threw it on the fire and said, 'We have put a distance between ourselves and Raimalard, and evaded pursuit for a day. Now, my lords, we must plan for the future. Where do you propose we should go?'

'I still think we'd be safe in Conches,' Ralph said.

'Who is the Duke's castellan?'

'Landric of Agys.'

Ivo blew out his cheeks. 'No. I remember the man. He'd give us to the Duke as soon as we crossed his drawbridge.'

'That,' said Curthose sadly, 'applies to every fortress in Normandy. Only the petty castles aren't kept by my father's garrisons. And the small ones are useless – we must find a place strong as Raimalard, or stronger.'

'We should go to France,' I suggested.

Curthose pursed his lips. 'Risky. King Philip is the Duke's over-lord – at least in theory – and the two have patched up peace since the defeat at Dol. Philip may find it politic to hand me over.'

There was a depressed silence. The heart of the fire collapsed in a shower of sparks; the forest's quiet darkness closed around our backs. I stared into the glowing embers, and felt thoroughly despondent. So much for my high ambitions, my quest for fortune and renown, my pragmatical decision to follow the Count of Maine. William of Evreux's prophecy was resolved into bitter truth. I had tried to steer Curthose from the disastrous course he followed, and had been defeated by the witless counsels of stupid men. Men like Ivo of Grantmesnil. I glanced at his brooding face, and wondered what he was thinking. Ivo had lost more than I ever hoped to possess: a great Honour, seven fiefs and the services of twenty knights. An immense stake flung carelessly into a hazardous gamble, and now forfeit. Ralph had squandered more – Conches was a greater barony than Grantmesnil – and that reluctantly, against his inclinations. Isabel had persuaded him, on her behalf and mine. Did he recognize the cause of his misfortune? I studied his face, and saw him look adoringly at Isabel across the fire. Almost I pitied him.

For Curthose I felt no sympathy. A weak, kindly, amiable man, totally unfitted by nature for his high position. You liked him; you could not admire him. He owed his downfall solely to himself. What use to follow him further? Easy to slip away by night. And then? A landless, destitute knight, without horse or armour, proscribed by the Duke, wandering from fief to fief, seeking to sell his sword to some minor lordling in return for food and shelter. Little better than a hired man-at-arms. No. I had to stay with Curthose, and try to rebuild his fortunes and my own. How?

There was also the matter of Isabel. It was strange, I reflected dully, how catastrophe quenched one's ardour.

Richer stood. 'We must set a watch,' he said quietly, and disappeared among the trees. Ivo watched him go. 'The Saracen has kept his armour,' he said without interest. 'Should we make him discard it?' Isabel said sharply, 'No. Let him be.' Ivo shrugged.

An inspiration, fleeting as a flame-spurt in the fire, sped through my mind. I caught and held it, turned it round and round in mental fingers and examined it. Poix. Why not? The danger was no greater – we had nothing to lose but our lives – and I would spit two birds on a single shaft: my lord's salvation and my own. Wiser, perhaps, not to put the plan plainly: the slightest opposition from Ralph or Ivo might discourage Curthose. One must dangle a juicier bait.

I kicked a cinder into the fire, and said, 'My lord count, it seems we shall find no haven in Normandy or France. There is but one alternative: we must make for Flanders, and seek shelter with Count Robert the Frisian.'

Curthose, half asleep, said drowsily, 'Flanders? God's wonders, Walter – all Normandy and Artois lie between!'

'We shall be taken long before we get there,' Ralph objected.

'If we wander the woods like outlaws,' I snapped, 'without purpose or destination, we shall certainly be captured!'

Ivo said briskly, 'Walter's right. We've got to go somewhere – why not Flanders? The Frisian owes no fealty to William: we shall be safe with him.'

Curthose lay on his side, scraped dead leaves beneath his head to make a pillow. 'I'm too tired to argue. We can but try. Let's see how we feel in the morning.' He sighed deeply and closed his eyes.

At moondawn I relieved Richer, and sat staring into the shadows, and listened to Ivo's snores.

2

Three months later we lay hidden in the forests near Evreux.

From Raimalard to Evreux, as the arrow flies, is barely sixteen leagues. We had turned and twisted, retraced our steps, made long detours; and often halted in concealment when horsemen ranged the neighbourhood, or exhaustion made us stop, or a source of victuals helped us to recover. Hunger, and the peril of armoured men, were unremitting enemies. Our money was long since spent; we lived like mendicants, poachers and outlaws. We begged at the doors of monasteries, craved food from village priests nearly as impoverished as ourselves. Richer's skilful archery also saved us from starvation; we ate the flesh of wolves and foxes, and stringy carcases of birds; once he killed a roe-deer and we feasted like kings for a week. In the beechwoods close to Ivri, desperate with hunger, we waylaid a paunchy abbot riding on a mule. He carried a little money, a bulging wineskin and a wallet of pastries, his attendant monk a loaf – plunder hardly worth the trouble of an ambush. We had to kill them lest they run to Ascelin Goel, who held Ivri, and bring his soldiers scouring the woods for outlaws. Ivo and I buried the bodies in shallow graves dug in the beechmast; he suggested we kept the mule, but I demurred: the beast would be a hindrance in the trackless tree-wastes where we lived. We slaughtered it, ate some, buried the rest and moved quickly from Ivri's marches. Because we had long protested that Richer's armour made our little company conspicuous, he cut a tunic from the abbot's robe and wore it over his mail.

We were bearded, shaggy-haired, alive with lice and fleas, our leather gambesons ripped by thorns and stained by the earth we slept on. Beneath the hair and dirt our faces were gaunt; the skin drooped in folds on Ivo's enormous frame; Isabel's cheeks were drawn and hollow. And yet, reduced by hard privation to the essential bone and gristle which wild animals need for the business of living, in this nadir of existence we stayed robust and healthy – except for one bad period when we starved for three long days.

A mood of desperate gaiety often lightened our travels: we felt we could sink no further, we could only rise, or die. The despair we had all experienced on the night after leaving Raimalard seldom returned: Curthose shed his dejection, remained resolute and cheerful; Ivo lived buoyantly from day to day and made light of all our hardships; Ralph was sometimes seen to smile. Isabel's quiet serenity seldom faltered. She became our cook, made bread when we stole flour, grilled meat when hunger or necessity did not compel us to eat it raw. Richer said less than anyone and did far more: to this day I do not know how he endured. He kept watch at night when the others were too spent to care; he scouted ahead by day when the way seemed doubtful or dangerous; he took his odd-shaped bow and hunted afar in the forests to find us food. Whenever we came near starving he produced a crust of bread, a sliver of dried fish or shred of meat – which he always gave to Isabel.

Evil stalked the inner forests, where people lived far from God. Once we found a carven altar, like the horror near Raimalard, rusted by old blood and garlanded with skulls. Later, a circle of leaning stones, which we came upon at dusk when marching late to reach a spring. There was fire within the stones, and voices chanting. We fled unseen into the dark. None of us slept that night.

South of Ivri we had entered a devastated area where, as I have mentioned, for three days we starved. This was a territory where strife seemed to spring spontaneously from the soil itself: a perpetual battleground for Melisent of Houdan and Fulcher of Anet, whose families had for years waged private war. Endless harryings had swept the land clean of tenement and tillage: there were piles of rubble where villages once had prospered, and the forest's green outriders swallowed untended fields. It was dangerous to travel in the open; you never knew when you might encounter raiders. Cowering in a ditch, we witnessed an affray, a swirling fight where a score of warriors clashed and hacked and bellowed, a rout and a chase that vanished in a dust-cloud, a dead man left on the ground. We searched the body hopefully, but found neither money nor food, and retreated quickly to the trees.

Even the forest was perilous: the survivors from the villages had made the woods their own and lived like wild creatures in the darkest depths. Occasionally we caught glimpses of half-naked bodies flitting among the tree-trunks, heard the twang of a bowstring – and quickly realized they disliked intruders. We tumbled into an ambuscade on a game-path which we followed, and were beset by hairy savages armed with reaping-hooks and clubs. Richer was struck by an arrow; only his armour saved him. The swords beat them off; they scuttled like weasels into the undergrowth whence they came, leaving a fetid body-stench and a crumpled corpse. For three days we wandered in this leaf-dark wilderness and never ate and seldom slept, for we sensed the hidden watchers in the trees and rested with swords unsheathed, searching the gloom through bloodshot, red-rimmed eyes.

Because survival depended on mutual protection we usually stayed together. But for various reasons – on watch, for purposes of nature, to collect wood for the fire and grass or bracken for our sleeping – we sometimes wandered apart. One day – I think it was after leaving Anet's marches: the memories of our daily vagrancies are blurred – I left the camp to forage grubs from tree-bark for our supper. I heard soft grunts and squeaks from a hazel copse, imagined a vole or hedgehog and crept near quietly to capture the animal.

Isabel and Curthose lay together in the undergrowth, and played the game of the two-backed beast.

Fury clutched me like a living hand, sweat started from my body. Certain he had taken her by force, I groped for my sword, began rising to my feet. Then I saw Isabel's face and the delirious ecstasy which glazed her eyes.

I crawled away from the copse, sick and shaken, venomously angry. My tearing rage overrode discretion: at that moment I wanted Curthose dead, although his being was vital to my plans for Poix. Yet a shred of caution remained: mine must not be the sword that killed him. Ralph sat apart, his tunic on his knees, picking dully at the vermin. I said between my teeth, 'You had better find your lady, else the antlers on your head will reach the stars.'

His hands were still. He looked at me sideways, his mouth trembled and he said, 'Who is it?'

'Curthose.'

Ralph plucked a louse from the hem, crushed it between thumb and finger, and resumed his search. 'I know.'

'Bowels of God! Is that all you say? Your wife swives squealing in the woods, and you —'

'Enough, Walter. This is my concern: let me resolve it after my fashion.'

'Resolve it —! Has your honour drowned in shame? You sit calmly while a man rides Isabel like a rutting stallion!'

He smiled crookedly. 'Men, Walter.'

I stared at him, my senses fogging. 'What do you mean?'

'Ivo also.'

'He has —'

'Yes. Often.'

I wiped my brow, and said spitefully, 'I suppose Richer takes his share as well?'

Ralph frowned. 'That infidel? No.' He dropped the tunic, crossed his hands and gazed at the ground. 'You are strangely unobservant, or else besotted in your love. This has been happening for weeks. What can I do? Must I fight you all, and try to kill you?'

'You could kill Isabel!'

Ralph shuddered. 'You don't understand, Walter. She is my world, my moon and stars and sunlight. Without her I am nothing, an empty husk. Isabel is wanton, a fever runs in her blood – that I have always known, and that I have accepted. Because your heart-beats hurt you, you don't tear out your heart.'

I said brutally, 'You might try cutting your throat.'

Ralph answered sadly, 'I've considered it – but then I should lose my love. Besides, I am a coward, as you've long suspected. No, Walter – I must endure.' He put a hand on my arm; roughly I shook it off. He flinched, and went on, 'This journey will come to an end, and with it our strange existence, living like animals rib to rib, with temptation carving gates for sin. Remember also this: Curthose and Ivo are knights; no knight can live for long without a woman. One must allow for nature.'

I hawked and spat. 'I've never met a complaisant husband. A new experience. And, if you survive to regain your fief, you will restore Isabel as chatelaine of Conches, and do her honour?'

'Just that, Walter.'

'Christ in heaven! The woman's betwitched you, as Mabille snared Hugh of Igé!'

'There's a difference between witchery and love, as you may find one day.' Ralph peered at my face, and added wretchedly, 'Have you . . . had her, Walter?'

I said coldly, 'Not yet. But I assure you I will.'

Isabel approached from the thickets, and seated herself demurely beside her lord. She looked happy and contented, and spoke to him softly.

I glared at her. She smiled sweetly.

3

With Evreux on the horizon, our bellies and purses empty, clothes in tatters and spirits low, Curthose decided we must find a civilized shelter. The thought of clean linen, a comfortable bed, wine and roasted meat beckoned him irresistibly: he pointed his nose to Evreux like a berselet scenting deer. 'Count William,' he asserted, 'was my friend. He'll not betray me if I throw myself on his mercy.'

I protested strongly. 'The count may not surrender you, Robert' – the rigorous months of wandering had planed the edges of formality – 'but Morin du Pin certainly will. An unbending man, ever mindful of his duty to the Duke.'

Curthose said testily, 'Then what do you suggest? We can't endure this existence indefinitely. Look at us!'

I looked, and saw a bunch of half-starved, ragged scarecrows, and understood his meaning. The year was turning; the chilly winds of autumn pierced our torn gambesons; winter was a menace we dared not think about.

I said thoughtfully, 'I once knew the lord of Guernan: Warin son of Fulk of Evreux. He holds the fief of his father, and owes no direct obligation to Duke William. It's worth trying. I shall go alone, and ask if he'll receive us.'

Curthose grumblingly assented. I unbuckled baldric and sword and handed them to Ivo: the villeins we resembled were never permitted arms. I found the track for Guernan, feeling naked and exposed, quaking when I met a pedlar or sighted peasants working in the fields. Three hours after noon I tramped through Guernan's straggling village, crossed the castle's drawbridge and bickered with a sentry at the gate. The man lounged on his spear and looked me up and down.

'Out, offal!' he said, scowling. 'What business can the likes of you have with Lord Warin?'

If I had not then seen a stooping figure crossing the ward I do not think I would ever have passed him. I called loudly.

'Hubert!'

The man stopped, surprised, and came to the gate. His face was thinner than I remembered, more sunken beneath the cheekbones, his shoulders bent. A sable streak still masked the ancient scar.

'Who calls?'

The soft, stammering voice vividly recalled my childhood in the apple-tree playground. I gripped his hands; the sentry frowned and raised his spear. I said urgently, 'Hubert, I am Walter of Poix. Don't you know me?' I thrust the hair from my forehead, parted my beard, and prayed for recognition.

Hubert smiled, spoke briefly to the man-at-arms, linked his arm in mine and led me inside the ward. He sat on the well-head and motioned me to sit beside him. 'What pretence is this?' he asked quietly. 'Walter of Poix was a ten-year child when he left Evreux – how could I know him now? Moreover, I have heard he died at Raimalard.'

'Hubert, listen.' I recounted events from my boyhood, incidents that only he and I could have known, described the bows he used to carve, the arrows he fletched, the crests he painted. Hubert watched me carefully, and at last he smiled.

'Do you believe me?'

'Yes . . . Tirel.' He felt my ragged garment, touched my beard. 'Why this? What misfortunes have afflicted you?'

I hesitated. 'Where is Warin?'

Hubert gestured to the wooden donjon. 'In the hall.'

I had had little contact with Warin during my days at Evreux. I remembered him as a hard, humourless individual whom children feared. I did not think the years would have softened him, and decided to enlist Hubert's help. Sitting on the well-head, the sunlight warming my back and encouraging a gnawing activity in the lice which infested my clothes, I described my companions, our travels and travails, and asked him to plead on our behalf for shelter in the castle. Hubert wagged his head doubtfully.

'My brother is a dour man. I shall try to persuade him.'

I basked in the sun and scratched. The sentry watched suspiciously, and spat when he caught my eye. Hubert signalled from the donjon; I climbed the ladder. Warin fiddled with a hauberk

103

spread on a table, trying to stitch a dangling mail-ring. He looked much as I remembered: a harsh vulturine face, the skin pitted and sallow, a taut slash of a mouth and fierce blue eyes. He rose to greet me, walking with a limp: a relic of the Duke's campaign in Maine.

'A pretty stew you bring me, Walter,' he stated uncompromisingly. 'You ask me to shelter fugitives hunted by the Duke. The Count of Maine, no less. This, you must know, I cannot do.'

I argued and pleaded, saying we should not stay long, that we required only time to recoup ourselves, restore our strength, obtain victuals, clothing and perhaps a little money before continuing our journey. Hubert added his persuasions. Warin listened, sucked his teeth, and said at last, 'Very well. Bring them in after dark: the watch will be instructed. You must all remain in hiding.'

I thanked him fervently, and departed for the forest glade where I had left my friends. That night I led them furtively within the castle. Warin bent his knee before the tattered vagabond who was Duke William's son, and set food and wine before us. We slept beneath a roof for the first time since leaving Raimalard.

4

We stayed at Guernan for nearly a month, and long before the end I was urging my companions to move. Curthose, rested and fed, shaved and resplendent in borrowed garments, was disinclined to exchange the comforts of castle life – such as they were, since Guernan was a tiny castle – for the hardships of the road. He basked all day in the ward or, when the weather turned cold, before the donjon's hearth-fire. Warin forbade us to go beyond the palisade, swore his garrison – a half-dozen men-at-arms – to secrecy, and pulled his chin anxiously when villeins entered the ward and saw us loitering there. Isabel made us conspicuous, a source of gossip: she wore man's clothing, but her sex was obvious.

Since that shocking discovery in the hazel copse, and Ralph's revelations, my relations with Isabel had been strained. The curtness, in truth, was all mine; she seemed happily unaware of anything wrong. And yet, I believe, she knew. With my eyes opened to her lechery I could not help watching when, making some common-place excuse, she left us, and observing whether Ivo or Curthose followed. One or the other often did. I felt miserable and heartsick, uncertain whether I hated her or loved her still. For the last I cannot account. At Raimalard and after, under stress from siege and starvation, I had thought my desire cooling – dalliance is not encouraged by fear and hunger. Now, aware that others shared her body, a mingling of lust and longing kindled my loins like fire whenever I saw her.

Richer, nowadays reticent and withdrawn, served Isabel attentively. His face was unreadable, but his vigilant eyes missed nothing, and I think he suffered.

A plague which struck Evreux, so Hubert told me, had killed Dame Orielde; on her death Dean Fulk joined Fromont in St Evroult's cloisters. 'I should have gone also,' Hubert said, smiling wryly, 'but I feel no compulsion to renounce the world. When my father departed I lost my home; Warin in his kindness took me in.' Hubert sometimes mounted guard and wore a hauberk – we had one false alarm: a ducal conroy mistaken for Goel's raiders – but his wound could not support a helmet and he went bare-headed, so that, white-haired and gentle, he looked like a saint in armour.

On a day when hoar-frost sparkled on the palisade stakes and rimed the puddles a messenger from Evreux sought Warin and spoke to him at length. Warin called us to the donjon. 'Tidings from Count William,' he said, frowning blackly. 'Your presence here, my lord of Maine, is known or at least suspected. The count sends this warning: Morin du Pin rides to Guernan on the morrow, bringing a troop of horse. If any strangers reside in the fief they had best leave quickly.'

'The Saints protect Count William!' Ivo exclaimed. 'Without his word we'd have waited like fowls for the plucking!'

Curthose said, 'He served me once. I liked him. God's miracles!' he added wearily. 'Must we start travelling again?'

'At once!' I said gladly. 'Lord Warin, will you supply our needs?'

Warin nodded. 'Everything I can. Money and food. I have no armour save my hauberk and Hubert's, and the sergeants' haubergeons. You can have them.'

'No armour,' Ivo said. 'Only gambesons, padded and quilted. And cloaks. Winter is here.'

'Will you take horses?'

Ivo shook his head. 'We enter the wilderness once more,' he answered grimly, 'and follow paths where horses cannot go, and so avoid pursuers. Come, my lord count, let us prepare ourselves.'

Curthose swallowed the dregs of his wine, and climbed reluctantly to his feet. We left Guernan in the darkness, as we had come. Hubert watched from the drawbridge, and lifted a hand in farewell, like a priestly benediction.

I never saw him again.

5

We travelled north and, between Gerberoî and Gournai, found a place they called Landelles.

The forest which surrounded it was trackless and entangled, the undergrowth so braided that from sunrise until sunset we hacked a passage with our swords. We emerged on a man-made clearing, and leaned panting on the hilts.

A tiny hamlet, lost amid towering trees: a dozen wattled huts, a little timber church, fields newly ploughed, pastures mottled by winter's yellowing grass. Smoke drifted from holes in thatch, spired like pale grey lances in the windless twilit air. Two hundred paces long, a little less wide, enclosed within serried tree-trunks like a looming palisade.

An aged priest tottered from the church: a bent, bony man, hawk-faced, his tonsure a dirty-white coronet surrounding a parchment skull. He paused at sight of the swords. Curthose ostentatiously sheathed his blade.

'Father, can you give us shelter for the night?'

The old man smiled and wiped a drip from his nose. 'Certainly, sirs. We seldom see strangers in Landelles.' A Poitevin accent twanged his French. 'My name is Serlo. Please enter my humble dwelling.'

He led us to a hovel slightly larger than the rest, past sullen peasants, a crone who muttered imprecations, a child who bawled and ran to his mother's skirts. The priest pushed open the door and called.

'Lesceline!'

The woman who bent beneath the lintel and stood bashfully before us was completely beautiful. Never have I seen such a perfect heart-shaped face, a complexion like creamed ivory tinged by the first flush of dawn. Wide violet eyes and tresses spun from gold, and a smile to melt your heart. Her robe was spotless, and she smelt deliciously of herbs and wood-smoke. I rocked on my heels. Curthose's eyes bulged from his head. Even Ivo, injured by deep experience in love and war, breathed deeply and combed fingers in his beard. Isabel scowled.

'My–um–housekeeper,' Serlo said. 'Lesceline, we have guests. Put another sestary of beans in the pot, my dear, and don't forget the salt.'

We ate hungrily, while the priest made conversation and inquired whence we came and who we were. We kept our identities secret, told a tale of pilgrims who had lost their way. Serlo pulled his ear, eyed the weapons, caught the glint of mail beneath Richer's tunic, and said no more. Curthose champed without tasting his food; his eyes followed Lesceline; he seemed moonstruck. We slept that night in the hut, divided by a cow, two sheep and a goat from Lesceline and Serlo at the farther end.

In the morning I bought food and made preparations for departure. Curthose watched silently, and finally said, 'Flanders is a long way away, and this is winter. Walter, I think we should rest here awhile.'

Nothing would move him. Ivo raised his eyebrows, jerked his head. I followed him outside. 'You're shooting broadheads against iron,' he said with a grin. 'The Count of Maine has fallen in love. I've seen it happen before. You won't separate him from that wench till he's drunk his fill.'

My heart sank. From Landelles we could reach Poix, my private destination, within days. 'She's a priest's concubine,' I said disgustedly. 'Are you saying that Curthose will risk his future, maybe his life, to bed a doxy?'

Ivo laughed. 'Exactly that. Don't you know him yet? Must admit I wouldn't mind a dip in that pond myself. There it is, Walter – you'll have to reconcile yourself to staying for a time. I'll investigate, and see how secure we are.'

The days passed, and then weeks. Ivo's inquiries revealed that the forest virtually severed Landelles from the outside world. Visitors were rare: an occasional traveller who lost his way and stumbled on it accidentally, as we had. The inhabitants seldom went abroad: the village was self-sufficient, if the winter were not too harsh. Richer, mistrustful of the peasants' tattle, vanished into the forest on reconnaissance, returning after two days' absence with his faith restored and the carcase of a buck. 'We're as safe here as anywhere,' he stated. 'Landelles is lost to the world.'

The cotters – a score all told – were at first reserved. Despite an unkempt appearance, our speech and bearing marked members of a caste they feared and hated. Gradually their suspicions thawed. Ralph, to occupy the time, cut stakes and built a fence to guard the winter barley against grazing beasts; Ivo and I chopped trees, collected firewood, and repaired the dilapidated church; Isabel collected pot-herbs, wove tunic and hose from wool-skeins. Richer's bow brought more meat to the villagers than they had tasted in their lives. Soon they recognized goodwill and, in their humble way, became our friends.

To this happy concord were two exceptions. Curthose lived in a dream of love, behaved like a man enchanted. With Lesceline he wandered hand in hand about the clearing, gazed into her eyes and whispered imbecilities. Soon the pair removed themselves to a separate hut, an unused, tumbledown shack no better than a cow pen – where they seemed supremely happy. You could get no sense out of Curthose in those days, no plans for the future, nothing – he seemed content to let the world go by. Serlo shrugged philosophically. 'It will pass,' he told me. 'I am old for the girl, and the blood runs hot in her veins. It will pass.' For a man of God, I reflected, he was most remarkably tolerant.

Inevitably, during that strange hiatus in our lives, during those dark afternoons when nights grew long, when time stood still and nothing mattered, I put the horns on Ralph. Roving the forest margins with Isabel in search of firewood, we found a sheltered hollow where dead bracken clustered deep. Isabel looked at the combe, and looked at me, and said, 'Walter, we have waited long enough.'

You whore, I thought: are you never satisfied? Then I saw her quivering lips, her yearning eyes; and my bitterness melted like wax in a furnace. I led her down the slope, wrapped my cloak around her and laid her in the ferns. I groped for the points of her hose, and touched her where I had touched her long ago. Isabel gasped, and gripped my body with arms and legs. Our loving was prolonged and violent, the crisis a savage cataclysm that left me limp and drained.

I rested on my back, an arm across my eyes, the scent of frosted herbage and wet earth in my nostrils, and said, 'Do you find me as mettlesome as the others?'

Isabel bent over me and stroked my hair. 'Hush, Walter. Why torture yourself? You are my dear and my love – the rest is trivial.'

I leaned on an elbow and gazed into the dark slanting eyes. 'Trivial? Thus you describe your harlotry? Three lovers have ground your buttocks – are they of no significance?'

'None – except you.' Isabel clasped her knees and stared at the naked tree-tops. 'I am what I am – I cannot help myself. Modesty, purity, chastity, continence – those virtues men seek in women you will not find in me. I think nature has created me more man than woman – do you insist on chastity in men?' She snapped her fingers in contempt. 'The priest Serlo, sworn to continence in God, yet keeps a concubine. I haven't seen you shrink from him.'

I said wonderingly, 'You demand for women a freedom and tolerance which the world won't – and can't – afford.'

'One day the world will have to,' said Isabel decisively. She rested her head on my chest and put her arms around me. 'Walter, can't you understand? Others have touched my body – only you have reached my heart.'

A stick snapped. I sat up hastily and arranged my tunic. Richer stood at the edge of the hollow, and regarded us impassively. He said without expression, 'Lord Ralph is coming this way.'

Richer could move in the forest soundlessly as a cat: he never trod on deadwood. With mingled gratitude and shame I saw in his hand a broken twig.

6

In February the snow fell, and then came frost, and winds that cut like swords. Landelles' inhabitants huddled in the huts round smoky fires, and fought the cold. Food ran short. Six extra mouths wasted the shallow margins the villagers held against emergencies; the grain pits emptied; the blackened slivers of meat vanished from the rafters where they hung. Two of the essential breeding-stock – a cow and a boar – perished in the bitter cold, and a new-born baby died. Curthose paid the old priest lavishly for what we took – but you can't eat deniers. Day after frozen day Richer took his bow to the forest, and saved us from starvation.

There was no question of travelling in these conditions, and I ceased harassing Curthose. Lesceline and he stayed cosily in bed beneath the fur of a bear which Richer killed at Christmas.

After ten weeks' suffering a warm wind blew and the snow melted. Serlo sent men to Gournai to buy provisions, replace the seed-corn we had eaten, the breeding-stock which died. The villagers seldom handled coins, and our money had made them rich. The scent of springtime made us restive; even Ralph was eager to go. Only Curthose, besotted with his wench, wanted to linger in Landelles. Flanders, for men afoot, was still remote: the thought of the journey appeared to daunt him.

His own idiocy compelled a move. At some time in the throes of love he had revealed his identity to Lesceline and, being a woman, she betrayed the secret to a cotter. The villagers who went to Gournai's market tattled; soon afterwards Richer reported strangers hovering in the skirts of the forest. 'Unarmoured, bearing weapons,' he said briefly. 'Sergeants by their mien.' I challenged Serlo, who confessed the consequences of Lesceline's indiscretion and thought the men were sent by Gerard of Gournai to verify the rumour. This was enough to frighten Curthose. He took a tearful leave of Lesceline; and when the hawthorn's leafbuds flaunted bronze-tipped cloven tongues we left Landelles.

Near Gaillefontaine the dust-plume of a conroy brushed our faces; we had to go to ground and double on our tracks. A full week afterwards I crawled to the crest of a rocky hillside and saw Poix embowered in a wooded vale.

Here was the seigniory I had travelled so far to win. The russet thatches of a sleepy town encircled a castled mound; smoke trickled lazily from rooftops; fields and vineyards climbed the slopes; cattle grazed in meadows that bordered a dawdling stream. A chapel bell tolled terce; the notes tingled on the sparkling air. This was a place of peace, a land unharried, a sanctuary from war. I looked for the marks of conflict – nettled mounds where houses had been, ash-grey fields unploughed and vineyards razed – and found none. Poix drowsed in green tranquillity.

Ivo, prone beside me, touched my shoulder. 'Your heritage, Walter,' he said, smiling. 'A prosperous place. A pity it's beyond your grasp.'

I said, 'I intend to have it. I'm going in now – alone if I must.'

That started an altercation. We crouched in a gorse thicket and quarrelled fiercely. 'We've struggled for months to avoid our enemies,' Curthose rasped, 'and now you propose to rattle a hornets' nest. God's wonders! How can four unarmoured men and a woman capture Poix?'

'We walk straight in,' I answered simply, 'and then I shall persuade my father.'

Ivo laughed. 'The lord of Poix, I have heard, is mad. Walter, you've inherited his malady.'

I said patiently, 'We are in France. King Philip is my father's suzerain – not Normandy. There's no obligation on the lord of Poix to deliver us to William. And I am, after all, his son.'

'Whom he doesn't recognize,' Ralph muttered.

I ignored him. 'Consider also this: isn't Robert of Maine a weighty counter in King Philip's hand, a means of putting pressure on the Duke? Will he willingly surrender so powerful a lever?'

'Am I to become a political pawn?' Curthose wondered aloud.

'Robert,' I told him, 'at the moment you're not even that. You're a fugitive and pauper. You can sink no lower. If you put yourself in Philip's power you at least regain importance and the value of your rank. You'll have built yourself a base, however shaky: a foundation whence you can negotiate.'

'Politics are beyond my ken,' said Ivo cheerfully. 'Walter, you've thought this out very thoroughly.'

There, I reflected, he spoke simple truth.

'I'd be safer in Flanders,' Curthose growled.

'You might,' I agreed. 'But Robert the Frisian is completely independent of both Normandy and France: Bavinchove settled that. You'd live in permanent exile, impotent and shabby, without hope ever of recovering your place.'

Curthose nibbled his nails, and mumbled in his beard. Ivo said, 'This is all very well, but first we must enter Poix. How do you suggest we start?'

I pointed through the gorse to the sunlit castle below. 'Poix is unused to warfare. Look – the bridge is down, the gates thrown wide and guarded by a single man-at-arms. The donjon door is open, the ladder set. We walk in and seize the donjon.'

'Not I,' said Curthose decidedly.

Ivo grinned. 'Many years ago,' he said reminiscently, 'Arnold of Echoufour with four men-at-arms took a castle garrisoned by sixty of Duke William's soldiers. I've a mind to see if we can do as well.'

'I'll come with you,' Richer said.

'And I,' said Isabel.

I looked at Ralph. He nodded gloomily.

'Are you deserting me?' Curthose demanded.

We regarded him silently.

'You're all demented!' he exploded. 'Very well. If we're going to die we might as well perish together!'

I gave instructions. We left the golden-speckled gorse, and walked openly down the hillside.

7

Cloaks concealed our baldrics and swords naked in the slings. We strolled through the little town, talking unconcernedly – my throat was dry and I could hardly speak – stopping to examine a huckster's wares, pressing against the house walls as an ox-cart creaked by. The carter called cheery greetings, thinking us some of his like. I paused at the lip of the drawbridge, my heart thudding painfully.

'Get on!' Ivo growled.

I crossed the bridge. The sentinel – a pink-cheeked, pleasant-seeming lad – leaned on his spear and chewed a straw.

'Your business?' he inquired.

I spitted him in the throat.

Curthose shouted hoarsely, 'Run!'

We pelted across the ward, swerving between huts and stables, stumbling over hay bales and saddlery and sacks. A woman dropped a bucket and fled screaming to the gate. A half-clothed sergeant ran from a barrack, lather on his face and razor still in hand. Helplessly he brandished the knife; Curthose smashed his sword-hilt in his face. There was shouting from the gate, and the patter of running feet. A sentry leaned from the battlements, face crimson in alarm, and raised a horn to his lips. From somewhere an arrow whipped; Ralph yelped and clutched an arm. Ivo, despite his bulk, bounded ahead, slid into the donjon's ditch and climbed the mound. Clutching grass tufts, we clambered on hands and knees, and reached the ladder's foot.

'Your privilege,' said Ivo gaily, and stood aside.

I swarmed upwards, sword clenched between my teeth. A face appeared at the doorway, mouth twisted in affright. An arrow thumped in the oak logs beside my head – never have I longed so much for mail-coat and ox-hide shield. I heard Richer's bowstring twang, a distant shriek; and tumbled through the entrance. Richer, climbing last, kicked the ladder away, slammed the door shut and dropped the bars. We stood in a line, swords levelled, and faced the room.

Trestles and benches on a rush-strewn floor. A daïs at the farther end, and a long elmwood table where, frozen in astonishment, were three men, a woman and a priest. A scullion cowered against a wall, a liam-hound lifted his head and bayed. Voices filtered from the floor above, and a call from the battlements.

'All yours, Ivo,' I panted. 'Come on, Richer!'

I ran up the steps, entered a room divided by a planked partition into bower and bedchamber. A handmaid clasped an armful of linen, a varlet made the bed. Richer flourished his sword in their faces, hissed imprecations in a foreign tongue. They fell on their knees and wailed. I mounted the ladder to the roof, thrust head and shoulders through the open trap. The sentry turned and hurled his spear; the point scored my forehead like a red-hot brand. I charged at him, beat down his dirk and hacked him dead beneath the ovens. No one else was there.

We returned quickly to the hall. Ivo stood on the dais, his sword-point resting lightly on a corpulent neck. Ralph and Curthose pointed their blades at the chests of the other two men. The woman, a blowsy slattern, sobbed quietly in a corner. The priest had his head on the table, and appeared to be praying. Isabel gasped when she saw me, for my face was a mask of blood.

'This fellow,' Ivo drawled, leaning gently on his hilt, 'seems to be the castellan. He is not, I think, your father.'

The man flinched from the prick, and cursed. He was short and enormously fat, a mound of flesh, his face a chalky bladder with one cheek hideously scarred: bone and flesh were crumpled into a seamed and puckered pit. The eye above was gone, leaving a wizened hollow like a husk of a blackened walnut. His tunic gaped on a chest with dugs like a farrowing sow.

I said, 'Your name?'

'Baudri of Pontoise,' he growled, 'King Philip's castellan of Poix.'

'And this?' I indicated Ralph's target, a bald, bearded man who eyed the blade beneath his nipple apprehensively.

'Grimond, my steward.'

'This?' A lean red-faced fellow wearing a green velvet surcoat, his hair and eyebrows pale as wheaten straw. He tapped his fingers lightly on the table, and seemed quite unperturbed.

'Delis of Carenci, holding a fief of Poix. And who, in the devil's name, are you?'

A rising tumult from the ward penetrated the donjon's oak-trunk walls. A ladder clattered against the door; someone hammered on the wood. 'Richer,' I commanded, 'up to the battlements quick. Discourage them.'

Richer ran lightly up the steps, plucking an arrow from his quiver as he went. To Baudri I said, 'First things first. Where is Lord Walter?'

'Who wants to know?'

'I am his son.'

The single eye swivelled to my blood-caked face, regarded me fixedly. 'I can trace no resemblance,' he observed drily. 'Perhaps —'

Ivo's point pricked his neck. 'Answer the question, friend.'

Baudri shrugged, jerked his thumb at the floor. 'Below.'

I stared. 'In the store-chamber?' For such was the basement floor of every donjon, a ration store, a cellar for wine, a lumber room, a black airless place where prisoners were chained and rats ran wild.

Baudri looked away. 'If you're indeed his son you won't like what you see. Lord Walter is very sick.'

The noise outside grew louder. An axe thudded in the door. A muffled yell, and the blows ceased. Ivo smiled. 'Richer's stung that fellow,' he said, 'but he can't hold them long. Not enough arrows. Baudri,' he added crisply, 'you must call them off.'

'And if I refuse?'

'You'll hang from a merlon, and your friends with you.'

Baudri resignedly lifted his shoulders, rose and waddled up the steps. With Ivo I took him to the battlements, and looked down. The ward seethed like a boiling cauldron. Sergeants climbed the mound, milled round the donjon's base. Bowmen ringed the palisade and sought with their shafts for Richer, who dodged from embrasure to embrasure and shot the men storming the portal. Arrows studded the merlons like reeds in a river.

Baudri crouched behind the oak and shouted. He owned a powerful voice, well suited to his frame. The tumult gradually stilled. Cautiously he showed himself, and spoke at length. The men-at-arms retreated from the mound and gathered in the ward, silent and perplexed. Archers unbent their bows and left the ramparts. Baudri pensively fingered his ancient wound, and said, 'Satisfied?' He looked at the body under the ovens, and added, 'Ilbert. A good lad. A shame you had to kill him.'

I said, 'Take me to Lord Walter.'

We left Richer on watch, and returned to the hall. Baudri bade the scullion kindle a torch and scuffed away the rushes which hid a panel in the floor. He lifted the flap and, torch in hand, inserted his colossal body into the opening. I followed him down a ladder into a dark, noisome chamber. Grain sacks climbed against one wooden wall, wine-casks lined another; spears, bowstaves, saddles and other litter cluttered the floor; a well-head gaped in the centre. The place smelt of musty corn, stale wine and used-up air. Baudri, breathing stertorously, waddled to a corner and held the torch on high.

An old man lay on a tumbled pallet. Long white hair, a matted and verminous beard. Spittle glinted on the strands. The face was hollow, emaciated to the bone, the skin livid and flaking. Wide, staring eyes, the pupils milky white, glittered in the torchlight. The old man muttered and hid his eyes with an arm shrunk and withered as a bark-stripped branch. A sickening stench, a mingling of ordure and corruption, hung about the shrivelled body.

'Lord Walter of Poix,' said Baudri.

I looked upon the broken ruins of my father. I felt no sorrow, no regret – I had never known this man who cast me out and tried to dishonour my birth. I knew instead a swelling rage that one of my blood should be treated so. Without conscious volition the sword lifted in my hand, prodded Baudri's belly. The light gleamed on its blood-streaked blade. I said through stiff lips, 'Why . . . like this?'

'He's been stark mad these four years past,' Baudri said.

'You pen him like an animal in a cage.' The point pierced Baudri's tunic, broke the skin. He yelped and backed away.

'Lord Walter must be kept in darkness – he can't bear light. Look!' The wasted creature on the pallet writhed and turned his head from the torch, arm over eyes, and uttered mewing cries like a new-born child.

'I think I must kill you, Baudri.' My muscles braced for the thrust; he felt the blade's tensing, and shrieked. A hand grasped my wrist. Ivo said, 'Steady, Walter. Remember your plan. The man's our hostage. No use dead.'

Unwillingly I lowered the sword. The fetor suddenly gripped my gullet, and made me gag. 'Out,' I mumbled. 'Out! Up to the hall.' In silence we climbed the ladder, inhaled the tainted air of the room above like fragrant scent. Ralph and Curthose still guarded the steward and Delis, and looked at us inquiringly. I leaned against the table, for my legs were shaking, and said to Baudri, 'Explain.'

He rubbed the slit where my sword had bitten, and answered sullenly, 'There's little else to tell. King Philip appointed me Poix's castellan many years since, because Poix is a marcher castle and vital to his frontiers. Lord Walter, even then, was an ailing man,

unfitted for the rigours of command. Then his reason left him, and
I . . .' Baudri hesitated, and continued, 'I think he will not live long.'

I said grimly, 'You have taken no pains to add to his years. Were
you not necessary for my purpose —'

Delis of Carenci said, 'You look like an outlaw loose from the
forest, and say you are Lord Walter's son. What proof have you?
And who are your friends?'

I indicated Curthose. 'This is Count Robert of Maine.'

Delis surveyed Curthose's bearded face and worn, soiled clothes,
and laughed. 'Why not the King of France? It were as easy to
believe!'

Curthose's ruddy face flushed a deeper red, his eyes sparkled and
he exploded in a fury befitting the Duke himself. 'You have my
knightly word, you dog! Is that not enough?' His sword blade
slammed the table. 'On your knees, garbage! On your knees – and do
me proper obeisance!'

They knelt before him, Baudri sulkily, Delis languidly serene.
Curthose said harshly, 'Can either of you hog's-spawn write?'

'No, my lord,' Baudri replied in a quavering voice.

'The priest,' said Delis, 'is lettered.'

Curthose jerked his head at the man, who jumped and dropped
the beads he fingered. 'Father, fetch quill and parchment, and set
down what I say.'

I scrutinized Count Robert in amazement. His uncertainty and
hesitations had dropped from him like an outworn cloak; he was
suddenly taut and vigorous, completely in command. It might have
been the Bastard speaking. If only, I thought sadly, Curthose were
always like this.

'Write thus,' he ordered. 'Robert Count of Maine to his suzerain
and liege lord Philip King of France. Greetings. Know ye by these
presents that I, your liegeman, estranged from my father William
Duke of Normandy, now rest in France's dominions, and in your
demesne castle of Poix await your behest as my fealty obliges. May
God and His Saints protect you. Robert to Philip. Farewell.'

The priest wrote laboriously, tongue between teeth. Curthose
snatched the quill and made his mark. The priest sanded the parchment, rolled and tied it. Curthose thrust the scroll under Baudri's
nose.

'Send this to the king,' he grated, 'by hand of a trusty messenger
on a speedy horse. Meanwhile we stay in this donjon, and you with
us, and answer for our safety with your head.'

Baudri opened the door and, with Ivo's point at his back, called from the portal. Curthose dropped into a chair.

'That should bring Philip running,' he grunted. He looked at the woman weeping in a corner, and his mouth softened. 'Stop snivelling, wench! Dry your tears, and bring me wine!'

Absently he caressed her thigh as she filled his cup.

8

The days went by. We lived penned within the donjon, mistrusting Baudri's sleek assurance that his garrison would not harm us if we entered the ward. Count Robert's spurt of energy was soon spent; he lowered the wine-casks' levels and swiftly bedded the flaxen slut: a village hind who was Baudri's favourite leman. Ivo hunted the donjon for armour, and discovered haubergeons and two hauberks. (Baudri's was useless – it could have clothed two ordinary men.) Ralph eyed his finds, and commented sourly, 'Much good may that do us! Five misfitting mail-coats against the army of France!' Nobody answered him: we all waited on the outcome of the hazard; and feared secretly that Philip would bring fire instead of friendship. On the sixth day my father died. The old man had sunk into a coma, and could no longer swallow the thin gruel which was all his food. I crossed his withered hands upon his breast, and left him. Baudri wanted to arrange his burying, and swore a truce. No one believed him. I closed the trapdoor leading to the basement, and replaced the rushes. Delis watched silently; then knelt and put his hands in mine. 'You are my liege lord, Walter of Poix,' he said. 'I do you homage for my fief Carenci.'

'If King Philip so affirms,' I said.

'If he affirms,' Ralph agreed sombrely. 'Your heritage, my lord of Poix, is trembling in the balance.'

On an afternoon three days later Richer called from the battlements. I looked out, and saw banners like plumes of fire on the bright horizon.

Chapter 6

1078–79

King Philip sent his heralds, and a salute to the Count of Maine. Preceded by knights in armour and followed by men-at-arms, his column flowed into Poix like a gorgeous sparkling river of silver and red and gold.

The king was rotund and jovial, pink-cheeked and going bald; his chins quivered when he laughed. Curthose met his liege lord at the gates, and made obeisance on bended knee. The two princes embraced and kissed, and together entered the donjon. The retinue found billets in the town; some pitched their tents in the meadows; for the king I cleared a space inside the ward and erected his pavilion, a flamboyant tasselled affair striped yellow and blue. A royal conroy took over guard from Baudri's men: only the king's guard watched over the king. This business done, and the company dispersed, I went into the donjon.

Baudri of Pontoise was not visible: I had clapped him in the store-chamber in company with my father's corpse.

Curthose talked amicably with Philip and his barons: Guy Count of Ponthieu, Simon of Neauflé, Robert Count of Meulan and lords of high degree. Wine trickled merrily from flagons into goblets; the talk was loud and cheerful, the atmosphere convivial. Presently Curthose beckoned and I knelt before the king.

'Sire, I present to you Walter, son of Walter of Poix, your liege-man lately dead. He has served me faithfully, my lord, and I commend him to your favour.'

Philip motioned me to stand. 'So? By lineage my vassal – yet I do not know you.' (I had waited on King Philip at banquets in Rouen's Tower.) 'You come opportunely, though rather late, to Poix. Why have you waited so long?'

I related, saving words, the long tale of my disinheritance, my upbringing at Evreux, service in Duke William's mesnie at Rouen and later under Curthose in Maine. Philip listened patiently, his black, intelligent eyes gleaming in folds of flesh. When I ended he said, 'Now, I suppose, you want to claim your heritage?'

'If it so pleases you, my lord king.'

Philip idly twisted a ring on his little finger. 'It's a little difficult. I'd half promised Poix to Helias of Gerberoi when Walter died – not knowing he had an heir. Gerberoi and Poix are neighbouring marcher castles: it's sometimes prudent to entrust important forts to a single hand.'

The blood drained from my heart like water in desert sand. I looked at the floor, studied the fresh-cut rushes in despair. Curthose said quietly, 'This boon I beg of you beyond all else, my lord: that you confirm Walter of Poix in his inheritance. He is a brave and trusty knight, as I have proved; he'll serve you faithfully as he has me.'

The king looked from Count Robert's face to mine, twirled the goblet between his fingers and considered. 'Be it so,' he said at last. 'Poix shall be yours, my lord: I shall bid my scribes prepare the covenant. Kneel, and give me fealty and homage for your fief.'

I put my hands between his, and swore the oath of allegiance; and blessed Curthose from the bottom of my soul. By his mediation he had acquitted all my services. It was as well: I never received any other reward from the Count of Maine.

'That castellan of mine,' Philip said, 'what's his name? – Baudri of Pontoise. I shall have to hang him. Can't have my castles taken in broad daylight by a handful of men. Very bad example. Where is he?'

I had given Baudri a deal of thought. Much as I should like to see him swing, he had commanded Poix for many years, knew the garrison, understood the workings of the demesne, the knights and people and priests. He would be valuable in managing the Honour: if I put him under obligation for his life he should serve me well. Therefore I craved his pardon from the king. Philip at first refused; but wine had made him affable, and in the end he yielded.

I ordered cattle to be killed, and organized a feast. It was midnight before the King of France and the Count of Maine, arms across each other's shoulders, reeled uproariously to bed.

I lay on a pallet in the bower, and listened to Ralph and Isabel making love in the bedchamber, and laughed aloud. I held in my hand King Philip's charter, sealed and witnessed by his barons. I was Walter surnamed Tirel, lord and suzerain of Poix. The future stretched before me like a highway to the stars.

On a windy April day I buried my father before the altar in the church, alongside his namesake and mine, the first lord of Poîx. The funeral's magnificence exceeded his degree: a king, the heir to Normandy and three counts followed the coffin. Candles spired smokily in incense-laden gloom; monks chanted dirges and King Philip's chaplain intoned the rites. When the obsequies were done the king summoned a formal council in his gay pavilion.

Philip came swiftly to the point.

'Count Robert,' he said, 'you seek from me, your suzerain, support against your father the Duke of Normandy, whose overlord I am. In brief, I'm required to help one vassal against another. Moreover – and I speak without intention of offence – the vassal I shall oppose is the most formidable in Neustria; whereas you, my lord, at present lack both influence and power. Such a course, you must agree, is hardly politic. Wouldn't it be wiser if I used my office to effect a reconciliation?'

Curthose stroked his fleshy nose. 'You can try – but you'll waste your words. I'm a rebel whom Duke William has hunted for half a year. Those who supported me are ruined men, their domains escheated, themselves banished or in hiding. You know the Duke, my lord: he doesn't easily forgive.'

'So! You'll have me believe your estrangement is complete and final. Therefore you can be restored only by force of arms. You ask, in short, that I make war on your behalf.' Philip leaned forward, his corpulent stomach pressed against the table. 'A perilous enterprise, my lord,' he said emphatically, 'and what profit will it bring me?'

Curthose lowered his eyes and plucked the tassel of his doublet. 'You hold my fealty,' he muttered. 'A suzerain has obligations to his liegeman —'

'True,' Philip interrupted softly. 'The Duke is also my liegeman.'

'A romantic fancy!' Curthose snapped. 'A figment of the laws of courtoisie! When has Normandy obeyed the beck of France? Not since Valesdunes!'

The king's eyes hardened into stony points, his mouth drooped at the corners. I read the danger signals, and cursed beneath my breath. I had rehearsed Curthose in the arguments he must use: the night's debauch had clearly quenched his memory. He was bent, instead, on antagonizing the only man who could help him. It was time to intervene.

'Your forgiveness, my lord king.' Philip turned his head, his plump face cold and hostile. 'There is a way to help my lord of Maine without your hand being obviously apparent.'

Philip looked at me with plain dislike. 'I am not afraid of showing my hand against Duke William.'

I swallowed. Curthose seemed to have offended him beyond re-covery. 'That, my lord, is evident to all the world. I was at Dol.' The king's expression softened; I plunged on desperately. 'But the scheme I have in mind – which the Count of Maine approves – demands that you keep at first in the background so that you may strike decisively – and profitably – when the moment's ripe.'

Philip leaned back in his chair, rested chin on hand and watched me carefully.

'Explain.'

'If, by your favour, you grant Count Robert custody of a marcher castle it will become a rallying-point for powerful barons who resent Duke William's rule.'

'What barons?' Philip looked pointedly at Ralph and Ivo. 'Neither wealth nor warriors,' he said sardonically, 'belong to those who've opposed the Duke.'

'There are many others,' I assured him. 'Mowbrai, Neufchatel, Breteuil – I could name a score. They will run to Count Robert's banner directly they think him strong.'

Philip's little eyes examined Curthose. 'Is this true?'

Count Robert nodded. 'I know the men he means. All have suffered some malfeasance from the Duke; all have plotted sedition in the past.'

'So!' Philip smoothed his mantle, sent me a hard, calculating glance. 'You collect these lords and their mesnies in a castle on my frontiers. What then?'

'They harry across the marches into Normandy, bringing devasta-tion to Duke William's vassals. The knowledge that Count Robert instigates the raids will stoke his anger. The Duke will summon his array and march against him.'

'Exactly.' Philip's voice was cold. 'And then a leaguer, and my seigniories destroyed. I recall you mentioned profit. I see none in this.'

I said quietly, 'With the Duke's armies contained by Count

Robert, you yourself, my lord, can strike from France and seize the Vexin.'

Philip's eyebrows climbed his forehead; he tapped fingers on the table; his gaze became remote. I read his thoughts plain as a familiar blazon on a painted shield. The Vexin, a marcher territory long disputed between Normandy and France, a battleground for generations past. Now, with no more opposition than a castle or two which held Duke William's writ, a chance was offered to grasp finally that debated land. King Philip bit his lip, and pondered deeply. Curthose caught my eye, and looked away; I read gratitude in his glance, and penitence for a brittle temper. All this he should have said himself.

The king sighed, and fingered his double chin. 'There are possibilities,' he admitted. 'The plan will need arrangement. To begin with: the castle. It must be far enough from the Vexin to prevent Duke William switching his forces quickly. It must be strong: if Count Robert's base is taken the whole enterprise collapses. What about Poix?'

This was the last thing I wanted – to see the Honour I had so lately won turned into a battleground. Revenues vanished where armies ravaged. I scratched my head, dismayed. Ivo scanned my face, grinned to himself, and said, 'Too small – a thimble for the forces we shall need. If you want advice about fortifications, my lord, send for Robert of Belesme. No man is more skilled in the art than he.'

'Belesme has made peace with my father,' Curthose said bitterly. 'He's less to be trusted than a usurer Jew.'

'He does me homage for seven castles,' said Philip thoughtfully, 'and would be wise to answer if I call him. A sensible suggestion, my lord of Grantmesnil. I shall send a message to Belesme.'

More discussion followed, and much argument, and guesses at the mesnies Mowbrai and Molines and other lords might bring, calculations of the rations for their sustenance, supplies of spearheads, arrows, bows and various accoutrements of war. Presently Curthose ran a tongue along his lips, looked pointedly at an alcove where the casks were kept. King Philip took the hint, and called for wine. Soon the talk drifted from weaponry to wenches, and the Count of Meulan told a story which made everybody laugh. I slipped unnoticed from the pavilion.

3

The entertainment of a royal retinue put a strain on Poix's resources. Baudri of Pontoise and his steward Grimond were useful: they knew the whereabouts of every secret granary, the hidden stores where cotters kept muids of wine, and extracted them remorselessly. The villeins suffered – an unfortunate introduction to my rule, which could not be helped. With Baudri I was direct and harsh, telling him baldly that he owed me his life. 'And while the king is here you'd better keep out of his sight,' I added forcefully, 'in case he changes his mind.' Baudri thankfully agreed, promised strict obedience and plunged happily into the work I heaped on his ursine shoulders. Though the peaceful years in Poix had blunted his warlike instincts, there was nothing he needed to learn about administering an Honour.

I rode to my dependent fiefs, petty estates whose revenues could just support a knight. Delis, at Carenci, occupied a wooden castle smaller than Warin's at Guernan: he alone maintained a following under arms, a handful of sergeants and bowmen. The others had reverted to the role of gentlemen farmers; they lived in halls of wattle and thatch, unfortified, the only soldier visible a watchman with a spear; and tended vines and worried about the harvest. I reminded my liegemen sternly of their obligations, warned they might soon be called to war, and recommended that they furbish their accoutrements and drill their men-at-arms. I left them shaken, and departed wondering: never in all my journeyings had I met a community so much at peace. I learned, years later, that similar tranquil territories were common in parts of England.

Isabel, before King Philip's advent, had made Baudri send to the town for female attire. I remembered a day when the donjon's floor was buried under robes and mantles, kerchiefs and ribbons and gold-embroidered surcoats whose sleeve-cuffs dangled from the wrist like silken waterfalls. Isabel fussed over the litter, picking and rejecting; a sempstress clucked behind her like an anxious hen. Afterwards she dressed as befitted the Lady of Conches – shedding, in my eyes, the allure that armour lent her. While Philip remained at Poix she stayed secluded, attending the daily meal, demurely taking her leave before wine flowed loose and chatter became bawdy. She was the only noble lady in the castle, but far from the only woman. They glutted the place. Baudri had kept a string of concubines, Grimond a couple; every sergeant, every bowman seemed to own a doxy who lived in a barrack, a store-hut or in odd corners of the ward. I banished most of this harlotry to the town – though Philip, camped in the ward, intercepted a red-haired beauty – keeping only the necessary washerwomen and kitchen-maids and a personable girl for my own amusement. Isabel slept with Ralph in the upper room; the castle was anyway too crowded for secret fornication.

Poix also was thronged; the king's knights and sergeants made the town their own, roistering noisily far into the dusk and, by day, creating tilt-yard and parade grounds in the fields, riding carelessly over sprouting barley and springing wheat. I was enraged; Baudri pursed his lips; but there was nothing we could do: Philip's men were beyond our ordering.

Released, after the king's coming, from confinement in the donjon, I was able, like Isabel, to attend to my own appearance. From face and neck I shaved the hair which all Norman warriors dislike intensely. I demanded from a reluctant Baudri the key to Poix's treasure coffer, and lavished deniers on a velvet paltock of chaumpan cloth, deerskin breeches, a sleeved and hooded braban chape, girdles of red silk studded with silver. From my new-found bounty I bought garments for Ivo and Ralph. Although Richer at last discarded his mail he eschewed finery, and wore a plain leather doublet and cross-strapped hose.

Armour was a problem. One of the two hauberks we had found had belonged to my father and fitted me tolerably well, but the gambeson was old and perished, the rings rusty. I sent it to an armourer for burnishing and repair. The other I gave to Ivo: the hauberk squeezed his body tighter than a skin; he wriggled his shoulders and emptied the air from his lungs. 'Can't lift an arm to hit anyone,' he wheezed. 'Can't breathe either – but it's better than nothing.' (The armourer, a dexterous fellow, inserted gussets from armpits to hem, and sewed mail-rings in the gaps.) Curthose was more fortunate: King Philip gave him a suit of mascled mail, shield and lance and battle saddle, and a sorrel destrier bred in Flanders.

Ralph had to be content with a sergeant's haubergeon. He ordered the armourer – on credit – to forge him a hauberk, but mail-making is a slow business and the summer was half done before the coat was ready.

Destriers were necessary as armour. The stables in the ward held thirty horses, among them Baudri's aged charger, huge and poorly trained. I found a well-shaped stallion in a merchant's yard in Poîx, and persuaded him to part with it for half its worth – the burgher, uncertain of his new lord's temper, was anxious to ingratiate himself. I lent Ivo money to buy a chestnut from King Philip's stud; Ralph made do with a lumbering beast in the castle stables. Richer's choice was odd: he picked a light-boned, short-backed palfrey, barely fourteen hands, and spent hours schooling it in the meadows. I watched him once: he had dropped the rein and tried to guide the horse with his legs alone. I shook my head, perplexed: the animal was far too light for a destrier, and no destrier was ever tutored thus.

4

At Pentecost Robert of Belesme arrived, attended by a constabular of knights and men-at-arms. I saw again the pallid, handsome face, green glinting eyes; and hated him with all my heart. I paid him formal courtesies and led him to the king. They conferred in the striped pavilion from none to vespers; I wandered on the ramparts and told myself I was not a young esquire, no longer subject to Black Robert's will as I had been at Rouen. Although he was become count since Mabille's death I was baron and Lord of Poix, a knight of like degree – and wondered why his presence still filled me with dread and loathing.

King Philip hailed me from the ward and said, 'My lord of Belesme wishes to inspect the defences.'

Did Philip still hanker after Poîx as a base for Curthose? Belesme walked the circuit of the ward, pushing at a palisade, plopping a pebble into the moat, surveying the gate and watch-towers. We climbed the ladder and examined the donjon from bottom to top, gazed finally from the battlements over twilit meadows. Belesme said contemptuously, 'This, sire, will not answer your purposes at all.'

I was thankful – and resented the sneering tone. So, obviously, did Philip; the castle, after all, was his. He answered stiffly, 'Poix has successfully endured leaguers in the past.'

Belesme said scornfully, 'Yes – half-hearted harryings by Stephen of Aumale. You'll have to withstand a full-blooded, vindictive war commanded by the Duke. Look!' He stabbed a finger into the dusk.

'A shallow moat, water barely arm's-length deep. A wooden palisade, indifferently repaired. No barbican at the gate.' He tapped an oak-trunk merlon. 'A wooden donjon, lacking bartizans, moss quilting the shingled roof. Finally' – he waved an arm at the hill-crests – 'high ground within mangonel range. The castle is a fire-trap, my lord – and anyway far too small.'

I glowered, only partly understanding Belesme's tirade: he used expressions I had never heard. Poix, in my judgement, was as strong as the average castle, stronger than most: no Tower of Rouen, certainly, nor perhaps a Raimalard. Philip, I think, was equally confounded; he said wryly, 'Lord Walter, you'll have to rebuild your castle. It seems, Count Robert, we must find another stronghold.'

Belesme said curtly, 'I've found it.'

'Where?'

'Gerberoi, five leagues south. I rested there last night. It's stone, all stone, and well designed. Give me a month and I'll make the place impregnable.'

The king crossed his arms on the battlements, and bent his head in thought. He said at length, 'My lord of Belesme, you are notably skilled in these matters – I should be foolish to spurn your advice. Pointless to stay here longer.' He looked at me and smiled. 'Lord Walter, I must leave you, and with me the Count of Maine. We march at dawn for Gerberoi.'

5

With the king's departure, and the certainty of summons of array before the year was out, I began ordering my muster. Besides six knights the Honour owed fifty men-at-arms; I chose the best from garrison and outlying fiefs, which left enough to guard the demesne. I inspected horses and equipment, paraded twice a week and prac-tised drills. I had hoped Richer would instruct the bowmen. He shrugged and said, 'What do I know of Frankish archery? My methods are different, and take years in the learning.' Richer had become withdrawn and solitary; he spoke little and seldom smiled. Since Isabel's reversion to feminine ways of life, picking at em-broidery with tirewomen at call, he no longer attended her. Instead he schooled his palfrey for hour after hour. From curiosity I often watched him: by midsummer Richer could control the horse by legs and weight alone. Once I saw him halt the palfrey, turn about and spring on an opposite course, all in one movement, all without touching the rein. Clever, I reflected – but quite pointless.

I supervised the bowmen's training and discovered crossly I was out of practice. The bowstaves in the armoury were mostly warped, the strings brittle, arrows distorted and apt to gad, the fletchings tattered. I set bowyers and fletchers to work, and replaced the stock. Ivo, hugely enthusiastic, drilled cavalry and foot; Delis came languidly from Carenci and proved himself a redoubtable fighter: he ran a course with Ivo and neatly unhorsed him. Ralph loitered, as it were, upon the fringes; he schooled his clumsy destrier and tilted at dummy and quintain. I would not have wagered a denier on his chance in battle.

I agreed with Ralph that Isabel should stay at Poix: indeed, there was nowhere else for her to go. I was glad Ralph had persuaded her – more likely she herself decided – that Gerberoi under siege was no place for high-born ladies, however hardy. Isabel assumed a natural place as chatelaine of Poix, ordering domestic matters and attending to our comfort. The donjon's interior, squalid under Baudri's reign, became clean and tidy; fresh rushes strewed the floors, brocaded hangings draped the walls, the servitors were deft. She remained friendly, a little aloof, perhaps ostentatiously considerate to Ralph. Neither Ivo nor I attempted any dalliance – we had other relaxations. Ralph worried about Baudri – a notorious lecher – who would become castellan again during my absence. I grinned at him.

'You misjudge your lady. But, if you think Isabel could be attracted by anyone so repulsive you'd better clap an iron belt around her loins.'

Ralph winced. Later I saw him whispering confidentially to a smith.

August was out, the harvest gathered, when a pursuivant from Gerberoi brought King Philip's call to arms. I summoned my liege-men, put all weapons to the grindstones, re-shod the horses, collected ox-carts for our baggage, loaded corn and wine and tents. On a morning drenched in sunlight we paraded in the ward: six knights, thirty sergeants, ten carts and a score of sutlers – and Richer. Pennons snapped and fluttered in the breeze, sunlight splintered stars from lance and helmet, horses snorted and curvetted. Every stable-boy and scullion thronged the ward; all Poix was in the streets to see us go. I looked proudly on my retinue, and found it good.

Isabel came to my stirrup, and gazed into my face.

'Farewell, Walter. May God and His Saints protect you!'

'Farewell, my lady,' I said jauntily. 'Keep Poix well for me while I am gone.'

Her face crumpled. She pressed my hand to her cheek.

'Tirel ... dear heart. Come back to me ... my love.'

Gently I drew my fingers from her clasp. Eyes were all around us: Ivo coughed, and glared ferociously at a smirking sergeant; Ralph frowningly picked a tangle in his horse's mane. I bent and whispered.

'Isabel ... still?'

Tears brimmed the slanting eyes which looked in mine. 'Now and always! Ah, Tirel ... will you be for ever blind?'

I lifted her hand to my lips, then I turned my horse and rode from Poix. The sun seemed to shine less warmly, a leaden dullness tinged the azure sky. Sorrow, remorse and a tangled skein of emotions conflicted in my mind. My young esquire Vauquelin – son of a vassal knight – had laced the helmet over-tight; I loosed the thongs and thrust it off. The wind's soft fingers stroked my hair; the coolness brought no comfort to my heart.

Once I had loved sweet Isabel of Montfort; for Isabel of Conches my love was dead.

6

At Gerberoi we came under Robert of Belesme's command and a discipline stricter than I had known since Rouen.

Helias and his forebears, Gerberoi's hereditary castellans, had over the generations converted the castle from a robbers' den to a fortress. Under Belesme's hand the fortress was become a citadel impregnable to all save treachery. Smooth, slippery flagstones, impossible to scale, revetted a mound which supported a smaller version of Rouen's Tower. An outer ward girdled the inner like a protective apron, both guarded by walls of stone and bastions which jutted like menacing fists. A stream, diverted, fed a moat you could cross only by swimming. From the moat the ground sloped to a plain where once the village stood. Belesme had razed the houses. 'The Bastard,' he explained tightly, 'would certainly burn them, then possibly attack under the smoke. Nor do I want a swarm of villeins clamouring for refuge.'

I met no fortifications so ingenious, so advanced, until years later I saw Gisors, which Belesme built from the foundations up.

We entered a fortress which was crowded though not crammed: Gerberoi could hold a thousand men, and before the end it did. In ward and donjon all was trim and organized; each soldier had his place, every animal its standing – it reminded me of Raimalard. Hugh had brought his mesnie from Neufchatel, William from Breteuil; Mowbrai and Molines were on the way. Simon of Neauflé gave me greeting; few other lords of France were there because King Philip's vassals gathered farther south at Pontoise for his thrust into the Vexin.

I found Curthose in the hall among a throng of stranger knights. Belesme, beside him, read aloud from a script a tally of knights and sergeants under arms. Curthose hailed me gaily, his rosy rugged features brisk and cheerful.

'The army gathers, Walter!' he exclaimed. 'Twelve barons and six hundred men already! Who would think the Duke so hated that half his lords are ready to break their vows? And more to come! My couriers bring promises of aid from Normandy and Brittany and Maine!'

'Promises aren't spears,' Belesme said coldly. 'Many we've approached have sent no answer. The Duke won't lack a following.' He rolled the parchment in his hands and sent me a chilly glance. 'Your mesnie, Lord Walter? How many men, how many horses?'

I told him. He flattened the scroll and wrote. Curthose watched admiringly. Belesme said, 'Rouse at prime. Stables, then drill till terce. Stables again at sext, followed by exercise at arms. You've brought sixty days' rations? Store them in the main granary: Helias is in charge. Send a sergeant to draw provender at vespers daily. Warn your men against thievery – already I've hanged two of Mowbrai's bowmen. That's all.'

I glared resentfully. 'My men know their drill – they've spent all summer training. I came to fight for the Count of Maine, not play at soldiers in the tilt-yards.'

'Yes, yes, Walter,' Curthose replied soothingly. 'I promise you plenty of fighting – but not just yet. Count Robert, you'd better explain our plans.'

Belesme sighed resignedly. 'The muster is not complete: we await more companies yet. Meanwhile we drill, and drill again: I'm not leading a half-trained rabble against Duke William's troops. In November —'

'The Duke,' I interrupted, 'has competent spies. He must know Count Robert's here, the castle full of soldiers. Do you imagine he'll wait until we're ready?'

'We are in France,' Belesme said patiently – a tutor-clerk enlightening a child. 'Duke William won't make war on France unless provoked. In November we provoke him. We harry into Normandy, and burn and rape and rob.'

'A bad season for campaigning.'

'Precisely,' Belesme sighed, 'and worse as the winter hardens. The Duke can't have an army mustered till December: he'll have to operate in frost and snow. Not exactly an advantage. We, on the other hand, live snug in Gerberoi. Meanwhile, my lord, you have a month to exercise your retinue.'

Day after day we practised evolutions of Belesme's devising. Many were novel. The purpose of armoured cavalry being to charge and shatter, cohesion at the point of impact is expedient. In fact the normal charge arrives in fragments. There are paladins who out-ride everyone, and hit the enemy first; there are knights less resolute, or their destriers possibly slower. Our mentors – Belesme's mercenary knights – relentlessly insisted that the line should start at a walk, progress through trot and canter to a gallop in the final fifty paces – thus striking like a solid iron flail, and not, as one sour-faced Angevin instructor put it, like a scurry of pattering hailstones. 'Fine in theory,' Ivo growled, sawing the mouth of an impatient destrier, 'but are we to crawl like snails while the arrows fly?' 'Duck your nasals behind your shield-rims!' the Angevin rapped. 'Arrows can't pierce your mail.'

Ivo was not the only grumbler. Knights are intolerant of control in battle. Moreover, every lord who led a mesnie considered it his right to organize, train and lead them according to his inclinations, and resented interference. It was a remarkable tribute to Belesme's personality and powers of persuasion that he convinced these arrogant men – myself among them – that his methods were right.

He went further, and made us practise wheels and turns no horseman had seen before. Knights in column of route march as they will, limited solely by the confines of road or track. Frequently they leave the column altogether, excitedly pursuing a hare, or galloping off to cast their hawks at a flighting pigeon. Belesme insisted we keep column of threes, forbade any but outriders to quit the files, and invented drills whereby columns could be quickly deployed to line in front or flank. We complained strenuously, heard his reasoning – always sound – muttered and obeyed.

I still disliked Belesme. Now I began to respect him.

Richer avoided these parades. I reproved him, and demanded his attendance. He answered calmly, 'Frankish battle-tactics are beyond my compass. I can't wield a lance, and this blade' – he tapped his curved, slender sword – 'is not forged for the shock of onset. My skills are different. Come, my lord – I'll show you.'

I followed to a stubble field beyond the dusty tilt-yards where conroys wheeled in complicated patterns. Small wooden blocks affixed to hazel wands studded the field at random. Richer deftly braced his bow – a thing I had never seen done on horseback.

'Stay here, my lord.'

Richer knotted his rein, dropped the loop over the pommel, cantered away. He turned at the end of the field, spurred the palfrey to a gallop, rode like a swerving tempest through the scattering of wands. The bow twanged like a lute-string to the cadence of his hoofbeats. The arrows flew. The palfrey jumped a ditch at the stubble's limits: Richer, facing backwards over his horse's rump, transfixed a block at thirty paces while his horse was in the air.

I rode slowly across the field, counting the arrows lodged in the marks. Fifteen, over a running course of half a bowshot. Fifteen shafts in a time while you might draw ten breaths – and all of them hits. From the saddle at a gallop it was quite incredible. I stared pop-eyed at Richer like a churl at a fairground freak.

He reined beside me, began silently to pull the piles from the wood. I said in wonder, 'A horsed bowman! A kind of warrior the world has never seen!'

Richer said, 'Not your world, my lord. This is the warfare of my people. By this skill we conquered kingdoms from Outremer to Gades.'

'Can you teach me?' I sensed a possibility, a sudden revolution in the art of war. 'Could you train a troop of mounted archers?'

Richer shrugged. 'It takes years of practising, my lord. Moreover, you need special horses: quick, handy ponies of the Moorish breed. This palfrey I have schooled' – he patted its neck affectionately – 'is far from perfect.'

'Seems good enough.' I toyed thoughtfully with a loose hauberk thong: Vauquelin, my vassal's son, was over-due for a rating. 'There's one drawback. An armoured knight is safe from your shafts.'

'We aim,' he answered mildly, 'at the horses.'

I had a quick uneasy vision of charging knights in line, a gadfly swarm of mounted archers, and destriers tumbling end over end. My notion might be double-edged: it required thought. I looked at Richer's bow. The stave, unbraced, had returned to its reflexed curve.

'Special bows, too,' I said. 'Can you make them?'

'In time, my lord.'

I left him, pondering; and never afterwards urged Richer to the drill-ground.

7

At Martinmas the raids began.

Robert of Belesme said, 'You will strike quickly, ruthlessly, and get away fast. Your object is destruction, not to fight. You'll take no prisoners nor bring back booty.'

He prepared each foray minutely, organizing constabulars down to the last man-at-arms, the ultimate palfrey. He chose routes and destinations, calculated time and space; and despatched raiding parties simultaneously to widely separated targets. 'Thereby creating diversions,' he observed, 'to prevent the enemy concentrating against a single sortie.'

On a grey November morning my retinue and William of Breteuil's mesnie – a company a hundred lances strong – left Gerberoi to ravage Gerard of Gournai's lands. We headed westwards for La Ferté, one of Gerard's castles: a dominant stronghold far beyond our testing. Nor did we intend to try – our objective was a petty fief held by a vassal knight.

A chilly sunrise lurked behind a sky of tarnished steel. The trees slid past like phantoms in a gossamer curtain of mist which beaded diamond droplets on armour-scales and helmets. We trotted fast in orderly files of three, outriders far in front and hidden in the mist. The music of a marching column re-echoed in the still cold air: creaking leather, jingling bits, the metallic swish and slither which armour makes. William of Breteuil – a hot-tempered, lowering man with a lantern jaw which the stubble shaded blue, the backs of his hand black-furred – scraped fingers across his lips, glanced anxiously at a pallid notch on the horizon which betrayed the hidden sun.

'Near terce, I fancy. We should be there by now.'

An outrider loomed from the mist, reined sliding on wheel-ruts ironed by frost. 'Moulicent is three bowshots on, my lord,' he announced.

'Right,' said William. He slipped the guige and enarmed his shield. 'Take your people through the centre, my lord, as we arranged; I'll seal the outskirts and work inwards.'

He bawled orders. His followers thudded from the road, forked right and left like prongs. An iron trident lunged at Moulicent. I swung an arm, increased the pace, burst through a thin birchwood belt and looked upon our prey.

Furrowed ploughland, vineyards like green-striped carpets and winter-bleached pastures embraced the tenement. The village street meandered like a muddy brook between cottages and huts, and ended below a stubby tower: the donjon of Moulicent's knight. A small monastery, a mere hermitage for monks, lifted greystone walls beyond the farthest field. It was a holy day; the tillage was nearly deserted; villagers thronged the street and an open square where hucksters cried their wares.

Into this peaceful pastoral we plunged like a raging torrent. Twenty horsemen galloped the street, killed all who came in the way. I lost my lance in a brawny priest, unscabbarded my sword and split a villein's head. At the tower's palisade I turned; two frightened soldiers closed the gate, a horn wailed hoarse alarm. No danger there; the castle could wait. We returned the way we came, and chased screaming men and women between the houses. Breteuil's horsemen crossed the fields from the flanks, spitted a bewildered ploughman, killed his oxen in the yoke and closed upon the slaughter. Soon none but the dead was left; the living moaned and cowered within their homes.

I said, 'Bring fire.'

Sergeants lit the brands they carried, cantered from roof to roof, shedding smoky trails, and touched them to the eaves. They battered window shutters and flung the torches in. Thatches smoked and spluttered, spurted fiery banners; a bitter stench of burning clogged the air. Smoke coils twined in writhing tendrils pursued by flames which clawed and crackled. Cinders sparkled redly in the haze; the heat scorched mail and leather. Peasants tumbled from doorways, sprawled on thresholds, plunged screeching from the furnace, clothes alight. The swords went hunting.

We breathed fire and could no longer stay.

'Away!' I shouted. 'Out to the fields!'

Mingled with Breteuil's men, we surrounded the flaming village and cut the fugitives down like conies when a barley field is reaped. Moulicent was a holocaust, collapsing in showers of flame, an incandescent pyre which roared like a gale. Breteuil rubbed smarting eyes and said, 'I'll sack the monastery. You attend to the vineyards.'

'The castle?' I asked.

Helmets peered from the battlements; an arrow curved in the air, fell short and thrummed in the grass. Breteuil scanned the puny donjon. 'Not worth the trouble of storming – let Gerard's castellan live to tell him the tale.'

Delis of Carenci dismounted a squad of sergeants, worked down the rows of vines and razed them to the roots. With the rest I scoured the fields, found wandering heads of kine. We slew them all.

William returned from the monastery, fondling a silver chalice. 'Not much in the way of loot,' he grumbled, 'and the house won't burn – all stone. Time to go.' A trumpeter lifted his horn and sounded Rally. Embers glowed in the grimy air; the smoke diffused an acrid smell, the stench of burning flesh. William said complacently, 'A good job done. Gerard's revenues from Moulicent are lost for years to come.'

We rode away.

Such was the pattern of harrying, this was the measure of death we brought.

8

In December the Duke of Normandy raised his banner at Aumale five leagues north, and sent summons of array to all his vassals. The raids from Gerberoi stopped, their purpose accomplished. Belesme probed cautiously across the march. Before Christmas patrols brought warning of the Duke's approach; by St Stephen's feast the fortress was beleaguered.

A strong and energetic garrison usually harasses the setting of the siege lines; but Belesme forbade interference. 'Let them be lulled,' he murmured, lounging at an embrasure, watching the trenches dug and mantlets built, 'and they'll make mistakes.' He shaded his eyes and gazed at a group of knights who rode the castle's circuit, keeping warily beyond bowshot; and pointed a slender finger. 'The Duke is there, making his reconnaissance. He's over fifty now, and not the man he was. Let's wait and see.'

The enemy wove his texture of investment; Belesme, an eagle watching fieldmice from a crag, observed each movement, plotted every trench and picket on a parchment sheet. He seldom left the battlements by day; at night he prowled the guard posts. The Duke raised mangonels, hurled boulders into the wards. Belesme smiled evilly, called carpenters and smiths, supervised the building of machines like enormous bows, powered by twisted ropes and braced by cranks. They shot long iron darts with great velocity and range. He mounted them in the bastions, and trained them on the mangonels. For three days the duel endured; then the mangonels stayed quiet.

The sky turned leaden grey, the weather bitter cold. Snow flurried the fields in streaks like feathery drifts. The tedium of leaguering, a chilly, stifling pall, settled on besiegers and besieged alike. Duke William's younger knights, bored by inaction, rode below the ramparts and shouted challenges to joust. Our own youthful paladins clamoured to take the gage; Belesme looked them over thoughtfully, selected a score by name and gave permission. When, horsed and armoured, I demanded to join the jousting he surveyed me frigidly. 'Dismount, my lord. No matter if these idiots get themselves killed – they're fodder for swords. You're more valuable – you sometimes think. Was not the whole conception of the campaign yours?'

Day by day, in interludes between rain and blizzards, brisk little tourneys flared beneath the ramparts. They became routine: at terce the drawbridge dropped and knights rode out and charged and chopped, six against six, ten against ten, according to mutual agreement. The sergeants lined the walls and cheered, and wagered on the courses. Four knights were killed, and others hurt. Nobody took prisoners or demanded ransoms: these were affairs of courtoisie, quite separate from the war. Belesme languidly ignored the mellays; he seemed concerned only with the timing. The gates were never opened before terce; trumpets called the jousters back at noon. Delis of Carenci – old enough to know better – once lingered overlong to finish a bout, and found the gates shut in his face. None of his pleadings persuaded Belesme to open; he spent the night with a friend in the enemy camp, returning on the morrow when the drawbridge dropped at terce. 'Christ's thorns, their tents are cold!' he told me. 'I don't envy Duke William's knights!'

The Duke made no attempt at an escalade; he seemed content to sit and starve Gerberoi out. We settled comfortably behind the walls, happily aware of the fortress's inviolability and twelve months' victuals held in store. Boredom was a more relentless enemy: there were brawls in the sergeants' barracks and quarrels in the hall. One ended in a killing, and a knightly body dangled from a gallows in the dawn. Such incidents enlivened the monotony. Knights gambled, drank, played checkers, visited the mews, exercised the destriers round a straw-track in the ward. Priests and pilgrims freely came and went; many of these holy men were spies in Philip's pay. I imagined Curthose awaited word of the king's assault in the Vexin – when he launched it the Duke must either raise the siege or attack. So, when Belesme called the barons to the donjon and made plain his mind I, like the rest, was stunned.

'My lords,' he said without preamble, 'the Duke is growing careless. The time has come to strike.'

Breteuil's jaw dropped; Hugh of Neufchatel gasped. Belesme examined his fingernails, and smiled.

'Every day they see our portals opened, and send knights to entertain our jousters. Except for them, and a ready squadron saddled under arms, Duke William's men stay warm within their tents. Tomorrow we shall send out every man we have and storm the camp.'

'M-madness!' Guy of Ponthieu stuttered. 'We're heavily outnumbered!'

'True. They have two thousand swords against our one. Surprise will level the odds.'

William of Breteuil looked frowningly at Curthose. 'My lord of Maine, has this lunacy your approval?'

Curthose shuffled his feet. 'Count Robert,' he said uncertainly, 'has persuaded me the plan is sound.'

'Do you approve?' Breteuil repeated. 'I must remind you,' he continued with a hostile glance at Belesme, 'that we risk our lives and lands on your behalf, and not —'

'I merely,' Belesme interrupted blandly, 'present a scheme which the Count of Maine himself propounded. Is that not so, my lord?'

Curthose inspected a garnet ring on his thumb, and murmured inaudibly, 'Yes. It is so.'

Nothing sounded more improbable – but the dice were shaken

and thrown. We had gathered at the Count of Maine's behest, and sworn obedience. The barons looked at one another, and muttered between their teeth. Breteuil sighed gustily, and said, 'Very well, my lord. Now, what are the details of this – um – operation?'

'These,' said Belesme. He leaned elbows on the table, and spoke for the turn of a sand-glass.

9

Snowflakes like wisps of wool wandered from black bloated clouds. The air was breathless, inert, laden with cold. I beat gloved hands on thighs, and shivered. The destrier sidled; my knee bumped Ivo's; he sent me a nervous grin.

Four hundred horsemen crammed the lower ward, muzzle to rump and knee to knee. The throng shifted and rustled, a grumble of sound like a distant storm. Noises gashed the murmuring: a screech of hoof on cobble, a monotonous pounding from the armourer's forge, a rattling bucket. My lance shaft slipped in ice-numbed fingers; I breathed an oath and changed the grip – we held the spears point-down lest the pennons show over the walls. Across a sea of helmets I saw Curthose's bulky shoulders near the gate. He spoke with Simon of Neauflé, nudged him in the ribs and cracked a jest. No tremors there. I envied him.

Behind us, in the upper ward, the footmen waited rank on rank.

The chapel bell tolled terce. Gate bars clanged from the sockets, the gates creaked slowly wide. The ropes of the drawbridge groaned on the windlass; the bridge descended like a falling spar. The jousting knights rode gaily out, singing and shouting war-cries, as was their wont. From Duke William's camp a flutter of pennons galloped to encounter them.

A clarion howled from the donjon.

I enarmed my shield, righted my lance and jostled to the gate, shouldered by eager horsemen. Like a foaming mill-race knights burst from the bridge, slid and skidded down the frozen slopes. Curthose twirled his lance, thrust the shaft thwartwise above his head. The riders reined, fanned right and left, formed line, moved forward at a walk, the horses fretting. More horsemen poured from the gate and ranked behind us: a second squadron which Robert of Mowbrai led. The lines wavered and gaped and clustered –

137

but there was no disorder. Belesme's relentless drilling had brought rewards.

Curthose pumped an arm; we started trotting. The roan stallion lunged and fought the bit, tossed his head and flecked spume on my shield. I shortened rein and spoke to him gently; the horse reared and plunged; the knight alongside cursed. Ivo glanced sideways, smiling broadly, his eyes alight beneath the nasal. 'Your ventail's loose,' he called. Young Vauquelin, I thought vaguely, must certainly be whipped.

Trumpets called afar, a plaint of mournful voices. I looked across the iron-ridged fields, speckled by frost-burned scrub. The Duke's jousters bolted homewards, lance butts thumping flanks. Tumult boiled in the camp; figures shrunk by distance careered from tents and horse-lines. Sergeants ran to the trenches, spears twinkled at the mantlets. A pennoned waterfall cascaded from the tents, deployed in a steel-tipped wall.

Duke William's ready squadron rode to meet us.

Curthose bellowed, waved his lance. I slipped the rein and cantered; the roan dropped his head and bore on the bit. Ivo laughed. 'Careful, Walter!' he shouted above the din. 'He's going to bolt!' The enemy horsemen crossed the entrenchments. They were a hundred paces distant, and closing fast.

Curthose stood in his stirrups, and pointed his spear to the sky.

I couched my lance, tucked shaft beneath armpit, straightened my legs and thrust hard on the stirrups. I lowered my head and nuzzled the shield; the nasal grated lightly on the rim. War-shouts blared in a rasping roar that drowned the stormwind hooves.

I breathed a silent prayer, and gave the roan his head.

You don't remember much about the climax of a charge – things happen far too fast. I recall a blazoned shield – chevrons or and argent – a lancehead bearing on my throat with the speed of a streak of light. A hurried tug at the rein, a shock that jarred my spine. The stallion staggered. My lance had snapped at the tang; I threw it away and groped for the sword. A spear-point scored my shield. I parried a darting blade, hacked at a passing helmet, met a laggard knight head-on and slashed his face. Then I was through.

The charge had spattered into separate groups who circled and shouted and slashed. Many had drunk their fill, and pelted from the fight – whether our own or the Duke's I could not tell: in armour all look alike. I was very near the entrenchments; arrows began to fly, and I lifted my shield. Mowbrai's squadron, away to the right, thundered upon the encampment. Footmen poured from the castle, serried the plain, advanced running in Mowbrai's wake. Gerberoi's mounted reserve, which Belesme himself commanded, ranked motionless below the drawbridge.

A riderless horse crashed my destrier's quarters and faced me towards the tents. A constabular burst from the camp and rode pell-mell for our battle.

A fresh onset – and we were unready.

Like waves which are spent the fighting was ebbing, for our numbers were greater than theirs. I bellowed for Robert of Maine, and gestured wildly. Bannerets saw the danger, shouted to disengage. Curthose emerged from a scuffle, face scarlet and shining with sweat. He roared commands. I ranged myself beside him; we formed a shaky line, and cantered to meet the threat.

It was, I noted thankfully, a tiny force, less than a score all told. They hit us in the centre; we closed from the flanks and beat upon their backs. A mist of battle, the breathing of men and horses, hung like a veil on the frozen air.

I bartered slash for slash with a green-helmeted knight, drove my point through his teeth and looked for Curthose. He circled warily around a squat, paunchy warrior who swung a mace, seeking an opening. The knight was slow, deliberate; his belly crammed the pommel, hindering his movements. Curthose feinted left and cut to the right. His blade clanged the fat knight's helmet, and he lurched from his horse, sprawled on the ground, scrabbled for his fallen mace. Curthose leaned from the saddle, his arm swinging up for the death-cut. A rider in banded mail spurred between them, shouting at the top of his voice.

'Robert! For the love of Christ! Would you kill the Duke?'

My blade, already falling, scraped the forearm of the band-mailed knight and sliced the bull-hide wrappings. He turned his head and looked straight in my face. Coif and nasal hid all but the 'cloven hoof,' but I saw his eyes. One blue, one amber.

Rufus!

My stomach curdled. The hilt dropped from my hand and dangled by the loop.

Curthose hesitated, lowered his blade, stared incredulously at the figure crouched beneath his hooves.

'God's miracles!' he breathed. 'I did not realize. His mail . . . I couldn't recognize . . .'

'Don't you know the coronet of Normandy?' Rufus pointed to a gold diadem encircling the helmet. He gripped his brother's arm. 'Robert, you must let him go!'

Two battling knights bumped my destrier and shook me in the saddle. A sword-edge, deflected from a shield, grazed my leg. I heeded it no more than the bite of a gnat. Curthose dismounted, raised his father to his feet. The Duke swayed, hands to head. Blood smeared his cheek. Knights surrounded him in a ring. There was no more fighting near us: the companions of Duke William's charge were dead or fleeing. Laboured breathing of men and horses rasped loudly in the stillness.

Curthose said unsteadily, 'Sire, I wounded and unhorsed you, and for that I am sorry. I beg you to believe I did not know my adversary. You are free to depart, my lord.'

Duke William wiped his face and dropped his hands. He spoke dazedly, mumbling his words.

'This battle ... is not ... half done. I shall be ... less merciful ... when you are taken.'

'Look behind you.' Curthose swung an arm and pointed. 'You are beaten, my lord,' he added gently.

The leaguer was smashed. Mowbrai's knights galloped through camp and siege lines, spearing and killing. Smoke billowed from blazing tents. Fugitives spurred to the faraway forests. Footmen from the castle ran for loot and slaughter.

'Go while you have time, my lord.' Curthose's eyes swept the ring of silent men. 'Grantmesnil, Poix, Breteuil – escort my father from the field.'

He helped the Duke to mount, and kissed his hand. William turned his horse without a word, and rode from the battle of Gerberoi.

10

Snowflakes drifted from an iron sky. Dried lather rippled the horses' coats like tide-marks. Leaning on their bits, they plodded towards the forest. The gash on my leg throbbed painfully beneath a crust of blood.

The Duke rode hunched in the saddle, helmet dangling on his back, a linen swathe around his greying head. He had not spoken since leaving Curthose. We left the frozen fields, and entered the forest's valance. A clarion called faintly from the castle. Rufus nursed his arm, which I had roughly bandaged with a strip torn from a dead knight's mantle. During the wrapping he had watched my hands; when I tied the knot he raised his eyes to my face.

'Walter, you have taken your . . . revenge,' he said softly. 'Is this enough?'

I found no words, and miserably bowed my head.

The Duke stared blindly into the distance. He said in a low voice, 'May the Curse of God and all His Saints rest forever on Robert of Maine! Never have I been so humiliated! Defeated, wounded, unhorsed! My own son!'

Unthinkingly he beat his knuckles on his cheek and winced. The pain enraged him.

'I promised him Normandy, fool that I was! I cannot break my word. But England he shall never have!'

He dropped the rein, and laid a hand on Rufus's arm. 'William, on the Cross of Christ I vow that England shall be yours when I am dead.'

I lifted my face to the sky. A snowflake nudged my brow like a cool caress.

Curthose had won his battle, and thereby lost a kingdom.

11

King Philip seized the Vexin; at Easter the princes made peace, and the war ended.

Duke William reluctantly granted amnesty to all the rebels, and restored their lands. Ivo departed joyfully to Grantmesnil, Curthose to Rouen where the Duke grudgingly received him. I returned to Poix soon after the battle. Ralph came with me, anxious to greet his lady and worrying, I believe, about the lecherous Baudri. When a courier knight brought him Duke William's pardon he informed Isabel, and prepared to leave for Conches.

She refused to go.

'I am happy at Poix, my lord,' she told him calmly, 'and here, by Lord Walter's leave, I stay. There is nothing for me in Conches.'

Ralph looked at me with hatred. 'Is this your doing?'

I spread my hands, confounded, knowing not what to say. 'My lady, my house is yours, your will is mine. But . . .' I stuttered into silence.

Isabel curtsied. 'Thank you, my lord.' I saw amusement in her eyes, and flushed.

Ralph said violently, 'By the belly of God, you bitch, if you won't come freely I shall bind and take you!'

'I think not, my lord. In Conches I am subject to your will – not here. For that very reason I shall not return.' Her voice hardened. 'Force me? You? My blood is Montfort – we are not easily compelled!'

I stared unhappily at a hanging on the bower wall, a tapestry of dragons intertwined. The devil take all women, I reflected: here was a complication which could lead only to trouble. Isabel was out of her mind: you couldn't defy your wedded lord like this! I prayed in my heart for Ralph to fulfil his threat. He rubbed his eyes, dragged fingers down his face.

'Have you considered the shame upon my House? Do you not fear God's vengeance, the anathema of Holy Church? Are you all strumpet, in thought and word and deed?'

'Calumny will not advance your cause, my lord. Nor will it change my mind. You'd better —'

'Silence, you slut!' Ralph stabbed a shaking finger. 'Do you think I shall consent to be openly disgraced, my dishonour noised abroad for all the world to hear? No! I've endured your furtive harlotries because – dear Christ! – I loved you. No more! You and your fancy man' – he glared at me with loathing – 'will find that Conches can wield a bitter sword!'

Ralph flung from the room. We heard him calling servants, shout for his horse, and listened to his hoofbeats pounding the bridge. Isabel smiled, and opened her arms.

'I was resolved to have you, Tirel,' was all she said.

Through all that sparkling Maytime I shared her bed in the bower, and tried strenuously to match her ardour. I do not think I succeeded. Isabel strove with all her might to revive a love that had died. 'Ralph is all bluster,' she once declared after a bout of naked wrestling in the dark. 'Do you fear his threats? – they're harmless as a baby's prattle.' She touched only part of my worries, the lesser part: Isabel did not recognize I no longer loved her. For me she was a fascinating concubine, delightfully skilled in her arts, a hoyden who warmed my loins but never my heart. I suppose I dissembled well – she seemed happy enough. Yet, despite Isabel's assurances, I was afraid of Ralph's reaction; I believed the man had been goaded beyond bearing.

I judged him right.

Our idyll lasted a month; then a sweating rider on a foam-flecked horse brought warning from Carenci. Delis was under siege, his corn in flames; the raiders followed fast. I sounded the alarm; my people flocked to the castle from field and town; before the last were in I raised the bridge, sent men-at-arms to battle stations. Barely in time: spears prickled the southern hill-crests as the gates clanged shut. I armed quickly, ran to the battlements. Isabel met me at the ladder's foot. Her face was white.

'Is it . . . Ralph?'

'Who else? Your pleasures,' I said stonily, 'are proving expensive.'

Horsemen, a little group, moved down the hillside, passed deserted houses, approached the gate. A knight in the van bore vine leaves on his lancehead; I called a warning to my bowmen, fingers itchy on the strings – men-at-arms mistrust the sign of truce. I left the donjon, crossed the ward, mounted a watch-tower beside the gate. The knight's lance slanted in salute.

'My lord would parley with the Lord of Poix.'

'Your lord?'

'The Count of Montfort.'

A slender, graceful figure spurred from the group, reined at the edge of the moat, swept back his helmet. 'Walter,' he called gaily, 'may I come in?'

'God's blood! Amauri!'

After a careful look around for lurking foemen – one cannot afford to be gullible – I had the drawbridge lowered, opened a postern. Amauri dismounted, entered the ward. I clasped his hands and heartily embraced him.

'Amauri! It's good to see you!'

He remained as I remembered, fair and golden, his skin roughened by wind and rain, the blue eyes laughing. He sat on a mounting-block, and scrubbed dust from his lips. I sent a sutler scurrying for wine.

'Count Amauri?'

'My father died two months ago,' he answered soberly. He drank, and looked at me over the rim of his cup. 'This is a broiling stew you've cooked for yourself, Walter. Where's that graceless sister of mine?'

'So!' I began to understand. 'Are you running errands for Ralph of Conches?'

'Not really. He's busy burning Carenci. Couldn't stop him – Ralph

143

seems vindictive. Your man in the donjon there is safe enough: giving as good as he gets. I thought I'd ride ahead and try to save more trouble.'

The sergeants on the palisades turned inquisitive heads. I snarled at them. 'Watch your fronts!'

Amauri tilted the cup, intently regarded the dregs soaking into gravel. 'You'd better tell me about it. I've only heard Ralph's side.'

I considered awhile; then told him all I thought he ought to know. I omitted Isabel's adulteries in the forests, omitted Ivo and the Count of Maine. He listened silently, eyes on the ground, stroking his fingertips together.

'She's determined to stay,' I finished lamely. 'To force her out would be discourteous.'

'Discourteous! Isabel's your leman,' said Amauri severely. 'The scandal rocks all Normandy. You've dishonoured Ralph and blackened Montfort's blazon. When he sought my aid I could do nothing but agree. We've brought two hundred spears against you.'

His companions, fearing treachery, shouted from the moat. Amauri strolled to the gate and reassured them, returned to the block, picked up his empty goblet. 'Good wine, this. Have you more? Well, old friend, what do you say?'

'Two hundred won't take Poix.'

Amauri swept a glance round palisade and donjon. 'Possibly not. But we'll ravage your demesne, destroy your other fiefs – Beaurain, Esquennes and Verton – and leave you ruined. Can you and Isabel exist on love alone?'

'I don't love her.'

The cup jumped in Amauri's hand, wine splashed his hauberk. 'St Mary Virgin! Then what's all this about? I thought —'

I shook my head. Amauri scrutinized my face. 'I see,' he said slowly, and sighed. 'Poor Isabel!' He ruminated a little, sipping his wine. 'You will let her go, if she is willing?'

'Yes.'

He rose briskly. 'I'd better talk to her.'

I led him to the donjon. Isabel waited in the bower, her face pale, the dark eyes haunted. Amauri bent his knee, surveyed her long and deliberately.

'Sister, I have come to save you from yourself. Will you hear me?'

A trace of pity tinged his tone.

I went below to the hall and paced the floor. Spears and bow-staves leaned against the walls – the armoury of alarm. Voices murmured from the floor above. I took up a dirk, thumbed the edge, gashed my skin and failed to feel the smart.

Footsteps rapped the stair.

Amauri said formally, 'My lady has decided to return to Conches. By your leave, Lord Walter, I shall escort her home.'

Isabel ignored me. She walked steadily to the door, her head high, face expressionless and strained. Amauri helped her down the ladder. I followed to the gate and crossed the bridge. An esquire surrendered Isabel his palfrey.

Amauri said, 'Farewell, Walter. I shall persuade Ralph – your fiefs will not be harried.'

'What did you tell her?'

Amauri, foot in stirrup, paused. 'Enough. I had to hurt her. She knows that you have . . . cooled. She realizes now that you rate the security of your demesnes higher than her love.' He swung to the saddle, and looked at me thoughtfully. 'If I were you, Walter, I'd not cross my sister's path again. The Montforts are a vengeful tribe.'

The cavalcade clattered away, trailing dust like a smoky plume. The spears that hovered on the hill-crests disappeared. I watched them fade, shame and relief contending in my mind.

Relief won.

No woman was worth losing Poix.

Chapter 7

1087-88

In a priory's austere dorter, eight years after Gerberoi's leaguer, I watched Duke William dying.

The stone walls glistened wetly; droplets trickled slimy tracks like creeping snails. Monks and knights, dark pillars in the gloom, waited silently in the shadows. Shutters that were closed and barred stifled the whisper of dawn; the air was stagnant, rank, and smelt of death. Candles lighted a bed and a gaunt face ravaged with pain. Duke William moaned, a high-pitched noise like the whine of a wounded dog. A priest knelt beside him, muttering prayers. Monks chanted in the chapel; low droning incantations craved God's mercy for their lord.

Rufus nudged my elbow, murmured in my ear. We left the chamber, walked along a stone-flagged corridor and stopped at an open doorway which spilled lamplight on the paving. He said, 'Why have you come to Rouen?'

The years had changed him, coarsened his ruddy features, sagged his jowls and robbed lustre from the golden hair, leaving it flat-yellow like September wheat. He was broader, heavier, more formidable – the youthful charm was gone.

I said, 'Your brother sent me when he heard the Duke was sick.'

'Why didn't Curthose come himself?'

I let the question go: Rufus knew the answer well. Robert's short-lived concord with Duke William after Gerberoi had ended in savage quarrels; Curthose fled to King Philip's court in Paris. There he stayed in exile over the years, pampered by the king – for he was still heir to Normandy – living a life of wagers, wenches, wine. A half-dozen times I had met him, sliding steadily downhill, a dissolute voluptuary who feared his father living and ardently wished him dead. Now the Duke's end was near: a mortal hurt at Mantes split his spleen. In a manner, I thought sadly, to me he owed his dying: the Duke was invading the Vexin which I had urged Philip to seize.

'My brother's fox,' said Rufus, 'nosing out the spoils for him to gobble?' Involuntarily I moved; he clapped me on the shoulder. 'No, Walter – put up your dagger: once of your steel is enough. You are loyal – a worthy trait – and obey the man you followed. A waning star: it's time you found a brighter to guide you.'

'Yourself?' I inquired coldly.

'Why not? You heard my father's testament. To Robert, Normandy. England is mine.' Exultation rang in his voice like the clang of blade on blade.

'There's also Henry.'

'Henry?' he said contemptuously. 'A disinherited prince. No, Walter. It's king or duke – whichever will pay you best. Think on it.'

'My fealty belongs to France.'

'Fat Philip? Nothing for you there. Come with me to England, Walter – I'll give you a handsome fief.' He read something in my eyes which stopped him dead. 'Is your loathing still alive? Does that foolery from our boyhood fester yet?'

The old fascination, the attachment born from youthful admiration, still fettered me like living chains. Revulsion fought affection. Was I tainted also by Rufus's perversion? I longed to take his hand, to call him friend – and shrank from my desire like a thing unclean.

'You haven't changed your . . . habits.'

Anger glinted in the parti-coloured eyes. 'Are you monk or knight? Do you live at Poix secluded from the world? By the Face, if you damn all sodomites you'll have few friends left in Normandy!'

He thrust me furiously aside, and pushed through the open door. A horn lantern hung from a beam and lighted the room. Metal clinked on metal. Iron-bound chests, lids open, lined the walls; on an ox-hide sheet on the floor were deniers piled in heaps. Servants knelt and counted. A clerk cut notches on a tally stick; another stood at a lectern, quill in hand, and scratched figures on parchment scrolls. Walter of Clare, Duke William's chancellor, stood watching with folded arms. Prince Henry squatted on his haunches, intent on the flickering fingers of the men who dribbled silver into leather bags.

Rufus said, 'Our father is not yet dead.'

Henry neither raised his eyes nor answered. Clare turned his head. He said in a tone of tired disgust, 'My lord secures his patrimony.

The Duke has spoken his will – I witness a fair division. It is a long task.'

'A long task. Five thousand pounds of silver deniers. You'll still be numbering at noon. Henry,' Rufus repeated, 'our father is not yet dead. Will you not attend him for a while?'

Prince Henry rose, the sinews cracking in his legs. He looked at Rufus impassively. His eyes were muddy pinpoints in a flat, round face.

'Is the Duke conscious?'

'No. It's unlikely he'll regain his senses before the end.'

'Then what use? I'm not a priest, to speed a witless soul into the dark.' He inspected the money at his feet. 'Has Robert come?'

I said, 'No, my lord. I am the Count of Maine's emissary.'

'A dutiful son,' Henry observed unemotionally. 'Yet our father has given him Normandy —'

'God save Normandy!' Rufus exclaimed.

'Exactly. Soon, perhaps, God may want our help. What do you think, brother? Do you believe Robert fit to rule his heritage?'

Clare stirred uneasily. 'My lords, this is hardly a proper discussion, while the Duke's spirit has not yet quit his body. I cannot —'

'Rest easy, my lord of Clare,' Henry said calmly. He pointed to the silver. 'This is all the Duke has left me. I have no lands, no corner of the earth to call my own, and no men bound by fealty in my service. None need be afraid of me. And I,' he added softly, 'need fear nobody.'

He squatted again on his haunches. The monotonous counting continued; the clerk's quill scraped the parchment. An errant whisper of air flickered the lantern's flame; shadows danced on the walls and little wave-points gleamed from the sea of silver. Far away in Rouen St Peter's bell tolled prime: the notes thrummed in the lamplit chamber like muted metallic strings.

Rufus jerked his chin; we walked through darkened corridors, left the cloisters, breathed deeply the dawn-fresh wind.

He said, 'That . . . Henry.'

'What of him?'

'You heard his threat?'

'Threat? I heard none.'

A gust swayed the treetops. Rufus shivered, and pulled closer his cloak. 'No? And yet – he carries menace within him like a dagger in the sheath.'

'A discomforting man,' I agreed. 'You never know his thoughts.'

148

Rufus squared his shoulders. He said confidently, 'Henry hasn't an arpent of land – without land a man is finished.'

I answered from deep experience. 'A landless knight has one ambition: to gain a fief. Prince Henry will never rest until he's won a heritage.'

'Who from? Me – or Robert? England or Normandy?' He gazed at a saffron ribbon which seamed the sky above Rouen's distant rooftops, and added softly, 'You're right, Walter. Henry will bear watching.'

A commotion rustled the cloisters, a patter of running feet, voices urgently calling. Men hurried past, dim fugitives in daybreak's dusk. A woman sobbed in the shadows; someone called a servant. A priest strode over the grass, head turning from side to side like a falcon questing sparrows. He found his quarry, fell on his knees at Rufus's feet. The tonsure flamed like a fiery crown.

Flambard said, 'My lord, the Duke is dead.'

Rufus bowed his head and signed himself. I thought for a moment he prayed. He dropped his hands to his sides. His face was triumphant, alive; steel clashed in the ring of his voice.

'Ranulf,' he said, 'we go at once to England. A kingdom is there for the taking.'

I turned away. Rufus caught my arm, looked steadfastly into my face.

'You won't come with me, Walter?'

I hesitated on the brink of outright refusal; but a wise man never closes all the options.

'Not now, my lord. Perhaps . . . later.'

2

Two leagues from Rouen I halted beneath a medlar tree and broke my fast. Vauquelin took bread and meat from saddlebags, spread a linen napkin on the grass. He still served me as esquire although of knightly age: Verton, an impoverished fief, could afford only one knight. I sat on a fallen log and chewed cold mutton, watched Delis scrape a pebble from his palfrey's hoof and told him, between mouthfuls, of Duke William's end. My men-at-arms, girths loosened, exchanged lurid tales of Rouen's brothels. Laughter crackled on the sunlit air. Dew lingered on the grass, gleamed like a million gems;

the medlar's leaves were faded to the shade of beaten bronze. I loosed the clasp of my mantle and bared my chest to the sun. Save for the sergeants we rode unmailed: never afterwards in Normandy did men cross their pales unarmoured.

The sentinel on the roadside called a warning. A column swung round the curve, outriders in the van. The leader wore an azure mantle, a gold-brocaded cap. Green eyes in an ivory face. I brushed crumbs from my tunic and stood.

Robert of Belesme reined his palfrey. 'Well met, Lord Walter! You come from Rouen? How fares the Duke?'

I said, 'He died at prime.'

Belesme's hand jabbed the bridle; the horse flinched and fretted. Absently he stroked its mane, stared at the medlar's branches.

'Dead? You have seen this yourself?'

'Not I.' I gestured the way we had come. 'If you doubt me, you'll find his corpse in Rouen.'

'I believe you.' Belesme's voice was a whisper, his gaze remote. 'Body of God, he's dead! At last! Who has Normandy's seisin?'

'Robert of Maine.'

'The drowsy count! He's in Rouen?'

'No. In France – Paris.'

Belesme's face changed. He thumped fist on thigh. 'I knew it! We've a fool for a duke, a sluggard too fond of his bed! I must hurry!' He wheeled his horse and roared at his men. 'About – turn about!'

I caught his rein. 'You'll not go to Rouen?'

'Rouen?' He laughed in my face. 'No, my lord. I ride for Alençon, Ballon, Belesme – to eject Duke William's garrisons and seize my own for my own. The balance of power has tipped – Belesme is riding high! Quick, before that dolt in France awakes! Let go!'

His whip slashed my wrist; I dropped the rein.

'Gallop!'

Pensively I contemplated the dust-haze that they left. Delis said, 'What does he intend, my lord?'

I said, 'Anarchy. Anarchy in Normandy.'

3

In the years since Gerberoi I had done much to strengthen Poïx.

Belesme's scathing condemnations and his skill in fortifying

Gerberoi convinced me that Poix by modern standards was no better than a cow pen. Wood was poor protection against the artillery he invented, and a standing invitation to assault by fire. During husbandry's off-seasons I set my villeins to rebuild the castle in stone. The nature of the ground forbade enlargement; nor was this desirable. My mesnie was insufficient to man extensive fortifications, and the ward could already shelter, with a squeeze, Poix's inhabitants in time of trouble. After three winters' work I owned a stone-built donjon with walls a bowstave thick; stone ramparts girdled the ward; a barbican guarded gate and drawbridge. I could do little to deepen the moat: the picks struck bed-rock four spans down. I doubled the width and scarped the banks.

The ward's stables and store rooms – thatched timber hutments – I replaced in stone; and sent wagons to Rouen for roofing tiles, since the craft was unknown at Poix. I raised a hall in the ward: an improvement on the donjon's cramped unwindowed chamber where torches sputtered day and night.

Meanwhile I made it my business to discover the state of relations between Poix and the landholders on her frontiers. I probed my marches, scrutinized my neighbours. Gerberoi's castellans had never quarrelled with Poix; Helias, last of the line, maintained the tradition. Northwards the county of Ponthieu began; Count Guy was France's vassal and no enemy to Poix. Due west across the frontier lay Aumale, Normandy's marcher fortress, the counterpart to mine. Count Stephen of Aumale, an amiable man, existed peaceably on his estates and, while the Duke still lived, desired no more than to hawk and hunt, journey to Rouen for Easter and Pentecost feasts, and obediently lead his mesnie when his suzerain went to war. Yet between the lords of Aumale and Poix an irritation festered like a suppurating sore, a complicated quarrel going back for many years. Needless to say it hinged on land: all private wars, in my experience, originate in land, however much the issue might become obscured later.

The dispute, stripped of diverse ramifications and complications, was simply this:

On the vaguely defined border between Normandy and France was a monastery called Bauquenci whose abbot recognized Poix's ruler as his overlord. Orbec, an adjoining fief, was held of Aumale by a knight called Landric who surrendered his manors to the monastery, pretending by this reverent act to secure his soul's salvation. (In fact minor lordlings often ceded their fiefs to Holy Church, because tenure from a monastery with no warlike obligations is a much softer choice than seisin from a fighting baron.) Since Bauquenci was held of Poix, Orbec slid into Poix's demesne, but Aumale claimed Landric's vassalage. Count Stephen demanded restitution; my father declined to rescind Landric's devout renunciation – Orbec, though small, was fertile – and an enduring quarrel was born.

Stephen unwontedly lost his temper, led raiders to Bauquenci, killed Landric, harried the monastery's land and annexed the fief. My father retaliated, was worsted in an inconclusive scuffle, and afterwards went mad. The abbot of Bauquenci sheltered Landric's heir and brooded over his wrongs. When King Philip gave me seisin of the Honour the abbot came and bitterly complained.

I am not the kind who rides breakneck to avenge imagined slights; and I gave the affair much thought. Aumale had certainly denied Landric's right to make his peace with God; he had furthermore despoiled sanctified land. The crux was Landric's allegiance; and here I fancied Stephen had right on his side. But the abbot was importunate; in the end I made him indite a reasoned statement of his cause and sent the writ to the count.

Count Stephen was in Rouen, attending on the Duke. His nephew, a youthful hothead, responded by raiding Bauquenci and carrying off two-score kine. This snapped my patience. I led out thirty horsemen, burned the standing corn on Landric's erstwhile fief and pillaged a steading. I was slow in getting away, hindered by the cattle that we drove. A constabular from Aumale intercepted our retreat and chased us into Poix. I lost three sergeants, the stolen cattle, and saw my vineyards ravaged. I chewed my nails and impotently raged.

Richer said, 'Aumale, my lord, can dispose three hundred men. You'll never prevail against him sword to sword.'

Richer, to my surprise, had not left Poix with Isabel. He offered no explanation; I sought none. He attained a status, gradually, between esquire and vassal knight, attending on my person in rivalry with Vauquelin, and supervising Poix's rebuilding. He also instructed bowmen, a select band, young men unprejudiced and eager. The older archers held no truck with Richer's pattern of training, with the outlandish reflexed bows he made from goat's horn, yew and sinew; and laughed at his attempts to teach his pupils to shoot from horseback. Here he admitted failure: the palfreys in Poix's stables were stubborn, thick-necked beasts, their mouths brazed by clod-fist sergeants.

I said, 'I was a fool to try. I let Aumale provoke me – and now I've a war on my hands.'

'Mounted bowmen,' Richer answered quietly, 'would shorten the odds.'

I stared at Count Stephen's horsemen who cantered into the distance, content with the havoc they had wrought. Smoke billowed from a burning barn, stray corpses dotted the fields. I said impatiently, 'So you repeatedly tell me. Where are they? Can you sow them in the ground and reap the crop? Your efforts aren't very successful!'

'Because I haven't the right kind of horse.' Richer pensively nibbled a finger. 'My lord, I advise you to make peace with the count. Meanwhile, by your leave, I shall return to Spain.'

I glared. 'Are you frightened of the consequence, of what Aumale may do? I can call upon King Philip's aid!'

'For private war?' Richer shook his head. 'Unlikely that he'd answer unless the count beleaguered Poix – and he won't risk war with France. No, my lord. Unless you settle with Count Stephen there'll be raid and counter-raid – and you'll always be outnumbered. Let me go to Spain and find means to redress the balance.'

'What means?'

'Horses of the Moorish blood, bred specially for war.'

I let him go, certain he would never return, sure his idea was futile. Meanwhile, raging inwardly, I accepted his advice and placated the Count of Aumale. I sent him a writ and the gift of a destrier, asserted my right to Landric's fief but asked for a two-year truce. Stephen, an amicable man – secretly annoyed, I think, with his fire-eating nephew – courteously assented. I continued to strengthen Poix; and ignored the persistent abbot.

Then a weapon was put into my hands which, helped by circumstance, not only resolved the business of Bauquenci but made my reputation formidable throughout Neustria.

In springtime Richer went away, and in springtime two years later he returned. I had almost forgotten him. He brought three companions of his race – swarthy, copper-skinned men – and forty horses. Most were stallions, with a sprinkling of mares. 'For,' he asserted, 'I intend to breed.' They were small – about fourteen hands – with long powerful quarters, sloping shoulders, sensitive concave faces: unlike our heavy-boned horses as berselets from liams. I examined them dubiously – they were hardly the war-horse stamp.

Richer stabled his charges in the ward and enlisted a troop of bowmen. He scoured the Honour for young freemen – villeins, naturally, were never armed – tested their horsemanship and made them live in the castle. The nucleus he had trained before had changed to orthodox archery and served in the castle garrison. This I did not regret: to my mind foot bowmen were essential, Richer's theories unproven. He began training his recruits, and because of my interest – I am, after all, named Tirel – I submitted to his instruction. My instinct for shooting remained; I had to unlearn everything else. Grip, draw and loose – all were different; strange were the reflexed composite bows and long light arrows. The Moorish draw I never mastered – string in crease of thumb, locked forefinger on thumbnail – which needed thumb-rings of bone or agate to prevent blistering. Richer sighed when I reverted to my old three-finger draw. 'You'll never make a master bowman thus, my lord.'

Nonetheless after two years' training I outshot my mounted archers save for Richer and his countrymen, whose skill nobody could match. I grouped in a six-span circle from three score paces, hit twelve out of twenty marks at a gallop. Soothing to one's vanity, valuable for hunting, impractical in battle: as a knight I always wielded sword and lance.

Meanwhile the tireless Richer instructed my smiths and armourers in the forging of chain-mesh mail. 'Scales and rings are rigid,' he declared. 'A bowman in the saddle must be supple – he has to bend and twist.' He evolved a kind of factory: the armour progressed along a row of workmen, each completing a different task. Richer equipped his bowmen with chain mail haubergeons, the first so armed in Neustria. Crusading knights, years later, brought meshed hauberks back from Outremer.

The Aumale truce expired before the troop was ready. Count Stephen made no move; I wanted to let the quarrel die, despite the abbot of Bauquenci's querulous complaints – a holy man's cupidity for land exceeds a knight's. But Aumale had given Orbec to a certain Rualed, a knight of erratic temper. One bright midsummer's day Rualed invaded Bauquenci, lifted all the sheep and wounded a monk. Honour demanded that I retaliate. My harrying swirled like a tide-rip to Orbec's palisade. Rualed could only watch, as earlier I had watched Count Stephen ruin my vines – we outnumbered Orbec's men-at-arms by five to one – and I retreated quickly to my marches unpursued. Then I made ready for reprisals, posted speedy horsemen on the Aumale road, summoned my liegemen from Beaurain, Carenci and Esquennes, and waited.

'Your archers had better prove themselves,' I growled at Richer, 'else we'll starve in Poix this winter.'

'No need to fret, my lord,' he answered quietly. 'I think you'll be surprised.'

I was.

The scouts reported a hundred swords approaching the march. I collected every man I had and went to stop them.

We clashed on open pastures at the edge of Esquennes. Stephen unhurriedly arranged his battle: forty knights and sergeants in the van, footmen in support, bowmen on the flanks. Six hundred paces away I did likewise with half his strength – except that Richer's bowmen were strung across my front. Aumale's clarion bellowed; his knights cantered to the charge.

Richer's archers swept to meet them like separate galloping bolts. At ultimate range they loosed, and loosed again. The arrows flew like hail. They checked and wheeled, pelted parallel to Aumale's line, bowstrings shrilling. With the lances a horse-length distant they swung on their hocks and fled, shooting backwards as they went. They cleared Count Stephen's front and poured arrows from the flanks.

Like corn-stalks sheared at the roots the charge collapsed.

I remembered a quick vision of destriers falling in waves. Here was harsh reality. No time for wonder. I hurled my twenty horsemen at the floundering, kicking shambles, speared dazed, dismounted knights, hacked cowering, flinching bodies. Delis encountered a knight whose horse had eluded the arrows; with a horizontal slash, like lopping a succulent leek, he sheared his foeman's head. The horse ran on with the body, spouting a scarlet jet; the head jumped to Delis's pommel, and glared angrily into his eyes.

Richer went to attend to the footmen. My men-at-arms ran to his help.

Within the time a man might arm himself the thing was over. Aumale's surviving knights, embattled in a ring, fell one by one. A knight with a broken sword called wearily for quarter. I lowered my lance and peered into his face.

'Count Stephen?'

'Stephen of Aumale. I yield to you, my lord.'

'Sound your clarion!' I said sharply; and beckoned my trumpet-bearer. The sooner the battle ended the better: I had no wish to lose valuable men. The horns wailed dolorously above the clang and shouting; gradually the fighting ceased, the sword blades drifted apart. My cavalry surrounded Aumale's shattered force; Richer's archers curvetted in a wider arc, bows flexed and arrows notched.

I said, 'I've no desire to make you prisoner, my lord count. Give me a hostage for your ransom, and go free.'

'How much do you demand?'

'Three hundred pounds of silver.'

Stephen nursed an arm a lance had bitten, and scowled. 'I have no choice. You may take my nephew Rotrou – if he's still alive.'

I stuck my lance in the ground, dismounted and said with a smile, 'And then the quarrel goes on, my lord – an irksome heritage for your heirs and mine. Were it not better to remove the cause? Instead of the ransom give me Orbec – it's worth but half.'

Count Stephen pondered. I studied his leathery face, the crinkles of humour at the corners of his eyes, and added gently, 'I shall take your hostage, and when your charter, sealed and attested, is in my hands, release him.'

The count sighed. 'Very well. It shall be done.' He looked at the dead and dying destriers sprawled chaotically across the field, sprouting arrows like hedgehog quills. Stephen compressed his lips, surveyed Richer's circling bowmen.

'You have a new and deadly weapon there, my lord of Poix.' Reluctantly he smiled. 'But I doubt you'll teach me the handling of it.'

Thus the affair was settled. I implemented Landric's will and gave Orbec to Bauquenci; the abbot settled Landric's son on the manor and everyone – except perhaps Aumale – was happy.

Richer merely said, 'Three hundred arrows spent to bring down forty horses. We'll have to do better than that.'

The fame of the fight, and of Richer's archers, spread widely through France and Normandy. Knights visited Poix from faraway castles to inspect this awesome weapon. King Philip, on progress from Ponthieu, demanded a demonstration, rubbed his nose and frowned. 'If others imitate you, Tirel' – the affair had revived my surname – 'we'll have to armour our destriers.' Certain knights were not so impressed. 'Mere pinpricks,' they scoffed. 'Your bowmen won't stand and fight.'

The sceptics were to meet their like in thousands, in Outremer ten years later at a place called Doryleum.

The barons who assembled at Rouen to witness Duke William's end hastened from his bedside when he died. The servitors seized silver, robes and furniture and left his body naked on the floor. At the funeral they tried to force the corpse inside a coffin far too short, and burst the bowels. The obsequies thereafter, I was told, were brief.

A new era dawned in Normandy.

The barons followed Robert of Belesme's example, pounced on their strongholds, expelled the ducal garrisons and installed their liegemen. Morin du Pin quit Evreux in a hurry; William's vassals regained Breteuil; even Ralph thrust the dead duke's men from Conches.

Thus established they looked about them, and remembered ancient quarrels which had been suppressed beneath the tight bandaging of Duke William's rule. Normandy sprouted private wars like grass-blades springing quickly after rain. Throughout the bitter winter refugees fled over the marches, knights wounded and disseized, villeins starved and wasted. The knights I sheltered and tended; the serfs belonged to others – I drove them out.

France on the whole stayed quiet. I had no fears for Poix. The castle I judged impregnable, and the archers' reputation discouraged casual raids. I heard that others tried to train horsed bowmen and had quit, discouraged, for lack of suitable palfreys.

To reward my services at Gerberoi King Philip gave me Achères on the Seine, a fief and castle owing three knights. I rarely visited Achères: twice yearly laden rounceys brought the revenues to Poix; Baudri, shovelling deniers into coffers, licked his lips. Baudri, over the years, had grown senile, his fat carcass monstrous, scarcely able to walk. With the priest as scribe he kept my accounts; the lank and gawky Vauquelin supervised the manors.

Occasionally I thought of Isabel, and wondered how she fared. I had no certain news: word travelled slowly in those troubled times; pedlars feared to travel, even priests. Knights returning from the wars brought rumours that Ralph had fallen out with his neighbour, my one-time guardian, William Count of Evreux; that the feud was fostered by rivalry and hatred between their ladies. I remembered that Countess Hawise had once had Isabel whipped, remembered Isabel's nature – and considered the rumour credible. The Lady of Conches, I reflected, liked to repay her debts. She owed me one. I smiled to myself. No reason I should ever see that beautiful vixen again.

I had another incentive to keep out of Isabel's way, for about this time I was married to Adelice of Clare, Richard of Bienfaite's daughter. My wife's father was Duke William's cousin, her grandfather Walter of Clare, Duke William's chancellor. The Duke himself, always interested in the affinities of his numerous relatives, concerned at the moment to strengthen his ties with France, decided on the Lord of Poix as a suitable husband. The match, in short, was one of those half-political unions common among noble families. I had no objection: Adelice brought me a substantial dowry and seisin of an English fief, Laingaham in Suffolk. She was a mouse-like maiden, comely without being beautiful, diligent in her duties, never meddlesome in my affairs – and has no bearing whatsoever on this history.

In this calm existence, like a stone in a tranquil pond, dropped a missive from Robert of Normandy.

I dismissed the priest who read it, dangled the parchment in my fingers and gazed thoughtfully into the fire. Curthose wanted help. The letter was enigmatic: he hinted at an enterprise and promised vast rewards. All the barons, so he said, were joining in the venture. Would I, his old companion in adversity, come to share the spoils? What venture, I wondered bleakly, could wrest spoils from ravaged Normandy?

The sergeants at a trestle down the hall bickered loudly over their dice. I silenced them abruptly, drew my chair closer to the hearth-fire and kicked a log ablaze. I wanted to think.

Why leave a secure home for uncertain gains? I had all that a man could want: wealth and leisure, a loyal and numerous retinue, horses and hounds, a wife and willing whores. Power? I had that also, within limits: I was a baron who led ten knights. I thought of Belesme and his fifty, of Breteuil with his seven castles; and pursed my lips. A petty baron by the measures of the great. Why was not Curthose more precise, what prizes could he offer? No harm in going to see, perhaps.

I sipped my wine, reflectively examined the fighting boar engraved upon the cup. I had grown overfond of wine, too fussy about my food. Tentatively, beneath the furred woollen cloak, I prodded my belly. Soft. Was I going to seed in peaceful Poix? I looked at the gross Baudri, snoring in a chair. Was I sliding down the selfsame hill?

My goblet sailed across the hall, hit Baudri in the face. He woke spluttering from his slumber. I rose to my feet and shouted for Vauquelin. Curthose promised spoil, and that meant war – you could not get it without. For a twelvemonth my sword was unblooded; I was sunk in stagnant sloth. Knights were made for fighting: why else did they exist?

5

The Tower of Rouen seemed shrunken since my youth. I explored the echoing halls, cavernous stone chambers, the mighty pillars and smelly dens where Amauri and I had slept. They still played, I noted happily, the game of middens. The seneschal who billeted my retinue said Curthose held a congress with his lords; after a bicker with the knight who guarded the door – a secret conclave, he declared – I entered the council chamber. Curthose sat enthroned, the barons lounged in chairs, petty lordlings perched on tables, leaned against pillars. Torches flared in cressets, candles cast a mellow light on tense, excited faces. Voices rattled in argument. I saw Ivo in the shadows and slid to a bench beside him. He grinned a welcome and whispered behind his hand.

'Duke Robert's hurled a boulder in the fishpond.'

'What has he said?'

'Listen.'

Robert of Belesme quelled the clacking voices. 'You propose, my lord, to invade England. Another Conquest? You'll challenge Rufus and all his baronage? A stiffer proposition than the thanes your father faced!'

I gasped and rocked on the bench. Ivo laughed at my expression.

'The English lords are on our side, ready to revolt.' Curthose's ruddy face was tired and strained; grey flecks like iron slivers speckled his temples. He gestured to a man who sat beside him. 'Bishop Odo has been writing to them for months. By Easter they'll be ready for rebellion.'

'Then this is my lord of Bayeux's idea?' said Belesme.

Curthose frowned. 'My uncle pointed out the merits,' he answered stiffly.

I scrutinized Odo of Bayeux's gaunt face and wary, roving eyes. The guiding hand was plain; such a daring concept was beyond Duke

Robert's invention. Had he agreed, I wondered, because the barons were tearing Normandy apart? Did Curthose hope to deport his turbulent nobles, quarter them on English fiefs, escheat their Norman domains and take them into his hand? A foolish aspiration – they'd hurry back in swarms. I thought of Rufus newly crowned, the holy oil still damp upon his brow, betrayed by all his vassals – and felt strangely sad.

Belesme stroked the silver lace that broidered his sable cloak, studied Curthose beneath his brows. 'And your part?'

'When the English barons rise we sail, land in southern England – why not Hastings? – and march on London.'

'Like a coulter ploughing sand?' Belesme inquired sardonically. 'None will oppose us?'

'Our friends hold castles on the route.' Odo's flat guttural voice. 'Pevensey' – he stuttered – 'these gob-stopping English names! Tonbridge and Rochester.' He looked speculatively at Belesme. 'We propose, my lord, to send you in advance to hold Rochester for us.'

'So?' Belesme raised his eyebrows, danced fingers on knee reflectively. He scanned the intent faces, caught William of Evreux's eye, saw Aumale's warning expression and said lazily, 'My lord duke, we wish to debate this matter among ourselves. With your permission —'

'Stay here.' Curthose rose abruptly, gathered his robe. 'I and my lord bishop will leave you to speak your minds.'

They left the chamber. Conflicting voices drowned the sentinel knight's salute. Acceptance and dissent whirled back and forth like missiles; knights hammered fists on table tops and shouted. Ivo yawned and yearned aloud for wine. Belesme listened silently, steepled fingertips to lips, his eyes derisive. I began to regret my coming, and longed for peaceful Poix.

William of Evreux scrubbed his grey, bristly head and said decisively, 'The crux is this, my lords. From Duke William – God rest his soul! – most of us held lands in both Normandy and England. His dominion now is divided. If we serve Rufus we offend Duke Robert. Give our fealty to Robert and we lose our English fiefs. There is your choice, my lords!'

'We all swore fealty to Robert during Duke William's lifetime: never to Rufus,' observed Ivo unexpectedly.

'Rufus,' Belesme drawled silkily, 'is hard and forceful, a fighter, a man to be feared. Whereas our Duke is, shall we say' – he fluttered an indolent hand – 'rather more pliable, more likely to accept our – um – wishes.'

The company digested the argument, and muttered among themselves. William of Breteuil said roughly, 'Let us support the man who already holds our fealty, whom we twist around our fingers like a sodden rag. I propose we follow Curthose with our mesnies!'

'And kill Rufus?' I asked in a strangled voice.

'Or depose him.'

Belesme said smoothly, 'You mentioned mesnies, my lord of Breteuil. Will you take *all* your men? I think it politic to leave strong garrisons to guard our castles. We trust each other, of course' – no irony in his tone – 'but another may be tempted.'

They took his meaning, and nodded wisely. Breteuil scratched the thick hair on the back of his hand and said, 'Then where will Duke Robert find his army?'

Belesme stood. 'He'll have to hire mercenaries. And so I shall inform him.'

6

I found Curthose on the ramparts, gazing across the moat. St Peter's bell tolled vespers. The evening was squally; the banner on the battlements streamed flat as a shield. Lights twinkled in Rouen's windows; mist skeins whipped by wind wreathed from the twilit river. Curthose beckoned me beyond earshot of his esquires and escort knight – a Duke of Normandy is never unattended.

'You owe me no fealty, Walter, you come in friendship. I'm glad. You'll be well rewarded – there's land going begging in England.'

'I ask for no requital in your service, my lord,' I said untruthfully. 'I answer when you call. But my retinue is small compared to lords who owe you service. Why did you —'

'You're famous, Walter.' A smile kindled the tired eyes, was gone like a fading spark. 'Stephen of Aumale – and others – tell tales of your mounted bowmen. A lethal weapon. I want them. I'll have to scrape, in truth, for every man I can get.'

A watering detail plodded from the river. Hooves thumped dully on sodden ground; mail rings glinted dimly in the dusk. Curthose watched them sightlessly, his face forlorn.

'I have to pay mercenaries, and the treasury is empty. Wars, devastation, ruin – my revenues shrunk to a trickle. And many expensive gifts, to keep my faithful vassals loyal.' His mouth twisted. 'I've had to sell part of the ducal domain.'

I regarded him compassionately, a man burdened beyond his strength, a duke without authority or resolution. Was this the man to lead another Conquest?

'Henry alone of all my lords possesses ready money – the heritage my father left. He refused a loan.' Curthose sighed. 'Knowing Henry, I was not surprised. I sold him Mont St Michel, Coutances and Avranches for three thousand pounds of silver.'

Henry had attended the council, saying nothing, seeing and hearing all.

'Then you'll find your mercenaries, my lord.'

'Yes.' The guard was closing the castle gate; a sergeant rated a man-at-arms who staggered home late from a tavern. 'Henry, landless, was impotent. A prince of the blood with three strong castles is a thorn to poison Normandy.'

7

I left all my knights and men-at-arms in Poix, and brought Richer and his archers to the army at St Valeri. Tents and pavilions crowded the beaches, dotted the inland dunes. Pennons fluttered from lances rooted in front of the canopies, and blazoned shields proclaimed each mesnie's lord. Knights in velvet mantles, scarlet and blue and green, strolled idly hawk on wrist along the tent-lanes. Sergeants in mail and leather-clad bowmen wandered in noisy groups; varlets hissed in the horse-lines; monks walked aloofly alone, black welts on a vivid mosaic. Garish colourful robes, like rainbows shivered in shards, enlivened the squalid wagon parks where the harlots lived.

Ships in rows were grounded on the sands; foresters felled trees; shipwrights and carpenters axed and planed and lopped, smiths hammered in the forges. I wandered lost among the tents, my retinue trailing behind, seeking a blazon I recognized. I found an orderly encampment sheltered under trees and was angrily repulsed by a black-browed knight. An altercation boiled, my hand rested on my sword. A familiar voice said, 'Come away, Walter. There's space beside my pitch.'

I snarled a final insult at the truculent knight and followed Ivo.

He said cheerfully, 'You wouldn't like it. That's the mercenaries' camp – Flemings, Bretons, Poitevins. Not our sort at all. Cut your throat for a denier and probably drink your blood.'

I encamped my men alongside Ivo's lines, picketed horses, pitched tents, watered and fed. Afterwards I strolled with Richer to the beach and inspected the ships. Richer speechlessly surveyed the slender vessels, tall curving prows and sternposts, the single masts.

'You can't put horses in these!' he said at last.

'It's been done before,' I retorted. 'Twenty-two years ago. We'll have to learn.'

Next day, and a week thereafter, we practised embarkation on transports moored in the shallows. These were modified to carry horses: flaps in the bulwarks opened outwards, making a ramp. Timbers set athwartships formed narrow stalls, five in the bows, five in the stern. (This for our smaller palfreys; the destriers' transports carried only six.) We spread sand thickly on the decks to give a standing, and shackled the horses taut. Ten palfreys, a crew of six and two bowmen to guard the horses packed the vessel tight as a barrel of pilchards. My horses filled three transports, the bowmen crammed a fourth.

Day after day, from all the encampments, men led horses to the sands, hauled them through the shallows, forced them up the ramps. Loose destriers galloped the foreshore, ears cocked, tails flaring high; cursing soldiers stumbled in pursuit. Order evolved from chaos; the animals lost their fear of sea and ships; we were allotted definite vessels and a place in the order of sailing.

Winter's greyness ebbed from the skies, springtime smiled on the beaches. A breeze rippled the sparkling water which was stippled with anchored ships. Ivo sat beside me on the beach, and looked unhappy. 'I've been appointed constable of the leading flight,' he announced gloomily. 'Your mesnie, mine, Breteuil's and a gang of Flemings – about three hundred in all. We've got our ships, and so has the second flight – Beaumont's. And that seems the lot.'

I scraped a seashell from the sand and held it to my ear. 'The army can't walk on water. We'll just have to wait till they've built enough ships.'

'Wait? Easter's a week away. Have you forgotten? The date for the English rebellion, which we're meant to support.'

'The shipwrights are slow,' I agreed. 'They need driving. William of Evreux commands at St Valeri – he's old for the job. Nobody's seen Curthose. Where is he?'

Ivo lobbed a pebble at a heap of seaweed. 'Rouen. Remember Lesceline? She appeared with a nine-year boy, and swore it was Robert's. Curthose had his doubts, put her to the proof – the ordeal by hot iron. Her hands were unscathed. Now he's acknowledged the child – and spends his time in bed begetting another.'

I dropped the shell, rested chin on hands. A thin gleaming line, bright as a sword, quivered between sea and sky. The tide was at the ebb, wavelets curled and rustled on the beach. A fishing boat rowed slowly across the bay; oars thumped in the rowlocks like muffled drums.

'Curthose,' I said. 'He'll sacrifice a kingdom for a woman's arms.'

'And us as well,' Ivo grunted. He scrambled to his feet, brushed sand from his mantle. 'One thing is certain: we won't be ready for the rising.'

Birdsong kindled the green-gold days of spring. The furious activity on the beaches faltered, the sense of urgency declined. I took my hawks to the woods, galloped berselets after hares. At evening knights gathered in pavilions, rolled dice and drank. The stews were busy; with Ivo I shared a doxy and kept her in my tent. Vague, garbled rumours filtered into the camp: the English barons had struck, the land was ablaze, Rufus on the run. Names rang like victorious clarions: Mowbrai, de Laci and Clare. It seemed they didn't need help.

A pursuivant from Rouen shattered our complacency. Count William's messengers hastily quartered the camp, summoned the lords to council. We gathered in an arc in front of the count's pavilion. He stood beneath his banner, twisting a parchment scroll between his hands. Lines of worry seamed a careworn face.

'Rufus has raised the English levies,' William of Evreux announced curtly. 'Thirty thousand men. He's taken Tonbridge; Arundel has submitted. He now besieges Pevensey, held by Robert of Mortain.'

The names meant nothing to me. I plucked a blade of dune-grass, chewed upon it thoughtfully and savoured the bitter taste. I knew a curious happiness, a hidden joy that welled like an underground spring. Rufus the paladin, a knight beset – and winning.

Count William said in a strained voice, 'Duke Robert decrees that the army sail immediately to relieve Pevensey.'

There was a laden silence.

'Do we swim?' wondered William of Breteuil. 'We have ships for a thousand men. What about the rest?'

Count William cleared his throat. 'Those that are ready sail. The rest will follow.'

Ivo gazed at the shipyards, at the skeleton hulls that towered like the bones of ancient dragons. 'When? At Michaelmas?' he inquired fiercely. 'You propose, my lord, to invade England with a thousand men. How —'

'I propose nothing. I give you the Duke's commands. Are you willing,' the count asked coldly, 'to defy him?'

8

A glittering, sun-drenched day, a brilliant gem on the necklet of a long hot summer.

I heeded it not. I crouched on a heaving deck, vomiting on the sanded planks, sickened by the stench of tar and brine. The sail bellied; a billow rolled under the keel, the crucifix carved on the sternpost climbed like a soaring hawk. I crawled urgently to the side, drooped on the row of shields and gazed miserably over the water.

The ship lagged in the rear of the fleet. During the night, creeping over a glassy sea in starlit darkness, ships had overtaken her, trailing stealthy wakes like luminous strings of pearls. I reviled the helmsman, a seamed white-headed rascal whose beard, mottled grey and russet, swept his chest like a rusted shield. 'She's a slow sailer, master,' Hardwin asserted. 'I can't go faster than my ship.' He hawked and spat over the side. 'In my boyhood I voyaged to Hastings. The Old Duke set us ashore where the enemy wasn't. Now you intend a landing where the English are ready and waiting.' His teeth gleamed whitely in the dark. 'Let the quick 'uns bear the brunt – you'll thank me later.'

A dawn wind blew from the south and lopped the sea. I then lost interest.

A hundred sails rode the tumbling waves like a flock of iridian gulls. The order of sailing was lost in the night, the flights were mingled together. Longships sped in the van, brimming with knights and sergeants, the fastest outreaching the rest. Far in the rear the transports wallowed, pale specks on an azure sea. Ivo's banner climbed to the masthead, a sign for his flight to rally and dress. A forlorn gesture -- the wind gave the ships a life of their own, a soul and a will beyond man's regulation.

Hardwin tugged his oar, studied the sail and shouted orders. Crewmen shouldered through archers thronging the hull, brusquely shoved them aside, hauled on ropes. The sail wavered, cracked like a riven tree-trunk, strained at the sheets. The rigging creaked; the vessel pitched and rolled. I clutched my throat, stared wretchedly at the racing water a sword-length from my face. Seaweed rocked on the swell, black and red and green.

The helmsman called and pointed. Richer touched my arm. His coppery face was wan; spray spangled his mail in glittering skeins.

'Land, my lord.'

Black-purple clouds like hanging hills, an opalescent haze, a long wavering shoreline honey-pale in noonday sun. I rose unsteadily, unhitched my shield from the row along the ship's side. Vauquelin's fingers flitted over helmet thongs and ventail; I pushed his busy hands aside and looked ahead. Vessels furrowed to the beaches, striped and checkered sails, yellow, blue and scarlet, a gaudy swarm of butterflies winging to the shore. I forced a way to the poop and croaked an order. Archers groped in wallets for bowstrings, braced the bows, elbows ramming ribs in the crowded hull. Vauquelin mouthed curses beneath his breath and unravelled a twisted guige. I gripped a mast-stay, shaded my eyes and saw the beaches plain.

The English beleaguering army, William of Evreux had said, would be taken by surprise.

He was wrong.

The throwing-arms of mangonels towered above the heat haze, and bannered pavilions clustered beyond Rufus's entrenchments. Pevensey's angular donjon climbed from the shore like a reef. In separate wings on either side an army thronged the shoreline, jagged broken masses like jetsam cast by a storm. Each wing held a front five bowshots long from water's edge to flood-tide's seawrack. Alien standards snapped on the wind, alien was the aspect of our enemy. I expected the iron-grey loom of knights, and oak-brown leather where spearmen stood. This array wore a gorgeous motley, twin flower-beds tipped with steel.

Beneath the castle a wide gap yawned, the beaches void of men, a beaten zone which Mortain's bowmen scourged.

The leading ships changed course. The pilots saw the empty strand and veered for the gap, converging like a duck flight after sunset. The ships closed one on another, the sails uniting in a wall which hid the beach. Hulls grated and cordage snapped; furious voices bellowed across the water. Hardwin hauled his sweep and swore. The ships on our flanks closed in; angrily the bearded seaman gestured them away. His eyes searched the serried hulls for a way to the beach.

None opened. On the wings the English swordsmen hovered like leaning cliffs.

I heard keels grate on shingle, saw hulls shudder to a halt. Knights jumped from the prows and stumbled, swords aloft, across the deserted sands beneath the castle walls. Mortain's men on the battlements saw them coming and cheered.

Clarions yelled in unison. The enemy's line erupted like a landslide torn from the beach.

My sickness vanished like mist in the noonday sun.

I shouted at the steersman, swung my arm and pointed out to sea. Hardwin tugged the sweep with all his strength, heels slipping on the deck. I seized the shaft and shoved. Slowly the head came round. The bow rasped another ship's quarter, strakes grated alongside. The sail spilled wind, flapped heavily and drooped. Crewmen loosened sheets. The ship lost way and rocked on the swell. The dragon figurehead snuffled the horizon.

I stared across the pooprail at the turmoil on the beaches.

Men fought ships in the shoals; the water churned like milk. Hands scrabbled on hulls; English axemen clambered inboard; their spearmen lunged at the shield-lined sides. Knights leaped from the decks and fought in the breakers, hacking and parrying in chest-deep water. The bowmen on Pevensey's battlements loosed desultory shafts, then eased their strings – impossible in that raging battle to distinguish friend from foe.

Ships from the rear sailed into the fight and rammed the sterns that rocked entangled, wedged, aswarm with men. Masts tumbled, sails shrouded decks, timbers cracked like twigs. Vessels drifted apart, trailing ropes and wreckage, the decks a swirling carnage. Knights embattled and exhausted cried for quarter; the English drove them overboard and watched their armour drown them.

'Are we,' asked Richer bleakly, 'going into that?'

No place for archers, I decided, pulling my lip. The tide was carrying us in; I spoke sharply to the helmsman, gestured seawards. Hardwin grinned agreement, called his crew. Oars rattled in the tholes and beat the water. The vessel gathered way, crawled from the turbulent beaches. We were not alone, I noticed, looking around: other laggards like ourselves clawed slowly out to sea.

Beyond a headland on our left more ships appeared.

Richer saw them first, and called. Hardwin rolled his eyes to heaven and muttered in his beard. 'Ours?' I asked hopefully. 'The transports?' 'English,' he grated. 'Say your prayers, master.' He shouted at the crewmen toiling at the sweeps.

'Row, you poxy sons of misbegotten whores! Row for your hell-born souls, else your guts will feed the fishes!'

I watched the scudding sails. Some turned towards the beaches to join the fight. Others headed for the ships rowing painfully out to sea. A hoy and a scarlet longship bore steadily on our quarter, pointing a little seawards to sever our retreat. Hardwin eyed them anxiously.

'They have the wind,' he growled. 'Master, we must alter course. You'll not see Normandy this night!'

He pulled the steering sweep and shouted orders. Crewmen dropped the oars, sprang to the sheets. The sail curved and bellied. The dragon's head wheeled round. The ship gathered way, water rippling at the prow. A beam wind canted the deck. We sailed parallel to a coastline rimed by breakers; smoke coils wreathed remotely from Pevensey's beach of slaughter – a sacrifice of broken ships, the pyre of Duke Robert's high ambitions.

Richer said, 'They're gaining.'

The scarlet longship cruised in our wake; the hoy had dropped behind, waves buffeting her clumsy bows. Hardwin shifted the sweep a fraction, combed fingers in his beard. 'A slow sailer, master. Perhaps you'll believe me now.' He pointed his chin to a cliff that jutted from the shore. 'They'll have us before we reach that head-land.'

'Richer,' I said, 'tell the bowmen to man the sides.'

It was an awkward, jostling business. Only half our men had room to line the sides and poop. The remainder crouched amidships, rib to rib, handed quivers to the others and drew their dirks. With the archers posted I looked astern. The hunter was creeping nearer, prow slicing through the waves and flinging spray. Fierce, bearded faces, iron caps and glinting spears. Voices hammered faintly, a thin thread of sound that wavered on the wind.

Hardwin thumped his oar. 'How do you want me to steer?'

'Just hold your course.'

Almost imperceptibly the longship overhauled us. I swallowed a lump in my throat, licked salt-caked lips. The waiting was hard to endure. Things happened so slowly at sea.

The scarlet hull was a bowshot distant.

'They've yawed on our larboard quarter,' Hardwin announced calmly.

The man talked gibberish, I thought testily.

The enemy prow slid away from our wake, drew steadily closer and lapped our stern. War-cries bayed above the wind, above the slapping waves and creaking timbers. Richer stirred uneasily, grumbled below his breath.

Half a bowshot.

'Nock your shafts!'

Arrows jumped from quivers, notched on strings. The archers lifted their bows, swayed on the lurching deck. A throwing-spear curved from the scarlet ship and thudded in the counter.

'Loose!'

Bowstrings thrummed and arrows whipped. The men flexed and loosed, notched and flexed and loosed. A sudden storm like driven sleet joined ship to ship, a transparent shimmering arch of feathered steel. The longship sheered away and the sail flapped loose.

'Poor shooting!' Richer observed critically.

You can't shoot well from a bucketing stance, nor promise to hit at sixty paces nor loose an arrow for every breath. Richer, a perfectionist, demanded exorbitant skill. The range was less than a spear-cast, the target a close-packed crew. I don't think a man in the longship was unwounded, and most of them died where they stood. She lost way; the helm-oar trailed like a broken wing. Bodies sagged like corn-sacks over the sides, slid into the water as the vessel rolled. Arrows thudded into lifeless flesh.

'Ease strings!'

The bowmen chattered and laughed, excitement swamping tension. Hardwin's eyes were alight with amazement. 'Never seen anything like it!' he crowed. 'And I saw the Bretons at Hastings!' He examined the distant hoy. 'I can outsail that hulk,' he declared, 'if they dare to follow.'

The hoy closed the stricken ship and dropped her sail. We saw her no more. Hardwin trimmed the sheets, edged farther from the coast. No other ships pursued us; we had the sea to ourselves. I sat on the forward end of the poop, legs dangling over the hold, and gave silent thanks to the saints for my deliverance. Hardwin hummed a tune; the ship lifted on the swell, wavecrests slapped the strakes.

'Where are you heading?' I asked idly.

'If the wind holds and don't shift we'll find Boulogne on this course. With luck.'

Richer said abruptly, 'The transports – and our horses! Can't we intercept them, turn them back?'

Hardwin looked at him with pity. 'Master, this is a ship. You can't sail into the wind!'

9

At evening the wind backed to the north and whipped spindrift from the wavetops. Hardwin ran before it, singing gaily: this, it seemed, was the course he wanted for St Valeri. During the night the wind-squalls roared to a gale; he furled the sail and the ship drove helplessly before the storm.

I cared not whether I lived or died. I shivered on the keel boards, deathly sick, soaked by spray and driving rain. Vauquelin unlaced my helmet, cradled me in his arms against the ship's demented lurching. In the grey of dawn she struck on a jagged shore, lay stranded and awash. Richer and Vauquelin dragged me to the land. I stumbled on a seaweed-slippery boulder and hit my head. The last vestiges of reason drowned in roaring darkness; I drifted endlessly on troubled rapids between sleep and waking, submerging into night, surfacing to dreams where eldritch faces hovered like wraiths and phantom voices called from far away.

Chapter 8

1088–91

Sunlight dappled the limewashed wall and lighted a ragged patch where plaster had cracked and fallen to expose the hazel-wand wattle. A blackbird perched on the casement's shutter and burbled his summertime song. Wheels rumbled on cobbles outside. I stared blankly at the thatch which bulged the rafters, and slowly turned my head. A shadow stirred at the window, hovered over the pallet.

'Richer,' I whispered.

His swarthy features crinkled in a smile. 'You know me at last, my lord. It's been a long time. I sometimes feared your wits had gone for good.'

'Where . . .'

'No questions yet. The fever, I think, has gone.' His hand touched my cheek. 'Yes – your blood has cooled. Could you eat, my lord?'

I felt hungry as a starving wolf, and nodded weakly. Richer stirred a wooden bowl. 'Barley gruel – you've taken nothing else this fortnight past.' He put an arm around my shoulders and raised me from the pillow. Greedily I swallowed the liquid. A few mouthfuls were enough; I pushed the spoon aside, felt the linen which bound my head.

'Richer,' I croaked, 'what has happened?'

He laid a finger on my lips. 'Hush, my lord. Better you should not speak. You nearly died – often I thought you gone. We struck on the Breton coast – do you remember? – a wild, deserted shore, and carried you here on a litter.'

'Here?'

'Coutances. You are lodged in a burgher's house in the town.'

Someone shouted in the street. The blackbird shrieked alarm and flew away. A sluggish memory stirred, flickered and caught alight.

'Coutances? A fief that Curthose sold . . . to Henry.'

Richer frowned. 'The prince is here.'

My head throbbed. I closed my eyes and tried to think. 'The bow-men,' I mumbled. 'Were they saved?'

'Five drowned. The rest are quartered in the castle – by Prince Henry's order. The palfreys are probably lost; though I've heard rumours that a handful of transports returned to St Valeri. I've sent to inquire.'

Remembrance returned in a blaze. There had been more than men's and horses' lives at stake – kingdoms trembled in the balance. I pushed aside the bedclothes, ignored the pain that stabbed my skull.

'Richer! The English rebellion! Is Rufus dead?'

He stroked the wolfskin coverlet which shone tawny bronze in the sunlight. 'No. King William lives, and is stronger yet. Mortain surrendered Pevensey when the landing failed. The king then beleaguered Rochester, and Belesme yielded. The barons submitted, the revolt is dead, England at peace.'

I rested my head on the pillow and stared at the rafters. A knot in the wood was shaped like a broken sceptre. So much for Robert's tilt at England's crown. Poor Curthose!

Richer rose and sauntered to the casement. A lime-branch nodded at the window; he plucked a leaf and rolled it between his fingers. 'There are things I do not understand, my lord. The prince has confined Vauquelin and your retinue in the castle. A sentinel guards your doorway night and day: he stands below the window now.' He smiled wryly.

'Does the prince mistrust me? I believe not. Then why this . . . consideration?'

Why indeed, I wondered dimly. I lay in Henry's hand. Surely no danger there? He had no reason for enmity; I scarcely knew him. He was Duke Robert's vassal, the duke my friend. Had he fallen out with Curthose? Even so, what could he want of me? King Philip was my suzerain; I owed fealty to nobody in Normandy.

Too difficult. I gave it up.

Richer flicked the crumpled leaf across the room. 'Prince Henry bade me bring him word when you were conscious.' He smoothed the pillow, drew the covers to my chin. 'I have been stupid to let you talk so much. It will be many days yet before you leave your bed.'

He closed the shutters. The room was dark and quiet; I drifted away on a rolling river of sleep.

Prince Henry said, 'Pevensey was a cauldron which boiled Duke
Robert's fantasy from the bones of hard reality. The skeleton of
truth lies bare for all the world to see. In brief, Lord Walter, times
have changed. Especially for you.'

I sat at the high table, on Henry's left. He beckoned a servitor to
fill my cup, went on gnawing a beef-bone. Gravy dribbled down his
chin. I pushed aside my trencher, dabbled fingers in an ewer
Vauquelin held, dried them on a napkin. My head ached – the wound
troubles me to this day – and hearth-smoke smarted my eyes. The
voices of Henry's liegemen clanged in the castle hall. A liam-hound
chained to a bench howled mournfully over the din. Except for a
face or two I knew none of the knights by sight: Bretons mostly, I
supposed, or mercenaries strayed from Duke Robert's disbanded
army.

I said, 'Why so, my lord? I was fortunate, my losses were trifling:
five bowmen drowned and ten good palfreys. The rest, I'm told,
await me at St Valeri – their transports survived the storm.'

Henry's fingernail searched his teeth; he spat out a shred of meat.
The dark crafty eyes rapidly examined my face, then slid away.
'You've lost a friend,' he stated flatly.

'Ivo? He's paid his ransom and returned to Grantmesnil.'

'Not he. Curthose.'

I stared astounded at his pasty face, the lank hair that fringed his
forehead. 'Why? How have I offended him?'

Henry leaned back in his chair and belched. 'The Duke is angry
with those who failed. He rants of cowardice – and worse. When
Rochester fell Rufus let Belesme return to Normandy – probably
glad to be rid of the man. Curthose promptly imprisoned him. The
charge was treachery. It didn't stick, and Belesme was freed. But
he's not the only one who's suffered from Duke Robert's spite.'

'I served him faithfully in a hopeless cause!'

Henry turned his bulky body, faced me squarely. 'Duke Robert,'
he answered stonily, 'says this of you. Tirel struck not a blow and
fled from the fight.'

A drunken sergeant sprawled across a trestle and grabbed his
neighbour by the throat. Before the brawl could develop a sentinel
stepped quickly from the door and banged his spear-shaft on the
drunkard's head. The man dropped limply beneath the table.

'If you go near Curthose,' Henry continued, 'he'll crack your skull like that.'

I said angrily, 'I had no mind for suicide. How can the Duke —'

'Save your excuses. It's not me you failed. However, it seems plain that you must find another prince to follow. In Curthose you have an enemy.'

'My suzerain is Philip of France. I need no other.'

'You forage wherever you think the pickings ripe.' Contempt was sharp in his voice; I flushed and held my temper. 'You're a hard, self-seeking man, my lord, holding what you have like a miser hoarding gold, but restless still for wealth and power. Why else did you make that hazardous voyage to England?'

Rage choked my throat; I rose to my feet. 'My lord, you are pleased to insult your guest. I beg leave —'

'Sit down!' His hand slapped the table; a goblet jumped and fell on its side. Wine spilled like a bloodstain across the wood and dripped to the rushes. 'What makes you think you are free to come and go as you please? You try my patience, Tirel!'

The threat was stark as a naked sword. I sank into my chair, stared blindly across the smoke-clouded hall. A mummer stood by the hearth-fire, juggling with silvered balls; knights lounged on the benches and jeered. Someone pushed him into the fire. The mummer screamed, rolled from the flames, frantically beating his burning clothes, and ran from the hall. The knights laughed uproariously, slapping their thighs and shouting.

I said dully, 'What do you intend for me, my lord?'

'Advice, no more.' Henry's face was bland, his tone soothing. 'You need another star to guide you – Pevensey shot Duke Robert's from the sky. He's finished; and Rufus seeks revenge. What Rufus seeks he finds; he'll wrest Normandy from Curthose before he's done. There's your star, Tirel – a sun that will blaze over Neustria.'

I wondered whether the wine had fogged my brain. The pain in my head was a jabbing torment. 'Your concern for my welfare is remarkable, my lord. Why should I follow the King of England?'

'He likes you.' Henry's fingers hovered over a platter, chose a sugared fig, popped it into his mouth. 'Rufus seeks a friendship you've refused. Why, Tirel?' He munched the sweetmeat, looked at me slyly. 'Few men reject the favours of a king.'

I said thinly, 'I have good reasons.'

Nobody ever heard Henry laugh: he came nearest to it then. 'Which I know well. You're over squeamish, Tirel.' His voice hardened. 'For your advantage, and mine, I want you to serve my brother.'

A long-haired, willowy esquire lolled against a table, strummed a lute, sang a roulade in a high, melodious voice. The noise around him stilled; knights turned on the benches to hear his song. I listened numbly, striving to make sense of Henry's words. Easy to understand my profit from Rufus's friendship – but where was Henry's gain?

I said, 'And if I refuse, my lord?'

'You remain in Coutances until you change your mind.'

The song ended. I held my head in my hands and studied the wine-stained table. A prisoner, cut off from the world, mouldering to decay in some noisome cell. I had seen it happen: Helias of Gerberoi had held for thirteen years a knight he hated; Belesme was reputed to keep a hundred captives in various castles; none knew whether the men still lived or had long since died. I looked at Henry's face, saw the merciless eyes, and shivered.

'You wish me to go to England?'

'Not so. Rufus is predictable: he will seek vengeance in kind for Duke Robert's abortive invasion. When Rufus comes to Normandy you will join him.'

I bowed my head. 'Very well, my lord.'

Henry said smoothly, 'I have, then, your given word. You will also swear an oath on holy relics.'

My anger spurted. 'Do you doubt me? You have little faith in knightly honour!'

'None whatever.' He jabbed a thumb at Vauquelin, attentive at my shoulder. 'Therefore you will also leave as hostage your esquire. When you enter Rufus's service he shall rejoin you. If you fail' – his glance was cold as a freezing wind – 'your liegeman will be blinded and castrated.'

Henry lifted a flagon and tilted it over my cup. 'We have exchanged promises, Tirel. Will you take some wine?'

3

Duke Robert besieged Brionne, so I turned southwards on the Evreux road.

The long journey from Coutances led through Normandy's

devastated heartlands. Day after day we passed burned-out villages, fields overgrown by nettles, corpses littering the wayside like dead leaves scattered by wind. The peasants left alive fled like wild animals when they saw us. The most resolute and desperate among these hunted serfs formed bands and lived in forests like the outlaws they became, and preyed on unwary stragglers from the ravaging troops who oppressed them. In an arm of the forest near Courci we chanced suddenly upon a score of these creatures gathered in a glade around a fire; they sped swiftly to the trees when we approached, leaving two naked bodies on the ground. I gazed, sickened, at the hacked and bloody flesh, the charred lumps grilling on red-hot embers. 'Starving,' Richer commented indifferently, 'so they fight their foes with their teeth as well as their hands.' One corpse had the bowels ripped, intestines trailed on the grass. 'Surely,' I mumbled, 'they don't eat . . .' Richer shook his head. 'Looking for money or jewels the man has swallowed – an old mercenary trick to safeguard loot.'

The stench corroded my nostrils for a league after Courci.

Soldiers we met in plenty: mesnies riding on a raid, roving mercenaries, vassals hastening to their lords' alarm-calls. If the outriders sighted them in time we kept away; those whom we met sheered respectfully aside when they recognized mounted bowmen – Tirel's archers, I realized, owned a fearsome reputation. I avoided castles: in those stormy days castellans kept strong garrisons, and I saw no need to tempt them. Hence, when my scouts brought word that the countryside around Brionne seethed with Duke Robert's troops I veered abruptly. It would be unwise, I reckoned, to encounter Curthose.

Evreux's demesnes were thoroughly harried, the gates closed; helmets studded the ramparts. An arrow whipped a warning; I lifted my helmet, showed my face, exchanged shouts with the guard commander. The bridge dropped, and I led my men across. Warin of Guernan met me at the gate. An arm was strapped to his side; a half-healed scar striped his jawbone from ear to chin. He answered my question tersely.

'Guernan's gone – stormed and burnt. I escaped by the skin of my teeth.'

'Hubert?'

Warin shrugged. 'Dead. A spear in the throat.'

I signed myself and breathed a prayer for my childhood's gentle mentor. All scattered now, I reflected sadly, those companions of the apple-tree playground: Amauri ruling a county, Isabel and Ralph my enemies. Now Hubert ...

'The count's in the donjon,' Warin said. 'I don't know why you've come, but he'll be glad to see you. We need every man we can get in Evreux these days.'

I left Richer to find stabling and quarters, and threaded the streets to the castle. Evreux swarmed: bustling men-at-arms, depressed-looking burghers, villeins fled from ruined homesteads, cattle lowing in yards, swine rooting in the gutters. A whole countryside was penned within the walls. Count William sat beside his lady in the hall, his knights around him. Nearly all were armoured, a garrison beset.

I bent my knee, and prayed permission to rest my horses awhile before leaving again for Poix. Count William said, 'You've brought your bowmen?'

'A score or so, my lord – those that returned from Pevensey.'

His haggard features lightened. 'Walter, we're in trouble and need help. This is the way of it.'

I listened in astonishment. The desolation in Count William's Honour was common to most of Normandy; seigniories where cattle peacefully grazed and villeins tilled the fields were rare as swallows in winter. I had assumed the damage was part of the random sense-less harryings in a country flayed by war, the work of hands in-different to the lords whose lands they ruined. A more particular origin engendered Evreux's wreckage.

'Ralph of Conches, allied with Robert of Belesme,' Count William said dejectedly. 'Belesme has quartered his mesnie in Conches; to-gether they have harried me for weeks.'

'For what reason —'

'Goaded by that hell-bitch Isabel!' the countess snapped. The years had scarcely touched Hawise's beauty; anger now graved fine lines on her lovely face. 'The woman declares she has a score to settle with Evreux!'

'With you, my lady,' the count corrected gently. 'She has made that plain – a requital for some fancied hurt in days gone by.'

Countess Hawise said between her teeth, 'The hurt was real enough and, by the Rood, I'll flay next time the skin from her living flesh!'

'If we can take her,' Count William murmured. 'We almost did in a skirmish a sennight since.'

'She still rides to war?' I asked incredulously.

'She charges armed and armoured at the head of her knights,' the countess said in a brittle voice. 'A godless, unnatural slut! She's given Ralph four children – the fathers are anyone's guess!'

I wondered why I felt an odd regret, a curious longing mixed with admiration. Isabel the shameless warrior – she seemed unaltered from the hoyden who had helped me capture Poix in years gone by. One does not so easily forget.

'Belesme and Conches combined are too strong for me to resist,' Count William said. 'I asked William of Breteuil for help. He refused. Then Ralph idiotically burnt a steading on Breteuil's demesne. William lost his temper, and is bringing men to Evreux to level the odds.' He looked at me hopefully. 'Your bowmen, Walter, will tilt them in my favour.'

I thought about it. Beyond the loot which pillaging Conches might bring there seemed no profit in the count's request. I wished no harm to Isabel; to Ralph I was quite indifferent. I marvelled briefly at Isabel's mettle in rousing her flaccid lord to despoil a powerful neighbour: such miracles smelt of witchcraft. How had she enticed Belesme? Those who fought Black Robert championed God against the Devil – but I was no crusader. Count William? Evreux had been my home, the count my patron. I owed a little to the past.

'Very well, my lord. I shall lend you aid.'

Richer, always a realist, deplored my verdict. He recognized the necessity of using his precious bowmen to defend my lands at Poix, saw sense in risking a sea voyage with the promise of fiefs to win, rejected outright their employment in an altruistic cause. 'War means casualties,' he grumbled. 'The horses we can replace from the stud at Poix, but bowmen take years to train.' I spoke of knightly obligations, and saw a satirical glint in his eye. I leaned heavily on Richer, he had become a trusted comrade; but I do not think he appreciated the codes which govern knights.

Count William waited for Breteuil, and meanwhile watched from the donjon the smoke of distant burnings. Not much was left to destroy; the little that remained the men from Conches remorselessly laid waste. The count frustratedly devoured his nails and uttered the kind of blasphemies which earns a hair-shirt penance. To divert his mind from his sorrows – and because I needed the wise old man's advice – I described my sojourn in Coutances, the singular oath Prince Henry had extracted, and asked if he could conjure a valid reason for Henry's insistence that I serve his brother. Count William brooded a while.

'Doesn't make much sense,' he admitted. 'Of course, Rufus is the coming man – he'll boot the Duke from Normandy before we're all much older. Is Henry promoting your advantage by making you serve a lord who'll twitch the strings of power?'

'I have no faith,' I answered grimly, 'in Prince Henry's benevolence.'

William pondered. 'Nor I, from what I hear.' He looked at a smoke cloud smudging the far horizon, and scowled. 'There goes La Lande: Belesme forgot, last week, to burn the manor. Why doesn't Breteuil hurry?' He crossed his arms on the battlements. 'Henry, you know, considers England his heritage by right. He was born in the realm; and he alone of the Conqueror's sons was born in the purple.'

'In the...?'

'Matilda bore Henry *after* Duke William was crowned king,' the count explained testily. 'Therefore by birth he's son of England's king. Not so Curthose and Rufus.'

'You think,' I said slowly, 'Henry is ambitious for the crown?'

'Of course. Particularly now that Duke Robert's attempt has failed. Unhappily for him, he'll have first to find a means to chop down Rufus.'

A curious notion began whirling in my head like a spiral of wind-driven dust. I stared unseeingly at the pyre that marked La Lande; incredible conceptions chased confusedly through my mind and settled in a cloud – a cloud night-black with treason and betrayal. I closed my eyes and saw behind the lids an image of stupendous evil, and shuddered like a palsy-stricken crone.

The count's hand clasped my shoulder. "What troubles you, Walter?'

I said thickly, 'Do you suppose Henry . . . sees in me . . . the instrument . . . he needs?'

'For what?' He looked at me vacantly. Understanding dawned in his eyes, then shock and horror. 'To murder Rufus? Christ's wounds, Walter, you must be mad! Think, man! You are bound by oath to enter Rufus's service. So be it. But what compulsion can Henry use to make you harm him?'

I lifted my helmet, let it dangle on the coif and rubbed my temples. The wound in my scalp, long healed, throbbed in time with my heartbeats. I felt like a fly entrapped in sticky, poisonous arabic. Utter nonsense – imagination was running riot. Henry's hold on me was gone directly I joined Rufus.

Count William said kindly, 'You'd better come below. It's that dent in your skull – apt to make you fanciful. Quite a common symptom. I remember a crack I got at Hastings . . .'

Still chattering, he guided me solicitously down the ladder.

4

William of Breteuil, taken at Pevensey, had depleted Breteuil's coffers to pay his ransom. Ralph's harrying had not helped his fortunes; William, avid for revenge, brought to Evreux a tetchy temper and two hundred men. He flaunted a wiry beard – surprising in a man so hidebound in the customs of Duke William's time. 'Fashionable in England,' he grunted. 'All the young sprigs round Rufus are sprouting hair. Disgusting habit – but saves the barber's time.' He was impatient to strike at Conches, quickly devised a scheme and allotted my archers – in whom he put no faith – a part in the operation. Two days after his coming he and Count William led five hundred swords to Conches.

We crossed the frontier and met the enemy in a loop of the river Iton, a flood-plain submerged in winter and a bog for the rest of the year. Conches' mesnie saw themselves outnumbered, hastily deployed in order of battle and awaited our attack: a clever move, for the marsh between the forces clogged a charge. Count William pinched his lip and chewed the problem; Breteuil, curbing a spirited destrier, pranced impatiently and urged an immediate onset. 'Even if we hit them at a trot,' he said, 'our numbers will bear them down.' The count scolded his rashness; the lords glared angrily eye to eye. I said, 'Light horsemen tread more easily in mire. Let my archers advance and scourge them; the enemy might break ranks to drive them off. Once started they won't stop.'

Count William nodded. 'Try it, Walter.'

Richer led the bowmen out. They wheeled parallel to the enemy's front, cantered slowly from right to left and loosed their arrows. We saw destriers slump to their knees, knights tumble over the pommels. The lance-line of Conches' knights rippled like wind-swept rushes.

Mounted knights are unaccustomed to sit helplessly immobile while arrows whip their ears and kill expensive destriers. Conches' bowmen were no deterrent: they shot at elusive targets and emptied a saddle or two. A single knight exploded from the ranks, levelled his lance and rode at his tormentors. Another followed, then a third. Within moments the remainder charged like a surge from a broken dam. Breteuil observed them frowningly, enarmed his shield, hefted his lance. 'We'll strike when the bog has slowed them.' He looked at me and grinned in his beard. 'Mounted bowmen have some uses after all!'

Richer and his archers fled to the flanks. Conches' heavy horses, disordered and entangled, plunged hock-deep in the slough. Count William beckoned his trumpeter, couched his lance. The clarion howled. A hundred armoured horsemen plunged into the mire and fell on the struggling knights.

I found the onset not to my taste. My destrier splashed in mud, faltered to a trot. Lances, to be effective, need velocity behind them; I threw mine down and drew my sword with scarcely time to ward a glancing cut. Someone behind me toppled the knight who dealt it; I spurred my flagging horse, edged to firmer ground on a flank. Both charges had squelched to a standstill, to a mellay in slow motion where destriers plodded laboriously and sweating knights lunged furiously at targets out of reach. Conches' men, outnumbered, wallowed soggily back on their tracks.

Stones grated beneath my hooves; I reined on a patch of gravel. In front of me Richer's bowmen harassed the enemy foot. I rode forward and called my name: a helmeted knight might be friend or foe and the shaft on Richer's string pointed at my breast. He gestured to the ridge where Conches' knights had stood before the onset.

'The lady Isabel is there, and Belesme,' he said incisively.

I shaded my eyes. The unbidden charge had left a group of armoured horsemen who stood like iron statues and surveyed the wreckage. In the marsh Count William's cavalry chased knights who pricked and plodded to outreach the searching swords. Conches' footmen viewed defeat, began to break and go – not for them the salve of ransom when the steel was at their throats. Clusters drifted from the battle line, flitted to the scrub.

The horsemen I was watching wheeled their mounts and fled.

'You're certain?' I snapped. Not that I doubted Richer: he had eyes like a stooping hawk.

'Isabel and Belesme,' he repeated.

'Come on!'

I skirted the morass and galloped for the woods which swallowed my quarry. Here, I thought happily, was a chance of solid gain from an unpromising adventure. Belesme's price in ransom exceeded all barons in Normandy – more than Duke Robert himself – and I would be rich for life. I entered the woodland's selvedge, sword swinging in my hand, and followed a straggling pathway beaten by hooves. Richer called a warning; the wind of my speed snored past my ears and drowned his cry. I caught a glimpse of a helmet ahead, and a horse's sweat-streaked quarters. .

The path swerved sharply through a blackthorn copse. I slewed round the bend, met shields and swords uplifted. 'Ambush!' I thought sickly; and tugged the rein. A shout, and sword blades falling. A clash which clanged my eardrums, drove daylight from the sky. I slid into the vortex, spun deeper into the depths.

'Tie them across the saddles. Be quick!'

Isabel's voice, dying reason said.

Then oblivion.

5

The smell was almost palpable, a suffocating blanket in the dark.

Damp earth and stagnant water. Ancient filth, fresh excrement and urine. The charnel stench of rotting flesh. The smell of fear.

We lived in darkness. Time held no meaning. The jailer's sputtering torch was the measure of existence: the torch he carried when he brought us food – thin gruel, dry bread and water in a pail. We scrabbled for the victuals, straining at the limits of the fetters. The rusty iron gnawed our wrists, scraped suppurating bracelets on the flesh. The jailer, a bearded Angevin, often placed the platter a careful handsbreadth out of reach, watched grinning while we scraped and clawed. His nose was gone: twin holes pitted the shrivelled skin.

The torch revealed our prison and the things abiding there. A cavern hollowed from the donjon's mound, stone-lined, stone-floored beneath the excrement of ages. Moisture glistened on the walls, dribbled in crooked rills. Rats squeaked and skittered in the dark; frequently we killed them, slamming fettered wrists upon the sound, breaking their backs. Then we tore the small squirming bodies and ate them, bones and fur and guts. At first it made me retch, for I knew how the creatures lived, the food they found. After a little while I was less fastidious.

We had company. Fettered upright against the opposite wall were things that had once been men. One was old, a yellowed skeleton disintegrating bone by bone. The skull had fallen, and grimaced on the floor. Two others were newly dead: the bodies hung in chains, flesh weeping from the bones in long white shreds which ripped softly loose and coiled on small mounds of ordure the living men had dropped.

The dead were dead, quiet decomposing friends, careless of the jailer's mete of food, no rivals in the fight to stay alive. We saw them only when the Angevin brought his torch, heard them only when the rats were feasting. More horrible was the man who shared our prison, a deformity who moved and spoke and never rested. He gabbled without end; he asked questions we left unanswered, mumbled prayers, songs, obscenities; and repeated over and over his hapless tale. A jester he had been, a purveyor of wit and bawdry, a buffoon in high favour in Conches' hall – until the day when, riding high in insolence and wine, he sang at a crowded banquet a chanson he had made, a song which hinted broadly at the Lady of Conches' whoredoms, a verse that blazoned plainly the horns on Lord Ralph's head.

Torchlight showed the requital. His hands and feet were severed, his eyes were festering pits. A tarnished hook protruded from a leather socket which cupped a forearm's stump: a clemency from his lord, the creature mouthed, so that he might feed himself and live to acquit his crime.

A torn and wizened wisp of a man, an object to be pitied – were it not for the hook. When food was brought he brandished the ugly weapon and kept us from the scraps until he had picked his choice. Otherwise he was harmless, a mumbling idiot. We heard him in the darkness sharpening his hook, grinding the point on stone and invoking heaven's favour for some enterprise I did not try to understand.

Time stood still, or passed, or retreated – a long blank wall fissured by the Angevin's torch. The stone chamber's stony coldness warned of summer's retreat: we shivered and plucked uselessly at the verminous rags which clothed us. At times I felt sanity slipping. Richer fought the madness; he wrapped me in his arms and murmured endearments and assurances. After he had calmed me he told tales of his native land, of Barbary and the Moors, of battles far away and paladins long dead. Even the jester ceased his ranting and craned to listen.

Once, recovering from a lunatic bout, I clung shuddering to Richer and said inanely, 'Will we rot here for ever? Are we forgotten?'

I heard him sigh. 'I am afraid,' he answered quietly, 'Belesme will remember.'

6

The flame of the jailer's torch, a harbinger of food, always started the saliva on my tongue. But this time he carried a mallet, struck the staples from the wall and roughly bade us follow him. I tried to walk; my legs yielded like sodden stalks and I slumped to my knees. The jailer cursed; Richer helped me to the lichened steps which led from the prison. The jester crawled on elbows and knees; the Angevin impatiently twined fingers in his hair and dragged him up the steps.

We entered the ground floor store room, stumbled between casks and bales and mounted a ladder. I faltered on the ascent; Richer, climbing below, guided my feet to the rungs. The jailer thrust open a trap, and we fell into clamour and light.

The blaze seared my eyeballs; for a moment I thought myself blinded. I lay face down and let the tumult thunder round my head, and peered through slitted eyelids, dazed and dazzled.

The hall of the donjon at Conches.

Lords and ladies richly dressed, velvet and silk and furs, candles spitting rainbow shards from jewelled rings and necklets, colours that danced and shimmered like a sunrise blurred by tears. Alien faces, hostile eyes and mouths that opened and shut on words which were lost in the din.

It had been very dark and quiet in the depths whence we had come.

'They seem hardly human! Which is Tirel?'

Laboriously I traced the voice. Red, curving lips, white teeth in a sun-tanned face, dark slanting eyes. The same yet not the same. Older, harsher, harder. Isabel leaned on Belesme's shoulder and played with the enamelled brooch which fastened his cloak. He smiled into her eyes and stroked her fingers.

'The thing on the left, my lady – he with the longest beard.'

'Faugh! They stink worse than the castle midden!'

'A song, Nivard, a song! I've spared your voice – let's hear you use it!' A shaking finger pointed at the jester squatting cross-legged on the rushes. Ralph was fatter, flabbier, and growing bald. Grease stained his chin and dribbled on his mantle. 'Quickly, Nivard – else I'll slit your tongue!'

The jester turned his sightless pits to Ralph. A quavering melody croaked between blackened teeth. 'Louder!' Ralph shouted. Isabel smiled, and fumbled shamelessly between Belesme's thighs.

Blearily I surveyed the hall.

Hearth-fire, candles, torches crackling in cressets. Esquires standing behind their lords. Three boys attended Ralph and Isabel: listlessly I scanned their faces. High cheekbones and slant eyes – Isabel's whelps, no matter who the sire. On a chair apart from the dais a tirewoman nursed an infant: the youngest, I concluded, of her bastard brood.

Nivard ended his pitiful song. Ralph raucously demanded more. Belesme said lazily, 'Enough of that mewling. I'd sooner hear a whetstone grind flawed iron. Poor sport, Ralph.' He whispered to an esquire; then said to the jailer, 'Strip them.'

The Angevin tore the rags and left us naked. Richer tried to resist; the man smashed a fist in his face and knocked him flat. Isabel pointed to my crotch, whispered to Belesme behind her hand, and laughed. I felt no shame, no emotion at all. A flea, exposed suddenly to the light, scuttled from ribs to armpit, and bit. I scratched abstractedly.

Belesme's esquire dropped garments at our feet. 'You need clothes,' his lord said, smiling. I donned a linen tunic and linen drawers such as peasants wear in winter beneath their kirtles. Richer dressed, and helped the jester. On Belesme's signal scullions carrying buckets came from the kitchen.

'You also require a bath,' Belesme murmured, and gestured to the servants.

They drenched us from head to foot, back and front. I cringed from the freezing shock; the linen clung to my skin.

'Take them away and dry them off,' said Belesme. He nodded to the jailer.

The Angevin drove us from the hall. Dragging Nivard, we climbed exhaustedly from floor to floor, and emerged upon the battlements. Sundown's lingering embers streaked the skyline, frost sparkled on the shingles of the roof. The sentinel stamped his feet and blew on his fingers, his breath a diaphanous veil.

'What's this?' he growled.

'My lord of Belesme demands his little jest,' the jailer said. 'Naught for you to do but watch them.'

He bound us one by one to merlons, choosing those that jutted beyond the roof. He tested the bonds and chuckled.

'A balmy night. Sleep well.'

The Angevin waved to the sentry and clattered down the ladder.

The cold advanced from the shadows, a clammy creeping tide. The sodden linen clung as Belesme intended, stiffened on my body and sucked the warmth from my skin. A prickling like icy daggers probed through flesh and bones, to the marrow within. I squirmed and wriggled my legs and arms as much as the ropes allowed, and hoped the meagre movement would warm my blood. After a time I stopped, for sensation fled from my limbs; I could not tell whether I moved or hung in the ropes inert. The linen, frozen rigid, crackled as I breathed.

A quavering discord climbed to the stars, a whispered croak like the rasping of flint on steel. The jester sang.

The cold became tangible, transmuted to solidity like walls which closed and crushed. I gulped air and swallowed ice. A languorous relaxation seeped through my frozen frame, a slow, enveloping lassitude that promised peace. The night revolved, whirled faster; the stars careered across the sky, trailing pendant flames.

Darkness swooped like a smothering pall.

'Walter!'

A voice from far away, from the other side of sanity.

'Walter! Wake! Wake!'

I tried to open my eyes. The lids were frozen shut.

'Sing, my lord! Sing!'

Richer, I thought dazedly. Through the fog which filled my head I heard his voice, a mumbling chant with neither tune nor words. The jester's chanson scraped in broken chords.

'Sing!'

A glimmering of reason stirred, a dying spark which lighted purpose. I fought the sleep which reared like a breaking wave, forced my jaws apart – and sang. Frozen and half alive, we sang. The stars wheeled in the heavens and moondawn paled the sky, and still we sang.

The sentry, back to the parapet, cradled his spear and watched. Once, I think, he crossed himself.

The jailer said disgustedly, 'Thought I'd got you off my hands. There's not many survives Count Robert's drench-and-dry!' He kicked the platter towards us, rammed the torch in a cresset. 'Leave you a light – you're having a visitor.'

I lay exhausted, drained by the agonized hours wherein life and warmth returned to frozen limbs, while I writhed in the fetters and cried aloud. I have no memory of the vigil's end: Richer said we stayed on the tower till dawn. The torture had mauled my body and deadened my mind: my body had recovered, my brain was a lifeless pulp, incapable of thought, reacting to physical needs like a beast of the fields. Eat, it commanded, drink, empty your bowels, sleep. Sometimes, like a murmur from the depths of space, it whispered longingly of death.

The jester's reason was gone. He chattered incessantly – imbecile, senseless ravings – and constantly sharpened his hook.

I leaned against the wall, head bowed, and stared at my shackled hands. A footstep scraped the stair. Richer's breath hissed sharply between his teeth. A shadow fell across my outstretched legs, a foot kicked mine. Unwillingly I looked up.

A shade from a world forgotten. What did she want in this vile den, breathing a stench which made her gag and cover her mouth with a kerchief? Away with you, my long-ago love – leave me to die in pain.

'Do not be afraid, Tirel. I come in mercy.'

Her eyes glittered, the torchlight painted scarlet daubs upon her cheeks. A fixed, unnatural smile, a twitching lip, speech slurred and indistinct. She swayed and leaned a hand against the wall. Drunk, I reflected vaguely, or drugged by the virulent herbs that witches use.

'You threw me away like a blunted sword, and broke my heart. I suffered tortures greater than I can ever make you suffer. Do you understand, Tirel? Do you realize why I punish you so?'

The jester's fetters clanked. He turned his blinded face, slid awkwardly towards her on his haunches. The chains checked him. He extended the hook like a searching fang.

'I am not a peasant slut to be flung like trash from a sated bed. My House is Montfort. We do not forgive. I demand vengeance, Tirel.'

The jester lunged to the length of his bonds. The chain leashed his ribs, drove the breath from his lungs. He collapsed like a broken puppet, head between knees, and sobbed.

'Now I have drunk my fill. Enough is enough.' A pleading note crept into her voice. 'Beg my forgiveness, Tirel. Crawl on your knees and kiss my feet. Humble yourself as I was humbled. Then, my childhood sweetheart, I may set you free.'

I gazed idly at my hands. My fingernails were overgrown, long broken yellowed talons. I scratched a vermin bite on my thigh: the skin peeled like leprous scurf. The jester's weeping picked at the silence.

'Answer me! Christ in heaven, are you dumb? Tirel, you loved me once. Am I not still desirable, still worthy of your body and bed? See, Tirel!'

Isabel stooped swiftly, gripped the hem of her robe and raised it to her shoulders.

Her body shone like ivory, the nipples were rosebuds crowning smooth round globes. I felt with revulsion a prickle of lust, a stirring in my loins like the drowsy slither of a sleeping reptile.

Richer strained at his bonds, his face contorted. He stretched out his arms, the pointing fingers splayed, and hissed a stream of invective in the language of his race. Isabel dropped her robe and shrank away.

I said wearily, 'Leave us, harlot. We have carrion enough for company – you smell no sweeter.'

She turned and stumbled blindly to the steps.

8

Stooped at the waist like a bent old man I hung from the rafters, suspended by the wrists which were tied behind my back. My toes just touched the ground, one foot at a time, never both together – that was the Angevin's cunning. You scrabbled the floor to cushion the pain, and felt an illusory solace when your toenails touched the rushes.

Richer dangled beside me.

The hall was nearly deserted. Belesme lounged on the dais, picking his teeth and scrutinizing the torture with an expert eye. Ralph belched into his wine. Isabel pointed embroidery on a tambour, intent upon her stitches, eyes veiled and face remote. A tirewoman sat apart, nursing Isabel's infant son who crowed happily on her lap. At the far end of the hall a group of men-at-arms whispered quietly among themselves.

Belesme said lazily, 'Are you ready to kneel before my lady and crave pardon?'

Richer's eyes were shut; he breathed sterterously. The agony tore like white-hot pincers; sweat trickled down my cheeks and dripped on my matted beard. The infant gurgled. The jester lay on his back and listened. He cocked his head to the sound, raised himself on his elbows, crawled closer.

Belesme frowned. 'You are obstinate, my friends. Lift them!'

The Angevin hauled. Pain whipped my shoulders, flamed in the joints. The room spun dizzily; a roaring filled my ears. I twirled slowly on the rope. Tears bursting from my eyelids forced them open, and I saw the jester.

He crouched beside the nurse. The woman, gaping, watched our dangling bodies. The baby, thumb in mouth, kicked unnoticed in her lap. Nivard the jester knelt beside her and stealthily touched the stump of his arm to the infant's belly.

He lifted the hook.

I tried to shout. My voice was a strangled grunt. Belesme laughed.

The hook hovered, flashed, and disembowelled Isabel's son.

A scarlet fountain drenched the nurse's robe. She gawked like a maniac at the horror in her lap, her teeth rattled and she strove to speak. Frenziedly she thrust the mess away. She fell on her side and screamed, and screamed again.

The table on the dais overturned with a crash. Sergeants ran from the door, surrounded the shrieking nurse and the jester who gibbered dementedly and flourished his crimsoned hook. A sword jumped from the sheath.

'Hold!'

Belesme's shout rang the rafters. His face was grey and terrible, his eyes like living fire. He strode to the awestruck men-at-arms and thrust them back, gazed at the dying child, his mouth working. He looked at the jester, and his teeth clamped shut.

'Bind him!'

Isabel sprawled motionless face-down across the fallen table. Ralph gobbled incoherently, eyes starting from his head, wine dribbling from his mouth. Belesme stooped over the yelling nurse and buffeted her face. The screaming stopped.

Richer groaned in the sudden silence. Belesme's glance flicked over him; he made a downward motion with his hand. The Angevin jumped to the ropes, lowered us to the floor. I curled up like a wounded hare while the agony throbbed and ebbed, and wandered into a sort of trance, an anodyne for pain. I heard from a hazy distance the jester's lunatic laugh, and Belesme's voice, harsh with menace, rasping orders. Someone forced me upright, shoved me across the hall, tottering like a cripple. The bustle of the castle ward, running feet and the noise of horses. Grass crisp beneath my naked feet, sunlight and air like wine, tall trees and a sapphire sky.

I had never thought to see these things again.

Men were busy in a meadow below the ramparts. Upon four powerful stallions, destriers by their stamp, they buckled the kind of harness which is used for pulling carts. I watched incuriously, revived by the sparkling air. Under Belesme's direction they led the horses apart, stood them facing outwards, four corners of a square. Sergeants mounted bareback, whips in hand.

What game was this, I wondered idly, and why were we brought to watch? Richer frowned and bit his lip, muttered something I could not catch.

Men-at-arms dragged the jester to the middle of the square and spread him on his back. They bound separate ropes above knees and elbows, led the ends to the horses and tied them to the harness.

Belesme raised an arm above his head, shouted and let it drop.

The destriers reared and plunged. The ropes tightened. The body in the centre jerked and lifted from the grass. The stallions momentarily checked, and strained against the harness. Their riders flailed the whips.

Nivard the jester shrieked, and split like a worm-eaten log. The horses, released from the load, bounced tattered lumps behind them.

Belesme sauntered from the meadow, stared me in the eyes. He was breathing quickly and his face was pale. 'A warning,' he said tightly, 'to any who seek revenge. If I believed you shared in this crime —!'

I tried to straighten my shoulders, flinched from the hurt. 'Rest easy. I do not slaughter children.'

'So speaks a knight in his pride.' Belesme looked at my wasted body; surprisingly a trace of pity flickered in his eyes. 'I have been compassionate, Tirel; I thought you had suffered enough, and wished to have you killed. My lady refused – she wants to prolong your misery. You seem to have offended her beyond forgiveness. I must leave you to her mercies: Conches holds nothing for me now.'

He turned and surveyed the field. The stallions had returned; sergeants dismounted and loosed the ropes, stepping carefully over the tendrils which slimed the grass. 'Too quick and easy a death,' he muttered. 'I was angry and impatient. He should have burned.'

Belesme put a hand to his face and rubbed his eyes.

'He should have burned. The dog slew my son.'

9

Richer's endurance faltered after Nivard's execution. For hours he lay prostrate in the dark and scarcely seemed to breathe. Alarmed by his stillness, I tried to rouse him, chattering foolishly of matters which might hold his interest, of archery and horses and the forging of chain-mesh mail. He seldom answered; I do not think he heard. Under the jailer's torch I anxiously examined Richer's face, the cheekbones splitting the skin and blank lustreless eyes. Despite our constant hunger he refused food; I forced water between his lips, put bread in his mouth. The morsels remained on his tongue and choked his breathing, so that I had hastily to pluck them out.

The silent lassitude gave place to fever; Richer moaned and threshed on the flags, rattled his chains and babbled in delirium. The fever brought raging thirst; I gave him all the water the Angevin brought, and myself licked the trickling walls. The rats attacked him in his helpless state; he seemed not to feel their teeth, so I listened for the gnawing and beat them off. I slept only fitfully, yet had to sleep, and while he was unguarded he lost much blood.

My friend was dying, and there was little I could do.

In desperation, knowing it useless, I begged the jailer for salves, for soothing draughts, even to send a priest skilled in the use of herbs. The man grunted and peered at Richer. 'He'll die,' he said indifferently, 'and so will you.' He jerked a thumb at the corpses on the wall – all skeletons by then; the rats had finished their work. 'No one gets out of here, dead or alive. Medicine!' He snorted derisively. 'The castle's beleaguered, men are wounded – we need the salves up top.'

It took time for his meaning to penetrate: coherent thought

became more difficult as time went by. In the depths below the donjon we heard nothing of the world outside; I strained my ears, imagined sounds of conflict like echoes ringing from distant hills. Echoes they remained; the noises, I decided, were in my head.

I had no measure of time save the Angevin's visits, which disciplined my stomach to routine. If he dallied hunger clawed. I now knew real starvation: quick gripings seized my belly and doubled me in pain. I managed to kill a rat, tore it apart and dribbled blood in Richer's mouth. But the animals had grown cunning and afterwards evaded my feeble snatches. The jailer never came, and I concluded dully we were left to starve. Richer sank into a stupor; only a flutter of breathing showed he lived.

I cannot remember when I finally surrendered, and waited quietly for death to come from the darkness.

10

Light stung my eyes; I put an arm across my face. Voices swelled and faded like music carried on wind. Noise and footsteps, the tapping of iron on stone, hands that grasped and lifted. The movement hurt; I besought them, whimpering, to let me lie.

'He's alive. Carry him gently. Ivo, bring the other.'

Amauri's voice, a whisper from long ago, a delusion conceived from anguish. I drifted away in dreams where I wandered with him hand in hand and lingered in an apple-tree's shade and talked with a white-haired knight who whittled bowstaves. The Tower of Rouen, and whisperings in the secret alcoves where we slept, a dim shuffling figure and frightened silence. Terror and exhaustion, and a man we feared. A boy who drowned in the Seine. 'You'll help me, Walter?' I help, Amauri? – you'll have no succour from ghosts. 'There's no help for anyone here, save in himself.' We are dead, my friend, and gone into the night.

A baldric dangled from the tent pole, a scabbarded sword and shield. A falcon-headed dragon, vert on azure. Mortain? No – his was gules, bend or. Aumale? To think was tiring: let it go. Rain pattered on the tent hide, trickled through a rent. The door flap lifted, slapped against a post; a wind-gust scattered raindrops on my cheek.

Amauri said, 'Awake, Walter? The Saints be praised – now you

192

can feed yourself. I'm an indifferent nursemaid: three days have been long enough.'

I drank the broth he held and tried to remember. Conches . . . the Angevin . . . starvation. 'Richer!' I cried. 'Is he dead?'

'The Saracen? No. He'll mend. Ivo cares for him in his pavilion.'

Ivo of Grantmesnil blundered into the tent, pushed back his helmet, shook water from his ears. 'Ha, Walter! Back in the land of the living? We'll soon have you on your feet!'

I looked at my wasted arms, thin as lance shafts, and said doubtfully, 'Soon? I feel weak as a day-old leveret. How is Richer?'

'He'll not draw a bow again,' Ivo said gruffly. 'Left arm torn from the socket, and healing poorly. Otherwise there's nothing much wrong with either of you that food and rest won't cure.'

I reclined on the pallet and examined the leaking roof. 'I don't understand. We were in prison —'

'Far too long.' Amauri frowned. 'After the battle of the marsh Count William besieged Conches and learnt you were imprisoned. No one willingly leaves a friend at Belesme's mercy. So the count offered ransom, promised to raise the siege in return for your release. Belesme merely laughed.'

'Not only Belesme, I think.'

Amauri snapped a loose thread from the coverlet. 'I'm aware of my sister's part in this, Walter. Don't rub it in – or say I didn't warn you, years ago. Eventually Count William had to lift the leaguer: Breteuil was in a hurry to get home. And so, for months, you were one of the scores of knights who rotted in Belesme's prisons.'

A wagon creaked past the tent, the oxen squelched in mud. The drover cracked a whip and loudly cursed his cattle. A sergeant bellowed orders in the distance.

'Breaking camp,' Ivo explained. 'We leave Conches tomorrow.' He grinned. 'You won't be sorry. If it weren't for Rufus you'd probably be there still.'

I stared. 'Rufus? From England? How —'

Ivo looked surprised. 'I'd forgotten how long you'd been out of the world. Rufus is in Normandy. Explain, Amauri – you talk better than I.'

Rufus, so Amauri related, had taken his revenge for Curthose's fruitless lunge at England's crown. Without setting foot in Normandy, using promises and bribery and blackmail – many Norman lords held English fiefs he threatened to escheat – he won to his side the barons east of Seine: Aumale, Eu, Gournai and many others. Then he brought an army across the sea.

'Curthose,' Ivo commented scornfully, 'refused to fight. Said he couldn't depend on anyone to support him.'

'Probably true,' said Amauri. 'So he met Rufus at Rouen and formally ceded the lands he had already lost. Rufus in return promised him aid in quelling the private wars which sundered Normandy.'

'The most rampant,' Ivo said, 'being the War of the Amazons.' He looked hopefully round the tent. 'Talking is thirsty work. Isn't there any wine in here?'

Amauri took a flagon from under my pallet, gave it to Ivo. 'I was keeping this for the invalid,' he said caustically. 'A mellow vintage to restore his strength. That, Walter, is the name they give to the dispute between Evreux and Conches, which everyone swears is kept alive by Isabel and Hawise.'

Ivo drank deeply and wiped his lips. 'A smooth wine,' he approved. 'Rather too strong for a sick man.' He took another gulp. 'By that time Ralph had the worst of it. The battle had depleted his retinue, and Count William's reprisals were destroying his fiefs. He asked Duke Robert's aid.' Ivo shrugged. 'You can imagine the answer he got. So, advised by Belesme, Ralph appealed to Rufus.'

'And here we are,' said Amauri.

I put a hand to my head. 'I don't follow. Why you, Amauri – a vassal of France? And Ivo, Duke Robert's liegeman?'

Ivo smiled widely. 'A rising sun is warmer than a falling star. We were both at Rufus's court, basking in the glow. The king wasn't much impressed by Ralph's appeal until I told him where you were. Amauri described vividly how Belesme's captives suffered. Rufus swore he'd have you out, provided a band of Flemings and sent us hotfoot to Conches.'

'To help Ralph,' I said, perplexed. 'Yet you beleaguered Conches?'

Amauri firmly removed the flagon from Ivo's grasp. 'My sister's doing. She refused to give you up. Isabel only surrendered when we stormed the ward. Ralph has now sworn fealty to Rufus; we leave the mercenaries to reinforce his garrison and discourage Evreux. The War of the Amazons, I think, is ended.' He trickled wine into a cup and added crossly, 'Ivo, you've left nothing but dregs!'

'And Belesme?'

'Slipped away before we arrived, I'm glad to say. If he'd been here we'd still be fighting.'

Ivo groped for his dangling helmet and set it on his head. 'I must see how Richer fares – time he was fed.' He looked at me sympathetically. 'Don't worry about him, Walter. I'll care for him well, and his arm will mend.'

'He's crippled because he served me,' I said bitterly. 'And another of my liegemen is endangered on my behalf. Rufus is in Normandy – and I didn't know. I have to redeem an oath – and rescue Vauquelin from Henry's clutches before he also is maimed for life.'

Amauri scrutinized me perplexedly. 'Vauquelin? I know nothing of this. What oath? Anyway, Walter, if you want to see Henry you'll have to move quickly. Curthose is determined to regain the fiefs he sold him; and Rufus apparently regards Henry as a menace. Together they are going to war against him.'

How, I wondered wearily, could I cope with these endless complications? Rufus in Normandy – and I had not gone to him as I had promised. I was weak and ill, incapable of travelling. Did Henry know of my imprisonment? Would he hold his hand? A wave of tiredness seeped through my limbs, my eyelids drooped. One fret persisted like a gnawing wound until sleep smothered thought.

Richer, my friend and vassal, was crippled in my service. Somehow I must save Vauquelin.

Chapter 9

1091

Amauri returned to Montfort. Ivo had me carried on a litter to Evreux, where Count William clicked his tongue when he saw my emaciated body. He put me in a bedchamber next to his bower in the donjon, found a horse-doctor skilled in healing and a buxom tirewoman to attend my needs. I insisted that Richer's pallet be placed alongside. His condition was worse than mine: the arm torn by Belesme's torture had not relapsed into the socket, and gave him constant pain.

It was vital I should get in touch with Henry; therefore I asked Ivo to lend a messenger. 'Anything to oblige a friend,' he said dubiously, 'but you'll need a constabular to get a message through. A single rider hasn't a chance.' He thought a little and added, 'There's another objection. I'm Duke Robert's man, and it might look suspicious if one of my liegemen was discovered communicating with the enemy. You see my point?' I saw, and ended my persuasion. Ivo grinned in relief, and left for Rouen.

Despite his pessimism I sent two messengers to Coutances, hardy horsemen chosen from my archers, whom Count William had quartered in Evreux. The first I never saw again, nor knew his fate; the second returned with a wound in his thigh and an ominous tale of scavenging peasants near Courci. I abandoned my efforts to reach Henry, and concentrated on recovering my strength.

Meanwhile I was destitute, owning neither money, arms nor warhorse, and turned to the count for help. He promised as much silver as I needed, said a destrier waited in the stables, and brought an armourer to measure for a hauberk. 'Allow an extra handsbreadth across the chest,' he told him. 'My lord is wasted.' I bade a clerk write a draft on my treasury at Achères; firmly he waved the scrip aside. 'You lost everything on my behalf,' Count William asserted gruffly. 'I can do no less than repay you.'

I quit the bed and exercised my shaky body in the ward, went farther afield to the meadows where I wandered as a boy. I felt strong enough at last to mount the destrier, and rode a course in the tilt-yard without falling. The armour dragged my shoulders, the lance handled like a tree-trunk, the helmet was a millstone on my head. Still too weak for war, but capable of travelling. I was in a fever to go, and overrode Count William's protests.

'If you must, you must,' he grunted. 'Do you want an escort? I'll give you some mounted sergeants.'

I shook my head. 'My bowmen will see me through. I leave Richer in your care, my lord: he is still unfit to move.'

'I'll look after him.' The wise old eyes surveyed me shrewdly. 'Not many men these days are so nice on points of honour, so careful to redeem an oath. Your experiences at Conches have changed you, Walter. You used to be no different from the rest: hard, ruthless, mindful of your own interests above all. You know well you can't trust Henry, yet you put your head in a noose to save your esquire.'

'I learned a little of comradeship and loyalty in Conches' donjon,' I answered sombrely.

I reached Torigni on a shining April morn; Coutances lay a short day's march ahead. In the woodlands which girded Torigni I encountered a hunting party, knights riding hawk on wrist. The merlins were not surprising – a hawk is much a part of one's equipment as a hauberk – but the lack of armour was: they were a long way from the castle to ride unarmed. They blenched a little when they saw the bowmen; I hastened to give friendly greeting, and inquired whether Henry still resided in Coutances. They looked astonished.

'Henry in Coutances?' said a gay young blade with tawny hair and a ruddy aquiline face. 'Not this fortnight past, my lord. Duke Robert and King William have wrested the prince's lands. Henry abandoned Coutances; Avranches surrendered; the prince is besieged in Mont St Michel.'

'He left no prisoners in Coutances?'

'None. The prince departed at leisure, before they invested the place.'

Christ's wounds, I thought, the Mont! I knew it by repute: an inaccessible fort surrounded by sea. How could I reach Henry? I thrust my lance in the ground, crossed hands on saddlebow and considered. 'How is the blockade set?' I asked hopelessly. A futile question: with Rufus in command not a mouse would slip the siege lines.

'Duke Robert holds Genets, the king Avranches,' the knight said. He looked at the little band of archers. 'You are, I think, Lord Walter of Poix – him they call Tirel?'

I assented listlessly, still striving to solve my problem. 'I have ridden many marches to find Prince Henry, through seigniories where men go always armed. Yet you —' I gestured to the silk and velvet mantles.

The knight laughed. 'King William controls Normandy from the Bessin to Avranchin: where his hand lies there's peace. Not a robber stirs, and none dares ride against his neighbour.' He drew a finger across his throat. 'Rufus wields swift justice!'

And in Rufus, I decided, lay my hope. I gave the falconers farewell and took the road for Avranches. Two days later, careful to avoid Genets where Curthose lived, I passed through an army encamped, traversed streets between narrow houses and gained admittance to the castle's crowded ward. England's dragon banner flapped above a chequered pavilion. A knight on guard at the doorway leaned on a naked sword and swore the king, in council, was engaged in business too important for disturbance. I heard inside the tent an angry, stammering voice, and pushed the obstinate knight aside.

Rufus hammered fist in palm, his fleshy features red with wrath. Curthose hunched in a chair and listened to the harangue, sulkily watching his brother beneath his brows. Barons and knights surrounded the pair.

Curthose said sullenly, 'I saw no harm. Henry sent a herald to Genets, asking for access to fresh water. Why should I deny him?'

'The garrison's wells have dried!' Rufus shouted. 'Then you let Henry's sutlers cross to the mainland for water, and order your sentinels not to interfere!'

'We are knights. We should prevail in valour, and not by using unfairly the vagaries of nature.'

'A fine fashion of making war! You'll next be sending him wine!'

Curthose suddenly smiled. 'I have. A tun of excellent Auvergne. William, would you let our brother die of thirst? Where shall we find another if we lose him?'

Rufus spluttered, lifted his hands helplessly and let them drop. Then, unwillingly, he grinned. 'Courtoisie has limits, Robert. We'll be here all summer if you behave like this. It must stop. No more watering details from St Michel!'

Curthose spread his hands. 'All right. Then the Mont will very soon fall.' He rose to his feet. 'I shall return to Genets and counter-mand the orders.'

He saw me on the way to the door and checked in his stride. His face stiffened and his eyes went cold. I kept my features still, and stared him out. 'Craven!' he whispered between his teeth.

Curthose spat deliberately at my feet, and stalked from the pavilion.

'What ails Robert?' Rufus asked. He peered at my face beneath the nasal. 'Walter!' He put both hands on my shoulders, rocked me back and forth. 'By the Face, a welcome sight! You're thinner – hardly surprising after long confinement in a prison: Belesme's at that! What are you doing here?'

'I come to thank you for your help, my lord, and beg a favour.'

'Anything, Walter: anything in my power! First let me promul-gate the orders of the day. There's a war on, though from Duke Robert's conduct you might not think it!'

I leaned against a tent-pole, studied the man I had last seen four years since at his father's deathbed, and listened to him speak. Kingship and adversity had hardened the florid face, carved furrows from mouth to nostrils, hung pouches beneath his eyes and firmed the mobile lips. Authority embraced him like a cloak. He dealt crisply with the knights who awaited orders, patiently unravelled problems, incisively dismissed inessentials. I began to understand the qualities a kingdom's government demanded, the faculty of decision, the knowledge of one's fellow men, the blending of steel and guile. In Rufus I saw a puissant king, a king in the Conqueror's mould.

The last banneret bowed and departed. Rufus blew out his cheeks and slapped his hands together. 'I've talked myself dry. fitzHamon,' he said to a lean, saturnine knight, 'let's have some wine. Robert' – this to the Count of Meulan, a grizzled, slit-eyed veteran – 'remind me to strengthen the detachment at Arderon. Now, Walter, what's your trouble?'

I hesitated. My request needed delicate framing: I could not reveal to Rufus the oath I had sworn to his brother, still less the tangled suspicions I had discussed with the Count of Evreux. The king, for political reasons, would readily war against Henry and deprive him of his castles; but to suggest to Rufus that Henry plotted his death would certainly estrange him and earn me his disfavour. I had, moreover, no whit of proof: it was sheerly a wild suspicion, which Count William had discredited. Therefore I told a lie: that when I lay in Henry's power after the shipwreck he had made me swear to serve him with my archers, and held my esquire hostage against redemption.

The tale sounded lame in my ears. Two bored household knights loitered in a corner and listened woodenly; a clerk's quill traced a charter – a king's campaigns must not disrupt a kingdom's ruling. Robert of Meulan's eyes rested sceptically on my face. Rufus looked frankly astounded. fitzHamon said quietly, 'Are you suggesting, my lord, that you be allowed to reinforce the enemy we are besieging?'

I answered wretchedly, 'Yes. Else my liegeman is mutilated.'

Meulan said in a rusty voice, 'An esquire's life against an army's vantage? You ask a great deal, my lord!'

Rufus held up a hand. 'There's more to it than that.' He tugged thoughtfully at his fingers, cracking the joints. 'A knight must keep his word, redeem his obligations. Would you willingly let a vassal lose his eyes? I think not.' He added sharply, 'How many bowmen do you lead?'

'A score.'

Rufus scratched his cheek. 'Nothing. A mere scantling. They can't alter the balance against us.'

'Lord Walter's mounted bowmen are not despicable,' Meulan warned.

'So I've heard.' He looked at me and smiled. 'Nevertheless, I won't take the responsibility for tarnishing your honour, Walter. You are free to pass the outposts with your men. fitzHamon, give him the watchword.'

'I will, my lord.' fitzHamon smiled ruefully. 'Prince Henry is fortunate in his foes: one sends him water, the other soldiers!'

Rufus laughed. 'Robert will chuckle when he hears – and reprimand me sharply.'

I knelt and touched my forehead on his hand. My eyes prickled; I felt ashamed and mean. Rufus gently put his fingers beneath my chin and raised my head.

'There's one condition, Walter.'

I quelled dismay. 'Yes, my lord?'

'When I have taken Mont St Michel – as I shall – you and your archers join my mesnie.'

A promise I had given to his enemy.

'Willingly, my lord.'

I waited for the tide to ebb, sent in the van an outrider whose spear bore green-leaf garlands and splashed across the sodden sands to Henry's fortress. After lengthy parleying at the gates the sign of truce prevailed; I was led to Henry's presence, bent my knee in the castle hall. Deep in conversation with Gilbert of Clare – that talkative, untrustworthy man who was my wife's brother – Henry ignored my entry and his seneschal's announcement. I was in no mood to endure discourtesy, and said harshly, 'My lord, I come to acquit my oath.'

The fish-like eyes surveyed me aloofly. 'You have tarried overlong, my lord of Poix.'

'I had no choice.' Briefly I told the tale of my long imprisonment. Henry listened silently, watching me the while and biting his nails.

'I heard rumours,' he observed. His glance wavered, and he added, 'A pity you come so late.'

I knew a stab of fear. 'Late? What do you mean, my lord? I left a hostage —'

Henry fluttered a hand. 'Afterwards. Why have you brought a mesnie – your famous archers?'

'A contrivance.' I related without pride the lies I had told Rufus, the regal generosity which let me pass the siege lines.

'Rufus's knightly courtoisie will trip him yet,' Henry commented tersely. He then plied me with stealthy inquiries concerning his enemies' dispositions and detachments and future plans.

'I had no chance to learn these things,' I answered impatiently. 'Nor am I a spy.'

'No? Yet it was a role I had in mind. You are bound, let me remind you, to join my brother's retinue.' He glanced swiftly at Clare, who returned a tiny nod. 'Once there you can serve me well – and the rewards, my lord, will be great.'

I felt the meshes of treachery entangling me. I braced my shoulders and said, 'I am committed to serve the king – and no one else.'

'Great rewards, Tirel,' Henry repeated persuasively. 'Money and lands, in Normandy and England. Possibly an English county: Laingaham is merely a beginning. Such prizes as no sensible man would refuse. In return for all these bounties I need only information, and later perhaps some small assistance in my plans.'

'You need not fear for your safety, brother.' A faint contempt edged Gilbert's voice.

'No!' My voice was hoarse and thick. 'I abide by my vow. I shall do no more!'

'You renounce enormous profits?' Henry sounded disconcerted. 'Your nature, Tirel, must have changed of late!'

I said with difficulty, 'I have discovered . . . constancy.' Fury suddenly drove out fear. 'You promise deniers and demesnes, my lord – you, a landless, impoverished prince! Will you conjure wealth from heaven? – you own not a whit on earth!'

A frozen anger glinted in Henry's eyes. 'You are more foolish than I supposed. You observe only the present, and distrust the future: a future which is mine – because I shall make it so! You under-estimate me, Tirel; and you will be sorry.'

'Your threats, my lord, are wasted. The king awaits me: you would be unwise to prevent my return.'

Henry smiled evilly. 'I have no intention of killing you, Tirel. You may still be useful, whether you will or no.' He pointed to the door. 'You have my permission to leave.'

'Not yet. You hold hostage my esquire, and your bond demands you deliver him.'

Henry watched me pleasurably, and showed his teeth in a smile. 'He died.'

I swayed on my feet, felt sickness surge in my throat. 'Dead? You swore —'

His tongue flickered like a yellow worm between his lips, the eyes were pitiless as steel. 'You came late, Tirel. I had no news, and concluded you were perfidious. And so —' Henry made a gesture, cruelly obscene, stabbing forked fingers to his eyes. 'Your man survived the blinding, but castration . . . not.'

I had a quick mental vision of Vauquelin, my devoted esquire, battle-follower and friend bleeding to an anguished death in some dark cell.

A red mist hazed my sight. I jumped towards him, fumbling at the sword hilt. Gilbert moved like a lightning blur, his shield crashed in my face. A guard knight seized my sword arm, his dagger-point pricked my neck. Henry watched unmoving, chin on hand. He flapped a hand to the doorway. They hustled me out and flung me down the ladder to the ward.

I was in a frenzy to be gone, to nurse my grief alone. But the tide was flooding; deep water engirdled the Mont and I could not leave till dawn. I lay amid my troop, staring at the stars, sleeping not at all. Moonlight flooded the ward, sparkled on the waves like crested spears, lighted plain as day the surf-line on the shore.

It was the darkest night of my life.

3

I led the archers from the castle; Henry waited by the gate. He beckoned me aside and stood at my stirrup. The sallow face was smiling, the eyes were wide and guileless. 'Walter,' he said briskly, 'I am sorry about your esquire. I thought you forsworn, and acted in a rage.'

'Your apologies, my lord,' I answered bleakly, 'will not restore Vauquelin to life.'

Henry lifted his shoulders. 'What is done is done. You cannot weep for ever. I offer you a boy to take his place, a noble youth well versed in arms and armour.'

Black anger shook me in the saddle. 'You traffic in bodies like a bailiff selling bondsmen! No! I have my own notions of requital for Vauquelin's killing.'

Knights clattered past, lances high, pennons snapping bravely in the breeze, and descended the steep twisting path from the Mont. Anxious for my troop which, riding on, had started to cross the sands, I asked sharply, 'Are you making a sally?'

'What?' He looked absently at the horsemen, and shook his head. 'They merely go to joust with enemy knights: a daily custom when the tide is out. Walter,' he continued, idly stroking my destrier's muzzle, 'I sometimes say much more than I mean. You must not think I intend any harm to Rufus. I promise you he holds my fealty.'

'Fealty —!' I laughed without mirth. 'You're fighting Rufus now!'

'Rufus is fighting me,' Henry answered mildly. 'I strive simply to hold the lands I bought of Robert: I did not seek this war.' A humourless smile parted the pale wet lips. 'A knight may not cravenly yield his seigniories and keep his honour. This Rufus understands: he respects the codes of courtoisie.'

I gathered the rein. 'The king is a trustful man. I shall try to shred his illusions.'

Henry watched me riding down the path. The smile had left his face.

The archers were far ahead, treading the same curving track I had followed to St Michel the previous day. The sands – a gleaming, flat expanse, speckled brown and silver like a sheet of mildewed leather – stretched unbroken to the mainland, to trees and scrub which rimmed the high-tide mark. Tents and pavilions dotted the faraway shoreline like scattered painted pebbles; gaudy banners, small as petals, fluttered in the wind. In the distance, right and left, knights capered and curvetted. I heard faintly the shouted challenges, saw them ride courses against opponents who cantered from the camps. They looked small as children's toys, tiny prancing figures shining in the sun.

I veered from the bowmen's circuitous track, followed a straighter course which I guessed would overtake them before Avranches. I rode solitary, eyes on the sea-rippled sand, thinking bitter thoughts.

I was utterly convinced that Henry plotted treason – and somewhere in the plot I had a place. I realized also that, for profound and elusive reasons, the conduct of my life was now transformed. Vauquelin's cruel death kindled in my mind an incandescent flame, a furnace that tempered a change which was wrought at Conches. I saw in front of me a single purpose: to guard the king from enemies he would not recognize, from men he believed his friends. All else became irrelevant.

Isabel's vengeance had not only savaged my body but bared my soul, exposing myself to myself, the avarice and selfishness, the ruthless pursuit of power. More pitiless in impact were dishonour and remorse. I had failed my liegemen, friends whom I, their suzerain, was bound to cherish and protect. One dead, the other maimed.

Then there was Rufus, the man himself, the peerless knight and splendid king. A flamboyant individual, generous and kind, hot-blooded but unmalicious. A valiant knight, a formidable fighter and leader of men, strict to observe his own knightly word and confiding without stint in the promises of others. A ruthless king convinced that neither human strength nor the powers of God and the Devil could or should withstand his will – but merciful and just to those he ruled. In the texture of his character as man and knight and king were threaded the strands of evil, the warp of unnatural vice. What did it matter? I could never condone his depravity – the thought of it made me retch – but the rest of him, the bravery and

204

honesty and truth, outweighed his single blemish. Since those long-ago days in Rouen I had resisted Rufus's attraction: now, as a kind of vindication, a sort of penance, I yielded to the pull.

I heard a distant shout and raised my head. A lone horseman cantered from a tent-clump, lance aloft, and spattered across the sands. A sea-pool crossed his path; he swerved around it, came nearer as I watched. I glanced expectantly around, hoping he coursed another knight. None was nearer than five bowshots. The pugnacious fool, I concluded sourly, was challenging me.

Running was unthinkable. Reluctantly I enarmed my shield, kicked the destrier to a trot. I searched the ground in front for pools and hollows; the sand stretched flat and level. My spurs pricked the horse's flanks, he snorted and broke to a canter. I shortened rein, wiped the palm of my lance-hand on his mane to remove the sweat, gripped the shaft and tested the balance.

The knight by now was close enough for me to see the colour of his mount, a strapping glossy-coated bay. The brute wallowed in his gait. A rolling destrier, as everyone knows, induces a wavering lance: my own charger, Count William's gift, rode true as a goose-fletched arrow.

From the tents behind my challenger men in mail were riding in his tracks.

The knight's legs closed on his horse, which sprang to a gallop, sand spurting beneath the hooves. The extra speed and effort made the animal lean crookedly on the bit and bear to the left. The rider struggled to right his alignment, the shield jolting on his rein-arm. My friend, I murmured grimly, a mule would serve you better.

I rammed in spurs, pressed hard on the irons, thrust spine against cantle and couched my lance. The knight's lance dipped and levelled; he shouted a raucous warcry that was tattered by the wind.

We rode against each other in the usual jousting fashion, near-side to nearside, shield to shield, so that shields could take the brunt and save mortal wounds. My lance was slanted across the withers, point aiming at his head, at the shining conical helmet which jutted above the shield rim. We hurtled on opposite courses to half a bowshot's length. His hoofbeats slapped the sand; the stallion fought the bit and foam-flecks flew from his mouth.

The blundering horse leaned more to the left and carried him into my path on the line for a head-on collision. I wrestled the rein and drove in a spur, swerved my charger over the line and canted my lance to the right. The knight sawed his rein, strove to alter his aim. My point took him full on the plastron.

The cantle rammed my backbone, the shaft shattered in my hand. I put both hands on the rein, heaved the destrier to a halt and turned about. The knight was dragged head-down, a foot entangled in the stirrup, his shoulders ploughing furrows in the sand. The leather broke; he thumped upon his back. I drew my sword, stood over him and raised the blade. The flat was turned towards him; I had no wish to kill the clumsy destrier's idiot owner.

The helmet shrouded his brow, the ventail shuttered mouth and chin, nasal hid nose and cheeks. The breath was driven from his lungs; his chest heaved and he gasped for air. His eyes opened; he saw the hovering blade and fought for words.

'Hold, rascal – hold! I am the king!'

The sword dropped from my hand. I swung quickly from the saddle. Frantically I fumbled at the plastron. The iron plate was dented but unbroken.

'My lord,' I cried, stricken, 'how badly are you hurt?'

'Winded,' Rufus panted. 'Nothing worse, I think. Help me up.'

He rocked on his feet, crouched hands on knees, and drew deep, shuddering breaths. I heard hoofbeats thudding closer. The knights who followed Rufus surrounded us in a ring, lances lowered, pointing at my body. Eyes glittered angrily beneath the helmets. A voice I know for Meulan's said furiously, 'You rogue! If you have harmed the king you die!'

Rufus, still bent double, wagged a hand. 'Let be! I am not hurt.' He straightened, and blearily surveyed me. 'Never before have I been unhorsed. Who is it struck me down?'

I twisted my helmet off. Rufus's eyes widened. 'By the Face! Tirel!' He began to laugh, the breath wheezing through his teeth. 'It's as well you're promised to my mesnie, your name already written in my book! You wield a pretty lance, my friend. I shouldn't care to number you among my foes!'

'I took you for a knight, my lord,' I said unhappily, 'and not for the king.'

'A knight I am,' said Rufus. 'Don't reproach yourself.' He contemplated his destrier wandering in the distance. 'Will someone catch that useless horse? I bought the brute this morning for fifteen marks – and I was swindled!'

We helped the king to horse, jogged towards Avranches. The tide was flooding; gleaming tongues of water chased across the sands and swirled around our feet. Rufus leaned from the saddle, laid his hand on mine.

'That's the second time you've tried to kill me, Walter. Remember Gerberoi? Better not try a third – you may be lucky!'

Dumbly I shook my head, and lifted his hand to my lips; and swore to myself by the Cross of Christ I would save King William Rufus from the brother who wanted him dead.

BOOK TWO

The Wolf Time

Wind time, Wolf time,
There shall come a year
When no man on earth
His brother man shall spare.

Prophecy from the old Norse Edda

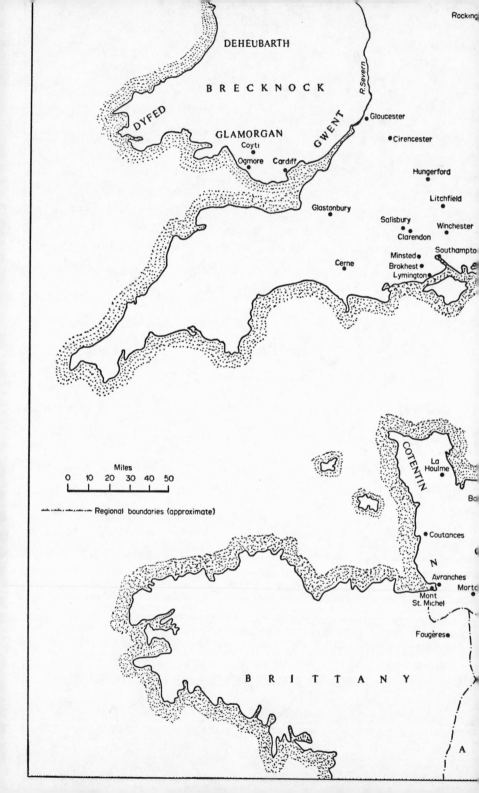

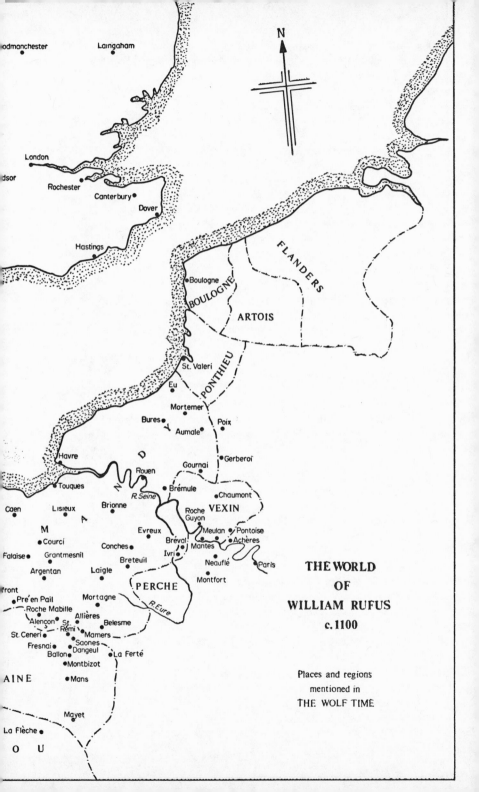

Prologue

THE island's pinnacles leaned against the evening glow. Cliffs climbed steeply from the sands, tapered to a spire thrusting skywards like a lifted sword; the rays of a dying sun spangled the gilded crucifix. Beneath the spire a castle crouched.

Mont St Michel.

The portals opened. Men in mail emerged from the gate, trooped down a twisting path and advanced across the sands. Horsemen rode in the van, infantry tramped behind, spears sloped, feet squelching in the wet.

A garrison, defeated, marched out with the honours of war.

Knights waited on the shore, lances slanted across saddle-bows, shields slung upon their backs. Two riders in front curbed fretting destriers, and observed silently the procession that threaded towards them. Royal emblems ringed their helmets, gold gem-studded coronets: William of England and Robert of Normandy.

The horseman who led the column stumbled on a pebble, cursed and jabbed the rein. The brute can barely stand, he thought: he has lived on nothing but seaweed since the fodder went. He glanced at the raking ribs and staring coats of the animals his companions rode. Starved out, he reflected, and forced to surrender. Starved out. When the wells dried they were done.

He spurred the horse to a trot, and rode alone to meet the victors waiting to receive him. He reined and drew his sword and held it out hilt foremost. Each formally touched the pommel.

King William smiled.

'Keep your sword, Henry.' He scrutinized shrewdly the pallid cheeks beneath the helmet, a face wasted by privation. 'You need food and wine, I think. Come, brother.'

The Conqueror's sons rode side by side through the conquering army.

*   *   *   *   *

It was raining in Caen, a steady dismal drizzle from a summer sky. Dawnlight crept reluctantly through the windows of St Stephen's Abbey, touched the congregation's shoulders in the nave, and retreated before the candles' spired splendour on the altar. The radiance lapped to the foremost ranks of the men who were gathered to hear mass, and kindled a shining flame on Robert's lambent coronet and bathed in glittering glory King William's jewelled crown.

William Rufus whispered to his brother. Duke Robert frowned.

Between nave and chancel soared their father's tomb, black marble carved and fretted, resplendent with precious stones, sapphire, jacinth and emerald, so that the sepulchre winked and sparkled. An epitaph graved in silver extolled the Conqueror's virtues. Rufus scanned the Latin verse incuriously; he had commissioned the tomb himself, delivering to the goldsmith silver and gold and gems. The king yawned behind his hand, and tried to recall the inscription which a clerk had once translated. He could remember only the last two lines.

'To Him Who rules on high he bowed his head,
And the proud king was numbered with the dead.'

Trite, Rufus decided. The priests for all their learning lacked the vivid imagery which burned in the minstrels' songs. He shifted his feet on the flagstones and stole a look at his brother. Robert joined fingertip to fingertip before his brow, and whispered the responses. The duke, he thought sardonically, had reason to pray: he needed all the help that heaven could give.

Rufus cricked his beefy neck and gazed at the roof where the rafters, springing from the trunks of vast stone pillars, interlaced in canopied gloom. Incense spiced the air and mingled with the smell of candle-wax and sweat. The abbot of St Stephen pronounced the benediction; the congregation knelt, robes and mantles rustled. A scabbard clanked on stone, a shoe grated on the flags. For a while they bowed in prayer, and their hands in the candled darkness flitted like pale grey moths in the sign of the Cross they worshipped.

Outside the abbey men-at-arms, sheltering beneath an elm clump, lolled on their spears and cursed the rain which trickled down the collars of their haubergeons. A banneret snapped an order, the men formed three-deep files and tramped slowly through the gateway. Behind them paced the rulers of Normandy and England, wide-shouldered burly men in fur-embroidered cloaks, crowns glistening on close-cropped heads, ruddy faces shining in the rain. Townsfolk bordered the street, cheered the duke they had seldom seen, and wondered which of the two he was. For in looks the princes were not unalike, red-skinned, square-jawed, rugged. The crown hid Rufus's yellow hair; streaks like scattered ash flecked Robert's temples. The duke was the shorter man – his cloak concealed the bandy legs which had earned him the nickname Curthose.

The constable of Caen's castle knelt before his suzerain and offered his sword. The royal brothers entered the hall, a long low building, shingle-roofed, stone walls lanced by narrow windows. A knight banneret, sword on shoulder, guarded the door and watched the company enter, a hundred or more, the lords of a thousand fiefs, proud men walking proudly, garbed in velvet mantles and tunics of silk and sendal, blue and crimson and green, a bishop's gilded mitre and, black threads in a blazoned tapestry, the cowled and silent monks.

The banneret closed the door and stood before it, blade point-down between his feet, hands resting on the quillons.

Chapter 1

1091

Ivo of Grantmesnil plucked my sleeve, a grin split his oak-brown face. He said, 'There's room on that bench if we're quick. And what is Walter of Poix, France's liege, doing in this assembly?'

I sometimes wondered that myself. During Mont St Michel's leaguer I had done duty in the siege lines with my little troop of archers; and had given the king my fealty but had not sworn homage — the suzerain from whom I held my lands was Philip of France. I was an ordinary knight in Rufus's household, living in his mesnie at his cost, and had not envisaged embroilment in those discussions of high polity which follow princely dissensions.

When lack of water forced the Mont to surrender Prince Henry remained with his brothers, honourably treated, all enmity apparently forgotten. The war was over, the curious war of the Conqueror's sons which started when Rufus invaded Normandy, abated when Duke Robert asked for terms, and smouldered anew in a joint campaign against Henry in the Mont. Duke and king returned to Rouen and chaffered throughout the summer over the treaty we were now assembled in Caen to witness.

Meanwhile Henry and Gilbert of Clare, that devious baron who advised him, slipped away to Brittany and wandered friendless and forsaken.

Towards the end of June Rufus had summoned me and said, 'Tirel, you must go to Brittany, find Henry and bring him here. I am told he is sheltering in a monastery near Fougères.'

Since I had once been Henry's prisoner, I had seen an aspect of his character he never revealed to Rufus, a vein of faithlessness and cruelty which made him different from his brothers: Rufus, an iron man, harsh, honourable and just; Robert, the drowsy duke, irresolute, kindly and lax. I was dismayed, and spoke without thinking.

'Is this wise, my lord?'

'Wise? What do you mean?' Rufus's eyebrows lifted, pale-yellow like wisps of straw. 'It's simply a matter of courtesy. I won't have him wandering the roads like a beggar, and living on the charity of monks!'

Impossible to tell him. Neither Rufus nor Curthose thought Henry dangerous: the only harm they saw in him was the blood that ran in his veins, the Conqueror's blood which gave him a claim to part of the Conqueror's realm. He was harmless, they believed, provided he was never allowed to handle the reins of power.

I had reason to know better. Henry was like a maggot, burrowing into decomposing bodies.

One does not immediately refuse a king's command. I left King William's busy council in the hall of Rouen's Tower and sought Count Robert of Meulan on the battlements. He was arguing amicably with Robert fitzHamon, and turned at my approach.

'The very man we want – a practised archer! Walter, fitzHamon swears an arrow shot from here could carry to the Seine's far bank. I say it's impossible!'

I glanced through an embrasure. 'About six hundred paces. No – not even with a candle-arrow and horn-backed bow. My lord —'

'There you are, fitzHamon. You owe me three deniers!' A smile creased his weather-worn face, the breeze stirred greying hair grown thick to cushion the helmet, cropped close on neck and temples. A crafty man, renowned in war and statecraft, a veteran of Hastings where he led five hundred knights. His deeds that day were famous, and never lacked the telling: the grizzled survivors of England's taking are all notorious bores. They have reason, I suppose: it was Christendom's greatest battle since the Saracens died at Tours – and I haven't forgotten Roncesvalles, which troubadours make such a song about, though no more than a rearguard skirmish.

fitzHamon fumbled ruefully in his wallet and clinked money into Meulan's wizened claw. 'No arguing with Tirel about bows and bowmen!' An arrow scar seared his falcon face from ear to chin; humour always lurked in the deep-blue eyes. Lord of Torigni and Creulli, he also held fiefs in England bestowed on him by Rufus. Although not a count, he ranked by possessions and power alongside counts.

These were William Rufus's closest friends and counsellors – which was why I needed their advice.

I said, 'My lords, the king has ordered me to find Prince Henry and persuade him to come to Rouen. This I do not think advisable.'

Meulan's eyes, slitted between lashless lids, examined me intently. 'No?' he inquired in a wooden voice. 'Why so?'

I said carefully, 'The prince, I believe, does not always seek the king's advantage. It were better he stayed away.'

fitzHamon inspected a ring on his middle finger, twisting the garnet stone to catch the light. 'Henry,' he said, 'has very little money and no land at all, no castles, no liegemen at his beck. Why do you think he can harm the King of England?'

A question I could not answer. I said haltingly, 'I have no proof -- only surmise. But I am utterly certain --' I stopped, and swallowed.

'Didn't Henry hold you captive for a time, and kill your esquire, Vauquelin?' fitzHamon asked. 'Perhaps, my lord of Poix, you're rather prejudiced.'

Meulan cackled like a laying hen. 'Enough of your baiting, Robert.' He looked at me benignly. 'I myself recommended that Henry be brought to Rouen.'

I said resignedly, 'You have your reasons, my lord. They are beyond my understanding.'

Meulan gazed across the roofs of Rouen. 'I am told that wolves will expel a rogue male from the pack, driving him out to forage as best he may. That same animal, often as not, hardened and matured by his solitary rigours, returns to his kindred and fights the leader for ascendancy. Usually he wins.'

He turned his head and stared me in the eyes. 'A lone wolf is a dangerous creature, Tirel. Go you now to Brittany, and find Prince Henry.'

Next day I departed, taking as escort my troop of mounted archers. The journey across Normandy in fair midsummer weather was not unpleasant; with Rufus's coming the anarchy which had savaged the land under Robert's rule had dwindled. The scars remained: the nettled mounds where villages once stood, weeds and thistles smothering the fields, skeletons mouldering in wayside ditches and furtive peasants lurking in the forests. But birds fluted in the hedgerows and flowers speckled the wastelands like gaudy scattered coins. I made no haste, and lingered at the night-halts, camping in the open or finding hospitality in castles on the way.

Near Grantmesnil I met my old friend Ivo roving with a conroy, armed and armoured, riding purposefully, clearly bent on business. The encounter was unexpected: our mesnies met in a woodland belt at a twist in the path, and for one chaotic instant there were shouts and stringing of bows, shields enarmed and lances levelled – in Robert Curthose's Normandy you assumed armed men were hostile. Ivo quickly recognized me despite the helmet's coif and nasal, since I led the only mounted archers existing at that time. We sorted the matter out, called our men to order and exchanged cheerful greetings. He was on his way, he said, to chastise an impertinent neighbour – the petty lord of a rickety wooden castle – who had dared to raid his demesne and lift some cattle.

I drank from Ivo's wineskin and wished him luck, and we went our ways.

After a week's leisurely riding we reached Fougères, where I quartered my troop in the town and, taking Berenger, my esquire, sauntered to the monastery and found the prior, a greasy monk whose eyes were puckered in folds of fat. He proved as evasive as he looked, and denied all knowledge of the prince I sought. My heart sank; I had no wish to hunt my quarry throughout Brittany. Our altercation attracted the abbot, a man of a different stamp, lean and direct in manner, who courteously inquired my business. I produced from my scrip the safe-conduct which Rufus had provided. The abbot examined the king's mark and seal, gravely inclined his head and invited me to follow. Through chapter-house and frater he led us to the cloister, where Henry lounged in a chair on a patch of grass. Gilbert of Clare sat on a stool beside him; a servant hovered at their backs.

I had not had speech with the prince since that evil day when I rode from Mont St Michel, leaving behind my esquire's corpse and much of my honour. I had not seen him since he led his men from the fortress a fortnight later. I felt now a coiling in my bowels, a mingling of the slimy skeins of fear and loathing. I hated him with all my heart, on my own behalf and that of the king whose fealty I owned.

I bent my knee and, with my gaze on the cloudless sky, luminous as thin blue glass, recited shortly my mission. Henry's chilly eyes, black and deadly as nightshade berries, slowly examined my face; no emotion stirred the suety features. He heard me out, looked at the scroll in my hand and said, 'You have written authority?'

I gave him the script which stated the purpose of my journey and forbade Duke Robert's lieges to offer me let or hindrance. Henry flattened the scroll and pretended to read. (I have since been told he is lettered, which I find hard to credit: neither of his brothers could read or cipher.) He pinched his pudgy chin between his fingers and said, 'Tell me the truth: why do my brothers want me?'

'I am merely a messenger, my lord. I have no place in the king's council, nor Duke Robert's. They are, I think, disposed kindly towards you, and wish you well.'

If only, I reflected savagely, I could tell him a dagger awaited his guts!

Henry slipped a hand beneath his tunic, open to the sun, and scratched his chest. The skin was white, like a serpent's belly, smooth and hairless as a woman's. He leaned forward and said in an iron voice, 'Why should I return to the men who plundered all I owned? Duke William died, and from all his domains accorded me naught but a little silver. Not a castle nor arpent of land, not a cottage to call my own. When Curthose needed money for his wars I gave him money, and took from him in pledge the county of Avranches.' Henry's voice rose, a bead of spittle trickled from the corner of his mouth. 'Afterwards, with his ally Rufus, he wrests from me again the fiefs he sold. The money I had is gone, the lands stolen. You behold in me, Tirel, an impoverished beggar, a disinherited prince.' He sank back in his chair and wiped his chin. The anger went from his face. 'Perhaps you think me justly requited for your wretched esquire's killing?'

Pigeons rose in a flock from the abbey's tower, wings snapping like breaking twigs, circled against the azure sky and settled on the grass within the cloister. I watched them unseeingly, and remembered how Henry, holding Vauquelin hostage, had blinded, castrated and killed him; and swallowed the lump in my throat.

Gilbert of Clare said harshly, 'Are you sent to take the prince by force?' Lines grooved his sunken cheeks from mouth to nostrils, lips thin as daggers, pale eyes in shadowed pits. He jerked his head towards the church. 'There is sanctuary, let me remind you! Will you risk anathema to snatch us from the altar?'

I answered tiredly, 'You judge King William by your own ignoble measure. There's no danger for you in Rouen – only a brotherly welcome. If you will not go I cannot compel you.'

'You'd be safer here, my lord,' said Clare.

Henry nodded, scrutinizing my face. For one false moment I knew a feeling of deliverance: this treacherous rogue would be kept far away from the king I intended to guard. A delusory hope: I had been ordered to fetch Henry; and Meulan, that cunning man, had given me the bait to tempt a wary fish. Unwillingly I spoke my piece.

'Rufus and Curthose debate a treaty to decide the provisions of peace. The war ended to the king's advantage: the duke must cede to the victor the territory he has won. Normandy is being divided. The bargaining continues; the terms are as yet unsettled. Is it wise, my lord, to shun a council where lands are being redistributed and fiefs are changing hands? Do you think your brothers can ignore your claims – if you are there to press them?'

The servitor brought wine. Henry sipped abstractedly, rolling the cup between his palms. Clare drained his goblet in a single gulp, and thumped the cup on the grass. 'You weave fantasies,' he rasped. 'Rufus and Curthose warred against my lord to filch the demesnes he held. Why should they now carve a moiety from Normandy and place it in his hands?'

I sighed inwardly; and trailed the second lure which Meulan had provided. 'There is also England,' I said gently. 'The lands your mother the queen Matilda bequeathed you in' – I stuttered, because the English came clumsily to my lips – 'in Gloucestershire and Cornwall. Will you renounce them to the king because you fear to face him?'

'Fear?' Henry's head snapped up. 'Guard your tongue, Tirel! I need fear no man, as I told you long ago. Only those who have much to lose need be afraid. I have nothing.'

He stared at the pigeons, tame birds from the monastery's dove-cots, strutting around his feet. 'My mother's bequest,' he muttered. 'I claimed the fiefs from Rufus when he was crowned. He promised me seisin as soon as he was settled. He was over-confident, was Rufus – the English rebellion that Curthose fostered in '88 nearly shook him from the throne.' A vicious satisfaction tinged his voice. 'But Curthose – ah, that flabby duke! – let Rufus deal the counter-stroke which brings him here today. I have heard nothing since.' Henry sent me a hostile look. 'You seem well informed about my English inheritance, Tirel. Does Rufus hold the lands on my behalf?'

I said what I thought was truth. 'He does, my lord.'

The cold eyes slid away; he pulled thoughtfully at the lank brown hair which fringed his brow. 'You are persuasive; your reasoning is sound. After all, I have little to lose – and I cannot believe my be-loved brothers will kill me. Yes. I shall come to Rouen.'

Clare thudded fist in palm. 'Foolhardiness, my lord! You may not be risking your life, but your freedom is at stake. A man may rot for years in the vaults beneath Rouen's Tower!'

'Rufus is too honourable, and Curthose would not dare. I know my brothers. You cannot dissuade me, Gilbert. We'll pack our trappings and depart.'

'Surely not with this man's rabble of archers?'

Henry's eyes travelled over me from head to foot; the pale wet lips smiled bleakly. 'No. I think my lord of Poix does not love me greatly. A pity if some unaccountable mishap prevented me reaching Rouen. You may go, Tirel, and inform your master I shall see him within the sennight.'

I bowed and left them.

2

I blinked in the blaze of light which flooded the hall of Caen's castle. A fire crackled in the central hearth; smoke coiled beneath the rafters and drifted through a smoke-hole in the roof. Torches sputtered in cressets, candles flared on tables. Chairs flanked two gilded thrones which dominated a dais at the end of the hall. Parchment scrolls and inkhorns, abaci, tablets and quills littered an elmwood table in front of the dais; benches lined the walls from end to end.

The princes gestured one to another, urging precedence in sitting, and sank into the thrones. The men who governed Curthose, and those who ruled England under Rufus, found places on the dais – the barons of wealth and castles and, more important, power. The rest were left to jostle to the benches, dividing right and left in a rustle of silken robes.

Ivo wedged his enormous rump on a crowded bench, waggled his hips like a dancer and forced a space. 'Here you are, Walter. Your pardon, my lord,' he added jovially to a neighbouring knight who glared at his intrusion. 'Can't help it, you know – I'm cursed with the biggest bum in Neustria!'

At opposite ends of the elmwood table stood Odo, Bishop of Bayeux, and Ranulf Flambard, now the Treasurer of England – delegates and spokesmen for duke and king respectively. Clerks beside them nervously arranged the parchments. Odo faced the room.

'We are assembled, my lords, to witness a covenant of peace which Normandy and England, in brotherly concordance, have agreed on so that strife between their realms may end for evermore.'

Beneath the glittering mitre Odo's wary, fox-like eyes roved quickly over his audience. 'You will hear the treaty's clauses one by one. If any should dissent, let him stand and state his reason.'

He held a scroll near his eyes – the end uncoiled to the floor – and began reading. Flambard bent his handsome head and followed the words on a duplicate script. Candlelight burnished the fiery hair which girdled his tonsure, and carved parallel valleys in the folds of his priestly robe. Odo spat the ornate Latin phrases in a brittle voice. Flambard, when he paused, translated his words into French.

'This is going to be a long business,' Ivo murmured.

I examined the faces on the dais. King William's men in a row beside him: all the lords of northern Normandy, with an outpost set at Conches, a quarter of the duchy under Rufus's dominion. Others also, lesser knights, lieges of the great. How had he done it? Not by force of arms, I recalled; not one of Duke Robert's vassals had lifted a hand against him.

Ivo followed my gaze. 'A precious gang of turncoats, all forsworn and false,' he whispered. 'Dazzled by King William's bribes – a mint of silver dribbled into greedy hands – and pulverized by his blackmail. They all hold fiefs in England which he threatened to escheat.' Ivo spat between his feet. 'Politics! The king's envoys tried their blandishments on me. Thank God I hold no more than a hamlet or two in Kent.'

Flambard's melodious voice, smooth as silk and deep as a bell, intoned a long translation: some drivel about ducal rights being kept as the Conqueror kept them. Waste of breath and parchment, I thought – only the duke himself, by the weight of his arm and the edge of his sword, could secure his dues from the turbulent men he led. Parchment and ink and seals meant nothing to them.

I inspected the faces I knew in the rank which supported Curthose: Count William of Evreux, old patron of my childhood; Gilbert of Laigle; William of Breteuil, a hairy man, his long lean jaw blue-stubbled, the backs of his hands black-furred; and Robert of Belesme lolling in his chair, playing idly with his girdle's silver tassel, eyes hooded in an alabaster face. Belesme, the flail of Normandy, dominating Duke Robert himself, the lord of thirty castles from La Ferté to Falaise, terrible and merciless and cruel beyond belief.

Where was Prince Henry?

Again I searched the faces on the dais, the ranks of the men who thronged the benches opposite. Not there. I found him at the end of the hall, alongside the dais but not upon it, seated on a chair whose lofty back and sculpted arms suggested a tawdry throne. His hands were folded in his lap, his expression neutral as his place.

Flambard and Bishop Odo chanted turn by turn like monks reciting versicles and responses during vespers in a chapel. They uttered vicious prohibitions against building unlicensed castles and insisted on the ducal claim to garrison private strongholds. Ivo shifted irritably. 'So much hot air. Directly Rufus leaves we'll do as we've always done since the Bastard died; stick castles wherever we like and refuse the duke's castellans. God's blood, I could do with a drink!'

The audience, in truth, was growing impatient. A fluttering like a wind-gust stirred the benches, feet scraped the rushes, legs were stretched and crossed, fingers twiddled buckles and embroidered belts. Rufus rolled his sceptre on his thigh and watched our faces; a smile twitched the full red lips. Curthose, chin in hand, listened frowningly to Flambard; his fingers tapped a rhythm on his knee. Henry lifted his gaze to the roof, and seemed lost in contemplation of the smoke skeins caressing the rafters.

Odo finished the scroll he read and plucked another from a clerk. Flambard, like a partner in a complicated dance, unrolled the duplicate. Ivo sighed windily. 'Not half-way through! My arse is sore as a virgin's crotch on her bridal night! How much longer must we endure?' He took no trouble to lower his voice; the knights near him grinned.

A tension like an overstrung lute-string twanged in Odo's voice, the parchment shook in his hands. The windy verbiage was ended; here was the crux, the harsh, hard facts we wanted to hear. The chatter faded and died; we waited for Flambard's rendering. The Treasurer laid down his script and spoke the words by rote.

'In return for promised services to be specified hereafter, Robert, Duke of Normandy, cedes to William, King of England, all of his dominion north of Seine and certain lesser seigniories which lie within the duchy. In proof of this agreement the lords of the lands concerned swear fealty and homage to the sovereign of England. Count Stephen of Aumale!'

Stephen rose stiffly, the muscles creaking in his legs, and knelt before the king. He bowed his greying head, put his hands between Rufus's palms and swore the oath of allegiance. The words murmured in the stillness like a prayer. The fire crackled, spat a glowing cinder which curved from the hearth and fell at Odo's feet. Viciously he stamped it into the rushes – looking, from his manner, as though he stamped on Aumale's neck.

'William, Count of Eu!'

The ritual flowed, the barons kneeling in turn to vow fealty to England: Conches and Gournai, Meulan and St Valeri, Courci and Mortain – men who willingly exchanged Duke Robert's flimsy rule for King William's iron hand. The hall was deadly quiet.

It is not every day you can witness a realm being sundered, and see wildly independent men pass submissively under the yoke.

fitzHamon, the last to swear, returned to his seat and fastidiously arranged his cloak. Odo beckoned Flambard to continue: a practical man, he was tired of proclaiming Latin which raked his throat and no one save the clerics understood. St Stephen's bell tolled sext; the rain had ceased; a watery noonday sun spilled through the windows. Flambard slid the parchment through his hands, found the place and read.

'In return for the domains thus ceded, William, King of England, pledges Robert, Duke of Normandy, that he will come to his aid against any who take arms against him, and will help to restore to Normandy the lands Duke William held, save those which, under the treaty, fall to King William himself.'

I remembered Maine, blazing in rebellion under Hugh of Este. Was Rufus pledging himself to war on Robert's behalf? The king seemed bored; impatiently he flicked a sweat bead from his brow. The hearth-fire, torches and candles overheated the room; girdles were loosed and mantles opened; an acrid smell of bodies tanged the air.

Flambard raised his head and spoke to the dais directly. 'That clause, my lords, concludes the agreement which apportions the seigniories of Normandy and England. Should any dissent let him rise and speak, or hereafter hold his peace.'

Eye avoided eye; some stared at the floor, others examined the smoky ceiling, the walls, the guttering candles. A swallow flew through a window, squeaked alarm and disappeared. Ivo whispered, 'How much would your neck be worth if you spoke?' I watched Henry, unmentioned in the treaty, and wondered what he thought. His hands stayed folded in his lap, the sallow face inscrutable.

'The pact, then, is agreed.' Flambard replaced the scroll on the table and took a shorter parchment from a clerk. Ivo groaned.

'The suzerains of Normandy and England pledge mutually that, if either should die without lawful issue during the lifetime of his brother, the survivor shall succeed to the whole of his dominions.'

Ivo's groan dissolved in a splutter. The chamber buzzed like a hive. Both rulers were unwed. Rufus had fathered no children – nor, with his perverted bent, were any likely. Curthose owned several bastards – I recalled Lesceline's brat, Richard, now twelve years old – but they were hardly lawful issue. The agreement shut them out.

It also shut out someone else.

When this sank in, everyone looked at Henry.

The prince sat awhile in thought, chin sunk on chest, rubbing his fingertips together. He pulled the mantle round his bulky body, stood and addressed his brothers in a calm, untroubled voice.

'My lords of Normandy and England, you have decided in your wisdom that none but you shall inherit Duke William's realm. Who am I to oppose a royal edict? You know full well I own neither funds nor fiefs nor following. I live on your kindly charity. But of one factor I must remind you.'

Not an eyelash stirred. Rufus watched Henry closely, his countenance benign; Curthose scowled at his hands.

'I am son of a crowned king of the English, born of his crowned lady on native soil, born, as they say, in the purple. You, my lords, in English eyes are foreign-born sons of a Norman duke and duchess. Under English law I am Aetheling, the lawful heir to England's throne.'

Rufus lost his benevolent look, his mouth tightened. 'Your claim is nonsense. The English, a conquered people, have no say in their government.'

'That I do not contest,' Henry answered mildly. 'I mention merely your subjects' customs – they may not regard with kindness my exclusion from succession.'

'I can deal with any unkindliness from the English,' said Rufus grimly. 'You dabble in dreams, my lord.'

'No. I have no false hopes. Any I ever held have died today. I ask for one favour alone: the seisin you promised of those English lands our mother bequeathed.'

Rufus lowered his eyes. 'Yes. There are complications. A legal issue – some confusion in the deeds. The chancellery clerks are debating.' He rapped the sceptre on his throne arm and said decisively, 'I suggest you come to England, so that together we may resolve the business.'

225

Henry searched his brother's face. At length he said, 'As you wish, sire.' He bent his knee and returned to his seat.

Bishop Odo faced the hall. 'You have heard, my lords, the heads of agreement, the clauses of the treaty read in full. Do you give assent?'

Voices rumbled in concurrence. Odo turned to the dais and addressed the sovereign princes.

'Your lieges accord acceptance. Do you ratify the pact, my lords of Normandy and England?'

Rufus and Curthose stood, and spoke in turn.

'Li rei le volt e grée.'

'Li deuc le volt e grée.'

The barons crowded the table to make their marks on the charter. Ivo gripped my arm.

'Out of here quick,' he said, 'before this mob drinks every tavern dry!'

So ended the Treaty of Caen, whose consequences linger to this hour when I speak, when the sovereigns who signed are lost to the world and Henry reigns triumphant.

3

King William lodged in the mansion of Theobald of Étampes near the Falaise gate. There, after breaking his fast, he held a daily conclave of his barons and advisers, interviewed envoys who brought tidings from his kingdom, listened to petitions and put his cross on charters. Household knights in turn stood guard on these occasions: the day following the treaty I waited, sword unsheathed, behind the king. Though no one yet had tried to murder Rufus, some strange individuals were allowed to attend his audiences – and the knight on duty was always alert. He now sat, chin in hand, and heard a clerk construe a dispatch from Walter Giffard, the chancellor who managed English affairs in Rufus's absence. The window shutters were opened wide, sunlight cascaded into the chamber and splashed angular golden pools on patterned Moorish druggets brought from Spain. Tapestries nailed to the walls portrayed Our Lord's entry into Jerusalem; a wind fanned the hangings and stirred the disciples' robes till they seemed to move and live. Amid this garish opulence – Theobald was a wealthy merchant – drab-gowned clerks at lecterns scratched busily on parchment; grave men in sober clothing conferred in quiet voices; a gold-bearded Englishman, talking to fitz-Hamon, stuttered broken French; and citizens from St Saëns, humbly attired, waited to complain against their lord's exactions. The clerk finished his reading. Rufus questioned the envoy, sharp probing queries, brief and to the point, and scratched his head. 'Trouble brewing in Wales – the marcher lords want help. Malcolm of Scotland moving south, despite his defeat in Northumbria three months ago. I must go to England quickly, else we'll have the Scots besieging York, the Welsh in Chester. Normandy must wait – we've tied the package tightly, the knots won't fray for a while.'

Rufus crooked a finger; a clerk came running, tablet ready, stylus poised. 'Orders! The army's encamped at Rouen under Robert of Mortain – he'll march forthwith for St Valeri. Warn the shipmasters in St Valeri they'll sail within a week. Horse transports and store ships harboured at Touques will join the fleet at once. We'll take everything we came with, plus the armaments and rations I stored in reserve at Bures: Mortain will pick them up on his way. Bures is too small to provide transport; he'll need to take unladen carts from Rouen. Have you got that down?'

Crisp, positive orders – a captain in command. The clerk nodded, scribbling rapidly. Rufus pondered. 'My household's hoys and longships are moored in Caen. I shall embark for England within, say, fourteen days, if the wind be fair. It can't be sooner,' he added thoughtfully. 'I have some persuasion to do. Mortain must encamp the army at Hastings and await me there. That's all.'

Rufus rose briskly and said, 'My lords, the audience is ended. You may withdraw.' The nobles strolled to the portal; the clerks gathered armfuls of scrolls and scurried from the room; the burghers from St Saëns, their complaints unheard, shuffled slowly out. Rufus saw their downcast faces and raised a hand. 'Do not despair, messires,' he called. 'Come again on the morrow – I vow I shall hear your plea before all else.' He smiled; and they saw that surpassing charm which made men love him; and went consoled.

Meulan said, 'You spoke of persuasion. Whom must you convince, my lord?'

'Curthose.' Rufus rubbed his fleshy nose. 'He must come with me to England, and persuade the rebels of '88 who still sulk in their castles, despite the thrashing they had, and dream of Normandy and England reunited. I'll have Curthose convince them, face to face, their dreams are over. And then the Scots. There's no point in fighting if I can get what I want without. Curthose and Malcolm are old friends; he's godfather to one of Scotland's children, and Malcolm did him homage in Duke William's time. A show of force, a healthy bribe and Robert's mediation ought to do the trick.'

I listened admiringly to statecraft in the making. Rufus had come a long way from the brawling esquire I knew in Rouen's Tower, the youth who offered to contradiction naught but a naked sword, the hothead who struck before he thought.

Meulan seemed unimpressed. 'Both are doubtful propositions, my lord. You rely too much on the duke's diplomacy. He's not famous for his powers of persuasion. I think you've a deeper motive.'

Rufus laughed. 'Useless to hide anything from you, Robert – you detect the workings of my mind like fish in a limpid pool.' He glanced rapidly round the room, empty save for fitzHamon, Meulan and myself. 'This must go no further. With Curthose gone from Normandy the old anarchy will rule again within a month. He'll leave Odo as his chancellor and regent – how can Bayeux cope with men like Robert of Belesme? How can anyone, come to that?'

fitzHamon looked perplexed. 'True enough. Yet I see no quick advantage in a Normandy torn by strife.'

'Not quick, Robert, not quick. We shall let the stew simmer awhile. And then —'

Meulan snapped his fingers. 'Of course! The treaty! You're pledged to help the duke against his vassals!'

Rufus nodded. 'Just so. To fulfil my oath I shall lawfully bring an army across the sea. Already I've got a quarter of Robert's duchy. Who knows what the next – strictly legal – invasion may win?'

Meulan smiled coldly. 'You keep me as an adviser, giving you the benefit of twenty years' experience in affairs of state. You need little instruction from me, my lord!'

'I'm learning.' Rufus sauntered to a window, gazed absently across Theobald's arbour. Sunlight wove a halo around his head. Wagon wheels rumbled distantly on Caen's cobbled streets. Rufus said musingly, 'There may be a sharp reaction from Philip of France.'

I uttered the thought that troubled me, the matter close to my heart. 'Prince Henry, my lord. What is your purpose in taking him to England?'

Rufus swung round. 'Henry? You touch a tender spot, Walter – an ulcer on my conscience. Henry is in for a shock. He thinks he's going to England to take seisin of our mother's lands – lands I've already granted to fitzHamon.'

I pictured the effect this duplicity would have on the vengeful man who sought England's throne, who I believed would commit any crime to gain his ends; and stared in horror.

Rufus spread his hands.

'What could I do? We've already seized Henry's demesnes in Normandy, and barred him from succession.' His voice hardened. 'You heard his claim at the council. Aetheling! Do you think I'd allow him a fief in England?'

I went as near as I dared to enlighten Rufus. 'The prince may seek revenge for this . . . trickery.'

'He can't. He's without influence or friends. Anyway,' he continued, a slight discomfort in his tone, 'all English land is mine by right; and I never confirmed his claim. I'll keep Henry at court and soothe his temper, find something to smooth his ruffled feathers. A friendly lad at heart: he's always on my side. Remember that affair at Laigle when we were boys?'

I remembered. Life was different then, Duke William still alive and England and Normandy one. Rufus still regarded Henry as the child who fought beside him at the top of a ladder. Would he never learn? At least I could protect him in England.

'Do you wish to embark my archers when we leave?'

'I don't want you in England, Walter – not yet.'

I gaped. 'Not . . . I don't understand, my lord. I'm in your household. How have I offended?'

'You haven't.' Rufus laid an arm across my shoulders. 'Walter, I must leave somebody in Normandy whom I can trust absolutely. Aumale, Eu, Gournai and the rest have sworn fealty – and will break their vows like sapless twigs whenever they find advantage.' fitzHamon looked offended; Meulan pursed his lips. Rufus laughed in their faces. 'Not you, my friends – I've seen to that. I keep you in .my council under my eye!' He squeezed my arm. 'Tirel, will you stay?'

A king's wish was an edict. So much for my schemes for guarding Rufus. I said dejectedly, 'What use can I be, my lord?'

'Abundant use. Your fiefs are in France, King Philip your overlord. You attend Philip's councils at Pentecost and Easter when he wears his crown in Paris, and listen to the gossip of his court. Philip, I believe, begins to realize my designs and may stir himself to action. He'll bear watching.'

'I am to spy upon my suzerain?' I said acidly.

Rufus dropped his arm from my shoulder, stumped to the window, plucked a rose that nodded in the casement and broodingly stripped the petals. He growled, 'Forget what I said. I ask nobody to smudge his honour.'

'You will do the king valuable service, my lord,' Meulan assured me seriously.

'Poix is near the Norman march,' fitzHamon added, 'Aumale's donjon barely four leagues distant. I respect your scruples but' – a smile lighted the hawklike face – 'you owe no obligation to our Norman lords. Surely you can gather knowledge of their doings – priests' tales and pedlars' tattle, news gleaned from wandering knights – which a trusty messenger may bring to England? We employ agents, of course, everywhere in Normandy and Maine.' He made a dismissive gesture. 'Low-born hirelings, inaccurate and unreliable. We need intelligence which is swift and true.'

The 'we' was significant: these three, between them, had discussed and decided my future. Absently I drew my sword a thumb's-breadth from the scabbard, fingered the hilt and tapped it home. I could refuse – and lose Rufus, the man I loved, the paladin I revered, the king who had rescued me from living death. Return to peaceful Poix and tend my vines, ride the fields and inspect the crops, hunt and fly my hawks? I had listened to councils of state and had dabbled briefly on the fringes of great affairs. Revert to a petty baron's existence, sinking into sloth and growing fat? The prospect stretched before me like a vista of eternity.

Drearily I assented. Rufus turned from the window, strode across the room and clasped my hand. Like a shock of the nerves I sensed again his scarcely controlled energy, a force on the edge of balance. He smiled broadly.

'This, Walter, I promise you'll never regret!'

God has not granted mortals the power to know the future. It is as well.

Chapter 2

1091–92

THE journey was uneventful; I rode unarmed. But near La Ferté I saw smoke on the horizon, grey-blue clouds from burning crops, and darker, sooty spirals which climbed from burning houses. I took hauberk, helmet and shield from a rouncey's panniers; Berenger helped me arm. Buildings and fields on fire signified a harrying, a raiding party loose; and one could not take chances.

Rufus had sailed a bare ten days before; and already the bonds of peace were wearing thin.

I crossed the French march and on an afternoon languorous with heat saw Poix cradled in her hills like a diadem in soft green velvet. I reined on the crest and surveyed the scene below, yellow cornfields ripening to harvest, vineyards striped dark green, a rivulet's silver ribbon curving through meadows speckled by grazing cattle. There was a church, and clustered rooftops dominated by a castle whose moat the streamlet fed.

Forty months had gone since I last saw Poix.

I had purposely sent no warning of my coming, and watched with interest the effect of our spears on the hillcrest. A sentry's warning, muted by distance, echoed across the vale. Huts and barracks in the ward erupted men who fled to battle stations, arming as they ran; sergeants by the drawbridge waited to turn the windlass. Like insects stirred by a stick serfs scurried from the fields, vanished among the houses, emerged again at the castle gate and jostled into the ward. A troop of horsemen burst from the gate, thundered over the draw-bridge and vanished into woodlands which mantled the opposite hillside. (I scratched my nose beneath the nasal – this was something new.) The drawbridge lifted, slammed on the lintel.

Before a priest could gabble a mass Poix was ready for war.

I remembered how, twelve years before, with only five companions — one a woman — I had surprised and taken Poix. My liegemen had learned the lesson.

231

We descended the slope towards the town. Half-way down I heard a shout; an arrow whispered past my head. Horsemen engraved the sky along the hillcrest we had left, a widely extended line, bowstrings flexed and arrows nocked. Again I heard the shout, and recognized the voice.

'Richer!' I bellowed. 'Richer! Ease your strings! It is I – Walter of Poix!'

A rider advanced cautiously down the hillside. He carried no bow, and guided his horse one-handed. I tugged my helmet off to show my face. He rapped a command; the archers' strings relaxed, arrows vanished into quivers. I looked at the thin brown face, the amber eyes spaced widely beside the nasal.

Richer the Saracen, my vassal and friend, companion in peace and war – once a bowman beyond compare.

No longer. His right shoulder was distorted, lumpy under the mail, the arm withered and strapped to his body. Never again would he draw a bow. I gripped the rein hand, which still remained to him.

'Why didn't you send outriders to herald your arrival?' he asked reproachfully. 'You were all but dead, my lord. If I'd not recognized your haubergeons —'

I blessed the chain-mesh my bowmen wore, still unique at that time among Christian armies. 'I thought to test your readiness. A mistake — you are much too alert. But this —' I indicated the men behind him — 'I saw you go from the ward and ride from the woods. The castle's defenders cut by half. Surely unwise?'

'Unprofitable to confine horsed bowmen behind walls. Better a quick sortie to catch the enemy unaware.' Richer smiled a little. 'As you were caught, my lord.'

We rode into the town and threaded deserted streets; frightened faces peered from windows, carts stood unattended, oxen in the shafts; swine rooted in the gutters, cattle wandered loose – all the signs of panic flight to safety in the castle. Richer went to the edge of the moat and called. The drawbridge rattled down and thudded into place. I dismounted in the ward, gave my horse to Berenger and greeted Poix's castellan: Delis of Carenci, a lanky, bony man, skin stretched tight on cheeks and temples, sleepy, slate-grey eyes.

He said, 'Welcome, my lord. It is fitting, I suppose, that you should cause the first alarm in Poix since you departed!'

He filled a beaker. I sat on a mounting block and sipped the wine, pressed from my own vines – a sweet, heady vintage resembling

Auvergne – and looked contentedly around. Horses whickered in the stables, nipping playfully the men who rubbed them down. Women emerged from barrack huts where they sheltered during the alarm – kitchen maids and washerwomen, sergeants' wives and doxies, and those who fled from the town when the clarion called. Men-at-arms relieved from battle stations strolled across the ward, unlacing haubergeons and helmets. Old soldiers paused expectantly, hoping for recognition: I lifted a hand and hailed them. 'Ha, Gervase! How fares your wife – any more twins?' 'Manier, you've put on weight: that haubergeon's splitting the seams!' They laughed and crowded round me, exchanging badinage and gossip.

Delis eyed Berenger, holding my horse and listening, and snapped, 'Slide the irons up the leathers, clot, and loosen girths! Have you forgotten your duties?' Delis had license to chide my esquire – young Berenger was his son.

I said, 'The first alarm, Delis? Not a single raid?'

'One only, hardly worth the name. Roving mercenaries dismissed from Duke Robert's army when the English invasion failed. They looted a Beaurain steading; Richer chased and killed them all but three, and recovered the spoil.'

'Tut! He let three escape?'

'No. He brought the rascals back. I hanged them,' said Delis simply, 'as an example.'

'No trouble from Aumale, Ponthieu, Gerberoi?'

'None. Our neighbour lords remember Richer's bowmen, the carnage they wrought in Aumale's ranks. Like dogs nosing a hedge-hog, they've decided Poix's too prickly to attack.'

I sat in the sun and finished my wine, talking idly to Delis and Richer, absorbing the joy of coming home. Delis grew terse as the talk continued; he seemed somehow discomposed. Richer became distrait, and I wondered why: you could never tell, from his face, what Richer thought.

Delis said awkwardly, 'Your lady awaits you in the donjon, my lord.'

God's blood – Adelice! I had clean forgotten.

I rose quickly, called Berenger, crossed the ditch at the foot of the mound and climbed a ladder's rungs to the donjon's single entrance. Servants in the hall were re-stacking spears and bowstaves. Berenger unlaced my helmet. I stooped and extended my arms; he dragged the hauberk from my body by the sleeves. A house-woman brought a basin and I washed the dust of travel, donned a velvet

233

mantle which Berenger found in a press. Clean and decently attired, I climbed a stairway to the bower.

Adelice, an arm around our son, curtsied solemnly. 'Welcome home, my lord.'

I lifted her hands to my lips. Time had not changed her looks, for she possessed the kind of features which the years treat lightly: an oval face, skin pink and white, curved rosy mouth, plump chin and wide brown eyes – comely without being beautiful. We were seven years wed, a marriage of convenience, a political match Duke William had arranged to strengthen his ties with France. Adelice of Clare brought me Laingaham as dowry – and also, far less welcome, kinship to brother Gilbert, Prince Henry's crony.

Adelice said, 'Your son, my lord.'

Hugh knelt; I lifted him and looked into his eyes. I had left a toddler; this six-year-old already had lost his puppy-fat, his body was light and bony in my hands. His face was the face of Poix, a mirror of mine: black haired, black eyed, a beaky nose and ivory skin. Only the mouth, the soft full lips, betrayed the blood of Clare.

I kissed the boy and set him down. Adelice presented her ladies: Rohaise, a sister widowed in Duke Robert's wars; Godeleve, a niece on the Bienfaite side; and three others whom I have forgotten. I scratched my cheek, embarrassed. Not since boyhood in Rouen's Tower had I mingled with noble ladies – and then they ignored me totally. Later with Curthose in Maine I had met rollicking, buxom wenches who did not disdain to bed a young esquire – but definitely not high-born. No women, for obvious reasons, cluttered Rufus's court at Caen. After a lifetime in camps and castles it seemed I must polish my manners.

Adelice saw me bothered – always she could read me plain as a shepherd reads the weather in the sky – and dismissed them to the tiring room. I slapped Hugh's rump and sent him scampering, placed Adelice in a chair and sat on a faldstool at her feet.

'Tell me, lady, how have matters gone at Poix?'

She accounted her stewardship, the chatelaine's part in a castle: servants' peccadilloes, furniture repaired, tapestries re-stitched, salting meat for winter, pedlars' exorbitant prices, the musty flour from last year's harvest, the scandal of the concubine who lived with the village priest. I listened with half an ear, my thoughts wandering to Rouen, to Caen, to Rufus and his brothers over the sea. My contentment drained like wine from a ruptured cask; I felt restless, irritable, trapped. Passive as floating driftwood I had eddied into a backwater far from history's rushing river, to the haven of Poix's tranquillity and peace like a smothering blanket.

Abruptly I rose from the stool and stalked to the bedchamber, unbuckling my belt as I went. Adelice followed without a word.

I stripped her clothes and swived her on the bed. Her body responded to mine with a curious submissiveness, as though her mind observed her physical antics, disapproved, and resigned itself to an instinct beyond control. Carnality with Adelice, as I now remembered, was like chewing glutinous porridge: a meal entirely tasteless. I finished and rolled on my back; she pulled the wolfskin coverlet to her chin, smiled and stroked my hair.

'Since you left me, Walter, I have lived on rumours – rumours that often asserted I was widowed. I heard you were drowned at sea, lost in the vaults of Conches, tormented by Belesme. I've questioned Richer – he is not forthcoming. What is the truth, my lord?'

I described my part in Duke Robert's invasion; the shipwreck that set me in Prince Henry's power; Evreux's raid on Conches, my capture after the Battle of the Marsh, imprisonment and torture. Then King William's intervention which secured my release, and Mont St Michel's siege. I said nothing concerning the commitment that brought me back to Poix, nor anything of my nagging suspicions of Henry.

'The princes,' I finished, 'are now in England, and Normandy's turbulent barons are sharpening their swords.'

Adelice picked a honeyed grape from a platter beside the bed and popped it in her mouth.

'God be praised,' she said, 'we live in peaceful France.'

2

Summer dissolved in rain and wind; winter's gales stripped autumn's lingering leaves; frost rimed the ploughlands' ridges. I rode much abroad, visiting my fiefs at Beaurain and Carenci, Verton and Esquennes, inspecting donjons and testing the defences of small wooden castles which were garrisoned by a knight or two and a handful of men-at-arms. They would never withstand a determined onslaught, nor was this intended: they were outposts designed to hold for a while until Poix — the stone-built bastion of my Honour — could sally and smash the invader. So tranquil was this corner of France that since I defeated Aumale my demesnes had never been ravaged: a record exceptional in both Normandy and France.

I supervised the vineyards' pruning, conned the steward's tallies and counted silver in his coffers, flew my hawks and hunted – the wolves were fierce that winter – shot a stag or two and tried to beget a child. I suspected Adelice used herbs to prevent conception. One son was not enough; children died easily, and Hugh was yet a child; warfare thinned young knighthood's ranks; only a numerous brood would ensure my line continued. I rated Adelice severely, bade her abstain from meat, burn candles to Our Lady. She endured my scoldings, promised all I demanded, yielded her passive body to our nightly tourneys – and obstinately kept her belly slim as a withered wineskin.

Delis returned to Carenci. I kept three knights in the household: two landless younger sons, the third a dour warrior whose fief Belesme had ravished – dependable men, agreeable comrades in chase and carousal. Richer none the less discreetly commanded the garrison. He exercised the men-at-arms, kept weapons ground to hairline edge, shield-hides oiled and armour burnished. He ran a smithy in the ward where workmen he had trained forged the flexible chain-mesh mail his archers wore. At first attracted by their pliancy and lightness, my knights and men-at-arms had doubtfully tried his haubergeons, swore them far too fragile, and stubbornly retained their discs and rings. Not till Jerusalem's taking was chain mail accepted in Neustria.

I took Richer into my confidence over Rufus's behest. A Saracen untrammelled by knightly codes, he saw nothing wrong in spying on knights, whether they be kings or counts or barons. He dismissed contemptuously the notion of intelligence from pedlars and the like. 'Gossip you'll get, no more, worth not a clove of garlic. We ourselves can watch our neighbour lords. Otherwise you want astute men serving in the mesnies of more distant fiefs: Breteuil, Laigle, Mans. I have plenty among my archers.'

'You can hardly plant my liegemen in stranger households,' I objected.

'They'll appear as deserters seeking service. Barons will gladly receive men who know the secrets of mounted archery.'

'Who will pass on their skills, and train bowmen to rival our own.

You've forged a transcendent weapon, the main reason for Poix's immunity. Why throw away the advantage?'

'Without Moorish horses,' Richer explained patiently, 'none may learn the art. Can you shoot from a lumbering destrier, or guide a Frankish palfrey without reins?'

You could not. Richer, the best horseman that ever I knew, had tried and failed. Therefore he had brought from Spain those light-boned, handy horses which Saracens use in war, which can stop and turn on a denier; and kept a breeding stud beyond the township's pale.

I said, 'You'll lose skilled men.'

'A dozen or so. I'll train others – and those we send can be quickly recalled at need. They'll remain your lieges, my lord, whoever they serve.'

I assented dubiously. Richer picked his agents, instructed them carefully and sent them to faraway fiefs. One vanished – possibly a brigands' victim – three returned, rejected by the lords whose services they sought; the rest sent information from baronies in Normandy and Maine, cryptic messages dictated to clerks and carried by pedlars. They revealed nothing startling. Hugh of Este sold Maine to Helias of La Flèche for ten thousand silver solidi; Helias maintained the county's independence. Bertrada, Countess of Anjou – Fulk's third wife – was tiring of her husband and enticing Philip of France. (Mere scandal, this; but it aroused my interest: Bertrada, by birth a Montfort, was Isabel of Conches's sister, that Isabel whom once I loved.) I forwarded these bits of news by mounted messengers to St Valeri. Whether they were valuable to Rufus I could not judge: I was simply performing a task he set.

The Scottish war, we learned, had gone as Rufus planned: after indecisive skirmishes the armies met at the Firth of Forth – whatever that may be – and Curthose, helped by Rufus's silver, extracted Malcolm's homage, his son as a hostage, and withdrawal to his own wild country. Of the Welsh wars I heard nothing; presumably the marcher lords had stemmed the tide. In London a tempest blew down seven churches and six hundred houses. Duke Robert returned to Normandy at Christmas.

Prince Henry was staying in England. I passed a sleepless night.

At Christmas I travelled to Paris, heard mass in Our Lady's church, attended the Great Council where the king wore his crown in state, and the four-days-long festivities that followed. The Countess of

Anjou was there, Count Fulk a sulky escort. Philip appeared moon-struck, unable to tear his eyes from Bertrada's lovely face, a face beautiful enough to enchant a king from his throne – as indeed in the end it did. Dark, slanting eyes, high cheekbones, wide curving mouth. A pain I believed forgotten stabbed like a twisting knife: she was Isabel of Conches in a softer, more voluptuous way.

Sternly I crushed my memories, and concentrated on my venison – rather tough – and bade Berenger fill my cup.

3

The remembrance lingered, persistent as a melody half forgotten. That, and other things, combined to prick me like a goaded ox until I made a decision which, on looking back, was certainly ill-judged. In vindication I can say only this: I was thirty years old, my life by normal odds three-quarters done, confined in sleepy Poix, remote from great affairs as a cloistered monk. I yearned for a part in a kingdom's ruling, for a finger in the pie that Rufus cooked: the reunion of Duke William's empire. I feared Henry, lurking like a viper poised to strike, and felt frustrated by my ignorance of his schemes. These worries nagged in the background and curdled my contentment.

In the foreground, the sight of Richer's crippled arm, and the fetter-scars banding my wrists and legs recalled a debt unpaid. Ralph of Conches had departed unscathed from burning Carenci's stead-ings; in Ralph's donjon Richer was maimed, we both suffered anguish and were left to die.

Honour demanded requital. I had done no fighting for months – and castle life in winter was abysmally monotonous.

I began, beyond all reason, to dream of Isabel, the woman I once loved and loved no longer. Certainly I loathed her: she had done her best to kill me, slowly and most painfully. I awoke from these dreams in a sweat; one night, half drowned in sleep, I called her name. Adelice stirred beside me, and touched my cheek. She knew much about Isabel of Conches, but said nothing; and presently I slept.

I have stated my excuses, and flimsy enough they are. The con-sequence remains. On a bitter February morning when frost bound the earth like stone I called Richer to the hall. I held my hands to the hearth-fire, staring into the flames, and said quietly, 'Directly the weather eases we lead a conroy to Conches.'

Richer said imperturbably, 'For what purpose, my lord?'

My eyes rested a moment on his crooked shoulder. I said, 'You could guess. We have an account to settle.'

Richer touched his arm. 'This is nothing – a casualty of war. You can't risk your fortunes to revenge a vassal's wounds.'

Even to Richer I was disinclined to explain my motives, which I did not fully understand myself. 'There will be no argument, my friend. We shall go to Conches and harry the land and speedily retreat. A quick in-and-out raid. The castle is beyond our grasp – we're not equipped for leaguers. Now let's make our plans.'

I called a varlet and filled a cup: useless to offer Richer wine – some quirk of his religion.

I said, 'The Honour owes twelve knights; we'll take ten, and our household knights. Thirteen in all. The fiefs can raise twenty men-at-arms; there are forty here and ten mounted sergeants. And all the fifty bowmen of your troop.'

Richer did mental sums. 'A hundred and thirty men. A powerful force, my lord. You'll leave Poix's demesnes defenceless?'

'Why not? Nobody threatens us; and we'll be gone for a fortnight or less.'

Richer nursed his arm – I wondered briefly how much pain his impassive demeanour concealed. 'Remember rounceys and ration carts, servitors and sutlers. You'll have two hundred men on the road all told.'

'So? A scantling. Belesme can put two thousand in the field.'

'You'll be traversing France during the close season for campaigning – and you'll not go unremarked. Every fief you cross will be alarmed, and news will travel ahead. Conches will be warned and waiting.'

I swallowed wine impatiently; Richer was in a carping mood. 'I see no alternative. What do you suggest?'

'Achères.'

I put down the cup and gazed at him, bemused. In return for my service at Gerberoi King Philip had given me seisin of Achères on the Seine, a petty fief that owed two knights. I saw the revenues accounted and took no further interest in the place.

'Achères,' he continued, 'is four days' march from Poix, three from Conches. Slow – but you're taking infantry and carts. Keep

239

your movements secret to the last, and make Achères your base for the leap on Conches.'

'You mean – send the conroys there in driblets over several days, a dozen men or so at a time, so they don't attract attention?'

'Exactly, my lord. And thence, untrammelled by baggage, you force a two days' march to Conches.'

Lucky I had the Saracen as friend: a soldier who could think as well as fight. I remembered his fighting days were done, and said, 'A pity you won't see the enterprise you've planned. We must put affairs in hand, organize small companies to march at two days' interval. Appoint bannerets for each. Summon Beaurain's lord, Carenci and the rest, and give them orders. Collect grain and fodder, requisition carts. Warn the castellan at Achères. Where's that priest? – tell him to bring quill and parchment!'

The fire was hot; I moved my chair away and opened my cloak. Preparing for war is more complicated than war itself – which the monks who scribble chronicles that describe huge armies marching seem always to forget.

4

I left last, leading a small constabular: all the footmen had already gone. We followed mostly those byways and forest tracks which I had learnt during my wanderings with Curthose. Yet we did not go unnoticed; continuous little parties moving in one direction during a season when travellers stayed at home were bound to arouse curiosity among suspicious barons. Near Gerberoi I encountered Helias abroad with a numerous mesnie: he loudly acclaimed a fortuitous meeting, politely escorted me across his seigniories and bade a sardonic farewell. Chaumont's lord Odmund-le-Vieux happened to be hunting in the woodlands where I followed a hidden track; his greeting was perfectly courteous, and he accompanied me for several hours lest I lose the way, explaining his thirty men-at-arms a precaution against brigands. I took consolation from the thought that a fortnight's wait in Achères would let speculation fade.

Achères' wooden donjon, a petty castle set to guard a ford, crowned a craggy promontory overlooking the Seine. Soldiers crammed the ward to bursting; tents and carts and horse-lines overflowed on fields surrounding the tiny village. It was fortunately a lonely place, a woodland curtain lapping closely round the clearing where the first warm winds of spring thawed pastureland and plough. I organized the last fast march to Conches, shedding carts and sutlers. On the second Sunday in Lent I started.

I knew the byways as a vixen knows her runs: tracks barely passable in single file, lost among briars and thorns – after leaving Bréval we scarcely saw the sky. By evening we forded the Eure and at nightfall camped deep in the forests beyond Ivri. This could be dangerous ground: Ascelin Goel, a short-tempered knight, was intolerant of strangers on his marches. The company I led could match any muster of Ascelin's – a merciless marauder, Ivri a robbers' eyrie – but a brawl would blazon my presence, the last thing I desired.

The footmen were exhausted, for we had come far and fast; stragglers trailed into camp throughout the night. We lighted no fires, supped on barley cakes and puddle water, posted sentries and slept in scattered groups among the trees.

At dawn we saddled up and laced our hauberks. The chosen targets for my raid, Monci and Medavi, were Conches's outermost hamlets, each guarded by a castle. Half my force I led against Medavi, the other marched on Monci under Delis of Carenci: simultaneous attacks designed to cause confusion and disperse retaliation. While Berenger's nimble fingers buckled my ventail – I remembered fleetingly my clumsy, beloved Vauquelin – I said to Delis, 'We separate when we leave the forest. You know your route?'

His destrier, brisked by an icy dawn-wind, bucked and tried to rear. Delis gentled him and answered, 'Certain. Four hours' march. We'll be there before terce.'

'A quick killing, remember. Burn, destroy and go. Don't let the men waste time on pillage. Leave the castle alone: Monci's single knight and ten men-at-arms won't worry you. If there's no pursuit we meet again here; otherwise make straight for Achères on your own.'

Delis lifted his lance in salute, and departed among the tree-trunks to find his conroy. An hour's marching brought us from the forest. I followed the track that led to Medavi, saw Delis's column veer to the left and disappear in morning mist. I led twelve knights and sergeants, twenty mounted bowmen and thirty men-at-arms. The horses moved at a stretching walk, as fast as the footmen could go.

Sunrise gilded the mist; the clammy skeins began to shred and lift, climbed in gossamer whorls, vanished in clear blue sky. We marched across open heathland. I felt exposed, sent outriders ahead and dropped a file to watch our rear. The vanguard flushed a sounder of boar; grey lumbering shapes fled over the track; and sternly I checked the knights who lifted lances. You cannot mix sport and war.

The sun climbed above the trees and warmed the riders' hands (the footmen were already sweating hard). A mavis sang a harmony to the music of our marching: creaking leather, the metallic slither of mail, the horses' jingling bridles. The vanguard caught a goatherd, a tattered creature cowering in a copse. I looked at the sergeant who held him and touched my throat: we were near Medavi, and could not afford forewarning.

The sergeant heaved the body behind a bush.

The track pierced straggling pinewoods and topped a long low ridge; beyond the hummock lay Medavi. I halted the column, rode to the spinney's edge, fallen needles deadening my hoofbeats. The village sprawled below, mud-walled hovels, a timber church, a gap-toothed palisade. The castle's wooden donjon jutted like a thick brown thumb. Cattle dotted the pastures, springtime's barley shaded the ploughland's green, and vineyards climbed a rocky slope. Quietly I summoned Fulcher of Beaurain and the sergeant Engelger who led the men-at-arms.

I pointed. 'You know what you have to do. Make sure of the granary, that reed-thatched barn by the church. Off you go.'

The knights left the spinney's margin, extended in line, cantered towards the village. Footmen descended the hillside at a run. Archers sped to positions on the arena's outer fringes and encircled Medavi's demesnes. With Berenger and a trumpeter I stayed on the ridge and watched.

In harrying a fief you hurt the enemy where it matters most – his coffers. Every landholding lord depends on revenues from his fiefs to feed his mesnie, pay his followers, keep what state he may. Destroy his crops and stock and villeins and his income for the year is gone. If the foray yielded loot so much the better – but only men like Ascelin Goel habitually harried for gain. I had no thought of plunder: we were too far from our base to carry off cattle and corn.

Medavi was carelessly guarded: my knights reached the nearest houses before the donjon's sentry collected his wits. Then a gong was beaten frenziedly and the gates of the ward were closed; spears twinkled on the ramparts. Herluin of Medavi would count the opposition before making a sally – a castellan's normal practice. I

242

reckoned on Herluin, his calculations done, staying prudently inside his fort – he was outnumbered five to one.

And so it proved: helplessly he saw his charge destroyed. The knights galloped between the houses, quartered yards and orchards, speared everyone they met. Men and women and children scurried from their hovels, ran to the fields, the church, dived into houses again like conies into burrows, anywhere to evade the plunging lances. The knights flushed women from the corners where they hid, rode infants into the mud. The footmen followed fast; the torches which they bore trailed smoky plumes; fires caught and crackled on the eaves, leapt in ravening tongues from house to house. The villagers fled from the flames to the fields; a woman burning like a torch reeled screaming over the pastures Knights remorselessly pursued, the bowmen barred escape. Corpses speckled the fields like crushed and trampled flowers.

I glanced at the sun, hazed by Medavi's pall, and said to Berenger, 'Nearing noon. Ride down: tell Fulcher and Engelger to deal with the vines and cattle.'

Berenger vanished in the smoke. Men-at-arms trudged to the vineyards, worked down the rows and slashed the stems; knights rounded up cattle and sheep, drew swords and slaughtered like butchers. The swine escaped to the woods: nimble-footed beasts and hard to catch. They and the horrified garrison, watching from the castle, were the only creatures alive I left in Medavi.

Richer was in part avenged.

I surveyed the carnage in the fields, the smoky pillar coiling to the sky, a beacon to warn the world. I judged it time to go – and saw a bowman on a lathered horse galloping the track from Monci. He reined in a scatter of pebbles.

'A constabular – about forty – riding fast. They're on my heels, my lord!'

I told the trumpeter to sound Recall. The horsemen gathered quickly, sword-blades clotted and hauberks streaked. The men-at-arms were slower, stumbling over ploughland. Lanceheads glittered on the Monci road. I cursed, and said to the blue-jowled rascal who led the archers, 'Pigot, go and harass them, delay them till we're mustered!'

Pigot shaded his eyes, stared hard at the distant riders. His lips parted in a grin, disclosing broken teeth. 'I don't think, my lord, that Lord Delis would welcome our arrows. He rides in the van – I can see the bull's-head blazon on his shield.'

I did not dispute his verdict – a master bowman's sight is keener than a hawk's. The column of knights and bowmen cantered up the slope. Delis smiled a greeting. 'Why have you disobeyed orders?' I blared. 'You should be on the road to Ivri! And what's happened to your footmen?'

'Safe enough,' Delis drawled. 'They left Monci an hour since and are well away. The village is burned. I come to tell you a constabular from Conches is riding here.'

'How do you know?'

'I left scouts to watch all roads from Conches. They reported thirty horsemen – knights and mounted sergeants – riding the Medavi track.' Delis slipped the lance shaft through his hand and examined the blood-caked pennon. 'I thought,' he added lazily, 'our forces might combine to rap their knuckles.'

A hundred against thirty. Worthwhile odds. Hastily I gathered my men in the pinewood and formed line of battle, knights in the centre, archers on the flanks. Behind them, riding palfreys, scantily armed with dirks and targes, a group of esquires waited to support their lords in combat, to drag them from the fighting were they wounded, re-mount them if unhorsed. Berenger's first battle – his face looked white and anxious. I recalled my blooding long ago, the sickening qualms, and grinned encouragement. He licked his lips, and tried to smile.

Hidden among the trees, the smoke from Medavi's pyre stinging our eyes, we lurked in ambuscade.

5

At a raking gallop the constabular burst from a thicket which masked the road, and rippled down the track that led to the fields. Delis enarmed his shield. 'Impetuous fellows,' he murmured. 'If they've galloped all the way from Conches their horses must be blown!'

I waited till the leaders left the ruined vineyard and started to cross the ploughland.

'Ride wide, Pigot! Go!'

The archers stormed from the flanks like curving menacing horns. Two bowshots from the enemy they dropped knotted reins on pommels, whipped arrows from quivers and nocked the strings. I heard warning shouts from Conches's knights, saw the column jostle to a halt, hooves slithering on stones, horses rearing and colliding. They swung on their hocks to meet the threat and formed a shaky line.

Then the tempest scourged them.

The horses suffered most, because bowmen trained by Richer avoided useless shots at arrow-proof shields and hauberks. Within an eyelid's blink the destriers sprouted barbs like feathered stickpins. They tumbled to their knees, or shied and tried to turn. A knight swung his horse and fled.

The archers swerved aside, shooting as they went, and left the enemy's ranks a splayed and tangled mess. The battleground was open for a charge. I checked my ventail strap, enarmed shield and hefted lance. My destrier plunged at the bit; I rammed in spurs and gave him his head.

An armoured avalanche swept headlong from the ridge.

Two hundred paces to ride. Our quarry gathered in a bunch, stumbling on fallen destriers, faltered into line and rode to meet us.

A hundred paces.

Thorn scrub gobbetted the ground, horses jinked and yawed, gaps opened in the line. Pennons snapped like whip-cracks in the tempest of our speed. The fleeter destriers drew ahead; Delis, twirling his lance, galloped level with my girths. 'Steady!' I shouted. 'Steady! Keep in line!' I could have saved my breath: charging knights brook no control. Delis laughed, closed his legs and forged in front.

Fifty paces.

The lances levelled. Conches's ragged ranks had raised a shambling gallop. I chose a knight on a chestnut stallion and swerved my horse on the line. Behind his destrier's nostrils I saw only a pointed helmet, painted green, a long shield lifted nasal high, a lance-head swooping at my throat. I straightened my legs in the stirrups, thrust spine against cantle and braced for the shock.

His point hit me on the helmet and tore it from my head. My lance shaft jarred and splintered. The impact wrenched me in the saddle, stabbed pain from wrist to shoulder. Meteors careered crazily across a sky that was suddenly black. The smell of sodden earth, grass prickling my face, a clanging in my eardrums. I grappled my reeling senses, set palms beneath my shoulders, heaved painfully to hands and knees. Hoofbeats thumped around me, a foreleg struck my thigh. The shouts and clashing of steel rang like noises heard through fog.

Unhorsed, I decided numbly. Up, Walter – the ground is no place in battle. I struggled to my feet, groped for my sword. The helmet hung on my back, half severed from the coif. I tried to set it on my head; my hand refused to obey. The shield dangled from the guige, I thrust forearm through the enarmes. Berenger's voice, muted, like a whisper from far away, his arm around my waist. Good lad, I thought dimly: a little late – now lead me from the shambles. I looked for my destrier, and saw instead a green-helmeted knight who tottered towards me sword in hand. Much too late, Berenger: you can't help me now. Feebly I pushed the boy aside – esquires do not fight knights – and strove to banish the mist that clouded my sight.

I drew my blade and fronted my shield. The sword weighed heavy as an oak branch, the ground rocked like a storm-tossed deck. The knight advanced to sword-length, lifted a wavering blade. The point shuddered and dropped; he uttered a noise like a croak.

'Tirel!'

I could not identify his face, masked by nasal, coif and ventail. I did not recall his blazon, a feathered dragon on a shield scored deeply by my lance. No matter – he meant to kill me: I had better take advantage of the opening he had left. I lunged for his ribs.

The thrust was weak as a kitten's dab: he warded on the forte, and disengaged. His blade descended on my shield rim, brushing my naked head. The cut glissaded harmlessly, no strength behind it. He was, I concluded thankfully, as paralysed as I. I feinted at his throat.

The fighting raged around us; we fought like men in a dream, bartering puny blows like insects trapped in honey. A riderless destrier knocked my enemy flat; I rested on the quillons while he clambered to his feet. Then, before his guard was up, I lifted the last of my strength and slammed him on the coif – a flat-bladed swipe, the hilt twisting in sweaty fingers. He grunted and dropped on his back.

I straddled his body, rested my point on his throat. His eyes looked into mine, dark and unafraid. He said, 'I yield, Tirel.'

'Who are you, my lord?'

He rolled his head from side to side. I bent and roughly wrenched the helmet off, stared stupidly at the mud-stained face. Icy talons squeezed my heart.

Delis, panting, reined beside me. 'All over,' he puffed. 'They've run. Left seven dead or wounded and ten prisoners – four of them knights. Might get a few deniers' ransom.'

I said nothing.

He peered at me, concerned. 'Are you hurt, my lord? I saw you fall, but couldn't help – someone was trying to cut my head off.' He looked indifferently at the figure sprawled at my feet. 'Who have you there?'

'Isabel,' I answered shakily. 'Lady Isabel of Conches.'

6

During the return to Achères I did not speak to her once. My head throbbed wickedly and I could not think. Old wounds were bleeding anew, old memories of pain and torture, humiliation of body and mind, the anguish Belesme had inflicted and Isabel condoned. I rode in the van, alone, unhelmeted to ease the ache, and spoke only to give such orders as were due. Berenger trotted at my destrier's quarters, watching me anxiously: I snapped when he tried to help. Delis chewed his lip and left me alone, casting occasional thoughtful looks at Isabel riding behind. Her face was pale – that silken suntanned skin that I remembered! – but she seemed unhurt. She rode a palfrey – the chestnut stallion had bolted – and talked unconcernedly with the guardian knights on either side, whose awed and deferent manner roused my silent fury. Every knight in Neustria admired Isabel; all knew she rode in armour when her vassals took the field, and fought like a maddened she-wolf in the clash of battle.

You've done it once too often, you bitch – and now what shall I do with you?

Ascelin Goel awaited us when we forded the Eure near Ivri. The need for secrecy was past, and I was in no mood to endure his tantrums. I bade archers string their bows and ride ahead; the lances followed. Ascelin counted heads, regarded his paltry retinue. A scowl contorted the lumpy features and pitted, greasy skin; his eyebrows twitched. He sent me an angry glare, and drew aside.

At vespers on the second day we reached Achères. I confined Isabel in the donjon, and found a slattern to attend her.

The conroys rested a day; then took the road to Poix. The sooner they went the better: an Honour stripped of its fighting men was always a temptation. Moreover, I expected Ralph to pursue his captive lady. I told Delis to be watchful and to warn Gerberoi in passing – Helias would always help me against Norman raids. The prisoner knights I freed on parole, demanding reasonable ransoms: they were landless, hired men. I gained six stalwart sergeants, taken on the field and given the summary choice of a slitted throat or service under my banner. There's no ransom for men-at-arms; a losing battle brings them either death or a change of lord.

I kept a dozen archers, and stayed in Achères.

The castle, as I have said, is small, the two-storied wooden donjon primitive and rude. Siege rations filled the ground floor store room: musty-smelling corn sacks, wine casks, salted meat, shield hides, spears and bowstaves. The upper floor, twelve paces square, comprised bedchamber and hall divided by a leather curtain. A trap in the ceiling – which functioned as a smoke hole – gave access by a ladder to the topmost floor, the donjon's battlemented fighting platform, itself shielded from the elements by a shingled roof. My castellan Baldwin of Achères vacated the donjon when Isabel arrived, and shifted quarters to an armoury in the ward.

When the conroys departed I told Berenger to take my baggage to the donjon. He dropped the helmet he was scouring, and stared round-eyed.

'But...' he stuttered. 'The Lady Isabel!'

Berenger had Delis's bony features and smooth, unblemished skin; his mother contributed a carrot-red tousled mop. A willing boy, skilled in the care of armour – Delis had trained him well – gangling as a puppy which cannot control its limbs, sometimes a little pert. I cuffed him lightly and said, 'Do as you're told – now!'

He called a servant; together they bore my baggage up the mound, climbed the ladder and disappeared inside the donjon. I heard voices raised in altercation. The servant tumbled down the ladder; then palliasse and panniers hurtled through the door; lastly Berenger, face fiery as his hair and swearing like a soldier.

I waited, grimly amused. Berenger shambled from the mound and said, 'The escalade failed, my lord.' He rubbed his neck ruefully. 'The enemy wields a strong right arm!'

'Well, let's see if a second assault will carry.' I picked up a plaited leather quirt, the sort that huntsmen use, and walked to the donjon. Berenger, gaping, watched me go.

I paused on the threshold. Sunlight filtering through the door revealed a squalid chamber, Baldwin's erstwhile residence – not a fastidious man. Gnawed bones from ancient meals nestled in dusty rushes on the floor. Chairs and three-legged stools nudged a wine-stained table, weapons and rusty haubergeons adorned rough oak-trunk walls. The bedchamber's leather curtain was torn and cracked; sacking draped the privy-vent. The place smelt stale and sour, old food, ordure and dirty clothing mingling in miasma. A suitable dwelling, I thought pleasurably, for Isabel of Conches.

She was seated in a chair, erect and tense, breathing quickly. A flush stained the prominent cheekbones, her eyes snapped fire. I surveyed her silently, idly swinging the whip, examining the coarse cary-cloth robe and cowhide shoes the woman had brought her, the glossy hair which fell unbound to her shoulders. I jutted my chin at the drab who cowered in a corner.

'Out!'

She fled from the room. Isabel said distantly, 'You send servants to invade this pigsty, then dismiss my woman. Your own presence is an insult worse than either.'

'Lady,' I said mildly, 'your predicament does not permit insolence.'

'Boorishness warrants rebuff. Why do you hold me thus? I offer ransom and parole according to knighthood's codes.'

'Do you believe,' I asked, 'I would accept a woman's promise? I am not so stupid. Ransom . . . possibly. How much do you offer?'

'A thousand pounds of silver.'

I shook my head sorrowfully. 'Such modesty becomes you but . . . you belittle your worth, my lady.'

'Must we chaffer like hucksters? What do you demand?'

'Five thousand pounds.'

Isabel stared. 'I am not the King of England! Impossible! The sum is thrice a decade of Conches's revenues!'

'Then,' I sighed, 'it seems you must remain here as my guest. A sordid dwelling, I admit – likely to become more cramped when I make my quarters here.'

'You will not —!'

'Why not, lady? The castle is mine.'

'Christ's blood!' Isabel clenched her teeth. 'Have you no courtesy, Tirel? Are you all mean-born peasant? This I shall not endure!'

I said gently, 'I endured worse – far worse – when you held me captive, lady. I was fettered. You are free. I was starved. You shall be fed. I lived in darkness. You may see the sun. I was tormented. You —'

'Ah, yes,' Isabel interrupted. A sneer twisted her mouth. 'Your Saracen – does he still wear Belesme's playful scars?'

Anger clawed my throat like fangs, bile soured my tongue.

'For that offence,' I whispered, 'I have sought requital. Now it is found.'

I stepped quickly round the table and seized her by the hair. Isabel turned her head and sank her teeth in my arm. I wrenched her from the chair, flung her face-down on the rushes.

The whip tore the flimsy robe and ripped her flesh. She cradled head in arms, fingers clutching nape. My arm rose and fell. Blood bubbled from the welts. She began screaming, and her body writhed. A battlement sentry's frightened face peered through the ceiling trap and hastily withdrew. I did not pause. I lashed her garments from her body, cut her back in strips. She ceased moaning and lay still.

I ran the quirt through my fingers, flicked blood on the floor, went heavily from the donjon, found the woman and curtly bade her attend her mistress. Berenger waited, eyes popping in a corpse-white face. Roughly I told him to find linen and bind my arm. 'Wash the wound well – it may be poisoned. A bitch-wolf's teeth.' He glanced at my face, averted his eyes and busied himself with the wrapping. His hands shook. I said, 'Prepare my quarters in the donjon. Take salves and linen also, then come away.'

I walked across the ward, found a quiet place concealed behind a stable, and vomited.

7

Isabel lay for days on her bed, and never spoke. The drab – reputedly a witch – succoured her tenderly, bathing and anointing the weals, swathing her body in linen. Certainly the woman was skilled in healing, and concocted soothing draughts from herbs gathered in the woods. I gave her silver, and promised a gallows if she failed.

I slept on a pallet beside Isabel's bed, the woman curled in a corner. Isabel seemed oblivious of my presence; she was turned within herself and nursed her pain. By day she gave no outward sign of anguish; at night I heard her weeping in the dark.

I lived mostly in the ward or on the battlements, staring morosely over the river. Springtime's emerald brilliance dusted the trees, birds shouted in the woods, the ploughs were out on Achères' starveling fields. I had no eyes for summer's heralds. The indolent Baldwin felt my forceful hand: I recalled the scanty garrison from the steadings where they lived, kept them stationed in the castle, posted double sentries and sent patrols across the river. I did not fear Ralph's reaction to Isabel's capture – nature had made Achères virtually impregnable – but one need not be taken unawares.

On the fourteenth day, roused by Berenger in the darkness before dawn, I saw in the candlelight that Isabel was watching. I shrugged into a tunic the esquire held, laced the points of my breeches and said, 'Are you recovered, my lady?'

'You have dealt me a hurt that will never heal.' Her voice was rough as a rusted blade dragged forcibly from the scabbard. 'The medicine I want you will not offer. Tirel, let me go.'

I shook my head. 'I know your medicine, lady – sharp-edged and barbed, the swords and spears of Conches. That draught I need not drink so long as I hold you hostage.'

'For ever? You know it impossible.'

'Time resolves all troubles. Meanwhile I recommend patience.'

I went about my business: a palisade's repair, and scarping the donjon ditch. At noon I found her seated cloak-wrapped in the hall, warming herself in sunlight that shafted through the doorway. The skin was taut on her cheekbones, her eyes were wide dark pools; raven hair enframed a pallid face. I had not broken my fast, and went hungrily to the victuals Berenger set on the table, tore bacon from the bone and stuffed my mouth. Men-at-arms clattered across the room, relieving the battlement watch, a servant stacked firewood beside the hearth, women scoured pans – there's no privacy in a castle. Isabel gazed over the ward to the river below, to a hoy that laboured against the current, oars thrashing crystal shards. She said meditatively, 'You hold a woman against her will. There's a word for that – the world calls it rape. Are you indifferent to the stain upon your honour?'

'You mistake your situation.' I waved the bacon bone emphatically. 'I took a knight in arms who yielded to my sword. I demand ransom for my prize, as courtoisie allows.'

'Does courtoisie permit that noble prisoners be flogged?'

I swigged wine. 'That was different. I whipped an insolent woman, as would any man of spirit.'

'A woman who unhorsed you,' she said softly. 'Walter of Poix, the famous jouster who once hurled Rufus from the saddle, prodded into the ground like a green esquire. By a woman. You lashed me out of spite, Tirel – not for revenge.'

I stared at her, astonished. 'If you believe that —!' I threw the bone to a liam that basked in the sun, and wiped my mouth. 'No matter. You also were unhorsed, and fortunate not to be killed. Are you not,' I added maliciously, 'becoming a little old for capering in armour?'

She said, unruffled, 'Two years older than yourself, my lord – not yet a crone. We bandy futile insults. If you insist I share your quarters, sleep beside you like a leman, we had better learn to live in amity.'

The first hint of resignation. I concealed relief, and said indifferently, 'Your delicacy surprises me, since once you were indeed my leman.'

Isabel flushed; her eyes sparked like spears. 'You dog —! How you could . . .' She covered her face in her hands, and said in a muffled voice, 'Must you savage my heart as well as my body?'

I looked at her under my eyebrows. Tears were but a weapon in a woman's armoury – and Isabel was not the weeping kind. I was not deceived, yet felt a whisper of remorse.

'I shall not goad you more. The bedchamber is yours; I'll quit the donjon.'

Isabel raised a tear-streaked face. 'What use? Who will credit, after all these days, that I had not shared your bed?'

Who indeed? Chastity was not a virtue which figured in Isabel of Conches's awesome reputation: I'd be just another lover on the string, another knight who planted horns on Lord Ralph's head. Where, incidentally, was Ralph?

'Your lord,' I said, 'is dallying overlong. I sent a demand for ransom a sennight since, and have had no word.'

Isabel looked at her hands. 'Ralph was following his merlin when his palfrey put a foot in a hole and threw him on his head. He was still senseless when you raided Medavi. Neither his steward nor castellan can take responsibility for so great a sum.'

This I had not known: it explained the lack of response – a conroy bent on vengeance – I daily expected from Conches. The liam-hound stretched and yawned, ambled over and laid his head on my knee. I fondled his ears abstractedly. I had stayed too long in Achères; it was time I returned to Poix, to the conduct of my Honour and my secret work for Rufus. I could not take Isabel – her presence in my mesnie would do Adelice dishonour. My purpose was accomplished: I had ravaged Ralph's demesnes and abased his lady. The interlude must end.

I slapped hands on knees and said, 'Then you may give parole, and depart whensoever you wish.'

Isabel plucked a thread from her cloak and examined it intently,
'You are generous, my lord. I must tarry a little longer: my back has
not quite recovered from your . . . attentions.'

That I knew for a lie; her woman had told me the scars were all
but healed. Isabel held me in a cleft, for I could not in decency
expel her while she still pretended illness. She looked me blandly in
the eye; I scowled and left her, vented my ill-humour on Berenger
and the varlets whom I ordered to clean the donjon, scour the filth
of years, strew fresh rushes and replace flea-ridden bedclothes. I
sent the slattern-witch to buy mantles and gowns and kirtles, the
best Achères afforded, and take them to her lady. If I had to go on
living with the wench, I thought moodily, at least I would live no
more in squalor.

At evening I avoided the donjon, eating instead with Baldwin in
his armoury quarters. Baldwin, a jovial rascal, rotund as a barrel,
crimson button nose glinting like a ruby sunk in suet, saw my evil
mood and plied the flagon freely. The meal ended in carousal; we
sang marching songs and bawdy verses ancient in Duke Rollo's time.
When starlight silvered the ward I swayed to my feet and mumbled,
'Time for bed. God send I can climb the ladder.'

Baldwin leered. 'I'd be up like a mummer's monkey for the lady
who waits atop!'

I said thickly, 'Careful, friend. Your mind is rancid as your wine.'

Berenger set my feet on the rungs, and disrobed me in the hall. I
parted the leather curtain. A candle burned on a coffer – the room
before had always been dark when I came to bed. Isabel lay on a
pallet, coverlet drawn to the eyes. I blinked around the chamber,
and said sharply, 'Where is the woman?'

'She is sick,' Isabel answered drowsily. 'I sent her away.'

I stumbled to my palliasse in a corner against the wall, conscious
of a nakedness the candlelight revealed. I flopped on the straw-
stuffed sacking, groped for the bearskin cover, and laid my head on
a baulk which served as pillow.

Isabel said, 'Will you not douse the candle?'

I climbed swearing from the bed, staggered across the room and
groped for the snuffer. The thing was in my hand, poised above the
flame – so nearly was I delivered! – when I chanced to raise my
eyes. Isabel's coverlet was gone; she lay on her back. The light
glowed golden on her body, on proud pointed breasts and shadowed
mysterious clefts in belly and loins. Her eyes held mine, and slowly
she lifted her hands.

I gave a stifled cry, and fled to her arms like a pigeon homing to roost.

The candle burned unheeded. Before it guttered and died I was again enslaved.

8

Winter perished early that year, but I had no eyes for springtime's beauty. My rapture was a flame, blinding, all-consuming; Isabel's love was vital to my being as the sap to a full-grown oak. She enthralled me like the enchantress I had once believed her to be.

We rode together in the woods, cast Baldwin's falcons at herons from the river's marshy reed-banks, hallooed the berselets after hares and rejoiced when the creatures escaped – the time was not made for killing. We took bread and meat and wine to sheltered dells, lay fingers intertwined upon the grass, watching the clouds drift by like the sails of lost white ships. A varlet held the horses, Berenger spread napkins, sat beside us and hummed cheerfully to himself. We did nothing that might shame him; our daytime dalliance was innocent as the butterflies sporting the sward.

Not so at night.

Isabel's skilful loving bound me in white-hot chains. Reason whispered she had known a string of lovers, from pages and young esquires to Robert of Belesme, who had taught her an erudition garnered from the stews. I crushed the thought, and plunged obliviously in burning depths.

'The past is scoured and gone, my sweet?'

'All gone, Walter. We begin anew.'

And so it was. The accounts were settled. I forgot the dark agonies of Conches's donjon, forgot Richer's maiming, forgot Poix and Ralph and Rufus, lived only in the present. Spring's fever warmed my blood, my love stayed with me night and day, I cared for nothing else.

Every idyll has an ending; mine lasted, I think, ten days. A galloper encountered us when riding from the castle, and announced a company approaching from Pontoise. This was not the direction whence I expected Ralph; and I hesitated, reluctant to forgo a day's delights. Caution prevailed; I retreated within the ward, sent Isabel to the donjon and manned the ramparts. Outriders climbed the castle's rocky hill and halted at the fosse. Their shields were slung aback and lances carried butt-end up. Heralds, I thought – but whose?

'Your business, my lords?' I called.

A knight answered formally, 'We announce King Philip of France, commanding entry to his domain in Achères, held of him by Walter Lord of Poix.'

One does not keep royalty waiting. I swiftly opened the gates, called Baldwin and Berenger and rode to meet my suzerain. Philip led his retinue, riding a fat ambling palfrey which wheezed beneath his weight, the bridle gemmed and gold-encrusted, a falcon gripping his wrist. I dismounted, knelt and kissed his stirrup. Sunlight polished the king's bald pate; dimples notched his plump pink cheeks. He said, 'We heard you were here, my lord, and turned aside in our progress towards Paris. It's a long time since I visited Achères.'

'I am honoured, sire. The castle, I fear, is small, hardly suitable . . . ' I noticed the lady who rode beside him, the ravishing face and sensuous body. Bertrada! God's bones, what a complication! '. . . totally unfitting,' I finished lamely, 'to house gentle ladies. Perhaps . . .'

'We bring pavilions in the train. Unfitting to house ladies, you say?' Philip laughed, his fat chins quivered. 'Is none living in Achères?'

Bertrada snickered. I flushed, and led them into the castle, called for chairs and wine and food. The king's seneschal looked distastefully around, bustled from the gate, halted the royal retinue outside and ordered pavilions to be pitched on the meadows. Philip's portly body fitted snugly in his chair, he supped wine and talked lightly to Bertrada seated beside him; a lady waited at her shoulder. Attendant barons in velvet cloaks cast supercilious eyes over Achères' puny ramparts. A steward placed a silver dish before the king, wheaten cakes and honey, sweetened figs and quinces. Berenger, kneeling, presented barley biscuits on a wooden board, the best that Achères' kitchens baked. Philip ignored his steward's platter, picked and nibbled a biscuit, finished his wine and smacked his lips.

'A good brew, my lord. Your own pressing?' He glanced slyly at the donjon, and added, 'Will the chatelaine of Achères not entertain us?'

Bertrada said directly, 'Where is my sister?'

'The Lady of Conches,' I answered stiffly, 'came here in armour, and lacks a proper wardrobe. She cannot dress in a manner befitting your presence, sire.'

'I did not believe Isabel so vain,' Bertrada said. 'If she won't show herself I had better find her. By your leave, my lord . . .' She rose and went to the mound, climbed the ladder gracefully. Philip chuckled.

'Let them cross sisterly swords. Walter, we must have a serious talk.' He waddled to the palisade, and laid jewel-studded fingers on my arm. 'You hide yourself in Achères and let the world go by. Meanwhile your little escapade has peppered political stewpots. It's time you sent the lady home.'

I said distinctly, 'I took Isabel of Conches in open battle, demanded ransom and offered parole. She is not held against her will.'

'That's the trouble.' Philip crumbled a biscuit and tempted a sparrow that chirped on a stake nearby. 'So humiliating for Ralph. He can't afford the ransom, and can't lead a mesnie to recover his lady by force – he's still abed, nursing a cracked skull. Just as well. If Normans crossed my march I'd have to interfere, and I don't want to get involved. You see my point?'

I saw. Major wars had often flared from private quarrels. Nor was Philip a belligerent man: like Rufus, though for different reasons, he preferred diplomacy. My temper prickled. Why should this indolent king, flaunting Fulk of Anjou's wife like a brazen trull, presume to rebuke my conduct?

I said stubbornly, 'When Isabel wishes to go she may. No one will take her forcibly.'

The sparrow perched on Philip's finger, and pecked from his palm. 'I have a way with birds, they come at my bidding . . . Walter, for Poix's seisin I hold your fealty and homage. Will you risk your Honour for a woman?'

The threat was plain. Time unreeled in a whirl, stopped and framed a mental picture ten years gone. The choice had then confronted me: Isabel or Poix. Cravenly I had yielded, humbled her and sent her from my house. Not again – not ever again. From that one act of selfishness had gushed a fount of pain.

I swallowed, and said, 'I know my duty to my suzerain, but in this, a private matter, I cannot acknowledge his precept.'

'Defiance, eh?' Philip closed his hand; the sparrow chirped indignantly and flew away. 'Must I escheat Poix?'

'Not without a fight, my lord.'

'Worse and worse.' The king rested shoulder blades against the palisade, spread arms along the top, surveyed a covey passing overhead. 'Never could tame starlings – far too independent. Like yourself, Walter: arrogant and quarrelsome. Did you know,' he added, 'that Ralph of Conches appealed to Rufus?'

My face betrayed astonishment. Philip said, 'Why not? Since Caen's treaty King William is his overlord. You've thrown a stone in a murky puddle: the ripples are spreading wide.'

'What was Rufus's . . . response?'

'Laughed himself sick, I'm told. He has little time for Ralph.' Philip giggled, trebling his chins. 'Nevertheless the man's his vassal, so he has to support him. Rufus wrote to me, your suzerain, and asked me to to – um – persuade you. So here,' he concluded amiably, 'I am.'

This changed the slant completely. Despite his threats fat Philip, I was sure, would never leaguer Poix on Conches's behalf. If matters came to the crunch and Ralph attacked he'd turn his back and let us fight it out. Rufus was something else: he kept his word. If Isabel were not surrendered I could expect King William's lieges at my walls – English feet on France's soil. Philip was bound to react; thus wars began. Must Isabel set kingdoms quarrelling? Could I fight Rufus, who truly held my faith?

Philip watched the struggle in my face. 'It's quite easy, Walter. Let the Lady Isabel return to Paris in my train, and stay a month or so in company with her sister. All very respectable; people will soon forget her interlude at Achères. Thus everyone's face is saved: you yield gracefully to your suzerain's wishes, Isabel lives discreetly at court, and Ralph eventually regains his lady.' He caught my hostile look. 'The raven calling the crow a Moor, you think? Not so. I shall wed the Countess of Anjou before summer's out. Well, what do you say?'

Isabel and Bertrada appeared at the donjon door, Isabel's woollen gown a sober contrast to her sister's gold-embroidered sendal. Philip levered his shoulders from the palisade. Isabel curtsied. The king said to Bertrada, 'Have you been sufficiently convincing?'

'I think she begins to see reason.'

Isabel smiled. 'It seems, Walter, our petty affairs are stirring kingdoms. Who'd have thought it? Had we not better ladle a little oil on stormy waters?'

'I am ready to fight the world on your behalf!'

'That I believe.' She took my hand and stroked my fingers. Philip quirked an eyebrow in amusement. 'And in doing so meet ruin and death. No, Walter. We have found happiness together; let's not destroy our memories.' She put her lips to my ear, and whispered, 'We must part, my love – but not, I swear, for long.'

I looked at Philip, who smiled benignly; at Bertrada's inscrutable face; at Isabel, and saw the promise in her eyes. A hopeless anger assailed me, a sense of loss, a certainty of rapture gone and never to be regained. I threw out my hands despairingly, and turned my back. Philip said, 'Then it is decided?'

'Yes.'

'The Saints be praised! A lot of trouble avoided. Where's the wine? – all this talking sands my throat!' He ambled to the flagons, drank deep and wiped his lips. 'That's better! Has the seneschal pitched camp? Tell him to strike the tents – we leave at once.'

Philip eyed me over the rim of his cup. 'I thought it would take far longer to make you both see sense. A persuasive lady, the Countess of Anjou, don't you think?'

Chapter 3

1092

IN a lowering temper I returned to Poix. Adelice perceived my mood and asked no questions, nor did I explain. As ever, she stayed tranquilly detached, disinclined to paddle in troubled waters. Provided she was left in peace to rule her domestic realm Adelice was happy to ignore my vagaries – she considered war and polity as beyond a woman's provenance. She was aware I had held Isabel captive; and she probably knew what followed. I did not inquire, and Adelice wisely held her tongue. Over-importunate ladies were sometimes harshly treated: it was at this time that Robert of Belesme consigned his wife to the vaults beneath his donjon, and Ingelran of Ferrières whipped Alberede from his gates. It was rash to cross quick-tempered knights – and Adelice had no wish to test my tolerance.

To Richer I merely said, 'I have paid the debt we owe. The tally is clean.' He answered nothing, but I saw a flash of pity in his eyes. Irritated for no reason I could name, I added roughly, 'Your hurt abides despite requital. I offer a salve: half the ransom which Conches will send.'

He said placidly, 'My lord, you are out of humour. Silver does not heal wounds. Let us forget what you have said.'

I felt oddly ashamed, and loosed my spleen in the tiltyard. If a woman could unhorse me it was time I furbished my skill. I ran a hundred courses and tilted at the quintain, spent hours fighting afoot with sword and shield. My day-to-day opponents were sergeants and household knights, redoubtable antagonists who soon began to find employment elsewhere when I rode down to the yard. I summoned Delis from Carenci: the third course left him senseless, blood running from his nostrils. Berenger revived him, bathing his face with vinegar. Since no more expert fighter existed on my Honour, few better in the kingdom, I concluded I had recovered my skill. I went on practising sporadically, and started training my son Hugh in horsemanship and swordplay.

In May a travelling tinker brought a message from Richer's agent in Domfront, a castled fief whose seisin Belesme held. Richer called a clerk, and found me in the riding school instructing Hugh. I lifted the boy from the palfrey's saddle, handed him a wooden sword and told him to practise cut and point. He trotted happily away and prodded a straw-stuffed dummy. The clerk read from a parchment strip.

'Richard Harecher and other burghers oppressed by Belesme's exactions seek aid to overthrow him. They talk of England.'

That was all: the usual guarded message to which I was accustomed, undirected and unsigned. I asked Richer, 'Whence does this come?'

'Domfront, my lord.'

'How can you tell? What indicates the source?'

Richer pointed to a cryptic mark below the writing. 'The sign I allotted Eudo when I sent him there.'

I snorted. 'This information seems futile as the rest we've had. Burghers trying to wrest a fief from Robert of Belesme! They've got a hope! Give it to a galloper and send it to St Valeri.'

I corrected Hugh's high-line thrust, and forgot the matter. Two weeks later my steward announced a knight who sought admittance. I sauntered to the gate – even in sleepy Poix armed parties, however small, are not received unscrutinized – and recognized Robert fitz-Hamon's arrow-scarred saturnine face. I led him within the hall, stabled his escort's horses and set food and drink before him. fitz-Hamon enjoyed his wine and talked of trifles; I forbore to probe. He was not the kind you cross-examined.

He surveyed a trio of archers rolling dice and said, 'That's a peculiar armour they wear. Where is it forged?'

'In my smithy.' I called a bowman over; fitzHamon fingered the mail. 'A complicated mesh,' he said. 'The linking must be difficult.' He dismissed the man with a gesture and glanced about the hall, thronged by knights and men-at-arms off duty, by scullions and serving-women. 'Will you show me how your haubergeons are fashioned?'

I took the hint. The hall was full of ears, whereas smithies are noisy places where secrets can pass unheard. I led him to an un-walled shed beside the gatehouse. A row of workmen stood at oaken tables ranged end to end beneath a roof supported on timber posts. Bellows roared a furnace in the centre; tongs and hammers, pincers and punches hung on racks. I said, 'We use a system of continuous production: each man performs an allotted task and passes it to the next. Here is the first stage.' A smith drew heated wire through a swage-hole shaped to flatten one side of the wire and round the other. fitzHamon watched attentively, and spoke without moving his eyes.

'I have come on a confidential mission, my lord, arising from your information concerning Domfront. The king sees a chance of advantage.'

With an effort of memory I recalled the message. 'Discontented townsfolk in a Belesme fief. It's not unknown. What use can it be to Rufus?'

fitzHamon moved along the row and stood behind a smith who coiled the swaged wire around an iron rod. 'Domfront's a half day's travel from the march of Maine.'

'Maine?' I said, startled. 'Maine is Duke Robert's problem – no concern to Rufus.'

'It will be one day.'

The next workman in the chain cut the coiled wire to form rings. fitzHamon slipped a ring on the tip of his finger. 'We've inquired about this Richard Harecher. He's a rich merchant, and commands the loyalty of Domfront's burghers. Belesme's tallages are ruining the trading community. Harecher and his fellows are ripe for rebellion.'

A smith annealed the rings piled at his elbow, and pincered them to overlap the ends. I said contemptuously, 'Like Conan in Rouen? You remember his fate!'

'Prince Henry threw him from the Tower. A badly organized uprising, betrayed to King William's foes beforehand. Bound to fail. This will not, for Rufus installs an envoy in Domfront who will time the citizens' revolt to coincide with the arrival of his army.'

A workman wielding punch and hammer flattened the overlapped ring ends. 'A dangerous trust,' I said, 'working under the enemy's nose. Do you realize that Domfront's castellan is Gunheir of Belesme, Count Robert's nephew? Who is the hardy fellow Rufus has in mind?'

'You, my lord.'

fitzHamon moved away, and leaned inquisitively over the shoulder of a man who punched rivet holes in the flattened joints. I followed in a daze, wondering whether the clang and clamour had sent my hearing awry. 'Don't you think,' I asked sarcastically, 'a baron of France hobnobbing with Domfront's burghers might arouse Gunheir's curiosity? I am not unknown in Normandy!'

An apprentice delicately forced a pointed rod inside each ring, opening it ready for linking, and passed them to the master armourer. 'Rufus suggests you go there in a merchant's guise and contact Harecher. Meanwhile Hugh of Avranches will enlist a mercenary force and keep them under his hand until the moment's ripe – that moment being your decision. This,' he continued, peering at the armourer's busy hands, 'is a very interesting process.'

The craftsman linked the rings and tapped the rivets home. The chain mail burgeoned like a silver sheet beneath his fingers. I said impatiently, 'A fantastic concept! Moreover, Hugh is old – he fought at Hastings – and not the man to lead a hazard like this!'

'Hugh,' said fitzHamon gently, 'won't command the force.'

'Then who will?'

'Prince Henry.'

The hammers clanged more loudly in my ears, the furnace roared like a gale. I drew fitzHamon from the shed, and said in a grating voice, 'What ploy is this, my lord? Who has persuaded the king to entrust such a dangerous venture to that . . .'

fitzHamon raised a warning hand; I stuttered into silence. He seated himself on the well head. 'Noisy in there,' he observed. 'A relief to be out of the din. The thing is this, my lord. Henry eventually discovered – as was inevitable – that Rufus gave me seisin of the English fiefs his mother bequeathed. He didn't create an uproar, for that is not Henry's way, but he left Rufus in no doubt that the king had broken his pledge.' fitzHamon traced a thumbnail along his jagged scar – a gesture habitual when he was deep in thought. 'Rufus feels guilty: he's sensitive on points of honour. In Domfront he finds a chance to win for his brother a fief he can call his own.'

'And an outpost, doubtless, in Duke Robert's realm!'

'That also,' fitzHamon answered easily. 'The snag, which Rufus can't or won't admit, is that in restoring Henry's independence he builds a base for treason.'

'So!' I exclaimed. 'You, as I do, believe that Henry —'

'Of course. The Count of Meulan and I tried hard to dissuade the king. Rufus thinks no ill of his brother, so one cannot argue plainly. In the end, seeing certain small advantages, we gave way.'

'I see no advantage whatsoever.'

fitzHamon picked up a pebble and dropped it into the well, cocked his head and listened for the splash. 'There are two. Henry is removed from Rufus's court – where already, I believe, he and the Clares conspire – and with luck he may be killed.'

'In taking Domfront?'

'Precisely.'

I examined carefully fitzHamon's face. The dark-blue eyes were guileless, a smile touched the corners of his lips. I shivered, though sunlight flooded the ward and the air was warm. He continued easily, 'Rufus believes you competent to execute his plan. Meulan and I know no one more devoted to the king. Will you, my lord, accept this charge on his behalf – and ours?'

A sergeant relieved the gate guard. Orders snapped and spear butts thumped the ground. Two knights rode over the drawbridge, hawks on wrists, berselets at their heels. A toddler chased a squawking hen, his mother grabbed and slapped him, the infant bawled. Wistfully I surveyed the familiar scene. Never had Poix seemed so desirable, so comforting and secure. Was I to leave this haven and abandon all I had won? All this for Rufus? No mortal deserved such sacrifice – the king demanded more than I could give.

'Yes,' I muttered. 'Yes. I'll go.'

2

I left secretly before daybreak, taking with me Richer and the bowman Pigot. We rode coarse-bred palfreys, deliberately left ungroomed; Pigot led a panniered mule which carried our scanty baggage. We wore linen breeches and loose-woven cloaks; and pulled the hoods around our heads. Except Pigot, who carried a dirk, we bore no weapons other than daggers. An itinerant merchant – not over-prosperous – led his modest train across Normandy's march.

I prefer to forget that journey. The Lord of Poix had hitherto ridden the roads as a baron well escorted. The difference now was vast. We met armed companies who thrust us rudely from the highway; humbly we gave them passage. Near Brémule we encountered robbers, ruined villeins lurking in a coppice, gaunt savages who wielded reaping hooks and staves. Pigot killed the leader and checked the rush; we fled like hunted hares, hammering unspurred heels on the palfreys' ribs. I ground my teeth in rage: the redoubtable Walter Tirel routed by half-armed villeins! Richer, when we reined three bowshots on, appeared quietly amused. 'Our disguise is patently authentic – and will kill us yet,' he observed ironically.

Pigot grouchily wiped his bloodied blade on the pack-mule's hide.

Because I avoided towns we rested at wayside inns or village taverns: leaf-thatched, verminous hovels. We supped coarse oat cakes and sour wine, slept on the floor or, in the better taverns, on prickly straw whose denizens kept us wakeful. Always we mounted guard in turns on the horses. We might have found better quarters, for I carried a purse beneath my tunic; but Richer, who had travelled the roads from Calais to Cordova, gauged exactly the accommodation which fitted our counterfeit station. 'We must not step out of character, my lord,' he assured me once when, after an exhausting day, I craved roast meat and mellow wine, 'else someone's interest will awaken. If you are questioned your bearing and mode of speech will instantly betray you.' Always, for this reason, Pigot bought supplies and haggled for our quarters.

A fortnight after leaving Poix we entered Domfront's gates. The town resembled Evreux, houses packed within ramparts partly palisaded, partly stone. Suburbs spilled beyond the pale. I scrutinized the castle, and misliked what I saw: an indomitable stone-walled stronghold, the donjon's topmost storey oaken-built. I found a middling hostelry and left Pigot to stable the horses. An inquiry at a tanner's stall directed us to Harecher's house, a mansion set back from an alley, overlooking a garden where blossom-spangled apple trees shaded scythe-shaven grass. A portly steward received us; I announced myself as Lambert of Amiens, a Ponthevin merchant seeking a trading permit in Domfront. The man accepted with alacrity the deniers I tendered, and led us to his master in the orchard.

Harecher was not what I expected. I had thought to meet a low-born tradesman, the familiar type who fawns on knights, cheats his fellows and whips his servants. I greeted instead a tall, thin man with a vulturine nose and bloodless lips and a skin like old bleached leather. His voice was resonant, the speech deliberate; dignity enfolded him.

I felt encouraged – the escapade might hold a little hope.

I asked for a trading permit, and begged admittance to the armourers' guild whose craft I feigned. Harecher listened in silence. He looked thoughtfully at Richer but made no remark: Saracens frequently travelled the roads of commerce. He dismissed the steward, led us to a bench beneath a cherry tree and said without preamble. 'Your accent is not of Ponthieu, your manner not a merchant's. Whence do you come? What is your purpose?'

The man's directness pierced my guard. I had intended to probe cautiously before revealing my identity. I knew nothing of Richard Harecher; when I discarded disguise I put my life in his hands. How far could I trust him? He watched my face and read my doubts. The pale lips smiled, and he said, 'My English commerce prospers. The ships have lately brought some interesting merchandise.'

I said, 'You have trustworthy connections oversea?'

'Sufficiently so. I receive cloth from Meulan's mills, hides from fitzHamon's yards, and I am presently negotiating a royal contract.'

'In which,' I stated, casting discretion aside, 'I am authorized to help. Have you had notice of my coming?'

'In a shipping manifest, prudently indited. I do not know your name, nor details of your . . . goods.'

Saving words, I told him. Harecher heard me out, eyes on the spring-green grass, long delicate fingers tearing a fallen blossom. At the end he said, 'I have made certain preparations, all that I safely can. A lot remains to be done. I think for safety's sake you and your men had best be quartered in my house. We shall have much to discuss, and constant traffic from here to the inn will attract attention. Gunheir of Belesme is a very inquisitive man, his spies active and alert. Guard your disguise, my lord.' His eyes twinkled. 'A rather less arrogant bearing and a soldier's slang might help!'

3

There followed a series of midnight debates with burghers in Harecher's house. The gatherings were small; to escape notice he summoned a few at a time. These tradesmen, by and large, were intelligent people, excited by the venture, not a little fearful of the consequence of failure. They had reason: Gunheir's gallows seldom stood unladen. I had not previously met merchants in the mass, and found their outlook strange. They were not impelled by motives which I easily understood; their honour was not insulted, nor their wives and daughters ravished; the little land they owned was never harried. They looked comfortable men, inclined to fat, cloaks woven from Canusian wool, tunics of finest linen. But their treasuries were dwindling, the profits cut. Belesme had doubled taxes, tallaged goods that were hitherto free, raised octroi duties and put a tax on wine.

What drove them was simple avarice, a united hatred of Belesme and a resolve to break his yoke.

With Harecher's help I extracted basic details of the aid that each could tender. Money, despite their grievances, was not a problem: an army could be paid from what they offered. And that was all. They lacked arms and armour, military training and the mental and physical toughness which carries men unflinching to a line of enemy shields. Harecher collected some ancient haubergeons, rusty dirks and spears; and had them stacked by night in his household cellars. I inspected gap-ringed armour, thumbed blunt and dented blades, bade Richer find a grindstone and Pigot sew new rings. The burghers apologized wanly: warfare was not their trade. Their armoury, I told them curtly, would hardly equip a gate guard. What, if their weapons were useless, could they raise in the way of men?

They all employed craftsmen, apprentices and packmen. Harecher made a catalogue, eliminated boys and dotards, and sieved the names to a scant twelve score. He divided them in companies by trades: cutlers and cordwainers, silversmiths and saddlers. The members of each guild worked close together, usually in the same street, which would ease the problem of assembly. He appointed leaders and distributed the arms – burnished and repaired but still hopelessly inadequate. For the rest, I declared moodily, they must find reaping hooks and pitchforks.

I inspected the town's defences. The roads from Caen and Avranches entered the palisade through gateways guarded by day and shut at sundown. Neither would withstand a surprise attack in strength. The trouble was the castle, sited midway in the town, whose donjon soared from a rocky hillock enclosed by a fosse and drystone walls. Gunheir, so Harecher told me, commanded a hundred men.

I remembered my half-armed tradesmen, and decided the work, if done at all, must be done by Count Hugh's soldiers. The sooner I saw him the better.

I journeyed to Avranches, a long day's ride from dawn to dusk. Count Hugh, already informed by Rufus of my task, waited impatiently. 'What kept you – Domfront's doxies? I'm told they're skilful sluts!' He was a grey, dried-up man, his face brown and wrinkled like an old walnut. 'Meanwhile I'm keeping five hundred mercenaries under arms and eating their heads off. A set of brawling rascals, mostly Angevins and Flemings. They pillage Avranches' taverns, rape the whores and never pay; the sooner I get shot of them the better I'll be pleased!'

'How many are mounted?'

'A score or so – all knights. Cavalry's no good for attacking castles.'

'Have you built a siege train?'

Hugh stared. 'Mangonels and belfrois? God's belly – no! You won't have time for a leaguer. Domfront must be stormed at once or taken not at all!' He continued less explosively, 'My lord, you misjudge the enterprise. If you don't surprise the donjon Gunheir will shut himself in and send for help. Belesme's nearest castle is Roche Mabille – two marches distant. Count Robert will muster his men and descend on your neck like a chopper!'

I agreed. I had long recognized that speed was vital – but a mangonel or two was always a help. 'The citizens are ready as they ever will be. I think we'll try an escalade in five days' time.'

Count Hugh cracked his knuckles. 'You'd better consult your commander. Henry's somewhere in the ward.' He lurched from the hall, leaning on a staff – Hugh was lamed at Hastings. 'Can't understand why Rufus puts an inexperienced youngster in charge of a hazard like this. I'm on the spot – a veteran of thirty years' service. Sheer favouritism, I call it!'

Henry was on the rampart, talking to Gilbert of Clare. His chilly eyes surveyed me, and he said in an empty voice, 'We're allies, Tirel. Who'd have thought it? How stands Domfront?'

I defined my strategy. 'The mercenaries are infantry, which means a two-day march. They'll move by night, halting the first dawn in Mortain's forest. During the second night they'll reach the woods which fringe Domfront's suburbs, where they'll lie concealed until the assault at terce.'

'Why keep them waiting for hours,' said Henry peevishly, 'chancing discovery by a roving swineherd, and warning sent to Gunheir? I favour an assault directly they arrive, when the gates are opened at dawn.'

'Not only will the garrison then be most alert, but still inside the castle,' I explained patiently. 'Afterwards they wander into the town, to shops and inns, and may be caught unaware before they regain the ward.'

'A sound argument,' Hugh murmured.

Henry said reluctantly, 'Very well. Then we lie in wait in the woodlands – how far from Domfront's walls?'

'About ten bowshots.'

Henry stroked the fringe of hair that fell to his eyebrows. 'So. Two thousand paces separate my force from its objective. Mercenaries won't run that far when they know there's a fight at the end – they'll save their breath for battle, and march. Meanwhile your citizens fight unaided. Will they hold?'

'That, my lord,' said I, 'is the gamble.'

4

I returned to Domfront and discussed the final details with Harecher and his leading burghers. I began to fear betrayal, because we had now to issue arms to individual townsmen and instruct them in their role. I passed two wakeful nights, and slept not at all in the long dark hours before the day of the rising.

At dawn I left my bed and prepared myself for onset. From the citizens' meagre armoury I had chosen a sergeant's haubergeon, a helmet, dirk and targe. I meant to avoid combat – but anywhere near fighting a knight without armour feels naked. Pigot found a boiled-leather cuirass and an iron cap; and I gave him money to buy a bow and shafts. He returned with his purchase and said contemptuously, 'The bowyers here use only elm and ash – I'm used to horn and sinew. This is a clumsy stave.'

I braced the bow and tested the draw. Pigot sniffed disparagingly. 'A linen string. They've never heard of silk or horsehair. Look at these arrows: ill-balanced and bound to gad.'

'Pigot,' I said, 'the shafts will flight true for twenty paces, which is all I'll need. Carry the bow braced and ready; stay close and guard my back.'

I told Richer that when the town gates opened he was to take the saddled palfreys to the suburb: if the business went awry I had no wish to be caught in Domfront. I donned my armour – the haubergeon flapped on my scrawny frame like a windless sail – and went to Harecher's hall to break my fast. The merchant wore an old-fashioned hauberk – the discs did not overlap – and was threading laces in a pointed helmet. A long shield lay on a table; new paint obscured the blazon. He caught my look, and said a little sadly, 'I was once a knight.'

Which explained a great deal about Harecher.

I ate without appetite, threw a cloak over my armour and went into the streets. Sunrise touched the banner that flapped lazily on the donjon; yawning shopkeepers opened shutters and arranged their wares; villeins slanting mattocks departed for the fields; ox-carts lumbered to the gates. I crossed the market place where hawkers were setting up stalls, and sauntered to the Avranches gate, open and jammed by traffic. A sentinel leaned on his spear; in the gatehouse, a stone-built hut, the guard boiled porridge on a smoky fire.

I retraced my steps to the castle, and leaned against a byre that edged the fields surrounding the fosse. A belt of wiry pasture-grass islanded the castle: Gunheir, a wise castellan, permitted no buildings within a bowshot of his ramparts. Sheep peacefully grazed the grass, the shepherd piped a plaintive tune upon his flute. The castle gate was open, the drawbridge down; a loaded haywain rumbled over the planks. Helmets gleamed on the gatehouse; I looked aloft to the donjon, and saw sunbeams spark from spearheads.

Men-at-arms from the castle, unarmed save for dirks, strolled among the people in the streets. They loitered in scattered groups, followed and observed by casual idlers who seemed to have time on their hands. The shops of the guilds were open and merchandise displayed; the salesmen curiously few, either old or very young.

Harecher was seated in his hall, and pensively observed a sand-glass. 'An hour to terce,' he said.

'Everything is normal at the gates. Gunheir's had no forewarning. Are your companies ready?'

'Ready? I suppose so – they have sent me word.' His smile was a mirthless grimace. 'I command shopkeepers, my lord, not battle-hardened warriors. I cannot vouch for their bearing when the steel begins to sing. Ready? Yes. A company is concealed in houses near the Avranches gate; another's hidden in the market, ready to scour the streets; the third in barns and byres opposite the drawbridge. All according to plan. You know the countersign?'

'Monjoie.'

We sat in uneasy silence, and listened to muted noises from the town. I tilted a flagon of wine, found swallowing difficult. Harecher watched the trickling sand. He rose and strapped the shield guige on his shoulder, slipped the baldric over his head, settled the scabbard on his hip.

'It is time. I lead the assault on the castle. Wish me well.'

'*Saluz aiez de Deu!*'

He crossed the yard and went openly into the street – a knight striding proudly into battle. I shed my cloak and walked quickly to the Avranches gate, Pigot padding behind. The crowds in the streets were sparser, less noisy, talking quietly in doorways.

I reached the gate-yard; and the bells of all the churches clanged for terce.

5

A mob erupted from the alleys and converged like tide-rips on the gate. The luckless sentry fumbled his spear; a pitchfork skewered his throat. A sergeant appeared at the gatehouse door, a porridge bowl clasped to his chest. He vanished under the trampling; I heard him shriek. They crowded into the guardroom and hacked the men-at-arms in pieces. One they spread on the cooking fire and held the plunging body while flames devoured his belly.

The gate was taken. I scrutinized the forested horizon, hoping to see the glint of sun on steel. Nothing. Villeins dotted the fields, plough teams halted, scythes inert, stunned into startled stillness by the clamour from the town.

The streets were pandemonium. Townsmen hunted Gunheir's soldiers as dogs hunt rats from sewers, chasing them up alleyways, flushing them from houses, hauling them from crannies where they hid. Furious little battles flowered in the wynds where desperate men, outnumbered, fought to save their lives. The pack closed hard upon them, spears outreaching dirks. The little groups died hard, fighting to the last, and barbarity was loosed upon their bodies. They were torn in bits, dismembered, their entrails ripped apart. A bloodied head was flourished on a spear. It had not been severed cleanly, gobbets dangled at the neck; brute force had wrenched it living from the shoulders.

I turned a narrow corner and entered the Street of Chandlers. Smoke drifted between the houses, a casement spurted flames. Someone in a hurry had scattered a hearth-fire's embers; if the fire were not quenched quickly the town would be ablaze. I sprinted to the doorway, heard shouting in the street, and the clatter of running men. A figure burst from the smoke, saw me and tried to swerve, slipped and tumbled at my feet. A boy, an esquire by his garb. I hauled him up and looked at his terrified face.

My heart lurched.

No time for speech. His hunters loomed from the smoke-veil, whooping and waving swords. I thrust the boy behind me, drew my dirk and shouted. The men came on, eyes blank and mouths contorted, maddened by the smell and taste of blood.

'Monjoie!' I yelled. 'Monjoie!'

They were deaf to reason, blind to everything but slaughter.

'Pigot!'

The bowman flexed, the string twanged twice. The third man tried to stop, his impetus carried him on and he sprawled on his back. His mouth was agape in alarm; I slipped my point between his teeth and buried the blade to the backbone.

Pigot grunted. 'A better stave than I thought. True at a scantling range.' He shouldered the bow, drew a dagger and went to cut his arrows from the bodies. I seized the boy by the hair and raised his face. His nose was bleeding, mud smeared his forehead. Those eyes, and the high-boned cheeks. . .

There was no doubt.

'Who are you?' I asked roughly.

'Gunheir of Belesme's esquire.'

'Your name?'

'Roger of Conches.'

I loosed my hold. The boy straightened his shoulders, frightened and near to tears, yet proud and a little defiant. Some twelve years old, I judged.

Isabel's son.

'Follow me,' I ordered, 'if you want to save your skin. Stay close.'

I hastened along the Street of Chandlers, leaving the fire to burn. We threaded a huddle of villeins' huts and stumbled through a muddy byre to the edge of the fields that ringed the castle.

A raging battle seethed at the drawbridge.

We had thrown against this place the bulk and the best of our men. A hundred shouting citizens struggled to enter the ward, a long congested column, the head rearing like a wave where it met the gateway's guardians. Stormers fell from the bridge, toppled into the fosse, scrabbled up the steep unyielding scarp, died on blades that flickered above the ramparts. Gunheir's soldiers blocked the gate, a solid armoured wall; bowmen on the palisade loosed shafts at the heaving mellay and picked off men at the edges as a child plucks the legs from a fly.

They strove to raise the drawbridge; I heard the windlass creak. Harecher in the forefront fought sword to sword with the guard, his blade carving arcs in the sunlight, his helmet a banner of flame. But the guard held firm, and the arrows flew, and corpses shallowed the fosse.

I looked huntedly to the road-gap that led to the Avranches gate. Where in Jesu's name was Henry and his hirelings?

Men-at-arms made a rush from the gate and forced the attackers back. The chains screeched on the ratchets, the bridge lifted a bowstave's height; townsmen left on the slanting planks slid helplessly into the maw. Harecher flung away his shield and leapt the gap. A score of his rabble followed. The bridge thudded down.

I heard hoofbeats above the din. Horsemen trotted to the fields. 'Stay here!' I told Pigot, running as I spoke. The leader soothed a restive charger and coolly surveyed the fight. I grabbed his knee, and gasped, 'Prince Henry?'

Ill-tempered eyes examined my face. 'Ha, Tirel!' said Gilbert of Clare. 'The prince sent the knights-banneret on and follows with his foot. He still has some way to go.' He looked at the roaring battle on the bridge. 'No place for cavalry, that. We'd better dismount.'

'Hurry!'

He gave orders. Knights clambered from saddles and handed reins to esquires. Clare dressed them carefully in line, looked again to the drawbridge, changed his mind and ranked them in troop of threes. I bit my knuckles. The bridge was lifting again. 'For the love of Christ be quick!' I said. Clare scowled. 'Do you teach me tactics? Out of my way!' He flourished his sword; the knights marched over the grass.

The garrison charged once more, and cleared the bridge. On the outer lip of the fosse they left ten men-at-arms, a suicide squad to hold the horde at bay. Behind this sacrifice the ratchets squealed, the bridge remorselessly lifted and slammed on the lintel beam. The mob closed on the gallant rearguard and cut them down. Half-way across the fields Clare halted his knights. He stuck his sword in the ground and leaned on the hilt and said, 'That seems to be that. No point in going farther. We're too few for an escalade.'

Arrows whipped and whirred, a shaft thumped my targe. I

answered bitterly, 'Had you been less leisurely, my lord —!' Clare regarded me with hatred. 'Excuses! Make them to the prince, not me!' The constabular turned about and tramped solemnly to the horses. The remnants of the stormers milled in front of the fosse; wounded crawled from the field, leaving slimy trails that glistened in the sun. Bodies were strewn like autumn leaves where the bridge had been. Men-at-arms lined the ramparts, brandished spears and howled derision. Bowmen went on shooting, and beat the survivors back. Soon they were running for cover in huts and byres.

I returned to Pigot, waiting in a cowshed, the boy shivering at his side. The archer's face was bitter. 'A close-run thing, my lord. Those laggard knights —!' I looked at Roger and forced a grin. 'Your friends have shut you out, my lad. Don't worry – I'll keep you safe.' He smiled wanly, and clenched his hands together to stop them shaking.

Harecher limped towards us, a dented helmet sitting skew-wise on his head, mail rings shorn at the shoulder, blood seeping through the gambeson. A broken sword hung loosely in his hand. He croaked, 'We failed – betrayed! Where are Prince Henry's men?'

From the quarter of the Avranches gate I heard voices chanting war-cries. The shouting swelled to a roar. An armoured river flowed from the houses and started to flood the fields. The Flemings' battle-shouts clanged like anvils: 'Arras! Arras!' Clare galloped to head them off, brandishing his sword. The yelling dwindled. The mercenaries halted, surveyed uncertainly the lowering donjon, spears foresting the battlements, the blank uplifted drawbridge.

Of the prince himself not a sign.

'There,' I answered tonelessly, 'are Henry's men.'

6

A council of war assembled in a barn overlooking the battlefield. Recriminations sputtered like sparks from a pitchpine torch. Henry sat on a manger, looking poisonous as henbane. 'You, Tirel,' he rasped. 'Explain yourself! Yours was the plan. How have you blundered – or was your failure worse than mere incompetence?'

'You've got the town.'

'God's death! What use is the town without the castle?'

'The burghers did all I demanded,' I answered angrily. 'They took the Avranches gate and opened the way to the ward. The fault was yours for dallying.'

'Dallying —! Have we wings? I sent the bannerets on!'

'A bunch of spineless sluggards!' I ignored Clare's angry growl, and added spitefully, 'Had you led the charge yourself, my lord, instead of sulking safely in the rear, your timing might have been better!'

Henry sent me a look which chilled my blood. 'My mother bore me a commander, not a man-at-arms,' he said between his teeth. 'Be very careful, Tirel! You have no friends here. I believe you false —'

'Dissension will get us nowhere,' Harecher put in tiredly. 'We must consider what's to be done. The castle stands inviolate; the siege lines must be set.'

'Counsel from a merchant garbed as a knight!' Henry rapped. 'Spurious as the goods you sell! How can five hundred soldiers leaguer Domfront?'

A fox-faced Flemish knight irritably tapped his shield. 'We've brought no siege train. Mangonels take days to build.'

'And days are what we haven't got,' said Clare. 'Already Gunheir's messenger will be riding to Roche Mabille.'

'The alternatives are plain,' I said. 'Either you attempt an immediate escalade, or quit the enterprise and march away.' I looked at Henry. 'The choice is yours.'

Harecher said quietly, a pleading note in his voice, 'If you abandon us, my lord, Belesme's reprisals will be hideous. Consider the men who fought for you.' He pointed to the bodies littering the fields. 'Have they died in vain?'

Henry glared vindictively. 'Your people didn't fight hard enough. Why should I squander my conroys to rescue cowardly tradesmen?'

Harecher's shoulders sagged. 'If I cannot persuade you . . .'

The Fleming said unexpectedly, 'Let's set the siege lines and probe the castle's defences – we may find a weakness somewhere. At the same time we'll patrol the road to the Roche. If Belesme sends a relieving force we'll have forewarning, and can raise the leaguer instantly and leave.'

Henry looked at him dubiously. 'You think that feasible?'

'It's the proper military solution, my lord,' the mercenary insisted.

Henry stared at the castle and said, 'Very well. We leaguer.' He walked from the barn, checked and said over his shoulder, 'Tirel, you have no more say in operations. Gilbert, give the orders for investment.'

The Fleming – a knight by courtesy: I doubt his forebears ever held land – surveyed Clare inimically. 'I don't need your directions. We know our work.'

So it proved. By nightfall trenches were dug, pickets posted and reserves disposed where sorties might be launched. They had to construct the siege works among houses fringing the fields: the open ground was a no-man's-land the garrison's bowmen ruled. Henry sent a herald demanding surrender: Gunheir returned defiance. Townsmen cleared the carnage in the streets – the fire had destroyed a house or two before burning out – and Harecher arranged a short-lived truce to recover the corpses garlanding the drawbridge.

Domfront licked her wounds, and mourned her dead in the dark.

I returned to a belated meal in Harecher's manse. The merchant had shed his battered armour. He picked listlessly at food, his eyes like shadowed pits in a haggard face. Richer, returned from the suburb, looked inquiringly at Roger. I related the day's events, and put the boy in his charge.

Richer said, 'What now, my lord? We may count, perhaps, on five days' grace before relief arrives. Will Prince Henry storm the castle?'

I shrugged. 'Unlikely. The besiegers are mercenaries, accustomed to weighing odds, averse to hopeless hazards. They've examined Domfront thoroughly, and dislike the view. That Fleming who commands them is simply going through the motions to pacify his employer.'

'Then what point in staying? Let us go back to Poix.'

'No. We will see the business out, and run when the others run.'

'So leaving us,' said Harecher, 'to Robert of Belesme and death in torment.'

'That,' I said gruffly, 'is the stake you wagered, the penalty for failure. Get out, friend – there's nothing to stop you going.'

Harecher regarded me stonily. 'Do you think, my lord, I would desert the men I led?'

'No. Grant me your pardon.' I scrubbed aching temples; the day had been long and gruelling. 'Roger, what shall we do with you? Do you want to wait for your friends from Roche Mabille?'

Food and rest and watered wine had returned colour to his cheeks. A personable lad, his body lithe and lean, dark hair sweeping his forehead, eyebrows quirking upwards at the corners, a firm decisive mouth. Isabel looked from his eyes. A draught wavered the candles, chased flickering tides of shadow and light across his face, rippled a

quick remembrance that came and went in a flash, an elusive likeness to another I had known. I tried to grasp the memory; it vanished
like a sunbeam quenched by clouds. I rubbed my head again: weari-
ness fostered illusions.

Roger said, 'By your favour, my lord, I had better remain with
you.' His voice faltered. 'I have seen today the consequence of
sack.'

'Your first taste of combat?'

He nodded silently and closed his eyes, saw searing pictures
behind the lids and opened them wide. I said, 'I can return you to
the castle under truce, if you wish.'

'I prefer not. Gunheir of Belesme is a ... brute.'

I recalled my youthful travails in Rouen's Tower, the savageries
that Robert of Belesme inflicted on esquires, and smiled sympathetically. 'A devil's brood, the House of Talvas. Very well. You
stay – we'll discuss your future later. And now to bed.'

7

At dawn I went to the siege lines. The pickets were alert, entrenchments manned, reserves stood ready under arms – daybreak was a
favourite time for sallies. A streak like tarnished copper smeared
the eastern sky, a lingering star gleamed pallidly in a velvet vault
above. The donjon reared like a massive crag; a hidden sun struck
sparks from battlements and ramparts. Dawnlight bred escalades,
and the garrison was vigilant.

I watched while the daylight strengthened and the dangerous
period passed: men-at-arms left sentries in the trenches, wandered
to the huts behind and lighted fires. A savoury smell of cooking
tickled my nostrils. I shared a Breton's breakfast – thick bacon slices,
grilled – and listened to lurid tales of the Conqueror's wars which
Pigot capped with fabulous yarns from dim campaigns. The Flemish
captain paused in passing, and helped himself to bacon.

'Will you attack today?' I asked.

'Not today nor any other,' he grunted. 'Storm that fortress? Look
at it!'

Pensively I regarded the donjon climbing in ascending tiers, grey
stone supporting the topmost storey's ribbed oak walls. A shingled
rooftop crowned the battlements. A tawny, furry pelt quilted the

shingles from eave to eave. I cupped my eyes and stared. Moss, the growth of years, and now bone-dry. There had been no rain for a month.

The idea exploded like a sunburst. I grabbed the Fleming's arm. 'A flaw – the vulnerable point in Domfront's donjon!'

His eyes followed my pointing hand. 'I see no weakness there.'

'How many bowmen in your conroys?'

'A hundred or so.'

Quickly I outlined my plan. The Fleming pinched his lip. 'Nothing is lost by failure,' I urged. 'This is no forlorn hope.'

'A last desperate fling before the siege is lifted.' The Fleming screwed red-rimmed eyes and contemplated the donjon. 'Yes. Definitely possible. We'll have to work like whipthonged villeins to get it done today. Have you told the prince?'

'No.' In Henry's view anything that bore my mark was damned before it was done. 'Go to him now – suggest the scheme as your own. He'll accept an expert's counsel.'

The mercenary departed at a run, and returned with Henry, Clare and the prince's household knights. They stood in a group, scanning the castle, shading eyes against the sunrise. The Fleming argued eloquently; and Henry nodded. I sidled from a sheepcote where I lurked and sent Pigot to summon Harecher. The Fleming assembled his bannerets in a haybarn, and said with a vulpine grin, 'Your royal friends, Lord Walter, have found other occupations. Yours is the conception – you'll explain it better than I. Anything I dislike I'll tell you quick enough!'

I defined the enterprise. The Fleming watched his captains' doubtful expressions, and snapped, 'The thing might work – I promise you that!' They looked at him and gave me full attention.

To Harecher I said, 'You'll muster every man to cut brushwood and bind fascines; collect hay and hurdles from the sheepfolds, and dump them in the market square for making mantlets. I'm sending soldiers to scour the town for braziers and tow – where do you store your fleeces? Pitch also we shall need, a cauldron to every brazier. Is that clear? Right – get moving! Meanwhile,' I told the Fleming, 'there'll be no traffic in the siege lines – all must be done behind the houses, screened from the castle. Bannerets, come with me!'

I led the knights on a circuit of the ramparts, keeping them concealed among the steadings that lapped the fields. I chose locations for the bowmen, a squad to each face of the donjon; and allotted a hidden area for the stormers to assemble. The Fleming listened approvingly, his pinched red face intent. When I finished he observed, 'You're wasted as a vassal knight, my lord – why not join the mercenaries, where merit earns you money? If I read your prince aright, you'll not get even gratitude!'

By noon the preliminaries were done: each banneret knew his task, every bowman his place in the plan. I went to goad the townsmen binding brushwood, to hurry the busy sergeants making mantlets; and saw that everything was sent to the places I appointed. Henry was around, examining the preparations. Though I took care to avoid him he saw me hurrying about; and presently Clare approached.

'The prince commanded that you should not interfere! By whose authority do you give directions?'

The fascines were not being tied as quickly as I wished; I was exasperated and in no mood to tolerate meddlers. 'By the authority of England's king,' I snarled, 'who ordered me on his brother's behalf to take Domfront. I'd welcome your room, my lord – you're in the way!'

'Whatever your instructions, Prince Henry commands in the field!'

'Then I trust he'll lead the storm. An escalade,' I said sardonically, 'is best encouraged from the front.'

Clare choked, and went furiously to Henry, who sent me an ugly look. But his malice no longer mattered. The outcome trembled on a hair: by nightfall Henry would be Domfront's lord or running for his life.

The noonday hours passed. Constantly I examined the donjon for signals of alarm: helmets gathered in a group, arms gesticulating, watches doubled, men at battle posts. The castle drowsed in the heat; sentries unconcernedly patrolled their beats. Sheltered by friendly houses, hidden by cotes and cowsheds, materials and men for Domfront's taking piled like flotsam leashed by a dam.

At vespers all was ready.

8

Bowmen behind mantlets advanced upon the castle. The heavy shields – hay packed and wadded between hurdles – were cumbersome and awkward in the handling; the men who bore them went at a snail-like shuffle. Their appearance hatched a clamour in the castle. Helmets thronged the battlements; spears twinkled on the ramparts. Bowstrings twanged and arrows whirred. The range at first was long, the shafts fell short; when the mantlets lumbered nearer arrows thudded in the hay. The bowmen carrying the shields pressed close against the frames and lowered their heads.

A fifty-pace advance brought the donjon within bowshot; and the archers propped the mantlets. They knelt, unquivered fire-arrows – tow soaked in pitch and wrapped beneath the barbs – lighted them from torches, stood and shot at the moss-furred roof. No need to linger over aiming: none could miss a mark so big. Arrows trailing fiery pennons thumped on shingles. A hundred tiny chimneys spired from the moss.

Water-soaked hides unrolled from embrasures and draped the topmost storey's oak-plank walls. When they realized that the walls were not our target a man-at-arms leaned outwards, clutched a merlon, wriggled perilously beyond the eaves and scanned the roof-top. He edged backwards into safety and we saw his vigorous gestures.

Men scrambled from embrasures and gripped the eaves. Lifted by their comrades round the legs, they clambered on the roof. There they beat with their hands the myriad minute fires spurting from the moss. Our bowmen grunted, felt for the killing arrows, notched and flexed and loosed. They had to stand and take deliberate aim; the enemy's counter-tempest beat about their heads and several bowmen fell. But four-score men were shooting at ten; the figures on the rooftop jerked in turn, slid scrabbling down the slope, tipped over the edge and smashed upon the mound a hundred spans below. An arrow through the belly pinned a sergeant to the shingles; he writhed on the roof like a fishhook-skewered worm.

The fire-arrows were spent. A lull descended on the fight, sundered by the snap and whip of desultory shafts, hammered by a tumult from the battlements. The separate coils of smoke united in a pillar, a blue-grey cloud pursued by fiery fangs. The men who lined the ward glanced anxiously behind them, for the donjon was their haven from the storm.

I crouched in a cowpen, watched the roof and prayed wordlessly for wind. The evening was warm and still; sunset painted splendour on the sky. The Fleming knelt beside me, and noisily sucked his teeth.

'The moss is burning,' he said. 'Will the shingles catch?'

The roof exploded in flame. Blazing streamers snapped like banners, smoke clouds volleyed in whorls. Above the crackle and din we heard the skewered sergeant's scream. Chaos reigned on the battlements; in the blink of an eye they were empty. I seized the Fleming's wrist.

'Loose the assault!'

'No. Wait.' He scrutinized the castle, puckering ferrety eyes, and continued reminiscently, 'In '90 Duke Robert besieged Brionne, and fired the donjon. I was there. There's worse to come.'

The roof collapsed in a salvo of sparks. Flames gnawed the wooden walls; livid rippling tongues licked down the sides; the planks began to burn. The topmost timbers glowed red-hot, embers sprayed like hurtling spears and showered the mound beneath. The Fleming called a warning to the knight who led the stormers.

'Soon they must evacuate. Then we go in.'

The donjon's portal opened, a ladder was pushed from the gap and lowered into place. Soldiers began descending, thronging the rungs. And the upper storey vanished in a giant whoosh of flame, an incandescent furnace bellowing wrath.

'What I was waiting for,' the Fleming remarked contentedly. 'The open door creates a draught.' He swung an arm and shouted, 'Now!'

The stormers, led by fascine carriers, sprinted across the open. The enemy on the ramparts, watching the inferno in horrified dismay, hardly noticed their approach. Faggots thumped in the ditch, the causeway mounted, mercenaries scrambled across, dirks between their teeth, swarmed over the drystone wall and streaked shouting into the ward.

I said to Pigot, 'Give me your bow and quiver.'

I plodded behind the charge, seeking among the crowd the man I wanted. Soldiers flooded the fields; knights and sergeants intermingled converged upon the causeway. Not all of Gunheir's men were taken by surprise: frenzied little battles flared across the paling; firelight flashed on swords like streaks of summer lightning. I came to the crossing place; trampled, sagging brushwood bridged the ditch, dead and wounded sprawled on the farther bank.

A trio of knights prepared to mount the wall. They lifted one amongst them and set him on the crest. He stood, regaining balance, black against the fire. I saw a bulky body and a blazon on the shield.

Henry's blazon.

I nocked an arrow, raised the stave and sighted between his shoulders. A dozen paces' range: the shaft would pierce his mail. 'Your requital, Vauquelin,' I breathed, and loosed.

The knight threw wide his arms and toppled inside the ward. A sweeping surge of men-at-arms, the last of the escalade, ran roaring over the faggots and shouldered me aside. I slipped and fell on my knees, and dropped the bow. Pigot pulled me up. His eyes were wide and his face aghast.

'My lord,' he mumbled, 'that was ...'

I smiled. 'Yes, Pigot. My life is in your hands. Will you betray me?'

His mouth worked soundlessly. He stooped and retrieved the bow, put it in my hand, paused and snatched the stave away. 'I'll carry this. It were better. If any saw ...' He glanced round fearfully.

'None would notice in this riot,' I said. 'Come. Let's cross.'

The drawbridge fell with a crash; the gates creaked open. Clarions yelled in the ward, shrilling above the tumult. 'Stand fast,' I interpreted. 'The garrison has surrendered.'

I walked across the bridge. The ward was all confusion, a bedlam of running men and crumpled bodies, a cauldron where carnage boiled. Mercenaries surrounded a group at the castle's well-head, brandished swords and howled invective. Embers sparked from the blazing donjon. The air was hot, heavy with fire, smelling of blood and sweat. A smoke haze veiled the dying sun, smudging the garish pageant that flamed across the horizon.

I pushed through the ring of soldiers and faced the prisoners they embayed: scarred and tattered men, armour cinder-scorched and torn. A knight in front threw down his sword and shouted, 'I yield! I yield, you rogues! Is there nobody here to control you?'

A broad, crouch-shouldered man, furious and fearless in the face of death. Green eyes glittered in a soot-streaked face. The Talvas mark. I said, 'Gunheir of Belesme?'

'Yes! Who are you?'

'Walter, Lord of Poix. You surrender?'

Angrily he surveyed me. 'You wear a sergeant's mail. How can I know you for a knight? I do not yield Domfront to varlets!'

The mercenaries pressed nearer, spears out-thrust. 'Kill the bastard! A Talvas! Split him apart! Tear his guts!'

I banged my shield in their faces. 'Hold! I claim him prisoner!'

281

The Fleming appeared – else I could not have held these battle-crazed soldiers avid for Gunheir's blood. He showered vicious expletives in the argot used by mercenaries. Sullenly the men backed down. I said to Gunheir, 'Sink your pride, my lord, if you wish to live. Follow me. Keep close.'

'To Prince Henry alone will I yield Domfront!'

The Fleming said casually, 'He's waiting by the gate.'

My mind went blank. I stared at him. 'Henry . . .'

The Fleming spat and ground the gob beneath his foot. 'By the gate. He entered last, after the place was taken.' Contempt soured his tone. 'The prince sets enormous value on his personal safety. How,' he asked of no one in particular, 'can one of the Conqueror's blood be so afraid?'

The Fleming beckoned Gunheir and the little band of captives, opened a path with the flat of his sword and led the way to the gate. I followed in a daze. Henry waited by the gatehouse, his mesnie knights around him, Clare standing at his side. I examined Henry's sallow face, the bulky frame, the mail and blazon – a fork-tailed serpent squirmed upon his shield – and rubbed smarting eyeballs.

Gunheir knelt before the prince. 'Domfront is yours, my lord. For myself I offer ransom.'

Henry said, 'That can wait. I hold you hostage against Count Robert's coming.'

Gunheir said gauntly, 'As you will. My life, in Belesme's eyes, weighs lightly in the scales against Domfront. I think, my lord, you hold a worthless counter.'

Henry strode into the ward, passing me without a glance. I went to the paling where the knight I shot had fallen. The body lay there still, face down, the feathered shaft protruding from his back. Pigot rolled him over. Sightless eyes in a livid face. A knight of Henry's mesnie: Goulafre of Maule – I had seen him at Avranches. The prince's height and build, the same insignia and mail – otherwise unalike.

Pigot closed the eyes and crossed himself. 'A decoy, my lord. Prince Henry takes every precaution.'

'He has reason – here is the evidence!'

I jumped, my nerves on edge. Clare stood behind us. 'How did you find Goulafre? Did you see him fall?'

'I saw him fall.'

'A careless shaft from a Breton bowman, doubtless?'

I gazed across the ward. The sun was gone. The donjon's flames quenched daylight's fading shreds; an evening breeze wafted cinders and the smell of fire. Voices hummed in the streets: the townsfolk, penned within doors during the assault, came forth to taste their new-won freedom.

'No,' I answered slowly. 'The shaft was truly aimed. Only the mark was false.'

9

Henry's hirelings garrisoned the castle, cleansed the stains of battle and hastily rebuilt the gutted donjon. Count Hugh brought reinforcements from Avranches: five-score knights and mounted sergeants, four hundred men-at-arms. Then patrols watching Roche Mabille reported an army marching: a thousand swords, they reckoned. Henry called to council his mesnie knights, Hugh's liegemen and the mercenary captains: a hundred knights thronged Domfront's hall. Expedients plausible, impossible and foolish were offered and rejected. The prince spoke little; his eyes searched the speakers' faces as if testing not only the proposals but the worth of the men who made them.

Hugh finally slapped his thighs and said impatiently, 'We talk in circles, my lords. Only three courses are feasible. First, we shut ourselves in the castle and stand a leaguer.'

'Then Belesme,' said Harecher, 'will destroy the town at leisure.'

'Correct. And you, my lord' – Hugh's eyebrows bristled at Henry – 'will inherit a damaged castle engirdled by ruins. Secondly, we can offer battle. Our numbers are roughly equal to Belesme's.'

'I am not inclined,' said Henry coldly, 'to gamble all I've won on a hazardous scuffle between equal forces.'

'Chancy affairs, battles,' the Fleming agreed. 'You never know how they'll go.'

'Right,' said Hugh. 'Which leaves the final course: to treat with Belesme.'

'A threadbare hope,' said Clare. 'Count Robert's not the type to yield his castles lightly. What have we to offer?'

'His nephew Gunheir's life,' said I.

'You heard Gunheir estimate his value!'

Hugh said smoothly, 'Also four thousand pounds of silver.'

Astonished faces looked at him. 'And where,' said Henry at last, will you find this sum, my lord?'

'I've brought the money from Avranches. With Domfront taken, Rufus foresaw that a salve must be provided to soothe Robert's injured pride.'

'You never told me this,' said Henry dangerously.

'The king hoped you'd compel Belesme by force of arms to accept his loss; and forbade me to reveal the offer until all else failed. It is, in truth, an enormous sum to squander. But now . . .' Hugh spread his hands. 'I think we should try this scheme, and send an embassy to Robert.'

'A perilous mission,' Clare said, frowning blackly. 'Belesme's temper won't be sweet: our messenger is like to lose his head. Whom shall we send?'

Henry surveyed the assembled knights. They avoided his look, fussily adjusted spur straps, stared at the ground. He looked at me speculatively.

'Tirel, I think,' he said. 'Unless you are afraid?'

'Not I, my lord.' I rose, and added pleasantly, 'Cowardice, like plague, spreads fast from a craven heart. My Saints are vigilant – the contagion passed me by. Not everyone, it seems, is so well protected.'

I left behind me in the hall a silence deep as the tomb.

10

Pigot and Richer rode beside me; men-at-arms escorted mules which varlets led. An outrider far in front bore a leaf-garlanded spear. In a secluded grove near Pré-en-Pail I concealed the mules and half the men-at-arms, leaving orders to return hotfoot to Domfront if I sent no word by sundown. We went faster when we had shed the mules; and a bowshot beyond Pré saw a dust haze lacing the clouds. Outriders trotted from the murk and surrounded my herald. I stopped and waited. Presently they led me to Robert of Belesme.

He sat a restive destrier, his helmet swinging by the coif. Hair glossy as black marble framed eyes like splintered emeralds.

'An embassy from Henry? I'm on my way to speak to him with swords! You'd better not delay me long, my lord!'

Quickly I stated my case. Belesme had lost Domfront; Prince Henry held the castle with forces equal to his own; a leaguer would be lengthy and expensive. We held captive Gunheir and his garrison

– those that survived the fighting – and would release the knights unransomed in return for Domfront's seisin.

The thin lips curled in scorn. 'Do you believe I prize so highly a bungling castellan's life? I shall hang him myself for yielding!'

His knights listened impatiently. They were riding to a fight that promised plunder, and the interruption irked them.

'By your favour, my lord of Belesme, a word alone.'

His mouth tightened. I realized he feared treachery: Black Robert trusted no one. I rammed my lance in the ground, unbuckled baldric, unsheathed dagger, gave the weapons to Richer and said quietly, 'You are safe from me, my lord.'

We rode a little apart and halted beside a muddied pool that edged the road. I said, 'You will never regain your fief. The fist that grips Domfront has England's arm behind it. Can you prevail against Rufus?'

Belesme slapped a horsefly on his destrier's neck and flicked it from his fingers. The tiny carcass curved and plopped in the water. 'You're talking rubbish. I ride to quell a gang of rebellious merchants, a rising fostered and supported by that hell-dog Hugh of Avranches. A local revolt – I've dealt with them before. Rufus has no hand in this. Nor, my lord of Poix, do I understand your part.'

Talking swiftly, I told him the whole story. 'England,' I ended, 'is resolved to hold Domfront: a stepping-stone for crossing into Maine. If you persist, my lord, you pit yourself against a kingdom's might. I do not decry your power – but can you win?'

Belesme ran a finger beneath his ventail, which seemed to discommode him. 'I have contended against princes. I fought Duke Robert —'

'And also Rufus,' I put in quietly. 'At Rochester. You remember the result?'

The count made guttural noises.

'You will not be the loser, my lord. King William is no robber baron. He offers recompense.'

Belesme's nose twitched like a brachet scenting deer. 'Recompense? What kind? Land? Money? Castles?'

'Money.'

'How much?'

'Four thousand pounds of silver.'

Count Robert blinked. 'God's navel! Rufus must wallow in wealth! The place is not worth half. Let me think.' Hand to mouth, he walked his horse away, slipped his rein and let the destrier snuffle the murky pool.

'Where is the silver?'

'When your seal is on the covenant, and witnessed by your barons, I will show you where it's hidden.'

He gave me a dubious look – Belesme judged others by his own mistrustful standards. But I stood completely at his mercy, and perfidy meant death – fifty blades would slice me into shreds. He assented with a grunt. Richer took from a scrip a parchment writ, from a saddlebag inkhorn and quill. The charter, prepared by Count Hugh's clerks, resigned to Henry Domfront's seisin, rights and revenues. I had learned the terms by rote, and quoted them aloud; Belesme could read and cipher and followed my words on the writ. He laid the parchment on his saddlebow and wrote his name: the lords of Perrie, Blève and Mamers – Belesme's vassals – made their marks. I tucked the scroll inside my hauberk.

'Follow me, my lord.' I smiled crookedly. 'You won't need an army at your back.'

Belesme signalled to his bannerets; a disappointed column turned about. He chose an escort; and I led the little party to the grove where the pack-mules waited. Belesme unstrapped the panniers and inspected the deniers piled within. His tongue flickered between his lips; he looked at me alertly. Clear as glass I read his mind: the charter was his for a slash; my life trembled on treachery's brink. But not even Robert Talvas might forswear his witnessed word – else property laws were meaningless and courtoisie was void.

On this slender hope I had staked my head.

Belesme looked at me straightly. 'None could doubt your courage, Walter Tirel. Why should you doubt my honour? Go in peace.'

II

Hugh of Avranches sat in Harecher's hall and fondled a cup of wine. I sprawled in a chair, wearied in mind and body: the stress of the last ten days was taking toll. Roger of Conches refilled Harecher's goblet – a nicely mannered boy, well trained: our cups were always brimming. Rain splattered the window shutters; a storm-wind pierced the chinks and streamed the candle flames.

Hugh suspended the charter between finger and thumb. 'It was bravely done, Walter. I confess I had not expected to greet you again.' He chuckled; a skein of wrinkles spoked from the corners of his eyes. 'The years must have mellowed Belesme! Our enterprise has ended well – and most of it your doing.'

'Prince Henry is . . . satisfied?'

Hugh lost his smile. 'No one can interpret Henry's thoughts.'

Harecher said, 'The prince has publicly pledged his oath to retain our laws and customs, and never relinquish Domfront.' (Henry kept his word: he holds the town to this day.)

'So. You've got rid of Belesme, Henry gains a fief and Rufus a stronghold. Everyone's happy except . . .'

Hugh looked at me kindly. 'The prince will offer you no favours, Walter.'

'I expected none.'

'You'll find Rufus less ungrateful. He wants you in England – I had a letter today. If you take my advice you'll go.'

I stared blearily into the candles and let the proposition sink into my tired mind. Why not? England, they said, was a tranquil land where men could ride unarmed. I felt suddenly sick of fighting. Save for the Honours that Rufus held, Neustria seethed with strife, a vat where warfare boiled and intrigue bubbled. Delis defended Poix – a faithful, dependable liege – so my fiefs were safe. Then there was Isabel. Must I – could I – sever the tie?

Roger bent to snuff a guttering wick. The light burnished his sun-tanned features and night-dark hair: a living portrait of the woman I loved. Again that transient memory teased me: a likeness to another from the past.

I took his hand.

'Will you, if your sire agrees, come with me to England?'

'Willingly, my lord!'

'Count Hugh,' I said to that wizened knight, 'I'll follow your advice.'

Chapter 4

1092

A BRAWLING wind chased clouds across the sun and dappled the
sea in green and purple patches. Breakers in successive lines, white-
maned like charging squadrons, lifted the keels of anchored ships
and kept them rocking. A chain of men, tunics girt waist-high, bore
baggage to a hoy moored in the shallows. Spray soaked them to the
shoulders, rimed their hair.

I sat on Boulogne's beach, and viewed the prospect with foreboding.

When the loading was almost finished I mounted a mariner's
back, rode staggering through the breakers, clambered aboard the
bouncing ship and wrung water from my robe. A berner clutching
brachets beneath his arms bundled the hounds on deck; an ostringer
climbed awkwardly aboard, a falcon nervously clawing his wrist. I
surveyed the crowded hull. Corded bundles crammed the stern; my
retinue filled prow and midships. Besides Richer I had brought Pigot
and six men-at-arms, Berenger and Roger and a household knight:
Lisiard of St Remi, a taciturn man whose fief Belesme had ravished.
My grooms and horses – a destrier and twelve palfreys – had already
sailed in a hoy equipped for the purpose: a speck on the tumbled
horizon marked their passage.

Drowned in the wind that thrummed the rigging, voices hailed
from the shore. Three monks of Benedictus stood like smoke-blacked
pillars among fisherfolk who watched the hoy's departure. The shipman said respectfully, 'The holy fathers seek a passage to England,
master. Is it your pleasure to let them board?'

The rocking deck had made me queasy. I rapped impatiently, 'Yes
– if the extra weight won't sink your hulk! Get them quickly
aboard and sail as soon as you can.' The shipman beckoned and
bellowed: two monks wrapped gowns round navels, carried the
third through the rollers and deposited him on the strakes. A frail,
aged man, hair snowy around his tonsure, brown watery eyes and

a face like crumpled parchment. He sat on a rope-bound bale, smiled thankfully and said, 'You've earned my gratitude, my son. I bought passage on another ship . . .' The roar of wind and water smothered his excuses; the anchored hoy yawed wickedly.

I hung miserably over the side and squinted at the surf.

The shipman chanted orders; the anchor swung aboard, oars rattled in the tholes and turned the prow to sea. The hoy rolled broadside on; the mast thrashed drunken circles on the sky. The seamen tugged with a will, and dragged the ship from the shallows. A green and crimson sail climbed to the masthead and bellied at the sheets. The hoy plunged madly on her course.

I voided my breakfast into the sea, and cradled head on arms.

The monk said hesitantly, 'I have a remedy for this sickness, my son.' From his gown he produced a silver phial of the kind that pilgrims use to carry holy water. 'An essence distilled from poppy seeds, quite harmless – an anodyne for rebellious stomachs.'

'Father,' I replied wretchedly, 'I would willingly swallow hemlock if it eased my suffering.' I drained the phial. 'I shall remember you in my prayers. What is your name, Father?'

'Anselm, Abbot of Bec.'

I tried to think of anything but the pitching ship and quick, unruly sea. Roger crouched at my feet, proffered a wineskin – rudely refused – and a napkin to wipe my mouth. Berenger draped a cloak around my shoulders. Devoted and willing esquires: they served my every need. Particularly Roger. My thoughts drifted to my meeting with his parents. From Domfront I had fetched a roundabout route, escorted by a constabular that Hugh of Avranches provided. My reception at Conches was mixed: Isabel all joyful radiance, Ralph in sulky wrath.

'You ride like a monarch on progress across my marches,' he snarled, 'careless of the hurts I've suffered at your hands. I've a mind to clap you again in the vault you know so well!'

I looked at his damp, protuberant eyes, wet lips and sloping chin. 'If you do,' I told him, 'you'll lose your son.'

'Roger?' said Isabel, startled. 'You've brought him from Domfront?'

'He's now half-way to Poix in Richer's charge. A hostage, you might say, for my safe-conduct in Conches.'

Ralph's lips quivered. 'An ignoble shift, my lord! A stripling's life protects your own!'

'Only a dolt puts a naked hand in a scorpion's nest. Roger is my glove.' (Which was true: but I had trusted more to Ralph's irresolute nature: another in his place would have cut my throat on sight.) 'I intend no harm to your son – much the reverse.'

Isabel looked at me strangely, a look I could not interpret, tinged as it was with a kind of secret amusement. 'Why have you come, my lord?' she asked quietly.

I gazed at the rafters of Conches's hall, where once I had hung head down in pain, and related the history of Domfront's leaguer – omitting certain details – and of Roger's rescue. Because Robert of Belesme swore his nephew's life was forfeit, Gunheir for his own protection had promised fealty to Prince Henry and became a household knight in Domfront's mesnie. Sons of baronial Houses did not serve landless knights: the esquire had lost his lord. What better, I inquired, than that Roger should serve in my retinue at England's court where, under King William's eye, he might win advancement – perhaps, in time, an English fief? Ralph, after all, was Rufus's man; and a liege's son in his suzerain's mesnie was favourably placed.

I oozed persuasion and conciliation. Isabel needed neither. Whipped by her arguments, Ralph reluctantly agreed: I realized incredulously that the wretched man still loved his wanton spouse and could, in the end, deny her nothing. Somewhere, hidden deep, there was iron in Ralph's soul, otherwise he could never have held his fiefs against the pitiless men who then tormented Normandy. To this day I stand astounded that a lord so supine kept his lands so long.

A racing wave flung sprindrift in my face. I tasted salt on my tongue, and wiped my eyes. Boulogne was far astern, Ponthieu's coast a hazy streak. The scarlet dragon that crested the prow cavorted wildly. Clouds sported around the sun, trailed tresses across the sky. Barely terce, I judged; and we would not berth till vespers. Holy Mary Virgin, give me strength! I flinched from a vicious roll – and felt the sickness easing. Maybe the abbot's potion worked.

I closed eyelids on the thrashing sea; my thoughts wandered back to Poix.

Adelice had greeted me in tremendous indignation: the steward, she swore, defrauded the coffers of revenues from our fleeces. I investigated my lady's charge, found it warranted, flogged the steward, severed his hands and banished him from my lands. She was utterly incurious about my activities in Normandy. I told her a little of Domfront's taking – she thought it a town in Anjou. Only in Roger of Conches did she show any interest: when I presented my new esquire her eyes dwelt long on his face. She turned his head to the light. 'A remarkable likeness,' Adelice murmured. 'The spit of the Lady Isabel,' I agreed. She sent me a peculiar look, opened her lips to speak and firmly closed them again. She amiably acquiesced in my plans for England; and ventured timidly to suggest she might join me later. For that, I told her gruffly, I could make no promise.

The hoy rose on a towering wave, and fell like a stooping hawk. I pushed away from the side, surveyed the distant coast, a ridge like a whitewashed fence surmounted by hanging clouds. The abbot touched my shoulder. 'Dover's cliffs,' he said. 'Has your sickness passed, my son?'

'It has passed. Yours was potent medicine. What vitally urgent mission compels you, Father Abbot, to cross this accursed sea?'

The old man sat beside me, and folded his gown over spindly shanks. 'The Abbey of Bec holds English lands at Deverel and Swinecombe. The royal tallages are heavy. I seek to persuade King William to lighten our burden.'

Rufus, I knew, disliked all priests save one: his treasurer Flambard. I considered it improbable that this fragile dotard – he was sixty if a day – would ever extract from that venal pair a single counterfeit coin.

'Have you visited England before?' I asked politely.

'Yes. In '78, when the Conqueror reigned. A lovely land – I'm happy to return. Duke William, a just and reverent ruler, gave me a gracious welcome. I fear my reception now may be harsh. The king's unlike his father.'

'Rufus,' I said warmly, 'is reputed just.'

'True. Also honourable and a peerless knight. Yet I doubt he holds the Church in much esteem.'

'He fears God, and maintains His right.'

'Rufus,' said Anselm serenely, 'fears neither God, nor man, nor the Devil.'

2

We rested the night at Dover – it took me years to pronounce these English names which I now produce so glibly – Richer hired carts and we took the road to London. Anselm travelled with us; he borrowed a mule and ambled along between his attendant monks. I found him strangely attractive, tolerant and wise – a contrast to the knights among whom I lived my life, different as a leveret from a leopard. His manner was engaging, his interests wide. Frequently he became abstracted, communing within himself as though the visible world were but a transitory shadow, the actions of its inhabitants a feverish dream. My questions roused him from his daydreams; for there was much in England's countryside I found surprising.

September's sunlight warmed our backs, and the trees wore summer's livery. The road climbed swelling downlands, skirted forests, traversed fields and farms. The harvest was all gathered, sheep grazed the stubble, plough teams turned the soil and cattle lowed in meadows. Strip-fields girdled villages like particoloured quilts. Peasants paused in their work to watch our passing, leaned on mattocks and called unintelligible greetings; children ran to the roadside and cadged titbits from the varlets. Once only, on all the road from Dover until Canterbury, I saw on an eminence the towering bulk of a donjon. These peasants lived unguarded, worked far from protective castles, indifferent to the distances which severed them from safety.

I remembered Normandy, her ravaged fields and ruined villages, the villeins who ran for refuge when they sighted steel, the shuttered forts that loomed on every hill, the steadings clustered fearfully beneath. Anselm studied my wonder, amusement in his eyes.

'In all Normandy or France,' I declared, 'you will find no man born of woman who is not shut up in a castle or a tower. But here —'

'Very different,' the abbot agreed. 'The reason is simply this: in England private warfare is illegal – one of Duke William's decrees, which is strictly enforced by his son.'

'How, then,' I protested, 'may a lord resolve a difference with his neighbour?'

'The king adjudicates in all disputes, according to law and custom. Consider, my son, the consequence of anarchy in Normandy: lords whose harried fields produce no revenues, who live only by looting their rivals, or on the ransoms of captured knights. Because England's barons get revenues from cultivated fields they have no need to pillage.'

The sun climbed high in the sky. I loosed my cloak and threw it to Roger. A linnet hovering in the transparent blue above carolled farewell to summer. We overtook pilgrims trudging in the dust; they gave us respectful passage and besought the abbot's blessing. Anselm signed the air and murmured Latin. I examined the band in passing:

fair-skinned, gold-haired men, burlier and taller than their fellows over the sea and much less servile in demeanour.

'Merchants?' I hazarded.

Anselm looked the party over. 'No. Men of the soil – ploughmen, millers, haywards. A reeve and, I think, a bailiff. People from some local Honour, journeying to Christ's Church for harvest thanksgiving.'

'They don't bear themselves like villeins.'

'They're not, my son – they're free. In Normandy as you know there are three classes of men: soldiers, priests and labourers. The labourers are villeins, bound in service to their lords; for, as it is truly said, *"Gent senz seignur sunt malement bailli."* But here you have the English, and therein lies the difference.'

Lucidly, with pauses while he fell a-dreaming, Anselm enlightened me about England. Duke William, he explained, conquered a land which contained two social classes: thegns and ceorls (unutterable English words!). In general the thegns were wealthy; while a ceorl could thrive and achieve the higher status – a feat impossible in Normandy. All ceorls were freemen: some owned land, others cultivated fields belonging to the thegns; all bore arms and none owed boon-work on their seigneurs' lands. The lowliest place was held by slaves – descendants of foreign invaders – who worked on the thegns' estates and corresponded to Neustria's villeins.

But the Conqueror imposed an alien system, a principle strange to England: that the king owned every arpent of land and leased them to his barons in return for military service. Estates were broken up, the thegns dispossessed; everyone moved down in the social scale; many impoverished ceorls accepted the boon-work stigma and therefore lost their freedom.

'Year by year,' Anselm lamented, 'more English husbandmen become what we call villeins. But a residue survives, sturdy freemen farmers who hang spears and iron caps above the hearth and serve at call in the fyrd.'

'The fyrd?'

'The English levies – those whom Rufus summoned in '88 to smash the Great Rebellion. Thirty thousand rallied to his standard. With these and a handful of knights the king defeated men like Mowbrai and Belesme, Montgommeri and Mortain; and saved his crown. Englishmen, though conquered, remain formidable warriors.'

'We beat them at Hastings,' I asserted; and hummed a derisive stave, a relict of the battle.

' "*Li Engleis sunt bon vantur, ne se sevent oster.*
Mielz sevent as gros hanaps beivre e gueisseillier." '
Anselm smiled. 'The English are indeed braggarts and gluttons and inveterate drunkards. Nevertheless I assure you they can fight.'

On Canterbury's outskirts the road was stopped by a concourse of monks and priests who were gathered to greet Anselm. They crowded round him, reverently touched his gown and kissed his feet. I waited, wondering. The frail little monk was apparently famous, his name renowned. He announced apologetically that his brethren insisted he break his journey, blessed me and bade farewell.

I slept in an inn at Rochester and crossed London bridge at noon next day.

The Tower's battlements reared four bowshots distant. We turned right-handed from the bridge and plunged into teeming streets. The world had spilled its peoples into London: Moors in feathered turbans, Ethiopians black as night, swarthy bearded Jews, slit-eyed yellow creatures from the lands of the rising sun, Saracens from Outremer and mariners of Spain. Among them stalked the English, the broidery's homespun weave.

Rouen I knew, and Paris: London was a universe in comparison.

I shall not describe the Tower: a replica of Rouen's, known to all. Inside the ward a counterfeit town clustered round a timbered hall – barrack huts and stables, granaries and kennels, armouries and mews. I shouldered through the crowd – men-at-arms and knights, lords, esquires and grooms – and went into the hall. A seneschal led me the chamber's length to Rufus on the dais.

He put his hands on my shoulders and rocked me back and forth. 'Walter! At last! For five years since my father died I've tempted you to England! At last! I shall not easily let you go! You've done me splendid service; I do not forget my friends.'

Rufus sent esquires scurrying for meat and wine. The barons at the table eyed me; I was a stranger clearly honoured by the king, possibly a rival in the race for royal favours. Some I already knew: Meulan's grizzled features smiled a welcome, I clasped fitzHamon's hand. I spoke the others fair, trying to remember names, bewildered by the noise and colour and light.

Candles flared in crystal lustres, though the sun had not yet set; torches sputtered in girandoles; a fire blazed on the hearth. The knights of the royal household talked loudly over their wine; servants and esquires scuttled beween the benches; a minstrel strummed a chanson on his lute, the melody faint as a dream, drowned in the surf of sound. Berselets snuffled bones among the rushes; a kitchen-maid squealed loudly when a man-at-arms pinched her thigh. Everywhere was colour: cloaks auburn and vermilion, mantles emerald and blue, and a coruscating brilliance of necklaces and gems. The hall was a peacock riot, azure, vert and gules, scented by wine and woodsmoke and the acrid smell of sweat.

I dwell upon this picture, familiar to any gentle man as the rivets in his helmet, because the gaiety and gaud made a stimulating contrast to Normandy's sombre halls where torches gleamed on armour more often than on silk. Rufus worshipped colour, fine cloth and precious stones, and demanded that his revelries – save one – be flooded in light.

The clefts of darkness I encountered later.

The king was in high good humour, laughter quaked his burly chest and his scarlet visage shone. His yellow hair fell shoulder length; this seemed the common mode: most knights had saved the barbers trouble. I fingered my bristled neck, shaved close in the Norman manner; and heard a snigger at my ear.

Golden threads embroidered Ranulf Flambard's priestly robe, miniver and vair trimmed collar and hem. The years had lent distinction to his haggardly handsome features, and stippled grey the flaming halo round his tonsure. 'Fashions change, my lord ' – he smiled – 'in hair and clothes and . . . conduct. Withhold your condemnation; do not judge too hastily. Much the same advice as I gave you years ago. Remember?'

I assented briefly and spoke of something else. Flambard wakened memories best forgotten.

The king inquired courteously about my journey. I described ruefully my sickness, and mentioned the Abbot of Bec. Rufus glowered.

'That scheming priest!' he snapped. 'So they've brought him over, have they? It's well you warned me!'

I let my astonishment show. 'Anselm only seeks remission of tallages on Bec's estates. What schemes could he have in mind? I think him a guileless man, a dreamer quite incapable of plots.'

'A pretext! Little do you know!' He beckoned Flambard; they put their heads together and talked in lowered voices.

I left the hall and sought my mesnie in the ward. The horses were stabled, Pigot and the men-at-arms housed in a barrack, grooms and servants sleeping where they could. Lisiard led me inside the Tower, up a stairway winding within tremendous walls, to a chamber full of knights and men-at-arms. He indicated an alcove by the door, and said morosely, 'This is where we sleep. I've known better in a bog-knight's donjon.' I laughed – Lisiard would have faulted paradise – and sent the boys for straw and sacking. We stretched upon the palliasses comfortably enough, shut our ears to gabbing voices, a raucous song a drunken knight was bawling, and settled down to sleep.

The esquires were tired and glad to relax; Lisiard lay like the dead, and soon was snoring; Richer alone seemed restless. He sat on the straw, his sound arm clasping his knees, and stared into the shadows which the single cresset cast. I touched his hand, and said, 'What ails you, friend?'

Richer turned his head. His eyes were unhappy. 'How long do you plan to serve the king, my lord?'

'How can I tell? For as long as he may need me.'

A knight relieved from vigil clanked across the flagstones, tripped on a recumbent form and swore. The Saracen watched him absently, and said, 'We must guard Roger and Berenger, my lord. This company smells of sin.'

3

I remained at Rufus's court; and he demanded my attendance at council and carouse, in banqueting and business. He loaded me with gifts; a bay destrier bred in Flanders, a mascled hauberk forged by Angevin smiths, furred cloaks and silken mantles, a sword of Spanish steel. He examined our squalid quarters in the Tower, and insisted that we sleep on quilted pallets in the passage outside his bedroom – a chamber on the topmost floor. I told Richer to shift our baggage; he demurred, and looked me straightly in the eye. I nibbled my thumb, made excuses to the king, and stayed where we were.

We rode hawking beyond the marshes that lapped the northern walls, and hunted boar in woodlands south of Southwark. Always Rufus showed me favour, called me friend and gossip. So long as no one crossed him he was rowdily good tempered, slapping his lords on the back, flinging a friendly arm about a shoulder, digging someone in the ribs.

Engaged in state affairs he became a different man. I came to know the council chamber well: a lofty, vaulted hall on the Tower's second floor. Garbed regally in ermined velvet, a gold diadem on his head, Rufus adjudicated tersely on law and life and death. Though in fiscal affairs he listened to Flambard's advice, he seldom consulted his council – and never offered reasons. He listened patiently to petitioners, his questions shrewd and pointed, like well directed arrows. But priestly opposition and infractions of forest law could engulf him in a fury terrible to see.

Twelve Englishmen were haled before him, accused of taking deer from Windsor forest. Rufus observed the law and delivered the men to judgement by ordeal of hot iron. On the third day they were brought to council; the bandages were loosed and their hands discovered unscathed. Rufus exploded, stammering in rage. 'Is t-this God's wilful verdict? By the Face, no longer will I t-trust an unjust judge! Let t-these scoundrels lose the hands that God has healed!'

The blasphemy stunned his councillors into silence.

When Anselm came to the Tower the king greeted him in friendly fashion, accepted the abbot's blessing and led him to the council table. They conversed amiably awhile. Then the king sent the sandglass a sidelong look – he had ordered the falcons for noon – and said pleasantly, 'How, Father Abbot, may we assist in any business that has brought you to our realm?'

Anselm hesitated. Even the bravest flinched from crossing Rufus. 'Sire, I must submit for your consideration that the tallages on Deverel and Swinecombe are unduly heavy.' A monk handed him a scroll, and Anselm read, 'Annually from Deverel a hundred muids of wine, of barley forty bushels...'

His voice droned on. I leaned elbows on the table, and watched dust-flecks dancing in sashes of sunlight flowing through high slim windows. Walter Giffard, the aged chancellor, began to snore; Meulan nodded slowly into slumber, the barons' rumps moved restlessly on hard oak chairs. Rufus listened intently, his eyes on Anselm's face; Flambard's aquiline features wore a wary expression. The abbot finished his statement. Flambard countered his points in turn; the argument dissolved into technicalities, in vine yields to the arpent and bushels to the hide. My thoughts returned to Isabel of Conches.

Anselm's voice recalled me. 'Let us leave it there, my lord. I must stay content with your remissions. They are little enough.' His smile was like a moon-gleam that briefly lighted an eroded land. 'There is a greater matter, surpassingly important, which my brothers of Canterbury have persuaded me, unworthy as I am, to press upon you.' He looked at the barons' bored and listless faces. 'May I speak plainly?'

'I hide no secrets from my lords of the council.' Rufus's voice was cold.

Dignity and purpose hardened Anselm's delicate features. 'I would fail in my duty, my lord, were I not to speak as I am bidden. What I must say affects both England's welfare and her king's spiritual salvation. The people of your realm, my lord, daily say things of you which in no way become your royal office. You have done grave wrong to Holy Church. England's subjects groan beneath your abuses. And you yourself, sire, conduct your life in a manner which befouls all that men hold sacred.'

Nobody blinked an eyelash. Slowly I drew in my breath, and soundlessly released it. Flambard regarded the abbot curiously; a hint of admiration glimmered briefly in his eyes. Rufus alternately spread his fingers and closed his fists. A vein throbbed in his temple.

He clasped his hands tightly together.

'I cannot help, Father Abbot,' he grated, 'what men choose to say of me. I can only suggest that so holy a man as you ought not to believe such stories. For the sake of my father and mother, who bestowed on you their friendship, I shall not answer in the fashion your insolence merits. You have leave to depart.'

Anselm rose. His legs were shaking. Saints who hazard martyrdom must sometimes be afraid. 'I shall pray for you, my son.'

'Pray yourself stupid!' Rufus answered violently. 'I shall live my life according to my will. No man's prayers will deflect my purpose!'

His monks supported Anselm to the door. Rufus strode from the chamber. The sentinel knight who guarded his throne clattered hastily in pursuit – the king was never unescorted. fitzHamon looked quizzically at Meulan, and jerked his head; they left together. The lords of the council conferred in a group, muttering and shaking their heads. Walter Giffard woke from his doze and rubbed rheumy eyes. I blew out my cheeks, and sank into a seat beside Flambard.

'What,' I asked, 'was all that about?'

The priest ceased scribbling on a tablet, dropped the stylus and said, 'Politics and finance mingled – the two can seldom be unravelled. Anselm's stirring a broiling stew, and is likely to scorch his fingers.'

I said feelingly, 'The man has enormous courage. To scold Rufus to his face —!'

'A paltry gesture. More important is that he's the keystone of a conspiracy – whether wittingly or not I'm still uncertain – woven by the bishops. They're trying to push him into Canterbury.'

I said, bewildered, 'Archbishop? Worthy, I would say, for primacy – the man's a saint in all but name. Why should Rufus —'

'For financial reasons,' Flambard said crossly. 'Can't you understand? All land belongs to the king. Bishops and abbots are among the realm's chief tenants, and receive their lands from the king. When a prelate dies his estates revert to Rufus, who alone has power to nominate a successor. If he delays the nomination those revenues flow into his coffers.'

I began to see light. 'So the longer that bishoprics and abbacies stay vacant, the greater the treasury's gain?'

'Exactly. You can't run a kingdom without money, and the king has huge expenses. Belesme's recompense for Domfront was but a tittle. Eventually, of course, the livings have to be filled – you can't, equally, run a kingdom without priests – so the king grants the land to the highest bidder. Very profitable: Herbert Losinga, Abbot of Ramsey, recently bought Thetford's see for a thousand silver pounds.'

'And Canterbury?'

'Vacant for the last four years, since Lanfranc died. The Church is outraged – you should see the reprimands from Rome! – the nobility is scandalized, and even the English murmur. Rufus merely laughs.'

'And will go on laughing!'

Absorbed in Flambard's revelations, I had not noticed the king's return. Rufus had recovered his temper; mirth peeped from the odd-coloured eyes. He clapped his treasurer's shoulder. 'Ranulf conceives these ploys; he has a genius for diverting money into my exchequer. Without him the realm would have been destitute long since. As for Canterbury —! Lanfranc was enough. I don't want another carping prelate peering over my shoulder and disparaging all I do. Anselm, that bishops' puppet, had better return to Bec before I run him out of England!'

I said, 'He's a saintly man, my lord, who I believe sees in the whole universe nothing real or valuable except the law of God.' (Earlier, against Anselm, I had taken Rufus's part; now I pleaded on the abbot's behalf – an ambiguity that endured throughout my relations with monk and king.) 'He has no ambition for this world's rewards and trophies.'

299

'Not for the archbishopric of Canterbury?' A sneer slithered through Rufus's words.

Flambard said disconcertingly, 'I think it's the last thing he wants.'

Rufus laughed. 'If Anselm had any hopes of Canterbury he'd clap his hands and run into my arms! Rather than make that snivelling monk archbishop, I'd take the pallium myself!'

I flinched a little. Flambard impassively closed his tablets. He was used to his master's blasphemies.

4

And now I must speak plainly of the company I kept.

I am not overly censorious; a lifetime spent in camp and castle planes the edges of fastidiousness. I know men who kill for fun, and torture for enjoyment, men who pillage churches and rape the Sisters of Christ. You could not live in Normandy without meeting knights like these, of whom the monarch and exemplar was Robert of Belesme. Every crime the law condemns, every sin that heaven forbids had passed in a sad procession before my eyes.

Including sodomy.

There are worse perversions: I have lived awhile among peasants and seen them practised. I do not condemn true pederasts, for God has as surely afflicted them as any leper. But I hate them for their proselytism, their insatiable appetite for corrupting others. I despise their victims, men whose tastes are natural but who experiment with sodomy's allures like timid bathers gingerly dipping their toes in icy water. When I contemplate their practices I want to vomit.

This said, I revered Rufus, king of perverts.

I was not blind to the malignant bane that flourished at his court, flaunted plain as poppies in a cornfield; yet I steadily ignored a depravity which, I decided, concerned me not at all.

I deceived myself.

One day Richer found me watching my destriers groomed; he led Berenger by the ear. 'Perhaps he'll obey your orders,' the Saracen said. 'The scamp won't heed my rating.'

He released his hold. Berenger sulkily rubbed his ear.

'What's the trouble, Richer?'

'Look at his hair!'

The carroty tresses fell to his shoulders. I touched a curl, and rubbed it between my fingers.

'God's face, it's crimped!'

'He used hot irons,' Richer agreed. 'I caught him.'

Berenger said sullenly, 'I follow the fashion, my lord. Is that wrong?' He gestured to the knights who strolled in the stable yard. 'Would you chastise everyone who wears long hair?'

I saw his point. The younger knights to a man flaunted hair as long as women's, parted from the crown and falling beside the forehead. Some sported wispy beards. That at least exceeded young Berenger's powers. I studied the affected gestures, mincing gait and rolling hips. A woman's walk. Anger closed my throat; the contagion was afflicting boys for whom I was responsible. I drew a dagger, thumbed the edge.

'Turn round!'

I sawed the precious tresses, which fluttered to the ground. The grooms relaxed their currying and snickered behind their hands. Berenger stood rock-still, his face aflame. Without benefit of water I scraped his nape and shaved the hair above his ears. Then I slapped him hard across the face.

'That for your idiocy! You are Carenci – will you ape the catamite?'

Berenger lifted his chin and stared me proudly in the eyes. 'I don't know what you mean, my lord.'

'Holy thorns!' I said, exasperated. 'Are you so innocent at twelve years' age?' I caught Richer's eye. 'Bring Roger.'

Richer shook his head. 'He is not —'

'Bring him!'

Berenger's fingers crept to the scarlet blot where I had hit him; tears filled his eyes. I turned hastily away, discovered an imaginary mud fleck beneath a stallion's stifle, and cursed the grooms. Richer returned with Roger. I led them out of earshot to a coign behind the stables, and leaned against a hitching-post.

'I will now,' I announced harshly, 'instruct you about sodomy.'

The diatribe that followed would have earned a bishop's approval; no hellfire-preaching priest could have been more damning. The esquires listened with starting eyes, Berenger partly aware, Roger quite confounded. I scanned those delicate features, and my heart contracted. Vehemence sharpened my words, fear gave point to my reasoning. From general exhortation I narrowed my condemnation, and censured notorious perverts, naming names.

Except Rufus.

I wiped the sweat from my face, dismissed Berenger and Roger, spoke seriously to Richer and went to find fitzHamon. For I was still afraid. The boys' dumbfounded expressions proclaimed their innocence: the taint had not yet touched them. I had opened their eyes; now I feared that natural curiosity – aided by invitation – might tempt them into sin.

fitzHamon was in an armoury, re-setting a loose topaz on the pommel of his sword. I put the problem baldly.

'You make a deal of pother over a common complaint.' The dark-blue eyes surveyed me with amusement. 'Sodomy is not rare in knighthood's ranks: you'll find it universal from Sicily to Sweden.'

'Never so unconfined as here at Rufus's court!'

'Maybe true.' The eagle face grew stern. 'Depravity blooms in pastures watered by royal example. Little we can do about it, Walter. The priests declaim and rant, and Rufus laughs. Either you must tolerate his ambience, or . . . There's nothing to hinder your going.'

'Nothing.' I looked away, and fiddled with the tassel of my robe. 'But . . . I wish to serve the king.'

fitzHamon glanced at me shrewdly. Idly he balanced the sword on the back of his hand. 'I see. Like all of us who loathe his vice you'r ˉnared by his attraction, by that courtoisie and honesty which draw men like a lodestone. Rufus has a single blemish; all else is pure gold. The paramount knight in Christendom, the most magnificent king.' He tapped the balanced blade. 'Weigh his fault against his virtues, and the scales ride never so high. Stay with him, Walter – you'll not be sorry.'

'I intend to. Meanwhile, how do I prevent my esquires being contaminated?'

fitzHamon smiled. 'We're not all pederasts. In fact they're a minority, though they seem prevalent as fleas in a he-goat's hide. There is, after all, a multitude of women at Rufus's court.'

'Of a kind. Where,' I said pointedly, 'is the Lady Sibyl?' (fitz-Hamon had married a Talvas, sister to Belesme.)

'Safely in Torigni,' said he suavely. 'Which doesn't affect the argument. High-born, virtuous ladies have nothing to fear from Rufus's minions.' He smiled broadly. 'Rather the reverse. About your esquires. I suggest you shift your quarters to my mesnie – we live alongside Peter's chapel. My knights and esquires, I promise you, are perfectly normal people.'

I accepted the offer, and told Richer to move our baggage. As befitted a puissant lord, fitzHamon's quarters, while not luxurious – the Tower was too stark for that – were comfortable and secluded, separated by curtains from armouries and store rooms. I closely scrutinized his mesnie. Although the younger members' barbering and clothing reflected the foppery which infested the court – young men are ever fashion's slaves – none was infected by the vice I dreaded.

Our union warmed my friendship with fitzHamon, a fellowship fostered by a mutual devotion to Rufus. At Advent, returning from Westminster after mass, he drew me from the road and said, 'How – um – fortunate that Prince Henry didn't fall in Domfront's fighting.'

Not even to fitzHamon, who had planted the seed, was I going to disclose my abortive effort to kill the prince. I said in a neutral tone, 'He took no risks.'

'That I have heard.' He stared at his palfrey's ears. 'So long as Henry lives the king will never be safe. There are . . . conspiracies.'

'The prince is in Normandy, and Clare with him. They can't harm Rufus across the sea.'

'Gilbert is not the only Clare.'

'You don't doubt Walter Giffard? He's Rufus's chancellor, and the Duke's before him – an old man nearing dotage!'

'Not Giffard; he's past the age for plotting, and loyal enough. But Roger of Clare is in England; Richard, a monk of Bec, attends Abbot Anselm at Canterbury.'

'Why,' I asked quietly, 'do you suspect the Clares – my lady's family?'

fitzHamon contemplated St Paul's spire lancing above London's rooftops, and stroked his scar. 'They're greedy, aspiring men who lack scope for ambition. The Clares can expect nothing from Rufus: he's never forgiven Gilbert for holding Tonbridge against him in the Great Rebellion. So they've hitched their wagon to Henry's star.'

'It doesn't mean they're trying to injure Rufus. Have you evidence?'

The cavalcade approached the wooden bridge that crossed the Fleet. fitzHamon swung his palfrey to the road. 'Nothing I can lay a finger on. But Meulan keeps his ear to the ground; and he's getting worried.' He shook his rein in exasperation. 'If only Rufus were not so trusting!'

We entered Ludgate; and snowflakes drifted lazily from the sky.

Rufus left the Tower to keep his Christmas court at Winchester. The king's progress resembled an invading army. In the van marched a mercenary conroy; then the king, his barons and knights, ladies, pages and esquires, a gaily chattering company a thousand paces long. The transport followed: two thousand carts and a thousand rounceys carrying tents, pavilions, ovens, mills, smithies, clothing, food and fodder; thirty mounted falconers, a hundred assorted hounds and a tramping host of servants. A mercenary rearguard ruthlessly whipped up stragglers. The procession filled two leagues of road from head to tail. Nor was this all: an advanced party always left at midnight, marched to the next day's camp site, spitlocked tent lines, cooked a meal and pitched pavilions. The king must rest in comfort directly he arrived.

We followed an ancient road the Romans built and none since then, apparently, had troubled to repair. A thaw had melted the snow; then frosty nights and sparkling days, clear blue skies and air like heady wine. Rufus rode hawk on wrist, boisterously gay, singing ribald songs and laughing at the stories Flambard told. I rode beside him, Berenger and Roger close behind.

Roger had struck acquaintance with a beautiful young knight who bestrode a spirited grey, and fervently admired the fellow's horsemanship. Because I mistrusted everyone – particularly handsome youths – who befriended my esquires I said to Richer, 'A stranger – I haven't seen his face about the Tower. Who is he?'

'William of Alderi, cousin and steward to Count William of Eu. A brave and spirited knight, I'm told.' Richer's tone was dry. 'They came but yesterday from Normandy.'

I made an excuse to speak to Alderi, and praised his prancing stallion. Tawny hair like rippling silk framed a fine-boned, flawless face and a skin like rose-flushed ivory. He wore modish clothes with a negligent air, a cold self-mocking elegance – though the long-lashed violet eyes were far from vague.

Rufus glanced at him casually; the hot eyes opened wide, and fastened in a speculative stare. An esquire summoned Alderi; all day they rode together and I dropped behind, displaced from my proud position at Rufus's side. fitzHamon, that worldly baron, poked my ribs and whispered, 'A new favourite. Don't look so sour, Walter – Rufus sees a trait in him you clearly lack. I wonder what it is?'

The progress halted at terce; a tented township arose round the king's travelling house: a timbered dwelling made in sections, easily erected and soon dismantled, divided into bedchamber and hall – a duplicate carried on wagons was ready to march at midnight. Pavilions blossomed in the meadows, tents and latrines and kitchens fruited like sudden toadstools. The mercenaries' tent lines surrounded the camp like a wall; pickets, patrols and sentinels guarded all approaches. Rufus held high revel in his house; Alderi sat beside him, Rufus chose savoury morsels and loaded them on his trencher. Always I was surprised by the food at Rufus's court: swans roasted and chervil-garnished, salmon stewed in wine, honeyed fruits and pastries, and mellow amber wine that held the scent of sun-drenched grapes. Not for him the graceless fare that castle cooks produced. Only the meats were blemished: Rufus liked raw beef, but his venison overdone.

Afterwards, with fitzHamon, I strolled to inspect the horses, and thence through the camp to a forest beyond the fields. The December day was waning, the sunset shed a coppery glow on winter's gaunt black trees. At the mercenaries' tent lines a sentinel barred the way. fitzHamon gave his name; the man examined our faces. 'Pass, my lords,' he said grumpily, 'but return by dusk. The pickets become edgy after dark – apt to shoot before they challenge.' We followed an ice-ridged path that wandered to the trees. 'Competent men, those mercenaries,' I observed. 'You'd think they guarded a beleaguered town.'

'In a sense they do. The '88 rebellion left its mark on Rufus. Hence the hirelings: a standing army quartered in royal castles across England. So long as the king employs them there can't be another rising: the barons are well aware the mercenaries can outfight them.'

'They must be mighty expensive.'

'Indeed. Another reason for Flambard's extortions.'

We entered a straggling woodland; frozen leaf mould crunched beneath our feet. Rooks circled the trees, their raucous cries forlorn on the still cold air. 'No private wars in England to subdue,' I mused, 'and no revolts. Rufus's barons must have an easy time. How do they acquit their obligations? Duke William demanded sixty days' annual service from all his vassals.'

'Mostly on castle guard in royal strongholds, and in everlasting wars with Welsh and Scots. Last summer —'

A shriek, and shouts, and distant crashes. Again the scream – a woman's voice – and babbling moans. I eased my dagger in the sheath; we ran through the wood. The trees opened on winter-bleached pasture and a plough-strip surrounding a steading. Men in iron caps and mail shirts flitted among the buildings, ransacked the cottage and flung chattels through the door. They drove cattle from a pinfold, herded sheep and hunted swine. A man in a peasant's tunic sprawled across a manger, his face a scarlet mangling. Terrified children huddled beside a cowpen, the eldest clutched an infant in her arms. Soldiers surrounded a hay truss where a woman lay spread-eagled. Her kirtle was dragged to her armpits, her head hung loosely, the eyes were wide and vacant. A man's haunches butted her loins. He finished and withdrew; another took his place. The girl – she was young and comely – jerked like a broken puppet.

I forced through a thorny barrier. fitzHamon gripped my arm. 'Steady, Walter! Those are mercenaries on the loose. Cut your throat for a straw!'

I shook him off. 'They must be stopped, and the king informed!'

'Rufus knows how they behave. Come back, Walter!' he called despairingly. 'God's blood,' he moaned, plunging after me, 'we'll both be dead by nightfall!'

The soldiers turned at my shout. The fellow who raped the girl slowly laced his hose-points, retrieved his targe and spear and walked to meet us. 'You intrude on private business, gossip,' he said unpleasantly – a Breton by his speech. His lips parted in an ugly grin; the teeth were brown and broken, his breath foul. 'Whence come you?' He examined my garb, and sneered. 'A cockerel knight, I fancy – one of our master's minions. Return to his pallet, sweetling, and keep your arsehole greased!'

The men beside him cackled. My dagger came out. 'For Christ's sake, Walter!' fitzHamon breathed. Anger trailed a bloodshot veil before my eyes. 'Release the girl!' I rasped. 'Restore the goods you've stolen, and get to camp!'

The Breton stared in disbelief, threw back his head and guffawed. 'A cocky callant,' he announced, 'who carols an insolent tune. Let's cut his balls, and hear him sing in treble!' His spear lifted; he took a pace towards me.

fitzHamon said steadily, 'I am Robert fitzHamon, lord of Torigni and Creulli, and Tewkesbury in England. You touch us at your peril, rogue – the king will have your head!'

'The king won't know – we'll bury you deep!'

They closed upon us, a dozen dangerous killers. The Breton's spearpoint levelled on my throat. A whirr and thump. His eyeball sprouted feathers. He fell at my feet, and whimpered before he died. A voice shouted from the trees. 'Stand fast, offal, else you're dead! My lords, this way.'

Pigot.

They backed away, eyes searching the darkening woods. A brawny soldier growled in his throat, lifted his sword and charged. An arrow pierced the hollow above his breastbone. He crumpled like an empty cornsack, and threshed on the grass.

'Any more for the gates of hell? My lords, come quickly!'

I looked at the wrecked steading. The girl sobbed wretchedly; the children crept from hiding and gathered round her. The husbandman was dead.

'Cover me, Pigot!' I called.

I circled the group of soldiers. The peasants could not understand my tongue, and cowered away. fitzHamon, breathing hard and cursing beneath his breath, herded them like sheep to the woodland's shelter. Pigot stood behind the brambles, bowstring drawn to his ear. He kept his eyes on the target, and said, 'I'll stay to discourage pursuit. On your way, my lords!'

Richer moved from a tree trunk, and beckoned silently. We hastened along the track, the peasant family following. Pigot, humming to himself, joined us at the mercenaries' tents, and swamped the sentinel's reproof with volleys of invective. Safely within the camp I eased the pace, and said, 'You saved our lives, you two. How did you —'

'I saw you go, and thought it best to follow.' Exasperation edged Richer's voice. 'When will you learn, my lord, there's no safety in the wild? No one wanders abroad unguarded.'

'This is England, not Normandy. I thought —'

'The Franks rule England; and wherever they go there's death. You have liegemen to protect you – use them!'

'A knight,' I answered loftily, 'should succour people in distress.'

'Courtoisie does not extend to villeins,' fitzHamon said. He looked at the shivering group. 'What shall we do with them?'

Pigot said, 'I'll take charge, my lord.' He spoke words in an alien tongue – men-at-arms are quick to learn a language. The girl threw herself at my feet and kissed my hands. 'A grateful trollop,' fitzHamon observed. 'You've made a conquest, Walter!'

I contemplated her thoughtfully. Behind the tear-smudged dirt were signs of beauty. It was days since I'd had a woman – the last in

a London stew. 'Feed her, clean her,' I told Pigot, 'and bring her later
to my tent.' The bowman smirked, and took the family off. We
walked past Rufus's house – a guard-knight stood at the door – and
encountered a little farther a cloaked and hooded figure, shadowy in
the twilight, pacing restlessly up and down.

fitzHamon peered beneath the cowl. 'My lord of Eu!' he exclaimed. 'Whom do you await on this chilly night? Come to my
pavilion – I've a wine to thaw your blood!'

Creases seamed a rugged face, a wart surmounted a bulbous nose,
hairs sprouted from the nostrils. His body was square and bulky, and
he rolled in his walk like a mariner. William of Eu grunted, and
grimaced at the wooden house. 'I await my steward,' he said in a
voice like rusty iron.

fitzHamon glanced at the silent building, the shuttered windows
which showed no light. 'Alderi? In there?'

A muted tinkle travelled from a village church. 'They ring for
vespers – he's been with the king since none. What am I to think?'

'Doubtless they discuss affairs of state,' fitzHamon suggested
gravely.

Eu made an indescribable noise. fitzHamon took his arm. 'Stupid
to linger here. Come and try that wine – you won't be disappointed.
Comfort yourself, my lord: it's always useful to own a liege who has
the – um – ear of the king.'

They vanished in the gloom. I went to my pavilion, feeling slightly
sick. Not till Pigot brought the English girl did I recover my spirits.
She was willing, though uncouth; and seemed a trifle sore.

6

'Mercenaries live for rape and pillage,' Rufus said, 'and get little
enough in England. Occasionally they rampage and do some damage.
It's best to turn a blinkered eye.'

'This, sire,' I told him respectfully, 'is what the English complain
of – what Anselm warned against.'

'That pious priest —! What do you suggest I do – hang the lot?
I'd have done it if they harmed you, but they only slew a peasant.
Your bowman killed a couple in requital – let it rest at that!'

'Sire, it's unwise —'

'Don't lecture me, Walter – I get enough from bishops! Robert

Bloet keeps on baiting me about Canterbury. God strike them all, I say!'

A solitary mallard sped across the sky. Rufus quickly loosed the jesses, cast his hawk, spurred his horse and followed across the heath.

So be it. England's affairs were none of mine; best keep my lips clamped tight.

Chapter 5

1092–93

THE king wore his crown at Christmas in the church of Holy Trinity. Winter closed upon the land.

Winchester is a foursquare ramparted town dominated by a stone-and-timber castle where Rufus made his quarters. I found lodgings for my mesnie in a leather merchant's house. Snow fell, and then hard frost; the cold was like a stony ringing void. Every day we exercised the horses, treading marbled trails in snow outside the walls; otherwise we stayed indoors, shuttered windows and stoked the fires. The king called me always to council, often to his table; I attended banquets which lasted from noon to twilight, long drawn tournaments of foolery and feasting, mummery, wine and song.

Anselm came from Canterbury to attend the convocation, and kept tactfully out of Rufus's way. I encountered him one bitter noonday crunching over the snow, his sandalled feet purple with cold; and persuaded him to my dwelling. The fire and hot mulled wine restored a little colour to his leaden face: I scolded him for wandering abroad in weather which kept sensible men within four walls.

'I go about God's business,' he protested. 'What does my comfort matter when the kingdom breeds corruption like a maggot-festered corpse?'

I said, 'How does that concern you? Father Abbot, the king is convinced the bishops intend seating you in Lanfranc's stall. Moreover he insists that you yourself are anxious for the primacy. What is the truth? If, as I think, the king is mistaken wouldn't it be best to return to Bec?'

Anselm warmed his bony fingers round the wine cup, and stared into the fire. 'Being neither deaf nor a fool, my son, I am quite aware of all these rumours. The king believes, and the bishops hope, that I am bent on Canterbury. All foolishness – the thing's impossible. I'm not King William's subject: my lord is Normandy's duke, my Father in God the archbishop of Rouen. Neither has given consent – how then can I aim at Canterbury? Finally' – he grasped my arm and looked me in the face – 'not for my soul's salvation would I accept! This you must believe. Can you see a man like me harnessed to William Rufus?'

One could not. I glanced at the sparse white hair and fragile features. Yet Anselm possessed an inner fire, a burning, bright conviction that radiated like strong sunlight through a meek and gentle bearing. He was no ordinary man. I liked and respected him, and feared a little for his safety. Rufus, badly crossed, was also far from ordinary. I could not conceive the king would do him bodily hurt – but there were other means of curbing a pestilent priest. The sooner they were parted the better for them both.

'Then go back to Normandy, Father!'

Anselm's lips closed firmly. 'No. I came solely, as you know, on Bec's affairs. Since then my eyes have seen the tribulations which scourge Holy Church. Abbacies lie vacant; and the king's simony so corrupts his clerks that they buy preferment. I must do what little I can to restore decency to the Church I serve.'

I shrugged, and ceased persuasion. If abbot and king collided I knew who would be most bruised – but there's no dissuading zealots.

'As you will. I shall try to convince the king his fears are baseless. Stay, Father, and share our meal. Friday, a fast day's dinner: only lentil broth. My servants found no fish in the market.'

Anselm pulled his fingers, and said abstractedly, 'If you would wait a little, there's a fine sturgeon on the way.'

He had retreated into one of his absent-minded trances, and I thought he drivelled. I told Roger to call varlets and serve the food. Anselm gazed at the fire, lost to the world. Someone hammered the door. A rough-looking man, cloak-muffled to the eyes, thrust a straw-wrapped bundle into Roger's arms and departed without a word. The esquire, puzzled, laid the package down and parted the straw. An appetizing fragrance filled the room – a sturgeon freshly broiled in savoury herbs.

Everyone looked at Anselm.

'This,' his attendant monk breathed unctuously, 'is miraculous!'

Lisiard – a credulous man – signed himself. I waited patiently for Anselm's explanation. He returned slowly from his day-dream, surveyed the fish and smiled.

'Now, my son, we may fare a little better.'

'Carve, Roger,' I ordered; and said to the abbot abruptly, 'How did you know, Father?'

He looked surprised. 'Know? I saw it here.' He tapped his brow. 'These visions sometimes come, wavering and transparent, like darkness moving in mist. Maybe,' he ended vaguely, 'a gift of God, perhaps a curse from Satan. I know not.'

Which is all the explanation I ever got. His monk noised the incident abroad, and it became one of many miracles credited to the Abbot of Bec.

I tried tentatively to convince Rufus that Anselm had no designs on Canterbury; and dropped the matter hastily when his crimson face grew redder and his hands began to clench. On this subject he was beyond reason. But sometimes a wicked humour tempered with justice his treatment of the Church he hated. Three monks came to Winchester seeking seisin of an abbacy which had long been vacant – Cerne, I think it was. The king lounged on his throne, chin propped in hand, and said laconically, 'Very well. What's it worth?'

After shocked protestations – clerks, I find, can be supreme hypocrites – a monk reluctantly proposed three hundred pounds of silver.

'Not enough,' said Rufus curtly; and cast an inquiring glance at his companions, one of whom said eagerly, 'If you make me abbot, sire, I'll pay four hundred!'

'Don't you think Cerne's worth more than that?' asked Rufus.

The first monk sulkily capped the offer. The king's eyes slid to his competitor, who raised the price. The bidding advanced to a thousand pounds; the brethren began sweating. Meanwhile the third man stood silently by, eyes downcast, hands hidden in his sleeves.

Rufus stabbed a finger and said scornfully, 'A paltry bid for a prosperous abbey! Surely you can do better?'

'I offer nothing,' the monk said simply. 'I have come merely to escort home with honour my new abbot, whoever he may be.'

The king looked at him hard. At last: 'You're my man. Go home, Father Abbot – Cerne is yours.'

The council laughed and applauded – except Flambard, who sorrowfully wagged his head.

2

Attendance at council and banquet meant that my esquires came frequently to the castle. I kept an eye on them at meals, for their place was behind my stool; if either dallied overlong in buttery or kitchen I sent the other swiftly to retrieve him. But esquires were not admitted to council in the donjon. During these lengthy sessions I sometimes wondered what the scamps were doing.

Curiosity turned to alarm when I discovered Alderi and the boys closeted in an empty guardroom. The gathering seemed innocent enough: Alderi, sword in hand, demonstrated a nearside cut and parry; the esquires in turn tried clumsily to emulate his skill. Affably I removed them; and thereafter insisted that Richer should accompany them whenever I went to council. To Berenger and Roger I said nothing: one could not forever be carping; and restrictions were likely to rouse a wayward disobedience which might spawn the dangers I feared.

My gambit did not answer. Richer said despondently, 'Alderi's a knight, and I am not. He regards me as a varlet, and sends me out of the room. Short of open defiance and a brawl where I must be beaten' – sadly he hefted his disabled arm – 'what would you have me do?'

'How does he treat them?'

'Openly and, so far as I can judge, without ill intent.' Richer paused. 'He seems genuinely friendly, anxious to earn their liking and respect – which certainly he's done. Alderi, my lord, is a most attractive man. Were it not ...'

'A debauched pervert,' I growled; and next time detailed Lisiard instead. Privately I warned him of his charge.

'God's teeth, I turn nursemaid!' he grunted morosely. Afterwards he observed, 'The fellow's persistent. Do you want me to fight him?'

I shuddered. Lisiard was a skilful swordsman: it were hardly politic for one of my mesnie to kill Rufus's favourite minion. I decided to settle Alderi myself. Pleading a flux in the bowels I left the council chamber early and tracked the three to the mews. Alderi fed a merlin, discoursing meanwhile on the art of casting into a wind. 'A slight forward throw from the wrist, not too sharp lest the hawk be unbalanced ...'

I dismissed my esquires, cleared jesses, hoods and leashes from a bench, seated myself and said without emphasis, 'My lord, I ask a favour: that you deprive yourself for the future of these youngsters' company.'

Alderi dexterously transferred the merlin from wrist to perch. 'I see no good reason,' he replied lazily, 'for doing so. Why do you ask?'

I scraped my feet in the sawdust, and felt my temper rising. 'Roger of Conches and Berenger of Carenci are my esquires – therefore I'm obliged to guard their welfare. I shall not stand idly by and see them ruined.'

'By me?' Alderi turned, a feathered hood in his hand. The violet eyes were scornful. 'You'd better make yourself plain, my lord – I don't like blunted shafts.'

I dropped a hand to my dagger. 'The barb must indeed be sharp, it seems, to pierce your hide. You want it plain. Very well. I do not tolerate sodomites who paw striplings in my care.'

Alderi slipped the hood on the merlin's head: neat, lissom movements that emphasized his grace. 'For that, one supposes, I should fight you,' he murmured, 'which is what you want. Contain your disappointment, my lord, because I shall do nothing of the kind. Nor do I intend to cease gossiping with your esquires.' The red lips curved in a smile. 'What will you do about it?'

I said furiously, 'If you hope to cower under the king's protection —'

Alderi looked bored. 'Not so. You misjudge Rufus, a knight who abides by knighthood's tenets: a man must stand on his own two feet and fight for himself. But you I will not challenge. We're on the same side.'

I glared at him, befogged. 'You talk in riddles, my lord.'

Alderi seemed surprised. 'You married a Clare – Adelice, wasn't it? Gilbert told me Prince Henry made you swear, years since, to enter Rufus's mesnie. Well, here you are. And so —'

He saw my look. His face went blank; the eyes were suddenly shuttered as though a screen had dropped. He bent and picked a dried mute from the sawdust, and flicked it away. The beautiful eyes were once more guileless.

'You're right, my lord – I'm talking nonsense. Unimportant tattle from the past. As for Berenger and Roger, you may set your mind at rest. I don't seduce children.'

I hardly heard him. An alarm call sang in my head like a tocsin sounding to arms. The years unrolled: I remembered Henry's coercion when he held me under duress: 'For your advantage, and mine, you must serve my brother.' And later, at Mont St Michel: 'Once there you can serve me well – and the rewards, my lord, will be great.' Then he killed my hostage and snapped the fetters which bound me: furiously I had renounced my oath. His answer, smiling spitefully: 'You may still be useful, whether you will or no.' Of my own free will I served in Rufus's mesnie: here, as Alderi said, I was. What evil did that sinister prince intend? Fetid as Satan's breath the winds of treachery whispered. I stared distractedly at Alderi, saw anxiety – the merest trace – lurking in his eyes; and pulled myself together. This was not the time, nor this the man, to answer the questions crowding my mind.

'I accept your word, my lord,' I said abruptly. 'It were better for your health that you should keep it.' And there I left him, thoughtfully plaiting a straw-wisp and watching my departure under silken lashes.

After two days' chaotic thinking I sought Meulan in the castle hall where the barons of the exchequer waited to audit accounts, led him to a quiet place and said, 'My lord, I'm bedevilled by doubt, and beg you to hear my cause – it may affect the king. I've no real warrant for my fears, but treason doesn't wait on hesitation —'

'Treason?' Meulan's eyes were icy slits in the weathered face. 'Whom do you suspect? Let's have it straight!'

I winced – could I accuse plainly on evidence so flimsy? 'What,' I said slowly, 'do you know of the Count of Eu, who lately come to England?'

'William?' Meulan passed a hand across his bristled chin. 'A rebel on Duke Robert's behalf in '88. Harried Gloucestershire and stormed Berkeley. Surrendered when the revolt was quashed; and Rufus banished him to Normandy. Swore allegiance to the king at Caen – his county's now an English bastion, himself a liege of England. You've got the wrong man, Walter, if you think —'

'I don't, my lord. The thing is this.' I related my promise to Henry, the renunciation after; and the queer remark that Alderi let drop. Meulan listened quietly, slowly stroking his jaw, the rasp like a stealthy rubbing of whetstone upon iron. 'That's all,' I ended. 'No more than a slender fancy. Perhaps I build a castle from an anthill.'

'Perhaps.' He surveyed me with a chilly glint in his eye. 'I had not realized you once avowed the prince. The bond, I hope, is broken?'

I held my temper. Meulan wove an intelligence network whose meshes tangled traitors: the king's spymaster must ever be distrustful. 'Broken indeed,' I answered shortly. 'My loyalties lie with Rufus.'

'You say it – I believe you. I know nothing against Count William or his steward. Perhaps I've been negligent. That can soon be cured.' His fingers gripped my wrist. 'You'll say naught of this to anyone, my lord!'

The chamber stirred, and chatter ceased. Rufus entered, crimson-robed and crowned, for this was a state occasion. He led the way from the hall to the vaults below. Meulan said, 'Stay, Walter, and attend the accounting. A tedious business, but you might find it enlightening.'

Winchester's castellan, in ceremonial armour, guarded an oaken door. He presented a key to the king; Rufus turned the lock and we entered a stone-walled cellar where England's treasure was kept.

The room extended beneath the donjon's whole foundations. Pillars supported a roof so low that a tall man bowed his head. Lanterns hung from rusty hooks, coffers climbed the wet-sheened walls in tiers; in the maws of bulging sacks jewels and silver glinted. There was a smell of mildewed leather, dampness and mouldering wood. At lecterns in the corners clerks waited with parchment scrolls. In the centre, raised on casks, stood a massive checkered board.

This was the king's exchequer.

Rufus sat in an ivory-inlaid chair. Chancellor, constable, chamberlains and marshal – the barons of the exchequer – stood around the board. Flambard gave a signal, and the auditing began.

'Revenues from reliefs.'

The Treasurer read names from a scroll, and a numeral for each. Clerks planked multicoloured counters on the squares. Rufus locked his fingers and watched intently.

'Reliefs are a principle evolved by Flambard,' Meulan whispered. 'Fiefs held by vassals are merely loanland, since all land, always, belongs to the king. Therefore when a vassal dies his fief reverts to Rufus. The new owner has to buy back the land.'

The last counter fell on the board. Flambard examined a script. 'Total receipts from redemptions —'

'You've forgotten Graeland of Thani,' Rufus interrupted. 'He died at Advent; I granted seisin to his son.'

Rufus in another guise: the sharp accountant.

'Joscelin can't raise the relief from revenues,' Flambard answered. 'He's trafficking with Jews, and promises payment by Easter.'

'That's his limit,' Rufus declared, 'else I'll disseize him.'

Clerks heaped counters on different squares. 'Credits from affirmations,' the Treasurer announced.

'Flambard revived an ancient law,' said Meulan, 'which decrees no wills are valid unless confirmed by the king. He inserted a small amendment: every affirmation needs a fee.'

'Does nobody protest?'

'Now and then. These tallages concern directly only the tenants-in-chief – taxation of the rich, you might say. They squeeze their vassals to find the money, so the barons get a reputation for rapacity – not Rufus.'

Meulan put his lips to my ear. 'Alderi has taken pains to attract the king's . . . attention. Yet from all I hear he's never been a pervert. Rather odd, don't you think?'

I searched his wrinkled face; the lantern's pallid light showed only boredom. 'To my thinking Alderi's a sodomite born and fostered.'

'Wrong. He used to have a womanizer's bent – hunted them in bed and out. A sudden change in habits. Most peculiar.'

The tortuous byways of Meulan's mind were beyond my following: I gave it up. Clerks shuffled counters from square to square in abstruse calculations. More discs were added, black in colour – 'records of expenditure,' Meulan said – and Flambard dictated figures. A monk at a separate table summarized the totals on sheepskins sewn end to end, rolling them down from the head as he worked so the parchment looked like a pipe.

'The Great Roll of the Exchequer,' Meulan commented. 'Nearly finished – the Saints be praised!'

Rufus, looking black, drummed fingers on his chair arms; Flambard pensively tapped counters on the board. 'Reserves are dripping away like grain from a leaking sack!' the king exclaimed. 'Expenditure has overtaken revenue. This, my lord of the treasury, is your responsibility! Will you see me beggared? What do you suggest?'

Flambard dropped the counters. 'Decrease one, sire, or increase the other. There's no different way.'

Rufus slammed a hand on the board; the counters leaped in the air. 'How may I cut expenses? Subsidies to my Norman vassals – can I buy their allegiance for less? Reduce the mercenaries, or slice their pay? – they'd vanish like rime in a thaw! And this year or the next I lead an army into Normandy – you can't conduct campaigns on a bag of silver!'

Flambard examined his fingernails, and bit a peeling cuticle. 'So we augment the revenues.' The drawl left his voice. 'Let's revise the land tax. Gelds are levied by the hide; but the English hide is variable: small for fertile land and large for wasteland. In effect, a tax on produce, not on land. I propose, sire, a universal hidage, based on the smallest measurement for fertile land.'

Rufus frowned and tried to follow the argument. His face cleared. 'I see. Most ingenious! Tax is still levied by the hide; you get more hidages and additional taxes!'

'Precisely, my lord. If you approve I'll have the decrees indited and sent to county sheriffs.'

'Certainly I approve! Have you calculated the extra revenue?'

'Naturally, sire. The tallages from land – a main source of exchequer income – will be more than doubled.'

'A scandalous impost which affects us all,' Meulan murmured. 'I shall really have to screw my tenants!'

4

In the Octave of Sexagesima Rufus moved to Alvestone, a royal house near Gloucester. There, after a banquet when he was more than usually merry, the king fell sick.

Rufus was never ill. He could gormandize like a glutton, drink like a thirsty boarhound and rise in the morning limpid-eyed and ruddy; he would hunt or hawk in snow and driving rain, return skin-wet and shivering and never contract a rheum. He seemed impervious to the ailments which strike less hardy men.

I hurried to his bedchamber where the lords were already gathered, silently watching the form that writhed on a pallet. A physician forced an evil-smelling draught between his lips.

'I don't like what I see,' fitzHamon muttered.

Pain twisted a mottled face; sweat glistened on his forehead and matted the yellow hair. I touched his cheek; the skin was burning. 'A colic?' I whispered.

'Something worse, I think. The leech fears a mortal swelling within the bowels.'

I knew that affliction, and had seen men suffer torment till the swollen organ burst. Then, invariably, they died. I scanned the small rough bedchamber – Alvestone was only a hunting lodge – and said, 'He must be taken to Gloucester, to better quarters and attendance. Here he will surely die.'

'So I think myself, and have given the seneschal orders.'

In a curtained litter Rufus was carried the half-day's march to

Gloucester – a gruesome journey, for he often shrieked in agony and tried to leap from the litter. With fitzHamon I walked alongside, and held him down. We had warned the king's castellan, who prepared a spacious chamber – fortunate in view of later events – on the donjon's topmost floor. There, on a swansdown pallet, we deposited the twitching body. Rufus sank into a coma, the breath rasping in his gullet. We called leeches from the abbey and women skilled in nursing from the lazars. They bathed the fevered form with vinegar and essences, forced the teeth apart and dribbled potions down his throat.

The king moaned, and rolled his head from side to side.

Meulan said, 'I believe he's dying. The barons and the bishops must be summoned to his passing.' He continued grimly, 'Strange legends farrow from the deaths of kings. The more witnesses the better.'

The lords of England came to the room in Gloucester, waited awhile to observe their suzerain's pain, departed and came again when they heard his state was worse. Cloaked and silent figures ringed the deathbed, priestly incantations murmured from wall to wall, a sour stench of sickness fouled the incense-laden air. When Lent was three days old the king recovered his senses, stared at the rafters above, moaned and scraped his belly. The prelates saw him conscious and crowded round the bedside, babbled exhortations and noisily urged repentance.

Lincoln's bishop waved a crucifix in front of the red-veined eyes.

'Repent, my son,' he crowed. 'Repent while you have time! Confess your sins, crave mercy from the Lord through Jesus Christ!'

I thrust Bloet away, shoved his brethren from the bed, dropped on my knees beside the king and took his hand. Slowly he turned his head; the glazed look left his eyes. 'Walter.' A fragile whisper faint as a sigh of death. I bent my head to his lips. 'I am . . . dying. Unshriven . . . unforgiven. Satan . . . howls for my . . . soul. Let me repent . . . confess.'

'The Bishop of Lincoln is here, my lord.'

His forehead wrinkled, he bared his teeth – the incorrigible Rufus showed in the face of death. 'That . . . wordy priest? No. Fetch . . . Anselm.'

Anselm was still at Alvestone; by morning he arrived, and I led him to the bedroom. Robert Bloet met us on the threshold, his countenance pallid and shocked. I gritted my teeth and steeled myself for the worst.

'I tried to confess the king,' Bloet said in a wavering voice. 'He cursed me!'

Rufus, I concluded, was improving.

Nevertheless he was still in pain and hardly able to speak. He recognized the abbot, lifted his hand and tried to smile. Anselm felt his brow, held his wrist and counted beneath his breath. He stripped the coverlet and gently touched the swollen belly, fingers smoothing the skin in feathery strokes. He replaced the ermine-tasselled sable and stirred a potion mixed from phials.

fitzHamon moved impatiently. 'Shrive him, Father, quick, before his soul has fled!'

Anselm poured the medicine into the beaker. 'The king won't die from this disease,' said he calmly. Rufus swallowed the draught, lay back and closed his eyes. Anselm bent over him, spoke quietly in his ear, a long murmurous exhortation. From time to time he paused, and Rufus nodded. The audience, ears pricked like roe deer scenting hunters, tried ardently to hear the abbot's whispers.

Anselm rose from the bedside, spoke in undertones to Bloet, his hands emphasizing points with little pecking gestures; and walked quietly to the door.

'You haven't shriven the king!' fitzHamon called angrily.

Anselm disappeared among the crowd that thronged the portal. Bloet announced exultantly, 'The king commands a proclamation made: his prisoners shall be freed, unlawful tallages remitted, abbacies and bishoprics restored to Holy Church! Taxes yet unpaid shall...'

A buzz of voices drowned his words. Disbelieving faces turned towards the bed. Rufus seemed unconscious or asleep. Flambard, looking furious, lost his arrogant composure; Meulan stroked his jaw and scanned the excited mob. 'Christ help the king's successor if all this really happens. He'll find an exhausted treasury and a host of traitors loosed!'

fitzHamon said, 'Vacant churches to be filled. I wonder who gets Canterbury?'

Bloet heard the remark; and consternation sagged his meaty cheeks. The primacy of England waited for the taking. He stumbled to the bed and stretched a hand to rouse the king. I seized his thumb and twisted it ungently.

'He sleeps – would you wake him into pain?'

Bloet looked at me with hatred, wrenched away and ran to the door. 'Anselm!' he called huntedly. 'Where's the abbot? Bring him back!'

They pulled Anselm into the room and dropped him on a stool. Lines were graven deeply on his face, the bones looked ready to split the skin. The bishops, arguing shrilly, gathered round him. Barons conversed loudly; clumping feet and clamorous voices jangled like a market place at noon. A bizarre deathbed for a king, I decided sourly.

Anselm's eyelids drooped; wearily he rolled his head from side to side. 'No. Rufus did not name the primate. The election should be done by Canterbury's monks.'

'Impossible!' Bloet shouted. 'Only the king can nominate the archbishop!'

'Then you must ask him.'

Bloet approached the bed.

'At your peril, priest!' I said without moving my lips.

fitzHamon stepped from the tester, spread fingers on the bishop's fleshy chest and pushed him back. Rufus stirred and groaned. Bloet saw the opened eyes, ducked beneath fitzHamon's arm and knelt beside the bed.

'Sire!' he said urgently. 'Sire – one restitution you must make, else your soul will lose salvation! Canterbury's archbishop – whom do you deem worthy?'

Meulan one side, I the other, thrust Bloet roughly away. He fell backwards on the floor. The struggle went unremarked; a hush fell on the room. Rufus lay unmoving, gazing at the ceiling. His eyes roved slowly across the eager faces, and settled on Anselm. You could hear a flea hop in the rushes, so quiet were they all.

Feebly Rufus lifted a hand, and pointed.

'I choose . . . this holy man . . . Anselm.'

A shout like a battle-yell rattled the chamber. Bishops and barons alike surrounded the Abbot of Bec, wrung his hand and thumped his shoulders. Bloet stayed on the floor, his fat face working; a tear rolled down his cheek. Rufus looked exhausted; he pointed his chin at the ceiling and drew quick shallow breaths.

'Must we tolerate these capers?' I called to Meulan across the bed.

The count shrugged.

Worse was to come.

Anselm's face was white as wheaten flour; he shook in every limb. 'No, no, no!' he bleated. 'I'm old, unversed in worldly affairs.

321

How can I rule the Church? Leave me in the peaceful abbey I love!'

'Guide us in the way of God: we ask no more!' demanded Durham's bishop – a gaunt, fanatical priest. 'All the rest you can safely leave to us!'

'You ask what I cannot grant! I owe obedience to another prince, to a Norman bishop, to the monks of Bec! How, without consent, may I cast aside my duties?'

Durham pointed to the bed. 'That man's tyranny drives Holy Church to perdition. Will you abandon her in her hour of need?'

I lost Anselm's answer in the hubbub. The bishops fell at his feet and bellowed implorations; Anselm knelt in front of them and begged them to leave him be. I watched the scene in disbelief, even the hardened Meulan looked astounded. Rufus opened his eyes and surveyed the shouting priests – did I catch an ironic glint?

Durham climbed creakily upright, retrieved his pastoral staff and strode to the bed. I moved to block him; Meulan touched my wrist.

'Let be. Rufus has consented.'

Durham said respectfully, 'Sire, will you invest your choice with the bishopric you have granted?'

The king murmured assent. Durham put the crook in Rufus's hand, and seized Anselm's arm. Others grabbed the abbot's gown and tried to drag him forward. Anselm hung back, resisting with all the strength in his puny frame. The struggle tempted a group of knights, who packed and shoved behind him. Everyone was shouting. You might have wondered whether a manic crowd was dragging a rational creature, or whether lucid men were hauling a raving lunatic.

Durham forced the abbot's hand to the crook in Rufus's grasp; Anselm kept his fingers tightly clenched. They strove to open his hand, and Anselm shrieked. The tussle swayed back and forth like a fairground riot. Durham prised Anselm's forefinger, hooked it round the staff, and held it there by force.

'Long live Canterbury!' roared the audience.

A monk chanted 'Te Deum'; others took it up. Singing at the tops of their voices the rabble carried Anselm from the room. I stared blearily at fitzHamon, who mopped his brow. Meulan gusted noisily through his nose. The bedclothes rustled. Rufus, wide awake, wore the ghost of a grin.

'God damned priests!' he whispered.

5

Whether spurred by the battle at his deathbed, or from Anselm's potions, or his own resilience, from that moment the king recovered. Before the end of Lent he was conducting the kingdom's business. The bedroom became chancellery and council, clamant with comings and goings. Anselm visited the patient daily and administered soothing draughts. Rufus said very little: none of us was certain that he remembered what had passed.

Anselm had no doubts. When the fever was finally gone he said, 'My election was invalid. Sire, you must undo what you have done – it were better for us both.'

'Never. I gave you face to face my spoken word. You're Canterbury's archbishop, and there's an end.'

Anselm threw up his hands. 'Do you know what you're at? You've harnessed an untamed bull and a feeble old sheep in the same plough under a single yoke. With what result? The bull will haul the sheep through thorns and thickets, and lacerate it till it bleeds to death!'

'It's done – let's hear no more.' Rufus clamped his teeth. 'A knight doesn't break his word.'

'I trust,' said Anselm sadly, 'you'll remember *all* the promises you made when you were sick. You pledged your troth, my lord, not to me but God.'

Rufus's laugh was bitter. 'God I hold beyond the bonds of courtoisie – I've suffered too much at His hands!'

Anselm clapped hands over ears, and looked ready to cry. Rufus looked at him coldly. 'It's as well, my lord of Canterbury, you should realize I avow no suzerain in heaven or on earth. With that understanding our alliance might be easier.'

Anselm tottered away. Rufus broodingly watched him go. 'Well, he's done it – he and those scheming bishops! I've lost Canterbury's revenues, and saddled myself with a saint! What promises was he maundering about? I remember none!'

Flambard said gloomily, 'You've filled all vacant abbacies, my lord, remitted certain tallages, and freed prisoners held for debt. The proclamation's out.'

'By the Face!' Rufus bolted upright, and clawed the coverlet. 'Withdraw it then – at once! I hereby revoke the decree!'

The dolour went from Flambard's features. 'It shall be done, my lord.'

And here was trouble, I thought. I glanced at fitzHamon and saw a cynical smile. Rufus caught the look, and furiously exploded. 'These are political promises – can't you see the difference? How can a king keep every pledge he makes? For Canterbury I gave my personal word – which I shall keep. For the rest – mere ink and parchment! A ruler cannot, and should not, honour inconvenient compacts. Especially,' he added, beginning to grin, 'when the reasons which compelled his promise no longer exist!'

fitzHamon laughed outright; Meulan smiled approvingly; and I saw a facet of statecraft I never knew existed.

6

By Easter the king had left his bed. He disciplined his victuals and drank sparingly of wine; otherwise his appetites recovered. Alderi, whom Meulan had banished from the sickroom, returned swaggering to court, fawned on Rufus in the daytime and was never seen at night. He sought out Berenger and Roger, or they him; the trio entertained themselves in stables, mews or tiltyard. I kept a watchful eye, and found nothing at which to cavil. The knight seemed honestly intent on burnishing their education in matters of hawk and hound, horsemanship and hauberks – a task, in truth, I should have done myself. My chance appearances at these diversions – a mime that secretly amused him – put me often in Alderi's company. Almost against my will I began to like him.

Rufus noticed Alderi's companions and called the boys to attend him. Gawky, flame-haired Berenger he ignored; but Roger clearly attracted him. He turned the esquire's face to the candles and said, 'The lad reminds me of someone. Ralph of Conches's son, you say? No, not he – nothing of those pulpy features here.' Lightly he stroked the raven hair, sat Roger by his side, talked genially of this and that, and recalled his own hard duties as the Duke's esquire in Rouen.

I watched this scene with growing unease; Alderi appeared even more unhappy. The violet eyes were troubled; he swept the esquires away like a rooster guarding her chicks, and afterwards kept them as far as he could from Rufus's sight. The king frustrated his diligence; frequently thereafter he summoned Roger to his table. Alderi, a hapless sentinel, stood dourly by and chewed his lip; sardonically I concluded that rivals were not to his taste.

An unlikely individual offered, as I thought, an answer to my troubles. On a blustery morning in March a ragbag mesnie entered Gloucester's gates; the leader announced himself as Jestin, Prince of Glamorgan, and sought audience of the king. Rufus, garbed in state, received him in the hall – 'got to impress these Welshmen,' was his comment – and learned through an interpreter that Jestin wanted help against one Rhys ap Tewdwr, King of Deheubarth, who had ravaged Jestin's lands and killed his brother.

Rufus scrutinized the Welshman: a beaky, hollow-faced man, his tunic shabby and threadbare with motheaten fur on the hem. His followers wore wolfskins, all were bearded to the eyes.

'I am inclined,' said he, 'to send you aid. If I do, what recompense can you offer?'

'All Rhys ap Tewdwr's treasure when you kill him.'

'He might be poor as a villein. No. Something more substantial – such as land.'

'You can take ap Tewdwr's land.'

Rufus's eyebrows climbed. 'In Deheubarth – a wilderness of mountains, rocks and bog? I'm not quite ignorant of Wales, my lord! I'll want better than that.' He smiled pleasantly on Jestin. 'There are fine fertile plains in Glamorgan.'

The Welshman lifted his chin. 'Have I wandered unbeknown into a market? Do princes haggle like hucksters selling fish?'

'Does the fellow think I'll help for nothing? No, idiot,' he snapped to the linguist: a priest from a parish in Gwent, 'don't translate that! Let me see.' Rufus rubbed his chin. 'There's a possibility here – a footing in Wales. I'm not yet hale enough to go myself, nor will I commit a major force to a doubtful venture. Ask him' – this to the priest – 'how many men he leads.'

Jestin promised a thousand. Rufus eyed the prince's ragged escort. 'Like these? They'll certainly need stiffening. I don't think . . .'

fitzHamon bent and whispered in his ear. The uncertainty faded from Rufus's face. 'Very well, Robert, if you think you can do it. I won't risk more than a dozen knights and five hundred men-at-arms. Choose hardy men; and promise the knights a fief apiece in Jestin's country.' He turned on the priest a steely eye. 'And don't translate that either!'

A seneschal housed Jestin's company; they lived in the ward for the next three days. fitzHamon chose a motley collection, mostly landless knights with a thirst for war and nothing to lose. I remember Pagan of Turberville, a pitiless fighter; and William of Londres, a knight of doubtful lineage and uncertain temper. Some brought useful mesnies, bowmen and men-at-arms, others merely servants and esquires. Rufus grudgingly released a mercenary conroy, truculent men who later gave more trouble than their worth.

I told fitzHamon I was coming, brooked no argument, and thankfully took my armour from the rack. Rufus tried to keep me, and wondered loudly why I sought a fief in Wales. He bade Roger a fond farewell, and lovingly ruffled his hair.

The evening before we marched the boy fell sick of a fever. Nothing serious, Richer averred: a chill that would answer to nursing. I thumped my brow. The main object of my going – apart from a craving for combat: I had not donned a hauberk for months – was to remove Roger beyond the king's caresses. Too late to change my decision; fitzHamon would never forgive me. Despondently I told Richer to stay and care for the lad, and issued a stringent warning.

The Saracen frowned. 'I'll do my best – but how can I deny the king?'

I thought the matter over; and reluctantly sought Alderi.

'I entrust Roger of Conches to your charge,' I told him bluntly, 'to safeguard while I'm gone.'

Alderi surveyed me coolly. 'I'm a knight, not a nursing-maid. I suggest you hire a drab.'

'This doesn't concern his sickness. You know very well what I fear.'

Alderi licked a fingertip and smoothed his eyebrow. 'Guard your tongue, my lord. Certain doubts are best unvoiced. Why ask me? Under the circumstances I find it strange.'

'You like Roger, and I believe . . .'

'Yes. He's a pleasant child. Liking,' he added languidly, 'is all. There's no more than that – which I think, oddly enough, you've realized. So be it. I shall keep him company, and see he doesn't pester Rufus overmuch.'

'You own my gratitude, my lord.'

And there, though ill content, I had to leave it.

We forded the Severn, followed a ruinous causewayed road across the plain and plunged into broken hills. Here the Roman highway ended; we threaded cattle-tracks and stony beds of streamlets swollen by rain. Stunted trees and thorn-scrub mantled the fells which marched alongside; every twist and hollow invited an ambuscade. fitzHamon fretted, augmented van- and rearguards, sent flankers blundering along the slopes. They made hard work of it and hindered our progress, already sufficiently slow.

Jestin viewed the precaution acidly, combed fingers in his beard and said, 'Needless. This is Gwent – my country. Your men are safe.'

fitzHamon looked at him sceptically, eyed the dangerous scarps and kept his guards in place.

Jestin's followers joined in driblets, appearing unannounced from gullies and copses, bringing sudden consternation to our tired flankers. Never had I seen such outlandish warriors: small, wiry men, woman-haired and bearded, garbed in skins and fleeces, some naked to the waist. Their chiefs wore iron caps and studded leather jerkins, and swaggered in this finery like coxcombs at a fair. They carried stabbing-swords and throwing spears and oblong leather targes. Some had lengthy staves. These confounded me – I could not believe the Welshmen fought with sticks. Pigot examined one of the shafts and discovered they were bows.

'How they brace and draw those poles – twice my bowstave's length – is past my understanding. Look at the arrow, my lord: long as a tall man's arm from fingertip to armpit. All right, rascal,' he told the suspicious Welshman who trotted beside his palfrey, 'take your arrow. I don't use boles for bowstaves, nor notch lance shafts on my string!'

Jestin's draggletail army darted happily about the hillsides which so impeded our men, wandered far ahead and loitered in the rear. Jestin, through the priest – a most unhappy clerk, yearning loudly for his parish by the Severn – assured us we were safe from ambuscade. fitzHamon withdrew the flankers, and brought van- and rearguards close.

'I don't trust these savages a finger-width,' he said, 'but if we keep the flankguards out we'll never reach our destination – a place with a name like a drunkard's belch.' Peevishly he jerked his head; raindrops flew like spray. 'When, in the Virgin's name, do this country's skies stop weeping? Another waterlogged camp tonight!'

Jestin, in the evening, called a council of war. Across a meagre fire which the drizzle slowly vanquished his chieftains faced our knights. We crouched beneath a leafless oak, cloaks drawn over our hauberks; for we had brought no tents: in this roadless desolation our baggage was borne on rounceys – a long, vulnerable string. Next morning, Jestin proclaimed, the army would cross his marches into Brecknock, a hostile realm which Rhys ap Tewdwr ruled. The trackway entered a country still more mountainous and rugged. We could be ambushed at every turn; the enemy's main forces might attack us unannounced. What plans, the Welshman inquired, had the Lord of Torigni in mind to ensure his army's safety and defeat Deheubarth's king?

'May Satan fry his soul!' fitzHamon growled. 'The rogue leads us into a wilderness, deposits us in mountains alive with enemies, then asks politely what we want to do. What do you advise, my lords?'

'I think,' said William of Londres, 'we run our heads in a noose. Get out while we can!'

'A craven's counsel!' said Pagan scornfully. 'Why retreat before we see a foeman's face? Keep going, I say!'

'If Tewdwr's men are anything like these,' said Lisiard, gesturing contemptuously to the chieftains opposite, 'we should smash them easily. I'm for marching on.'

A wind gust thrashed the branches overhead and spattered raindrops down my neck. Testily I pulled the cloak around my throat. 'If we retreat, these ruffians will betray us. Possibly they'll join their enemies – who knows what the Welsh will do? – and harry us all the way back. Better to advance.'

After a wordy argument the other knights concurred. 'Very well,' fitzHamon said. 'On we go. Now to concoct a battle plan with our – um – allies. Ho, priest! Tell Jestin this.'

We sat on the squelching ground and grew steadily wetter. fitzHamon, through the interpreter, sifted the prince's proposals: a Welshman, I concluded, invariably used ten words when one would do. His chieftains shared the discussion; the council clucked like a chicken-run. The drizzle increased to a downpour. fitzHamon at last said tiredly, 'Jestin's certain we'll meet Tewdwr's men tomorrow. This, therefore, seems to be the plan. The Welsh will provide scouts and outguards. They'll send a striking force ahead to find the foe and then, by feigning flight, draw them on our lances. We march in the closest order, cavalry in the van. The baggage stays here under guard. Has anyone,' he concluded bitterly, 'charged up mountainsides before?'

I beckoned Lisiard and went to the gully where my mesnie huddled under shelters built from tree boughs, saddles and horse rugs. The horses picketed nearby champed forage our allies had provided: disgustedly I fingered parched and brittle grass, and ordered an extra feed from the oats we carried on rounceys.

'Fodder's running low,' Lisiard said sombrely. 'Only two days' feeding left – provided we cut the ration. The rounceys already exist on hay alone.'

I eased the helmet from my brow. 'Tomorrow will decide the outcome one way or the other. After that we'll either be dead or sacking the enemy's granaries.'

Berenger pulled the hauberk over my head, stripped me to the skin and towelled my chilly body, found me breeks and tunic nearly dry. I tunnelled beneath a saddle-cloth shelter, and donned my sodden cloak. Berenger scrubbed my rust-flecked mail; Pigot brought food in a wooden bowl; we supped the steaming broth and examined the scene morosely.

Twilight shadowed a narrow valley curtained by scudding clouds; camp fires flickered like candles glimpsed through tears, bivouacs humped the ground like scattered chunky boulders, the figures of men and horses loomed like wraiths. The hills were rocky battlements; mist wreaths shrouded the crests.

Lisiard gloomily surveyed the slopes. 'I must borrow an angel's wings and sew them to my destrier. Here's no fighting-ground for knights.'

A manifest fact. I settled myself for sleep.

8

We marched at dawn. The rain had stopped; the mist became more dense. We rode in column of threes, myself in the foremost rank with Lisiard and fitzHamon. Behind us clattered the horsemen, then tramped men-at-arms, a long brown winding column, the rearmost lost in mist. Somewhere ahead the Welshmen skipped; their flankers' calling rang among the crags. fitzHamon searched the hill-slopes, and muttered under his breath. I cursed my Flemish destrier – Rufus's gift – which kept stumbling over the stones, and held my rein hand taut. Palpable as spiders' webs, the mist-veil swirled and brushed our faces.

Shouts echoed in the hills. fitzHamon hefted his lance, enarmed his shield. 'Jestin's found his foe. We ought to see them soon.'

Figures clad in furry pelts came tumbling down the hillsides, zig-zagged through the scrub and scurried towards the column. Several carried scarlet rags on spears – a recognition blazon fitzHamon had devised.

'Our own flankers. They haven't stood for long. Tewdwr's men will be close behind.' fitzHamon called to the horsemen: 'Halt! Front left and right!'

Welshmen fled to the trackway, and gestured urgently to the scarps whence they had come. We peered at the mist-clad slopes, seeking their pursuers, heard high-pitched yells and battlecries – but saw not a living creature. We nuzzled shield rims, balanced lances, and waited with nerves at stretch.

Whutt!

'Navel of Christ, what's that?'

Whutt! Whutt!

Someone screamed. A destrier reared; the files bucketed sideways. I goggled in disbelief. Feathers jutted from a shield, a barb bristled on the owner's back. The shaft had skewered hide and mail and flesh and bone like so much flimsy parchment. Hauberks were proof against arrows – what sorcery was this?

Whutt!

A sound like a muffled whipcrack, like no arrow I ever heard – and plenty had passed my ears. Another agonized cry. A destrier streaked from the ranks; the rider dropped his lance and clutched his thigh. An arrow pinned him to the saddle, piercing hauberk-skirt and leg, alva and horse's ribs. The destrier faltered in his stride, and tumbled end over end. The knight, still pinned in place, shrieked as the cantle crushed him.

The column began to disintegrate: soldiers scattered from the track, and sought shelter in bush and boulder from the flaying remorseless shafts. Our cavalry milled in confusion, hugging their worthless shields.

I bridled my panicky destrier, who was doing his best to bolt. My fingers slipped on the rein: Berenger, I thought vaguely, had over-oiled the leather, tomorrow he'll be whipped. The animal bumped fitzHamon's and nearly tipped him from the saddle; he cursed me roundly.

'We're trapped in an ambuscade!' I yelled. 'Must we die like Roland's men?'

'There's one way out – straight on!'

fitzHamon bawled commands, and lifted his lance on high. 'Keep close!' I called to Berenger, whose eyes were wide and scared. We followed in disarray, crouching over saddle-bows, lance-shafts flogging flanks. A galloping rabble thundered along the vale. The footmen, seeing us go, followed fast as the ground would let them. We left them far behind, curtained in the mist.

The valley tapered to a cleft. The pass disgorged a mob which ran towards us. I steadied my destrier, levelled my lance, saw scarlet shreds on spears. fitzHamon hauled his rein, his destrier's hooves scraped sparks from the stones.

'Where are you going?' he shouted. 'Where in hell is the enemy?'

The Welshmen trotted past him, took no heed.

'They're pretending flight,' I said. 'This is the force that trailed their cloaks to entice ap Tewdwr on.'

'Pretending —!' fitzHamon gritted.

Jestin appeared at his side, bareback on a shaggy pony hardly bigger than a goat. He pointed behind and volleyed words.

fitzHamon shook his head despairingly. 'I think he means the enemy's on his tail. Holy Jesu, what a place to meet them! Come on!'

We pursued him through the pass, the horses slipping and sliding on the pebbled bed of a stream. The gorge widened, and opened on a plain, a bowl enclosed by hills.

Across the flats the Welsh advanced in a broad brown spate. The bulk was footmen: chieftains riding ponies chanted exhortations. The nearest spears were four-score paces distant.

fitzHamon pulled to a halt, and looked at the enemy grimly. He turned his head and surveyed his little force – forty panting men and blowing horses.

'No use waiting,' he said crisply. 'Form line!'

We jostled into a ragged rank, knights clustered in the centre, sergeants on the wings.

'Ride knee to knee. Whatever you do, don't scatter!'

He pointed his lance to the sky.

'Charge!'

We had breath enough to raise a shout, and pelted through the scrub. We heard the deadly arrows whip; Lisiard cried and fell. I jerked my rein and closed the gap, Pagan at my knee. My shield rim clinked the.nasal, I yelled curses as I rode, the oaths resounded hollow from the shield-hide.

The enemy's onset faltered; they turned and tried to run. We were on them before they knew it, and rode them down like chaff.

My lance-shaft snapped in a naked chest; I drew my sword and slashed, felt the edge carve flesh like melting cheese and judder on a breastbone. The blade was wedged in the body, and almost lugged me from the saddle. I wrenched it free and drove the point through a mouth that yelled in fright; took a bearded head with a sideways cut which jumped it from the shoulders. The Welshmen parted before us as corn goes down to the sickle; we rode through the horde from front to rear in a pounding torrent of steel.

fitzHamon slowed and swung about. The charge had dishevelled our line, no longer an armoured flail. The enemy ran for the hills; the margins of the swathe we had cut dissolved like snow in the sun.

'Hunt and kill!' fitzHamon panted. 'Every man for himself!'

I collected my tired destrier, overtook a limping fugitive and clove his skull to the teeth. A man on a hairy pony checked when he heard my hoofbeats, turned his mount and faced me. The point of a throwing-spear scored my shield. He followed the throw on his silly pony, shouting and waving an axe. I parried and straightened my arm; his speed sank the blade to the forte. He tumbled to the ground, and wrapped arms round my destrier's foreleg. The animal shied and tried to rear. I leaned from the saddle and hacked him rib from rib.

Berenger, behind, was quietly sick.

The tumultuous ride from the ambush had so exhausted the horses they could hardly go out of a trot. Many of the Welsh we hunted reached flinty slanting screes where we could not chase them. Jestin's warriors burst from the gorge, scattered across the plain and quested the hills for their quarry. Our footmen followed; mercenaries broke from the ranks and raked the bodies for booty. A futile search: the carcases were bare of loot as the rocks they lived in.

I kicked my drooping destrier to the knights around fitzHamon, who pushed the helmet from his head and wiped the sweat from his face.

'Presumably a victory – and the easiest of battles. The Welsh, I thought, were meant to be doughty fighters.'

'They've never seen a charge of armoured knights – it's broken many better men than they.' I slid from the saddle, handed the rein to Berenger, and cleaned my blade on a dead man's fox-pelt. 'Now they know – and won't easily be caught in the open again. How in future, mailed and mounted, will we reach them in their crags?'

I plodded over the battleground, looking for Lisiard's corpse. Mercenaries were searching bodies; our allies hunted the wounded, and atrociously despatched them by thrusting spears up buttocks. I turned two dead knights over before I found him, the shield fastened to his body by an arrow. The barb protruded from his back. Lisiard's eyes were open and he muttered curses. I knelt beside him, and felt beneath the shield for the point of entry. Not a mortal wound: the shaft had pierced his shoulder below the collar-bone.

'Clench your teeth,' I ordered. 'This will hurt.'

With my dagger I sawed the arrow between shield and hauberk – an awkward task which made him writhe – turned him over, hacked off the barb and pulled the shaft from the wound. Lisiard yelped and fainted, which made my succouring easier. I unlaced his helmet, dragged the hauberk over his head – Berenger came and helped – tore his tunic in strips and plugged the bleeding holes.

Lisiard came to his senses, went on swearing.

'Up you get,' I told him briskly. 'All you need is a cup of wine and a good long rest.'

Lisiard drained the wineskin Berenger carried. The echoes of the killing in the hills were growing fainter. Men-at-arms and Welshmen roved the carcase-littered plain. Jestin arrived on his pony, carrying by the hair a dripping head. He threw it on the ground, where it rolled face-up.

'Rhys ap Tewdwr,' he proclaimed triumphantly. 'Myself I slew him!'

I heard the priest's translation, recognized the warrior who had run himself on my sword, shut my lips and let the wretched princeling enjoy his glorious moment.

'We camp here,' fitzHamon stated. 'Tomorrow we go south.'

'But why?' Jestin waved his arms expansively. 'All Brecknock is yours!'

fitzHamon inspected the wilderness around, the moisture-curtained hills and stony scarps. 'You'd want a hundred hides to pasture a single cow. With a little searching,' he told Jestin smoothly, 'I'm sure we'll find richer land.'

At sunrise we departed, and left the carrion to the crows.

9

After three days' march we emerged from the hills, traversed a fertile plain – the Vale of Glamorgan – and halted by the sea at a starveling fishing village they called Cardiff. 'Here,' fitzHamon said, 'I shall build my castle. The Vale from Gwent to Dyfed, from the mountains to the sea is mine by right of conquest and King William's warrant.'

When Jestin understood this claim his rage was sweet to behold. He spluttered till the dribble flecked his beard. 'Norman robbers and ruffians! Will you partition my realm? All Glamorgan will rise to drive you out!'

'Indeed?' fitzHamon drawled. 'You may have trouble, friend. The Vale is cavalry country – no devil-sent mountains here. Do you wish to perish like Tewdwr and his men? We leave you Gwent and all the northern hills – Brecknock too, which hereby I renounce.' His voice hardened. 'Go, Jestin Prince of Glamorgan – voice no more empty threats! King William's aid, you'll find, is never cheap!'

Jestin departed fuming. Meanwhile the mercenaries, who had hardly seen a woman for a fortnight, comprehensively ravished every female old enough to be entered. The fishermen promptly fled; fitzHamon, vastly annoyed – he needed labour to build his castle, villeins to tend his fields and was fond of fish – hanged three men-at-arms and drove the rest to build the fort. Within a week they raised a mound by a shallow river called Taff, planted a wooden donjon, dug ditches and fenced a ward. fitzHamon left a hundred men and traversed the Vale. He chose strategical vantage points and sited castles; to each he allotted land, to each he appointed a lord and a stalwart garrison. Pagan did homage for Coyti, Londres was granted Ogmore.

I offered Lisiard release from his fealty if he coveted land in Wales. He answered grumpily, 'I've sworn an oath to wrest, one day, St Remi from Belesme. That's task enough for any man; I don't want any distractions.' A reluctant smile crinkled the cadaverous features. 'I'm content enough in your mesnie, my lord, despite' – he touched a bandaged shoulder – 'your service being highly dangerous!'

fitzHamon naturally offered me a fief; courteously I declined. I deemed my possessions sufficient, my overlords various enough. Poix's Honour and Achères I held of France, Laingaham from Clare and through him Rufus. A tenancy in this faraway land and homage to fitzHamon roused needless complications. Glamorgan was a very long way from France.

Pigot had stolen a Welshman's bow, and waxed enthusiastic. 'A devastating weapon!' he declared. 'Nothing can withstand it.' He nocked an arrow – we were walking Cardiff's circuit, watching the ditch being scarped – and aimed at the palisade. The arrow thrummed in the wood.

'Come and see!'

We clambered in and out of the moat, and inspected the stake he hit. Fresh-hewn oak four fingers thick: the barb had gone clean through.

'Enormous penetration!' Pigot exulted. 'No armour ever forged will stop it.'

I looked at the clumsy bowstave, tall as the man himself. 'My archers are mounted, Pigot – that bow is far too cumbersome to use on horseback.'

'Agreed, my lord. But infantry so armed could counter knights.'

'Exactly. That's the reason I dislike it. Why introduce a weapon which might destroy our knights' supremacy? Besides, you'll never alter the Norman archer's traditions – remember the trouble Richer had recruiting his mounted bowmen? Burn it, Pigot, and bury the ashes deep!'

Pigot grumbled – and obeyed. Nevertheless I had an uneasy feeling that at some time in the future the paladins of courtoisie would fall before the long bow.

10

I left fitzHamon in Cardiff, taking my mesnie and the mercenaries Rufus had loaned. After a troublesome march through coastlands – the soldiers bent on pillage and hard to restrain – I reached Gloucester early in May to confront a situation both abominable and dangerous.

Chapter 6

1093–94

Richer's face wore a look of blank despair. He said in a toneless voice, 'Roger's gone. He's living in the castle.'

The ground heaved under my feet. 'How . . . long?'

'Two days.' The Saracen was near weeping. 'My lord, I could do nothing. The king sent knights to fetch him.'

I looked at the livid weal a whipthong had left on his face. 'Alderi – have you seen him?'

'Yes. I followed Roger. Alderi saw my wounds, and ordered me from the castle. I begged his help. He answered that knight-errants were unfashionable. He was . . . flippant.'

I loosed the shield guige and, mailed as I was, ran through Gloucester's streets to the castle. The hall was almost empty; someone told me the king was hunting. I searched behind pillars, scoured side-rooms, found Alderi in a garderobe teaching Roger the slip-knots used for liams' leashes. The knight lifted a hand in greeting, and continued his instructions. 'Pass one end through the loop, thus, and pull the bight taut . . .'

I took Roger's cheeks between my palms and lifted his face.

'Are you . . . well?'

'Why not, my lord? The fever went weeks ago.' The laughing eyes were guileless, frank . . . unscathed. He lifted my hand to his lips in a gesture of homage and love. 'It's good to see you back. I have served the king' – a touch of pride – 'while you were gone.'

I swallowed, and glanced at Alderi, intent on an intricate knot. 'By your favour, a word . . .'

'Yes. It's time.' Alderi snapped the twine. 'Roger, go now to Gaimard the fewterer: tell him from me to show you the bonds that couple berselets. I've forgotten them.' He slapped the boy's shoulder affectionately. 'Off you go!'

Alderi regarded me quizzically. A silver fillet bound his hair, gold threads embroidered a silken paltock, fine-meshed woollen hose embraced his legs like skin. He wore gilded shoes, long-pointed, the points turned up like scorpions' tails. Alderi caught my mordant glance, and lazily stretched his legs. 'Unusual, aren't they?' he murmured. 'The latest rage. Fulk of Anjou started it, I'm told – simply because of his bunions.'

'Why,' I said between my teeth, 'is Roger in the castle? You gave your word —'

'I said I'd try.' Alderi bent and fingered the tips of his ridiculous shoes. 'If they made them longer still,' he said pensively, 'one could tie the points to one's legs with neat little golden chains. Very smart.' In the same reflective voice he added, 'You'll have to take the boy away, my lord.'

'What has happened?'

'Rufus's ardour outruns his discretion. I fear he's fallen in love. He's now decided Roger must sleep in the castle. And so . . .' He hunched his shoulders.

I gulped. 'Did Roger share the king's . . . bedchamber?'

'Very nearly. I had to feign hysterics. My dear,' he minced, 'you never saw such a scene! The jealous lover callously rebuffed, and striving to oust his rival. For quiet's sake Rufus sent Roger out.'

'Doesn't the boy realize . . . has he no idea?'

Alderi dropped his affectation. 'I don't think so,' he said soberly. 'Roger's remarkably innocent, despite your lecturing. Oh, yes, I know about that – he asked me to elucidate certain . . . obscurities.' Alderi smiled. 'Certainly he came to the right man. However, I believe he's no more than flattered by the king's attentions. What esquire wouldn't be?'

'Is Rufus still chasing him?'

'Yes. It's all very inconvenient,' Alderi drawled. 'I can't pretend to throw spasms every night of my life. And I'm not going to quarrel with Rufus.' His tone was definite. 'Go away, my lord, and take your mesnie with you – if the king allows.'

I left him admiring his shoes and wandered into the ward. I leaned on the palisade and tried to arrange my thoughts. Once more the blemish that stained the man must send me away from Rufus. I recalled the revelation, two decades before, when Rufus first disclosed his loathsome bent: a disaster which severed our friendship for eighteen years. Must I be banished again, and break the vow I had sworn to myself to shield him from secret enemies? I rested head on hands and groaned: a nearby sentry leaned on his spear and eyed me in astonishment. Should I feign ignorance of the king's attempt to seduce my esquire – return the lad to Conches, inventing some excuse, and remain at court myself? No – it would not answer. Everyone had seen the king's infatuation; his quarry's blatant flight would become a general jest and provoke him beyond forgiveness. His rancour would fall on me; and that I could not endure. I had hitched my wagon to Rufus's star and the traces were soldered fast.

Moreover, despite his disgusting vice I loved him.

A rowdy cavalcade wended through the streets: laughing, mired men on steaming horses, hounds running at their heels, huntsmen in leaf-green livery, a red deer's carcase slung across a pony. Rufus rode in front, white teeth gleaming in a scarlet face; he lifted a spiralled horn and blew the menée. The cortege entered the ward; stablemen ran to the horses, berners collected hounds. Rufus dismounted, spanned the dead buck's antlers, and boisterously slapped a verderer's back. He showed an overreach to the strapper holding his horse, wagged an admonishing finger and ambled across the wooden bridge that leaped the donjon's ditch.

I waited on the rampart, giving time for the fuss to abate; and followed Rufus to the hall. He sat slantwise on a table, swinging a leg, gulping from a gold-rimmed drink-horn. Mud stars splotched his tunic, brambles had scarred long calfhide boots. I edged through the chattering crowd, conspicuous in my mail, and bent my knee. Rufus waved his drink-horn, splashing wine on deerskin breeches, and roared greeting.

'Walter! Back from the wilds – haven't you had time to unarm? You've won me a county in Wales, so fitzHamon's missives said! A taciturn fellow; his reports are short as a hedge-priest's mass! A cup of wine, my friend! Sit here' – he patted the table – 'and tell me all the details.'

I sipped my wine, and spoke of Brecknock's battle, ap Tewdwr's death and Glamorgan's taking. Barons crowded round to hear, smelling of horses' sweat and rain-damp leather. I ended my account, drew in my breath and said, 'With your permission, sire, I must shortly leave you.'

'Hey?' Rufus buried his nose in the cup. 'What's this? Why must you go?'

'My fief at Laingaham,' I said lamely – I had invented no better excuse, 'demands attention. The steward swindles the revenues, the fields are badly tilled. And so . . .' My voice trailed off.

Rufus drained his horn to the dregs and cast it on the floor. He took my arm and led me out of earshot. 'Now, Walter, tell me your troubles and stop babbling about insolvent fiefs. Is it Poix? If Eu's vassals or Aumale's have harried your lands I'll cut their bollocks!'

'Neither, my lord. I spoke truth. For nine months I've lived in England without visiting my English manor. Surely it's time . . .'

Rufus gave me a searching look.

'Well, I won't stop you, Walter – but I shall miss you.' He strolled three paces away and stepped decisively back. 'That esquire of yours – Roger of Conches – will stay in my mesnie. I've taken a fancy to the lad: he promises well, and he'll find advantage at my court.'

I pretended surprise. 'The boy is indeed honoured, my lord. I shall send to Conches and seek permission from his lord.'

'Permission?' Rufus's fingers curled: storm-warnings of a royal rage fluttered up the mast. 'You need none – it is my will!'

'Courtoisie demands it, sire. Roger's entrusted to my charge. You don't barter a baron's son like a bonded serf!'

'By the Face!' He lifted a fist. 'Do you defy me? You presume too far on friendship, Tirel! You'll send that boy to the castle before you go!'

I swallowed my spittle, and said in a shaky voice, 'No. I shall not.'

Rufus lowered his hand. His words came out in a whisper, hissing between the teeth. 'So. It's that again. You've heard . . . rumours.' He stamped away, scraped fingernail on an arras draping the wall, traced the antlers of a hart being torn at prise. 'True enough. Walter, I love Roger. Will you never understand? Haven't you loved women, known the longing and the glory and the pain? Can't you see that this . . .'

Forcibly he ripped a trailing thread from the tapestry. 'No, you can't – nor do I care! This remains, my lord of Poix: go when and where you like – take Roger at your peril!'

Rufus strode away and shouted for wine. I found my hands were shaking. Alderi lounged by the portal. He said lightly, 'You look pale, my lord. I watched that little encounter: Rufus in a rage is a chastening experience. What was the outcome of your . . . dispute?'

'Unhappy. The king won't let Roger go.'

Alderi twined a glossy curl around a finger. 'Oh. What, then, will you do?'

'Get out as fast as I can.'

'Very wise. The nearest port for Normandy's Southampton. Meanwhile,' he added coyly, 'I'll try to soothe my suzerain. My boyish charms might turn his mind from your esquire. We shall see.'

I left abruptly, feeling sick, and collected Roger quickly from his conference with the fewterer.

2

Within an hour I was on the road.

We faced a three-day ride, moving at the fastest pace the horses could make. I offered no explanation: nobody asked questions. Lisiard gloomily saddled the horses; Richer looked once at my face, kept his countenance inscrutable and coped with the rounceys' panniers. Roger and Berenger quickly unarmed me, clothed me in breeks and hose. We took the long straight road called Ermin by the English, reached Cirencester at dusk and quartered in a tavern.

I feared pursuit and capture; I dreaded the king's requital. I was not afraid for my life because Rufus, however angry, could not gratuitously kill King Philip's barons. But imprisonment needed little excuse or none; at Conches I had suffered a donjon's vaults and the silent, singing blackness which sends your reason tottering. I wanted no more of that. An unheralded flight might give me a day's-march start; my horses were sound and speedy enough to outstrip the king's pursuit.

I aimed next day for Hungerford. The way was dry and dusty; summer squandered sunlight on the land; the fields were emerald stripes on flowered carpets; lime trees shivered shining leaves like scales of viridian mail. We made good marching, canter and trot and walk. Climbing the scarp from the vale I saw, far back, a swiftly moving dust-cloud on the road. No normal traveller gallops; hastily I led my retinue to a thorn grove's shelter.

Three riders on lathered horses climbed the hill. The foremost carried a gonfanon that whipped in the downland wind.

'King's messengers riding post,' I said. 'Do they carry commands to stop us?'

'Probably riding on other business,' asserted Lisiard, unwontedly optimistic.

'Assume the worst,' I answered. 'Where will they find men to take us? Not Hungerford – a bog-knight's castle. Winchester's the place: we'll have to skirt it.'

'Better take to the byways now.'

'And slow the pace to a crawl? No, We'll stick to the road and wait at Hungerford tonight.'

At evening I rode into the village, sword-hand ready, met none but a careless soldier and villeins homing from the fields. Splashing across the ford we saw a cavalcade approaching; I drew my sword and hid it beneath my cloak. Knights in garish mantles, men-at-arms and ox-carts: clearly a lord on passage – not a company sent to seize us. We drew aside to give them way, and scrutinized their faces.

I nearly fell from my horse.

In leather doublet and breeches, a feather in her cap, rode Isabel of Conches. I spurred my horse and babbled, knowing not what I said. The slanting eyes were opened wide; she dropped her rein and reached out both her hands.

'Tirel! I thought you at Rufus's court! We're on our way . . .' She saw the sword in my hand, and laughed. 'Do you greet me with steel, my lord, after all these months?'

Clumsily I sheathed the blade; my hands were trembling. I bent and kissed her fingers. 'Why you have come, or whence, I know not, lady – but by the Rood, the Saints themselves have brought you! A God-sent answer to a prayer I never made!'

'What prayer? What's all this?' Ralph of Conches came sidling up, displeasure in his puffy face. 'Greetings, my lord of Poix,' he said without enthusiasm. 'Whither are you bound?'

I called Roger, who came shyly forward and bowed to his lord and lady. 'Your son, my lady, I deliver him to your charge – guard him well!'

Isabel frowned. 'I don't understand, Walter. Why? Has the child been wayward?'

Horses sidled and fretted; the knights of Conches's retinue looked longingly to Hungerford's donjon; men-at-arms examined the houses for sign of a bush. Ralph testily waved them on. 'Give my salutations to the castle's lord, crave quarters for knights and ladies,' he told his steward, 'and room in the ward for the rest. Now, my lord, explain yourself. Why do you rudely shed your esquire, like a bailiff ridding his fields of a useless serf?'

I hardly heard his jabbering. Ralph was Rufus's man: why was he in England, what his destination?

'Where are you bound?' I asked sharply.

'Gloucester, to wait upon the king.'

And here was a stew. Disastrous to return Roger to the perils he had left. Not even Rufus would pluck the boy from his parents – but why renew temptation? God knew how Ralph would behave when he heard the truth. The weakling lord of Conches was unpredictable when angered – and the insult to his son would unscabbard the tamest sword. And if Ralph abjured his fealty the king lost a base in Normandy.

I seized on an easy falsehood. 'I go to Laingaham – a dull, forsaken spot. No place for a spirited lad, my lord; he'd be better off with you.'

'Laingaham?' Ralph looked at the setting sun and got his bearings. 'A long way off course, aren't you?' He shook his bridle. 'We can't stand here for ever – let's see what hospitality that starveling fort can offer. I wager we bed with fleas tonight!'

Ralph's misgivings were justified: a cramped and squalid donjon, an austere meal, the knight an uncouth Poitevin of uncertain lineage. Afterwards, lauding my Flemish destrier, I took Isabel to see the paragon. Hurriedly, hating the need – sodomy is not a subject one discusses with gentle ladies – I told her all the truth. Isabel, quite unshocked, stroked the destrier's mane and heard me out in silence.

'We met king's messengers galloping the road near Litchfield,' she said coolly. 'Riding, so they said, to Southampton to stop a thief. Your flight to Normandy is blocked.' She pulled her lip. 'If Roger returns to Gloucester we walk wide-eyed into quicksands. Why not go to your fief, as you pretended?'

'The king's writ runs in Laingaham.'

'Would Rufus wrench a son from his mother's arms?'

I gaped at her, bemused.

'Yes.' She smiled at my bewilderment. 'That's the key to unlock this maze. I must come to Laingaham.' She studied my stunned expression, and her mouth went soft. 'I shall not find your company intolerable, my lord.'

'But . . . what will you tell Ralph?'

'Some plausible excuse – he values my advice. I'll say Roger hated the court, but is happy in your mesnie. For myself – I yearn for my child, and wish to be with him.'

'Ralph is like to seek me sword in hand!'

Isabel's lip curled. 'Do leverets grow wings, does dawnlight shine in the west?' She sent me a provocative glance. 'His fears are ground-less. I shall be well escorted, my lord, by knights and ladies in waiting.'

Ralph, snorting and suspicious, came grumbling to the stable. Isabel smiled at him sweetly, and praised the stallion's points. Her lord grunted, gave me a scowl and led her away.

At morning, wearing a baffled look, Ralph conducted his retinue along the road called Ermin. Isabel's followers leavened my mesnie; and we headed north.

3

Laingaham is a secluded hamlet set in a rolling plain which is quilted by forests and woodlands. A mouldering wooden donjon crowned an eminence west of the village, a relic of Gilbert's father, Richard of Bienfaite, who built the fort without Duke William's license. The Duke was disagreeable; Richard abandoned his castle and raised a fortified hall on the flats below: a commodious timbered building nudged by kitchens, stables and granaries; a palisade and ditch encircled the whole. The peasants' dwellings neighboured a tiny church; pasturelands and fields lapped southwards to a stream.

Such was Laingaham, which came to me by dowry.

A gallery at an end of the hall led to a bower: here I quartered Isabel and her ladies – three sprightly maidens of vivacious bent: Isabel could never stand dullards. Her tirewomen lived within call beneath the gallery. Richer, Lisiard and Conches's knights – two companionable men, fond of drink and dicing – the esquires and I myself slept as usual in the hall. Richer found me a testered pallet, and set it in a corner free from draughts. Lisiard eyed this luxury, swore I was going soft.

My relations with Isabel assumed a hue of chastity befitting any monk. After a passionate bout in the bower, nearly disrupted by a serving wench, we concluded that conditions were against us. Dalliance, in short, was difficult. Almost imperceptibly, without a word being spoken, we came to accept the pass, Isabel wryly, myself most grudgingly. In truth we were both in our thirties, past our prime, and youth's hot-blooded ardours beckoned less imperiously. So I worshipped from afar, and she seemed serenely content: like ships after stormy voyaging we lay becalmed in a haven.

Nevertheless I did not live like a hermit. The girl I had rescued from the mercenaries had attached herself to my mesnie, become my willing leman and extremely fluent in French. She slept often in my comfortable pallet – Lisiard complained our loving kept him wakeful. There were also ardent sluts in hall and hamlet: nowadays, I am told, swarthy, beak-nosed, grey-eyed children play in Laingaham's meadows.

The summer flowed peacefully past like a limpid, dawdling brook. Small pebbles from the outer world dropped sometimes in the water, and stirred hardly a ripple. We learned from Ralph's infrequent letters that Rufus made his summer progress and had come to Rockingham. Ralph repeatedly demanded that his lady join him; Isabel, by the steward's hand, sent soothing answers. 'Though,' she told me, 'I can't live here for ever. When summer's out I must go.' I felt a clutch at my heart; and chid myself for illusions.

All dreams end in the dawn-wind.

My lady's lovely sister Bertrada, Anjou's countess, wed her king among the Church's execrations. Philip, we heard, was shirking his kingly duties, steadily shedding responsibility on the shoulders of Louis his son – a cold, arrogant young man I much disliked – granting him the Vexin county and important fiefs. This news seriously concerned me: my affable overlord's power appeared to be waning. It occurred to me that I ought to visit Poix and see for myself the trend of Philip's court.

August's steamy rain gave way to September's mists. Robert Count of Meulan unexpectedly arrived, passing on his way to visit a Norfolk fief. I gave him a fitting welcome, food and wine and quarters; he stayed three days. He brought gossip from the court, and something more than gossip. After a midday meal, when servants had cleared the table and left sweetmeats in silver platters, Meulan chose a quince and said, 'Among other things, Anselm and Rufus again crossed swords.'

'Will the abbot never stay content? He's got Canterbury – what more does he want?'

'Rufus made him archbishop – which was all he promised.' Meulan laughed. 'Anselm found himself holding a mitre and pastoral staff, and nothing more: Rufus retained seisin of the lands that Lanfranc held.'

'It's the king's right: he owns all land.'

'So Rufus argued. They had a row: Anselm mild and obstinate, the king fuming. In the end Rufus yielded – and made the archbishop do him homage for Canterbury's manors. Anselm didn't like that much.'

'So now they're reconciled?'

'Almost. Not quite.' Meulan popped a fig in his mouth. 'Anselm started another hare. He wanted to recognize Pope Urban, which touched Rufus on the raw. He reminded Anselm forcibly of Duke William's hard insistence that no pope is acknowledged in England unless the king consents. The rule still held. He also asked sarcastically which pretender Anselm favoured: Urban or Clement.'

'A valid question. We've had two popes in Christendom for seven years.'

'Rufus won't have either. Anselm, luckily, saw he'd gone too far, was likely to batter his head to bits on an iron wall; and quietly dropped the point. I doubt we've heard the last of that, knowing Anselm's perseverance. Some would call it mulishness.'

Meulan took a napkin his esquire tendered, and wiped his hands. 'There's another matter, Walter, best said in private. Shall we ride your fields? – I have a mind to see your husbandry: it's long since I tended a fief.'

Thunderheads climbed a leaden sky, the air held the smell of rain. The harvest was all garnered; plough teams furrowed the stubble. Meulan dismounted, and crumbled a clod in his hand. 'Heavy soil,' he commented. 'Rich and fertile. Productive as the ground where William Count of Eu is planting seeds. The crop, I'm afraid, will be none but tares.'

Meulan's unusual obliquity measured his disquiet – he was not given to parables. 'Count William?' I inquired patiently. 'What has he done?'

Meulan dropped the clod and dusted his hands. 'He's playing on the king's ambition: to re-unite the lands his father ruled. He persuades Rufus that Normandy's in ferment, anarchy rife, Curthose a duke of straw – all true – and urges an invasion.'

'From what you say the time seems ripe. Why are you opposed?'

Meulan set foot in the stirrup, and heaved himself to the saddle. 'You haven't harvested the beans in the field beyond the meadow. Let's examine the yield. Why? Because Curthose offers Philip a secret pact, a Norman–French alliance to kill or capture Rufus. Belesme has promised support; he'll bring two thousand lances. The pot is on the boil. They *want* Rufus to land in Normandy, to encircle him and crush him. Eu provides the incitement, prickling and persistent. For my money he's an agent Curthose sent.'

'You've warned the king?'

'I and fitzHamon both, separately and together. You know Rufus: he laughs and calls us fainthearts. He thinks he can defeat all

Christendom in arms.' Meulan plucked a pod and sniffed. 'Time you gathered these: here's signs of mildew.'

'So Rufus musters his array?'

'Not yet. He's pulled both ways, by me and William of Eu. Only one thing really holds him: his knightly word to Robert Curthose under Caen's treaty.' Meulan felt the bit. 'Home, Walter; there's rain on the way. To my thinking Curthose will spring the trap by denouncing the treaty.'

We walked our horses towards the hall. Meulan flicked his whip at a villein who leaned on a mattock to watch us pass. 'Your serfs are given to idling – you should keep their noses down. How much longer will you stay sequestered here?'

'A month, maybe. I'm considering going to Poix.'

'Don't do that. Return to court. Rufus has forgotten his grudge – his rages never last. He's been asking after you, and clearly repines your going. As for the cause of your quarrel' – an ironic smile bared yellow fangs – 'Alderi's back in the – ah – saddle, and brooks no rivals. Besides, the weft of this plot lacks certain essential threads; you may trace the missing pieces I can't find.'

I said thinly, 'I wondered at Henry's part. Where is he?'

'Still in Domfront, astride the palisade, waiting to jump on the side where the grass is greenest. He won't commit himself; and my spies can't track the string that leads to Curthose. The prince is a cunning rogue,' he conceded glumly.

We surrendered our horses to strappers and ran for shelter in the hall; lightning scrawled the sky and the rain fell down like lances. We drank long and deep that night; Meulan, mellowed by wine, expansively exhorted me to rejoin Rufus. I havered, and promised nothing.

While Laingaham held Isabel no mortal power would move me.

4

Soon after Meulan's departure my lady announced she would rejoin Ralph, then with Rufus at Rockingham. Vigorously I protested; Isabel said firmly, 'No, Walter. I must go. Ralph is pricked beyond endurance. Even the king has twitted him – so Meulan said – inquiring of his lords at large where the Lady of Conches is nesting. Do you want him running here with swords?'

'The prospect doesn't make me quail,' I said sourly. 'Moreover Ralph worries without reason. Your knights and ladies can attest his honour's safe.'

'Truly – but the world smells scandal and whispers tales. The golden days are ended, Walter. We have known contentment here, my love – never,' said Isabel wistfully, 'have I been so happy as at Laingaham. Let it end without strife or rancour.'

I sadly commanded the steward to muster carts and oxen. A vexing problem – almost forgotten – suddenly twitched my memory. 'What,' I asked Isabel, 'will you do with Roger? He must not return to court!'

'Of course not,' said she, wide-eyed. 'He stays with you.'

'I may travel to France and afterwards – possibly – wait on Rufus. Better, my lady, that Roger return to Conches.'

Isabel shook her head. 'If he goes anywhere, Walter, it ought to be Poix – to your Honour, not Ralph's; in your charge, not the Lord of Conches's.'

'Why, in the Virgin's name —'

Isabel came close – we talked beside a window in the bower; her ladies, clucking, folded garments in wicker panniers – and took my face between her hands. 'How is it possible, my sweet, you do not know? Can you really be so blind?' She lifted a mirror from a tiring chest, and held the silver square before my eyes. 'Look on yourself, my lord!'

I saw a lean, pale, hook-nosed face, thin bitter lips, black-browed steel-grey eyes. 'There's one image, Walter. Don't you see another?' Isabel pointed to Roger, ramming kerchiefs in a satchel.

I stared at the boy, bewildered. His eyes belonged to Isabel, slanting upwards at the corners; high cheekbones reflected hers, and shining jet-black hair. The disparities struck like a blow: the long hard line of the jaw, thin high-bridged nose and taut, intractable mouth.

I turned on my lady a shocked and rigid face.

'Yes . . . I see. When did . . . this . . .'

Isabel caressed my cheek. 'At Poix, Walter, during those faraway days when we renounced the world for love. Before Ralph with brother Amauri brought lances and the threat of fire, and you weighed your Honour against our love – and sent me away.'

I wiped my forehead. 'All done. The debt is paid. Close the coffer, turn the key, forget the gall it holds. You sprinkle salt on ancient wounds, my lady.'

Isabel put her arms around my neck, her lips very close to mine. Her breath was warm, and sweet as new-mown hay. Her ladies' industry faltered, they peeped and smirked; Roger dropped the garment he was folding. Isabel embraced me, careless of their scrutiny, and whispered in my ear. 'Take our son, my dearest, keep him always. Send him, if you must, to Poix. It is fitting he should flower into manhood at the place where I . . . conceived him.'

Passionately I kissed her – to the devil with the women. She beckoned Roger, who looked doubtfully from Isabel's face to mine. 'You stay in Lord Walter's mesnie,' she told him quietly, 'and obey his will in all things till you're knighted.'

The boy's face cleared. 'My lady, I wish for nothing better.'

'You may have to remain in Poix when Lord Walter returns to England.'

Roger's mouth drooped. 'That I shall not like. Not Poix, I mean,' he amended hastily, 'but separation from my lord.' He considered a little, finger to lip. 'Will Berenger be there?'

I smiled. 'I'll see you're not parted from that red-haired scamp. His father is Poix's castellan; he'll look after the pair of you – and I wish him luck!'

Some day, I supposed, Roger must learn the truth.

5

I crossed the sea on a squally October day and was thoroughly ill. The road from St Valeri wound peacefully through Ponthieu, a county Guy ruled firmly, holding steadfastly aloof from French and Norman quarrels. Yet the contrast after England was like going from a garden to a guardroom: hauberks rode the highways; the marks of warfare seared the land. I had almost forgotten the timorous half-starved villeins who hid like startled mice from the spearhead's glint. I remembered tranquil England, the land that Rufus ruled, and the peasants who paused in their labour to greet us as we passed.

Poix rested undisturbed, serene as a cloistered nunnery. Delis complained he was growing fat, so quiet was his life. Nothing, he said boredly, had disturbed the stilly routine; no more than an outlaw band which raided a steading at Orbec. 'That was five months ago,' said Delis. 'Their corpses still droop from the gallows; we've caught no more to replace them.'

Adelice welcomed me gladly, her placid face unwontedly alive. In the bedchamber I dutifully paid tribute to her body – and closed my mind on memories of hard, lithe, passionate limbs. Afterwards I sensed a restlessness beneath her calm demeanour; often I caught her eyes upon me, hesitant and doubtful. Adelice never complained – she knew I hated peevishness – and firmly swallowed grievances before they could be uttered. At last, finding me benevolent after a rousing day with hounds, she said timidly, 'May I accompany you to Laingaham, my lord?'

I checked a curt refusal. Why not? My destiny lay with Rufus, whatever chasms opened on the path, whatever vagaries of his character or mine severed transiently our friendship. Inevitably to Rufus, as a river flows to the sea, I must return. Poix would see me little, Laingaham had become my English home. The household needed a woman's care; Isabel, I thought miserably, would never go there again.

'Why, certainly, my lady – such was always my intention.'

I was startled by the happiness in Adelice's eyes, and the grateful hand she laid on mine.

I had promised Roger that Berenger stayed in Poix; so I needed a new esquire. Briefly I considered Hugh, now rising eight, and killed the thought – the child was far too handsome. Warned by bitter experience I chose Berlai of Beaurain, a vassal's eldest son: an ugly, blotch-skinned lad who squinted vilely. Rufus was fastidious, Berlai in appearance quite repulsive – though he proved a skilled and willing esquire. Then I listed a mesnie, more numerous than the handful I had taken a year before.

Delis listened to the names, and observed, 'Better not remove too many.'

'Why so? Our neighbour lords have promised truce.'

'A courier from Paris arrived this morning.' Delis beckoned the priest, and flicked a scroll across the table. 'Read, Father.'

The missive, under Philip's seal, commanded an array of arms at any time after Christmas, and named Mantes for the muster.

'A warning order,' Delis drawled. 'I wonder what the king intends.'

Here was confirmation of the secret pact that Philip and Curthose made. I tugged my ear, perplexed. I had intended visiting Philip before I left; certainly he would then reveal his plans, expecting me in person to bring my conroys. Thus I should be committed; for the king's liege, knowing his mind, could not brazenly join the foe he meant to fight. Wiser, I decided, to avoid Paris, feign ignorance and, when Philip called the muster, let Delis lead my men.

The idea of deserting Rufus never entered my head.

'In that case,' I told Delis, 'I'll take only the mounted archers. They're a private body – separate from the lances owed to the king.'

I was worried about Richer. Since his failure to guard Roger the Saracen had become taciturn and withdrawn. I realized he took his discomfiture hardly, thinking himself forsworn; repeatedly I rallied him and told him to forget a misfortune he could not possibly have prevented. He stroked his withered arm, and his eyes were bitter.

'I can neither wield a sword nor draw a bow, my lord – and I blundered in my trust. What use am I? I think it best, with your consent, I return to Spain and live my crippled life among my people.'

The man was maimed in my service; I felt like weeping. 'For that, my permission will ever be wanting.' I put an arm about his shoulder. 'We've been comrades in war and adversity for many years; I've leaned on your advice and friendship. Poix's knights and men-at-arms will fight my battles – you can give me more, far more, than a ready sword or twanging bowstring. I embark, old friend, on perilous waters where the way is dark and stormy; I shall need your skilful touch on the steering-oar.' I took his hand. 'Your archers go to England – how can you stay behind?'

Tears stood in Richer's eyes. He bowed his head. 'Very well, my lord. I follow wherever you go.'

6

A turbulent winter storm delayed us at St Valeri; on New Year's Day I reeled ashore at Dover. While resting at an inn a journeying knight informed me that Curthose after Christmas sent defiance to King William, denounced the Caen treaty and declared his brother truthless. Rufus, highly delighted, sent couriers bidding his vassals ride to his banner at Hastings.

What Meulan prophesied had come to pass.

I despatched Adelice to Laingaham, and rode at speed for Gloucester where Rufus held his court. The town seethed in warlike ferment; gaily-mantled cavalcades, hawk on wrist and hound at heel, were scarce as flowers in winter – armoured knights and wagon trains jostled the narrow streets. I shouldered a way to the castle's hall, and loitered quietly behind a pillar. More provident, I reckoned, to spy the land unnoticed. The hall was crowded and clamorous, a bustle of comings and goings. Rufus sat on the dais, gay in purple tunic and crimson chape; his barons clustered round him like bees on a gorgeous flower. Daggers pinned a map to the table; Rufus plucked a quill and scrawled his marching lines and strategy. He looked buoyant, tremendously vital, his energy vibrating like rays from a burning sun.

Across the restless room, above the sea of heads, his eyes looked up and locked with mine.

Rufus dropped the quill, climbed slowly to his feet, and advanced across the hall. The throng gave way before him, thus a lane was carved between us. The furrows from his nostrils dragged the corners of his mouth. I kept my features still, and held his hostile gaze. A muscle started quivering in my leg.

'So. My errant lord of Poix, returned like a dog to his vomit. And what have you to say?'

'I serve in your household, sire, my name written in your book. I return where I belong.'

'You went without my permit!' Rufus snapped. The lines round his mouth relaxed; he dropped his voice. 'What lord allows his knights to come and go when they please, and depart if some . . . quirk . . . offends them? Not I, my lord, I promise you!'

'I avow my offence. But . . . I was provoked beyond bearing.'

Rufus flushed. 'Does one rust fleck rot the hauberk, one blemish blight the fruit? Will you always judge me by your monkish canons?'

'Never more, my lord, I swear.'

His eyes dwelt upon my face, as though probing through flesh and bone to reach my innermost mind. 'You swore fealty, Tirel.' His voice was soft, the anger gone. 'I believed you had broken your word – a knight's unforgiveable sin. I see I'm wrong.' He gripped my arm. 'By the Face, I'm glad! I wouldn't lose your trust for a thousand pounds in gold! You've come at a happy moment; weighty matters are in train, a war's afoot. I'll need your voice in council.'

Hand on arm he led me to the dais. The barons murmured together; they'd expected a royal tantrum but saw reconciliation. Rufus smiled impudently, and whispered in my ear, 'Where have you hidden that attractive boy?'

'Safely in Poix, my lord,' I answered woodenly.

'Foiled, by God! Cheer up, Walter – don't look so stern! Tell you what – to soothe your solemn principles I'll have a woman tonight!' His nostrils twitched, as if he had scented carrion. 'Faugh! Perhaps not, after all – a far too gruesome penance!'

7

The army assembled at Hastings, the wind blew strong from the south, for six weeks we were stormbound; and Anselm crossed the king.

In the origin of the quarrel the archbishop was at fault. Rufus's tenants-in-chief financed the expedition, the king quoting as precedent Normandy's contributions to the Conqueror's invasion. Barons and bishops gave all their fiefs afforded – Flambard saw to that – and Rufus in exchange remitted some of their service dues in knights and men-at-arms. Mercenaries fought his wars: he wanted wages rather than warriors. Therefore, when Flambard said that Anselm sent a mere five hundred silver pounds the king was very angry.

'What can Canterbury afford?'

'Two thousand pounds at least,' the Treasurer said contemptuously. 'This offer is nothing but an insult.'

'Send it back,' said Rufus tartly, 'and summon Anselm.'

The archbishop entered the royal pavilion, and tottered to a chair. The wayward tempest bellied the walls, rustled the rushes, plucked smoke from a red-hot brazier. Rufus strode about the tent. Anselm watched him, waited for the outburst, and finally said mildly, 'Why, my lord, do you refuse my gift?'

Rufus checked his pacing and glared. 'A paltry sum – a mockery!'

'Better a willing scantling than a fortune under duress. Nor, my lord,' Anselm went on warmly, 'will I further oppress my tenants – while you held Canterbury's manors you wrung them dry. They've been stripped to the skin; would you flay them alive?'

'Humbug! Your liegemen aren't impoverished – they can raise far more!'

Anselm surveyed him benignly. 'You may indeed be right – but I give what my conscience allows. The Church's goods aren't meant to be used for war, especially not a war against Duke Robert, once my worldly suzerain.'

'Do you dictate my conduct of state affairs?' Rufus blared.

Anselm looked horrified. 'Never, my lord! I merely offer advice. No good will come of this war that you intend.'

Rufus sneered. 'Are you a man of battle, to read a campaign's guidance? Enough of this bickering! Will you or will you not give me Canterbury's dues?'

Anselm's watery eyes were mournful. 'Five hundred pounds, no more. Already from the abbeys and the churches you persist in holding vacant you've extracted enough to ransom the Holy City. No more, my lord!'

'By the Face! Are not the abbeys mine? You do as you choose with your manors, shall I not do what I wish with my abbeys?'

'God's houses belong to God – they're not yours to despoil for war.'

Rufus ground his teeth. 'Insolence! Lanfranc would never have dared to taunt my father thus! Lavish with your sermons, niggardly with money – I want neither! Get out!'

He thrust a shaking finger towards the doorway. Anselm rose and shuffled out, supported by his monks. Speedily I followed. The wind whirled sand in spirals, breakers clawed the beaches, spray-salt smarted my eyes. I said to the old man pleadingly, 'My lord archbishop, must you purposely incense the king? What hope for England's realm if church and state are at odds? Try to be more politic, I beseech you!'

Anger shook Anselm's lips; they were dry and cracked. 'Must polity crush honour? Is the king's friendship bought and sold like merchandise at market? Do I buy his favour for fifteen hundred pounds? My son, you should know me better!'

I watched him stumbling over the dunes, wind whipping the foam-white hair. Meulan came to my side. 'Why should Anselm say no good will come of the war?'

'I don't know. He has visions, sees things in his head. Let's hope his angels, just this once, have erred.'

Anselm compounded his offence by preaching, in the newly-built Abbey of Battle, a ferocious Lenten sermon which rebuked King William's minions, condemned their effeminate garb, chastised their mincing gait and trounced their long twined hair. Openly he railed against the foulness of Rufus's court. The king himself was not at mass; when told of Anselm's diatribe he swore like a Breton bowman. 'I hate that meddling monk! Day by day I loathe him more! If he's waiting to bless our departure you can tell him he's wasting his time. I'd rather Satan's maledictions than all his blasted prayers!'

The archbishop, in truth, was baiting Rufus beyond reason. Fearing a confrontation when the king, his temper gone, might be goaded into sacrilege, I urged Anselm to depart. He murmured of his duty; forcibly I told him that no priest could function from the Tower's vaults, which was where he was heading. Anselm scratched his tonsure, sighed sorrowfully and agreed. With Canterbury's brethren in his train, he went from Hastings.

The breach between king and prelate yawned like a ravine.

Ralph of Conches was among the barons who wiled away those stormy days at Hastings. I avoided his company; he showed no want of mine. I took Ralph's enmity as a matter of course: the man had reason. Though I was far from the only knight who had grafted the horns which soared from his head I rode most often on the antlers; for riddance of this burden Ralph burned candles to his Saints.

Once, exercising our horses, I encountered him at sunrise on the beach; penned in a narrow sand-strip by the tide we perforce rode side by side. I made casual conversation, Ralph replied unamiably, cursed the ice-barbed wind that stared the horses' coats and said, 'I thank you, my lord, for the hospitality you afforded my lady at Laingaham.' He spoke reluctantly, his tone ungracious.

'The Lady Isabel's presence did my household honour.'

'Maybe.' Ralph spat sand from his mouth, and wrapped the paltock closer around his shoulders. 'Hitherto honour has been prominently lacking in your conduct. But for once, so I'm informed, you behaved decently.'

I wondered fleetingly whether the pompous idiot suspected Roger's sireing. 'Your lady would have it so,' I said brutally. 'Impute to me no virtues. Isabel holds me in thrall, in bond to the crook of her finger.'

Ralph nodded sombrely. 'As she holds me – else long since I'd have slit her throat. You're the last of her many lovers, the only fawning hound that remains of the dog-pack once at her heels. Curthose, Grantmesnil, Belesme, all the rest – they've let the scent go cold. Will you never lift your nose and slink sated to your kennel?'

A gust tore the cap from my head and sent it skittering over the shingle. Berlai dismounted hastily and scuttled in pursuit. Wind hunted the breakers shorewards, ripped spindrift from the crests; the ships plunged like restive stallions, plucking at their anchors.

I turned my horse. 'Time to go back. You mouth insults, my lord of Conches, and lack the resolution to back your petulance with steel. I'm willing to engage you with mesnies at our backs or singly, lance to lance. You've only to say the word.'

'Fight the man who unhorsed Rufus?' Ralph laughed harshly. 'Would suicide further my cause, and keep Isabel from your bed?'

'In that case shut your mouth, lest I deliver an open gage which you couldn't in honour refuse. Let be, Ralph. We're both enmeshed in toils that will hold us till we die – like flies entrapped in honey our struggles sink us deeper. Best to cease struggling.' My destrier plunged and bore on the bit; I kicked him into a trot. 'Where does Isabel dwell while you're in Normandy?'

'While we're in Normandy,' Ralph corrected. 'At a lorimer's house in Winchester. Had you been staying in England I'd have sent her straight to Conches.'

'I think you misjudge your lady.'

'Perhaps,' Ralph answered dourly, 'but not you.'

A few days later the wind veered and blew from the north; joyfully Rufus ordered the encampment struck and horses and baggage embarked. On the evening before we were due to sail I walked with Meulan over Hastings' famous field. The count led me here and there, pointing where the Bretons broke and fled, where the English levies charged, and the evil Malfosse, grave of valiant knights. 'The ground's altered,' he said. 'The apple-trees's been chopped; monastery and abbey usurp the Fighting Man where the valour of the English and all their glory raged. If you had seen the field at dusk, the corpses heaped and the wounded crying . . .'

I tried to look interested; but I had heard the tale many times before: a perennial reminiscence that ageing warriors told.

'A spy from Rouen landed today,' Meulan continued, his tone unchanged. 'The rumour is confirmed: Philip's on the march to support Duke Robert.'

My boredom vanished like morning mist.

'An awkward situation for you, Walter. Philip is your suzerain.'

'Yours also,' I reminded him.

'I hold land in Rufus's Normandy, in Rufus's England, in Philip's France. Rufus has two-thirds of me, Philip one. There's the difference. But you – will you oppose your liege?'

I bit my lip. 'I've foreseen this pass since first you said King Philip might join the duke. It makes no difference. I follow Rufus.'

'You put your Honour at risk. Philip is likely to escheat Poix.'

'Of that I'm well aware. I follow Rufus.'

It was not to be. We returned to the camp, to palliasses laid in the open, since all the tents were struck. A chamberlain roved the lines, called my name and brought a summons from the king. Rufus sprawled on a heap of straw; a lantern tinged his face a deeper red and turned his hair to molten gold. 'Ha, Walter! You've heard Philip's taken the field?'

'Yes, my lord.'

'Well, you stay in England. Mustn't fight your overlord. A pity – I'd have liked you at my side, and to have seen your archers at work.'

I said desperately, 'You own my fealty, sire, and I'm ready to serve you in battle.'

Rufus looked shocked. 'But you owe Philip fealty *and* homage. A knight can't break his vows! That sort of thing brings courtoisie in disrepute – and I won't have it!'

I gestured helplessly. 'I've counted the cost —'

'That's not the point! Losing Poix is a trifle compared to the stain on your blazon. I won't be responsible for smirching your honour! You will *not* embark tomorrow, Walter. There's plenty of work in England: Giffard rules the council in my absence, Flambard becomes chancellor; they'll value your help.' Rufus peered at my face; the lantern's wavering flame lit the wretchedness in my eyes. His voice softened. 'You can serve me better here, my friend. Brave knights are two a denier, but a loyal and cunning counsellor is worth a monarch's ransom.'

Ralph overtook me as I trudged unhappily over the dunes to my retinue's bivouac. His face was stark; a muscle twitched the corner of his mouth.

'You're not going,' he stated flatly.

'No.'

He crossed arms across his chest, hugging himself in misery. 'I leave Isabel to your lechery, leave you rutting like fevered swine —'

'Have done!' I rapped. 'I shall not approach your lady – you have my word! Would I dishonour a knight while he fights for Rufus?'

I left him staring in the dark; and went to bid my followers disembark our baggage.

A dawn-wind carried the fleet to sea. I stood on the beach and watched the sails grow smaller, like petals blown across luminous blue-green glass.

The weeks went by. Couriers brought messages from Normandy: Rufus's campaigning prospered. He gained his ends by silver rather than sieges: he bought wavering lords to his side and put mercenaries in their castles. Thus he won La Houlme, which William Peverel held, and Argentan from Roger of Poitou. Helias of St Saëns refused a bribe for Bures; the king compelled a surrender and took the garrison prisoner.

The tide then turned against him.

Curthose and King Philip jointly besieged Argentan; the castle yielded bloodlessly on the leaguer's opening day. Seventy knights were seized and held for ransom. Curthose marched west and stormed La Houlme, taking eight hundred prisoners, including fifty knights. The victories spread despondency like a suppurating plague. Vacillating lords whose loyalties Rufus had bought remembered themselves forsworn and renewed fealty to Curthose.

Thereafter every courier brought Flambard demands for money.

Rufus's bribes were expensive; and unpaid mercenaries soon desert. Moreover the king insisted that knights taken while in his service be ransomed at his cost: a principle his enemies ignored. Flambard levied heavy gelds, doubled reliefs and taxes, and demanded additional aids from abbeys and Honours. But the streams that fed the treasury dwindled to a trickle; and the floors of the coffers were scraped to gather the last of the deniers. Rufus still clamoured for more.

By August the chests were empty, for Flambard shipped the money to Normandy as fast as the gelds came in. At a council held in Winchester he pithily stated the crisis.

'The reserves are gone; our revenues can finance the war no longer. My lords, I invite your suggestions.'

Old Walter Giffard said sleepily, 'The situation's impossible. Rufus must abandon his campaign.'

'Which means that we, his counsellors in England, have failed the king,' said I. 'No! We've got to find something. What drains the king's resources? Ransoms, bribes and mercenaries' pay. You'll never persuade Rufus to leave his knights imprisoned. Bribes – a political weapon – he can't relinquish. Why not send him soldiers to replace his expensive hirelings? What about the English levy?'

Flambard sat up straight, a sparkle in his eye. 'The fyrd! I'd never considered that.' He brooded, deep in thought. 'My lord,' he said at last, 'I think you've found the answer. We'll write the king immediately: the muster requires his seal.'

Rufus sent his writ, and summons of array went out to all the shires. At Walter Giffard's behest I dictated harbourmasters' orders, calling ships from every port from Lymington to Dover. Twenty thousand English gathered at Hastings. I rode there when the wind was fair and the army ready to sail. Encampments mottled the dunes, warriors crowded the beaches, a north wind breathed, the sea was calm – and utterly bare of ships.

I galloped to the pavilion where Flambard lodged, and found him examining a scroll bearing Rufus's seal. I gestured seawards to the empty waters. 'The fleet! Have the orders gone astray?'

'No, my lord,' said Flambard smoothly. 'I countermanded them.' I struggled furiously for words.

Flambard tapped the parchment in his hand. 'The king's warrant. The fyrd is not going to Normandy, and so I shall inform them.' He beckoned a clerk. 'Admit the thegns.'

Twenty bearded warriors stooped beneath the lintel. Stalwart, flaxen men, they were – the captains of the host – in scaled and mascled armour, helmets horned and pointed, broad two-handed swords and long-staved, dangerous axes. They frowned on Flambard, for they accounted him – not Rufus – the author of all the extortions that bore upon their people. The chancellor, unperturbed, told a scribe to translate the writ.

An astonishment matching my own crept slowly over their faces. They spoke angrily among themselves; a blue-eyed giant strode to Flambard, hand on hilt. The guard-knight stepped between them and drew his sword. Flambard flapped his hand and gestured the knight aside.

'Tell them,' he ordered the scribe, 'that this is a royal command – not mine. Consider a little. The corn is ripe for harvest – would the levies rather risk their heads in Normandy than reap their fields at home? The king considers his subjects' welfare. Isn't the maintenance money a fair exchange?'

The thegns grumbled angrily among themselves, and left the pavilion. I gathered they accepted the chancellor's proposal, whatever it might be. I looked at Flambard.

'Explain!'

Gleefully he rubbed his hands together. 'Simple, my lord. Every man in the levy brings six-score deniers for his maintenance on

campaign – a sum the shires contribute. The king has commanded
they give him the money and then return to their homes.' He smiled
widely. 'Twenty thousand men: I shall send Rufus ten thousand
pounds of silver!'

'An infamous trick! Does Rufus countenance this?'

Flambard's eyes gleamed wickedly. 'You sowed, my lord, the seed
of inspiration; I matured the plant; the king has culled the flower.
And why not? It's money he wants – not men!'

The war went on. Belesme, playing a hand of his own, ravaged
Normandy from Roche Mabille: Prince Henry, safe in Domfront,
sent not a man to hold him. Rufus, harassed by Duke Robert's
troops, retreated north of Seine and shut himself in Eu. The allies,
duke and king, marched to leaguer him. Before the siege lines closed
Rufus's harbingers sought Philip; a little later laden rounceys
brought him half the English shires' silver. Philip counted the
deniers, smacked his lips – and led his army back to France and his
lecherous Queen Bertrada.

Shorn of his ally's help, Curthose retreated to Rouen. The campaign dwindled to stalemate, to inconclusive skirmishes and
ineffectual harryings. The Norman lords resumed their private
quarrels, the raids and burnings which the war had sometimes
hindered. Belesme stormed La Ferté-Maci, almost on Domfront's
doorstep; Rufus, highly annoyed, commanded Henry to Eu to explain
his indolence. The king sent ships to bring him – Duke Robert's men
held Normandy, and none might cross by land.

Henry embarked at Avranches, bade the shipman alter course and
sail forthwith for England. Flambard sent word of his landing. I
left Laingaham in a hurry, and sped south over wintry roads.

Chapter 7

1094–96

Fast as I went, Rufus was there before me.

Snowdrifts streaked the Tower's ward; a wind that carried daggers streamed the banner on the battlements: King William's rampant dragon snapped defiance at the sky. A human chain bore baggage from the wharves: furniture, panniers, tents, hauberks, saddles and bales of cloth. Strappers led frisky horses released from the ships' confinement. Soldiers hunted quarters; knights roved the Tower's chambers. Chamberlains and stewards hurried from floor to floor, struggling to pluck order from the chaos.

In the chamber used for banquets Rufus sawed venison and stuffed gobbets in his mouth. His barons thronged the tables, eating and drinking hard; knights clattered about the hall, bellowing for scullions. All were hungry after the crossing, for food is scarce on ships. A little apart Prince Henry sat, the food untouched before him, his pale round face inscrutable and eyes like cold wet stones.

I bent my knee to Rufus, who waved his knife and said indistinctly, 'Well met, Walter! A cup of wine! How prospers Laingaham?'

'Well, my lord. I am late in my attendance – I had not expected your coming.'

Rufus drank from a goblet and cleared his mouth. 'We landed an hour since: a smooth passage sped by a following wind. The fleet leaves Valeri tomorrow and moors at Dover. I came ahead in haste, sailed straight to London. Giffard had sent me news that needed attention.'

He shot a glance at Henry, who returned his look impassively.

'The war's ended.' Rufus scowled. 'A thorough mess: I bit off more than I could chew. Talk of chewing,' he added, hacking at the meat, 'this venison's almost raw! The Tower's cooks want flogging – they know I like it done!' He spiked a hunk on the point of his knife and popped it into his mouth; the juice ran down his chin. 'France and Normandy combined were stronger than I reckoned; and Curthose, for a change, waged war like a raging lion. Some sorcerer must have peddled him an elixir of energy! An unprofitable campaign: I've won an extra castle or two and return to a ransacked treasury.'

But the king looked far from downcast. The scarlet face was cheerful, his manner brisk and vigorous. He washed and dried his hands, and swilled his mouth with wine. 'To the council chamber, Walter: we've something to discuss.' He left the table, his brawny body lurching as though still aboard a ship. I climbed a winding stairway set in the Tower's walls; Prince Henry followed, with Eu and Clare and the lords of the inner council.

Windows shed ribands of sunlight which painted gilded patterns on the flagstones; a hearth-fire billowed smoke that drifted in transparent scarves below the rafters. Voices echoed hollow among the pillars: the chamber, usually thronged, held less than a dozen men. Rufus flopped on the throne at the table's head – a mighty oaken board with bronze and ebony inlay, legs carved like spiralled towers. We seated ourselves haphazard on stools and tall-backed chairs, Henry farthest from the king.

Rufus linked his fingers, pressed his thumbs together, and looked fixedly at his brother.

'I won for you Domfront, my lord,' he said in formal tones, 'sent silver for your maintenance and soldiers for your garrison. For that you yield me fealty and homage. Yet in nine months of warfare, when I was sorely pressed, you made not a move to help me. How,' Rufus ended mildly, 'do you explain your peculiar lethargy?'

Henry smoothed the hair that fringed his forehead. 'I led five hundred men, Belesme two thousand. I never favour odds of four to one.'

'Caution is a quality of captains,' Rufus silkily agreed. 'But Belesme roved far afield, his mesnie supporting Curthose – he was at Argentan's re-taking. Could you not at least have harried his lands in hope of enticing him back?'

'And risk being cut off from Domfront?' A strain like a tensioned bowstring quivered in Henry's voice. 'Belesme moves fast when his demesnes are at risk!'

Meulan said, 'While Black Robert stormed St Ceneri you could have taken Roche Mabille. The castle was well-nigh empty!'

'Information which I lacked.' Henry snarled. 'To you, my lord, I owe no explanations!'

Clare banged his fists together. 'I'd have you remember that all

Normandy separates Domfront and Eu, a land which for most of the war the enemy controlled. How, twelve marches distant, could we match our schemes with yours? Could five hundred men alone defeat Duke Robert? Not that, nor twenty times as many – he's Normandy's master today!'

Rufus reddened, and swallowed the gibe. 'A plausible excuse. For the moment, let it go. There's another point I don't quite understand. I commanded your presence in Eu, brother, and sent ships. You put to sea and came to England. Why?'

'The wind changed,' said Henry blandly.

Rufus sucked his breath between his teeth. I glanced at the others. Eu's weather-browned face, seamed like seasoned oak, was tense and wary. Alderi lolled in a chair, buffing his nails with a silken kerchief. Flambard tapped a sapphire which hung from a golden collar.

A sparrow twittered at a casement, flew across the room and perched upon a lectern. Rufus watched it with empty eyes, breathed deep and mastered his rage.

'The vanes at Eu were steady this fortnight past. The winds off Avranches must be strangely variable. Have you,' said Rufus softly, 'no better reason for defying your liege's order?'

Henry tapped fingertips together, his face expressionless. 'None.'

The sparrow chirped, and flew through a window. Rufus thumped his fist on the table. 'If a banneret of mercenaries acted thus he'd be hanged for cowardice and mutiny! This chance I give you, brother, to redeem yourself. You'll return to Domfront on the tide and hold the town on my behalf. You say your force is puny – I'll send five hundred more! The baron who advises you' – he glared angrily at Gilbert of Clare – 'is lavish with excuses, impoverished in valour. He'll stay in England to recoup his courage!'

Gilbert jumped to his feet, and groped for his dagger. The duty knight behind the king reached quickly for his sword-hilt. Rufus leaned on his hands, and glowered in Gilbert's eyes. 'Would you draw in your suzerain's presence?' he asked dangerously. 'Men have died for less! Sit you down!'

Clare's furrowed face looked shrunken. He said, 'With your permission, sire . . .'; and walked stiffly from the room. Rufus, brooding, watched him go.

The king addressed his brother. 'A ship lies moored at the wharf. At none the tide will turn. Your fief, my lord, awaits your care.'

Nobody looked at Henry. The prince was caught in a cloven stick:

although akin to sovereigns he was merely a petty baron holding a single fief – if he refused submission the Tower's vaults awaited. But the Conqueror's blood ran in Henry's veins. Surely he would not accept this pitiless dismissal, ejected from the realm he craved like a peculant reeve from a parish?

Henry twisted a ring on his thumb, and sat quietly thinking. He raised his head, and spoke without emphasis.

'As you will, my lord. I return to Domfront.' He gathered his cloak, bowed to his brother and went.

Years afterwards I realized that this tame acceptance of abasement was the shrewdest and most crucial move on Henry's road to the throne.

Rufus blew out his cheeks, subsided in his chair, and told Flambard to state the treasury's accounts. Meulan caught my eye, sauntered to the fire and spread his hands to the blaze.

'Well, I've managed that. The king took a deal of persuading.'

'Henry,' I said, 'has at last forfeited Rufus's trust.'

'He still trusts Henry – don't deceive yourself. Rufus has boundless faith in knightly honour: he accepts all gentle men as true, and is hurt when they prove forsworn. No – I've played only on the prince's indolence, his incompetence in waging war; and imputed much of the blame to Clare, an inept counsellor. I dared to go no further: to hint at Henry's treachery might well have cost my head. Rufus, in fact, believes he does his brother a useful service in sending him to Normandy to retrieve his reputation.'

'Clare also should have gone. A dangerous man.'

'Dangerous indeed – and useful to us in England. Gilbert's hasty and impetuous: he may leave a trail to follow.' Meulan ruminated. 'I never suggested to Rufus that Clare lacked courage. The king is quick in judging men – he may be right.'

I gestured to William of Eu. 'Count William – you thought him faithless. Has your opinion changed?'

'I still believe him secretly Duke Robert's man. Of solid proof there's none. Intelligence flowed to Curthose throughout the war from Rufus's headquarters, which was one reason for Duke Robert's success. I never found the source.' Meulan crossly kicked a log into the fire. 'There's conspiracy in the air – I smelt it like putrid meat – strands of parallel plots ravelling gradually into a rope. Eu and Curthose, Henry and Clare – where's the link that joins them?'

I left Count Robert brooding over the flames, and overtook Alderi descending the winding stairs. An arrow-slit lighted his beautiful face, burnished the tawny hair. He said lightly, 'How fares your esquire, my lord?'

'Roger? He's well, enjoying himself in Poix. I have to thank you for . . . pacifying the king after I removed the boy from Gloucester.'

Alderi yawned, and tapped fingers on his teeth. 'A scantling – think it nothing. And now I bid farewell, my lord – I doubt we shall meet again.'

I stared. 'You're leaving Rufus?'

'My task,' he replied enigmatically, 'is done. And the king, I think, is finding me less attractive – best to leave before I'm booted out. It will be a change,' said Alderi boredly, 'to bed a woman again.'

He walked gracefully down the steps, stroking his elegant curls. I sniffed the scent he used, a lingering waft of roses, and pondered over his words. I began to wonder dimly whether I had judged Alderi wrongly – a doubt which had no bearing on his vices.

At compline, in St Peter's chapel, Meulan whispered in my ear. 'The link we sought is in the forging. Gilbert, Eu and Alderi have ridden for the north.'

The antiphons of nocturn surged to a crescendo like the wind of a gathering storm.

2

The king rode on progress to Rockingham, a castle in Northamptonshire. Duke William had built the donjon and extended the ward to a sluggish stream which flowed beneath the height. You guessed vainly the Conqueror's motive: the place lacked tactical vantage, commanded no prosperous town, no strategic pass or ford. But Rockingham stood in a forest's heart, and the forest was full of game.

Rufus enjoyed this wild retreat, both because of the hunting and the jousts he arranged on a meadow beside the stream. Only urgent affairs of state pursued him here; he regarded Rockingham as a haven from his duties. So Anselm's arrival from Canterbury displeased the king intensely – he was leaving for a tourney where the knights already waited.

'Can't Anselm leave me in peace? Tirel, go and find out what he's after. Meulan, tell the marshal we'll have to delay the courses – there's nothing but trouble whenever that man casts up!'

I greeted the archbishop, inquired after his health, the travails of his journey, and came gradually to the point – you cannot be abrupt with a quiet man like Anselm. He answered, 'I seek the king's permission for a journey to Rome for the pallium.'

And here was trouble. That paltry strip of embroidered cloth was an emblem of papal authority – and a scarlet rag to the bull that was William Rufus.

I said earnestly, 'My lord, you know that request will anger the king. Must you rend a half-healed scar and poison the wound afresh? You're Canterbury's archbishop, recognized by king and people as England's Father in God. Why do you need Rome's credentials?'

The watery eyes showed mild surprise. 'None has held Canterbury's throne without the pallium.' He fluttered his fingers. 'Except Stigand – whose example I cannot admire.'

I pleaded and cajoled, for this was a sticking-point, a condition Rufus would never accept. The old man's face grew obstinate, the pallid lips closed firmly.

'I beg you, my lord, to convey my request to the king.'

I told Rufus, expected an explosion, and saw instead the ruddy face grow thoughtful. 'With a little preparation I'll toss Anselm on the horns.' Mailed as he was for the tourney, Rufus clanked to the chapel where Anselm waited with his monks, and stood before the archbishop, hands on hips.

'I hear what you propose, and understand your ruse: you're trying to make the English Church a vassal of Rome. I tell you now, as I've told you before, that the pope's recognition in England requires the king's agreement. I do not agree, my lord of Canterbury, and there's an end to it!'

'You're unreasonable, sire. I want merely to follow the pattern my predecessors set. Lanfranc brought his pallium from Rome with Duke William's full permission.'

'Lanfranc,' Rufus gritted, 'bowed to my father's will, and put his interests before the pope's. Can you say as much?'

'I have plighted you my troth, my lord,' said Anselm placidly.

'Yet to Rome you also swear obedience! How may a man obey two masters?'

'I made my vows to Urban long ago, when abbot of Bec. Would you have me forsworn?'

Rufus curled his fingers; he, of all men, was the last to urge a man to break his troth. He said in a choking voice, 'Whatever oaths you gave in the past confer no right to bring to this realm the badge of papal authority. I'll not have Rome on my back!'

'You refuse to let me go?' said Anselm.

The anger left Rufus's face, his eyes were cold and hard. 'It is not my will, nor was it my father's, to allow England's people to call any man pope without their suzerain's leave. You seek to usurp this right – you might as well take my crown. I propose, my lord archbishop, to summon an assembly, the bishops and the barons, to give judgement on the matter. You'll not return to Canterbury until the council's ended!'

Rufus stamped from the chapel, shouted for his destrier and rode to the field of tourney. There, in a swirling mellay, thirty knights a side, he let his sword relieve his feelings and dismounted five opponents. Afterwards, in jovial mood, he dictated mandates to his lieges lay and clerical. 'This will settle Anselm once for all,' he declared, wriggling from his hauberk. 'I'll have a word with the bishops and remind them of their duty. They'll dance to my commands like a mummer's bear to the pipe! And by the Face, why not? – aren't they my lieges? Why should Anselm seek a higher degree? God curse the man! Walter, did you see the way I toppled Bigod – a nearside feint and a backhand slash?'

Riding from the ends of England, barons and bishops assembled. Rufus conferred privately with each bishop as he arrived. The king seemed highly satisfied, and rubbed his hands together.

The hall in Rockingham's ward was connected by a corridor to the chapel: here the council gathered, Anselm and his monks inside the chapel, king and barons in the hall. The bishops, apparently neutral, sat on stools that lined the passage walls. Therefore Rufus and his adversary were seldom face to face: each side discussed the other's points and spokesmen carried the answers. I shall not try to relate – nor can I remember – the endless legal points they discussed, the delicate canons of logic.

Anselm affirmed his cause; Rufus replied bluntly that allegiance to England's king and obedience to Urban could not go together. Thus was stated clearly the point for the council's decision: could Anselm at the same time keep his plighted troth to Rufus and his plighted obedience to Rome?

William of Durham declared the bishops' opinion. 'I have no advice to give you, my lord archbishop, but that you obey the king's will. If you draw distinctions and reservations, if you plead any call on God's behalf against the king we, the prelacy of England, can give you no support.'

'Am I to accept,' said Anselm benignly, 'that God's will must yield to the king's?'

Durham stuttered. 'You evade the point at issue. Your divided fealty —'

'On the contrary, my lord of Durham, it's the nub of the whole discussion. I give obedience to the Vicar of Christ in the things of God, in earthly dignities to England's king.'

'You have not answered the charge. I can't convey your quibbling to the king!'

'No?' Anselm tottered to his feet. 'Then I'll do so myself.'

He shuffled across the chapel, past the rows of silent bishops and into the torch-lit chamber where barons whispered behind their hands and Rufus, on the dais, stonily watched him approach. Anselm, in quavering tones, repeated his assertion.

'You say nothing new,' Rufus snapped, 'and every word displeases me.' He pointed a hand. 'Go to your place.'

A rustle like a wandering wind stirred the crowded benches. The barons saw the frail old man dismissed like a worthless scullion: it was then, I think, opinion started to swing in Anselm's favour. The archbishop turned and stumbled to the chapel, a monk supporting him on either hand.

Rufus gave Durham a furious look. 'You promised to judge and condemn him, according to my will! Fulfil your pledge, my lord – delay no more!'

Durham stalked to the chapel. 'My lord archbishop,' he said, 'you try to take from the king his dignity and rights. Submit a proper answer to the charge, or presently expect a verdict which will chastise your presumption!'

'The council,' said Anselm wearily, 'is assembled to decide a point of law. No arguments have been heard and nothing proved. How then can I be judged?'

Anselm closed his eyes, appeared to doze – and produced the plea which shattered Rufus's case.

'An archbishop of Canterbury may not be condemned on any charge by any judge save the pope.'

'I can't refute him,' Durham told the king. 'His statement rests on Holy Writ and St Peter's authority.'

'God's Face! If you knew his cause inviolate why did you let me begin the suit? Now what can we do?'

Argument raged furiously. The bishops made suggestions which Rufus tore in shreds, for every one admitted Anselm's claim. The barons listened to sophistries of law and scripture far beyond their grasp. Meulan observed bitterly, 'We weave a spider's web to entangle him; then Anselm breathes a word and puffs it apart!'

I peered into the chapel: the archbishop drooped in a chair, hands folded in his lap, and slept like a tired child.

Durham at last said sullenly, 'We can't refute him. I suggest you remove him by force, my lord, deprive him of ring and staff and banish him from the kingdom.'

The proposal was unfortunate. The barons rumbled. A doctrine that the king might disseize at his pleasure the kingdom's premier vassal could be dangerous to counts as well as bishops. Heads were shaken, lips were pursed.

Rufus glared ferociously.

'I command you to withdraw your fealty from Anselm, as the bishops have done already, so that he may know he lacks supporters throughout the realm!'

His edict stirred a storm. The barons conferred, crossed the hall to consult their friends, argued and gesticulated in a rising gale of sound. fitzHamon lounged on Rufus's left, watching the confusion with an ironic glint in his eye. Meulan listened coldly to the hubbub, and stroked his jaw. I leaned against Rufus's chair-back, and knew the king defeated.

Roger Bigod gave the verdict which finally crumbled his hopes.

'We are not the archbishop's men,' he said carefully. 'We can't withdraw from him a fealty we've never sworn. Yet, though Anselm is not our lord, we cannot decline his leadership in spiritual affairs, for he's Canterbury's archbishop whom you yourself, our suzerain, appointed.'

Rufus stared at the hands which clutched his knees. I saw his shoulders shaking, a vein in his temple throbbing, a rising tide of colour suffusing neck and cheeks. An outburst was impending – and the barons would bear the brunt. This was not the moment to estrange his loyal lieges: strange rumours of conspiracy were travelling from the north, and the king might soon be needing every sword that he could find. Hurriedly I whispered in his ear.

'Hold your temper, sire! You are stronger than any one baron – but not all of them together. Would you set the lords of England firmly on Anselm's side? Thus you'd fan dissension – and remember '88!'

Rufus turned his head and stared at me blindly. He gazed around the hall, dwelling on the faces waiting tensely for his answer. He crooked a finger, beckoned Durham.

'Tell Anselm I withdraw from him all faith and friendship, all protection in my kingdom, all duty to his place.' He continued in a voice like clashing swords, 'Those who want my favour had better heed my will!'

The king walked from the hall with never a glance to left or right. Hastily I followed, for Rufus's mood was such that he might do something disastrous. He called for wine, perched on a table's edge and downed the draught in a gulp. The savage lines in his face relaxed, the viciousness went from his eyes. He put down the cup with a satisfied sigh, and clapped my shoulder.

'You were right to check me, Walter. Fatal to antagonize my vassals.' He listened, brooding, to the council's clamour. 'They're probably discussing what I'll do next – the affair can't rest as it is. Anselm undoubtedly thinks he's won. Not so. I have a trick or two in hand which might surprise him.'

Rufus smiled maliciously.

'I myself will send for the pallium to bestow on the Archbishop of Canterbury. Urban will think it's for Anselm. I'll give it to another – possibly William of Durham, despite his useless pleading.'

He looked ruefully into the empty goblet.

'It means accepting the pope – but it's worth it to spite that hell-spawned monk!'

3

Even Meulan failed to recognize the ten footsore foreign merchants as harbingers of rebellion.

They had travelled from Northumbria, and begged to petition the king: a tale of theft and pillage, ships burned and cargoes plundered. Robert Mowbrai, Count of Northumbria, they said woefully, had attacked them anchored in a haven on his coasts, and despoiled them of all they had.

Rufus frowned at the plaintive Norsemen. 'Mowbrai, that sombre man! What's got into his head? Hasn't he enough to do in keeping out the Scots?' He added decisively, 'He's broken the king's peace. Send him orders under my seal to restore what he has taken.'

We all forgot the matter, except the merchants, who lingered at the court – the king passed Lent at Windsor – and after four weeks' waiting sought audience again. Rufus asked the chancery clerks for Robert Mowbrai's answer; they hunted among the parchments and declared that none was sent. The messenger was summoned – a sergeant of the household – who swore he had delivered the script to Mowbrai's hands.

'Didn't you wait for an answer?' Rufus demanded.

The sergeant replied timidly that Mowbrai listened to a priest's translation, snatched the scroll from his hands and ripped it across and across. 'Return,' he had told the messenger, 'tell Rufus that's his answer.' The sergeant, unsurprisingly, shrank from delivering the count's defiance to a king so hot as Rufus. I could not blame him.

Nor did Rufus. He scratched his ribs and thought it over. 'Unlike Mowbrai,' he said, 'surly though he is. Someone's pricking him: we'll soon find out. Send messengers riding post – knights, not sergeants – arraigning him for robbery; and order him to Windsor for answering the charge.' He surveyed the merchants, standing patiently before him and trying to follow the exchanges in an alien tongue. 'Extracting recompense from Mowbrai looks like being a lengthy process. I'll restore your losses. Make your account to the chancellor. Ranulf!'

Flambard took quill and parchment, heard sceptically the merchants' lavish tallies and accorded half they asked.

The charge evoked an answer: Mowbrai demanded hostages from Rufus and safe-conduct back to his county whatever the trial's outcome. The king's temper snapped like a brittle twig; he crushed the scroll in his hand and strode shouting to the door. 'Meulan! Call an array! I'll lay a lash on Mowbrai's back he won't forget for years!'

Such was the edict, and no one argued. But armies are not gathered in a day. Springtime sprinkled flowers on Windsor's meadows before the conroys came from Anglia and Devon, Derbyshire and Kent – the lords of England marching to the muster. Rufus fumed impatiently and spent hours among the tent lines in the fields: always was he happiest in the company of soldiers.

On a morning when the sunlight spangled diamonds on the dew he strolled beside the river, accompanied by myself and a guardian knight. Rufus bent and plucked a kingcup from the reeds, and twirled the stem between his fingers.

'Roger Bigod's mesnie to come, and Laci's – then we go,' he said contentedly.

Meulan cantered across the meadow, slid from the saddle, hooked the rein over his arm and said, 'Evil news, sire. Mowbrai is not alone.'

Rufus sniffed the scentless flower. 'Who else?'

'These have joined him: William of Eu, Roger of Laci, Gilbert of Clare.'

'Clare? You surprise me – I'd not have thought he had the guts. No more?'

Meulan braced himself. 'One. William of Alderi.'

Rufus's face contorted as though a swordpoint pierced his heart. He stared blankly over the river, sparkling in the sun, dawn-mist rising in gossamer threads tinged yellow and pink and green.

'Alderi.'

His fingers tore the kingcup. During those silent moments, while golden petals fluttered on the grass, a kindness went from Rufus, a clemency and trustingness he never quite recovered. He ground the shredded flower beneath his heel.

'We tarry no more for Laci. Has Bigod come?'

Meulan shook his head. 'There's worse yet. Curthose gathers ships at Havre, an army on the beaches.'

'Invasion. A concerted plan – Mowbrai and my brother.' Rufus spoke jerkily, his features haggard. 'A landing in the south, rebellion in the north – my forces torn apart. Call a council of war, my lord – we need to plan afresh.'

The council met in Windsor's donjon: Rufus put the crisis to his lords. The king's verdict was brisk and forcible. 'We face the same predicament as the English before the Conquest. We'll use Count Harold's strategy, go north and trounce the rebels, return by rapid marches and face our Norman foes.'

'You'll leave the south defenceless?' Meulan asked.

I said, 'Call out the levy, sire.'

Rufus grunted approvingly. 'That we'll do, and leave all Kent and Sussex in their charge. Summon fitzHamon from Wales, put him in command. I'll leave him, too, the Kentish knights and a stiffening of mercenaries.'

Speed was vital. The tent rows checkering Windsor's meadows vanished overnight: laden carts and wagons took their place. I sent a galloper to Laingaham, calling Richer and his archers: they joined us on the march near Godmanchester. Rufus gratefully pressed my

371

hand when he saw the light-boned horses and supple link-mesh haubergeons. My fealty owed no service in knights and men-at-arms.

Laboriously, far too slowly, chained by the creaking wagons, the army wound its way along the Roman road to the north.

4

Three weeks later the vanguard entered the woodlands north of Durham.

We were now in hostile country, approaching Mowbrai's frontiers. The army marched in warlike order, guards to front and flanks, a rearguard shepherding wagons and mules and sutlers. Far in front, outriders to the host, I led my mounted archers in a swathe across the road: Rufus had soon recognized that light, quick-moving horsemen made better scouts than men-at-arms on plodding palfreys. He sent me off, that midsummer dawn, with a hearty slap on the back.

'Laci's holding Newcastle, only a day's march on; so keep your eyes skinned, Walter!' He was happy at the likelihood of fighting, yet rode unmailed in the van despite his lords' remonstrances. 'I'll arm when I hear your bowstrings twang!'

'And if you fall into ambuscade you're dead in the twitch of an eye,' said I dourly.

'That's what you're there to prevent, Walter! Away with you!'

A belt of woodland lay like a green-leaf cliff across the way. My archers approached the spinneys warily: a couple probed each coppice while others rode the fringes, arrows nocked. I watched them from the road, a little in rear of the line, Richer at my side. The sun climbed red from the skyline, promising heat and sweat. A sepia haze in rear marked the army's passage; flank guards on the moorlands trailed gauzy banners of dust. So it had been since crossing Tees: a daylong march in the sunlight, baking in our hauberks, a country bare of enemy, larks trilling in the sky.

Richer suddenly halted. 'Steel in that copse on the left.' He shaded his eyes. 'A glint, no more – then gone. Yes, there it is again. Ambush, I think, my lord.'

I hollered warning to the nearest bowmen, plunged from the road and cantered towards the trees. I had missed the ominous gleam, but trusted Richer's vigilance – he had eyes like a questing hawk. The

372

bowmen closed upon us; Richer spurred to a gallop; we followed in his dust and entered a tangled thicket where brambles laced the gaps between the trees. I lifted shield to nasal, stared anxiously over the rim and caught the sheen of armour behind an oak. A man stepped clear – a knight by his mail – and lifted high his arms.

'I yield, my lord!'

The bowmen were tense and nervous; an arrow thumped his hauberk. He staggered and hugged his chest. I circled my horse behind him, set swordpoint on his nape. 'Out! Move fast!' Point on spine I hustled the knight from the dangerous trees to the open heath. He stumbled in his running, hindered by the hauberk. I kept him trotting remorselessly beyond bowshot of the woods, and watched him drop on hands and knees, hanging his head and gasping.

'Your title,' I demanded.

'Take me . . . to the . . . king.'

Richer jumped from the saddle, hooked fingers beneath the nasal and wrenched the helmet off.

Gilbert of Clare.

I slung my shield aback, and dismounted sword in hand. 'A traitor,' I said pleasantly. 'There's no clemency for vermin.' The dangling helmet left his neck exposed; I lifted my sword for the slash. Gilbert screamed.

'I yield!' he babbled. 'You can't kill . . . ransom . . . the king's life . . . I can save him!'

I rested the sword on his neck. 'A coward – as Rufus judged. Buy your life with betrayal, then, my lord – it seems your habit. What danger threatens the king?'

'Take me to Rufus!'

The edge sawed his neck, blood spurted brightly. Gilbert screeched.

'Mercy, for the love of Christ! An ambuscade in the woods – three hundred lances!'

'Richer,' I said sharply, 'halt the archers short of the trees!' But Richer was already horsed and gone, a fleeting feather of dust, to save his bowmen's skins. 'Pigot, gallop! Tell the king to go no farther!'

I prodded the weeping Gilbert, who pawed his neck and chest – the barb had struck his plastron, bruised the breastbone. Rufus was struggling into his hauberk. A scarlet face emerged from the coif and said, 'What's the trouble, Walter? Who's that you've got?

God's face – Clare! The treacherous son of a bastard's slut – why haven't you killed him?'

'He's brought warning of an ambush, sire – and I think he can tell us more.'

An esquire laced Rufus's helmet, another buckled the ventail across his chin; he held out his arms for the bullhide wrappings. 'My baldric's twisted, Herluin – pull it straight.' He looked about and pointed. 'There's a fine tall tree over there. Fetch a rope.'

I said, 'Clare yielded of his own accord, without resistance. I wonder why.'

Rufus looked at the wretched man who knelt at his feet. 'Stop snivelling, rogue! Why did you give yourself up?'

Gilbert said brokenly, 'The design is shattered. Duke Robert has abandoned his invasion. The ships he gathered at Havre are being dispersed, his army is disbanding. The weight of your sword will fall on us alone – how can we withstand you?'

'How indeed?' said Rufus thinly. An esquire brought his destrier, the king tried girth and bit, set foot in the stirrup. 'So the rats scuttle back to their holes. How typical of Curthose, wavering like a willow in the wind!' He swung to the saddle, enarmed shield, and tried his lance's balance. 'Keep your life, Lord Gilbert – your blood would foul a sword, your neck's not worth a rope. Send him to the wagons, tie him to a wheel and let him walk.'

Rufus shaded his eyes and examined the distant tree-wall, the twinkling points of light where Richer's bowmen waited. 'Ambush in the woods, you say? Come on – let's rattle them out!'

5

Roger of Laci held Newcastle, a fortress by the Tyne. By the rules of Norman warfare we should have destroyed the village, burned the crops, killed the villeins and raped the women: this was Mowbrai's county, and he warred against his lord. But Rufus regarded Northumbria as part of the realm he ruled, and threatened ferocious penalties to any who harmed his subjects. Of course his foragers scoured the granaries, emptied the peasants' grain-pits, corralled cattle and sheep and swine – the army had to eat.

The villeins might starve next winter, but none died then by the sword.

The king set siege lines round the castle and sent a herald demanding surrender. Laci returned defiance. Rufus frowned at the massive donjon. 'Likely a lengthy leaguer, provided they have the heart. Still, there's no great hurry now that Curthose sulks in Rouen.'

In truth, the king's relentless energy, stoked by the Norman threat, dwindled to a flicker. He seemed reluctant to press Newcastle hard, unwilling to see it fall and open the way to Bamburgh, the last of Mowbrai's strongholds. The restless urge which during the march had sent him riding the column from head to tail, rating laggards, herding stragglers, testing the out-guards' vigilance; and, in camp, impelled him round the outposts after dark, bantering with the men-at-arms and sharing their sour wine – that driving vigour abated. He left Meulan and myself to organize the siege lines, took hounds and huntsmen, rode abroad – and cursed his rampant soldiery who had driven the game away.

Alderi and Eu supported Count Robert in Bamburgh.

Rufus's indecision had no influence on Meulan. He plotted the trench lines tight – not a mouse could wriggle through – sent men to the woods for timber and chivied the engineers. Within a week his engines ringed the donjon, boulders battered the walls from dawn till dusk, arrows harassed the garrison and fire-shafts burned their huts. I urged Meulan to let me lead an escalade. That grizzled old man of Hastings tried to scratch an armpit through his mail – we were all full lousy by then – and wagged his head. 'Not yet. I know Laci. He's not the sort to stand for long the battering he's getting. We'll try him again in a day or so.'

The count sent heralds, who brought back Laci's answer: he wanted passage for a messenger to Mowbrai, to state his plight and ask for help. Laci promised surrender if Mowbrai failed to send relief within thirty days. 'We're hunting rebels,' Meulan growled. 'The rules of formal war are out. Who does he think he's dealing with? Robert Curthose?' He threatened an escalade with everything he had and death for every knight and sergeant who resisted.

Roger yielded on condition his life was spared.

We hauled Rufus from a stag hunt to get his confirmation. The king said sulkily, 'Laci's a nithing – let him live. Clap fetters on him and keep him in the donjon. Clare also – he'll welcome another craven.'

Tynemouth and Bamburgh remained. The king sent Meulan and two thousand men to leaguer Tynemouth, and pressed north with the bulk of his army. On a thundery day in August he came to

375

Mowbrai's stronghold. We looked the castle over, and disliked the view. A monstrous hewn-stone donjon climbed from precipitous cliffs; between the sea and the castle's ramparts a desert of sand dunes rolled. Within the rocky fortress, which we knew had never been taken, Northumbria kept the pick of his knights and a thousand stalwart men.

Rufus shed his languor, rode the castle's circuit and appointed lines of leaguer. He was gripped by a restless vehemence, seemed mad to finish the siege. He refused to send in heralds. 'Mowbrai and Eu are men forsworn. They won't surrender – they can't. So why waste time?'

The lines were barely set when he wanted an instant storm. I persuaded him to wait, to follow the rules of warfare and soften the castle first. Mangonels were built, and battered away for a week; bowmen behind mantlets sprayed fire on the fort. We might as well have pelted it with feathers. The castle was rock, all rock; the mangonels' boulders burst on walls that were harder than they. Bamburgh could neither be broken nor burnt. Short of starving the garrison out – which the king impatiently rejected – there was nothing for it but an escalade.

The barons huffed and puffed, and swore it a lunatic venture. The vertical cliffs were unscalable: the only point of entry was a flight of steps on the southwest side, carved from solid rock. A bastion guarded the top, where a postern pierced the ramparts. Rufus asked for volunteers, and got an icy response; he then chose knights by name, the strongest and most valiant. I heard my title called – and went quick to a priest for shriving.

All the bowmen in the army were assigned to cover the storm, and mangonels were shifted to focus on the gate – obvious preparations which the enemy observed. When everything was ready the king assembled his knights and declared he would lead the attack. I waited till they left his tent, and said, 'Sire, this is foolishness. You must not risk your head.'

Rufus eyed me fiercely. 'Do I order others to go where I dare not go myself? You judge me strangely, Walter!'

'If you're killed, my lord, who will take England's seisin? Curthose? Henry? Even Mowbrai?'

'God's face, what does it matter? At Hastings my father charged in the van, himself cut down Count Harold. When has the blood of Normandy chilled at the sight of steel?'

I clenched my hands so tightly that the nails bit into the palms.

'You'll meet your enemies face to face.' I tried to steady my voice. 'Will you strike down . . . Alderi?'

Rufus reached for my throat. 'You dare . . . utter that name . . . to me!' His voice was like the whisper of a sword that slid from the scabbard. He hit me across the face. I staggered – and quenched my savage anger. None had struck me thus since I was knighted – nor ever has again.

I said through rigid lips, 'You do yourself dishonour. I said what I said for your own salvation – and you know the reason well.'

Rufus glared at me, breathing fast. He turned his back and touched a hauberk that dangled from a rack, and spoke with face averted, fingering the scales.

'So be it. You lead the stormers. Now leave me.'

I went from the tent unsteadily, sweat prickling my brow. Looking after Rufus was wearing to the nerves.

Dawn was dark and sultry; dingy clouds like coffin palls draped a hidden sunrise. Bamburgh loomed on the lightening sky like a massive carven mountain. We waited behind the mantlets, five hundred knights and sergeants, an iron column in files of three, the widest the steps would pass. I rested on the quillons of my sword and watched the ground between my feet. When I could distinguish a grasstuft's separate fronds I beckoned to the trumpeter. The clarion bayed like a hunting wolf.

Bowmen manned the mantlets, notched and flexed and loosed. Throwing-arms banged on stop-beams, boulders whirred through the air. I fronted my shield, peered over the rim and balanced sword on shoulder. The stormers tramped to the castle, stumbling on half-seen tussocks, slipping on the stones. Only a bowshot's march, it was – and arrows flayed each step.

By the time I reached the foot of the cliff I wore three shafts in my shield. The knights who had started beside me were gone; two others had taken their places. The close-knit files were scattered, bodies marked our passage like bundles dropped from a cart. Helmets studded the ramparts, arrows whipped like hail, throwing-spears curved in glittering arcs. The din of battle roared like a breaking wave.

The stairway curved before me, the steps worn hollow by myriad feet. Burning cinders showered from the bastion at the top, from braziers up-ended. An ember stung my sword hand. I breathed a prayer and jumped for the steps. My feet slid apart as though jerked by ropes. I crashed on my face, smelt rancid fat.

The treads were greased a finger's-depth in lard.

The valour of the knights who followed saved my life. They trampled over my body, cramming on and shouting, fell one upon another, a heaving armoured mantle which crushed me on the stone. They had mounted half the steps when the bastion's defenders tilted a heavy cauldron.

The scalding oil cascaded in a steaming ochre flood. Battlecries shredded in screams. I writhed beneath the bodies, and felt fire sear my face. Panic loosed my bowels, I struggled like a lunatic, tore myself free and fled. An arrow punched my spine and drove the breath from my lungs. I faced about, my shield had gone, I scooped the targe of a fallen sergeant.

The tail of the steps was carnage. Blackened creatures crawled and mewed, and died when the arrows struck. Knights and sergeants ran from the stairs of slaughter. I reached the line of mantlets, cowered beside the bowmen, dribbled into my ventail and nursed my burning cheek.

Richer said, 'A hopeless venture, doomed from the start. Where are you hurt, my lord?' He smelt the stench of shame, pulled off my shoes and breeches, scrubbed my thighs one-handed; then left the mantlets' shelter, stripped a dead knight's breeks and dressed me. I crouched shuddering, head in hands.

The Saracen led me to Rufus, who had watched the rout from a hillock. He leaned on his shield, arms crossed on the top, his expression forbidding.

'You failed, my lord.'

The scald on my cheek was a fiery brand, the dent in my back a stabbing ache – I carry the scars today. I said wearily, 'Every assault will likewise fail. Bamburgh is impregnable.'

Rufus looked at the corpse-strewn land beyond the mantlets, at the dead men choking the stairway. 'Two hundred killed, and nothing gained. The fault is mine. No more escalades. I'll build a counter-castle, and wear the rascals down.'

6

A fortress such as Bamburgh was not to be held by a hutment: Rufus raised an enormous mound, dug a fosse that was sheer and deep. On the summit he planted a donjon with walls two oak-trunks thick. At the end of a fortnight's labour the castle glowered defiance at Bamburgh's towering pile five hundred paces away.

'I'll call it Malvoisin,' said Rufus. 'The Evil Neighbour.'

In September Tynemouth fell; Meulan and his army joined the king at Bamburgh. fitzHamon, returned from Kent because Duke Robert's threat was lifted, became constable of Newcastle. Then a courier of calamity came riding hard from Wales: the Welsh had stormed Montgommeri and slaughtered Count Hugh's men. The tedious work of leaguering had wearied Rufus; he eagerly seized the pretext and decided to march to Wales.

'We've taken two of Mowbrai's castles and hold him penned in the third. He'll have to surrender in time: the revolt is virtually broken. So,' he told Meulan, 'I'll leave you sixty knights, eight hundred men-at-arms and victuals for a year; and take the rest of the army to teach the Welsh a lesson!'

Rufus marched away, and never saw Bamburgh again. Mowbrai, watching his conroys go, loosed a sally to surprise them. But Rufus, expecting exactly that, had left a powerful rearguard which pounced on the count's constabulars and hunted them back to the castle. Manning Malvoisin's battlements, we cheered as the rout fled past.

'Rufus reads his enemy's mind as a monk reads Latin script,' Meulan observed. 'Mowbrai's taken an ugly knock: I doubt he'll risk his nose again.'

He was right. The rock-strewn waste between the castles stayed empty of all save seagulls. We settled down to starve the enemy out.

It was dreary work. Howling winds hurled rainstorms from the sea; the donjon's unseasoned oak-trunks shrank; the gusts came through like spears. The rain found holes in the barrack-huts' thatch; stables let wind and water; the horses shivered and coughed, and some of them died. There was little entertainment in that bleak, deserted countryside; we tried to hunt and hawk, but the game was sparse. We rode under Bamburgh's cliffs and challenged Mowbrai's knights to jousts; and were answered by jibes and arrows. So between excursions to the pickets, and patrolling on the roads, we huddled in cloaks in the donjon's hall, heaped faggots on the fire and drank and rolled the dice.

November came with a blizzard which streaked the moorlands white. We caught a few deserters: they reported Mowbrai resolute, his henchmen Eu and Alderi determined not to yield. The levels in

Malvoisin's wine casks fell like an ebbing tide; the gambling grew wilder, the stabbing-fights more frequent; and Meulan built a gallows beyond the gate. Winter, dank and desolate, yawned before us. The storm-swept castles watched each other like dogs snarling over a bone.

'This could go on for ever,' I told Meulan while we peered through whirling snowflakes at Bamburgh's walls. 'Neither can make a move. How shall we break the deadlock?'

Meulan sniffed and wiped a drip from his nose. 'There's a way I've long debated, involving treachery and lies. Let's leave these frozen battlements – come below.'

We sat on stools in the hall and warmed ourselves at the fire. Meulan swallowed wine and said, 'The idea is this,' and spoke at length in a quiet voice.

I listened in growing doubt. 'Treachery indeed! The king wouldn't use such a trick.'

'Belly of God!' said Meulan. 'Must conquest wait on courtoisie? Sink your scruples, Walter! fitzHamon has a part in this chicanery: let him decide.'

At dawn, with a ten-man escort, I took the southward road; at vespers, on foundered horses, weary and chilled to the bone, we entered Newcastle's gates. fitzHamon plied food and wine, bade servants stoke the fire till it roared. 'You've ridden like a saint pursued by fiends. What's the trouble – has Malvoisin gone?' He peered at the scar on my cheek, gleaming stickily in the firelight. 'I'll give you a salve for that – it's going bad.'

I huddled close to the flames and, between mouthfuls, outlined Meulan's ruse. fitzHamon stared in amazement.

'I'm to pretend,' he said at last, 'disloyalty to the king, and offer Mowbrai shelter and the protection of my garrison. Leaving aside my danger if the plan miscarries – forsworn in my suzerain's eyes – Mowbrai would never believe it. The whole world knows me resolute for Rufus.'

'Meulan's word and mine stand proof on your behalf. It's not Mowbrai you'll have to convince, but Clare. It shouldn't be difficult. He's a frightened man, wild to save his skin. Where is he?'

fitzHamon jabbed a thumb at the floor. 'In the vaults below, chained as Rufus ordered.' The lean, engaging face looked troubled. 'It might work. Anything is worth trying to end the stalemate at Bamburgh. Remember, however plausible I am, Gilbert could pretend to agree and then warn Mowbrai of the trick.'

'So nothing is won – and nothing lost.' I stood up stiffly, the arrow wound in my back a gnawing torment. 'Send me word of Gilbert's coming and we'll let him pass the outposts. Tomorrow I return – and we'll need fresh horses.'

Five nights later a lone rider slipped stealthily past the pickets, who watched the shadowy figure go and wondered at their orders. Thereafter I slept by day, and waited armed and armoured from dusk till daylight in Malvoisin's ward, a constabular ready beside me, horses saddled. A week went by. Meulan opined that Clare suspected fitzHamon or Mowbrai doubted Clare; the plan had foundered on distrust.

On Christmas Eve a galloper from a picket on the Newcastle road called from the lip of the fosse that horsemen were riding south.

I mounted quick, the bridge slammed down, the constabular thundered out. The night was clear and bitter cold, starry and tin-selled with frost. We got to the road and rammed in spurs and settled down to ride.

We had the advantage. Mowbrai – I hoped it was he – could not gallop all the way to Newcastle – but we could press the pace until we caught him. Press I did, at a swinging canter, hooves sliding in steel-hard ruts, starring ice-sheathed puddles. The breathing of men and horses clothed the troop in mist. No one spoke except for curses when somebody's destrier skidded; hoofbeats pounded, leather creaked, scabbards clattered and mail rings clinked – a drumming like a stormwind's roll that echoed afar in the dark.

Lisiard saw the quarry first, a faraway glint in the gloom. He pointed his lance; we closed our legs and drove the horses faster. I heard a shout and the noise of hooves, saw sparks spray bright as they reined. Starshine winked on helmets. They plunged from the road and vanished in trees.

A narrow track showed the way they had gone. We followed at a trot, lances balanced, alert for ambush. The path ended at a grassy clearing where buildings clustered in a group. Loose horses, stirrups dangling, wandered in the open: I counted six. Cautiously we rode a circuit of the houses.

The place was a little monastery, a secluded hermitage for a handful of monks. A chapel's lancet windows vented yellow slivers on the grass; inside was the thresh of turmoil, and high protesting voices and the hard rough words of knights. I dismounted, sword in hand, and tried the door. The bars were down.

'They've gone to ground,' said Lisiard. 'We'll have to winkle them out.'

I dismounted the constabular – twenty swords, all knights – and tethered the horses. The chapel was detached from the other buildings, and had but the single door. I rummaged in an outhouse, found an axe. The knights gathered round the portal.

'Whoever you have to kill,' I reminded, 'Mowbrai is taken alive!'

A banneret hacked the door; our shoulders hurled it down. I entered at a run, shield fronted, sword held high. Blades hammered on the hide, a point glissaded off my helmet. The knights piled in behind me, shouting and swinging their swords.

The light in the chapel was blinding to my dark-accustomed eyes: candles blazed on the altar like a forest of burning spears. Midnight mass, I remembered vaguely, between parrying a cut and lunging: today was born our Saviour to purge the world from sin. Monks cowered against the walls and scuttled like terrified mice. At the ends of our blades six blazoned shields backed slowly towards the Rood. The clash and screech of steel on steel, the crunch of sword on shield, the shouting and laboured breathing and the cry of mortal hurt echoed between the sacred walls like a demons' paean from hell.

By the time they were forced to the altar only a couple remained. On one of the shields glared Mowbrai's blazon: a boar's head tushed and snarling. We held them in an iron ring, trapped between Cross and Christians.

I lowered my sword and said, 'My lord of Northumbria – yield!'

The answer was a ferocious lunge that almost reached my nasal. I warded – a frantic slash – and spun the blade from his hand. I rested my point on the cleft above his breastbone.

'Do you yield, my lord?'

Mowbrai bowed his head, loosed the enarmes of his shield, spread empty hands.

7

I shall not dwell long on Robert Mowbrai, Count of Northumbria, a man who has small bearing on my history: a bludgeon in the hands of cleverer men. We took him to Malvoisin, and led him thence to Bamburgh's walls, a halter round his neck and fetters on his wrists.

Beyond bowshot of the gate we stopped and sent a herald, ivy gar-landing his lance in sign of truce. Mowbrai stared on the ground, dejection wilting the tall gaunt frame, his heavy pock-marked face a mask of sullen despair. Sergeants planted a brazier before him, thrust rods in glowing charcoal. Mowbrai looked at the pointed irons, and closed his eyes.

The herald delivered his ultimatum – surrender, or behold your liege lord's blinding – and waited by the steps where black and shrivelled corpses littered the ground in heaps. A frost-wind blew from the sea, fanned the brazier's fire, lifted sand-puffs from the dunes and fluttered the cloaks of the knights. Bamburgh's lords debated. Only Eu, we heard long after, counselled defiance; Mow-brai's vassals, appalled at the threat, overbore him to a man and accepted Meulan's terms. The boar's-head banner fluttered down the staff on Bamburgh's donjon.

Meulan allowed no honours of war: the garrison marched out unarmoured and unarmed. Mowbrai's knights he treated courteously as lieges obeying their lord, fixed their ransoms and offered parole. I thought the count too trustful.

'Rebels one and all, my lord – can you afford to loose them?'

'Rufus would treat them so,' said Meulan bluntly. 'They're knights and men of honour. Let them go.'

There was no accounting for Meulan. He had trapped Mowbrai by an underhand trick which Rufus would never have counten-anced; yet assumed his prisoners' conduct to accord with Rufus's codes.

Alderi and the Count of Eu came last in the sad procession. Eu's desolate expression declared the fate he expected. Meulan said in an icy voice, 'I hold you prisoner, my lord, at mercy for the king.' He jerked his head at a sergeant. 'The chains.' Eu held out his arms, and iron clinked on his wrists.

The rigours of a siege had wasted Alderi's features, the lustre had gone from his hair, the violet eyes were bloodshot. He had shed his studied indolence and mannered affectations, bore himself straight as an ashwood spear and looked at his captor calmly. A singular flash of compassion flickered in Meulan's eyes. He said quietly, 'Though your treachery is plain I would, if it were possible, set you free. You know, I think, the vengeance that awaits you.'

Alderi smiled. 'I hold no silly illusions,' he answered lightly. 'My life henceforth is short.'

Alderi lived for a month, but I did not see him die.

The arrow from Bamburgh's bowman had driven the mail rings a thumb's length into my back. A petty wound, though painful, and I gave it small attention. The hurt refused to heal, and became a festering pit whence issued daily enough pus to fill a goose's egg. Berlai swabbed and cleaned it, stuffed salves into the hole and swathed linen about my ribs. The wound showed signs of healing, until the wrench in warding Mowbrai's thrust opened it again.

On the southward march from Bamburgh I lasted for fourteen days. Then a raging fever racked me, and my head seemed to float from my shoulders. At the ford in Godmanchester I tumbled from the saddle; the water on my burning skin was cool as a soothing balm. I hurtled into a darkness shot with pain and evil dreams.

Strange creatures peopled my nightmares: double-headed dragons, Satan horned and grinning, gibbering ghosts of knights with cindered faces, Mowbrai's wild-boar charging from his shield. My body fried in a furnace till consciousness was vanquished and I slid again to the depths. I rolled in slime at the bottom, drifted to the surface and faces that I knew: Isabel and Adelice remote among the stars, insubstantial visions which melted in my hands.

I wept bitterly, and floated into the void.

The light was hurting my eyes. Somebody whimpered like a beaten dog. Then Richer's voice, a murmur from far away. 'My lord has wakened. Make the posset ready.' A cup at my lips, warm liquid in my mouth. A brown face close to mine, a real face, lean and hard, no phantom spun from dreams. I tried to speak. 'Lie still, my lord. The worst is past.' I stared blankly at adze-planed rafters, sagging thatch, an arras draping a wall where a knight charged lance in rest. A memory stirred and was quickly gone, like a ripple of sun on water. Isabel stooped over me, her face serious and sad.

I knew that I dreamed again, and closed my eyes and slept.

Buttresses of sunlight painted gold upon the rushes. Cautiously I moved my head – and the nightmares fled to the shades. I lay on a pallet in Laingaham's bower; Adelice sat at the bedside. She stroked my fingers – thin and wasted like the hand of a week-old corpse – and said, 'I burned a hundred candles to the Virgin; she has listened to my prayers and given me back your life.' Tears gathered in her eyes. 'My lord, I thought I had lost you – so often you nearly died.'

I croaked, 'The sickness ... how long ...'

'Peasants harrow the fields, the hawthorn buds are springing green. You'll never fight a longer battle, my lord. Had it not been for Richer's skill, and my lady —'

Footsteps rustled the rushes, and I heard the swish of silk. Isabel stood by the pallet; cool fingers touched my brow. 'The fever's gone for good,' she said. 'I'll bid Berlai bring your gruel – it's all you've taken for weeks. Tomorrow, perhaps, a morsel of bread and meat.'

I felt weak as a day-old puppy, brain flaccid as my limbs. Adelice saw the question in my eyes.

'My lady of Conches was told you were near to death, and in two days rode from Winchester to Laingaham. She left her retinue far behind and arrived alone.'

'Killed two horses on the way.' Isabel smiled. 'I have an eye on two fine palfreys in your stable – stallions of Richer's breeding.'

'My lady is skilled in salves and healing,' said Adelice. 'She and Richer saved you – not I.'

'Your wits have gone astray,' Isabel told her briskly. 'Your nursing pulled him through: not for an hour together did you leave his bed. And Rufus sent his physician, who helped a little.'

They smiled upon each other in perfect understanding. Surmise tossed in my mind like waves on a stormy sea. Placid though Adelice was, how could she accept my leman in her home? She knew I was Isabel's lover – indeed the whole of Normandy prattled our turbulent wooing. Every knight kept doxies in his castle – handsome sluts and village drabs – to entertain his idleness and spice his revels. His lady, were she wise, just closed her eyes. But Isabel was noble, her battles and loves notorious, a legend in her lifetime and a target for womanly spite. Yet Adelice plainly welcomed her. What magical charm had fused in friendship two such different women?

I gave it up, and thought vaguely back to the past, the leaguers in Northumbria, to Rufus and the rebels. It seemed an age ago, an aeon cleft by canyons wherein I fought with devils.

'What happened to Mowbrai ... Eu ...'

'Later,' said Isabel firmly. 'Much later. Where's Berlai and the gruel – is the boy asleep?' She went to the door and called.

Adelice bent and kissed my lips.

Slowly my strength returned; and after a fortnight's cossetting I insisted on leaving my bed. I basked in April sunlight in the yard, a cloak around my shoulders and a bearskin wrapping my legs. I lazed all day in an indolent trance, and slept like a hog at night. My questions went unheeded; the women pretended ignorance of Rufus and his doings. Richer told me a little: stray morsels garnered from pedlars, disconnected fragments which made no sensible story. The little I heard I did not like: the king had shown a ferocity quite alien to his nature. Then fitzHamon came to Laingaham, sent by Rufus to learn my state. I sat him down in the sunshine and demanded an accounting.

'An ugly story,' fitzHamon said. 'Rufus summoned all his barons and tried the rebels in Salisbury. The trial was a farce, of course – the men were taken sword in hand, blatant in their guilt. The king condemned them out of hand.

'Mowbrai went to Windsor's donjon – he'll never see daylight again.' (He lives in durance as I speak, a score of winters later.) 'Rufus escheated Laci's lands and banished him from England. These were the lesser villains, mere tools in the plotters' hands.'

fitzHamon sighed. His manner became hesitant, like a man avowing shameful crimes.

'Meulan – um – questioned Eu and Alderi. Neither was unduly obstinate. Eu confessed the whole conspiracy; Curthose's the invention, his the guiding hand. Alderi admitted spying for Curthose before and during the Norman war. Having gained the king's – um – confidence, the rest was easy.'

I said thinly, 'Alderi embraced sodomy to help his spying?'

'Just so.' fitzHamon abstractedly picked his teeth. 'To give Eu credit, he hated his steward's debauchery. But you can't control a fanatic – which Alderi became. To gain his ends he yielded open-eyed to Rufus's corruption; the more Rufus used his body the more he loathed him.'

'Meulan told the king all this?'

'He had to.'

'How did Rufus ... react?'

'Like a furnace sheathed in ice, outwardly cold and hard but his anger incandescent. The fire consumed his victims.' fitzHamon watched a starling flock that circled behind a plough. 'A knight, one Geoffrey of Baynard, appealed Eu of treason. A put-up job: Bay-

nard's a famous swordsman.' fitzHamon looked at me wryly. 'I
believe Rufus would have chosen you had you been there. Well, the
only answer to an appeal is trial by battle. They fought on Salisbury's
plain. Eu was a little . . . weak . . . after his interrogation: Baynard
disarmed and wounded him.'

'He was then imprisoned?'

'No. In open view on the plain a hangman castrated the count and
gouged his eyes.'

I felt a pang of sorrow – not on Eu's behalf, but for the clemency
and justice which Rufus seemed to have lost.

'And Alderi?'

'Several knights begged Rufus for his life – Alderi was popular at
court. Nothing would move the king. He had Alderi stripped naked,
scourged at every church in Salisbury and hanged on the highest
gibbet his carpenters could make. Higher,' said fitzHamon, 'than the
minster's spire. His body dangles yet.'

My throat was dry; I called Berlai and ordered wine. A woodman
drove an ox-cart into the yard, unloaded faggots bound with hazel
switches, and bore them to the shed by the forge where firewood
was stacked. A cockerel scratched on the midden, flaunted his
comb and crowed. Clouds scudded across the sky; the sun had gone
and the wind was cold.

I shivered.

'What of Clare?'

fitzHamon shrugged. 'Pardoned. He had surrendered voluntarily,
Rufus judged, and purged his offence by revealing the ambush.
Gilbert's gone to Henry in Domfront.'

fitzHamon rose from his stool, sauntered to the well-head and
gazed into the depths. He returned and said, 'Your springs are low
this year: the water is only four spans deep. So – the plot and the
plotters are finished: the king is riding high.'

'Except for Henry.'

'If he were indeed involved – but the proof is wanting. He's a lone
wolf now, his friends imprisoned or dead. Can Henry play the hand
on his own?'

'You forget his brother, Robert Curthose.'

fitzHamon stared. 'Is Laingaham so far from the world? Has word
not reached you of Pope Urban's preaching? He's calling a crusade
to win the Holy City, and Duke Robert has taken the Cross.'

fitzHamon drained his wine, and set down the empty cup.

'Normandy, like an overripe plum, is falling in Rufus's lap.'

Chapter 8

1096-97

I SUGGESTED going to London with fitzHamon, and brought a storm about my ears. Adelice wept and swore me unfit to journey a bowshot's length; Isabel called me an idiot; Richer observed bleakly he would prepare a litter to bring me back and a coffin for my bury- ing. fitzHamon smiled and told me to curb my impatience: nothing important would happen before midsummer. I railed against them all, ordered a palfrey to be saddled – and fell from the animal's back before I reached the wheatfields.

Recovery was a slow and arduous process. I had to learn to walk before I could ride. With my ladies on either hand I strolled the meadows, rambling farther day by day, until strength returned to my rickety legs and flesh to my wasted frame. Then, on an ambling palfrey, I rode gingerly abroad, inspected the springing barley and cattle calving in the meadows. In maytime, greatly daring, I cast a hawk at a heron, followed at a canter and saw her stoop and kill. When roses sprinkled the hedgerows I donned a padded gambeson, hefted a blunted sword and challenged Lisiard to combat in the yard beside the midden. Considerately he softened his blows, avoided hitting my helmet and dented only my shield.

Progress afterwards was swift. I tilted daily at the quintain, gal- loped an assault course and murdered straw-stuffed dummies. Then I tackled living targets, rode courses against Lisiard and the knights of Isabel's mesnie, suffered some nasty knocks and heavy falls. On Barnabas' Day I unhorsed them all in turn.

I felt ready again to face the world, the world of knights where a man survived by the strength of his arm and the swoop of his sword.

Sunlight gilded peaceful summer days. The hall was full of women: Adelice's ladies and tirewomen and those whom Isabel brought; the room beneath the gallery was crammed as a Benedict nunnery. With my lady I slept in the bower; Isabel's chamber was divided from

388

our pallet by curtains of arras and hide. This was nothing new in halls and castles, but I found at times the situation delicate. Adelice, though placid, was noisy in her loving and squealed like a slaughtered pig in the throes of crisis. Sometimes I heard a chuckle beyond the curtain.

Once, riding to hawk for mallard near the stream, I tried to extract from Isabel a reason for the friendliness, near to devotion, that Adelice accorded her. Isabel answered frankly.

'When I came to Laingaham Adelice was desperate and you were all but dead. She'd have sold herself to Satan had he saved you. At first, I think, she didn't realize fully who I was – merely another helpmate in the struggle for your life. I found a salve that cooled your blood; the fever afterwards waned. Adelice is . . . grateful.'

I pulled behind a hedge, examined the streamlet's reed-fringed banks, saw a ripple and green-blue flash. 'Duck lurking by the willows, Berlai. Go flush them.' I loosed the merlin's jesses and balanced her on my wrist. 'I still don't understand. Adelice knows our history, and she's a Clare – tolerance is a virtue flowing thinly in their blood.'

Isabel sighed. 'Early in our loving I often reproached your blindness: never would you recognize that of all the knights who swived me you alone had touched my heart. Like a thundercloud hiding the sun that blindness still afflicts you.'

Berlai crawled to the reeds, rose and flapped his arms. Mallard skittered from the water and curved above the willows. I cast the hawk. 'They'll follow the stream. Let's ride the banks.' We cantered across the meadow, watching the fleeting specks. 'You talk in riddles, my lady: your hands have cradled my heart for twenty-five years.'

Isabel said fiercely, 'And Adelice's heart and soul are rushes beneath your feet, a sacrifice for your burning! Have you never guessed that beside the flame of her love mine is no more than a candle?'

The merlin stooped like a falling stone – and missed. I cursed, and took the lure from Berlai. 'No,' I answered sullenly, 'I did not know. Adelice is a dutiful wife, a pleasant, tranquil lady – and wears a mask like a triple-hide shield to guard her mind from the world. How was I to tell?'

Isabel sniffed. 'Men – God help us all! You don't appreciate your luck, my lord: a devoted woman for wife and the Lady of Conches your lover!'

'Lover!' I displayed the lure; the merlin – a bird of Richer's training – settled fussily on my wrist and preened her feathers. 'Two years and more since we have bedded!'

Isabel smiled slowly. 'You gave a promise to Ralph; and I, with no words spoken, have likewise promised Adelice. At Laingaham she owns no rival.'

My lady gave us greeting in the yard; I took her hands and gazed into her eyes. She smiled and touched my cheek, and inquired after our sport. Perplexedly I shook my head, and went to the hall.

Ralph arrived a few days later. During the Norman war he had held Conches for Rufus, was never attacked, and did nothing to attract Duke Robert's attention. Afterwards, at Rufus's behest, he stayed lest Curthose, intending an English invasion, might think it worth his while to eliminate an enemy fortress in his rear. When the duke revoked his plans Ralph returned hotfoot, and was highly displeased to find his lady ensconced again at Laingaham. He plainly disbelieved she had come to attend my illness.

'Ill?' he growled, eyeing me across the goblet he held to his lips. 'Seldom have I seen a man in better health. What foolery is this?'

Patiently I explained, and described the debt I owed. The hostility melted from his face; he leaned to my ear and murmured, 'Your vow ...'

'Intact,' I assured him; and added amiably, 'Of course now you're in England I'm no longer bound.'

Ralph spluttered in his wine. 'You dare —!' He banged his cup on the table. 'With thanks for your hospitality, my lord, and gratitude for harbouring my lady, we must leave you. Rufus calls his vassal lords to London.'

'I've had no word.'

'Why should you?' said Ralph maliciously. 'You're not Rufus's liege. You owe him neither fealty nor homage.'

'The king has my faith.'

Ralph sneered. 'For what it's worth. Only homage counts – the service oath for land. You've done no homage for Laingaham.'

'None. The fief belongs to my lady, a dowry grant through Clare.'

'Exactly. You're France's vassal, not England's; yet you hold a place in Rufus's councils alongside Meulan and fitzHamon, lords who lead a hundred knights; and you lead what – a score? Why should Rufus favour one of Philip's lesser lieges?'

'I've known him for twenty years and more – since we were esquires.'

'Ah!' Ralph leered. 'Since you were boys, in fact. Perhaps the services you render him are ... boyish?'

I sent him a look. Ralph blinked; his little fish-mouth quivered. I said quietly, 'Be careful, my lord. You're my guest – don't step beyond the bounds of hospitality.'

Ralph sat shaking in his chair, looking as though he had barely escaped some fearful cataclysm. A knight of Isabel's mesnie sang a chanson to his lute in a low melodious voice.

> *'Biau fut li tans, resplandissent li jor;*
> *Ces eues doces reperent en vigor,*
> *Foillissent bois e traient a verdor ...'*

2

The Lord of Conches found lodgings for his retinue in Eastcheap; I gave Isabel farewell and hurried to the Tower. At a window bay in the council hall Rufus gossiped with his lords. Flambard sat at the inlaid table, surrounded by clerks and servants; abaci, scrolls and tablets littered the board; before him hovered a restless crowd, knights and monks and stewards, bailiffs from petty fiefs and a covey of black-robed Jews. A knight clanked down a leather bag; deniers spilled from the mouth.

'Four pounds,' he said determinedly. 'It's all my fief affords – last year's harvest rotted in the fields.'

Flambard consulted a parchment. 'Your Honour owes two knights,' said he smoothly. 'The geld demands three silver pounds for every knight enfeoffed. Two pounds more, my lord of Bochesorne.'

The knight – I knew him by sight: the squint-eyed Humphrey Visdelou – gesticulated furiously. 'I've scraped my coffers clean! Can I conjure deniers from the air?'

Flambard scratched a note on the scroll. 'Four pounds delivered, two to come. Go home and squeeze your bailiff, my lord!'

Rufus gripped my hands. 'The Devil nearly claimed you – I'd given you up for lost. Your guardian saint was wakeful, and plucked you from his furnace – or did you see, in your illness, visionary harps and angels chanting psalms? Hell's gates and heaven's portals – both are absurdities conjured by priests! Kings and counts and cotters all go into the night like sandgrains scattered by wind. God's face, I preach like a prior! Sit beside me, friend, and tell me your news.'

'Little enough, sire, and none important. I'm told the wind sets fair for Normandy.' I indicated Flambard's reluctant donors. 'A levy?'

'Yes. Another geld on all my vassals – the heaviest yet. I have to raise a pledge: ten thousand silver marks. This, if you haven't heard, is the way of it.'

Urban's discourse, it appeared, had so uplifted Curthose that he promised to take the Cross and sweep from the Holy City the Saracens who held it. 'An opportune bolt-hole for Robert,' said Rufus sourly. 'Despite his success in keeping me out two summers ago he's lost his grip on Normandy. The strongholds north of Seine are mine, Helias of La Flèche holds Maine, and everywhere else his barons are fighting private wars. The duchy seethes in anarchy. So he's scuttling out, dishonoured, to seek honour in Outremer.'

Rufus watched an abbot who haggled with Flambard. Covertly I scrutinized the king: the heavy face was creased about the jowls, his eyes were pouched and bloodshot, streaks like ashes flecked the yellow hair. Thirty-eight summers had seen him; he had aged another ten since the gibbet soared at Salisbury.

'All very fine and holy,' Rufus said, 'but you can't crusade without money: a Norman duke must lead a powerful mesnie. Robert's hoard is empty, so he sent to me. Ten thousand marks, he wanted. I demanded Normandy as pledge.'

The argumentative abbot had exhausted Flambard's patience. The chancellor clapped his hands together and barked, 'Haven't you chests full of dead men's bones wrought about with gold and silver? Melt down your chalices, good father abbot, prise the jewels from your shrines and crosses! Two hundred pounds, your abbey owes – and every denier you'll deliver!'

Rufus grunted approvingly. 'These miserly monks! Well, Curthose agreed – Normandy is mine for the next three years, or longer if he loiters in Outremer. To get his duchy back he's got to repay the loan.' Rufus smiled. 'Will Curthose find ten thousand marks in Jerusalem's spoils?'

I said curiously, 'You feel no call yourself, my lord, to take the Cross?'

Rufus shouted with laughter. 'I, the enemy of God, to march in the cause of God? Your wits are wandering, my friend! Outremer is far away and very hard to win. I stay to reap wealth and power from a man whose lunacy inspires errands which yield neither! When Robert's gone in autumn I shall take Normandy's seisin!'

Triumph blazed like beacons in his eyes. 'Normandy, Walter, is mine – and never will I let it go!'

3

In August the king moved to Windsor. His restless energy seldom allowed him to linger long in any one place – Rufus was never happy save when he was himself moving and keeping everyone else in motion. There he received in private a guileful, smooth-tongued Italian, one Cardinal Walter from Rome – the outcome of a secret deputation Rufus had sent to the pope, a mission led by William of Warelwast, a clerk in the royal chancery.

Although I had heard vaguely of Warelwast's journey I had no inkling of its purpose: Rufus revealed the mission to nobody but Meulan. Warelwast travelled to Rome with a train of laden mules whose burdens clinked as they plodded. He had audience with Pope Urban, and returned with the mules unladen and the cardinal for company.

Warelwast avoided Canterbury and Anselm, came by devious ways to Windsor and presented his prize to Rufus. The king summoned his inner council – fitzHamon, Flambard, Meulan and myself – sent the clerks outside, closed doors and mounted guards. The cardinal, hands hidden in his sleeves, imperturbably surveyed these preparations. He pouted his mouth perpetually above a dimpled chin; the muddy eyes looked no one in the face. I distrusted him on sight.

Not so, apparently, Rufus, who treated the cardinal affably. When the politenesses were finished he came swiftly to the point.

'His Holiness looks favourably on my plea?'

'He is willing to grant you, sire, a legatine authority to bestow on Canterbury's archbishop the badge of papal authority.'

'On the primate?' Rufus coughed. 'Did Pope Urban specify —'

'No names were mentioned, sire!' Warelwast said sharply.

'Quite so.' Rufus looked inquiringly at the cardinal. 'You have brought the pallium?'

'I have.'

Cardinal Walter scrutinized the ceiling, apparently admiring the vaulting's delicate tracery. Rufus waited, curbing his impatience.

'The sooner you deliver it ...'

'There is, naturally, a condition.'

Rufus blinked. 'I offered – ah – concessions to His Holiness which he graciously accepted. I thought the bargain concluded, the terms agreed. What more does he want?'

'Only that you recognize his authority in England, and yield obedience to the pope as St Peter's true successor.'

Rufus smiled relief. 'Of course. That was implicit in our agreement. Warelwast, you made my covenant clear?'

'I did, sire.' He surveyed the cardinal with a kind of puzzled dislike. 'The pope, in my hearing, assented.'

Cardinal Walter withdrew his hands from his sleeves, and carefully steepled his fingers. 'Sire, His Holiness desires that a proclamation should be made throughout your realm, acknowledging him as Vicar of Christ and England's spiritual liege.'

The muscles on Rufus's jawbone bulged like walnuts. 'Is my word not enough for Urban? Must I give him written bonds like a haggling Jew? God's blood, my lord, he's dealing with a knight!'

The cardinal's eyes slid swiftly away to examine the ceiling. 'The pope has often dealt with knights,' he answered tonelessly, 'and finds the results discouraging. My instructions, sire, are definite – else the contract is cancelled.'

Rufus regarded him angrily. 'Very well. It shall be done. And now – the pallium!'

'When the proclamation is written and sealed, my lord.'

'Call your clerks, Ranulf!' Rufus roared. 'Parchment, ink and wax! Prepare a script to satisfy the cardinal!'

Flambard summoned scribes, and dictated while they wrote. Rufus stamped impatiently around the room, stared from an open window, tapped fingers on the mullion. Meulan went to him and spoke in lowered tones. I could not hear what he whispered, but his face was grave with warning.

'This is what we agreed,' Rufus said loudly. 'I cannot believe him treacherous.'

Flambard sanded the scrolls. The king scrawled his cross. Flambard threaded linen strips through slits in the parchment, joined the ends and melted wax upon them, imprinted on the blobs the royal seal – King William mailed and mounted. Rufus contemptuously tossed the scroll to Cardinal Walter.

'There's your proclamation, my lord cardinal. Are you now content?'

'This will be read throughout the kingdom?'

'You have my word.'

The cardinal groped in his robe, and produced a bundle wrapped in deerskin. Rufus ripped the stitches; a crumpled woollen band, crucifix-embroidered, unfolded in his hands.

'The pallium,' said the cardinal calmly. 'To be bestowed on Anselm.'

Rufus's head recoiled as though struck by an unseen fist. He said in strangled tones, 'What is this? Anselm? He's no part of the bargain!'

'Bargain?' The cardinal's voice was cold as a northern wind. 'The Vicar of Christ is not a huckster to peddle his wares in the market. He sent the pallium for Canterbury's archbishop.'

'Anselm,' Warelwast cut in angrily, 'was never mentioned!'

'Not by name,' the cardinal agreed. 'Nevertheless he is England's primate – to whom alone Pope Urban grants the pallium.'

'This is trickery!' Rufus shouted. 'By the Holy Face of Lucca, you'll win nothing from your deceit!' He scooped the scroll from the table, and ripped the skin across.

Cardinal Walter said evenly, 'You'll break your knightly word, my lord, written and sealed before witnesses?'

The parchment fluttered from Rufus's hand. He stared at the cardinal's greasy face. 'I'll not be bound! I'll not give this . . . this rag' – he hurled the pallium on the floor – 'to that malignant monk!'

Cardinal Walter smoothed his robe, and stood. 'Urban authorizes nothing else. You'll defy the pope – to whom you've sworn submission and acknowledged as Father in Christ? I think not, my lord.'

He tapped his knuckles on the table. 'For your future guidance, sire: in bargaining a covenant the form of words is important!'

4

Over Rouen's greystone battlements a dragon banner floated. King William had come to Normandy for seisin of the duchy.

His liegemen gathered; and pavilions spread like a rainbow quilt across the meadows. Rufus greeted the lords as they came, held riotous banquets night after night and tourneys and hunts by day. Not since the Conqueror's time had Rouen seen such revelries. The king postponed from day to day the critical assembly where the barons must pledge allegiance. Meulan fretfully urged Rufus to call the assembly; and fitzHamon observed ironically that the sooner his foes declared themselves the better for everyone's peace.

I asked Meulan why he delayed.

'He's sounding out the two great lords whose refusal to swear homage could plunge Normandy into chaos: Count Helias of Maine and Robert of Belesme. Both appear to be havering. Either's defiance means war – and we can't afford war as yet. Curthose pouched ten thousand marks, and drained the English treasury.' Meulan blew his nose, and wiped fingers on his breeks. 'The duke's away to Outremer by now; marching, so I'm told, in a haze of wine and wenches.'

The Lord and Lady of Conches lived in a pavilion on the encampment's fringe. Despite Ralph's chilly welcome I visited them often, gossiped away the hours, listened idly to Conches's knights relating ancient legends – splendid tales of Rollo's deeds and Roland's dauntless paladins. Isabel encouraged these fables, and applauded the knights who chanted verses they themselves invented. She gathered round her from different mesnies a covey of warbling songbirds. Derisively I eyed her strumming fops: the hands of knights are made by God for holding swords – not lutes. Encountering them in tourneys I soon revised my judgement: the songsters' lances struck more truely than the notes they trilled.

This was an aspect of Isabel's nature I had not seen. I knew the whiplike Amazon who led her knights in battle – but who was this dreamy woman listening entranced to songs that Charlemagne sang?

During this strange hiatus when nothing seemed to happen except tourneys fought at noontide and feasting half the night, a craving for Isabel's body awoke like a raging thirst. I think the urge was fomented by overmuch food and wine; seldom, in the crowded camp, could you pass a baron's pavilion without being hauled inside to taste his vintage. I tried to quench my lust in Rouen's stews, and in brothels behind the wagon-lines where doxies flaunted their wares. Nothing would answer; I left these squalid conflicts more ravenous than before.

While exercising the horses I found by chance a deserted hermitage: a tumbledown stone-built hut secluded in a coppice.

Later I returned with servants, cleared the litter, swept the room, and spread bearskin druggets on the floor. On a sunlit afternoon I persuaded Isabel to try my sorrel destrier – spoil of a recent tourney, won from a Gascon knight – and led her out on the Gournai road, Berlai trotting behind. We discussed the destrier's points, Rufus's feats in tourney, Belesme's disdainful arrogance, and the splendid wines at Robert fitzHamon's table. I turned from the road at the coppice, and led her to the hut without a word. Isabel scanned the ivy-draped walls, the wooden door askew on its hinges. She sent me a sidelong glance, and laughter danced in her eyes.

'How did you find this mansion, Walter? A veritable palace – fit for a king and queen! Who will brush away the cobwebs and kill the rats?'

'The place is clean, my lady.'

Isabel slipped from the saddle, pushed open the rickety door and peeped inside. She put a hand to her mouth, and looked askance at Berlai.

'He is safe,' I said.

I told Berlai to take the horses and keep watch on the path. Amazement sat in his ugly face; he squinted so violently that the pupils well-nigh vanished beneath his nose. I put a finger to my lip. Berlai goggled, mouth agape. A faithful esquire, he was; somewhat wanting in the brain.

Isabel lay on the bearskins, hands clasped behind her head, and gazed at the rotting rafters and mildewed thatch. I looked at the lean lithe body, and felt a prickling burn my skin. Her slanting eyes smiled into mine, a flush crept over the smooth tanned cheeks.

'Why do you dally, Walter? Have Rouen's doxies drained you?'

I flung myself beside her, plucked her tunic's laces and stripped my lady bare.

A shaft of sunlight pierced the crooked door, slowly climbed the walls, slanted on the rafters and was gone. A pigeon clattered to roost, crooned softly on the roof. Remote as a voice from a distant star a chapel bell tolled vespers.

I went no more to Rouen's stews.

In the castle hall Duke Robert's barons paid homage to William, Duke and King.

A seneschal called titles, a roll like battle clarions: Mortemer and Laigle, Torigni and Mortain, Grantmesnil and Blois – their sons had hammered Christendom from Syracuse to Leith. Rufus, crowned and sceptred, took their hands in his and heard their vows. He gathered between his palms the lands his father ruled, an empire from Northumbria to Maine.

'Helias, Count of Maine.'

A lanky, loose-limbed frame; square-jawed swarthy features, deepset amber eyes. An ancient mace wound cratered his cheek, a dark-brown pit, the edges puckered. Everyone watched him stalk to the throne; the hall was deathly quiet.

Rufus gripped the sceptre tightly, his lips downturned at the corners.

'My lord,' he said in a neutral tone, 'you rebelled against my brother and abjured Normandy's dominion. Will you restore your faith to me, who holds his place?'

'Sire, I give you my fealty. I crave your friendship as my seigneur, and wish to serve you well in peace and war.'

A whisper like a wandering wind-breath rustled through the hall, a collective sigh that spelled relief. Or was it disappointment?

'Kneel, then, Helias of La Flèche, and swear your oath.'

Like a warrior facing a lance-line Helias braced his shoulders. 'I have taken the Cross. Tell me this, my lord: shall I depart for Outremer assured of your goodwill, certain that my county rests safely in your hands?'

'Your county?' The king's eyes glittered. 'You took Maine from Normandy by force, my lord: the land belongs to the realm my father held. You'll do homage for Maine, acknowledge me your overlord, Mans and the county mine. Then go wheresoever you will.'

Helias touched the sunken scar on his cheek. 'For five years I've held Maine: the county is mine by right. Fulk of Anjou claimed Maine's seisin: I resisted his demand. Robert Duke of Normandy brought swords across my marches: I defeated him in battle.' Helias clenched his hands. 'Sire, I hold that both these claims have lapsed.

I promise fealty and friendship – but I will not swear you homage for my lands!'

The sceptre slipped through Rufus's fingers; he gripped the end like a club. 'Whatever my father held I'll also hold. Surrender your county, my lord!'

A note of desperation trembled in Helias's voice. 'Sire, I am sworn to the Cross! Let me go in peace, and offer me no threats! Will you war on a pilgrim vowed to the cause of Christ? Rather than that, I pray you, submit the issue to your council, let your barons judge my claim!'

Rufus's shoulders heaved. He faced Helias like a charging boar.

'Spears and swords and arrows will plead my cause against you! I've no mind to fight crusaders – but rebels I'll hunt to the ground! Get you to your citadel, repair your broken walls – soon I'll bring to Maine a thousand pennoned lances!'

Helias stared at the king – a wondering gaze as though he looked on a being from an alien world. 'Your reputation doesn't belie you, sire. So be it. You've declared war. I wear a pilgrim's Cross; that Cross I shall mark on my shield – and the world will know you fight a sworn crusader!'

He walked proudly from the hall. Rufus shuddered with rage, and hammered the sceptre's boss on his thigh. Meulan bent and whispered swiftly, 'Better to take him now, and nip rebellion at the root.'

The flush receded from Rufus's face; the shaking stopped; he clenched his teeth. 'Don't talk nonsense, Robert. The fellow's got safe-conduct. I can't touch him.' He looked at the seneschal. 'Is Helias the last to swear?'

A baron strolled to the dais and knelt gracefully at Rufus's feet. Green eyes in an ivory face. Garbed all in lavender velvet, tunic, mantle and breeks, silver threads embroidering collar and hem. A golden chain engirdled his throat; a turquoise blazed on the pendant.

Robert Count of Belesme.

Rufus eyed him warily. Debating in his council he had said – and we agreed – that of all the Norman barons Belesme's allegiance was most valuable – and equally improbable. He ruled his Honours like an independent prince, had served Curthose when it suited, fighting mostly for himself, dominating half Duke Robert's realm. An unpredictable ally – and a very dangerous enemy.

Rufus forced a smile.

'You promise fealty, my lord – *and* homage for your lands?'

'Both, sire.' A smile curled the dagger-thin lips. Without hesitation he put his hands in the king's and murmured the oath.

'Guillaume de Engleterre, jo sui vostre liges hum par fei e par humage.'

Belesme rose, and fastidiously brushed his knees. 'The thing is this, my lord,' he explained languidly. 'I heard your altercation with the Count of Maine. You've got a war on your hands. I've been fighting him for years – his borders march with mine just south of Perche – and can't make any progress. But you'll find my experience useful; and I'll welcome your support. Together we'll plunder Maine and give Helias the boot.'

Even Meulan, that imperturbable man, gaped at Belesme's effrontery. Rufus opened and closed his mouth, and said through his teeth, 'Maine belongs to Normandy. I don't pillage my own dominions.'

'No?' Belesme admired his fingernails. 'A laudable sentiment – Curthose was less meticulous. However, queer things happen in war. When do you intend invading Maine, my lord?'

'Not this year.' Rufus chewed his thumb, remembering his empty coffers, Flambard's gloomy accounting and Meulan's warnings. England was impoverished. 'Perhaps next autumn.'

'A year to wait.' Belesme idly swung his girdle's silver tassel. 'Rather a pity – Helias will have time and enough to prepare. Ah, well. Whenever you send your summons, sire, I'll muster my conroys.'

He bowed and sauntered away.

To give Black Robert his due he kept his oath: never till Rufus died did he unscabbard a sword on England.

6

The king wintered in Normandy; and passed the months persuading his newly-sworn liegemen that an iron fist had supplanted Duke Robert's flabby hand.

He revived the Conqueror's practice and sent vassal knights and mercenaries to garrison vital strongholds. By Christmas he controlled the most important castles: Gournai and Aumale, Argentan and Evreux and others throughout the land. He could not forbid private war: a tradition enshrined in Normandy since Duke Rollo's time. Instead he decreed that disputes be brought to his court: only if his mediation failed could neighbours resort to war.

One or two barons ignored his warning, believing Rufus's injunctions as hollow as his brother's. Ascelin Goel of Ivri suffered from this delusion, and led his men to harry Breteuil's demesnes. To Ascelin's distress constabulars from Evreux, Conches and Laigle closed quickly on his raiders, slaughtered half and hunted the rest to Ivri's gates. Ascelin surveyed the army leaguering his castle, counted his depleted garrison, and prudently surrendered. Rufus imposed a heavy fine; his mercenaries occupied Ivri.

Normandy's turbulent warlords scratched their heads and wondered. If Rufus could persuade his vassals – who usually watched delightedly while a rival ruined another – to unite against a marauder the good old days were gone. So, in fact, they were – while Rufus governed Normandy private warfare lapsed.

At Easter he returned to England, Ralph and Isabel to Conches; and I visited Poix. All was peaceful and secure; I lingered till the sowing was done, then followed the king to London. The Tower was half deserted: Rufus waged war in Wales.

By midsummer he was back, claiming the Welsh were trounced – and barely controlled a smouldering rage which burst like a boil one noonday over the dice.

'That abominable archbishop! Deliberately he mocks me, flaunts his insolence in my face! What in Satan's name can I do to curb him?'

I wondered how the fragile man of peace could so violently annoy a king engaged in a frontier war. Cardinal Walter, after his swindle, had given Anselm the pallium; and Rufus had sworn he would never set eyes on the archbishop's face again. Nor, since then, had they met.

'Twenty knights he owes me!' Rufus, fuming, rattled the dice. 'A pair of deuces – my luck's clean out! Twenty indeed he sent to Wales – a ragamuffin pack! Some so old they could hardly ride; the rest hadn't couched a lance in years – fat and bloated farmers! Hauberks patched and weapons rusted; spavined, gaunt-ribbed destriers, unfit to draw a cart. And the men-at-arms in the mesnies were an antiquated rabble!'

'Kent is a peaceful county.' I rolled the dice – a double trey – and Rufus grimaced. 'Canterbury's knights have probably done nothing more serious than castle guard in all their lives. Anselm, by his calling, is hardly able to judge —'

'He'll do me right!' Rufus stormed. 'The law, for once, is on my side – I'll bring a case against him to the council!'

Another confrontation loomed – and the king had never won yet. Better perhaps to mediate: Rufus's grounds, on sight, seemed irrefutable; but Anselm could produce surprising weapons – and I wanted to save my friend another humbling.

'If you agree, sire, I'll take your complaint to the archbishop and seek redress.'

Rufus bristled. 'You're too friendly with that pernicious monk! Blandishment and promises are all you'd get, and a cunning reason to excuse himself. Here's a chance to twist his neck, and I'll not lose it!'

'Wiser to test his defences first, before you launch your storm. Will you let me see him?'

Rufus threw the dice, and grunted satisfaction. 'Quint and trey – you'll not beat that! Go if you must,' he added. 'You'll make no difference to the charge I'll bring!'

7

I rode to Canterbury, taking none but Richer and a servant. Anselm received me in the chapter, surrounded by his monks, listening to a prior reading Holy Writ. He wore a threadbare gown, and cobbled sandals on his feet; the conflicts of his office showed plainly in his face. The skin was grey and wizened, his cheeks and temples hollow, veins like thin blue threads meandered across his skull. I knelt and received his blessing, and asked for private speech. He wafted the monks away. I set a stool beside him and stated Rufus's charge, the threat of a cause in council. Anselm gazed at the candles; his eyes looked tired and lost.

'What can I know,' he said exhaustedly, 'of horses and swords and soldiers? Canterbury's knights hold tenure by finding their own accoutrements. Am I a banneret, to check gambesons and girths?'

The prior continued to intone his texts. His voice drowned Anselm's murmur; I cupped an ear to hear him.

'The king holds his lords responsible for the mesnies they send to his service. He is set on restitution – and in this the law supports him.'

'What penalty can Rufus inflict?'

'An amercement, heavy or light, according to his temper.'

The archbishop closed his eyes. The lids were almost transparent, thin as butterflies' wings. 'Another depredation of the Church's goods. I think I have had enough of courts and kings, the world which calls on men of God to fight their worldly battles, and persecutes them harshly if swords are a little blunt or saddle-leather cracked. I am weary of England and her king and everything to do with her.'

'You're Archbishop of Canterbury,' I reminded him sharply.

'In that office I have failed. The king has not restored to Holy Church the abbeys he has stolen, his court is a stinking cess-pit, his subjects groan in his grasp.' Anselm pressed fingers to temples, torment in his face. 'My soul is sick. I must go to Rome, to that blessed haven of rest from England's sorrows, and seek from the pope encouragement and help.'

'The king,' I said bluntly, 'will never give you leave.'

'Then I will go without. On Rome my heart is set.'

I recognized the obstinate tone in his voice, the determined ring which showed his mind decided. The prior's Latin droned like a buzzing bee; I shut my ears and pondered.

Anselm's craving for Rome sprang not from episcopal duty – as when he wanted to fetch the pallium – but from caprice. He might rightly ask for permission, which Rufus at discretion could refuse or grant. Certainly he would refuse. Anselm wished to consult the pope because the king had threatened a suit: an appeal, in short, to Urban from Rufus's authority in a matter purely temporal. No sovereign ruler – Rufus least of all – would allow papal interference in a secular dispute between lord and vassal.

The archbishop, I decided, was digging a pit for himself.

I opened my mouth to point his error; then shut my teeth so firmly that I bit my tongue. If Anselm persisted – and he would – Rufus might justly strip his prelacy and banish him from the realm: a chance he'd jump at readily as a cat on a wandering mouse. Would it not be politic to let things take their course? Archbishop and king would never be reconciled; while England held them both there'd be no end to the strife. I looked at the old man thoughtfully. Try to prevent his whim? Useless: his mind was set; and worse – I'd do the king disservice.

Best to encourage Anselm, let him tumble into the pit.

I rose. 'I came to advise submission, because England's laws sustain the king's demand. Nevertheless you insist on seeking

Urban's counsel. If you wish to set pope against king, there's no more I can say. Farewell, my lord.'

I kissed his ring. The prior's reading drowned the archbishop's answer: I gave the loud-mouthed monk a malevolent look as I left.

When Rufus heard Anselm's intention his eyes widened; a smile spread slowly across his face, he slapped his hands together. 'By the Holy Face,' he roared, 'I've got him!'

Messengers rode to Canterbury, and called Anselm to the Tower for answering the charge.

I shall not recall the details – the hearing lasted three long days. Anselm, weary to death, spoke in a voice so faint the council could hardly hear him: desperate and exhausted, he seemed bent on his own destruction. Rufus, to give him credit, forbore from harrying his victim, stated calmly his demands and lucidly framed his case. He wanted restitution, a mere two hundred pounds. Anselm refused: the money belonged to the Church, and was not his to give. Rufus coldly emphasized that he transgressed the laws of seisin, which required proper service for the holding of a fief. Anselm denied the charge: he had sent the knights he owed; their accoutrements and training were not his liability. If Rufus pressed the penalty he wanted the pope's advice: Urban alone could sanction amercement paid from the Church's funds.

Rufus smiled forbiddingly, like a man who sees his enemy ride headlong into an ambush.

'I do not consent to your going.'

Anselm insisted. With or without the king's authority he would travel to Rome.

Rufus consulted his barons and bishops. They agreed that by custom, law and usage Anselm had no right to withhold amercement, nor journey abroad on a secular errand without the king's permission – which was wholly true. The archbishop had no case.

Rufus addressed him quietly.

'You are resolute in your intention?'

'I am resolute,' said Anselm faintly.

'Then go – and there you stay. You will never return to England.'

Anselm's face was the face of a corpse. He shuffled painfully to the dais, tripped upon the edge and collapsed on a bench beside the king.

'My lord,' he whispered, 'I bid you farewell. If I could have gone with your goodwill . . .' Tears trickled down his cheeks. 'Now, for the last time, I offer you my blessing – if you do not refuse it.'

404

The triumph went from Rufus's face, almost he looked ashamed.
'I refuse not your blessing.'

The king bowed his head; Anselm signed the air and murmured benediction. He tottered slowly from the chamber; Canterbury's black-robed monks followed him like a funeral train. I felt a prickling in my eyes, and sniffed and rubbed my nose. Meulan eyed me derisively.

'Weeping for a saint's departure? You're in the wrong country, Walter!'

8

At Rufus's command I returned to Poix.

Delis kept my Honour safe. During the war he had led in King Philip's army the mesnie I owed for my seisin – twelve knights and seventy men-at-arms – and lost two sergeants killed. 'There were no real battles,' Delis lazily explained. 'March and counter-march, a siege or two – we helped in Argentan's taking – and garrisoning castles. Duke Robert did most of the work; Philip somehow contrived to be generally late for the fighting. His son is a hell-bent hothead, always looking for trouble; fortunately our conroys never marched in Louis's train. We acquired a little loot – not much – and trundled happily home.'

Delis had taken Roger and Berenger to war, and conceded that the esquires had borne themselves well. Both were rising seventeen, strapping lusty youths nearly ready for knighting. But knights from noble Houses needed destriers, armour and land. I had no manors to bestow; all my Honour's fiefs were already held. Delis said carelessly, 'Berenger inherits Carenci: he'll not be for ever landless. For a destrier he can have the bay stallion I acquired when Argentan fell. Armour is difficult: a hauberk's cost will swallow two years' harvests, and mildew ruined the summer's corn. I suppose —'

'Send Berenger to the master-smith and get him measured. I'll give him the hauberk when I knight him.'

I could not so easily settle Roger's future. Ostensibly Conches's son, he was not my vassal; Ralph should arrange his knighting and give him seisin of a fief. Ralph's demesnes exceeded mine by far; and somewhere in his Honours there'd be manors wanting lords. Roger must return to Conches. I looked sadly at the features which reflected Isabel's likeness, and found the prospect hard. None the less for the boy's own good it had to be done; and I decided to take him with me on the mission that Rufus demanded.

Hugh, eleven years old, was growing sinewy and lean, strong beyond his years, entirely devoted to skill-at-arms and horses. 'Spends all his day in the saddle,' Delis said, 'and when he's not astride a horse he's in the tiltyard fighting some unlucky sergeant. Neither Berenger nor Roger like opposing him in courses – he'll have them both unhorsed before he's very much older.'

I scrutinized my son. He passed his days in lowly company: men-at-arms and ostringers and fewterers; his speech was coarse and manners rough. He was developing into the kind of man you met in solitary castles, or commanding mercenary conroys: uncouth knights whose only skill was a swift and ready sword. Hugh as Lord of Poix would speak with kings and princes; and Rufus's court had taught me there was more to knightly behaviour than knocking men off horses. Hugh wanted, in truth, a woman's care: someone to teach him manners.

Adelice came happily to Poix. She looked aghast at her rowdy son, and took him in hand at once. Hugh, thoroughly disgusted, learned anew to wait at table, to ride attendance on a lady in the chase, to make a bed and fold a mantle. When Adelice gave him a lute he violently rebelled and ran to me for succour. Sternly I admonished him. 'A proper knight must be able to strum a roulade and compose verses to his tunes.'

Hugh studied me speculatively; laughter lighted his beak-nosed face. 'Very well, my lord.' He held out the lute. 'Will you show me how it's done?'

I discovered urgent business that demanded swift attention.

Halfway along the Paris road I heard King Philip had gone to Mantes, and followed him there. The town which killed the Conqueror had never quite recovered from his army's vengeful sack; the rampart's compass was smaller; broken, nettled mounds – relics of thriving suburbs – mottled the land beyond. The castle since its burning had been rebuilt in stone, and the ward enlarged. Even so, I thought Mantes a restricted place for the King of France's court; and wondered – because Philip loved luxury – why he stayed uncomfortably away from Paris.

My suzerain was enjoying the sunlight on the battlements. Philip was fatter than ever; a belly like a wine-cask strained his girdle; scanty silvery hair tasselled a shining pate, a skein of threadlike veins raddled the pendulous cheeks. The queen was seated beside him, idly studying a missal. The years had spared Bertrada's beauty, though an unfamiliar sullenness graved lines on the ravishing face. Prince Louis leaned on a merlon, gazing over the town; barons and ladies lounged in the shade, sweltering beneath the shingled roof. Philip, I remembered, revelled in heat.

I bent my knee, exchanged courtesies of greeting; and inquired whether a plague had driven the court from Paris. Philip chuckled, quivering his chins.

'A plague indeed – a pestilence of priests. We shelter here like fugitives, because there are fewer priests in Mantes. Surely you have heard about our hounding by the Church?'

Bertrada closed the missal with a snap that split the vellum.

'A papal persecution,' she said in a steely voice. 'The pope threatens his anathema on a marriage he calls adulterous. No priest will hear our prayers, none will hold for us a mass.' She gestured to the handful of attendants. 'This is all our court. Urban's denunciations have so terrified our lieges that few will share our table.'

Philip patted her hand. 'There, my dear. Why distress yourself? Was our marriage not worth a mass or two?'

Louis, still scanning the landscape, said tonelessly, 'Your union *was* adulterous – why rail at the priests?' His eyes were pale, expressionless, the mouth a grey-lipped slit, his face a parchment skull, black stubble shading the jaws. 'Fulk of Anjou – your lawful husband, my lady queen – is still alive. My mother you shut in Montreuil's donjon – and she died there *after* you were wed. How can any Christian believe your marriage valid?'

The king said sharply, 'Enough, Louis! Why should you grumble? Since the barons seem reluctant to heed my mandates France's rule is virtually in your hands.'

Louis crossed arms on a merlon, and watched a raven circling the tower. 'But not entirely. Divided counsels, my lord, at a perilous time for France. We've acquired a greedy neighbour. Rufus has ambitions Curthose lacked.'

The talk was taking an awkward turn for the message I had to deliver. I said hastily, 'Sire, I carry on King William's behalf a proposal touching your marches. If I may deliver his word in private, to you and your council —'

Philip waved a hand. 'You behold my council around you.' He groped in a platter, and munched a honeyed apricot. 'No secrets here. What does Rufus say?'

Pointless to soften the blow. I said, 'King William gained England by inheritance. Normandy is now in his hands. The king, my lord, is determined to win the lands his father held.'

Philip spat out the apricot stone. 'He'll have to fight for Maine, if I know anything of Helias.'

'Maine is not the only county where Normandy once held sway. There's also the Vexin.'

Philip choked on his mouthful. Louis ceased contemplating the countryside, and leaned his back on the battlements. His eyes were pebbles in a death's-head.

I swallowed, and continued, 'King William solemnly requests that you cede Pontoise, Chaumont and Mantes, and all the fiefs between: the lands that once the Conqueror ruled. For this he is ready to pay a fair indemnity.'

'Ah.' Philip's fingers wandered to the platter; he chose a fig and held it to his lips. 'How much?'

'Not for all the wealth in England!' Louis's elbows thrust him from the merlon; threateningly he stood above his father, his lips taut as a trap. 'Yield Pontoise – a sword-point in the heart of France? Surrender the Vexin's fortresses, our bastions against Normandy's greed? God's blood, my lord of Poix – you ask for nothing less than France's independence!'

Philip nibbled the fig. 'Normandy held them once,' he murmured placatingly. 'Perhaps, if sufficient recompense . . .'

Louis looked at the king with loathing. 'Not for a world of silver and gold! The Vexin belongs to France!'

Philip stroked Bertrada's hand. 'It seems a pity. What do you say, my love?'

She sent Louis a venomous glance beneath her lashes. 'Does the prince dictate your pleasure, my lord? He must know the sequel to refusing Rufus.' She flipped the missal's pages, and said in a brittle tone, 'However, in this instance I believe him right. Without the Vexin France is lost.'

The king looked at me sadly. 'There's your answer, Walter. How much, incidentally, was Rufus offering?'

'Ten thousand marks: the sum he gave for Normandy.'

King Philip licked his lips, and regarded his son malignantly. 'Worth it, I'd have said. However . . . And what will Rufus do when he learns I've turned him down?'

I said steadily, 'Sire, I am not authorized to carry threats.'

Philip seemed amused. 'Hardly. After all, you're still my vassal, although —'

'We ride for Paris tomorrow!' the prince interrupted. 'The barons must hear this ultimatum, and the realm be readied for war!'

King Philip heaved to his feet, and clasped his sagging paunch. 'Gets his zeal from his mother, not from me!' He surveyed me disconsolately. 'You'll not bear arms against me, Walter?'

I knelt and kissed my suzerain's pudgy hand.

'Never, my lord.'

At dawn my retinue accompanied Philip's cavalcade as far as the turn to Conches. When Mantes' gates slammed shut behind us the castle's chapel bell began a frenzied tolling. The ringing was repeated by the bells of all the churches; the air reverberated; echoes rolled like thunder over the hills. Philip looked at his queen, and smiled wryly.

'Do you hear, my beauty, how they drive us away?'

I remembered then the priestly belief that bells banished devils and pestilence.

9

I halted briefly at Conches, and delivered Roger to the man who believed himself his father. Ralph swore Roger should be knighted by nobody less than Rufus. He then stared hard at the youthful face – he had last seen Roger at Hungerford, four years before – and looked at me. The years had wrought a change in the young man's features, emphasized the eagle nose, tufted more the eyebrows, hardened mouth and jaw. Jet-dark eyes and high-boned cheeks declared his mother's blood: the House of Poix had firmly stamped the rest. Ralph sent me a bewildered look, gazed forlornly at Isabel, dropped his hand from Roger's arm and faltered away.

'Ralph realizes the truth,' I said. 'Will he disinherit . . .'

'So blazon his shame – and mine?' Isabel's voice was hard. 'I doubt it. My lord of Conches has worn his horns for twenty years: he ought to be accustomed to the weight.'

I felt pity for Ralph's wretchedness; and breathed a thankful prayer that heaven's sweet deliverance had saved me, long ago, from wedding Isabel of Montfort.

I reached Winchester by Michaelmas, and told Rufus the mission had failed. He was unsurprised. 'There was just a chance that Philip might take a silver-baited hook. He loves money more than honour; I've bribed him often before.'

'Philip is king in name, no more. Louis is the enemy you'll fight.'

'Young and inexperienced – a banneret apeing his betters. This means parallel wars, as I expected: twin campaigns against France and Maine. Money – money and mercenaries: I need them both by the sackful!' He smiled crookedly. 'I've recovered Canterbury's revenues now that Anselm's gone, which makes a useful start. fitz-Hamon's left for Kent to smarten those slovenly knights. They won't know what's hit them!'

At Winchester, London and Windsor the king held numerous councils, debated with English and Norman lords the double war he intended. From the meetings – sometimes stormy – a strategy emerged. Rufus mustered for the eastward thrust the barons north of Seine; the lords of central Normandy would lead an army into Maine. The English barons – lesser lords who held no Norman fiefs – he divided between the two. He left in place his marcher lords on the Welsh and Scottish borders, and proceeded to strip from England the vassals who guarded his castles. I considered this dangerous, and told him so.

Rufus bared his teeth. 'Since Mowbrai's revolt and the rebels' fate do you think anyone will challenge my rule? Do you, Walter?'

Memory haunted his eyes. 'Nobody would dare,' I said. 'I spoke foolishly, my lord.'

Rufus decided to conduct the Vexin war himself; to Robert of Belesme he entrusted the Maine campaign. Through autumn and early winter the barons assembled their mesnies, drilled knights and men-at-arms, sharpened swords and mended mail, collected corn and wine and tents. Meulan crossed to Havre, seized every cart in the countryside and a thousand mules and oxen to transport the army's baggage. The king's writ went to the southern ports; shipmen hoisted sails and brought the hoys to Hastings. Constabulars and conroys tramped the roads from every county, and converged like crows on carrion at the fields round Battle Abbey. Meanwhile all across Normandy, from Mortemer to Mortagne, baronial mesnies marched to the points of muster; Rouen for King William's force, Alençon for Belesme's.

No one argued with Belesme: the saturnine count dozed openly while the barons discussed the Vexin, and urbanely refused to disclose his schemes for Maine's invasion. 'Send half the mesnies to Mamers: here is the list' – he flipped a scrip on the table – 'and half to Alençon. Afterwards the strategy is mine.' Rufus regarded him doubtfully, and caught a warning glint in the emerald eyes.

'I find in war,' Belesme said smoothly, 'secrecy is vital. If my hauberk knew my plans I'd cast it into the furnace.'

Rufus found time to allot my part in the war. 'You can't fight France, Walter,' he said, 'and so, if you agree, I'll send you to Belesme. Moreover,' he added meditatively, 'it might be prudent for a faithful friend to observe Black Robert's antics. Normandy's transcendent soldier – but tortuous as a viper and far more vicious.'

'You've provided him an army to fight his bitterest foe. Belesme won't miss the chance of crushing Helias.'

'Maybe. Now,' said Rufus busily, 'where's that report on Neauflé's garrison?'

Thus, like a sergeant accepting a banneret's orders, I submitted meekly to King William's bidding. Rufus had no right to command my bowmen's service – I was France's vassal and, indeed, my mesnie under Delis later fought at Philip's side – yet I never thought to disobey his will.

I think, had Rufus asked, I'd have gone to his bed.

10

At Advent the army sailed. I saw my archers disembark, led horses ashore through surf, and found the wagons which Meulan had gathered on the dunes. We stayed encamped two days at Havre, sorting out the conroys and loading carts – we carried two months' rations, so the peasants of Rufus's Normandy were safe from pillage on the march.

We took the long road south through Lisieux and Argentan. December's rainstorms lashed the column, sheened haubergeons and helmets, and turned the track to a greasy river churned by wheels and feet. We endured a sennight's misery, drenched in camp at night and mired to the eyebrows on the road. The sight of Alençon's donjon gladdened four thousand hearts.

I squatted on a corn sack in the ward, scraping mud-stars from my face while Berlai unlaced my hauberk and sorrowfully clicked his tongue at the burnishing task in prospect. Belesme sauntered from the donjon, elegant in purple cloak and silken tunic, and paused before me, hands on hips.

'Not overmuch prinking, my lord,' he drawled. 'You've another

411

day's ride tomorrow. I'm sending you on to our farthermost outpost, a place of danger and honour.'

'God's bones!' I swore disgustedly. 'Where's that?'

'Saones,' Belesme murmured, and strolled away.

I stripped the hauberk, and gratefully swallowed wine that Richer brought. It were better I had mounted then and there, and ridden fast to safety and salvation.

Chapter 9

1097–98

'WHAT'S the good of mounted archers in a castle?'

Belesme had not bothered to inform me he had appointed Ralph of Conches as Saones' castellan; but there he was, sucking his teeth and watching my men ride over the drawbridge.

'None,' I answered unpleasantly, 'but surely you'll venture now and then outside the walls? Or won't you?'

The castle gripped a spur commanding a plain which rolled south-wards into Maine. The donjon, a four-sided stone-built tower, stood on a natural mound; the drystone walls of the ward surmounted a deep, dry fosse. Within the ramparts were stables and barracks and granaries; rubble-paved alleys divided the buildings like the streets of a miniature town. The ward was a hive of noise and bustle: bellows roared in smithies, hammers clanged on anvils, soldiers whetted weapons and sang ribald songs. Knights exercised their destriers on a straw-track hugging the ramparts: Saones, deep in the enemy's march, allowed no casual wandering in the hostile land outside.

A Breton quartering master – one of Rufus's hirelings – allotted my troop a stable and an open space nearby where the bowmen pitched their tents. Richer saw to the carts' unloading, stacked corn sacks in a granary and posted a sentry – mercenaries are rampant thieves. I beckoned Lisiard and Berlai and went to search for quarters.

The donjon's lowest storey – prison and store-room both – lacked doors and windows; a ladder climbed from the mound to a door on the middle floor. We paused on the threshold to accustom our eyes to the gloom. Arrow slits admitted a miserly light: the room was all but dark. It was twenty paces square and filled the entire floor; oaken pillars braced the battlements' floor above. Smoke from a central hearth blanketed the rafters and wreathed through a trap that gave to the battlements. The hall was unpartitioned, no rushes on the wooden floor, no arras on the walls. A privy concealed by an ox-hide curtain vented a piercing stench. Benches and wine-stained trestles crowded the middle; hauberks dangled on wall-racks, helmets were spiked on pegs; and swords and bow-staves leaned against the stone. The chamber smelt of excrement and sweat, leather-grease and smoke.

Here lived and slept a hundred knights and esquires. The castle was stripped for war; comfort had no place.

We squeezed between knights who sat on the floor and gambled or leaned against pillars and gossiped. Finding a sleeping place was a matter of luck and bluster. Berlai dumped my bundle in a chink between a wine cask and a woodstack. 'Not there, by your leave,' a knight called pleasantly. 'That's the corner I lay my head.' I was weary from a chilly ride, and opened my mouth to argue. Someone put a hand on my arm: a slim knight dressed in brown, tanned deerskin tunic, calfhide boots and breeches.

Isabel said, 'There's space beside our pallets near the door.'

I stuttered, lost for words. Berlai quickly lugged our baggage to the gap she pointed; if we all three slept on our sides we could just fit in. Roger greeted me happily, resplendent in gleaming hauberk, so proud of his new-won mail he could not bear to put it off. 'Ralph knighted him a sennight since,' Isabel said. 'Roger was too impatient to wait for Rufus's sword.'

'And what, my lady,' I said crustily, 'are you doing in this galerie?'

Isabel pointed to the ceiling. 'Let's go to the battlements. My throat is sore from talking above this din.'

We climbed the ladder, spluttered in the smoke skeins swirling from below, and mounted to the roof. This was the fighting platform, the castle's final pinnacle. Merlons and embrasures jutted beyond a steep-pitched roof; along one side the ovens were ranged, where scullions were baking bread and meat. Beside them, ranked in rows, stood cauldrons filled with oil and fire-pans full of lead bars, ready for boiling and melting to incinerate escaladers. Sentries at corner embrasures nursed their spears and damned the wind; knights escaped from the stink below hugged cloaks around their shoulders.

We sheltered behind a merlon. Isabel said, 'Why so angry, Walter? I've always ridden to war with Conches's mesnie.'

'War? You've scuffled with your neighbours, fought in petty skirmishes. This,' I said sternly, 'is something different: a major war where kingdoms lie at stake – no place for wilful hoydens apeing knights.'

Isabel laughed. 'Were the lances blunt when Poïx came harrying Conches? Are the blades more keenly honed because Rufus conquers Maine? The risks are the same, dear Walter, however impressive the war.' She raised my hand to her lips; the touch was soft and glowing, like a rosebud warmed by sun. 'Would you have me brood in a bower, spinning wool and pointing embroidery, while Roger draws his sword for the first time since his knighting?'

I stared across the sombre landscape. The ground fell away in a rock-strewn slope from the castle's foot to the plain below, where a rivulet welled to a lake. The water reflected leaden clouds which trailed transparent skirts. The country unrolled like a map to the far horizon: a wind-tossed forest ocean engirdling grassy islands bleached by frost. On the forest's rim a dark hump loomed like a rock in a surging sea.

Isabel followed my gaze. 'Dangeul,' she said. 'Count Helias's foremost fortress, the counterpart to Saones. Only two leagues distant – a block on the road to Mans.'

'A block indeed, if Dangeul's men are resolute.' Raindrops spattered the battlements; I drew her under the roof. 'Belesme has mustered his army. What, now, is his strategy?'

Isabel explained. Black Robert held his strongest forces at Mamers and Alençon, base-points of a triangle whose apex here at Saones pierced deep in the hide of Maine. Within this fort-barbed arrowhead he garrisoned smaller castles – St Remi and Allières – to guard his supply lines; and intended raiding far into enemy country, by-passing Dangeul and Ballon and Helias's other outposts, avoiding leaguers, fanning the fires of havoc till they scorched the walls of Mans. Belesme hoped that Helias, made desperate by devastation, would in the end be forced to offer battle – and be crushed by our greater numbers.

'Belesme's certainly an expert in harrying,' I ruminated, 'and raids are hard to counter unless you have forewarning. But a battle —!' I shook my head. 'Except for Gerberoi – which was only a rout – Neustria's knights have not seen a battle since the Conqueror went to Hastings.'

Which was truth. Warfare's nature had gradually changed since the lance-lines met head-on at Valesdunes. Defence, in the form of castles, blunted all attacks. You sallied out and did what damage you could; then scuttled inside your walls when the foeman came for revenge. War was raid and leaguer, the victor the man who lost the fewest castles.

Wind whipped smoke from the ovens; the banner above the battlements crackled like a greenwood fire. I glanced once more at Dangeul's louring bulk, and took Isabel below.

2

The raids began.

Belesme directed targets and diversions, sent guides to lead constabulars by devious hidden ways. From Christmas until Lent I rode the forest tracks at the head of ten-score warriors, penetrating deeper and deeper, descending on some helpless hamlet, scattering villeins and slaughtering kine. Day after day, week after week, the smoke from burning villages climbed above the forests.

Belesme insisted that we ran no risks which might result in losses. So whenever I saw an enemy helm I turned about and ran: the constabulars fled loose-reined till Saones' tower showed. Once, on our farthest irruption, Mans' turrets broke the horizon: we had come six leagues from Saones without seeing a hostile spear. During those winter weeks marauders went from Saones and from Mamers, from St Remi and Le Val, and met no more opposition than wandering patrols. The credit was Belesme's: he chose divergent routes, sent parallel raids and cunning feints, and directed every detail to the ultimate man-at-arms.

Helias had no answer; to counter our irruptions he needed luck or information: he seemed unequipped with either.

Until Lent.

I led my men at a swinging trot to a settlement east of Ballon – forty mounted bowmen and an Angevin constabular. We followed a track through trees, a drove road made by peasants. Outriders probed ahead; the column, in double files, trod fetlock-deep in the muffling mould a thousand autumns had shed.

Richer touched my rein hand. 'Someone in that coppice on our left.'

I saw a figure flitting through the trees, half hidden by boles and undergrowth. It fled across a grassy dell and plunged into bushes beyond – a tattered bearded creature, naked to the waist. 'A villein dispossessed,' I said, 'living wild in the forest. After all our harrying there must be a lot like him.' I looked at the sun. 'Near terce – we should be nearly there.'

We crossed a tongue of open ground between two forest tentacles

416

– a boggy, reed-speared patch; rank water splashed my face. I stared anxiously around: the open was always dangerous.

Richer said, 'There he is again.'

A man in a ragged tunic, glimpsed at a spinney's edge. 'Another hind,' I answered. 'Not the same. We move too fast for the rascal behind to pace us.' The figure dodged through saplings, keeping parallel to our course, and disappeared. I closed my legs on my destrier's flanks, and gratefully entered a woodland's shelter.

Twice more we spotted peasants lurking beside our course, running level awhile and vanishing like wraiths. Uneasily, not knowing why – villeins could not harm us – I sent a sergeant hunting when yet another showed. He rejoined the column panting, wiped blood from a cheek a bramble had torn and said, 'Lost him. I saw a second in the trees ahead. Why do villeins roam the forest in ones and twos?'

'Nothing to fret about,' I answered curtly – and was worried without knowing why. Anything odd in this perilous country made one nervous. We left the forest's valance, and started to cross a heathland slanting to a crest. The hamlet we had come to burn lay just beyond.

A sunken roadway cleft the heath, a trench that hedgerows fringed: hazel, briar and thorn. The outriders urged their horses through the hedge. I heard them shout; they tugged the reins and tried to turn. The roadway suddenly sprouted spears like rushes in a river.

Ambush!

I whirled my lance in the signal for turning about. Richer quickly arrayed his archers to cover our retreat. The column jostled and split apart, horses spun on their hocks. Knights and sergeants intermingled stampeded to the haven of the woodlands they had left.

Horsemen appeared from the trees on either flank. Their lances levelled. I swung my head from side to side, judging speed and distance. They would strike us before we gained the woods and ride us down like sheep.

I stood in my stirrups and yelled, and flourished my lance to the right where the enemy were nearest. A dozen or so of the bolting mercenaries attended my frantic shouts, and checked and wheeled their destriers. I gathered them fast in a jagged line and rode to meet the charge.

We barely had time to break to a gallop before the constabular hit us. The pace of the charge had disordered their line: we rode for the gaps and thrust as we closed. My point caught a knight on the nasal and gouged an eye from his head. The impact wrenched the lance from rest: I rammed the butt in a sergeant's face and groped for my hilt. A mace blow slammed my shoulder blades and drove the breath from my lungs. I crouched gasping over the horse's withers, and felt for my sword. A knight in a yellow helmet crashed into my destrier's quarters. He lifted his blade for a vertical slash, the edge nearly touching his spine. My neck was bent like a felon's awaiting the headsman's stroke.

The sword clanged my helmet and slithered harmlessly aside. A blade protruded from yellow-helmet's mouth like an elongated tongue, blood spurted between his teeth. Lisiard twisted his sword and tugged it free. He grabbed my rein. 'Out of this,' he grunted. 'Dig your spurs in deep.'

My destrier plunged at the kick; Lisiard hauled it to the nearest trees. A sergeant pursued us, brandishing his dirk. Lisiard turned and faced him, sword uplifted. He swerved and galloped off to look for easier prey. We stopped in a hollow brimmed with bushes.

Blearily I surveyed the rout.

From the sunken roadway footmen advanced at a run. Richer had left them, to deal with the knights who attacked from the left. His archers streamed across their front, shooting as they rode – too late to stop the charge from reaching our routed remnants. There was carnage on the heath, a slaughter of the fugitives, and furious little mellays where survivors stood and fought. I saw no quarter given: knights who yielded died.

Richer collected his scattered archers and led them to the woods, loosing arrows as they went. Not all escaped: chain-meshed figures clutching bowstaves grovelled in the heather.

'Rouse up, my lord!' said Lisiard. 'We'll be taken if we linger.'

We pounded through the forest's depths, a wilderness far from tracks, and used our swords to cut through matted undergrowth. We collected other survivors; many were wounded, and two fell dying from the saddle. Somewhere south of Saones we regained the track, and met Richer at the head of his troop, a bandage swathing his face. 'Only a scrape,' he said. 'I was lucky it wasn't worse. I reckon half our company is lost.' My back throbbed fiercely where the mace had struck; perhaps the arrow wound that Bamburgh gave me was re-opened. Miserably I wondered how Helias had known where to find us.

Ralph waited at the drawbridge. He scanned my depleted following; anxiety bulged the eyes that asked a wordless question.

'Ambush,' I said laconically. 'They knew exactly where and when we'd come.'

Ralph's face was the colour of dough. 'You too?' he wailed. 'Are there spies in Saones who give Helias forewarning? Robert of Courci —'

I said sharply, 'He led a parallel raid to Beaumont. Was he also trapped?'

'Yes. His retinue – what was left – came in an hour ago. Two ambuscades in a single day. How can they know?'

I left Ralph counting heads and totting up the losses; and found Courci in the donjon lugubriously examining a deeply dented helmet. 'Courci's smithy forges matchless steel,' he said, 'else my brains were larding a ditch in Maine!' Brown eyes twinkled cheerfully in a ruddy full-fleshed face. 'I hear you also met misfortune?'

'We were snared and routed. Tell me, my lord – did you see peasants along your line of march?'

Courci tossed the helmet to an esquire. 'Take it to an armourer, Guibert: tell him to flatten the dent.' He pressed a forefinger to a broken nose, and splayed the boneless gristle across his face. 'Now I come to think of it, we did – several. Wanderers we have rendered homeless. Thought nothing of it.'

'Ever noticed them before, on previous harryings?'

'Can't say I have.'

'That's it, then.' I wriggled my shoulders, trying to slake the pain. 'Helias has mobilized every villein in the countryside to track our companies and send him word. Henceforth we're going to find our raids expensive.'

3

So it proved. Helias had drawn an invisible frontier through Dangeul; beyond that line his peasants followed and observed us. Sooner or later the enemy lay in wait, lining hedgerows, guarding fords, manning the dangerous turns on forest tracks. Twice more I led marauders out, met ambuscades and fled. Other knights fared likewise: Ralph himself scraped home to Saones, reins flapping his destrier's neck, and left twenty liegemen dead. (Isabel rode on this escapade. Furiously I rated her; she laughed and swore she'd enjoyed nothing so much since unhorsing me at Medavi.)

In short, Black Robert's harriers were generally trapped and checked. We could have sent stronger detachments and fought it out; but that crossed Belesme's strategy: he wished to conserve his strength for the final battle. The issue depended on ruining Maine until Helias was driven to fight; now his devastated county stayed more or less inviolate.

Belesme came to Saones and called a council of war. His serenity was ruffled, the green eyes quick and restless, the lines from mouth to nostril deeply grooved. He said, 'My lords, the war is grinding to a stop. Moreover, day by day our losses mount; the enemy inflicts more casualties than we on him. We're losing the initiative – and must regain it.'

'Change your strategy,' said Ralph. 'We nibble Maine's demesnes, burn unimportant hamlets, all in the hope of bringing the count to battle. He won't be tempted. Why not gather all our men and march on Mans?'

Belesme looked at him scornfully. 'Leave Dangeul and Ballon un-taken in our rear? Leaguer Mans – while Helias ranges Maine unscathed? A ten-year-old esquire knows better the rules of war!'

Ralph flushed. 'A decision must be forced – time is no longer on our side. The countryside lies derelict, vines uprooted, corn unsown and cattle killed. Our foragers find nothing, and rations are running short.'

'True enough,' I said. 'Already the destriers live on hay – and the sutlers demand ten deniers to buy a quartern of oats.'

Courci said breezily, 'So we're heading for starvation, while Helias whittles our forces. Better ask Rufus to send us supplies and soldiers.'

'Better to bay the moon,' Belesme declared. 'The Vexin war fares badly; Rufus's hands are full. He's taken Roche Guyon; Count Robert gave him Meulan. And there his victories end. Chaumont and Pontoise stand; Prince Louis with five hundred knights harasses him unceasingly.'

A breeze from the open doorway swirled smoke around his face. Belesme coughed, and fanned his hands. 'We must get to the roots, my lords, and dig them out. Why is Helias winning? Because his intelligence learns our moves: that peasant swarm which tracks you in the forests. They must be . . . deterred.'

He joined his fingertips together, and propped them under his chin. 'These are your instructions. Send out your constabulars, attract the spies, capture them and then return to Saones. No more than that – no pressing into Maine and falling into ambuscades. When you have taken fifty – alive, you understand – then send me word.'

'Fifty!' I exclaimed. 'What's the use? Helias can set a thousand on our trails!'

Belesme rose from the chair. 'Fifty,' he said softly, 'will be enough.' His eyes were cold and cruel. 'Villeins are quite easily discouraged.'

4

The companies rode out: decoys to lure bondsmen, no longer bent on war. It was hard to take a quarry so elusive; we saw them often enough, but pursuing them in a wilderness they knew better than the animals proved wearisome and difficult. A dozen forays seized a dozen; we'd still be hunting at Christmas.

Richer proposed a solution. He split his mounted archers among different constabulars: the light and nimble horses moved handily through obstacles which defeated lumbering destriers and iron-mouthed sergeants' palfreys. At sight of a peasant spy they sped in chase to the woods, jinked like coursing hares between the trees and rode the fugitives down.

By Easter three-score hinds were crammed in Saones' vaults. Ralph sent word to Belesme.

Black Robert came to Saones, and descended to the chamber where our prisoners were packed so tightly they could neither sit nor lie. Delicately he pinched his nostrils: the stench was vile. 'Ten will make a beginning,' he observed. 'Bring them out.' Roped together wrist to wrist, the emaciated creatures were hauled to the ward and crouched blinking in the daylight. Belesme lazily examined them – a cat with a stricken prey.

'Send axemen to the woods. I want straight lance-length trunks, no thicker than your fingers can encompass. Birchwood saplings, I have found, answer the purpose best. And make ready a constabular: we shall soon be riding out.' When the spars were brought he bade carpenters strip the bark and adze the ends to points. Then they were bound in sheaves and carried by men-at-arms.

Belesme took the Dangeul road, the captives stumbling alongside, roped to a sergeant's stirrup. I wondered at his rashness: we avoided open highways on our forays into Maine. Black Robert hummed a tune, moving easily in the saddle, his hauberk smooth and taut as a panther's pelt. The enemy's trackers flitted among the trees; Dangeul's wooden tower loomed closer at every stride. I fiddled with my plastron, feeling naked and exposed.

Belesme halted the column. His hand made downward motions, and the men dismounted. The road snaked over grassland, and was ridged by tall earth banks. Ralph, nervous as I, rapidly despatched pickets to front and flanks and rear. Belesme surveyed the precautions, a twisted smile on his lips. 'This will do,' he said. 'An open place which none can miss. Plant the stakes.'

Sergeants plunged the spars in the banks, and forced them down till half their length was sunk. They set five each side of the road, with a five-pace gap between. Belesme strolled along them, testing their firmness. He crooked a finger.

'Bring the first.'

They dragged a villein to the roadside and stripped him naked. Belesme gave his orders, whispering under his breath. Two sergeants gripped the peasant's hips and hoisted him above a stake until his crotch was level with the tip. He bleated piteously, bewildered, still uncertain of his fate. A third man poised his anus above the barb. He pressed the heels of his hands on the buttocks, prised open the cleft between, carefully inserted the point.

Belesme smiled, and clapped his hands.

They hauled downwards on the wretch's thighs, and the stake pierced home to his bowels. He squirmed and coiled his legs around the pole, his head flung back, mouth gaping to the sky. His back was arched like a bowstave, he clawed both hands on his rump.

Belesme's tongue crept between his lips, and licked in turn the corners of his mouth.

One by one they impaled the peasants. A cacophony of agony shivered the sun-bright air. I felt the vomit rising, hastily loosed my ventail and retched between my legs. Ralph squatted on the ground, and mumbled to himself. Lisiard swayed on his shield, studying the roadway's ruts: I think he prayed. The men-at-arms stared silently, eyes round and faces strained. Our horses, scenting blood, sidled and stamped their feet.

The last was done, dragged moaning to his stake. The posts bore hideous burdens that uttered bestial noises. Belesme sighed deeply. His eyes were blank, unfocused; a sweat-bead coursed his cheek. He said dreamily, 'A present for Dangeul. Mount and away, before they arrive to admire the gift.'

On the journey back he woke from his trance and said, 'You have seen the remedy for our troubles. Take out the others: impale them on the roads to Ballon, Montbizot and Fresnai. The villeins will learn the cost of spying, Helias lose his watchers.'

We did as Black Robert commanded. In the end I observed it unmoved, hardened to the spectacle, reminding myself that these were bondsmen, hardly human kind. God is sometimes merciful, and blunts our sense of pity.

Within a week we rode unhindered, foraying into Maine.

5

Helias sent heralds to Belesme.

He offered battle on the plain between Dangeul and Saones, and promised to bring to his standard every spear he could command. Belesme counted on his fingers. 'Let me see. Helias has his mesnie, presently quartered in Mans; and those of Gaufrid of Mayenne, Ralph of Fresnai, Rotrou of Montfort. Several others – lesser barons. Two thousand at the most, and I can put four thousand in the field. Helias lays his head in the leopard's jaws.' He gave the heralds a courteous answer, and named the day of meeting.

Belesme stripped Mamers and Alençon of all but the minimum garrisons. The conroys converged on Saones; in the castle, already crammed, soldiers and horses and baggage were jammed tightly as grapes in a vat. Ralph extended the ward, and surrounded the whole with a rock-built rampart. The site included the village church, soon profaned by knights who quartered themselves inside. Mercenaries from Mamers speedily looted the village and raped the peasant wenches who had not already fled.

Prince Henry came from Domfront, leading thirty knights. There was a brash confidence about Henry, a touch of swagger in his bearing: the renewal of Rufus's trust had lent him new authority. He ejected the knights from the church, put his mesnie in their place, installed a bevy of bawds from his wagon train and conducted lurid orgies. The priest unwisely complained to Belesme – and was chained in the castle vaults.

Scouts sent to Dangeul's marches reported Helias mustering.

Belesme explored beyond the lake, and returned in thoughtful mood. 'There's a height there we must take,' he declared, 'else Helias will have an advantage. According to the terms agreed neither army marches before sunrise on the day. I think we must anticipate a little.' He called the barons to council and described his plans. Here I will not discuss them – they become apparent later. But while disposing retinues he relegated my archers to Henry's squadron in reserve.

Vehemently I protested.

'You don't understand their function, my lord. Mounted bowmen should harass the enemy before battle is joined.'

'Gadfly tactics,' Belesme said coldly, 'likely to provoke an attack, as happened indeed when you goaded my knights near Conches. Remember? No – I shall have the advantage in numbers and ground, and will do the attacking myself.'

'Then Richer will lead my mesnie. I'll stand in the line.'

'That's your affair,' Belesme observed dismissively.

I went to Ralph and asked leave for Lisiard and myself to fight beneath his banner. Bemusedly he agreed, his mind distracted by arrangements for the morrow – complicated problems always tied his brain in knots. I helped to contrive an order of march, and to fix a scale of rations. In the midst of devising the battle ranks I saw Isabel garbed in mail and listening attentively. I looked at her clinging hauberk, chain-meshed like my archers' armour.

'You are not,' I said incredulously, 'really intending to come?'

'I told you I was,' she said composedly. 'My mind is not easily changed.'

I turned furiously to Ralph. 'You must forbid this madness!'

Ralph squatted on his haunches, playing with pebbles in the dust. 'Bowmen in the lead, thus,' he muttered, altering a pebble's place, 'then Courci's knights, so . . .' He looked up. 'What's that? Isabel? You should know by now that when her mind is set all the hounds of hell won't turn her from her purpose. Save your breath, my lord. Now,' he murmured, returning to his stones, 'men-at-arms in the rearmost rank, like that . . .'

We marched at evening. A mellow sunlight washed the fields and hazed a glittering curtain on the dust of the army's passing. Behind wagon train and rearguard Saones' portals thudded shut; from battlements and ward the garrison anxiously watched our going: on our well-being theirs depended. The league-long column splashed through the rivulet's ford, tramped between the road banks where the villeins had been impaled – the bodies long since gone, taken by their friends – and mounted a gentle slope. On a rounded crest the vanguard halted; bannerets guided the conroys to left and right. Ralph's mesnie held the centre; Robert of Courci's men were mustered under his banner. We dismounted, sent the horses away to a coppice far in rear, trampled the lumpy grass-grown ground and examined the position.

Three thousand knights and men-at-arms, a broad and murmurous band of steel eight hundred paces long, stood on the top of a long low hump which ridged the plain like a frozen wave. The forest's tendrils touched the wings, a screen against outflanking. In rear, two bowshots distant, Belesme posted his reserves: separate mounted squadrons stationed behind the flanks, the right in Henry's keeping, the other in his own. We heard their hammers clinking as they picketed the horses. In front the land fell sharply to the forest before Dangeul: a red-cross banner, barely discernible, flapped on the donjon's battlements.

'A good place to defend,' Ralph considered. 'An assault must climb to find us, and the ground' – he waved a hand to the scrub-raddled slope – 'is nasty going for an uphill cavalry charge. Why does Belesme insist on attacking?'

'Downhill for us, to speed our onset – even if afoot. Otherwise . . .' I looked at Dangeul's donjon. 'I wonder what Helias thinks of our stolen march?'

We were not left long in doubt. A herald knight came galloping from the forest, brandishing a leaf-swathed lance to proclaim his peaceful errand. He reined in a flurry of dust in front of Ralph.

'Word from Helias Count of Maine for Robert Count of Belesme!'

'And here I am,' said Belesme, sauntering through the ranks. 'What irks my lord of Maine?'

'He says this. In marching before the day agreed you have broken your vow and disgraced your knighthood. He arraigns you for your perfidy!'

Belesme surveyed him balefully. 'I'm waging war, not playing at checkers. Would Helias have me recall my army – a piece moved out of turn? Tell your lord he may sleep in peace: my men will move no farther until he offers battle.'

The herald swept his helmet from his head. Flaxen hair lay flat on his skull, a purple birthmark blemished the side of a high-coloured, bony countenance. 'How shall Count Helias trust a perjurer's word? He'll at once array his army to watch you through the night! I am

Payn of Montdoubleau. Mark my face and blazon' – he fronted a painted shield – 'for tomorrow I shall seek you!'

A dust-plume trailed his going. 'If threats were swords,' Belesme said contemplatively, 'I'd have died long since.' He scanned Ralph's dispositions. 'Extend your right a trifle, my lord – there's a gap between you and the Bretons. We sleep where we are for the night; at cockcrow we advance.'

He strolled away. The sun was setting; shadows like indigo pools advanced from the forest's fringes; a gold and scarlet brilliance burned the sky. Noises carried clearly: a stallion's neigh from the horse-lines, the rhythmic clink of a farrier's maul, a water-cart's screeching axles bringing the casks from the springs. The sounds of a bivouacked army grumbled along the ridge: shouts and songs and laughter, the whisper and hiss of steel. Fires were glowing rubies pricking the dusk like stars; a hundred wavering spires of smoke speared the windless air.

The rhythm of marching warriors hammered from afar. A fading twilight lighted spears and helmets on the road which pierced the trees a thousand paces ahead. Sentinels shouted alarm: men stood and girded weapons; bannerets called orders and ranged the ranks in line. Pickets on the slopes below strung bows and nocked their arrows.

We waited tensely.

Helias's column left the road and marched parallel to our front. Their voices tinkled faintly, commands and oaths and yells. Maine's army formed array and settled for the night, a dark and menacing mass five hundred paces away. Our companies returned to scrape the cooking-pots, and find hollows on the stony ridge for sleeping.

Ralph tore a hunk of salted pork and stuffed it in his mouth.

'Helias's counter-measure – he doesn't trust Belesme a bowstring's breadth. Stupid, really – nobody fights at night. Where's my cloak? – it's cold now the sun is down.'

I chewed the stringy mutton that Berlai cooked – he was more adroit with armour than a skillet. Roger chattered excitedly, full of zest and nervousness in prospect of his battle. Firelight flushed the lean young face, struck sparks from the deep-set eyes. I looked upon him lovingly, and spoke severely. 'You'll fight on my left – my shield will guard your open side. And keep in rank – knights who lose their dressing leave openings for swords. Be wary of the spearmen; their reach is longer than yours.'

He tucked his hands between his knees to hide a tremor. I tried to remember how I felt when first I faced an enemy. Where was it? Holy Saints! – this very place, twenty-two years ago, when I struck down Viger of Dangeul and took his horse and armour. I could not recall my feelings, cicatrized by endless fighting since.

Courage in battle, I reflected, was simply a matter of habit.

We sprawled round the dying fire, and talked of anything but the morrow. Stars studded a blue-black vault; moondawn lifted a burnished shield behind Dangeul's stark black tower. Ralph stretched his arms. 'Time for sleep.' He rolled himself in his cloak beneath a stunted thorn bush, and soon was snoring. Roger lay on his back and stared at the stars. 'Close your eyes,' I told him softly, 'think of running water, count the ripples as they pass.'

I stretched myself beside Isabel, flung my cloak across us both and took her in my arms. Her body moulded mine; the mail rings clinked and scraped. After a time her limbs relaxed. I dozed restlessly, in fits and starts.

I was wakened by Isabel's shivering. I raised myself on an elbow, and peered into her face. She clung and spoke in my ear, a whisper faint as a lisp of leaves. 'A hideous dream! I'm frightened, Walter, tortured by foreboding. There was so much . . . blood. Dead faces that I knew.' She clutched me fiercely. 'Take me, sweetling, take me *now*! Evil marches with the dawn, and dawn is very near.'

I looked cautiously around. Moonlight sprinkled silvered dust on recumbent bodies lying in rows like a battle-line felled by spears. A sergeant threshed an arm and shouted in his sleep; the conroy's sentinel crouched on his spear and crooned a song to himself.

I rearranged the cloak.

Swiving, clad in armour, is a complicated business – but it can be done.

6

Berlai roused me at dawn, gave me a leather cup and a wheaten biscuit. Isabel had gone in the darkness. All around me half-seen figures stamped their feet and buckled on mail, hawking and coughing and spitting. The moon had set; the stars were cooling embers that faded, blinked and died; a sheen like rust-streaked iron smeared the eastern sky.

Ralph's face was grey in the dawnlight, his eyes were sad and haunted.

'I heard you.'

There was nothing to say. I stared across his shoulder to the enemy lines, a black welt scarring the shadows, where torches flared and faraway voices murmured. I swallowed my food, the crumbs rough in my gullet, and poured the wine-cup's dregs on the grass.

'To the uttermost end you've spared me no dishonour.' He spoke calmly, without emphasis, like a priest reciting a litany. 'Through all the years you've trodden my name in the mud, losing never a chance to nail more antlers on my horns. In field and hall and bower you've rutted with my lady. And now, on the eve of battle —!' He peered into my face, as if seeking there the solving of a puzzle. 'Are you all filthiness and lust? Have you no decency at all?'

From Dangeul's donjon a trumpet wailed, a muted moan remote as a prayer from hell. I said, 'Always you've possessed a remedy for your troubles.' My finger touched the pommel of his sword. 'Has it rusted in the scabbard all these years? You won't show me the point – why not turn it on yourself?'

Tears glistened in Ralph's eyes. His hands opened in a blindfold gesture, and he blundered away. Berlai waited patiently to arm me. He re-threaded the hauberk thongs and pulled them tight, tested cross-straps in my helmet's crown, fitted it on my head, nasal exactly central, laced the coif and buckled the ventail over my chin. He wrapped bull-hide straps around my forearms and knotted the tapes, draped baldric over my shoulder, settled the sword hilt snugly against my hip. I discarded the shield-guige, a hindrance when you fought on foot.

A bronze and saffron splendour flared from a hidden sun, kindled the dew-gemmed grass and sluiced a roseate flood on the plain that sloped to the enemy. Barons and bannerets ordered their arrays, hurried along the lines, pushed soldiers into place. Servants and sutlers swarmed to the rear, ox-carts lurched on the humpy ground and drovers flailed their whips – they would not pause before Saones' gates. Bowmen braced their staves, ran fletchings through their fingers, smoothed the feathers precisely and tested points on thumbs.

Ralph was lost to his duties, leaning on his shield, eyes brooding into the distance. With Robert of Courci I checked our mesnies: knights in the foremost rank, sergeants in the second; leather-clad, iron-capped men-at-arms were marshalled in the third. Esquires lurked in rear; their business not to fight but to save their masters' skins. In front of all the bowmen stood in little groups from wing to wing.

I patted Roger's shoulder, and tongued his baldric three holes tighter. 'Who's your esquire, lad? – the oaf doesn't know his job!' He gulped and tried to smile.

Isabel's face was pale beneath the tan. I scanned the chain-mesh hauberk that embraced her slender body, mistrusting the armour's temper despite evidence proved by my archers. Her shield was light, a single hide, suited to her strength. Under-armoured and poorly armed, I concluded sourly: I'd have to protect my lady as well as defend myself.

The sun rose over the treetops; clouds like milky smoke-puffs drifted across the sky. High time we moved – else Helias might fore-stall us. I took my place in the ranks. On our left was Waci's mesnie, on the right a Breton conroy. Hugging the ridge's ground-swells, the battle-line beyond them curved like an iron-scaled reptile. A hundred paces behind each wing the cavalry squadrons mustered: Prince Henry's scarlet banner and Black Robert's sable guidon. Maine's order resembled ours: a long dismounted battle line with cavalry guarding the flanks. Such was the pattern for set encounters – no captain until Henry, at Tinchebrai eight years later, ventured to disturb it.

Belesme and a brace of knights, the sole horsemen on the ridge, came riding down the ranks. He stopped and shaded his eyes.

'Maine's sheep await our shearing. Advance the bowmen!'

Archers trickled down the slope and halted just in bowshot of the enemy. Helias's bowmen marched towards us, gained their range and stopped. The movements were a prelude, like the opening steps of a ritual dance. We nuzzled our shields and cowered.

Arrows whirred and thumped in hide, somebody shrieked and fell. Belesme sat his horse like a graven rock, shield dangling on the guige. A barb nicked his destrier's stifle, the stallion shied and reared. Impatiently he curbed it, drew sword and held it high.

Swords rasped from a thousand scabbards in a thousand glittering arcs.

'Ralph!' I called urgently. 'Take your place!'

Like a man in a dream he entered the ranks and stood on his lady's right. Belesme whirled his blade in a circle, and the trumpets shouted again.

Roger was at my shield arm, Isabel brushed my sword. We tramped down the slope to test the might of Maine.

Gorse and elder stippled the ground and disordered the ranks. The unwieldy battle-line eddied and bulged like a wave that was spent on a shelving beach. The enemy bowmen retreated, skipped for shelter in their line, knelt behind the front rank's legs and went on shooting. The shafts did little damage: provided you fronted your shield and kept your head well down you were fairly safe.

The Welshmen's murderous arrows – God be thanked – remained in Wales.

I rested sword on shoulder, and began to sweat. Walking in armour is uncomfortable work. I glanced at my flankers. Roger's face was white and set, a muscle quivered in his jaw. Her targe hid all but Isabel's eyes, narrowed against the sun. Ralph wore a rapt expression, like a martyr going to the stake, his shield at a slovenly angle, exposing most of his body. I reached my sword and tapped the hide to waken him. He took no notice.

We covered half the distance, and saw the enemy clear: a palisade of painted shields topped by pointed helmets. Among the motley devices – saltires and serpents, chevrons and bars – were scarlet crosses on white, the pilgrim's blazon Helias's mesnie flaunted. The line was still as a granite cliff, and sword-blades peeped from the shields.

'Close in! Close in! Close on the centre!'

Bannerets shouted and waved their swords, striving to order the ranks. Arrows smacked on hide like the patter of hail on thatch.

The Bretons, flayed beyond bearing, broke from the line and charged; and we hurled ourselves at the foe.

Hurled? Indeed I brag a little – the years embroider memory. You can't sprint far in armour with a shield across your body. In fact we went at a shambling trot, and some of us tripped and fell. Perhaps eagerness blinded these knights to the boulders, perhaps they stumbled on nothing. Courage is a variable virtue. For myself, I edged right-handed as I ran, swung an arm across Isabel's nasal and strenuously thrust her back. I heard a furious squawk.

Then we crashed the shield-wall.

They gave before the brunt; and sergeants in the second rank pressed targes on knightly backs. I clashed the shield of a knight in a chequered helmet, shoved myself away and swung my sword. He warded thwartwise, lunged as the blades glissaded. I caught the point on forte, reversed and smashed the pommel in his face. The nasal saved him; he spat out broken teeth and thrust at my throat. I deflected on the quillons, switched parry into cut, scraped the patchwork helmet. He grimaced through a mask of blood, and backed beyond reach.

I looked quickly to right and left.

The battle-line was broken into individual duels. Knights hacked at one another like woodmen hewing trees. The battle's diapason was the din of a hundred smithies, a crazy metallic clanging underscored by human voices: sergeants' encouraging barks and knights' diminishing war-cries – men wrapped in mortal combat need all their breath for fighting.

Roger bravely held his own, exchanging cut and parry with a ponderous, bow-legged knight who wheezed like a punctured bellows. Isabel leapt into line beside me, twirling her silly sword; I swung my shield and promptly hurled her back. Ralph fought in silent fury, straddling a fallen knight, his sword a darting lightning-flash that scorched his opponents' ears. Even as I watched his adversary ran.

The series of single combats, like water-drops running together, coalesced in whirling mellays. I bartered blows with a band-mailed knight who swung an axe at my head. I ducked the slash; he lifted the haft for a vertical cut and I rammed my point in his armpit. The sweat ran down my body, my sword arm ached from fingertips to shoulder. Here and there the fighters drew apart and rested panting on their swords.

Our main attack was checked, the enemy still unbroken. Where in Christ's name was the cavalry?

They arrived on the thought – and were not our own. A torrent of pennoned lances fell like a steel-tipped avalanche on the battle-line's rearmost ranks. The neighing of maddened stallions blared a new note in the tumult. I saw horsemen straight behind me, spearing our men-at-arms, and tottered back to help them.

The clamour and the turmoil spoke disaster. So thought the Breton mercenaries: they turned and fled. Where the fight had raged on our mesnie's right was a trampled grassy gap; horsemen began to fill the space and batter the open flank.

Time to go. Where was Belesme's cavalry, where Prince Henry's squadron?

I seized Robert of Courci's arm and shouted in his ear. 'Disengage! Form a ring! Withdraw!' He wiped a sweating face and bawled

431

orders. I ran from man to man, yelling above the noise, clawed at armoured bodies and shoved them into place. Slowly we formed an irregular oval, knights on the outer ring.

Step by step we backed from the fight.

For the span of a hundred paces we were almost unmolested. Maine's battle line, I think, was thankful to see us go. Individual riders came and prodded at our shields; jadedly we beat them off. I had time to look about and seek my friends. Isabel's chain-mesh moved at the rim, Roger on her sword hand. Ralph was a little apart, between Robert of Courci and Lisiard. I slipped through the crowded men-at-arms and stood at Isabel's side. She looked at me defiantly, daring me to move her. I forced a smile.

'You may stay in line. We need every sword we have.'

Everywhere along the front our conroys retreated, some in orderly formation and others fleeing in rout. Only on the left the fighting raged unchecked; Maine's cavalry ringed our mesnies there and stabbed and hacked and killed.

They were fully engaged and occupied, a target for surprise.

Where was Belesme?

He came down the hill like a river in spate at the head of ten-score spears. Destriers stretched their necks and raced, lances swooped and levelled. The squadron crashed on the left flank battle and shattered it in shards.

'Late – but effective,' I grunted. 'Now for Henry's constabulars, and we may beat Helias yet.'

I looked to the ridge where we mustered at dawn – it seemed an aeon ago. Henry's horse had advanced to the crest, blazoned shields and steel in line, pennons alive in the wind.

'What's he waiting for?' Lisiard asked plaintively.

A constabular circled our flank, cutting our retreat, formed line and charged. The onset slithered to a halt – few destriers can be made to ride down shields – and lances thrust and swords descended.

We held them for a while, but the mellay attracted knights who had broken our right and roved the field in pursuit. The orb was soon surrounded, and we fought to stay alive. They charged, withdrew, and charged again. A mace blow snapped my sword; I groped in the dust and found an axe and cleft a destrier's poll. Exhaustion trembled my legs, the axe was a tree in my hands; my movements were slow, like a tired old man. The ring contracted, shedding bodies at the edges like an onion peeling skin.

We were hopelessly embayed; the end was not far off.

A knight rode out from the mob around us, lifted his lance and called. 'You are lost, my lords! Will you yield?' I scanned his eagle blazon – Payn of Montdoubleau, who had brought Helias's defiance.

Ralph made a noise in his throat, a prayer that died on a sob. He stumbled forward, sword on shoulder, shield-point trailing the ground. Payn thought him a herald, and slanted his lance athwart his horse's withers and warily watched him approach.

Ralph halted, lifted his sword and slashed the destrier's neck. He loosed the hilt and stood, arms dangling by his sides, shield wide, and braced his shoulders.

Payn said something savage, swiftly recovered his lance and speared him through the chest.

Roger shouted and broke from the ranks. I tried to grab him and missed, and ran calling in his wake. The knight saw a second attacker, released the embedded lance and whipped his sword from the scabbard.

He met my son head-on and cut him to the breastbone.

I cannot recall what happened next. Lisiard described, long after, how I dropped my shield and leapt at Payn and dragged him from the saddle. How I lifted the axe and cleft his skull, seared head from neck, sliced the body, blow after blow, till the ribs were mashed in the entrails. How he and Berlai dragged me raving like a maniac to the shelter of our shields.

I remember Isabel's face, the anguish in her eyes.

The lances closed again. I poised my dripping axe and waited numbly for the finish.

From Prince Henry's stagnant squadron flowed a silvery stream of horsemen which split into separate galloping jets and lapped our enemies' backs. Bowstrings thrummed and arrows whipped, destriers folded like pole-axed steers and ploughed to the ground in volleys of dust. The knights who hacked our shield-wall turned and bolted. Chain-meshed bowmen circled the orb, called my name and the name of Conches, rode close to the weary survivors.

A skewbald palfrey knocked me staggering. 'Quick, my lord!' said Richer.

I gathered the shreds of my strength and threw Isabel over his cantle. Richer cursed in the tongue of his race, pricked the horse and fled. A bowman dismounted beside me, heaved me to the saddle and jumped upon the crupper. 'You steer, my lord!' cried Pigot. 'I'll get this sluggard moving.' He beat bowstave on the palfrey's ribs; I turned his head to the ridge.

They saved a dozen knights and esquires, Berlai and Courci among them. Rescuers and rescued paused on the crest and viewed the vista of defeat. Helias's battle line advanced on lingering knots of resistance harried by his knights. Belesme's cavalry had vanished, carrying all before them, hunting their antagonists through and beyond the forest. (Later I was told they galloped around Dangeul, exchanging futile insults with the soldiers on the ramparts.) On the ridge's shoulder Henry's squadron lingered, bannerols fluttering proudly, a hollow, wasted vaunt.

They turned and trotted calmly from the field.

'Either imbecile or craven,' Richer said. 'His barons urged an onset when they saw the Bretons break. He sat his horse and answered never a word.'

My throat was parched, my tongue like gritty wool. 'Yet you came to our help,' I mumbled.

'I saw you overwhelmed, and left unbidden.' Richer smiled crookedly. 'You'll have to avert the prince's wrath. Come, my lord, we cannot dawdle here.' He pointed to the battlefield: enemy bannerets gathered their men and approached the ridge. 'They're mounting a pursuit.'

He spoke to Isabel over his shoulder. 'We're making for the trees. Hold tight, my lady, and beware the branches.'

We cantered from the ridge. Nearly half the horses carried double burdens and wandered in their stride; the pace was slow. Before the forest hid us there were helmets on the skyline.

8

We crossed a grassy glade and heard riders thudding through the woods behind us. Pigot thrashed his bowstave on the palfrey's flanks. The horse shuddered, bore on the bit and faltered to a trot.

I reined and fell from the saddle.

'Richer!' I croaked. 'Dismount the men who ride discumbered, and send the others on. We'll set an ambush here at the edge of the trees.'

Richer's orders crackled. He jumped from the horse, put Isabel in the saddle, the reins in her hands. Her eyes were blank and empty beneath the helmet. 'Wake up, lady!' Richer snapped. He turned fiercely on Pigot. 'Who told you to dismount? Escort the Lady Isabel and take her safe to Saones!'

Pigot looked at my empty scabbard, thrust bow and quiver in my hands. 'You'll need these, my lord. Straight shooting and good fortune!' He wheeled his palfrey and pounded after his charge.

We left the horses hidden in scrub – they were trained to stand – and lay flat in a bracken screen which fringed the glade. I fumbled nock to string, my fingers stiff and clumsy. Voices called from the woods in front, and horsemen burst from the trees.

Eight of them, all knights. They extended in the open, and spurred their horses faster. The leader wore a scarlet cross in splendour on his shield, and shrilled a huntsman's holla. Richer let them come within forty paces.

'Now!'

I stood and flexed and loosed, whipped arrow from quiver and nocked and flexed and loosed. The strings of twenty bowstaves twanged; threescore shafts had gone before your heart beat thrice. Destriers tumbled and riders sprawled on the grass. Only two survived the tempest, wrenched their reins and fled.

The red cross knight lay prone, winded and crying for breath. Another moaned and clawed his face; an arrow skewered his jaw. The rest closed shoulder to shoulder, sword in hand. We stepped from hiding, made an arc around them, arrows nocked and strings at stretch.

'Throw down your swords,' I called.

They hesitated, glowering defiance.

'Loose!' I said to a bowman at my side.

An eyeball bristled a feathered shaft; the knight crumpled where he stood and died without a sound.

'Your swords.'

They let the weapons fall. A knight in jazerant armour gestured to the gasping figure on the ground. 'I am Hervi of Montfort, standard bearer to my lord. I may not leave him thus.'

'Your lord?'

'Helias Count of Maine.'

The breath whistled through my teeth. I went quickly to the red cross knight, turned him over, ripped the helmet from his head. A square-jawed, swarthy face, a mace wound scarring his cheek. Helias indeed – a prize to snatch salvation from disaster. I faced his knights.

'Your parole, my lords, on promise of ransom. Otherwise —' I pointed to the archers, bowstrings drawn to their ears.

Sullenly they yielded. Hervi lifted Helias to horse, and held him in the saddle. We hustled through the woods, our speed reduced by the prisoners trotting alongside.

No one else pursued us. Saones' bells were tolling sext when we thankfully passed the gates.

Helias was shaken by his fall, but otherwise unhurt. I made him comfortable in the hall, told an esquire to strip his armour, and gave him meat and wine. Tentatively, a smile wrinkling his leathery features, he suggested I release him for two thousand deniers' ransom. I laughed without amusement.

'Your capture is worth a county, my lord – as you know well. Who can hold Maine against Rufus now that you are taken?'

I discovered Isabel in an empty stable, with Berlai in attendance. She stared fixedly at nothing, and shook all over. I forced wine between her lips; her teeth chattered on the cup. She looked at me 'Sin,' she mouthed. 'The wages of sin.'

I shook my love by the shoulders; her head wagged drunkenly, the tears fell ever faster. 'God has taken vengeance, and damned my soul to hell.'

I laid her on a heap of straw, spread a cloak on her shivering body, left Berlai on watch and plodded to the ramparts.

All afternoon the debris of defeat trickled into Saones. Henry had arrived long since; shouts and drunken laughter racketed from the church. At none Belesme rode in, his ivory face a coldly furious mask. I went to his stirrup and told him Helias was taken. The anger fled from his eyes; he gazed at me in wonder.

'Belly of God!' he breathed. 'We've won after all!'

At evening the army of Maine marched up, clamoured around the walls, sent a herald demanding surrender on pain of a forceful leaguer and no quarter when they stormed. Belesme put a halter round Helias's neck – courteously asking pardon for the inconvenience – and led the count to a watch-tower beside the gate. The rope was tied to a beam; Belesme lounged beside his captive, a friendly arm about his shoulders, ready to nudge him into eternity. Helias stood unflinchingly, and smiled at his wrathful liegemen. But the argument was conclusive, and the enemy marched away.

Wagons left at dawn to scour corpses from the battlefield, and returned with what was left of Ralph and Roger, the bodies stripped

by pillagers and naked. I could not bear to put them in the churchyard Henry's men defiled; and found a quiet place beneath a lime
tree near the lake. Here I buried, side by side, my son and the man
I had wronged. I strewed rose petals on the mound, and stood for a
long time thinking dead-dark thoughts.

Lisiard touched my arm and led me away.

I had not told Isabel. She lay in the stable, mumbling to herself
and fingering a rosary.

Chapter 10

1098–99

Four days later I took the road for Rouen.

The war in Maine was finished; with Helias taken his liegemen had nothing to fight for, and his barons and knights began dispersing to their homes, leaving garrisons in Mans and the outlying castles. Belesme briefly considered an invasion, eyed his shaken forces and rejected the idea: Mans was a nut too tough to crack unaided. He tried persuading Helias to order the town's surrender, and backed his arguments with threats of torture. The count smilingly refused. 'I don't fear your menaces, my lord of Belesme,' he said. 'You would never dare to harm a prize so valuable to Rufus.'

Belesme scowled; and ordered me to escort Helias to Rouen, taking Conches's leaderless mesnie as an extra guard.

I was glad to leave Saones and its memories of defeat and bitter loss. We went slowly, at the footmen's pace, baggage carts creaking behind, and marched no more than four leagues in the day – golden days, sun-drenched from dawn till dusk, summer's livery clothing the trees, the sky at night a maze of glittering stars. I rode at Helias's side, and found him a pleasant companion, his outlook strangely simple for a man whose ambitions aspired to ruling Maine. He believed himself the county's rightful lord, and explained at length why this was so, asserting his twofold connection with Herbert Wake-dog and the old Counts of Maine, and his purchase of the county from the unpopular Hugh of Este.

'But the king has me in his hands, and Maine's independence is coming to an end.' Thoughtfully he stroked his palfrey's mane. 'Will Rufus kill me, do you think?'

I was shocked. 'Never, my lord! Christendom holds no knight more honourable, none more valiant to defend the codes of courtoisie. You must not judge the king by Belesme, who will gladly forgo ransoms for the fun of tormenting his prisoners. You'll be decently treated, as befitting your rank; although, naturally, held in some restraint, perhaps banished to England or sent on the crusade to which you're sworn.'

'In knightly conduct Rufus owns a stainless reputation,' Helias agreed, 'yet men do peculiar things when counties are at stake; and his temper is, to say the least, uncertain. Well, we shall see.' A pheasant whirred from a wayside bush and made his palfrey shy; skilfully he gentled it. 'Talking of the crusade, have you heard if Antioch is still besieged?'

We discoursed affably while the sun-bleached road slid away beneath our hooves. Helias presented no problem; he had given his parole and, being the man he was, would not dream of trying to escape.

Isabel was another matter.

The valorous lady who had led her knights to war was now carried in a curtained litter borne by varlets: the first time, I was certain, she had ever travelled thus. From the rabble of bawds and trollops who followed the troops to Saones I had picked two hags of the better sort, bade them wait upon my lady, and put Berlai in charge. Isabel was recovered from the palsy that afflicted her at Saones, no longer lay for hours, staring-eyed and trembling, and spoke sensibly to her attendants and took the food and drink they gave her. She was not sick in body, but something had happened to her mind: a remote abstraction encased her like an invisible sheet of ice. I tried to penetrate the barrier, spoke to her often, avoiding mention of those I had buried by the lake, and strove to arouse her interest in happenings on the march, during peaceful interludes while we camped at night and men-at-arms sang songs around the fires. She answered civilly, as to a stranger making polite conversation. She left the litter only for calls of nature, and a little exercise at evening, accompanied by her women and the watchful Berlai, and travelled always with the curtains drawn.

Once in desperation I took her hand; she did not try to resist; her fingers rested coldly in my palm and her face remained expressionless as an image carved above a minster's portal. Shaken, I released her; the hand I had relinquished returned to the rosary lying always on her breast.

There were silver streaks in her hair, and shadows dark as night beneath her eyes.

Prince Henry, with Clare and a bevy of knights, overtook us on Mortagne's outskirts. They were travelling fast; Henry paused only to exchange greetings with my distinguished prisoner, sent me a

439

hostile look, and passed on. 'He's going to make excuses to his brother,' I remarked bitterly, 'before another version of his conduct reaches Rouen. Why didn't he advance? I've seen Henry twice in battle, and believe him craven. His conroys arrived late in Domfront's taking; when eventually they attacked he loitered in the rear. Never have I seen a man so determined to stay alive.'

Helias made deprecating noises. 'I don't know your prince; but surely one of the Conqueror's blood would never flinch from steel?'

'How else can you account for his behaviour?' I wrapped a scarf around my mouth; a dust-pall raised by Henry's retinue shrouded the road ahead. 'I grant you he's inherited all Duke William's other attributes: he's cunning, ruthless, unscrupulous and cruel. And of late,' I added contemptuously, 'the prince has become a notable lecher, wielding his prick more readily than his sword.'

Our journeying was undisturbed, the way peaceful as a lane in southern England; and I consigned my hauberk to a baggage cart. Many quarrelsome neighbours had gone to Outremer, and Rufus's forceful measures had all but quelled private warfare; so villeins were leaving the forests whence they preyed on unarmed travellers and were returning to nettle-grown fields and ruined huts. We saw ploughs at work on earth unfurrowed since the Conqueror died; and villages rebuilding where none had lived for a decade. The swathe of Rufus's armies marching to the Vexin cut well to the north, beyond Seine; and in any case he would permit no pillaging within Normandy, whatever havoc he might wreak on Philip's marches.

It was difficult to remember that hardly ten leagues south the land was devastation and men rode sword in hand.

On the fourth day we reached Breteuil. Lord William, that hairy, irascible knight who years before had shared with me Moulicent's sacking, was somewhere in the Vexin fighting Louis. His castellan received us courteously and offered quarters in the castle. I was stabling the horses when Berlai told me Isabel wanted speech.

She lay on a pallet in the bower, surrounded by Breteuil's ladies, who fussed about with simples and nauseous possets.

'You sent for me, my lady?'

'I go no farther, Walter.' Her lips barely moved on the words.

I thought her overcome by the journey's rigours, and spoke coaxingly. 'Conches is only a half day's march ahead. Rest here awhile, if you wish, until you've recovered your strength.' In a wan attempt at jesting I added, 'The delay won't matter – Helias, I am sure, is in no great hurry to meet Rufus.'

'I shall never return to Conches.'

I looked at her haunted face, the eyes fixed on the rafters. 'Then where, my lady? You cannot stay here for ever.'

'I can. There is a convent of nuns at Breteuil.'

Her wits, I decided, were wandering. The women stood agog, ears pricked like inquisitive cows. Brusquely, lacking courtesy, I ushered them from the room, slammed the door and returned to Isabel's bed. 'Whatever foolishness is this? Nuns can care for you no better than your people at Conches, restore your health no sooner.' I purposely spoke sharply, trying to break that cold indifference of despair.

'My body no longer matters – a corrupt and lustful carcase fit only for the crows. In a House of God my soul may find salvation and my sins in time be purged.'

I still did not realize her meaning. 'Then summon a priest, confess and endure his penance, and so find absolution.'

Isabel slowly turned her head. I recoiled from the agony in her eyes. 'Don't you understand?' she whispered. 'God's wrath has punished me for a lifetime's wanton sinfulness, for harlotry and cruelty and killing. My lord and my son are dead, taken to requite my wickedness, a penalty I must endure all my life, a burden I cannot support alone, unaided by the mercy our Saviour affords to sinners.'

'Surely this retribution – if you so regard it – is more than enough to purge a world of vice? Your debts are paid!'

'It is no more than a warning, Heaven's final ultimatum. Unless I mend my ways and turn to God the remorse I must bear throughout my earthly days will be gaiety and joy beside the torments my soul will suffer in hell's everlasting fires.' Tears welled in her eyes. 'I cannot bear it, Walter. I must renounce the world.'

At last I understood. 'You will enter this nunnery?' I asked incredulously.

Isabel nodded weakly. 'I beg you, Walter, send for the lady abbess, so that I may persuade her.'

I cannot remember exactly what I said. On my knees beside the pallet I besought her to change her mind, recalled that she had other sons to carry on Ralph's name, boys who needed a mother's guidance, and a castle wanting a chatelaine. I ranted like a madman, blasphemed against a vengeful God who demanded such reprisals, and assured her His ghastly revenge had already purged her sins.

Isabel lay still as a corpse, eyes closed, tears trickling down her temples. In the end I dropped head in hands, and tried to stifle my sobs.

The room was very quiet; a caged linnet by the window uttered little twittering cries.

I felt a touch on my hair. Isabel said softly, 'Summon the abbess, Walter.'

I stumbled to the door, turned with my hand on the latch and looked for the last time on my love. A smile flickered on her lips; compassion lingered like a fading spark in the wide dark eyes.

'Farewell . . . beloved.'

The words were faint as a rustle of leaves – and to this day ring like clarions in my head.

2

The abbess at Breteuil willingly received a high-born, wealthy novice who shed lustre and lucre both upon her convent. Count Helias therefore found me a morose companion during the three-day march to Rouen. A considerate man, and fundamentally gentle, he respected my league-long silences, never mentioned women, and discoursed on hawks and hunting. He knew well the cause of my misery: the stormy history of my love for Isabel of Conches was notorious throughout Neustria, had even been set to verse and sung in castle halls by wandering trouvères. And the news that the wanton, warlike Isabel, repenting of her wrongdoings, had resolved to take the veil provided a resounding epilogue.

Isabel was gone, and a twenty-year chapter in my life had closed.

A league from Rouen I sent outriders to warn the castellan that Helias of La Flèche was on his way. Consequently, after crossing St Sever's bridge, people crammed the streets, all eager to behold the rebel count who had routed Normandy's army; knights and men-at-arms and servants thronged the castle ward. Helias bore himself proudly, his lanky frame erect in the saddle, and stared haughtily ahead. Only a severed muscle that quivered in the mace scar on his cheek betrayed his stress.

I had imagined the king to be warring in the Vexin, and almost fell from my horse in surprise when I saw the familiar thickset figure standing hands on hips before the donjon's portal. The scarlet face looked fierce; sunlight spun a flaming halo around the yellow hair. I led my prisoner up the mound, and bent my knee. Rufus offered me a friendly hand, but never took his eyes from Helias. The count made no obeisance, and met the king's glare with a slight smile on his lips.

'I have you, my lord!' said Rufus.

'I lie at your mercy, sire,' Helias agreed amiably.

Rufus's mouth trembled in the stammer that betokened a royal rage. I felt a stab of fear, and glanced uneasily at the gallows that reared beyond the ramparts. Knowing the king so jealous of his honour I had assured Helias his life was safe – but Rufus in a fury was often unpredictable.

Incredibly he smiled, and clapped both hands on his captive's shoulders.

'I hear you gave Belesme the thrashing of his life, and that against greater odds. Come inside, my lord; take a cup of wine and tell me how you did it! You too, Walter, so I'll have the losers' version!'

The hall was thronged, all the lords were there: Meulan and fitzHamon, Evreux and Breteuil. Prince Henry perched on a table, twiddling a wine cup in his fingers, whispering to Clare. Rufus sat Helias in a place of honour beside him, commanded goblets to be filled and offered honeyed figs. 'You're my prisoner, of course,' he told the count cheerfully, 'and there's no question of ransom, so your stay will be prolonged. Still, it's unnecessary to make you uncomfortable. Presumably I have your parole? Good! Then you'll have a pleasant chamber next the bower with no more than a sentry at the door – just for form's sake.'

I left them talking, and edged through the crowd to Meulan, who listened dourly to something fitzHamon said. I gestured to the teeming hall.

'Why are the lords of the Vexin army gathered in Rouen? Have you won the war?'

Meulan snorted. 'Far from it. We failed to take Pontoise and got a bloody nose at Chaumont – the garrison's bowmen sallied and dismounted thirty-score knights. Aimed at the horses, killed the lot. Copying your archers' methods, Walter. Very effective.' He rubbed his greying stubble. 'Now we've withdrawn to lick our wounds and wonder what to do next.'

'I wouldn't have thought King Philip so resolute a captain.'

'Philip? France's barons won't follow an excommunicated king. He's had nothing to do with it. Lives in Paris with his whore Bertrada. No – it's that son of his, Louis, who directed the campaign. He wages war like an outlaw chieftain: sudden raids and quick retreats. They say he leads a mere five hundred knights. I don't believe it!'

'I suppose,' said fitzHamon lightly, 'he'll boast until his deathbed of how he vanquished Rufus, the paladin of our age.'

'The king will try again,' Meulan asserted. 'Now Helias is taken he can use the army in Maine. What really happened in that disastrous battle near Saones, Walter? We've heard Henry's tale, beautifully slanted to account for his constabulars alone escaping intact. What's the truth?'

I described the fight in detail, sparing nothing of Henry's inertia, though careful not to hint the cause was cowardice. fitzHamon stroked the arrow scar seaming his jaw.

'Yes,' he murmured. 'Rather different. According to Henry, he saw your battle-line broken and surrounded, Belesme's cavalry gone helter-skelter in a futile charge, and pulled his squadron from the field barely in time to avoid destruction. Whereas if he'd charged with Belesme you might have won the day. *Very* different.'

'He got his story in first,' Meulan snapped, 'and convinced Rufus it's the truth: an astute captain saving his troops to fight another day. The king has restored to him Coutances and Avranches, and made him Count of the Cotentin. Our Henry,' he added bitterly, 'has never known higher favour.'

I looked warily about, and whispered in Meulan's ear, 'Is the prince now satisfied? The old suspicions, the smell of sedition, the secret conspiracies – have they gone?'

'I don't know,' said Meulan irritably. 'I've been fighting a war; my spies couldn't reach me; the threads are broken. Henry – and that rascal Clare – could be plotting arrant treason, and I'd still be in the dark.' He looked at me with a dawning light in his crafty eyes. 'You've been in this from the beginning, Walter, since Domfront and beyond. Would you consider offering to serve in Henry's mesnie?'

'The Saints forbid!' I stared at him, aghast. 'I hate the man, and he loathes my guts. He wouldn't have me.'

'So?' The old warrior regarded me beneath his hoary eyebrows. 'You could be very useful, established in Henry's household. Think it over, Walter.'

'Tirel!' A roar from the high table, and Rufus's beckoning arm. I went speedily to the king, and grasped the goblet thrust in my hand. 'Lord Helias has described his battle. Now tell me your side. What went wrong?'

For the second time I related the rout at Saones: a much amended version, for Henry brooded within earshot, his sallow face intent, the cold eyes hard as flints. I omitted all mention of our right-flank cavalry; and saw, at the end, a sardonic smile playing on Henry's lips, and a derisive glint in his eye. I disliked my timid discretion – but what else could I say? Henry had established himself in Rufus's esteem: none but a madman would name the prince a coward to his brother's face.

'Interesting,' Rufus observed. 'A sound battle plan – shattered by those dastardly Bretons. I'll have their bannerets broken. I had not known,' he went on, 'until my – er – guest here so informed me, that you yourself took Lord Helias. You've done me valiant service, Walter; this I shall not forget.'

I bowed and withdrew. A hand tapped my shoulder; I saw a lean and ruddy countenance, hair pale as wheaten straw.

'Delis! What are you doing here?'

'Captured,' said the Lord of Carenci tiredly, 'in a futile skirmish near Pontoise. I rode my destrier into a bog, and William of Breteuil took me easily.'

'Why have you not paid ransom?'

'Breteuil demands five hundred deniers – more than my fief affords. Rufus offered to pay it himself if I entered his service. I had to refuse. Hardly fitting for the leader of Poix's mesnie to change sides. Especially,' he continued, lazily amused, 'when the Lord of Poix himself is fighting on Normandy's behalf. It might snap Louis's temper – he's king in all but name – and cause him to escheat your Honour.'

'Five hundred deniers.' I pondered, rubbing my head. 'It's a lot, but I suppose I shall have to find it if the state of my coffers allows. How have the harvests been?'

'Only moderate. You'd better leave me languishing in Breteuil's donjon till the war is over. They might exchange prisoners at the end.'

'Don't talk nonsense!'

I led him to the dais, knelt before Rufus and said formally, 'Sire, I beg leave to ransom this my vassal Delis of Carenci, taken in fight by Breteuil's lord.'

445

'Carenci?' Rufus gulped wine; he was on his second flagon and in amiable mood. 'I didn't realize he was your man, Walter. What does Breteuil want? – I can't remember.'

I told him. Rufus belched. 'Quite expensive – William always was a grasping man.' He signalled to a clerk and said, 'Father Restould, indite authority to the treasurer for five hundred deniers' payment to Lord William of Breteuil.' He turned on me a beaming face. 'There you are, Walter – your liege is free. No call for thanks: I owe you this and more.'

Can you wonder that, in spite of all his failings, Rufus commanded devotion in the knights who served him?

Varlets placed trestles in preparation for midday dinner, clattering among the throng, rudely pushing knights aside; and set platters on the boards. So many mighty lords were there that I, a petty baron, was relegated by stewards to a table below the dais. The banquet – it was nothing less – wended a lengthy course: pigeons baked in bread, venison roast and garnished, lampreys broiled in wine, sweet pasties and much besides. Minstrels strummed their lutes and chanted ballads of the wars, a tumbler wrapped his ankles round his neck and rolled like a hoop on the rushes between the tables. The shouts for wine grew frequent, the talking boisterous; raucous singing drowned the minstrels' voices. The prelates took the hint and left; pages escorted their mistresses – the ladies of Rouen's garrison – to quarters in the bower.

Rufus's face shone red as a setting sun; he hammered dagger-hilt on table in time to a marching song.

A travel-stained courier, dust-caked to the eyebrows, burst between the sentries at the portal, limped to the high table, leaned across the board and spoke quickly to the king. Rufus's face went purple; he drove his dagger-point deep into the wood. Gradually the clamour stilled, heads turned towards the dais; a lute string thrummed like a wasp-drone in the silence.

'B-by the F-face!' Rufus stammered. 'Word from B-belesme!' His face worked furiously. 'Fulk of Anjou has taken Mans, and claims Maine for his own!'

A rising wind of whispering murmured through the hall. Rufus hit the embedded dagger, snapped the blade.

'It's all to be done again!'

Helias's shoulders shook; he chuckled, struggled to command his features, collapsed in helpless laughter. Rufus glowered, hands on chair arms, a leopard ready to spring. Slowly he relaxed, glaring at his prisoner. The anger left his face, a smile twitched his mouth. The king slapped his knees and began to laugh.

Helias of La Flèche and Rufus faced each other, both bellowing with incoherent mirth.

3

The banquet ended abruptly; by vespers Rufus's couriers were out, riding hard through the short summer night to call his vassals to a muster at Alençon.

A new war was afoot – or, more properly, the old war had revived. I went to my lodgings in a mercer's house, sat on a bench in the yard beneath an apple tree and there, while evening shadows gathered, considered what I should do.

The king had declared his intention of leading the campaign himself: my rational course was to follow him to Maine. I remembered those old battle grounds, the charred and desolate steadings, corpses rotting in the fields. The trodden heath near Saones, a grave beneath a tree, and a lady immured for life. Revulsion shook me like an ague; I pressed fingers on my temples and stared blindly into the dusk.

Maine was not for me.

Then what? I might return to Poix, resume the conduct of an Honour which, for love of Rufus, I had neglected far too long. But while France was waging war I could not revert to a peaceful life, overseeing the harvest and the culling of the vines – Louis would expect me with my mesnie in his train. More strife, more carnage, more fear and pain and stress.

I bit my lip and tasted the rusty tang of blood. Twilight faded, the darkness deepened. Wool-bales stacked in the mercer's yard assumed peculiar shapes, like bodies heaped in piles where a battle-line once had stood.

It seems an odd confession for a knight; but after a lifetime's fighting I was sick of warfare.

I had lost Isabel. What remained? England, Laingaham – and Adelice. A sudden yearning for her tranquillity swept my senses like a flood, a longing to run into her arms as an infant flies to its mother. Tears prickled my eyes; I strove to regain my manhood. Walter Lord of Poix, veteran of mellays and leaguers by the score – crying in the dark like a frightened child!

447

St Peter's bell tolled compline, a requiem for the dying day. Misery descended like a falling cliff; I cradled head in arms and wept aloud.

From this welter of self-pity and remorse I rose resolved to follow Rufus into Maine.

4

By dawn the king was gone from Rouen, riding to Alençon. A bustle of departure fermented in the ward; wagons rumbled over the draw-bridge, knights clambered into saddles, the tramp of men-at-arms re-echoed in the streets. Meulan was in the donjon, grouchily examining a loose rivet in his shield and rating his esquire. 'Take it to the armourer,' he growled, 'before the whole contraption falls to pieces. Good day to you, Walter. Where's your horse? We leave at terce, if this rabble can sort itself out. Never seen the king in such a hurry. Will you ride with me?'

'Willingly, my lord.' I noticed Henry on the rampart, talking idly to Clare. 'The prince displays no urgency. Does he follow later?'

Meulan compressed his lips. 'Yesterday you left the castle early, and missed the last development. Henry, at Rufus's bidding, goes to England. A Welsh revolt, apparently, and Hugh of Shrewsbury killed. The king is sending his brother to rally the marcher lords.'

'So.' Pensively I regarded the Count of the Cotentin. The pasty face was animated, his gestures unusually brisk. 'Henry loose in England. Do you approve?'

'Of course not!' Meulan said disgustedly. 'I tried to persuade Rufus that the prince would be better employed in leading his mesnie to Mans. Waste of breath. Henry proposed the idea; Rufus thought it excellent. That was that.'

His cunning old eyes were slits in the grizzled face.

'Have you considered the suggestion I made yesterday, Walter? It's more than ever necessary that somebody should watch Henry.'

I said bleakly, 'Not I. Find your own spies, my lord: it's no work for a knight.'

Meulan looked disappointed. 'As you will. But you'd never do the king a better service.'

I wandered away, crossed the ward to the stables, gave Richer instructions to saddle-up and load the archers' baggage. A strapper bitted my palfrey; Berlai folded blankets on my destrier's back, carefully settled the cumbrous battle-saddle, tightened girths and handed the leading-rein to a bowman – only the most impoverished knights rode their destriers on a march. Lisiard fussily stowed his hauberk in a chest; Delis, ready mounted, gave me farewell: he would reach Poix two days later. 'Don't get captured again, my friend,' I warned him. 'The king won't ransom you twice!'

He laughed, and rode away.

I walked through the gate, sauntered along the Street of Weavers towards the mercer's house where my servants awaited orders, and stepped aside to give passage to a doddering monk supported on each hand by black Benedictines.

'Lord Walter!'

I stopped, and peered beneath the cowl.

'Body of God! Anselm!'

He put back the hood. The fine-boned countenance was more frail than I remembered, the straggling white locks sparser.

'Must you greet me with blasphemy, my son, after all these months?' he asked in smiling reproof. 'How fares Poix, and your lady?'

'Well enough, Father. What are you doing in Rouen? I had not thought you so rash as to stay ...'

'In a town where Rufus dwells?' Anselm wagged his head. 'It matters not at all. He probably knows I'm here, and doesn't bother. In his eyes I'm no longer England's archbishop, and have ceased to count. Why should he pursue me? The king, whatever his faults, is not vindictive.'

A summer shower spattered raindrops on the cobbles. I said, 'Shelter in my lodging, Father – it's only a few paces on. I have not yet broken fast: will you share the wine and pork that waits me?'

I settled the old man in a chair, the silent monks like sentinels at his shoulder, and gave him a cup of wine, for he would not eat. He described his travels since the king expelled him, his journey to Rome and interview with Pope Urban, who had forbidden him, whatever Rufus's edict, to resign Canterbury's see. 'I'm an archbishop lacking an abbey,' he commented placidly. In turn I related the history of the war in Maine and told how Ralph and Roger died. Hesitantly I mentioned Isabel's renunciation, the words stumbling on my tongue, for the wound still hurt like fire.

'The Lady of Conches,' said Anselm, 'will reform her life and persevere worthily in the fear of the Lord, and so find salvation. To this you must become reconciled, my son, and put away your memories of the past.'

Smug advice, I thought impatiently, from a saintly man of God. Anselm saw the resentment in my face, and touched my hand. 'You are not blameless in this matter, yet your penance is far less than hers. Be thankful for God's mercy, and bear with grace the tiny trials you suffer.' He looked at me keenly. 'You are troubled in other ways, my son. Will you not tell me?'

Thus encouraged I poured out to him, as to a confessor, the anguished doubts which had afflicted me in the mercer's yard, and the wayward resolution which was leading me to Maine. He looked perplexed.

'I do not understand why you follow the king against your inclination. You are not his man.'

'I swore an oath, many years since, to serve Rufus and protect him from a hidden enemy.'

Anselm said, 'You mean his brother Henry.'

I gaped at him, astounded. 'When did you learn . . .'

He smiled sadly. 'The prince has sent me secret emissaries, smooth-tongued men who believe me the king's implacable foe, who cautiously probe my bent and suggest I use my influence with the pope. They want Rufus excommunicated, and promise a great reward: the restoration of my see.'

'You know that is impossible while Rufus lives!'

'True. But what if Rufus dies?'

'Stark treason! You refused?'

'Of course.' Anselm sighed. 'If only it were possible to undo the treaty signed at Caen in '91 . . . Had Rufus and Curthose not agreed that each should be the other's heir if either died childless, so excluding Henry from succession . . . The prince is determined to win the land he regards as his rightful heritage – and Rufus stands in the way. I am fearful . . .'

I clasped my hands tightly together. 'Then you realize why I must stay with the king?'

Anselm closed his eyes. The lids were delicate, minutely veined, sere as autumn leaves. 'There's no danger for him in Maine, nor anywhere save England.' He spoke very quietly, his lips scarcely moving. 'Sunlight . . . trees . . . a running stag . . . death coming on the wind . . . death . . .'

Terror prickled my skin in a myriad frozen barbs. Hardly breathing, I watched the fragile face, and felt the sweat start on my brow.

Anselm opened his eyes, and said in a matter-of-fact tone, 'Go to England, Walter. There your destiny awaits you.'

5

Meulan had gone from the castle; fitzHamon, marshalling the rearmost conroys, was on the point of departure. I told him, saving words, of my change in plan. Briskly I countermanded my orders to Richer. Pigot led the archers back to Poix, and delivered a message to my lady. Within a week Hugh and Adelice joined me; with Richer, Lisiard, Berlai, a score of men-at-arms and servants we left for Havre.

We waited there a fortnight, bound by contrary winds; and reached Laingaham while the harvest was being gathered.

Henry, I learned, had gone to Wales. The Welsh would keep him occupied for many weeks; and my anxiety abated. The manor's calm routine enfolded me like a comfortable robe; I rode the fields and cast my hawks, played checkers and rolled dice with Lisiard at evening; and found solace for my tormented heart in Adelice's sweet affection.

She listened to my troubles, soothed my hurt – and never spoke of Isabel again.

Gales and rainstorms heralded summer's passing. News filtered slowly from the outer world. Rufus, we heard, led a tempestuous campaign in Maine, took Mans and forced Count Fulk to sue for peace. The treaty freed all prisoners on both sides: Helias returned to his family fief on the Angevin border. It was said that he asked leave to enter the king's service, keeping his rank of count but relinquishing his claim to Maine until, by some signal exploit on Rufus's behalf, he should be deemed fitting to receive the county as a grant from the king's free will. Rufus seemed disposed to agree; Meulan, fearing lest Helias, admitted to the royal councils, might displace him as the king's advisor in chief, persuaded a refusal.

Helias replied defiantly: he would at some time in the future pursue his claim with spears. The king lost his temper, told Helias to do his worst and expect no mercy when he failed.

Anyone else would have answered the count's defiance with death or blinding – but the treaty pledged Rufus's knightly word, and Helias went unscathed.

At Advent Henry returned from Wales and settled at Clarendon, a hunting lodge in the New Forest where the king allowed him residence – the Count of the Cotentin still held no land in England. It was time to move closer to my quarry. I summoned Richer and Berlai and rode to Winchester, one day's march from Clarendon across the forest's breadth.

Ranulf Flambard held magnificent state in the castle, as befitted the priest who ruled England while Rufus waged his wars. A steward led me to the chancellor's private chamber on the topmost floor, a room luxuriously furnished: tapestries draped the walls, my feet trod gorgeous druggets woven by Spanish Moors, and beeswax candles flared in silver sconces. Resplendent in a sky-blue silken mantle, Flambard greeted me genially – but the handsome face looked haggard, the luminous eyes were bloodshot. He wore the marks of a man who lived under constant stress.

'It becomes everlastingly more difficult to meet the king's demands,' he explained. 'Every ship from Normandy brings couriers seeking money. I've tallaged the kingdom almost dry. Landholders, as you know, meet the gelds from their vassals' produce, selling corn and fleeces to pay the levies I impose. Peasants bear the brunt; they lose the very food they need for living. There's famine in many counties; villeins desert the manors to seek a living where they can, regardless of the maiming if they're caught.'

I forbore to ask how much of the taxes supported the chancellor's opulence; and said, 'His subjects must be cursing the king.'

Flambard laughed without mirth. 'Not so. The English believe no ill of Rufus. Their hatred focuses on me, whom they regard as the source of all their troubles. I'm the best-loathed man in England.' He lifted his shoulders. 'I can bear it – I obey the king's behest, which is all that matters.'

I said, 'Mans is taken, the war ended – the king's demands will surely cease.'

Flambard raised his eyebrows. 'Don't you know? Rufus is still fighting. He's found an ally: William Duke of Aquitaine. Together they're advancing on the Vexin from the south, harrying the lands round Montfort – which they've failed to take. A winter campaign, probably doomed to failure, and disastrously expensive.'

I clucked sympathetically; and considered how best to broach the object of my visit. I was never certain how far Meulan and fitz-

Hamon took the chancellor into their confidence over Henry. I brushed my doubts aside, and told him plain the tale from start to finish. Flambard listened silently, his eyes hooded, a finger stroking his mantle's gold embroidery. 'And so,' I concluded lamely, 'I have to find a means of keeping watch upon the prince.'

Flambard plucked a hair from his fiery tonsure and held it to the light. 'A spy in his household, in fact,' he said reflectively. 'Someone unknown to him, unnoticeable, anonymous. Who better than a priest? They go anywhere without remark.'

'You have a clerk in mind? He must be intelligent, discreet, and utterly reliable.'

'My chancellery contains no other kind,' said Flambard curtly. He held the hair in a candle's flame, and watched it crisp to his fingers. 'A grey one,' he explained. 'I hate the scars of age. Incidentally, did you know there's another Clare at Clarendon – Roger, Gilbert's brother? The vultures are flocking. Very well. I'll send a man there after Christmas. He'll report direct to me – you can't read, can you? – and I'll tell you all he sends.'

I rose from my comfortable chair, padded with silken cushions. 'You've earned my gratitude. How much,' I added curiously, 'did you know of Prince Henry's conspiracies?'

'Everything, my lord,' he assured me gravely.

6

I stayed at Winchester, enduring a winter more severe than the oldest dotard remembered. Snow blanketed the land from horizon to grey horizon. Cattle froze in byres, and villeins died in ditches; wolf packs roved round Winchester's moat and attacked anything that moved. Rivers were solid ice, roads impassable drifts; pedlars and pack-trains ceased to travel and commerce came to a stand. The townspeople, like a garrison beleaguered, stayed within the walls, huddled over fires, and fought the bitter cold.

Under these extremes I expected little news from Clarendon. From St Stephen's day till Lent the clerk sent only two reports, both brief and uninformative. One odd feature was common to both: Henry, despite the weather, braved cold and wolves and rode out often in the forest, always taking Clare and a warden named as Ranulf. He did not hunt – impossible in such conditions – but roamed the glades and tracks, as if seeking to unravel the forest's convolutions. Which was unlike Henry, I considered – his was not the kind of character that invited physical rigours.

I could read nothing sinister in this unusual quirk, and dismissed it from my mind.

On Our Lady's Day a warm wind breathed from the south, the snow melted and the rivers ran in flood. The king returned from Normandy, wore his crown at Westminster for the Pentecost feast, and made a royal progress thence to Clarendon. From Winchester I travelled in his train; and on this blustery sunlit day in June, garbed ready for the hunt, he basked in the lodge's forecourt and reminiscently discussed the inconclusive war in France.

'Louis never offered open battle, and his castles were impregnable,' said Rufus morosely. 'Particularly Montfort, which Count Amauri held valiantly – do you remember him, Walter, from our fledgling days in Rouen? We harried to Seine and beyond, got some paltry loot and a few indifferent ransoms. The war could have dragged on all summer; so I thought it best to declare a truce.' He looked at the sun. 'Are the horses saddled, Henry, and the beaters stationed? It's time we made a start.'

A verderer said respectfully, 'The prince has ridden ahead, sire, to make all ready for the drive.'

I surveyed the barons who waited in the forecourt, missed Clare's surly visage, and felt suddenly uneasy.

'Has Lord Gilbert gone with the prince?'

'Aye, my lord.'

Be reasonable, I told myself: on a sunlit noonday how can they hurt a king surrounded by the nobles of his household? I remembered the clerk's reports, which had flowed more frequently since the snow had gone. They held nothing to incriminate Henry, no tales of secret conclaves or mysterious gatherings by night, nothing to connect him with discontented barons ripe for revolt. That was what I looked for, and I was both relieved and disappointed. The clerk, a conscientious man, reported all he knew, however trifling; and like recurring staves in a tuneless song came repetitive reports of Henry's explorations in the forest, meeting verderers and wardens, and his eagerness to learn the hunt routines in every baily. I had puzzled over this, and found no sense; now, like a moonshaft lighting a murky night, a frightening solution stared me in the face.

Though the day was bright as a burnished blade, in the forest's tree-dark coverts a hunter stood alone, concealed from driven deer and hidden from his friends.

'Henry's very zealous,' Rufus said testily. 'Can't he leave arrangements to the wardens?'

I walked quickly to the horses held by strappers in a line before the thatched and timbered house – the hall of an English thegn before the Conquest. Curtly I bade Richer mount, and made for the gated palisade which girdled outhouses and hall. Rufus was on his feet, examining a bowstave; he raised his head as I passed.

'Where are you off to, Walter? What's the hurry?'

I waved an arm, passed the gate and kicked my horse to a gallop. The forest's tendrils embraced Clarendon; a broad beaten track led us straight into the depths. Mighty aisles of oak and ash reared close on either hand; the path narrowed, wound like a drunkard's road between undergrowth and bracken and flowered elder bushes stippled white. Above the hooves I heard the wind-gusts whooping; tree-tops swayed and threshed; and the sun cascaded puddles like spilt gold upon the grass.

The trackway forked. I halted, fuming. Richer said, 'Whoever you're after has gone this way.' He pointed to the ground. 'Hoof-prints fresh since the rain at dawn.'

We trailed the marks that pocked last winter's leaf-fall. I eased to a trot, pulled to a walk, ears pricked and eyes alert. The track tapered to a horse-width, bordered by thorn and bramble; a briar-spur tugged my chape. I heard a voice ahead, and jabbed the bit.

'Hold my horse.'

I dismounted, crept through the undergrowth, cursing softly when the brambles ripped my face. The path ended on a grassy glade, a ride the verderers created: axe-hewn tree stumps jutted among the tussocks. A killing-ground for hunters, where beaters drove the deer from the clustered trees beyond, and bowmen stood in the undergrowth where I crouched. I went on hands and knees behind some fretted briars.

At half a bowshot's distance Prince Henry sat his palfrey beneath an elm tree, holding a riderless horse. Gilbert paced the grass, counting aloud as he went. He stopped and called, his voice muffled by the wind.

'Forty.'

Henry gestured to right and left. Clare went to a gap in the foliage, an alcove between a blackthorn bush and sapling oak, a perfect hide for a hunter to lie in wait. Thence he stepped the range to a similar gap, a space which bracken concealed.

'Sixty.'

'Too far even for a tirel,' Henry called. 'Find a nearer space.'

I heard a rustle in the bushes, climbed quickly to my feet, saw a wiry figure clad in the green-dyed leather jerkin and breeks the wardens wore. A brown-haired, swarthy face, mean-mouthed and bushy browed, pale blue hostile eyes. A bowstave, ready braced, dangled from his shoulder; a hand rested on the dagger at his belt. His eyes examined me swiftly; despite mired clothes and thorn-ripped face he recognized my quality.

I kept my voice low. 'Who are you?'

'Ranulf of Aix, king's warden in Clarendon's baily. Why, my lord, do you creep about the forest like a hunting stoat?'

Anger conquered my discomposure: sergeants do not question knights. 'Curb your insolence, rascal! I do what I do. Out of my way!'

I moved to pass him. The dagger-point scraped my chest. 'Not so fast,' he grunted. 'We'll see what my lords yonder have to say.'

He opened his mouth to shout.

'Be still,' said Richer, 'else you die.' His dagger pricked the warden's neck in the hollow at the base of his skull. 'Mount and away, my lord! Shall I kill this rogue?'

A warden slain on his beat would raise a hue and cry unmatched in the Forest's annals. 'God's belly, no!' I snapped. 'Hold him till I'm clear.' I ran to the palfreys hitched to a branch, mounted quick and fled along the track. On the sough of the wind I heard a yell; presently Richer, flogging his horse, overtook me at the fork.

'You should have let me cut his throat,' he observed calmly. 'He'll describe you to the prince, who will know that you were watching. I'm in the dark, my lord. Won't you tell me what this is about?'

Treachery and treason, a blurred miasma, shadowy, still unproven. 'Later, Richer.' My mind revolved the problems like a wagon-wheel creaking endlessly to nowhere. Tell the king that Henry planned his murder? On what proof? A man pacing distances between the hunters' hides? Innocent enough, surely? What had Henry said? 'Too far even for a tirel.' He meant a marksman, a sharpshooter – that was what my nickname signified. Too far for what – killing range? Alike for man or stag: nothing to be plucked from words, no hard evidence from deeds.

I thumped my forehead, almost weeping in frustration. Was I inventing malignancy where none existed? No! I was utterly sure that danger threatened the king.

A cavalcade approached along the track, Rufus at the head. I braced my shoulders, rode to meet him, resolved to give him warning, endure disbelief and wrath, and maybe worse.

Rufus said, 'Been in the Forest, Walter? I hope you haven't disturbed the game!'

I gulped, and began to speak. A rider on a sweat-streaked horse shouldered through the retinue: a king's messenger from the gonfanon he bore. He tendered a small cylinder, calfskin-wrapped and neatly sewn.

'From Southampton, sire. A courier on a hoy from Havre delivered this at dawn, and protested uttermost urgency!'

Rufus tore the stitches, and stared blankly at the script. 'What a time to receive despatches!' He swung in the saddle and bawled, 'Can anyone here read?'

Knightly heads were shaken. A mule ambled past the files, a short plump man aback, a priestly habit tucked about his thighs. 'I am a clerk, sire,' he said humbly. He took the scroll which Rufus thankfully proffered, and scanned the writing. Priests were rare in hunting parties: idly I examined him. A round, unremarkable face, dimpled chin, guileless eyes and a balding head – no bristles on his tonsure. Not the type, I thought, to enjoy a day in the woods. For a moment he raised his eyes from the scroll and caught my glance. No flicker of expression showed, no hint of recognition – but I knew.

Flambard's spy, relentless in his mission.

He read the stilted phrases inscribed in clerical French. 'Robert Count of Meulan to his suzerain William of England. Greeting. This from Robert of Belesme, presently at Alençon. Helias of La Flèche, mustering his liegemen, has taken Ballon, Dangeul, Mans, and beleaguers Saones. Belesme beseeches aid, his men outnumbered. I pray you send forthwith a writ of array. Robert to William. Farewell. Given at Rouen this Octave of the Trinity.'

Rufus's eyes bulged, he thumped his fist on the saddlebow. 'Helias! The Devil take him!' He clenched both hands and beat them on his thighs. 'By the Holy Face of Lucca, will I never be done with Maine?'

Like a radiant beam from heaven I saw Providence offering help. I said feverishly, 'Sire, you must leave at once for Normandy!

Helias, left unhindered, will conquer all the county! At Saones he crushed Belesme – will you endure a second defeat? Go to Normandy, my lord, call the barons to your banner!'

The fury gradually ebbed from Rufus's eyes. 'By the Thorns, Walter, you're right! It's time I dealt with Helias once for all! I'll tear his eyes and bowels!' He turned upon his retinue, who listened open-mouthed. 'Let us go beyond the seas and help our friends!'

Rufus swung the horse on its hocks. The barons, quite confounded, looked blankly at one another. 'Come on, Walter,' said fitzHamon glumly. 'I truly believe he's heading for Southampton. He mustn't ride alone.'

We galloped after the king. A handful of lords made to follow, reined dubiously and watched us go, scratching bewildered heads. An esquire persisted, riding on our heels – a comely rose-pink youth, Rufus's current favourite.

Deliverance. Thankfulness coursed like warm wine through my veins, and so relaxed my tension that I watered in my breeks.

7

The arrow flies six leagues from Clarendon to Southampton: the straggling lanes we followed made it eight. Rufus went at a swinging canter, reins loose on his palfrey's neck, and sang lustily as he rode. fitzHamon, with a face like stone, rode at his bridle hand; once he interrupted the king's carolling to say, 'This haste is needless, my lord. Why not wait to gather a mesnie? You shouldn't be left without men.'

'I *am* left without men,' said Rufus happily. 'Except for you, my friends. Don't worry – more await me on the other side.'

The trackways pierced the Forest – that wilderness of trees whose menace shrouds my history's final pages, whose shadow fell forever on my life. We threaded clearings humped by ivied mounds: relics of the hamlets Duke William had destroyed to make his chases. The Forest, mauled by wind, roared like a lion embayed; tree boughs swayed and creaked; an elm splintered at the bole and crashed across our path, panicking the horses and unseating the pretty esquire. Clouds raced across the sky, piled high on the horizon, mounted and hid the sun. Rufus stopped singing. We rode unspeaking, collecting the flagging horses between bit and spur, shoulders hunched against the squalls.

We clattered to the waterfront as the bells were pealing vespers, the palfreys stumbling in their gait and hanging on the bits. Ships were moored at the wharfside and anchored in the river, plunging at the cables. Whitecaps ripped the Itchen's waters; beyond the river's crescent I glimpsed the open sea, a spouting, wind-rent waste.

'A headlong ride to no purpose,' said fitzHamon acidly. 'None will put to sea in this.'

Rufus slipped from the saddle and strode to a bearded shipmaster unloading bales from a hoy – a crazy, aged ship she was, broad-beamed, three horse-lengths long, sail patched and timbers flaking. Rufus hailed him loudly.

'Ho, master! Will you take me now to Normandy?'

The man looked up, hugging a sackcloth bundle and swaying to the vessel's movement. His face was sunburnt, deeply seamed, the furrows rimed by salt. A scarlet kerchief swathed his head, tied in a knot at the nape. He smiled broadly, white teeth in a chestnut beard, and answered in uncouth French, the patois used by sailors who ply the narrow seas.

'In a northerly gale? The wind has addled your head!'

Rufus jumped into the ship, and clapped him on the shoulder. 'Come, man – you'll be well rewarded. I am the king.'

The shipmaster slung the package to a crewman on the wharf. 'Stack it near that bollard, Gudrun.' He bent to lift another. 'And I'm the pope. You're standing on my cargo – move aside.'

'What is your name?'

The man heaved a bale to his shoulder. 'Inquisitive, aren't you? Ulward, freeman of Rye. Satisfied? Now go away.'

'Look at me, Ulward!' said Rufus fiercely. 'Don't the English know their king?'

'King be —' He stared hard at Rufus, and sucked in his breath. 'Jesu! It is! I once saw you embark at Havre.' The bundle thudded on the strakes; he fell to his knees. 'Forgive me, my lord! I didn't —'

'No matter,' said Rufus breezily. 'Now will you take me across?'

'Impossible, sire!' Ulward waved a hand to the gale-lashed river. 'Look at it! And we're in harbour, sheltered from the blast! The sea outside is a boiling fury!'

'I never yet heard of a king being drowned!' cried Rufus. 'Come on, Ulward: get your crew aboard and loose your moorings.' The bantering note went from his voice. 'This is a command, friend: disobey me at your peril!'

Ulward made a hopeless gesture; and called orders to his men. A seaman cast off the stern rope. The other man dropped his jaw, sent a frightened glance at the waves and the forest's wind-tossed trees, and scampered from the wharf.

Rufus laughed.

'We're short of a crewman.' He scanned the three of us standing on the wharfside, gazing down into the hull. 'Who will take his place?'

fitzHamon tightened his lips, drew chape around his shoulders and stepped aboard. The esquire swallowed, looked longingly at the safe and solid land, clambered reluctantly over the side, slipped on a greasy plank and landed in a heap. The seaman loosed the head rope, and leapt nimbly amidships; Ulward, swearing beneath his breath, rammed a pole against a bollard. A gap opened between ship and shore, a space where water plucked and spurted. Rufus gripped a mast-stay, and looked at me in wonder.

'Aren't you coming, Walter?'

I held his eyes, wishing helplessly I could make him understand. Anselm's voice was in my ears, a whisper in the gale. 'No danger ... none anywhere save England.' I had seen the peril close, smelt its fetor like a clammy breath.

I must stay and grapple the renegades who threatened the man I loved.

The hoy drifted into the stream; Ulward jumped to the steering oar. The sail jerkily mounted the mast, flapped and bellied. Rufus's face changed; a wounded look showed briefly in his eyes, and then an angry flash. He turned his back, hauled savagely on the sheets. The bows met a foam-smeared roller, swooped high like a rearing horse. Rolling in vicious wind-chopped breakers, the hoy crawled round the river's curve, a speck in a weltering waste, and vanished from my sight.

This was the duty my oath imposed – and the king believed me faithless. Sprindrift stung my eyes to tears. Blindly I remounted, and rode back to face his enemies.

Rufus landed safe at Touques, mustered a vast army, drove Helias from Mans and chased him into Mayet. The castle stubbornly resisted, and all the escalades failed. But Maine had been re-conquered, Helias rendered impotent: Rufus harried his demesnes and lifted Mayet's siege.

At Michaelmas the king returned to England; and saw Normandy never again.

Chapter 11

1099–1100

I STAYED snug in Winchester while Rufus fought in Maine.

At the time of Mayet's siege Flambard called me to the castle. He wore a garish mantle and a gloomy expression, and said, 'For four weeks past I haven't heard from my clerk at Clarendon.'

'He has never provided any worthwhile information. Perhaps he's nothing useful to report.'

'It's worse than that. After a fortnight's silence I sent a man to Clarendon to make discreet inquiries. He says the priest has vanished.'

'Possibly gone on pilgrimage to a holy shrine. There's one quite near at Glastonbury – St Joseph's.'

'A chancellery clerk entrusted with a mission?' Flambard inquired grimly. 'I train them better than that. No. I'm certain his spying was discovered, and Henry . . .' He snapped his fingers.

I said curtly, 'We must replace him.'

'After this warning, a second stranger prying in Henry's household wouldn't last the turn of a sandglass. I'll send no more – the chancellery is understaffed as it is.'

Despite my pleas Flambard remained unmoved. I returned to the tavern where I lived and wondered what to do. With Meulan and fitzHamon in Normandy, and the chancellor holding aloof, I felt hopelessly alone. I remembered Meulan's hint that I should seek a place in Henry's mesnie, and for a few despondent moments revolved it in my mind. I dismissed the notion. Apart from our mutual hatred, Henry must certainly know from Ranulf of Aix that I had spied on him in the Forest – how to explain *that* incident away? The prince's suspicions were fully aroused; he would be more than ever wary of newcomers in his retinue.

I clutched my head. Somehow I must keep in contact with this evil man.

Richer entered the room, bearing platters for our meal. He scanned my face and said, 'What ails you, my lord?'

A craving to share my burden made me say, 'Do you recall, Richer, the day you wanted to kill the warden?'

'Clearly. I still think you mistaken in letting him live, since Prince Henry is obviously your enemy.'

'Not mine alone. This is the way of it, Richer.'

He listened to the story of my ten-year mission, the duty – self-imposed – that I had vowed, the diaphanous veil of plots I strove to rend. 'Worse than all,' I ended, 'the king I guard believes me faithless – I deserted him on danger's brink.'

'Then leave him,' said Richer brutally. 'Return to France, and send a letter disclosing your suspicions.'

I said miserably, 'I can't. Nor would the king heed a deserter's warning.'

Compassion softened Richer's taut expression. 'Till lately the bonds of your devotion have drawn you towards separate goals: Isabel of Conches and England's king. Now, with the lady lost, the skeins have united in a single unbreakable rope which ties you to the king. Cut it, my lord. You lie in greater peril than you think. Prince Henry knows from the warden that you've discovered his bent. He'll not hesitate to sweep you from his path.'

'No. I don't fear Henry.'

'I do. Unless you're very careful he'll snare you yet. He must, as you say, be watched.' Richer stroked the strap which bound his withered arm, and said casually, 'I'll go into the Forest, and shadow him when he rides.'

I protested stubbornly. A stranger to the wilderness, he did not know the wardens' haunts, the verderers' patrols; and would certainly be caught. Forest law dealt hardily with vagrants. Nor, I added, looking at his maiming, could he properly defend himself.

Richer said calmly, 'I don't walk on my arms, nor shall I need to fight, for none will see me. I can move in the woods more stealthily than the creatures which inhabit them.'

This I knew to be true, remembering our wanderings in Normandy's haunted tree-wastes after Raimalard long ago. For want of a better contrivance I let him have his way.

Richer submerged in the Forest, and lived in the wild like an animal. Every sennight he reappeared, collected food, changed torn and mired garments, told me his news and vanished. The sum of his reports was sparse: Henry roamed the coverts with Gilbert and brother Roger, studied rides and drives, and fostered friendliness with verderers and wardens. He had lately made his quarters at a hunting lodge near Minsted, three leagues south from Clarendon, and pursued his freakish wanderings in the woodlands round about.

When Rufus returned from Maine the prince was bound to wait on him; he left the Forest for London, and hastily I followed. Richer, thin as a famished berselet from his hardships, unobtrusively rejoined my household. His conclusions marched with mine, and were equally indefinite: all Henry's schemes now centred in the Forest, but exactly what they were we could not guess. Of one thing I was certain: the king must not hunt there unprotected.

I had to establish myself again in Rufus's esteem, so presented myself at the Tower and told the marshal I wanted audience. I feared a curt refusal; to my relief the knight returned and led me to the battlements where Rufus conversed with his lords. I knew them all save one: a blond-haired youth with a profile like an angel, an alabaster skin that roses tinged, and a smile to melt your heart. That smile . . . a memory flickered and died. Rufus treated him genially; I wondered if his looks had won for him the king's peculiar favours.

Rufus ignored my presence, though the marshal announced my name. I lingered uneasily on the outer fringe of barons, and endured the questioning glances which the king's indifference brought – I was known to all as one of his closest friends. fitzHamon saw my distress, and whispered in his ear. Rufus lifted his head; his features were set in rigid lines and his eyes wore a bitter look. He crooked a finger. I went to him on shaking legs, and bent my knee.

'Well, my lord of Poix?'

'I come to renew my fealty, sire.'

'A little late, aren't you? I've been three months warring in Maine – and didn't notice you among my loyal lieges!'

'I was ill, my lord.' A lie, and Rufus knew it.

'Humph! All that time? You could have joined me when your malady mended. What kept you away?' The king leaned forward, and anger sharpened his voice. 'Was it shame?'

'I do not understand you, sire.'

I understood only too well.

The barons spoke in whispers, ears cocked to Rufus's spleen, possibly not displeased to hear a favourite set down. Rufus stood abruptly. 'There's a matter to be resolved between us, Tirel. Come here.' He stalked to the battlements, crossed forearms on an embrasure, and scowled across London's rooftops. 'You abandoned me at Southampton. Why? Were you afraid?'

A deliberate insult, as he certainly was aware. He also knew that a knight whose valour was belied must answer the taunt with steel. But this was Rufus: one did not draw on the king. Yet I flushed resentfully; my sword hand went involuntarily to my hip, dropped empty away. Save for a dagger you went unarmed in courtly dress.

Rufus saw the gesture; a muscle tightened on his jaw, and then his face relaxed. 'An unworthy jibe. Forget it was said. You haven't answered the question. Why did you refuse to board that leaky ship?'

I said unhappily, 'I had good reason, sire, which I cannot explain.'

He gave me a searching look. 'You try me hard, Walter. Henry avers you are in some way disloyal; and your conduct doesn't help me disbelieve him.'

I beat my fist on a merlon, and said passionately, 'Sire, I assure you my heart and soul and body are yours, my life lies on the altar of your service! Have I ever failed you, save in this?'

For ten heartbeats Rufus held my eyes; then he touched my hand.

'No. Never. So I'll let this go, and invent a pretext to save your face. I don't believe in nursing grudges.' He linked an arm in mine, drew me towards the avidly watching barons, and said smilingly, 'My lord of Poix has confessed his fault. He's laid so low by a bouncing ship that he cannot, even for my sake, challenge a stormy sea. I must forgive him – I've seen men utterly prostrate after the smoothest voyage.' He peeked at me slyly. 'My physician, Walter, will stir a potion to bind your queasy stomach when next we have to cross.'

The lords smiled and murmured, and gathered unctuously around the outcast restored to favour. Rufus took the handsome young knight by the hand.

'Walter, meet a stranger at my court: Richard, Duke Robert's son, come to serve me while his father fights the Turks.'

Richard's smile sent memory winging back across the years, to my wanderings with Curthose, a hamlet embowered in forest, an old priest's concubine whom Curthose stole and bedded. Richard, the radiant Lesceline's child, a bastard the duke acknowledged and had brought up at his court.

I said, 'Once I knew your mother – the loveliest lady I have ever seen.'

Richard said soberly, 'She retired to a convent, and died there five years since.'

Farewell, Lesceline of Landelles, leman to priest and duke. The world is an uglier place without you, and Curthose a poorer man.

'Tomorrow,' said Rufus, 'I leave on progress to Winchester and Gloucester.' He looked at me inquiringly. 'You'll come, Walter, in my train?'

'Sire,' I said fervently, 'wherever you go I follow.'

2

Henceforth I dwelt at court, following Rufus's restless roving from Westminster to Winchester, to Rockingham and Gloucester, all places where we rested awhile and beguiled the days in hunting, hawks and tourneys. The kindom dozed in peace – even the Welsh were quiet – Normandy was safe and Maine subdued.

William King of England, Christendom's puissant lord, had reached the summit of achievement. He was amiable and gracious in those days. Having realized all ambitions – save for France – he stayed content.

Not till a hunt near Clarendon did I learn he yearned for more.

Rufus fought in the tourneys and received his share of buffets; usually I rode at his sword-hand and warded the fiercer slashes. My attentions were so persistent that Rufus became irritable. 'Stop cosseting me like a suckling child!' he protested during a breather in a tournament at Gloucester. 'I can well look after myself, and give better than I get.' Which was true enough: knights tended to avoid the red king's blusterous onsets and his bruising sword. Nor did they fancy my point and edge – fitzHamon alone unhorsed me once, catching me unaware. When Rufus and I fought side by side we had to seek opponents.

The mellays were harmless affairs of blunted swords and mazered lances. A thoughtless stroke might break a royal bone, but none could easily do Rufus mortal hurt, nor, were he successful, would his reckoning be light. But peril crouched like a wolf in wait when we hunted driven deer: the hunters stood in hides alone, often masked from their companions. I never stood in the line of bow-men; invariably I skulked in undergrowth behind Rufus's hide, far enough away to avoid alarming the stag but sufficiently close to keep the king in sight.

This habit also annoyed him. 'You're the best marksman at court, probably in the kingdom,' he complained. 'I want venison for my table, to feed my hungry household – five hundred flapping bellies. Why don't you take a bow and do your part?' I pleaded a strained shoulder, then rheumatics in my wrist; finally I bandaged my draw-hand and swore to a festering cut. Rufus grumbled roundly; I stub-bornly persisted.

In all the hunting drives from Rockingham and Alvestone and lodges in the Forest I never loosed an arrow.

From Clarendon, on an April day, we hunted deer with hounds. The king rode out from the thegn's old hall, heading a company five-score strong: barons, knights and esquires, verderers, varlets and huntsmen. Fewterers mustered brachets: small shag-coated hounds to find and follow the scent. A berner, promoted huntsman since a kennel brawl maimed his master, held on coupled leashes a dozen heavy liams used for killing the stag at bay. Ranulf of Aix, the baily's warden, guided the procession to the thickets where harts were harboured.

Hoar frost's glittering mildew rimed the twigs; sundawn thawed the leaflets into sprays of diamond dew. The air was crisp, like cold rare wine; a charcoal burner's fire wafted a scent of woodsmoke. Rufus slapped his palfrey's neck. 'By the Face,' he crowed, 'it's good to be alive!'

Henry's eyelids flickered; his lips shut tight.

Ranulf examined the ground on the edge of a hawthorn spinney. 'Fresh slots, done in the hour,' he told the king. 'Your leave to loose the brachets, sire?'

'Let them go,' said Rufus.

The fewterer swung his arm and hollered. The pack broke from his horse's feet, a rippling tan cascade. They threw their tongues and pelted into the trees. Riders curbed restless horses, shortened reins and looked towards the king. Rufus controlled a prancing palfrey, and waited till the tail hounds vanished. He eased the rein and cracked his whip.

'You may ride, my lords!'

The cavalcade galloped behind the king, a train broadening to the skirts like a meteor's flaring tail. The cry of the hounds grew fainter, splintered by the trees; occasionally we glimpsed a brachet's fleeting stern. I flanked Rufus's near quarter, Henry on his off, fitzHamon in the rear. Gilbert of Clare cursed a hard-mouthed stallion and sawed the bit; Roger – bony nosed, a lean hard jaw and colourless, burnt-out eyes – jeered at his brother's antics. Richard's supple body flowed in fluid rhythm to the lunge of a flea-bitten grey.

We entered denser forest. Oak and ash trees clustered close, their branches sweeping low. Rufus went at a headlong pace, loose-reined, and whirled his whip. Horsemen swerved between the boles and ducked beneath the boughs.

A branch brushed Rufus's head.

A sickening thought recalled another Richard, the Conqueror's second son, killed in this very forest nineteen years before – a hanging hazel branch had pierced his belly. I yelled at the top of my voice.

'Be careful, my lord!'

Rufus brandished the whip, and laughed. Henry glanced at me sideways, hatred in his eyes.

We hurtled across a ride, met a grass-patch, brilliant green. Ranulf guided us across a bog which sucked at our horses' hooves. The brachets' cry was nearer, the chase-note changed to a frantic yelping.

Ranulf said, 'The hart is embayed, my lord.'

We threaded an aspen copse and entered a narrow clearing where tree-trunks broken by gales had tumbled crosswise. Elder scrub and bramble screened the fallen logs. The little brachets scurried around and yowled frustration to the skies. One bolder than his brethren squirmed inside, yelped and tumbled out, his rib bones white in a red-lipped gash.

'A brave fighting stag,' said Rufus. 'Bring on the liams!'

Ranulf raised a horn and sounded a triple-note call. Hunters ringed the mound to discourage the stag from breaking. Soon the berner came, panting from his running, hounds tugging at the leashes. Rufus signed permission, and he slipped the couples.

The heavy rust-brown liams crashed the braided brambles like longships breasting breakers. Undergrowth heaved and crackled, hounds snarled and worried, a stag trumpeted defiantly, a dog squealed in mortal pain. The brambles parted; a hart burst into the open, liams hanging on his quarters and tearing at his shoulders. Dragging the mauling burdens he blundered a dozen paces. His enemies swarmed over him, and ripped and tore.

Ranulf slipped from his horse, jumped in and flashed a knife. The antlered head reared proudly, and thumped on the grass. While Ranulf kept the hounds at bay Rufus dismounted and spanned the head.

'Sixteen points. A fine beast, in his prime. Sound the moots.'

Four long horn blasts echoed through the woods. The berner paunched the hart, and flung offal to the hounds in the custom of the curée. He severed head and tail, to be borne before the king returning from his hunt.

Rufus wiped a shining brow. 'Enough for the day, my lords. Where are we? – I don't recognize this corner of the Forest. Lead on, Ranulf, show the way. Henry, Robert, Walter – ride with me.' The crimson features crinkled in a laugh. 'I've taken more than a stag this day, and you had better hear.'

We walked our horses through the spinneys, tracking Ranulf and a varlet who carried the bloodied trophies. The lords kept a tactful distance and loudly discussed the hunt. Rufus glanced across his shoulder, and said jubilantly, 'Keep this to yourselves, my friends: I don't want it noised abroad. William Duke of Aquitaine is pledging me his duchy!'

fitzHamon whistled between his teeth; Henry's mouth fell open.

I recalled what I knew of the duke: a giddy young man who dabbled a little in poetry and wallowed deep in women. It was said he built a convent at Niort, put trollops in the cells disguised as nuns, and thoroughly enjoyed his private brothel. After prisoning his duchess he ravished a vassal's lady, installed her as his leman and painted her portrait on his shield, declaring he would carry her in battle as she carried him in bed.

All gossip, this: I cannot warrant its truth.

'William told me when he joined me in the Vexin,' Rufus continued, 'that he wanted to go crusading, but couldn't raise money enough to equip his troops. I offered a loan; and we've been quietly negotiating ever since. This morning Meulan's courier delivered the duke's decision: I lend him what he needs, and receive in pledge his duchy.'

'The same arrangement you made with Curthose,' said Henry thinly.

'The same.' Rufus's eyes glittered. 'I have Normandy and Maine; soon Aquitaine is mine. Anjou remains. Between Aquitaine and Maine, the hammer and the anvil. I'll beat the county flat and render Fulk my vassal!'

Henry steered his palfrey round a puddle. 'Dominion from Pentland to the Pyrenees. Is that what you're after, brother?'

Sunlight lanced the tree-tops, sprinkled gold on Rufus's hair, softened the furrowed harshness of his face. 'That and more,' he said. 'Why should I stop at the Alps? I can win the greatest empire since Charlemagne ruled Christendom!'

fitzHamon looked at me sideways. The same doubt filled our minds: Rufus's vaulting ambition leaped the boundaries of reality. Would Apulia and Sicily and France stand meekly by while England riveted shackles on the world?

Henry said, 'Lands pledged can be redeemed. Jerusalem has fallen, crusaders quit Outremer. How can you hold Normandy when Robert claims redemption?'

'What with?' Rufus sneered. 'The spoils from Jerusalem's sack? He won't extract ten thousand marks from that!' He bared his teeth, and said in an iron voice, 'Not twice as much, nor all the swords in Neustria will compel me to yield a hide of the lands I hold!'

We left the Forest's margins, saw Clarendon's timber walls and grey thatched roof. Ranulf put the horn to his lips and blew the menée.

3

After Easter word reached England that Robert Curthose, returning from crusade, had tarried in Apulia and wedded Sibyl of Conversana, Duke Robert Guiscard's grandniece.

'And that's put a falcon in the dovecote,' fitzHamon told me during the Pentecost feast in Westminster Hall. 'They say the lady's dowry is more than enough for Curthose to redeem his duchy. Which is not Rufus's idea at all!'

Idly I surveyed the splendid scene, all the baronage of England, great and small, gathered to do homage to their king. A multitude of candles and torches aflame in cressets shed a mellow light on rainbow mantles, costly furs, jewels and golden collars. At the pinnacle of this pageantry, a lion in his pride, Rufus blazed enthroned, crimson-robed and crowned, surrounded by his counts and mitred prelates.

I said, 'Remember Caen's treaty? Curthose married may beget a son who becomes heir to both England and Normandy. Do you think Rufus will denounce the pact?'

'No. His word is pledged. Nor will the king easily surrender Normandy.' fitzHamon caressed his scar. 'A pretty problem. I wonder what he'll do.'

'He may take a wife,' I suggested, 'and breed a whelp to oust Duke Robert's brat.'

fitzHamon laughed. 'Then will the heavens fall!' He lowered his voice and added, 'Have you considered how this crisis affects our comrade yonder?'

I looked at the dais where Henry lounged beside his brother, listening to the talk and saying little. 'The prince is no worse off. He holds lands in the Cotentin, none in England – and landless here he remains.'

fitzHamon tutted. 'Stir your brains up, Walter! Don't you realize that if Curthose sires an heir he finishes for ever Henry's hopes of inheritance when *both* his brothers are dead, and drowns his high ambitions like kittens in a bucket?'

'It alters nothing. He has long been scheming for England's rule. The plots will doubtless simmer – and we must go on keeping guard.'

fitzHamon pinched a guttering candle, and wiped a sooty thumb on the board. 'We'll want our wits about us. If Henry's to act he must do it soon – before Robert reaches Normandy.' Nervously he crumbled a hunk of bread. 'I wish to God Meulan were here. We need his crafty counsel.'

But Meulan remained in Rouen, Rufus's regent in Normandy. fitzHamon stood. 'I must go back to the high table. Think well on what I've said, Walter – I feel time is getting short.'

He went to take his place among his peers. I made disjointed conversation with a baron from Northumbria, my mind elsewhere, disturbed by fitzHamon's conclusions.

I decided to stay closer to the king than the shirt he wore.

4

The very next day my resolve was shattered. While tilting at the dummies my destrier slipped on a greasy patch and rolled me in the mud. My knee was badly wrenched; I could neither walk nor ride.

Rufus announced his departure for Winchester, and sent harbingers ahead to ready the forest wardens for a shoot of driven deer.

I was carried in a litter among the baggage wagons, pestered by the escort's banneret – a mercenary from Poitou – who related windy stories of his feats in France and Maine. I listened with half an ear, rehearsing various ways to guard the king. There was only one choice.

Arrived at the tavern where I lodged I summoned Richer.

'He leaves at daybreak for the Ampfield baily, less than an hour's ride, and returns when the drives are over. Ride in his train, Richer, and never let him out of your sight, neither on the march nor in the Forest.'

'How,' said Richer mildly, 'can I lurk within sight of the king while he's standing in the hide? The wardens will send me sharply about my business.'

'You're known to be my man, the king and his attendants see you always at my side – they won't think your presence strange. As for the foresters, use arrogance and bluff – even, if you have to, your skilfulness in woodcraft.'

Richer saddled his palfrey in the darkness before dawn, and joined the hunting party at the castle. I could not eat the bread and bacon Berlai brought to break my fast, had my pallet carried to the tavern's stable yard, watched the horses groomed – and waited. The sun crawled over an azure sky, shadows shifted slowly on the cobbles; every hour Berlai changed the compress on my knee. I rated him unreasonably, for his was a gentle touch and he hurt me not at all. He could not understand my mood, and looked like a beaten dog.

Evening's wash of silver paled the golden day. A faraway clatter of hoofbeats hammered the streets. Richer entered the yard, and gave his palfrey to a strapper. I saw his face – and panic drove a clenched fist into my stomach. He sank exhaustedly on a hay bale beside my pallet, and gazed for ten long moments at the ground between his feet.

'Lord Richard is dead.'

I let my breath out slowly, like a vintner pouring Falernian drop by drop. On the dregs of my lungs I said, 'Jesu mercy! Duke Robert's bastard! I feared . . .'

'The king,' said Richer wearily. 'I know. I think you'll find small comfort in Richard's killing.'

'Killing?'

'Indeed.' He plucked a straw from the bale, began one-handed to plait the stem in complicated patterns. 'It happened thus. On the second drive, deep in Ampfield's woods, King William chose a stand ensconced in a thicket of birch. Before the beat began he decided his hide ill-placed: a bramble clump, he grumbled, obscured his view. He changed position, quickly, with the hunter on his right, Lord Richard.'

Richer tied a knot in his straw. The stem broke; he dropped it and chose another.

'When the king moved I moved also, crouching in the bracken thirty paces behind. I could see him clearly, but not the hide he had left, where Lord Richard took his place. The foliage was dense; the bowmen, I believe, hidden one from another.'

The strapper grooming Richer's palfrey crossed the yard and sorrowfully reported an overreach, near fore. The Saracen nodded absently; impatiently I waved the man away.

'The drive started. The beaters were incompetent, far too noisy: the deer came out in a rush, bucks and does together. Arrows flew haphazard, and flicked across the ride. I crept nearer to the king. He loosed and felled a buck, a well-placed shoulder shot. Then it was over, and fewterers slipped hounds to track the wounded deer.'

The sun had gone, sinking behind the castle in a gold and crimson holocaust which bathed the stones in blood. A drunken man-at-arms staggered from the tavern, fumbled at his breeches and pissed against a wall.

'Someone shouted. Men went running to the place where Lord Richard stood for the drive. He was still there, dead as carrion, an arrow through his temples.'

I said from an arid throat, 'An accident.'

'So everyone assumed,' Richer answered dryly. 'But the bowman from a hide alongside mounted his horse and fled.' Richer paused. 'One Alberic, a knight of Henry's household. They let him go. Doubtless he'll find sanctuary in a monastery or church and nobody will force him out. He's guilty of naught save a random shaft. Why should he – or anyone else – deliberately kill Lord Richard?'

'There's no reason. A bastard severed from succession, no menace to the great. Everyone liked him; he had no enemies. It was pure mischance.'

'Have you convinced yourself?' asked Richer quietly.

I stared into gathering shadows. The strapper finished his work, set a bar across the stall and clumped from the yard. A trumpet moaned from the castle, mounting the second watch. The sounds and scents of a town at evening wafted on the wind: villeins tramping home from the fields, a wagon's screeching axles, a reek of privies and sewers and, remote as a cry from the rim of the world, a liturgy's doleful chant.

'They have laid my lord in St Peter's abbey, and there they mourn him.' Richer rose stiffly, walked to the stable and examined the palfrey's pastern. 'Nothing but a scratch – he'll trot sound tomorrow.'

I said, 'Who saw Richard take Rufus's place?'

'Very few. The king's esquire, waiting behind the hide. Lord Richard's. A forester in attendance. Myself. It was done in a trice.' Richer abstractedly unbuckled the strap that bound his withered arm. The limb swung stiffly, like a dead bough moved by wind. 'They both wore leather jerkins, russet-brown. Both are fair-haired men, and much of a height. Don't deceive yourself, my lord. An accident indeed – which someone regrets for a different cause.'

I stared at the luminous sky, saw evil stalk from the shades and swell across the heavens like monstrous storm-dark clouds. I said in a stifled voice, 'They will try again. And I lie here crippled, useless, while the wolf-pack's cry draws nearer.'

'They'll have to run mute awhile if they mean to kill in the forests,' said Richer bluntly. 'In mourning for his kinsman the king has closed the chases until the Fence Month is past and the does have done their calving. I doubt he'll hunt again till August.'

'The Saints be praised!'

'All your Christian seraphims,' said Richer gravely, 'would not have saved Lord Richard's life today. Who can ward an arrow flying from nowhere?'

I put my face in my hands, and closed my eyes.

5

The king must be warned.

After a night of horrible dreams where formless demons gibbered, I decided to seek Flambard's advice. On Berlai's arm I hobbled to the castle, found the chancellor in his resplendent chamber and related Richer's story. He was loth to believe Richard's killing other than a hazard of the chase: an explanation everyone accepted. I

474

spoke forcibly and fiercely. He heard me out, chin propped upon his hand; then remarked inconsequentially that in reward for faithful service Rufus had granted him Durham's see. 'I had to pay a relief,' he said ruefully. 'The king gives nothing away.'

'My lord bishop,' I said roughly, 'you wander from the point!'

'Not at all.' Flambard smiled. 'As a prelate of the Church I can command her servants. Listen.'

He expounded his proposals. Rufus, although Godless, a scoffer and disbeliever, was not free from superstition and that uneasy fear of Fortune's malice known to everyone who risks his life in battle. Flambard suggested playing upon this weakness. He would send to the king from time to time holy men declaring dire prophecies -- monks and priests and hermits, the kind whom visions visited. 'They will foretell nothing definite,' Flambard cautioned, 'nothing to implicate Prince Henry and his cronies – I don't want any more clerics murdered – nor compromise the Church. We bishops,' said he loftily, 'stand aloof from worldly wickedness.'

'If that's the best you can invent,' I answered listlessly, 'you'll waste time and clerical shoe-leather. Rufus is not the man to credit dreamers.'

'Maybe – but repeated warnings may move him to take precautions. Remember this, my lord,' he added seriously, 'every mortal being is afraid of death.'

6

And now I must describe how my world collapsed around my ears, my honour trailed in ordure, and the king I loved was slaughtered.

All Christendom knows the story in various garbled versions. Credulous monks spoil parchment with the fables told by pedlars; then history mouths as sober fact the chronicles they write. Merchants carry the tale to the seas that border the earth, and tangle the telling in passing. Knights gossip in castle halls on winter evenings, stitch embroidery on narration; and trouvères overhearing rhyme fantasies in their songs.

Lies, all lies. This, I swear by the Holy Rood, is absolute truth.

At terce on August's opening day the king set out from Winchester with a company ten-score strong: lords of the hunting party, stewards, esquires and varlets, and a mercenary constabular to guard him on the way. By middle afternoon we reached the Minsted baily, and entered a hunting manor called Malvoute.

From here, long years before, Richard son of the Conqueror had ridden to eternity. Rumour said the duke had razed a church to build the lodge; so the curse of God was laid upon it, and retribution followed sure as leaf-fall follows harvest. Afterwards Duke William never used Malvoute, and bestowed upon the house its sinister name. The buildings began crumbling until Rufus, deriding the legend, had them put in order.

When Duke William built the manor the English were still distrusted, so he raised a stone-built donjon, a lopped stump two floors high, and ringed the tower and ward with ditch and wall. Because defences were superfluous when Rufus repaired Malvoute he made windows in the donjon and an entrance at ground level. The rampart's fallen boulders nestled in grass and bindweed, and ash stakes toothed the gaps. The Forest swarmed around it like a blackly menacing army; the glade seemed always shadowed, always dark.

Servants had been sent ahead to garnish the place for the king. In the bustle of arrival and the rush for sleeping quarters I lost Rufus for a time. I saw my horses safely stabled, a hut allotted to my varlets and room for Richer and Berlai in a guard house by the gate.

I discovered the king in a little garden that spread from the donjon's base, a pleasaunce which a holly hedge surrounded. Mallows glowed pink and purple, poppies flaunted scarlet crowns, and the grass was newly scythed. Rufus discussed the morrow's drives with an attentive group of verderers and wardens.

'The Brokhest beat is usually productive,' he declared. 'Barely an hour's ride; we can start the hunt at prime. What reports of the deer?'

'Harts are harboured in Ramnor Wood, others in Balmer thicket. You'll not lack for sport, my lord,' the Minsted warden asserted.

'Good. Are the hides ready?'

'Yes. We'll need nine bows, my lord.'

'And nine we have!'

I said, 'I shall not shoot, sire.'

'Ah, Walter!' Rufus said explosively. 'Can't you shed this fad? What fun do you get creeping about the undergrowth? Carry a bow like any normal man!'

Another voice said, 'Many fine heads may be lost through a gap in the line, my lord.'

Ranulf of Aix. The spiteful face looked strained.

'Why are you here?' I demanded. 'What hand does Clarendon's warden have in ordering Minsted's drives?'

Gilbert of Clare said brusquely, 'None of your business, my lord! Ranulf knows every covert in the Forest, and has come from Clarendon to lend us his experience.'

I caught a sour look from Minsted's warden, ousted from authority; and said, 'Never before has an alien warden —'

'What matter?' Rufus snapped. 'The more skilled wardens the better. Now, the beats at Brokhest. Nine bows are essential?'

'Nine, no less, my lord,' Ranulf replied.

'That's it, then. Walter, you'll stand in line.'

'Sire, I beseech you —'

'Don't argue!' Rufus blared. 'Why should my sport be ruined because of your senseless whims? Do as I tell you!'

When the king used that tone the bravest blenched. I bowed my head to hide the despair in my face.

'I will, my lord.'

A satisfied smirk crossed Henry's lips. I looked at him in hate; and went quickly in search of Richer.

The king called for dinner at none, ate little and drank less: his habit on the eve of hunting or of war. He strolled in the ward at evening, spoke graciously to stablehands and soldiers; and at sundown went to his chamber. This was a kind of gallery reached by a ladder, formed by removing half the donjon's upper floor, shielded from the hall below by leather curtains. His esquires disrobed him; a chamberlain descended to inform us the king would sleep. Stewards peremptorily hushed the servants' chatter; knights went whispering to pallets in the hall.

Silence enfolded Malvoute like a shroud. From far away a wolf howled in the Forest.

I dreamed that I cringed in a noisome pit, naked and alone. Bestial faces peered from the rim, shadowy and indistinct, like coin heads rubbed by time. I trod on slimy things that writhed, and clawed at slimy walls, struggling to answer a distant call, a voice that cried for salvation. The calling ripped the mantle of sleep and clanged in my ears like bells.

'*M'aidez!*'

I leaped to Rufus's ladder, bumping bodies in the dark. The duty knight on guard at the foot hurtled into the chamber, drawing his sword. I followed close, clutching his hauberk's skirt. The knight looked fiercely around, searching the gloom for foes. Starshine bled from a window, dimly lighted Rufus on the bed. He groaned and clutched his belly.

'Lights!' I bawled. 'Bring lights!'

Someone fired a torch and handed it up the ladder. Lords crowded into the room, naked as they slept. Rufus writhed, knees curled to his chest, and bit the pillow.

'Pain,' he moaned. 'Such pain!'

'Find a leech!' fitzHamon barked.

An esquire departed running. We stood helplessly and watched the king. Eye avoided eye; one thought was in every head. Unlike barons such as Belesme, whose enemies were legion, Rufus scorned tasters, swearing they soured his victuals. Furtively I examined the faces dappled by wavering torchlight. No elucidation there. Clare looked disconcerted, Henry stunned.

The leech was hustled in, a wizened little pop-eyed man nursing a bag of simples. He demanded candles brought, held a taper close, prodded Rufus's belly, wiped spittle from his tongue and held it near the flame. He mumbled to himself, dived into his satchel, stirred a draught, forced the oily liquid down an unwilling throat, stood back and wiped his hands.

'Bring a privy pan,' he squeaked; and watched his taper burn. 'Now!'

Rufus heaved and yelped. The leech deftly slid the pan beneath his rump. A vile stench soiled the air. The king vomited; a yellow lumpy dribble clotted his hairy chest. Esquires cleansed him, and changed bedclothes.

The leech examined the excrement, and said complacently, 'The malignant humours are out. My lord will soon be well.'

fitzHamon wiped Rufus's forehead, wet with sweat. The king weakly clutched his hand.

'Stay with me, Robert.'

'That I will, sire,' fitzHamon said. He turned on the cluster of nobles, all stark as a witches' coven. 'Pray leave us, my lords. Poix, Breteuil – I need your help to tend the king.'

Henry stepped to the bed. fitzHamon faced him, stared him down. The prince turned slowly away, and left the room.

Servants brought our garments, hastily we dressed. By a single candle's light we kept our watch. The leech crouched in a corner. A clogging stench of sickness lingered like a fog. Rufus tossed on the bed, presently dozed restlessly and muttered in his dreams.

The long dark hours passed.

Dawnglow quenched the candle. I lifted an aching head, caught fitzHamon's eye, and put hand to mouth in a mime of eating.

'No. It couldn't be. Not poison.' Exhaustedly fitzHamon dragged a hand across his face. 'I've pondered it all night. If he were suspected of killing his brother nobody – neither the bishops, nor the barons, nor the English – would accept Henry as king. Therefore Rufus's death must appear plainly accidental.' Desperation shook his voice. 'May God and His Saints defend him!'

Breteuil, open-mouthed, watched fitzHamon kneel and pray.

8

The king slept late. A little after prime I remembered the hunt at Brokhest. No question of that. I descended blear-eyed to the ward where stablehands held horses ready saddled. The lords, conversing in undertones, turned heads at my approach. 'The king lies abed,' I told them. 'The start must be delayed. I doubt, in truth, that he will hunt today.'

Henry walked towards me, halted straddle-legged and furious. He slapped his whip in the palm of his hand. 'Is this your verdict or my brother's? What says the leech? You take too much on yourself, my lord!' He made to pass me. 'I will speak with the king myself!'

I fondled my dagger hilt and said softly, 'He's asleep. None will disturb him.'

Henry's nostrils flared – for an instant I thought he would strike me. Abruptly he beckoned Clare and strode away. I returned to the bedchamber.

Rufus was awake, limp and listless but little the worse. 'My mouth's like a badger's arsehole,' he grunted. 'Give me wine.' The leech clucked disapprovingly, mixed a cup of milk and water. Rufus swallowed the draught and said, 'It was the beef at dinner. I thought it tainted at the time. Will somebody whip the sutler?'

Clearly the king was mending. fitzHamon took me to the ward, leaving Breteuil on watch with the leech and a brace of esquires. He inhaled the freshness of the morning air and stretched his arms. 'Everyone ate the same food. Did you notice anything wrong with the beef, Walter?'

I shook my head.

A sentry at the gate rammed his spearshaft across a monk's fat chest and said in a Burgundian brogue, 'Out, Father! None may enter here.'

The monk lifted hands to the skies and bleated, 'I carry vital news! I must have speech with the king! Let me pass!'

The sentinel stayed adamant; the argument waxed louder. We strolled across. fitzHamon said, 'What are your tidings, Father? If they're sufficiently urgent I'll tell the king.'

'Ah, my lord!' A mouth like a wet rosebud pinched between plump white cheeks, brown pouches under his eyes. 'I've dreamed a terrible dream, an omen of catastrophe, a prediction touching the king! He must be told!'

'Tell me,' said fitzHamon firmly.

The monk wavered; then spouted words. Out of the spate I netted a jumbled tale of crucifix and church, an idol on an altar which Rufus jumped upon and gnawed until the effigy kicked like a mule and knocked him flat. He lay prostrate, the monk whispered fearfully, and flames belched from his mouth.

A nonsensical farrago. Surely Flambard's spurious prophets could concoct something better than this? fitzHamon, though ignorant of the Bishop of Durham's ruses, thought likewise.

'A nightmare indeed, but hardly deserving the king's attention.' With a straight face he continued, 'Unwatered wine on an overfed stomach is apt to disturb one's sleep.'

The monk's twaddle was better than nothing. I murmured, 'Tell Rufus.'

fitzHamon regarded me curiously, saw something in my eyes, and jerked a thumb to the donjon. Rufus was propped on pillows against the tester, the greyness gone from his face. fitzHamon, smiling broadly, repeated the monk's story.

Rufus grinned.

'Another? The fourth in a month – these clerks do nothing but dream! Send him packing!' The grin faded; his fingers plucked the coverlet; he gazed at a wash of sunlight that cascaded through the window. For the first and only time I saw fear in Rufus's eyes.

'Wait! He's a monk, and dreams for money. Give him a hundred shillings.'

The sum made fitzHamon gasp. The king had been impressed; Flambard's ploy, I mused, could be gradually succeeding. The king might soon be induced to take more thought for his safety, to be more careful of the men who called him friend.

Rufus flung the covers aside. 'I'm getting up, Manier,' he told an esquire, 'bring my clothes. Set a chair in the hall, away from draughts.'

There was no restraining him. The barons gathered round, full of praise for his recovery. The morning went in idle gossip, Rufus rather taciturn but obviously feeling more himself. The day's hunting seemed forgotten, for which I was heartily thankful.

Gilbert of Laigle, a rugged, beetle-browed knight who once had governed Mans on Rufus's behalf, mentioned Aquitaine's pledging, now an open secret at the court – Rufus, often reticent about setbacks to his polities, could never hug good fortune to his chest. The king declared negotiations prospered, an instalment of the loan already sent, William busy mustering his crusaders. He repeated his intention of marching to the Alps as soon as William left for Outremer.

My earlier doubts recurred; mildly I reminded him that the lords of France and Burgundy might well oppose his plans. Rufus replied sulkily, 'Oh, stow your gab, Walter! Aquitaine by Christmas will be mine; I shall hold the feast at Poitiers. Then we will see.' He patted his stomach. 'Nothing since yesterday's dinner, and that I lost! Bid the stewards lay the table.'

He ate voraciously. Unwise, I thought, to shovel chunks of undercooked meat inside an empty belly; the leech in the background wrung his hands and tried to catch my eye. But nobody could coddle Rufus: he responded harshly to advice about himself. I quietly told his esquire to cut the mutton small, and hoped for the best.

More disturbing were the quantities he drank. Henry, sitting beside him, kept his goblet filled and encouraged him to drink, swearing the wine would settle a turbulent stomach. Rufus shed his moroseness, grew affable and talkative.

Henry, choosing his moment, suggested that after all they might hunt that day.

Rufus pursed his lips. 'Too late for Brokhest – we wouldn't arrive till sundown. Anyway, I don't feel like riding far.'

Henry looked at the Clares; the trio left the table and went to the ward. On pretext of easing my bladder I trailed them to the stables, and saw a vehement debate with Ranulf of Aix and Minsted's warden. Presently they returned, and Henry said, 'The warden reports some splendid stags harboured in Striknage Wood. A mere ten bowshots' ride; then a short walk to the stands. He can organize a drive within the hour.'

'A pity to lose a hunt on a day so fine as this,' Roger of Clare observed.

Laigle patted his paunch and hiccuped. 'We could do with some exercise – I'm full of wind as a ranting priest!'

'We haven't had a hunt since May,' Gilbert stated. 'I've forgotten the taste of venison.'

The king looked uncertainly from one to the other. fitzHamon said hardily, 'Rash to venture out directly after your sickness, sire. You should try to look after yourself.'

That, unhappily, decided Rufus. 'D'you think I'm a puling woman, to droop all day because I've had the gripes?' He drained his cup and slammed it on the table. 'Right! Send the beaters out, and have the horses saddled!'

I saw triumph flash in Henry's eyes. He walked quickly from the hall.

9

Esquires garbed the king for hunting. He donned a linen tunic and supple buckskin breeks. Over all he wore a sleeveless calfhide jerkin – leather sleeves encumber a bowman's draw. He sat and stretched his legs for an esquire to lace his boots, and jovially cursed the boy for drawing the thongs too tight. He chaffered with his lords, who boisterously answered his jests. Rufus, in great good humour, had shed the effects of his malady.

Ranulf of Aix entered from the ward, ushering a varlet nursing a sheaf of arrows. 'Rotrou the fletcher, sire,' he said deferentially, 'begs you will accept these shafts turned specially for your use.'

I recognized the man, one of the armourer's staff which travelled with the household. He knelt and presented six birchwood arrows. Rufus poised one on his finger to check the balance, spun a second on thumb- and fingernail to test the straightness; and grunted approval.

'Good work, Rotrou – these won't gad.' He picked a pair from the sheaf and held them out. 'Here, Walter – these are yours. A peerless marksman deserves the finest arrows.'

I took the shafts, careful not to ruffle the goose-wing fletchings. Pale yellow, six hands long, the barbs five fingers' length and two in width. Three scarlet bands ringed the shaftments above the fletchings: the royal crest reserved for Rufus's arrows. I touched a thumb to the pile; the point was needle-sharp and pricked my skin.

'They'll fly true, my lord. I could not want better.'

Rufus stamped his feet, and lightly cuffed the esquire. 'Still laced over-tight, you scoundrel! No matter – we can't dally longer.' He bustled to the ward where stablemen held horses and huntsmen and foresters waited.

I handed the arrows to Berlai; he put them in my quiver with the rest and mounted his palfrey; a brace of bowstaves slanted across his shoulder. I spoke quickly to Richer, three whispered words. He climbed to horse. We followed the cavalcade through the gate, reined sharply when it checked, and craned to see the cause. A monk barred Rufus's way, and flourished a parchment scrip.

'God's face!' cried the king. 'How many more? What's that you bring?'

'Word from Serlo, St Peter's abbot at Gloucester. Tidings of dire import, sire!'

'Monks bring nothing else!' Tetchily he bridled a curvetting horse. 'Read, man – read it!'

From the rear of the procession I could not properly hear the cleric's homily: some ominous dream, I gathered, touching the king's doom-laden destiny, a reckoning for sin. When the whining voice had faltered to the end Rufus's laughter brayed.

'Serlo is soft in the head, writing me the nightmares of his snoring monks! Does he think I'm a gullible Englishman to be scared by wheezing old men? Stand aside, Father, else I'll ride you down!'

He urged his horse, still laughing. William, *li rei rus*, in his forty-third year and thirteenth of his reign, rode gaily to his death.

10

At once the Forest hemmed us in. Minsted's warden rode in front, and after a little way held up his hand. 'Here we dismount, my lords, lest the clatter alarm the deer. Henceforth we must keep our voices down.'

We consigned the palfreys to horseholders who accompanied the party. I took a bow from Berlai, strapped a quiver to my belt, and curved the elmwood stave across my knee to test the flexion. A favourite bow with a powerful draw, it shot a hunting arrow to kill at ninety paces. Berlai produced two plaited linen bowstrings; I tucked them in a wallet.

Rufus said, 'Henry, you'll be on my right, Walter on my left.'

He did me honour. Wardens naturally placed the king in the best position, where most of the game would run and sport was brisk. Hence stands on his flanks were eagerly sought. I inclined a grateful head, and glanced at Richer. His eyelids flickered.

Henry said, 'By your leave, William, I'll go farther down, nearer the right-flank bow. The stags are apt to break wide there, and run aslant the ride.'

An odd excuse. Stags turning wide? Red deer kept to the runs their ancestors had trodden – verderers could predict the line they'd take to a spear's-length either way. Why was Henry anxious to keep beyond bowshot of his brother?

'As you wish,' said Rufus grumpily. 'You'll miss a lot of shooting. Gilbert, take the hide on my right.'

Covertly I scrutinized Clare, seeking his reaction. The lined, sunken features betrayed no feeling at all; studiously he quivered arrows one by one.

The warden allotted the remaining hides, and appointed foresters to guide each bowman to his place. fitzHamon, I recall, was on my left, Roger next his brother to the right, Breteuil beyond. The rest I cannot remember, nor is it significant.

There were nine bows in the line. One was deadly.

The party scattered, trailing separate game-paths leading to the hides, keeping downwind of the harbourage lest the deer should get the vent. Woodmen waited beside the paths, and after we had passed cast down the blinks: branches interlaced to hinder the flight of wounded stags for hounds to catch them. They worked skilfully and quick; the barriers fell in place without a sound.

I trudged a narrow track; a century's dry dead-leaf fall crackled beneath my feet; elder's withering flower-heads brushed my ribs. My guide slipped through the shrubbery with a forester's practised silence; Berlai came behind, clumping the brittle mould. A stone's-cast to my right, hidden by trees and undergrowth, Rufus swished

484

through ferns, the warden as his leader, an esquire carrying his bows. Richer, I hoped with all my heart, was tracking him in rear. fitzHamon moved farther off; I could neither see nor hear him.

We were drawing close to the deer, and no one spoke.

A chill like an icy wind-gust bristled my scalp. Where was Clarendon's stealthy warden? I'd not set eyes on Ranulf of Aix since we left Malvoute.

I restrained an urge to shout for Richer. Too late now. A peril unaccounted for, loose somewhere in the Forest.

The forester paused in his stride, put finger to lip and pointed to a cranny sliced in the scrub. Between an elder tree and aspen I stepped into a crevice cleared of brushwood, screened by shrubs and brambles. I stamped my feet to firm the footing, and looked about.

Before me an open glade sloped gently to Striknage Wood – a cage of seagreen caverns pierced by sunset's brazen spears. Ferns and brushwood tasselled the tree-wall sixty paces distant. I could not see Rufus's hide – an elbow of the thicket bulged between – but heard him stamp the ground as I had done, and judged him over-near, not more than thirty paces. Fifty were more usual between stands: perhaps the woodland's conformation allowed no choice. Nor could I glimpse fitzHamon, hidden farther on my left; nor sight another bowman in the line. The cavity enclosed me like the palms of close-cupped hands, the fingers stretched to give me a view ahead.

Berlai and the forester concealed themselves in holly clumps behind the hide. I took a bowstring from my pouch, braced the bow, drew three arrows from the quiver, considered briefly which to nock. Best to use a crested shaft – Rufus would think me graceless if I failed to flight his gift. I nocked a scarlet-banded arrow and waited, bow held low, my fingers on the string.

A setting sun flung shadows like fallen towers across the glade. A squirrel frisked in the aspen boughs, scurried down the trunk, flirted his brush and vanished. Pigeons sailed to roost, wings clacking as they perched. The elder's rankness tickled my nostrils, and I fought a sneeze.

Voices murmured far in the heart of Striknage. The beaters knew their work, talking quietly as they went, urging the deer towards the hides at a slow and steady pace. Often I had stood in drives where they shouted and clattered sticks, stampeding the stags on a line of flustered bows.

I lifted the stave and flexed, drew and eased the string, eyed a furrow in the trees where I judged a deer path ended, a gap directly in front of Rufus's stand.

A stag trotted from the opening, his auburn coat aflame in the sun, and halted, antlers poised, and snuffed the air.

A bowstring twanged. An arrow flashed like a golden streak and scored the animal's ribs. Idiot Rufus, I said to myself: a head-on shot at fifty paces. Why didn't you wait?

The red stag leapt and swerved, came running straight towards me. Another frontal shot. I drew the string to my ear and sighted, hoping the beast would turn his flank.

'Shoot, Walter, shoot!' Rufus howled. 'Else my stag will be gone to the devil!'

A royal command. I loosed.

As the fletching passed the bowstave my target stumbled in his running and dropped his head. Antlers hid the chest at which I aimed. My arrow glanced from a beztine – *snick!* – and flicked to the right. The stag jinked and fled along the glade. I cursed and groped in my quiver, heard a bowstring thrum, lifted my head too late to see the arrow fly.

Gone beyond your range, Rufus – why waste shafts?

Voices gabbled from his hide, the esquire's shrilling shout and the forester's hoarse call. Trampling feet and the snap of breaking branches. A wail that echoed across the glade and soared above the tree-tops.

'The king is stricken!'

I dropped the bow and ran.

Rufus lay chest-down. The crown of his head was grinding the ground, his body curved to the scrabbling toes. Spasms jerked the buttocks in a hideous sexual travesty. A groan rattled deep in his throat. The rump arched higher. A quick convulsion stretched the body flat. It threshed once, twitched, and moved no more.

Manier the esquire clapped the back of his hand to his mouth and bit the bones. The forester, eyes starting, backed away, treading cautiously like one who walks in quicksands. Voices rang the glade, and the patter of running feet.

I tumbled on my knees beside the king, gripped his shoulders and turned him over. Glazing sightless eyes, a bitten tongue protruding between his teeth. A worm of blood writhed lazily from his mouth. A broken arrow jutted from his chest; his fingers clenched the splintered shaft.

Three scarlet bands adorned it, just above the fletching.

A pulse thumped in my head like drums beating from afar, booming louder as they neared. I crouched across the body.

Henry said, 'You shot him.'

Still kneeling, I looked up. The lords surrounded the corpse, their faces gaunt, appalled. fitzHamon swayed and seemed on the point of falling. Ranulf of Aix leaned on a bowstave; his legs trembled and he licked his lips. Henry, hands on hips, stared down at his brother. His features were white as milk, but showed neither shock nor grief.

He stepped across the body, thrust a hand in my quiver, shook the arrows to the ground, and retrieved a banded shaft.

'One gone.' He pointed to the broken stick in Rufus's hand. 'That is yours?'

I nodded dumbly.

Henry twirled the arrow in his fingers. 'What happened?'

'Mischance,' I mumbled. 'The shaft glanced . . . and then . . . I don't know . . . I could not see . . .'

Memory twitched my jangling nerves. One man had certainly seen. I looked wildly around. Foresters and beaters sprinkled the glade, immobile as the trees, terror in their stance. A stag sped unremarked across the open. Ranulf blankly watched its flight. His face was ashen grey.

Where was Richer?

Henry said, 'Bear witness, my lords. Tirel, by his own admission, killed the king.'

The pounding in my ears grew stronger, tramping through my head like marching feet. 'Christ forgive me!' I cried. 'Sooner would I burn in hell than this . . .'

'You'll burn,' said Henry flatly. Forcibly he flung the arrow down. 'My lords, what shall we do with him?'

'Mishap,' Breteuil mumbled. 'Let him go.'

Laigle growled agreement. Gilbert of Clare glanced quickly at his brother.

'Provided the Lord of Poix instantly quits England,' Roger said.

fitzHamon said nothing. He held both hands to his face, and cried like a child.

Richer ran from the hawthorn thicket which bordered Rufus's hide. Thorns had ripped his garments, earthstains spattered knees and arms. He slid to a stop, and began to speak.

'My lord . . '

Henry silently surveyed him. All the evil in the world fermented in his stare. Richer's mouth went slack. The Saracen looked cowed.

'Your pardon . . . it was nothing . . .'

The tension drained from Henry's features – a gambler saw a dangerous hazard won. He said in a grating voice, 'Get out, Tirel. Leave this land. You have grace till morrow's prime; then I'll hunt you down with swords.'

I climbed to my feet. My legs were frail as grass-stalks. I looked down on the paladin I had slain.

An insect crawled across a staring eye. I stooped and brushed it away.

II

Twilight faded and darkness deepened, a pall for my sombre thoughts. Our hoofbeats hammered loud in a sleeping world. An hour after midnight by the stars I heard the distant rustle of breakers brushing Southampton's shore. On the outskirts of the port Berlai's palfrey cast a shoe; we stopped at a wayside smithy, roused the smith, and leaned wearily on our horses while he worked.

Richer fumbled in his tunic, put something in my hand.

'Here is your arrow.'

I held it near the furnace glare, saw scarlet bands and a steelbright barb, undimmed.

'Your shaft went wide of the king,' said Richer woodenly. 'I crawled into the undergrowth and found it.'

Stars whirled madly across the sky; the smithy's pebbled standing rocked beneath my feet.

'Why did you not speak?'

Richer said in a tired voice, 'The king is dead, and Henry is king. I was afraid to die.'

In the void of night where sea met sky a silvery banner unfurled and falsely heralded dawn. The radiance bathed my hands, and washed them clean.

Author's Postscript

'King William, in hunting, from his own men was by an arrow offshot.'

That, in an English chronicler's words, is really all that is known about Rufus's death.

Almost all contemporary writers name Walter Tirel as his killer, a few are non-committal, one accuses a shadowy character called Ranulf of Aix. None described his death as other than accidental. Not one so much as hints that Henry had a hand in it.

The theory of Henry's complicity has been evolved by later historians; their reasons are best summarized by Dr A. L. Poole in Volume 3 of *The Oxford History of England*:

'Henry . . . had most to gain by his brother's death. His actions seem to be premeditated: wholly disregarding his dead brother, he rode straight for Winchester, seized the treasury . . . and . . . three days after the death of Rufus, he was crowned at Westminster. Finally . . . when his position on the throne was assured, he treated the family of Clare with marked favour. There is, at the least, enough evidence to arouse the suspicion that the sudden end of Rufus was the result of a conspiracy . . . of which Henry himself was cognizant.'

Moreover Walter Tirel, who lived to a ripe old age (he died on crusade in Palestine some time after 1134), swore to the end of his days – 'when he had nothing either to fear or hope' – that he did not shoot William Rufus.

Glossary

arpent	A measure of land, about an acre.
baldric	Belt worn pendent from one shoulder to carry a sword.
banneret	Knight commanding 10 or 20 knights and/or men-at-arms.
barbican	Projecting watch-tower over castle gate.
bastion	Projecting tower in a fortified wall.
berner	Feeder of hounds.
berselet	A hound, rather like a greyhound, which hunts by sight.
braban	A Flemish cloth.
brachet	A hound which hunts by scent.
cantle	The back arch of a saddle.
cary	A coarse cloth.
castellan	Knight custodian of a castle.
chape	A short cape.
chaumpan	Cloth woven in E. France.
coif	Extension of hauberk, attached to helmet, to protect the neck and ears.
compline	Last service of the Catholic daily office, about 9 p.m.
conroy	A mixed force, cavalry and infantry, about 50 strong.
constabular	A body of cavalry 10 or 20 strong.
courtoisie	Chivalry.
denier	A silver coin, the only coin in circulation at this time. Marks, shillings, pounds were token expressions.

destrier	A war-horse.
donjon	The main tower or keep of a castle, surmounting a high mound.
enarmed	Shield gripped by straps on inner side.
escalade	Scaling of the walls of a fortress in attack.
escheat	Confiscate.
fascine	Long cylindrical faggot of bound brushwood.
fewterer	Keeper of hounds.
fistmele	Distance from bowstring to inner side of grip (width of fist with fully extended thumb).
fletching	Feathering of arrow.
forte	Strongest part of a sword-blade, nearest the hilt.
gabion	Cylindrical wicker basket filled with earth.
gad	Erratic or unsteady flight of an arrow.
gambeson	Military tunic of leather or thick cloth, sometimes padded, often worn beneath hauberk.
guige	Shoulder-strap supporting the shield when not enarmed.
haubergeon	Short, sleeveless mail-coat, extending to hips or mid-thigh.
hauberk	A knee-length mail-coat worn by knights.
hide	Measure of land area, varying from 40 to 120 acres.
Honour	A seigniory of several manors held under one lord.
jazerant	Mail covered with small overlapping metal plates.
league	About 3 statute miles.
liam	Heavily-built hound, generally used for starting the quarry.
man-at-arms	Any soldier, mounted or afoot (other than bowmen), under the rank of knight.

mangonel	A siege-engine for casting stones.
manse	Mansion-house.
mantlet	A moveable shield or screen to protect attackers.
mascled	Mail covered with small lozenge-shaped pieces of metal, not overlapping.
merlon	The part of a battlement between two embrasures.
mesnie	Entourage or following of a lord.
metheglin	Mead.
miniver	A variegated fur.
motte	Castle mound, natural or artificial, on which the donjon is built.
muids	Measures of wine.
Neustria	An area corresponding roughly with Normandy, Maine and northern France.
nithing	A vile coward, an outcast.
nock	The notch of an arrow.
none	Fourth service of the Catholic daily office, about 3 p.m.
octroi	A tax levied on articles entering a town.
paladin	A knightly hero, a renowned champion.
palfrey	A riding horse or hack.
paltock	A short coat.
pile	Arrowhead.
plastron	A rectangular iron breastplate worn beneath the hauberk.
prime	First service of the Catholic daily office, about 6 a.m.
quillons	The cross-guards of a sword.
quintain	Target mounted on a post, to be tilted at with lances.
reeve	Minor official appointed by a lord to oversee his workmen.
rouncey	A pack-horse.
seisin	Possession of feudal property

sendal	A fine silk.
sergeant	A tenant by service, usually military, under the rank of knight.
sestary	A measure of volume, about 1 ½ pints.
sext	Third service of the Catholic daily office, noon.
stave	The body of a bow.
stele	Body of an arrow between nock and tip.
sutler	A camp follower who sells provisions.
tang	Extension of lance-head, securing it to shaft.
terce	Second service of the Catholic daily office, about 9 a.m.
vair	A fur obtained from squirrels.
ventail	Flap of mail buckled across chin and mouth.
verderers	Officials of the royal forests, with particular responsibility for the greenwood (vert).
ward	Outer fortified part of a castle, extending from the donjon.